KU-538-420

Penguin Books

TANDIA

Bryce Courtenay is the bestselling author of *The Power of One*, *Tandia*, *April Fool's Day*, *The Potato Factory*, *Tommo & Hawk*, *Jessica*, *Solomon's Song*, *A Recipe for Dreaming*, *The Family Frying Pan*, *The Night Country*, *Smoky Joe's Café*, *Four Fires*, *Matthew Flinders' Cat*, *Brother Fish*, *Whitethorn*, *Sylvia*, *The Persimmon Tree* and *Fishing for Stars*.

The Power of One is also available in an edition for younger readers, and *Jessica* has been made into an award-winning television miniseries.

Bryce Courtenay lives in the Southern Highlands, New South Wales.

Further information about the
author can be found at
brycecourtenay.com

Bryce Courtenay

TANDIA

PENGUIN BOOKS

PENGUIN BOOKS

Published by the Penguin Group
Penguin Group (Australia)
250 Camberwell Road, Camberwell, Victoria 3124, Australia
(a division of Pearson Australia Group Pty Ltd)
Penguin Group (USA) Inc.
375 Hudson Street, New York, New York 10014, USA
Penguin Group (Canada)
90 Eglinton Avenue East, Suite 700, Toronto ON M4P 2Y3, Canada
(a division of Pearson Penguin Canada Inc.)
Penguin Books Ltd
80 Strand, London WC2R 0RL, England
Penguin Ireland
25 St Stephen's Green, Dublin 2, Ireland
(a division of Penguin Books Ltd)
Penguin Books India Pvt Ltd
11 Community Centre, Panchsheel Park, New Delhi – 110 017, India
Penguin Group (NZ)
67 Apollo Drive, Rosedale, North Shore 0632, New Zealand
(a division of Pearson New Zealand Ltd)
Penguin Books (South Africa) (Pty) Ltd
24 Sturdee Avenue, Rosebank, Johannesburg 2196, South Africa

Penguin Books Ltd, Registered Offices: 80 Strand, London WC2R 0RL, England

First published by William Heinemann Australia, 1992
First published by Penguin Books Australia Ltd, 1997
This edition published by Penguin Group (Australia), 2006

5 7 9 10 8 6

Copyright © Bryce Courtenay 1992

Cover design by Debra Billson © Penguin Group (Australia)
Cover photographs by Stuart McClymont/Getty Images and Simon Wilkinson/Getty Images
Typeset in 10/12.5 pt Sabon by Post Pre-press Group, Brisbane, Queensland
Printed and bound in Australia by McPherson's Printing Group, Maryborough, Victoria

National Library of Australia
Cataloguing-in-Publication data:

Courtenay, Bryce, 1933– .
Tandia.
ISBN 978 0 14 300454 7.
I. Title.
A823.3

penguin.com.au

Together since the world began,
the madman and the lover.

*Discovered by Allied troops written
on a latrine wall at Dachau*

As a great admirer of the work of Dame Elizabeth Frink I have put many of her observations concerning her art into the dialogue which comes from the character Harriet in my novel. I have also used the concept of the walking Madonna, Frink's work of acknowledged genius done for Salisbury Cathedral. Other than these obvious, and I hope complimentary, references, the character Harriet is not intended in any way whatsoever to depict Dame Elizabeth, who is not known personally to me. All the other characters, unless they are mentioned specifically by name as public figures of the time, are entirely fictional.

One

On the morning she was raped Tandia had risen just before dawn and come back to the graveside to pay her proper respects to Patel. Someone had been there before her. She looked at the grass around the grave but only her own footprints showed on its wet, dew-frosted surface. They must have come last night.

Tandia had been the last to leave the funeral on the previous evening, just a little after sunset when the cicadas in the dusty mimosa trees around the cemetery had suddenly shut down. She'd watched the two black grave diggers working to fill the hole. As they sliced their long-handled shovels into the red clay they chanted a soft urgent rhythm. When they'd heaped the soil high enough and patted it down and rounded it properly, one of them, using the back of his shovel, drove a crude wooden cross into the comfortable looking mound of soil. They departed still singing softly, shovels across their sweat-wet shoulders, their diminishing shapes outlined against the red sun.

Tandia had arranged all the wreaths over the bare mound of earth. Directly under the wooden cross she'd placed a large bunch of Easter lilies wrapped in cellophane. The card, pinned to the broad satin ribbon, read: 'REST IN PEACE, PATEL. POLICE BOYS' BOXING CLUB.'

Now, someone had moved the Easter lilies to the side to make a place at the foot of the cross for a small Indian oil lamp with a bright blue flame that burned perfectly still, as though frozen in the pewter light. Beside it stood a tiny brass vase from which burned four sticks of incense, and around the cross hung a bright garland of miniature orange and yellow marigolds.

Tandia watched as tiny puffs of grey smoke broke away from the sticks. The incense made a warm smell in the dawn air, a little bit of home comfort for Natkin Patel, South Africa's best-known Indian boxing referee, who had been born a Hindu and who died a Christian.

Tandia wondered about the appearance of the Indian stuff on Patel's grave. Was Patel already a Christian when he had put his curry sausage into her black mother? Or did it happen only after she was born? Which God was going to punish him for bringing a bastard mixed-race child into the world? Do you suppose the Gods keep score? When you turn your back on one God and choose another, does the old God demand vengeance? Or would the Lord Krishna, Patel's old God, be satisfied with a garland of miniature marigolds, four sticks of incense burning in a cheap brass vase and a lighted oil lamp? A careful person like Patel would not have wanted to take any chances. For damn sure, he would have decided it couldn't hurt to leave both gates to paradise a little open. That was Patel all right. He'd always liked to make arrangements a long way ahead.

Patel would have liked the funeral. Quite a lot of white people came. Also, of course, important leaders of the Durban Indian community. Because he was Church of England, which is a pretty rare thing to be when you are a South African Indian, and because he was well respected by the police, they had given permission for his lying-in to take place at Kruger's Funeral Parlour.

Kruger said he was prepared to make this concession for a boxing referee and coach who, even if he was an Indian, was greatly respected and a good type of man. Nevertheless, allowing a dead Indian to be laid out for inspection in a whites-only funeral parlour was a very brave and honourable thing for him to do. To show their appreciation, Mrs Patel and the two boys, Teddy and Billy, had asked Kruger, along with Captain Vermaak, president of the Police Boys' Boxing Club, to be pall bearers.

Lying in the small funeral parlour in his expensive stinkwood coffin, arms crossed, eyes closed, his curry-coloured skin with its tiny indented smallpox scars losing its sheen, Patel looked different. It was his hair; it was no longer parted the way he always wore it, pasted down with Brylcreem so that the roadway down the centre of the scalp was precise, not a single hair trespassing to the other side. Kruger, who should have known better, had parted Patel's hair with a side parting. Patel looked like a stranger.

Patel was Tandia's only loved one. If you could call him that. He hadn't even touched her since she was six years old. She knew that as a baby he'd loved her, she knew that for sure. Now, before he was dead that is, she didn't think so. Maybe he just felt guilty. Although guilty was perhaps the wrong word. More like ashamed. Ashamed that a person like him had sunk so low as to do it to a kaffir woman. She loved him anyway.

Tandia had always thought the time would come when he'd love her again. When she was grown up, after she'd done all the things he wanted her to do, then there would be a reconciliation. He would recognise that he had a clever daughter as well as two fat legitimate sons who were, anyway, a load of rubbish. It wasn't fair! Patel just wasn't the sort who would go and drop dead on a person. Especially in the boxing ring with white people standing all around. He would rather die than have a thing like that happen to him.

The morning of his death, when he'd appeared at the back steps for his boots, he'd been his usual self, the smooth skin on his forehead glowing, his hair oiled and parted perfectly in the middle, the pleats in his gaberdine trousers sharp as a knife and his heavily starched white shirt crackling as he pulled his boots on. That morning he'd been a million miles from being dead.

Yesterday, after the first few Indians had gone into the funeral parlour they came back out into the bright sunshine, but instead of saying nothing, like people do at such times, everyone was whispering about the wrong parting of Patel's hair. 'What can you expect? Isn't that typical of the whites to bugger up an important thing like a person's hair!' Of course the whisper didn't get to where Mr Kruger was standing under a big old fig tree with all the other white people from the boxing club.

Tandia waited until the last mourner had come out of the parlour. She stood beside the coffin and looked furtively up at the white funeral attendant in the frock coat and cravat who stood watch beside Patel's dead body. He was young and fat and his face was covered in acne scars and purplish bumps where the acne still bothered him. He didn't look too dangerous; still, you never knew with those young white guys. What if she acted brave as anything?

Just the thought of going up to this oozey white person made Tandia's mouth go dry. If Patel was alive he would have been able to do it. He was always boasting that he was well known in white circles. As a small child Tandia had thought he said white *circus*. For years she imagined Patel was some sort of performer, an acrobat or something. But now there was nobody who would be game enough to take the matter up with Mr Kruger. She'd watched the Indian mourners as they came out of the little chapel; one thing was for sure, none of them was going to make a fuss about Patel's hair.

Tandia moved up to the fat white man in the frock coat. 'Excuse me, *meneer*.'

'Can I help you?' She was surprised he spoke English; she'd expected him to be an Afrikaner.

Despite her boldness, the dryness in Tandia's mouth stopped her next words. She had first to work her tongue around the top of her mouth before she spoke again. 'Excuse me, sir, you combed his hair all wrong. It should be parted down the middle.'

There was a moment's silence as the attendant looked at Patel and then back at Tandia. 'That's not my job.' He turned and, pointing to heavy red velvet drapes that hung from the ceiling to the floor and formed the rear wall of the chapel, he added, 'The corpses, I mean the passed-away persons, they all done by Mr Kruger, the boss. I just stand by the coffin, you understand?' He leant forward, his voice almost a whisper. 'I'm just here in case someone gets hysterical and flings themselves on the body.' His voice was surprisingly high and whiney, and he was plainly as intimidated by these surroundings as Tandia. 'Please don't make trouble, this is the first time I done this job.' He shrugged his shoulders and the nape of his frock coat rose up to his ears and then fell back again. 'That's why Mr Kruger gave me only a coolie funeral.'

Tandia smiled up at him. He was a dumbbell but she sensed he meant no harm and this gave her the confidence she needed to continue. 'Tell me, please, have you got a comb?'

'Yes, of course.' The big man brought his hands up and patted both sides of his breast frantically, producing a small black comb from his top left pocket. The movement was amazingly quick for such a big, slow-thinking man.

Struggling to remain calm, Tandia said, 'Perhaps, maybe you could comb my father's hair with a middle parting?' She smiled. 'Please, so he dies happy?'

'No way!' He pulled back in alarm. 'No, man, I can't do that. I don't do the touching. I don't touch no stiffs, I can't do what you asking me. No bladdy way!'

Tandia snatched the comb from his hand and quickly combed Natkin Patel's stiff hair over his eyes. Swallowing her panic, she said to herself, 'Please God forgive me, I'm only doing this so he dies happy, he was a very proud man!' She drew the small comb down the centre of the cold scalp; it was like parting a doll's hair on a papier-mâché head. But Patel's hair had been lacquered to keep it in place. 'Please God, make it lie down!' she pleaded. Frantic, she flung the comb down on his chest and used the palms of her hands to smooth the hair down on either side of his skull. Patel's head was icy cold to her touch and she gave a short, involuntary shiver. It still wasn't perfect, but it looked okay, much more like the real Patel; like he'd been asleep and mussed it up a bit.

The white man at her side cleared his throat. 'Come, hurry up, *jong*. I got to close the lid now.'

Tandia nodded. 'Thank you, sir, he can rest in peace now.'

Reaching behind a vase of gladioli he brought out a large screwdriver. 'Ag, man, he's dead anyway, I don't see what his hair has got to do with anything.' From his trouser pocket he produced a large brass screw and, closing the lid of the coffin, he inserted the screw into the keyhole of the brass locking-plate and screwed it shut. Tandia remembered she'd left his comb resting on Patel's beautifully starched shirtfront. It was too late to rescue it and she hoped the attendant wouldn't remember. It was a cheap comb anyway; for sixpence you could buy one like it anywhere.

The funeral parlour attendant replaced the screwdriver and moved over to the rear wall of the chapel where he pulled open the drapes to reveal a large, round-shouldered radiogram. He pushed a small lever on the turntable and the record arm rose. Removing the record and blowing on it quickly, he flipped it onto the reverse side and re-positioned it. Then he pushed down on the lever again and the arm rose slowly, swung above the turning record and plunged downwards. With a slight crackle of static, the needle came to rest in a groove and almost immediately the strains of a Bach funeral cantata filled the small room. The big man rolled his eyes and let out a huge sigh of relief. In his anxiety to get his routine right he appeared to have forgotten about Tandia. He jerked the curtain together and moved hurriedly towards the closed chapel doors, pausing only to adjust his coat, pulling simultaneously at both sides of his lapels. Taking a deep breath, he straightened up, lifted his chin and swung the doors inwards so that the organ music could escape into the sunshine.

Tandia slipped quietly behind the curtain where she watched as the light flooded into the dark funeral parlour. She could see Teddy and Billy, the two Patel boys, coming up the steps followed by Kruger and Captain Vermaak. Behind them came four Indian friends of Patel. They all had their hands clasped as they walked over to Patel's coffin and took up their positions. The organ music rose to a crescendo and Kruger nodded to the attendant who, in turn, nodded back to the pall bearers who hoisted Patel's stinkwood coffin onto their shoulders and carried it slowly back towards the door. Billy and Teddy on either side at the front led the coffin out and the attendant, looking pleased that he'd pulled it all off successfully, brought up the rear.

Tandia forbade herself to cry at the funeral. Crying was the biggest mistake she could make in front of Mrs Patel. If Mrs Patel saw her crying she knew what she'd be thinking. 'That coloured bitch is trying to show more grief than his proper family!' By closely observing the business of death, her mind stayed busy and she was able to push her sorrow aside by crowding it with detail.

Tandia often did this. When a thing got too hard to bear or if it began to crowd her emotionally, she would do what she thought of as 'thinking a thing inside out'.

When, for instance, they started to throw handfuls of earth over Patel's coffin it was such a personal and private thing to do that her grief threatened to overwhelm her. She wanted to rush forward and put her own handful of red clay over Patel, to stand over his grave and weep for him. But she dared not move

8

forward. She hadn't been invited to the funeral and she had fully expected Mrs Patel or Billy or Teddy to send her home when she turned up at the parlour. Now she crowded in the details, the droning on of the minister, all the dust-to-dust and ashes-to-ashes stuff, people fidgeting, the Indian guests awkward when the Bible was being read. She watched from the very edge of the mourners, too far away to see into the open hole and positioned so as not to be seen by Mrs Patel or her two fat sons, who were having a really good time sniffling and blowing into their hankies, which was a big, fat laugh, because everyone knew they hated Patel. He wanted them to be boxers but they'd both turned out soft and fat and scared of their own shadows.

Anyone watching the funeral would have picked her out quite easily. At nearly sixteen she was tall and slim for her age and was becoming everything Patel had said she would be. Tandia was not aware of her beauty. Her green eyes, small, straight Indian nose, skin the colour of bluegum honey, beautiful bone structure, full lips and close-cropped peppercorn hair were a cultural corruption, an act of sin. To see her extraordinary beauty you needed eyes that made no racial judgement and there were few of those in South Africa.

Now, she stood at Patel's graveside just as dawn was breaking. In Tandia's mind she had come to have a good talk to him. It had almost been dark by the time she'd completed decorating his grave with the wreaths the previous evening and she hadn't been able to say goodbye properly. She had planned a conversation which she could never have hoped to have with him while he had been alive. But overnight, as she lay in her iron cot in the shed, his death had built a bridge, a place to cross so that she could reach him. In death Patel became the father he had never been in life.

Earlier, as she made her way to the cemetery, she had even tried using the various words for father in her mind. She'd tried the three conventional versions, throwing back her head and saying them out loud, testing them out on the stars in the pre-dawn sky. 'Father!' It sounded awfully posh. Patel was definitely not a 'Father'. 'Dad?' Could she ever have a relationship as casual as such a marvellous, warm, taken-for-granted word? She tried the third, 'Daddy'. She liked it best because it was so patently a contradiction of the relationship she had had with Patel. Except for when she was very small, when she would sit on his knee and he would absently stroke her tiny shoulder and talk to people about her green eyes. At that time the word had been possible and now that Patel was dead she wanted it returned to her.

But Natkin Patel the small printing shop owner, first-class Indian person, illegitimate curry sausage user, policeman's friend, who was well known in white circles, was still too soon buried for any of these names to work very well.

Tandia's final image of Patel was him sitting on the steps of the back *stoep* not even acknowledging her as she handed him the boots she'd carefully polished. But she knew time and several visits to the cemetery would soften the hard edges of the reality. She would now have someone to whom she could talk, with whom she could share her loneliness, and onto whom she could focus her abundant but unrequited love.

The curious invention of making Patel alive now that he was dead so pleased Tandia that she had momentarily postponed the fear she felt at the prospect of being thrown out on the street when she returned home at sunrise. But now that fear returned. If, as she had decided, she would use Patel's graveside for really important conversations, none was more important than the one she brought with her on this first cold dawn morning.

Tandia finally came to grips with the thing on her mind. The thing she wakened to every day of her life as long as she could remember. The thing she never said aloud, but was now going to ask Patel here in the Indian cemetery with the dew clouding the cellophane wrappings around the Easter lilies and with the pungent smell of the incense filling the air.

In the Indian Christian cemetery there was plenty of room between the graves for patches of grass, dandelion and blackjack to grow. Not many Indians died Christians, so you could pick and choose your spot. Mrs Patel chose a lot about fifteen feet from a grave which boasted a six-foot marble cross and belonged to T. W. Nepul, who had been a wealthy merchant and important spokesman for the Durban Indian community. It was said also that he had been a personal friend of General Smuts. She liked the idea of her own husband being close to a bit of gratuitous wealth and prestige. If a person could pick any spot in the graveyard, as Patel himself would have said, 'Dammit, man, it doesn't do any harm to be always with the best people.'

'What am I?' Tandia began. 'Am I Indian? Or am I a kaffir?' She talked directly to the mound of earth at her feet. 'Please, Patel, what will I do now, you must tell me, please?'

She paused as though waiting for him to answer; then she continued. 'Do you think because I'm mixed race I'm a coloured? I don't want to be a coloured. Also, not a black person. Patel, can I please be an Indian when I grow up? Mrs Patel doesn't like me. When she throws me out and I have to get a passbook from the police, can I tell them I am your daughter, that I'm an Indian girl?'

With Patel's death Tandia knew things were going to be very difficult for her. When she got back to the house in Booth Street she expected no mercy from Mrs Patel. Would she simply send her packing? Kick her out of the only home she had ever known, the dark little corrugated-iron shed in the back yard? In her imagination Tandia could hear the old woman's voice. 'Go on, *voetsak*! Take your things and get out of my house!' Surely she wouldn't do that? She must give her a chance to find a job first!

Mrs Patel was an ignorant woman. She couldn't read or write and hadn't taken up Christianity like her husband. Her own religion commanded absolute obedience to Patel, but she had been deeply disturbed by his change of faith. The Patel caste is a religious one. Other castes may change, could change, but not a Patel. It was a hugely offensive thing to have done to his caste. Especially as Patel's religious zeal was shown to be less one of burning faith than of a desire to achieve assimilation into the European genre. Being a Hindu required her to forgive him everything, even sleeping with a black woman. Now, with Patel dead, the shackles of fidelity and obedience were undone; now she was in control.

From the very beginning Mrs Patel couldn't do anything about the black child her husband had spawned. Natkin Patel wanted his bastard daughter and he seemed to feel an attachment to the plump honey-skinned baby that he'd never felt for his two sons.

'See,' he said, picking her up, 'the skin is soft like velvet, darker, maybe a little darker, but not so black as a kaffir. I'm telling you, man, this one is lucky, bladdy lucky. Look! Green eyes! An Indian and a kaffir mix and, goodness me, out come green eyes!'

Patel was a good cut-man in the ring and so fancied himself a bit medically minded. 'How can it be? You mix a black with an Indian; one thing is certain . . .' he paused for effect, 'all dark eyes, every bugger has dark eyes. Tell me, hey? Where have you seen a green-eyed kaffir or an Indian? I'm telling you, not even so many white people have green eyes.' He absent-mindedly stroked the baby. 'Usually with kaffirs you get gene swamp.' 'Gene swamp' was Patel's very own expression; he'd invented it to explain why mixed marriages between blacks and whites didn't work. 'The ugliness of the kaffir comes out and nothing good of the white or the Indian is left.' He bounced Tandia on his knee. 'But not this one, hey? I'm telling you something for nothing, except for her hair, which I got to admit is a kaffir's hair, this one is going to be very, very pretty.'

Mrs Patel said nothing, her humiliation greater than she believed she could bear. Patel wasn't even ashamed! He talked openly to people about his bastard daughter. It wasn't respectful. It wasn't fair. She'd done her job as a good wife and given him two sons to look after his old age and no silly daughters to bleed him dry with wedding dowries, and in return he insulted her name and her race.

She would suck her dislike for Tandia through her gold teeth. 'Sies, man, how could you love that?' At least she didn't have to have his shame in the house. Tandia lived in the corrugated-iron shed in the back with her kaffir mother. When Tandia was five her mother died quite suddenly. Her death came as somewhat of a surprise to the neighbourhood, for she was a robust and happy woman who performed the task of servant to the Patel household with cheerfulness and energy.

Nobody knew about the poisoning of Tandia's mother, but then again, everybody knew. The police, of course, treated it just like another dead black person. It happened all the time. Maybe even some money changed hands? Patel was well known in boxing circles, white boxing circles, where the police were very big. He could easily have paid someone not to look too closely.

Tandia had grown up with the story of her mother's death. It remained street gossip for years, and there was no doubt in her mind that Mrs Patel had been responsible. She had no evidence to prove it, but she knew the woman's hate was big enough.

The hurt at being hated so much by Mrs Patel had only been bearable when Tandia took it out of herself and turned it inside out, turned Mrs Patel into an ignorant but honest and jealous woman who had been cheated by her husband.

Deep in thought, Tandia was unaware of the two men creeping up behind her in the cemetery. She sensed their presence too late. Her left arm was grabbed from behind and twisted painfully behind her back.

'Don't struggle, kaffir, or I break your bladdy arm, you hear?'

She felt the cold metal of the handcuff as it snapped around her wrist. Her free arm was pulled behind her and the second metal bracelet snapped onto it. She didn't scream at first, her shock was too great. But then it came, the pitch so high its beginning was silent, a rasp of cold air pulled into her epiglottis. The scream cut across the misty, dew-soaked cemetery; it may even have reached half a mile away to where the cement-block houses of the new Indian township began. But it had no second breath, no second pull of fright. A hard hand slammed across her mouth, the signet ring striking her front teeth. Her head pushed downwards, they raced towards the headstone, the force of the man propelling her impossible to resist. Instinctively she brought her shoulder around to take the brunt of the crash as her slim body slammed into the cold marble cross.

The grip on her mouth and neck loosened and then her attacker released her altogether. Her knees buckled and she started to fall. A hand grabbed the chain connecting her handcuffs and broke her fall, allowing her to sink to her knees. She didn't feel the metal band being loosened from her left wrist and was barely conscious of her arms being brought around the base of the cross and of the handcuff snapping around her wrist again. Her attacker stood directly behind her, working purposefully.

'That's right, kaffir, in the doggy position, you people like that, hey?' He gave two sharp barks, 'Woof woof!' Tandia heard a short laugh and for the first time became aware that a second man was present. The cotton shirt she was wearing was bunched and a hand pulled at her bloomers. It was the feeling of the elastic pulling over her thighs that brought her back to her senses. She kicked out with her left foot and connected with the squatting policeman's thigh, knocking him over.

'Fok! The black bitch has dirtied my uniform!' He reached out and, grabbing her ankle, jerked her leg straight. With her knees no longer supporting her, Tandia crashed onto her stomach. Straddling her the policeman pulled her bloomers down. Then he brought his hands under her hips and jerked her back to her former kneeling position. He was a strong man, but now he panted slightly from the effort and he spoke in short, sharp bursts. 'You dirty my nice clean uniform, hey. I got to teach you some manners, man. Kicking with your dirty kaffir feet. That's not nice, you hear!'

Tandia heard the click of his belt buckle. 'Don't move. You hear? Stay jus' like that.' His voice was steadier now, more confident. She heard the second man laugh. 'Take your boots off, man, your trousers won't go over your boots, *domkop*!' The man behind her gave a grunt, then another as the second boot came away; then came his voice again, light, almost flippant. 'First you got to learn not to kick your betters!' She felt the sting of the leather belt even before her mind registered its sound on her buttocks. The belt came down twice more, each lash followed by a grunt from the policeman. Tandia screamed; the pain was terrible. 'Coming, ready or not!' She felt his hands on either side of her thighs pull her back up, then a brutal thrust and a sharp pain. She gasped and let out another scream. The policeman slipped one hand around her waist holding her hard against him and clamped the other over her mouth. His grip was too tight for her to bite his fleshy, nicotine-smelling palm.

'Jesus, a virgin! The-black-bitch-is-a-fucking-virgin!' The repeated force of the body slamming into her was synchronised with his voice. She fought for breath, snorting through her nostrils. Nothing else mattered, not the pain, nothing; he was suffocating her and she was fighting to get enough air to stay alive.

Suddenly, the hand over her mouth relaxed and the grotesque presence dismounted. Tandia remained very still. Panting, but very still, her eyes tightly closed. She was aware, for the first time, of the taste of blood in her mouth. It was the only thing that seemed real. She held on to it. The salty, normal taste of blood kept her from passing out. Would they kill her? Not if she didn't look. Not if they knew she hadn't seen their faces. Tandia, who had so often wondered whether her life was worth anything, suddenly knew she wanted to live.

'Hey, Geldenhuis? C'mon, your turn. Nice tight pussy. A very recent virgin. Guaranteed only one owner!'

'Don't use my name in front of the kaffir girl! I don't fuck kaffirs.'

There was a moment's pause. 'Ja, is that so? How come then, you always like to watch?'

'C'mon, hurry up, jong, it's already half past six. We got to report.' Nervous anger strained the second man's voice. 'We only came to pay our respects to old Patel!'

The policeman who had raped her was breathing less heavily now, aware perhaps that he had upset his superior. He changed the subject. 'What's going to happen about your title fight with Gideon Mandoma now Patel's dead?'

Geldenhuis didn't answer. '*Kom! Maok you, jong!* It's nearly bladdy sunrise!'

Tandia felt the sudden downward pressure of a boot in the small of her back. 'Nice one! Her black arse looks like a hot cross bun.' She lay absolutely still, the gravel chips cut into her stomach and her arms pulled painfully as the handcuffs looped around the cross held her rigid. Her shift remained bunched above her waist. Tandia kept her eyes tightly shut even after she heard the soft click of the key and felt the handcuffs removed from her wrists and her ankles.

She lay there as though dead, not a muscle moving. Inside her head she screamed, *'Please God, don't let them kill me!'*

Tandia felt the sudden downward pressure of the boot again, this time on the base of her neck. 'Don't open your eyes, kaffir, not for a long time, not for ten minutes, you hear?' It was the voice of the second man, the one called Geldenhuis. The pressure increased and her head was pushed into the ground. 'Hey! You! Kaffir! I asked you, do you hear?'

'Yes, *baas*,' she sobbed.

The boot twisted into her neck, sending a sharp stab of pain down her spine. *'Ja dankie, baas!'* the voice demanded. She felt his hand tug at her shift and pull it down over her thighs.

'Yes, thank you, baas,' Tandia whimpered.

'You report this you dead meat!'

Tandia lay there for a long time. The sun came up and took the morning cold away but she kept her eyes shut. She was a kaffir, that at least had been decided.

Tandia opened one eye. It focussed on a willy wagtail sitting on a half-fallen tombstone ten feet from where she lay. Cut into the pocked cement tombstone she read the words, 'Dearly beloved', but the remainder of the writing on the lopsided tombstone was covered with dry lichen.

The willy's tail was going up and down, regular as a metronome. A tiny breeze caught and ruffled the white feathers on its breast. It cocked its head slightly and looked at her without curiosity. Then it flew away and rested on the temporary wooden cross on Patel's grave. But it didn't stay long; its tail only went up and down three or four times before it took off again. Maybe because of the incense? Can birds smell? Tandia didn't know.

All the tears, the bitter child tears were over. The white man had decided for her. She was a stinking black kaffir who had had her buttocks parted by a white man's hands.

Tandia's world crumbled. The small amount of self-esteem she had harvested out of her childhood had come from her efforts at school. Now, with Patel dead, there would be no more school. She had been crushed, she was suddenly no better than the lowest black person. A stinking, dirty kaffir!

Tandia lay very still and let the hate come in. Let the hate spread, enter her salty, blood-rinsed mouth and creep down her dry throat and into her chest and down, down, down, to congeal in her stomach so that she thought for a moment she would vomit. She gulped, but she held the hate down. She held it until it spread throughout her whole body. And then, only then, when she knew it would never leave her, Tandia allowed herself to weep again.

This time it was a cry that started on the surface like a child crying and then burned deeper and deeper so that it ended up a whimper, hardly a cry at all. It was only then, when the crying was leached out of her, that the fear came, it rose up in her breast until she could contain it no longer. 'Patel!' she screamed. 'Why did you have to die!' At almost sixteen, life as a kaffir had begun for Tandia.

Two

The afternoon was well advanced when Peekay wakened. Despite the lateness of the day the heat beat down on the tin roof of the round miner's hut, his home for nearly sixteen months.

It would be another month before the rains came to the Northern Rhodesian Copperbelt. One morning he'd come up from underground, his ears ringing from a night spent blasting rock, and it would be there: the hot, dry, insect-crackling night would have turned into a perfectly still, rain-misted morning. He'd remove his hard hat, unclip his miner's lamp, place it into the recharging rack, and walk out and stand with his face held up to the pewter-coloured sky, allowing the soft drizzle to drench him, his body soaking up the first cool, wet morning for nine months. It felt so good and clean, like the beginning of the world.

But mostly the Copperbelt was like now, this last afternoon. His skin itched and felt clammy, beads of perspiration ran down his armpits, and the sheet on which he lay was damp.

Peekay stared at the ceiling fan above him. Fixed from the centre of the cone-shaped roof, it rotated in jerky movements, like a man with a slight limp forced to run for the bus. He searched around the perimeter of the fan until he found the blowfly. Almost always there was a blowfly, a big fat one with a shiny body the colours of oil spilled on water. He watched as, sensing the danger, it banked away from the fan to crash straight into the finger of God, a coil of yellow fly-paper which dangled from the ceiling.

Sweat trickled down Peekay's chest and a painful erection aimed its barrel directly at him. Virginity was a real bastard. He imagined his pointing cannon putting an end to his misery, firing directly at him, the ball whistling across his belly, over the rise of his chest, entering just under his chin, up through the roof of his mouth, the grapeshot exploding inside his head and scrambling his brains. The headline in the *Copperbelt News*: COCK CANNON KILLS OXFORD MAN IN MINING DISASTER!

His hands were swollen from the fight with the giant Botha in the Crud Bar the previous afternoon. The big man had tried to kill him in what had turned out to be an unfair contest. The huge, clumsy Afrikaner diamond driller, driven insane with the pain of a powder-head-ache, caused by the gelignite he'd sniffed in the course of his job, and attempting to drink himself into oblivion, and a young, fast and angry welterweight.

Peekay dwelt on the history which had brought the confrontation about: the tiny Afrikaans boarding school where, thirteen years earlier, a frightened five year old had been thrown in a backveld school system designed to foster a hate for the English. Here Botha, the fourteen year old who ruled the school and who was known as the Judge, had set about persecuting the defenceless English-speaking child.

The effect of the Judge's persecution never left Peekay and his hate had erupted on a hot afternoon a thousand miles from where it had begun. Peekay burned with mortification as he recalled his blinding anger, how he'd removed a razor-sharp pocket knife from his trousers and, straddling the unconscious Botha, had used the blade to cancel the crude swastika tattooed high up on his left arm. The retribution he'd etched with Botha's blood had been more than simple revenge; was he, too, infected with the same sick violence his childhood tormentor had shown towards him? How else could he explain the fight, this savage, appalling action?

For sixteen months Peekay had risked his life nightly blasting on a grizzly in the mines; now, as he was about to leave, like the fly banking to avoid the fan, he'd flown into the finger of God.

Peekay was tired. At eighteen he ached inside with a tiredness which stretched back to the boarding school when the Judge had tried to break his small spirit. He'd barely survived that year and in the process had learned how to camouflage himself, how to protect his fragile ego. He'd never again entirely emerged from the camouflage.

Some of us hide by being so utterly normal, a digit in a sea of equal numbers; others hide out in front. Peekay had turned his childhood trauma into a succession of conquests. Only he was aware that the gifted, confident child others perceived was inwardly fearful of the retribution which came from failure. He had determined never to be beaten again, either physically or mentally. When he fought the Judge he was fighting himself.

He rose slowly from his sweat-soaked bed. He glanced down at his rigid member. This! This is a part of it! The sex urge constantly overtook him and numbed his mind. He thought of the French and Belgian whores who came over from the Congo in a chartered DC 3 every three weeks to 'service' the miners. Peekay didn't want the first time to be with a whore, having to pay for it. But now, after yesterday, he wondered why. He wasn't really any different. When it all boiled down, the law degree he was planning to take at Oxford wasn't going to turn him into a civilised man; underneath he was a cruel, animal bastard like the rest of them.

Peekay had imposed a number of conditions on the method of his deflowering. These sexual aspirations had been brought about very largely as a consequence of having read the entire collection of Mickey Spillane detective stories which he'd inherited from the previous occupant of the hut. The neatly stacked paperbacks with their lurid dime-store covers were arranged along the ledge of the only window in the hut, almost as though the books had become a part of the window. Peekay's resolve to eschew the French whores and wait until the real thing came along had been confirmed when he read how Mike Hammer, Spillane's detective hero, had seduced a beautiful and sexy heiress. He'd read that Hammer slipped his rough hands, more accustomed to fondling the butt of a snub-nosed forty-five, through the pink ribbon straps of her night lingerie, peeling them slowly over her perfect shoulders. Then he took her into his arms. Her skin was as smooth as whipped cream on a satin bedspread.

It was the final sentence which had set Peekay's blood racing. He resolved to keep his virginity intact until life delivered him just such a whipped-cream experience. For he'd convinced himself that if he could achieve a single act of perfect lovemaking, all his carnal desire would melt away and manhood would click into place like a well-oiled rifle bolt.

At eighteen Peekay was Amateur Lightweight Boxing Champion of South Africa, undefeated in one hundred and sixteen fights. He'd set his sights on becoming professional Welterweight Champion of the world.

As if this wasn't enough, he wanted more. He had brains to spare, more than he could possibly need to be a world champ, which he correctly saw as something you became and, in a matter of two or three years, were no longer. For his *real* future he had decided to read law at Oxford.

Peekay was aware these two ambitions were somewhat incompatible. But for almost as long as he could remember he'd been two people, or put more precisely, the same person who was thought about quite differently by two sets of people. There were those who talked about his being a future world champion and who had never heard of Oxford; and those who knew him as a brain, a small-town kid, the son of a widowed dressmaker, who had made them proud by winning a scholarship to a private school for the sons of the rich and who now had a place at Oxford University.

Somehow Peekay had managed to keep both groups in his life happy. He was highly ingenuous and people took to him easily, often taking strength from him as well as becoming loyal either to the boxer or to the brain, one or the other aspect of his personal disguise.

Only Hymie Levy, Peekay's beloved friend, believed with him that both ambitions were possible and not contradictory.

Peekay had met Hymie on their first day at boarding school and they'd remained friends. Hymie was the son of a Jew who had fled Poland just prior to Hitler's invasion and who had become a millionaire carpet manufacturer and retailer. Despite being born rich, Hymie was street smart, a loner who was naturally cautious and usually two steps ahead of most people in the thinking department. Where Peekay reached out, Hymie pulled back. Where Peekay accepted, Hymie questioned. Where Peekay trusted, Hymie was suspicious. Peekay's defence system, born out of his early boarding-school experience, made him a quiet sort of person. Hymie adopted loudness as his defence. The poor boy and the rich, the Jew and the Gentile. Together they made a formidable combination.

Parted for the year and a half Peekay had been in the mines, the bond between them was, if anything, stronger. They thought of themselves as a duo and even, in the long term, inseparable. They would both graduate in law; Hymie would manage Peekay to a world championship fight, and eventually they would practise together in Johannesburg. While Peekay had been earning money in the copper mines to pay his own way through university, Hymie had already started at Oxford.

Peekay walked over to the small paraffin fridge which stood directly under the window. He withdrew two small metal trays of ice each marked with a band-aid and sandwiched his erection between them. The shock of the ice cold contact made him jump but it worked every time and after only a few moments he returned the ice trays to the fridge. Then he pulled on a slightly sweaty jockstrap and a pair of boxing shorts and stepped up to the speedball which hung from a central rafter just below the fan.

He began to work the beautiful tear-shaped leather

ball, ignoring the pain from his swollen hands. The beautiful drumming rat-tat-tat-tat of his fists on the leather ball soon calmed his mind; although he hadn't fought for nearly eighteen months, he knew he hadn't lost any speed. His body was harder than it had ever been and his mind, after working a grizzly, was a good deal tougher. A couple of months sparring with good partners and his timing would be right on the button. He'd be ready for his first fight in England.

After twenty minutes at the speedball Peekay's entire body was a lather of sweat. But he felt good, clean. He couldn't undo yesterday. He'd go over to the cottage hospital and see Botha. Explain to him. Apologise. It probably wouldn't help but he'd do it anyway. The Boer bastard would be surprised, think Peekay was going soft; what had happened to him in the fight was fair in the violent kind of world they both shared.

He walked over to the door and took a towel from a hook. Slipping off his boxing shorts and jockstrap, he wrapped the threadbare towel around his waist and left the hut to walk over to the shower block. Tonight was his last shift underground. After tonight, the next time he went underground would be in a London tube. For some days Peekay had been trying to keep down his excitement, but now it rose in him, tingled inside of him ignoring his attempt to push it away. He did a spontaneous little dance in the dust.

Hymie met Peekay at Southampton where the Union Castle liner docked. They looked an odd combination; the blue-eyed Peekay in a cheap suit, carrying a battered suitcase, his body tanned and hard, his crew-cut just beginning to grow out; and Hymie, dark-eyed, pudgy and pale-faced, in corduroys, duffel coat and college scarf, his dark hair worn just short of a mane. They climbed into Hymie's little tan Ford Prefect and set off for Oxford.

Peekay, who had expected to find a bleak, cold England, was not prepared for the sublime shock of a perfect late September day. The idea of four distinct seasons had always fascinated him; it was tidy, clean and precise, the habits of an old and fastidious land. Now, in this quiet coming to the end of summer, there was a kind of purity which Africa could never possess, like the organ notes in a Bach cantata. Here no dust-devils danced across the cracked red earth, mocking the day-after-day thunder of Mojaji's drums as they attempted to beat the spring rains from a brazen, remorseless African sky. In this brassed and yellow autumn afternoon, England was more than Peekay had ever imagined.

Three

Tandia arrived back at the Booth Street house before Mrs Patel had risen. She moved painfully over to the yard tap and washed the red cemetery clay from her feet and legs. Then she filled a four-gallon paraffin tin bucket and carried it into the shed where she poured the cold water into a large white enamel basin. She undressed slowly, pulling the cotton shift carefully over her bruised body. With a cloth she rinsed in the bucket she wiped as much of the blood away as she could see before she squatted in the basin to bathe. The skin around her wrists had been rubbed away and in some places the handcuffs had cut deeply into the flesh so that each time she put her hands into the basin the water around her wrists stained pink. The cruel welts made by the policeman's belt still burned her buttocks and when she wiped tenderly over them there was blood on the cloth, although whether from the welts or from the other place she couldn't be certain.

Up to this moment Tandia's life had been a dichotomy, a two-person affair. She would return home from school and take off her white blouse and gym frock, her short white socks and shiny black shoes, and change into a servant's cotton shift and blue beret. Then she'd wash and hang out her school uniform to dry; later, before she went to bed, she would starch and iron it when she did Patel's shirts. This personal task completed, she would change from a bright little Indian schoolgirl into the Patels' black servant. It was an emotional journey Tandia made every day of her life and one which she walked with a terrible loneliness.

As a child she had cried the loneliness out of her system as she lay in the dark on a coir mattress in the hot shed. She could remember thinking that even the rats that scurried across the corrugated-iron roof above her head had mothers and fathers. She only had Patel whom she was allowed to call Patel, and not 'baas', like a kaffir, but not daddy either, like a proper daughter.

Her bath completed, Tandia wrapped her towel around her torso and dragged the basin which was almost two feet in diameter to the doorway, tipping its contents into the dusty back yard. The water splashed, runneled and rushed for a few feet before being sucked into the dry earth. Moments later only a damp stain showed where it had been, and that too would soon disappear, baked dry in the hot mid-October sun.

Tandia returned the basin to its place under her iron cot, and she applied a damp cloth to her swollen eyes and mouth. Then she dressed slowly, not only because of the pain but also because she sensed that the ritual of changing from servant to schoolgirl, a moment which every school morning of her life she had cherished, might be coming to an end. Her blouse crackled with the starch, just the way Patel's shirts did, and the freshly washed and ironed gym frock fell neatly on her trim body. Her back hurt as she bent down to put on her white socks and tie the laces of her brightly polished shoes. She would say nothing of her early-morning graveside visit to say goodbye to Patel. If she told the old woman anything it would only give her yet another reason to throw her onto the street. 'Please God, let her tell me I can stay,' Tandia prayed. 'I'll do anything, anything she says. Just let me stay and finish school next year.'

Just as she did every day Tandia crossed the yard and climbed the steps onto the stoep and entered the kitchen to make breakfast. The old woman was sitting at the kitchen table shelling peas. She was wearing her deep purple sari, always a bad sign; purple was a colour that made Mrs Patel very cranky. Shelling peas was Tandia's work and her heart sank.

'Good morning Mrs Patel,' she said brightly as she reached behind the door for the apron she wore to protect her school uniform. Then she crossed the kitchen, tying the apron as she walked toward the stove to fetch the kettle for morning chat.

'Where you think you going, hey?' Mrs Patel did not look up as she spoke so she didn't see Tandia replace the kettle and, turning from the stove, lower her head and clasp her hands in fear. Nor did she wait for Tandia's reply. She had rehearsed her speech a dozen times and she wanted it to come out just the way she had thought it. 'You think we got money for school now that Mr Patel is dead, you think that?'

She looked up for the first time, her eyes shining with malice. 'You mad, you hear! You nothing but a stinking kaffir. Go! Get out of my house. You got one hour, then you out. Get out of that school uniform, it's mine now, you hear?' She paused, sucking air through her gold teeth. 'You a dirty kaffir going to an Indian school. You who is not even a Hindu!' Her body juddered at the ecstasy of the moment for which she had waited so long. 'What do you think the mothers of the Indian girls think of me, hey? "That Mrs Patel from Booth Street,"' she mimicked, '"she sends her husband's kaffir bastard to a good Indian school!"' She paused to catch her breath. 'I waited a long time, now it's my turn!' Rising from the kitchen chair she pointed to the kitchen door. 'Get out of my house, kaffir!' Lifting the white enamel colander from the table she hurled it at Tandia. The colander hit Tandia's shoulder and fell to the cement floor, clattering amongst the bouncing, scattering, gleefully escaping peas.

Tandia looked up at the old woman. The blow from the dish hadn't hurt her, but somehow its impact had strengthened her nerve, so that she now stood her ground. Yesterday she would have fled in tears. But a lot had happened since yesterday. She had grown up and learned the true meaning of hate. Not the soulful badly-done-by kind of hate she had nursed in childhood nor the deep resentment she felt for the old lady, but a new kind which burned inside her guts so fiercely it felt as though it was stripping away the lining of her stomach. She had also learned the power of a naked threat. The power contained in the voice of a policeman called Geldenhuis when he said, 'You report this and you dead meat!'

Tandia looked up at the old woman, with the new hate and the power she now borrowed from the memory of the policeman's voice. Her voice was even and she spoke slowly. 'One day I am going to get even, I don't care how long it takes.' She paused. 'For my mother and for me also. I swear it on my mother's grave!' She pointed at Mrs Patel. 'You better pray to Arthie Paraschatie to protect you, because one day, sure as God, I'm coming back to get you!'

At the mention of Arthie Paraschatie, the Hindu Mother of God, Mrs Patel drew back. 'My sons will beat you, you hear! Do not come back to this house. You stay away, or I call the police!'

Tandia picked up the colander and, taking it by the handles she placed it upside down over the old lady's head and patted it twice. 'Goodbye, you old witch! Good riddance to bad rubbish!' Whereupon she turned and walked from the kitchen.

No sooner had she got to the back yard than her newly gained courage collapsed. She thought of rushing back to ask forgiveness from the old woman, beg a little time, a few days to get a pass and find somewhere she could live. But she knew it was useless; even this would be denied her by the triumphant old bitch. She wiped her tears and entered the shed and pulled the large enamel basin out from under the cot.

Tandia knew enough to realise that her life, despite Mrs Patel, despite the loneliness, had been a fortunate one by the standards of a great many Indian and coloured families and almost all the urban black ones. Natkin Patel had been, by Durban Indian standards, a wealthy man and he had used his wealth and position to give her a chance in life.

She had expected Mrs Patel to send her packing and after Patel's funeral she'd worked out a plan. She had five pounds exactly, an amount that had taken her nearly ten years to save. She would take the bus to Clairwood; blacks as well as Indians lived there. At Clairwood or perhaps Jacobs, she would find a nice clean black family with whom she could board. Her five pounds would buy her food and board for six weeks and leave enough over for train fares so she could go in to town to look for a job. She would be sure to find a job of some sort in that time. She could clean, cook – Indian food anyway – wash and iron and work a sewing machine, so she could work as a housemaid or she might even get a job as a junior clerk or a sales assistant in an Indian shop in Victoria Street. She spoke both Tamil and Hindi as well as Zulu and, of course, Afrikaans and English, so that should help a lot. Before she had fallen asleep the night before, Tandia had decided that she wasn't entirely helpless and that when she got settled she'd complete her matriculation at night school or by correspondence school.

But now, back in the tin shed, a terrible fear struck her and Tandia started to cry again. She had used the last scrap of her courage in the kitchen with the old lady; she had no more left as she began to pack her things into the basin. Her stomach churned and she realised she hadn't eaten since lunch the previous day when the old lady had locked the house up to go to the funeral and removed the key from its usual hiding place under a loose brick in the back wall. Tandia packed her school books first, then leaving one cotton shirt on the bed she rolled the other two up and placed them in the basin. Mrs Patel hadn't said anything about shoes so, technically, she was entitled to take them. She left them on but removed her blouse, gym frock and school beret and hung them together with her spare blouse on a wire hanger which she then hung on a nail protruding from one of the two wooden roof beams a foot above her head.

It didn't take long to pack away the fifteen years of her life. She had accumulated almost nothing of personal value other than a few trinkets, ribbons and bits and pieces which were all contained in a biscuit tin. The last thing she packed was a small kewpie doll someone had given Patel for her when she was a small child. The paintwork on its face had almost totally rubbed off and only a suggestion remained of the doll's large, wide-open painted blue eyes and red bow lips. She'd named the doll Apple Sammy, although she'd long since forgotten why she'd given it a boy's name or even such a silly one. The worn but much loved little doll had rested on her bed for as long as she could remember and now she hugged it briefly, wrapped it carefully in the third cotton shift and put it into the basin. She now set the basin into the centre of a square of cheesecloth and, in the African style, drew the corners over the top and knotted them.

Tandia, an African of very recent persuasion, did not know how to hoist the basin onto her head and walk away, straight-backed and proud with her hips and arms swinging free. She managed to carry the basin out of the shed into the yard where she set it down. It was much too heavy to continue to carry in her arms, and she quickly decided she would have to fashion a head cloth and rest the basin on it, keeping it steady by holding on to either side.

Tandia returned to the shed to fetch the blue servant's beret for this purpose. As she entered she was struck by the sight of her gym frock and blouse and her school beret hanging from the hook. Through her teary eyes it looked as though she herself was hanging from the nail. The shock she felt caused her hiccups to stop and a surge of anger overcame her. She reached out and lifted the kerosene lamp from the shelf above her iron bed and, removing the fluted glass from the kerosene bowl, she unscrewed the wick and sprinkled methylated spirits over her school uniform. The duality of her life was over.

Tandia carried the paraffin-soaked gym frock, blouse and school beret out into the yard and hung them from the clothes line. Lighting the end of the paraffin-soaked wick from the lamp, she set her school uniform alight. She waited long enough to make sure the flame from the wick had caught; then, on a sudden impulse, she retrieved her school beret and replaced it on the burning hanger with her blue servant's one. Quickly she pulled the paraffin-splashed beret over her hair. Then crouching down on her haunches with her back held straight she carefully lifted the basin onto her head and rising slowly to a standing position walked out of the back gate without looking back.

Tandia had only gone a few yards down the alley when she heard the old woman screaming blue murder. 'Fire! Fire! My house is on fire! Come quick, she's burning down my house! Somebody, come quick!'

'See ya later alligator!' Tandia shouted back to her. She knew the washing line was well away from anything and that there was no possible chance of the house or anything else other than her past life catching alight, and for a moment she enjoyed the old woman's distress. But suddenly that petty victory tasted bitter in her mouth and she knew she had made a devastating mistake.

The bus stop was no more than half a mile from Booth Street but it took Tandia almost fifteen minutes to approach it. The large enamel basin was balanced precariously on her head and her neck and back hurt but she was too concerned with getting it to the bus stop to let the pain intrude. A hundred yards from the deserted stop she saw the bus approaching. Tandia started to trot awkwardly towards it but soon realised that she would be unable to cover the distance in time. She stopped and freed one hand from the rim of the basin to signal the Indian driver to stop. Running late for school, she'd done the same thing a hundred times before and she recognised the driver as someone who had often stopped for her. But now he looked blankly back at the young black girl with a large basin on her head and the big Leyland bus roared past her in a cloud of dust.

Dismayed, Tandia turned suddenly in the direction of the departing bus and the basin slipped and toppled to the road. Her books and belongings broke through the cheesecloth covering and scattered across the roadway. A *bakkie* following closely behind the bus caught the biscuit tin with all her precious bits and pieces and squashed it flat under its rear tyre; another wheel caught two of her textbooks. The driver gave a short impatient honk on his horn and accelerated away.

Tandia was too spent for tears. She began to gather her things together. It seemed imposible to her that it was only just approaching nine o'clock in the morning. She was beyond thinking rationally, simply holding on to the single idea that she must take the bus to Clairwood and find somewhere to stay.

On her haunches on the side of the road, she placed the last of her books back into the now chipped and slightly misshapen basin. Cocooned in her misery, she wasn't aware of an approaching vehicle until she heard the sudden scrunch of its front tyres. She looked up as the van slowed beside her and its passenger door swung open. A pair of black boots landed on the road even before the *kwela-kwela* had come to a complete stop.

The policeman leaned down, and jerked Tandia sharply to her feet. Tandia cried out in pain as the black policeman gripped her lacerated wrists. 'What is your name?' he demanded. Tandia stared dumbly back at him, her mouth slightly open, unaware of the tears running down her face. The policeman must have felt a wetness in the palm of his right hand for he suddenly released his grip and looked down. The sight of the blood on his hand seemed to make him even more angry. With a look of contempt he reached out and wiped his hand on the front of her shift allowing it to come to rest between her small breasts. Whereupon he gave her a sharp, impatient push and swiped her across the top of her head, removing her beret which fell onto the roadway. 'What is your name, *umFazi*?'

The driver of the police van, a white officer, leaned across. 'Hey, you kaffir! Is your name Patel? Tandia Patel?'

Tandia, her fear and confusion showing, nodded dumbly. The police officer glanced at his wristwatch. 'You don't look like a kaffir, more like a coloured. How come you got the same name as the complainant, she said you was a black person.' He didn't wait for her reply. 'Anyway, whatever you are, you under arrest, you hear?' He jerked his head, indicating the black policeman. 'Arrest her, but make quick, it's already long past nine o'clock, we supposed to knock off an hour ago, now I got to write up a fokking charge sheet.'

For the second time that day Tandia felt a pair of cold handcuffs dose around her wrists. The black man now seemed oblivious to the condition of her wrists and snapped the handcuffs firmly shut. He appeared not to notice as Tandia winced from the pain. Pointing to the back of the van he gave her a sharp shove between her shoulder blades. Despite her terror Tandia could think only of her books.

'Bring my things, please,' she said in Zulu. The black policeman ignored her and hastily unlocked the padlock on the van door and swung the van doors open. He gave her a perfunctory push. Tandia, desperate for her books, resisted. 'My basin, you must bring my basin!' she begged. The black man pushed her harder this time and unable to grasp onto anything she fell over the tailgate.

'Get in before I hurt you!' he hissed. 'Can't you see the baas is in a hurry?' Then he turned to retrieve the battered basin.

'Fok! Make quick, jong!' the white officer shouted from the front of the van.

The policeman hurriedly slid the heavy basin into the back of the van and slammed the two doors shut. The police van had already started to move when she heard the clunk as the passenger door closed.

At first the interior of the van seemed completely dark and Tandia lay on the floor until her eyes adjusted. Then she crawled awkwardly on her elbows and knees towards the basin. Her knees hurt and she began to feel the loss of circulation in her hands because of the handcuffs. A narrow bench ran the length of each side of the van and Tandia used the one nearest to the basin to pull herself up onto her haunches; then she pushed her back against the bench so that she could maintain her balance as the van jolted and picked its way along the rutted township road. A sudden jerk of the van sent her sprawling. She regained her balance with difficulty and managed to pull herself up onto the bench where she was able to look directly down into the basin. The cover had been torn from her Latin primer and her algebra textbook was broken in half, but her other books seemed intact.

She looked to see if her brown school beret was in the basin but it wasn't. It had been left on the roadside together with the squashed biscuit tin. With her beret the last of Tandia's self-esteem was gone.

Tandia's arrest had happened so unexpectedly she hadn't really connected it to a cause. Now she realised that Mrs Patel must have called the police. The stupid, ignorant old woman had accused her of trying to burn the house down. Tandia began to sob. Her small, sweet, innocent revenge was going to send her to prison where no one would find her and she was certain to die.

As she sobbed she felt herself grow angry, stupidly angry at Natkin Patel for dropping dead without warning her. One minute he was there in all his shiny, clean self-importance, the next he was gone before she got her proper chance in life.

Tandia's ego was too fragile to carry her anger for Patel for long. Now her despair turned inwards onto herself. She had been stupid to burn her gym frock. Childishly stupid. She had allowed her emotions to show, had put them on display and they had been used against her. Through her despair came the tremulous conviction that she would never again allow her emotions to be the mistress of her actions.

By the time the police van drew up behind the Cato Manor police station Tandia had regained her composure somewhat. She waited in the back of the stationary van for what seemed like an age before she heard the bolt slide open and the double doors of the paddy wagon opened to reveal the black constable again.

Tandia was led into the charge room to find the police officer who had driven the van seated at a small table opposite which stood a smaller chair. It reminded Tandia of a classroom chair, a thought which somehow increased her anxiety. Resting on the table was a type-writer, patches of wear showing through its black paint.

The white policeman looked up from the report he appeared to be reading and followed Tandia with his eyes as the black man instructed her to stand beside the chair. Then he removed her handcuffs and quickly left the room.

Tandia had never ached as much in her life and despite the intimidating chair and her sore bottom, she longed to sit down. The white officer dropped his gaze again and continued to read. She clasped her hands behind her back and surreptitiously attempted to rub the circulation back into them.

Finally the white officer glanced up at her and then back at the paper in his hand. 'Can you write your name?' he asked in Afrikaans.

'Ja, meneer,' Tandia replied. The policeman looked up in surprise. He had probably expected her to call him 'baas', or even to deny any knowledge of the *taal*.

He placed the document on the table facing Tandia, opened it and indicated a place at the bottom of the third page. Then he reached into the pocket of his khaki tunic and withdrew a blue Croxley fountain pen. 'Then sign,' he instructed, holding the pen out for Tandia. Tandia reached out to take the pen but the circulation had not yet fully returned to her hand and, unable to grasp it, she dropped it to the table. A momentary flash of anger showed in the white man's eyes but he quickly concealed it and gave a sigh of impatience. 'No funny buggers, you hear? Jus' sign the charge sheet.'

Tandia felt a lump in her throat as she tried to speak. Finally in a small, frightened voice she managed to ask, 'What does it say, meneer? Can I read it please?'

The police officer snatched the report from the table.

Pushing his chair back he began to fan himself with it. 'It's just an ordinary charge report, you sign it now, okay?' He kept his voice low as he half rose from the chair and leaned forward to place the report back on the table in front of her, but the threat in it was unmistakable.

Tandia swallowed hard, moving her tongue across the roof of her mouth to get her saliva working. 'Please, meneer, I must read it,' she said in a barely audible voice.

This time the policeman sprang from his chair and grabbing the report he thrust it at Tandia so that the paper was only inches from her face. 'What's that you saying, kaffir?' He pulled the paper back from her face and began to jab at it with his right index finger. 'We got all your paticklers here! You trying to be cheeky, hey? You charged with arson, you hear? You know what is arson? You tried to burn down the house of your employer! That's a very serious offence!'

His hand opened suddenly and he smacked Tandia hard across the face. The small chair toppled as she staggered backwards trying to maintain her balance. 'Don't fok with me, kaffir! You sign, jong, or you in the deep shit, you hear?'

He dropped the sheet of paper at her feet and lowered himself back onto his chair. 'Pick it up!' He pointed at the fallen chair. Sobbing Tandia righted the chair; she was still seeing stars from his blow. 'The paper also!' he shouted.

She felt faint and could barely see it on the floor. Her hands shook so violently she had to make several attempts to grip the edge of the charge sheet. She held it out to the policeman who snatched it from her and dropped it onto the table. Then he picked up the pen.

To Tandia's surprise he now spoke softly. 'C'mon, man, now sign. It's late, I want to go home, I'm already an hour and a half late, I want to go home and have my breakfast.'

Tandia burst into tears. The police officer leapt from his chair and struck her a violent blow on the side of her face, knocking her over and sending her sprawling across the polished cement floor.

Seemingly in an instant, he was at her side. 'Fok you, kaffir! Get up!' He bent down and grabbed her arm and pulled, but Tandia resisted and the white man released his grip on her bleeding wrist. 'Fok! Get up! I haven't got all day!' It was then that she noticed the dirt on his trousers, a soil mark just above his knees where she had kicked him in the cemetery. A moment later he drove his boot into her kidneys. Tandia screamed then gave a low moan and passed out.

She came to as she was being dragged by two black policemen along a long corridor. Tandia tasted blood and she tasted the hate and she kept her eyes tightly closed. They came to a halt and she was lowered to the floor. Her face still stung from the violent slap she had received and the polished cement floor was cool on her bruised cheek. She heard the slight rattle of keys and the sigh of a heavy door opening, then she was picked up again and lowered to the floor of the cell.

Long after she'd heard the clunk of the door closing and the rattle of the keys as she was locked in, Tandia continued to lie with her cheek pressed against the cool cement floor of the dark cell. She was like one of those stick insects that continues to play dead long after its attacker has lost interest in it. Eventually she opened her eyes, raised herself to a sitting position and looked around the small cell. It contained a bench which ran the length of one wall. A toilet bucket sat in one corner smelling sharply of disinfectant. On the floor beside the bucket lay a single scrap of newspaper. A light bulb, protected by a cover made of heavy wire mesh, was set into the ceiling at least twelve feet above her. The light was off and the only light coming into the cell was from a small barred window about ten feet from the floor. The effect was like being thrown into an empty well or a dark pit.

Tandia rose and sat on the bench. The fact that she was alone and the shouting had stopped was an enormous relief, but she was too numbed to think. She vaguely sensed that it was a useless pursuit anyway. The act of thinking suggests there are choices and she was beginning to realise that for a black person the choices are almost non-existent.

Tandia wondered briefly about the welfare of her basin, though now it seemed to represent a life which had been taken from her. The idea that she could educate herself in an environment where mere survival took all the energy she possessed suddenly seemed ridiculous. After the events of the past few hours Tandia was prepared to give up even before she got started.

After a while, when she had become accustomed to the dark cell, Tandia lay down on the bench and gazed up at the square of light coming through the window. Beyond it she could see a patch of blue sky and, just cutting into the frame, the white crescent of a day moon.

She must have dozed off for a while, for she was startled to hear the key in the door. It opened only slightly and she heard the scrape of a tin plate as it was pushed into the cell. Tandia waited until the key had been turned and removed from the lock before moving to the doorway. Two hunks of white bread and a tin mug of cold black tea rested on the plate. The bread was stale but not too bad when she washed it down with the bitter-tasting tea.

Having eaten for the first time since noon the previous day Tandia felt stronger. She looked up through the small window to find that the day moon had disappeared and the sky seemed a lighter blue. It was past noon, she thought. The bread and tea must have been lunch.

But Tandia was wrong. She had slept most of the day and it was now five in the evening. She was not to know that the meal she had just eaten was all she was entitled to receive over a twenty-four hour period. A district police station is not equipped with cooking facilities and besides, any policeman will tell you, a hungry kaffir is a more cooperative one.

The sleep had stiffened her and she became aware of just how badly she hurt. The pain seemed to have seeped into her bones and into her spirit and she felt utterly miserable. Now, having eaten, her bowels needed to work and she was forced to use the foul-smelling bucket in the corner. She used up the small square of newspaper, praying that she would not need to go again.

Hitching up her bloomers, she felt the small knotted square of cloth pinned inside them, which contained her money – the five one-pound notes which made up her lifetime savings. Tandia felt a sudden surge of hope: she would offer to pay for the gym frock, to compensate Mrs Patel. Then maybe they would just give her a beating and not send her to gaol. After what she had been through she could take the *sjambok*. In the end it would be a small price to pay for her freedom and she knew that rather than go to gaol, she would take any punishment, no matter how severe.

Hope is a flame that kindles new expectations by grasping at passing straws. The food and the sleep allowed Tandia to hope just a little. She had a chance if she could stay out of prison.

The blue framed square of light above her head began to darken and the cell was in almost total darkness before the lone ceiling light came on. The weak bulb made the cell no brighter than it had been during the day, but the absence of the comforting square of sky at the window made Tandia's new-found optimism soon collapse. Her bruised little body was hurting all over and no matter how she sat or lay she was in pain.

There was a sudden rattle at the door followed by the sound of a woman swearing in a mixture of Zulu and English. Then followed a sharp expletive from a male voice. The cell door swung open and a black woman was pushed in and the door closed behind her. The woman appeared not to have seen Tandia, imagining herself alone in the cell. She leaned with her back against the heavy door, swaying slightly, obviously drunk, her chin resting on her large breast. She wore a half-smile and her nose was bleeding slightly. She sniffed and then wiped her nose by running the top of her index finger past both nostrils, across the back of her hand and back again pulling the blood and mucus back into her nose. Then she examined the blood on her hand, brought her hand to her mouth and slowly, like a cat licking its fur, she licked the blood clean, starting at the tip of her index finger and working back across her hand.

The woman was perhaps in her mid twenties, broad-hipped and with a bottom that protruded enormously in the short, tight knitted skirt she wore. Tandia, who had grown accustomed to the dim light, could see her quite clearly. She had a broad, almost flat face and she wore bright red lipstick which gave her thick lips an added fleshiness so they looked like raw meat. The trickle of blood had reappeared at both nostrils and added to her carnivorous appearance. To Tandia, she looked as though she was getting ready to eat somebody.

The woman, bringing both her hands up to her mouth, suddenly retched. Half-stooped, she lurched over to the bucket in the corner and threw up. The sour smell of stomach-fermented kaffir beer filled the cell. The woman was sick three more times, the noise of her spitting and hawking filling the small cell. Finally she turned from the bucket and straightened up. She was panting from the effort of throwing up and her carnivorous lipstick was now smeared across her face. Steadying herself by placing her hand on the wall, she wiped her eyes with her free hand and looked about her. It was then that she saw a frightened Tandia hunched in the darkest corner of the cell.

'Shit! Who you?' She wasn't really asking a question and her flat gaze was not in the least curious. She withdrew her hand from the wall which caused her to lurch slightly forward. 'Don't fuck with me, you hear!' Her words seemed to upset her balance and she fell two steps backwards until her shoulders bumped into the wall, whereupon she gave a soft groan and slid slowly to the floor beside the bucket, one fat arm coming to rest inside it. In moments she began to snore. The tight skirt had ridden up her thighs and Tandia now saw that she wore nothing underneath.

Tandia didn't know what to do. She sat in the dark

corner, one arm drawing her legs up against her chest, the fist of her free hand in her mouth in an attempt to hold back the panic she felt rising within her. After a while her breathing calmed a little. What should she do? If she took the woman's arm out of the shit bucket she was fearful that she might wake and beat her up. Her sense of survival told her to leave things as they were and her sensibilities, already deeply offended, told her that she could not do so, that the mess in the bucket was in part her doing.

Tandia waited until she was sure the woman was not likely to wake from her drunken sleep and crept over to the bucket. The woman's hand rested on the bottom, covered in shit and vomit. Gagging as she lifted the arm out of the mess, she rested it on the floor beside her and carefully removed the *doek* the woman wore tied around her head. Using the head cloth she wiped the foul-smelling hand and arm clean. Tandia's heart leapt with fear as the woman gave a sudden groan, sighed deeply and, lifting her arm, dropped it back in the bucket. Tandia pulled back in horror; the stench was overpowering. She began to cry softly.

After a while she dried her tears. She was crying too much. Crying was an indulgence she would have to learn to do without. She now realised that the woman had passed out and was unlikely to be roused, so she moved over to her again. Once again she removed the woman's hand from the slop bucket and wiped it as clean as she was able, using the now soiled doek. Then she dragged the unconscious woman clear so that she lay on her side with her lipstick smeared cheek against the cement floor. This seemed to stop her snoring.

Several hours seemed to pass in the stinking cell and Tandia, when she felt she could bear it no longer, would concentrate on the tiny window until she could make out the pinprick of stars in the tiny square of darkness. She imagined how fresh and clean it was out there with the stars, how some of the air from the space surrounding them was finding its way into her miserable cell. She was not sleepy and her body ached in even more places when she lay down. Besides, the idea that the woman might wake while she was asleep made her fearful of closing her eyes even as she sat. She conjugated the verb 'lacrimare', 'to cry', in imperfect, future, future perfect and past perfect. Patel had always stressed that she must be good at Latin; he dreamed that she would go on to become a lawyer. She went on to irregular verbs with funny endings and then recited her personal and relative pronouns. 'Qui, quae, quo, quod,' she whispered to herself. It was strangely comforting to be using her mind and she challenged herself to remember Book Four of Virgil's *Aeneid*, especially the part where Aeneas enters the underworld and finds himself in the Elysian Fields. That was her set text in the end-of-year Latin exam, which she would now never take.

It must have been quite late when Tandia heard the rattle of the key in the door of the cell. A black constable appeared and without even glancing at the sleeping woman beckoned Tandia to come out of the cell. He was a much older man than the policeman who had arrested her earlier in the day. 'Down there, but wait first.' He spoke quietly and locked the cell door as Tandia waited for him. The light in the corridor was much brighter than in the cell and she held her wrists out to him for the handcuffs. He looked at her swollen and cut wrists and then up at her face. The expression in his eyes was not unkind and he shook his head once and clicked his tongue in sympathy. Then he pointed down the corridor and nodded for her to start walking. 'Go to the end of the passage, the last door on the left.'

Tandia's rubber-soled school shoes made almost no sound on the cement, but when the policeman turned to follow her the metal tips on the heel and toe caps of his boots sent a clicking metallic sound racing down ahead of her to the end of the passageway.

Tandia turned at the last door on the left and found herself back in the charge room. She hesitated at the door and waited for the black constable to catch up. Seated on the table, with his legs swinging over the side, was a white policeman she had not seen before. She felt enormous relief that it wasn't the same police officer who had so intimidated her when she had been brought in.

The man seated on the table didn't look up. But, aware that she stood at the door, he pointed to the larger of the two chairs, the one which had been previously used by the other policeman. The white officer sat on the end of the table and Tandia was brought to the chair by the black constable. 'Sit.' He indicated the chair beside her.

'Ja, sit, please,' the white officer added quietly. Tandia, as though afraid to make the slightest sound, lowered herself slowly into the same chair used by her white tormentor of the morning. She noted that the seated police officer held the charge sheet in his right hand and that the typewriter still stood at the opposite end of the table from where he sat. Apart from the three words, the white police officer remained silent, swinging his legs and blowing a tuneless whistle. Not as much a whistle as the controlled breathiness a person affects when they appear lost in their own thoughts. Tandia grew more and more apprehensive as she waited. The black constable had taken up a position at the door with his legs apart and his hands clasped behind his back. He seemed relaxed and uninterested, his eyes turned downwards.

After a while Tandia, who had kept her eyes downcast, ventured a glance at the white man seated on the table. He was small for a policeman. She was used to thinking of size in the boxing parlance used by Natkin Patel, and she judged him to be a welterweight. Tandia was used to the policemen around Cato Manor where white police sergeants were generally much older men. This one wore a crew cut with a clipped, blond moustache and seemed to be in his early twenties. His nose had been broken more than once which gave his boyish face a slightly romantic appearance. He looked clean and tough sitting there looking down at the floor. He turned suddenly and looked at her and before she dropped her gaze she saw his eyes. They were very pale blue, like a favourite blue cotton shirt that has been washed a thousand times. His eyes didn't look tough at all and Tandia's heart skipped a beat. Perhaps it wasn't going to be like the other one.

'You see this?' he said, lifting what looked like the charge sheet Tandia had refused to sign earlier. Tandia nodded, afraid to speak. Then he brought his free hand up and tore the sheet of paper in two. At the sound of the paper tearing, Tandia looked up in surprise. He placed the two pieces together and tore them down the centre once again. Then he dropped the pieces on the floor under his feet. 'You Patel's daughter, aren't you?' He didn't wait for her confirmation before continuing. 'He was a good guy. A bladdy good ref, even a good coach.' He paused, thinking for a moment, 'Ja, I can say it for sure, when it came to boxing, he really knew his onions.' He glanced up at Tandia, the beginnings of a smile on his face, 'You his daughter, hey. Maybe he was a Indian, but sometimes you've got to make exceptions, Patel was a good guy.' He paused, 'Ja, he was definitely a good guy.' Unlike the previous police officer he spoke in English, though it was at once obvious he was an Afrikaner. He glanced up at Tandia quickly and then back at the floor. 'Ag jong, I suppose you people also got feelings, I'm sorry about his death, you hear?' Then he added again, 'He was a okay guy.'

Tandia sat looking down at her hands. 'Please, sir, I will pay back the money for the gym frock, I have enough money!' She was surprised at her own audacity.

The policeman's pale blue eyes seemed to stare at something beyond her, as though he saw things in the air behind her back. 'Ag, that!' He pointed to the scraps of paper on the floor. 'That's all finish and *klaar*.'

Tandia's green eyes were questioning and she was very close to tears. Before she could speak he shrugged and then added, 'It's the least we can do. Boxing's like that, sometimes there's no colour bar. In boxing Patel was a real white man.'

'Thank you, sir,' Tandia said quietly, and then added, 'Am I free to go now?'

The policeman seemed not to hear and turned his torso slightly to face her. He wore a boyish grin as he spoke. 'Lucky you didn't sign the charge sheet this morning hey? Once you sign, there's no turning back, proceedings have to happen, you got to go in front of the magistrate.' He glanced abruptly at his watch and then turned and looked towards the door and nodded. 'You go out there now, I'm telling you, jong, you'll be back here quick smart. It's nearly twelve o'clock in the night and you haven't got a pass.' He grinned. 'A police patrol would pick you up in no time flat. Better you stay here tonight hey?'

Tandia looked up at him fearfully, her heart beating wildly. 'Please, sir, do not take me back to that cell, there is a woman there!'

The white sergeant fumed and looked enquiringly at the black constable at the door. 'A shebeen prostitute, she is drunk, sir,' the black man answered.

The sergeant turned back to Tandia. 'Ja, I know what you mean.' He looked up at Tandia suddenly. 'This gym frock, the one you burned. What school was that?'

'Durban Indian Girls' High School, sir,' Tandia replied. She looked up at the policeman, 'I will pay for it, for everything.'

The white policeman gave a low whistle as though he was impressed. 'Ja, I already heard of that school. That's the one down at Brighton le Sands.' He paused. 'I'm not from Durban myself you understand.' He said this as though to indicate that he was superior to the local police product. 'I come from Jo'burg, they don't have such a thing as a Indian private school in Johannesburg. There are not so many rich Indians there, because, you see, we got the Jews.' He gave a short, bitter snort. 'The Jews are even better at rooking the public than the coolies.'

'Yes, sir,' Tandia said softly.

'An' now you not going there no more, hey?'

'No, sir.'

'At this school, do the girls talk about . . . you know, sex?'

Tandia looked up, shocked. 'No, sir! Never, sir! On my word of honour!' She was aware of her sudden outburst and lowered her voice. 'It is forbidden, sir.'

The police officer's eyes resumed their faraway look,

but his voice was suddenly hard. 'Has a man ever done it to you?'

The shock of the question caused Tandia to gasp. She could feel the panic beginning to suffocate her and she was breathing hard, her face deeply blushed.

The black policeman's voice speaking in Zulu came suddenly from the direction of the door. 'You do not have to answer that, umFazi. Do not answer him, it is better you start to cry.'

The white policeman turned furiously to the door. His look was met by the impassive face of the black constable. 'Hey, jong, what did you say to her?'

The black policeman looked directly back at the white man. 'I said she must be quick and answer the questions, sir.'

Tandia began to sob. Quiet little sobs which shook her shoulders and could barely be heard. 'Listen, you black bastard, when I want you to speak, I'll ask, you hear?' the white officer snapped.

The black policeman pulled himself to attention, 'Yes, sir!' he replied in an automatic way. His eyes held steady as he met the white sergeant's angry glare.

The white policeman turned away. 'Cheeky bladdy kaffir,' he said as though to himself. Then he called, 'Okay, take her back to the cell. I can't interrogate a subject who is crying.' He jumped from the table and started towards the door.

Tandia rose from her chair quickly, 'Please, sir. You said I was free, sir!' she cried, beginning to follow after him across the room.

The white policeman whirled around to face her. 'Who said that?' he cried angrily. He turned back to the constable at the door. 'Did I say that?' He turned again, pointing an accusing finger at Tandia. 'Did I say this black person was free?' Tandia was unable to meet his gaze and lowered her eyes. 'You won't answer my questions. That is not cooperating with the police. Now, all of a sudden you want to go free. I am a police officer and I am asking you questions in the course of my duty. You refuse to answer!' His pale blue eyes were flecked with cold, bright anger and a small muscle in the left side of his cheek jerked suddenly.

'No, sir, I have not done this thing. I am a good girl, sir,' Tandia burst out.

'You are lying!' The white man shouted, pointing to the smaller of the two chairs. 'Sit there!'

Tandia sat down and covered her face with her hands, trying hard to stifle her sobbing.

The black constable took a step towards her. 'I will take her back to the cell now, sergeant?'

'I thought I told you to mind your own bladdy business, constable? You speak again, you on report, you hear?' He turned to Tandia. 'I haven't got all night to waste. I asked you nicely, now I'm going to ask you one more time. Have you had sexual intercourse with a man?'

Tandia pulled her hands away from her face. 'I was raped! This morning I was raped!' she sobbed.

The white officer allowed Tandia to cry for a few moments. He walked back to the table and lifted himself back onto it. This time he sat directly in front of her. Tandia's eyes were level with the table top, so now when she raised them she looked directly into the white man's crotch. Seated like this, his presence was hugely threatening; his legs swung casually, one on either side of the small chair, seeming to trap her between them.

Tandia tried to sniff away her tears and suddenly

started to hiccup. The white police officer called over to the constable, 'Hey, Matembu. That's your name, isn't it? Bring some water, make quick!'

The black policeman left the room and returned shortly with a tin mug of water. The sergeant took it from him and held the mug out to Tandia. 'Here, take it, drink, you'll feel better.' His voice was conciliatory. She took the mug from him and holding her nose she drank deeply until the mug was empty. In order to avoid his crotch and look into his face she was forced to pull her head back.

'Thank you, sir,' she said in a voice barely above a whisper. She put the mug down beside her chair.

'It works with me like that also, funny, isn't it?' the police officer said in a friendly voice.

Tandia nodded dumbly, then she sniffed and knuckled her tears away. Her nose was running and she didn't know what to do about it. The white policeman turned to the constable once again. 'Go in the lavatory, bring some paper.'

The black policeman returned and placed a roll of lavatory paper on the end of the table. 'Take it,' the white policeman said, 'blow your nose.'

Tandia was obliged to rise from the small chair and reach past the white officer to get the roll. As she did so his legs closed around her thighs just for a moment then he released her again. It was a crude, intimate gesture yet so quick that she wondered for a second whether it had happened at all. Her heart beat wildly as she sat back in the small chair. Eyes lowered, she unwound a length of toilet paper, tore it off the roll and proceeded to wipe her nose and then blow it hard. The paper was hard and unyielding, not suitable for the task she was using it for. Having cleared her nose somewhat

Tandia was forced to hold the sticky mess in her closed hand.

The police sergeant leaned backwards on his hands opening his crotch even further. 'Did you report this rape to the police?' he asked.

'No, sir,' Tandia replied softly.

'And where did this rape take place, and what time also?'

Tandia spoke in small sobs. 'This morning. About six o'clock. At the Indian cemetery. Where, where ... they buried Mr Patel!'

'The person who you said raped you. Can you describe this man to me?'

'There were two of them, but I did not see them,' Tandia sniffed.

The sergeant raised his eyebrows, his voice affecting surprise. 'Now all of a sudden it's two men, hey! Two men raped you, but you didn't see them? How can this be? It is already light by six o'clock?'

'From behind, they grabbed me from behind. Only one raped me.' Tandia shuddered involuntarily.

The sergeant leaned forward and folded his arms across his chest, rocking slightly. 'This is a very curious business. They raped you in broad daylight, or one of them did anyway, and you didn't see them?'

'He told me to shut my eyes. Also the other one said if I opened my eyes he would kill me. I was very afraid!' How could she tell him that they had been policemen? He wouldn't believe her and any chance she had of getting off would be destroyed forever.

'And you didn't report this to the police?'

'No, no sir.'

'Why not? Don't you know it is against the law not to report a crime?'

'I was too afraid, sir,' Tandia replied softly.

'Afraid? All of a sudden you're afraid of the police? Innocent people got no reason to be afraid of the police. You prefer a rapist to a member of the Sou' African police force?'

'No, sir. I was very frightened, sir. I didn't know what to do, I didn't want to make any more trouble!'

'Oh, I see, you were already in trouble. What trouble is this? Tell me. What sort of trouble were you already in?'

'About Patel. Mrs Patel was going to kick me out.' Tandia whimpered, looking up and appealing to him with her eyes. 'She hates me.'

There was a long pause as the policeman appeared to be thinking. When at length he spoke there was a hard edge to his voice. 'I think you lying, you hear? You lying to me, jong.'

Tandia looked up in alarm. 'No, sir! It is true! I will swear on the Bible!'

The white man had the distant look in his eyes again, as though he could read things dancing in the air. When at last he spoke his voice was quiet. 'You a whore. A black whore who does it for money in the cemetery. Sies, man. Did you do it in the cemetery next to the grave where your father was buried?'

'No, no!' Tandia cried. And then she froze and her eyes widened in alarm. It had taken all this time to sink in. The voice, the frightening voice after the boot had rested on her neck as she lay at the foot of the marble cross, it belonged to the one in the graveyard who had been called Geldenhuis. It was Geldenhuis who was questioning her.

Tandia knew she was utterly and devastatingly beaten, that if she admitted she knew him she wouldn't leave the police station alive.

Geldenhuis changed tack suddenly. 'This money, you said you had to pay for a new gym frock? Where did you get this money?'

'It was mine, sir. I saved it for ten years.'

His voice suddenly boomed above her. 'You got this money from being a prostitute! You went to the coolie cemetery before school, most likely lots of times, and you did it there! You think I am stupid or something?'

'No, sir. It's not true, sir.'

'What is true and what is not true is not for you or me to say, it is only for the magistrate to decide. Where is this five pounds?' he said suddenly.

'I have it here,' Tandia whimpered.

The policeman stretched out his hand, 'Give it here,' he demanded.

Tandia knew she was badly trapped. 'I cannot show it to you, sir,' she whispered.

'You have this money concealed on your person, but you cannot produce it? Let me ask you a question. If you went to the lavatory, could you produce it then?'

Tandia said nothing.

'I see, the police know about these things. It is called a body search. Do you know who keeps their money in such a place?'

Again Tandia remained silent.

'Whores! That is the place prostitutes keep their money!'

'It is not what you think!' Tandia blurted out. She was distressed beyond tears. Geldenhuis had completely broken through her defences. If she took the money out of her bloomers right there in front of him, it would prove very little except that she was brazen enough to lift her skirt and put her hand down her pants. In his eyes this would only condemn her further.

Tandia turned to look towards the black constable, but he immediately averted his eyes. She was beyond his help.

Geldenhuis lowered himself from the table and walked round to sit on the chair opposite her and called for the black constable to place the typewriter in front of him.

From a drawer in the table he removed a charge sheet and rolled it into the typewriter. He typed 'PATEL, Tandia', deliberately, using only two fingers, stopping when he had completed the two words. He then looked up casually at Tandia. 'Your address, what is your address?' he demanded.

'I have no address, sir,' Tandia replied.

'Vagrant,' the sergeant said, typing out the word slowly using only one finger to select each letter. 'No fixed address,' he said again deliberately pecking out the words on the typewriter. Then he looked up, leaned forward and placed his elbows on the table. 'Do you know what I'm doing?' he asked.

As he typed Tandia had torn off a length of toilet paper and blown her nose and attempted to wipe her tears. Her eyes were red-rimmed and swollen and her pretty little face was bruised and sore. She nodded her head in reply to Geldenhuis.

'I'm charging you with a one seven five, soliciting in a public place.' He shook his head as though regretting the need for what he was doing. 'It's so easy, you know. All you got to do is tell me the truth and you can go.' He cleared his throat, 'Look at me please,' he instructed. Tandia looked up at Geldenhuis across the table. He smiled and spread his hands and turned his palms upwards. 'Just tell me you did it in the cemetery and got paid for it, that's all. I'm a man of my word, just say, "Yes. Yes I did it, sergeant," and we won't lay a charge, you hear. You can leave the station with no police record. You know what it means to have a police record, don't you?'

Tandia's hands were on her lap curled around several messy scrunched balls of toilet paper and now she fixed her eyes on her clenched fists and remained silent. If she told a lie and said she was a whore, she was free, her life could begin again. If she maintained her innocence who was going to believe her? Who would believe that over ten years she had saved every penny, tickey and sixpence she had earned at Patel's printing shop, for getting the lunches for the men or running an errand or writing a letter for someone who couldn't write until she had five pounds of her own? If she admitted the truth, that it was two policeman who had raped her and that Geldenhuis was one of them she would not be alive for long, that was for sure. She was conscious of the white man looking down at her, fixing her with his pale eyes, eyes which she now perceived as more deadly than a snake. Tandia raised her head slowly until she looked directly at Geldenhuis. 'I will say it,' she said, and began to weep softly.

'No, man, saying it is not enough. I will write it down and then you will sign it, you hear?' Geldenhuis tried hard to conceal the triumph in his voice. He had broken her. He felt his erection grow almost to the point of release. Maybe she was only a schoolgirl but she wasn't stupid. What he had done required skill, real brains. He had won. It was better even than boxing.

Tandia knew she was hopelessly trapped. The last time she had refused to sign she had been hit and kicked unconscious and thrown into that foul-smelling cell. The thought of what Geldenhuis would do to her if she withheld her signature was almost more than she could bear.

This time the keys rattled along at a fair pace. He stopped once near the end. 'What is your Christian name, Matembu?' he asked the black policeman at the door.

The black constable straightened up. 'My name is Joshua, sir.'

Geldenhuis typed and removed the paper from the typewriter. He handed it to Tandia across the table. 'You read it first, then you sign it,' he said lightly.

Tandia, her hands shaking visibly, started to read the confession.

> *I, Tandia Patel, whose signature appears below, do knowingly and freely admit, in the presence of Sergeant J. T. Geldenhuis, a police officer stationed at the Cato Manor Police Station, that I did solicit for the purposes of sexual intercourse, two male persons unknown to me in the location of the Clairwood Indian Cemetery at approximately 6 a.m. on the 17th day of October 95. And I further state that I did perform sexual intercourse with one of these men in return for the payment of the sum of five shillings.*
>
> > *Signed: (Miss) ....*
> > *Tandia Patel. Date: ....*
> > *Witness: (Sergeant) ....*
> > *Jannie Teunis Geldenhuis ....*
> > *Witness: (Constable) ....*
> > *Joshua Matembu*

As Tandia read the piece Geldenhuis had written she couldn't think beyond the fact that it spelled freedom. She had been raped, violated and beaten. She was exhausted and humiliated and her body ached from the beating it had taken over the past eighteen hours. The niceties of moral rectitude taught so steadfastly at Durban Indian Girls' High School had no validity in her present circumstances. A refusal to sign the confession would do nothing for her self-respect nor did it even serve the useful purpose of adding to her hate. She became aware of Geldenhuis staring at her and when she had finished reading she looked up into his pale blue eyes. 'I will sign it,' she whispered again.

Geldenhuis said nothing. He was in control of himself again. He merely handed her his expensive fountain pen. Tandia's chair was too low for her to sign the paper while seated. She released the sticky balls of toilet paper in her hand and dropped them beside her chair and wiped her hand surreptitiously on the back of her shift. Then she rose and, crouching over the table, shakily signed the confession.

Tandia remained standing as Geldenhuis reached over and lifted the paper. He drew it towards him as though he was going to kiss it, but instead, he blew briefly on Tandia's signature and then waved it in the air. He then took the pen and signed the document himself. He called over to the black policeman, 'Hey, Matembu, come and sign your name.'

The black constable walked reluctantly over to the table. 'I not want sign this paper, sir. This bad paper.'

The white sergeant didn't look up. 'Sign it, man, you a material witness,' he said impatiently.

'This paper, sir, it not for charge sheet. I do not want sign this paper,' Matembu persisted.

Geldenhuis shot from his chair, 'I'm not bladdy asking you, I'm telling you! It's a fucking order, you hear!' He proffered his pen and moved Tandia's confession over to the edge of the table where the black man stood.

The black policeman took the pen and slowly signed his name and returned the pen to the sergeant. 'I will get her things, sir. The umFazi has a basin. I will get the keys from the desk sergeant, sir?'

'Ja, orright, also a police car, tell the sergeant I need a police car for only one hour.'

The black man turned to go and then turned to Geldenhuis. 'It is very, very late, sir. I must ask the desk sergeant for a police pass if the umFazi is going to be released on the street tonight.'

'Just get her things, you hear? She will not need a pass.' Geldenhuis folded Tandia's confession carefully. The black policeman looked hesitant. 'I'm telling you, man, she won't need a pass!'

'Please, sir, I have signed the paper. You said you would let me go if I signed that paper,' Tandia begged.

Geldenhuis stood with his hands on his hips. 'Where would you go? You have nowhere to go.' He glanced at his watch. 'It is one o'clock in the night, there are bad people out there.' He undid the button on the right breast pocket of his tunic and took out his wallet, then he carefully slipped the folded confession into it. 'I will keep this, you hear? I can use it any time I want, you understand? Any time. It is a legal document.' He spoke quietly with no threat in his voice, which, to Tandia, now seemed more threatening than had he shouted at her.

Geldenhuis placed the wallet back in the pocket of his khaki tunic and fastened the polished button. 'Sit,' he commanded, indicating the bigger chair once again. 'Sit, I want to have a nice little talk with you.'

Tandia did as she was told. She was filled with despair. She'd signed his paper and now he wasn't going to let her go. Or was he? He'd asked Matembu to get her things but he wouldn't authorise a late-night pass. Geldenhuis again sat sideways on the table, one elbow resting on the typewriter. He was relaxed, even friendly. 'You know something, Tandia?' It was the first time he had used her name in conversation. 'You are what in the police we call a *swart slimmetjie*, a clever black. And your kind, the *swart slimmetjie*, your kind we hate the most. You got a bit of education, you too smart for your own bladdy good. If I let you just walk out the station tonight, I'm telling you, jong, you'll be back in no time flat.'

'No, sir, I won't be back. I do not ever want to see this place ever again!'

Geldenhuis sighed, as though he was trying to explain something to a backward child. 'Ag, ja, man, you can try, but I'm telling you, it will be no good. No matter how hard you try, we will bring you back. We keep our eye on all the clever ones. You see, sooner or later they join the ANC. I'm telling you, jong, a black kaffir with an education is a dangerous person in the hands of the ANC.'

Tandia looked down into her lap, afraid to meet his eyes, the blue eyes that saw everything.

Geldenhuis tapped the wallet in his breast pocket. 'Now you know why I got this piece of paper. That's one reason.' He paused and then said, 'Look at me.' Tandia lifted her frightened gaze to his face. 'I want to help you. You want to know why because?' Tandia did not reply and once again lowered her eyes. 'Look at me, dammit,' Geldenhuis rapped. Then, as suddenly he smiled again. 'Natkin Patel showed me a lot of things that made me a better boxer.' He paused and brought one leg up so that his heel rested on the edge of the table, his hands capping his knee. 'Do you know about boxing?'

'Only a little bit,' Tandia sniffed. Geldenhuis nodded and continued, 'Next month I fight a Zulu boxer called Mandoma. He fights in the Transvaal and he's very good. Patel trained me for this fight which is for the South African professional welterweight title. He has seen Mandoma fight lots of times and he thinks I can beat him. I think so also.' Geldenhuis stopped talking and seemed to be lost in his own thoughts.

Tandia knew what Geldenhuis was talking about. Some years previously Patel had been called up to Johannesburg to referee a fight which took place in Sophiatown under unusual circumstances between Gideon Mandoma and a white schoolboy. Though both fighters were only in their teens at the time, Natkin had been impressed with what he saw. From that point on he had followed Mandoma's career in the ring.

If Patel had been helping to prepare Geldenhuis for a fight with Mandoma, Tandia thought, then the white policeman must be a very classy fighter. What's more, he had the hate. Patel always said that to be a champion, a boxer has to have the hate. Tandia knew at first hand that Geldenhuis had the hate.

Geldenhuis spoke at last. 'You see, I owe Patel. So I will help you. I will pay my debt, you hear?'

'Thank you, sir,' Tandia said, trying to conceal the fright in her voice. She wanted nothing more from the monster who sat on the table beside her. No matter how dangerous it was outside on the streets, it was better than being in this room with this white man who totally controlled her.

'I will help you, and you can help the police. Would you like to help the police?'

Tandia did not reply and Geldenhuis took her silence to mean that she would cooperate. 'You see, if you help the police, then you safe, as a *swart slimmetjie,* you safe.' He grinned suddenly. 'You on our side, man!'

Tandia waited for the trap to close. 'What must I do, sir?' she asked in an uncertain voice.

'Ag, easy stuff. I will take you to this place where you can stay. They will give you work also. It is a woman who owes me a favour.'

Tandia sensed the plan Geldenhuis had hatched in his head was important to him and she grew a little bolder. 'What must I do for the police at this place?'

'People will come. Sometimes Indian people, rich Indian people. Sometimes white people. Also important rich ones. You will watch and you will learn who they are and you will tell me what they do and say.'

'What kind of place is this place?'

'Ag, you know, it is place where they have women, where men go sometimes.'

The trap had been sprung! Geldenhuis was going to find her a place in a brothel. Tandia looked up at the white man, her distress plain. The police sergeant had a smile on his face and he absently tapped the outline of his wallet in the breast pocket of his tunic.

He jumped from the table and straightened the tunic of his uniform by pulling it down first from the front and then the back and smoothing the waist with his palms. 'I will speak to my friend.' He beckoned to Tandia. 'Come, I must take your fingerprints and then we go, hey?'

Four

Wisps of early morning mist sat on the surface of the Cherwell as Peekay and Hymie walked across Magdalen bridge. Hymie's car was parked in a small garage he'd rented just behind the grammar school. Despite the pale sunshine, Peekay's blood, still thin from the tropics, made it feel like the dead of winter to him. He was grateful for the fur-lined leather gloves Hymie had tossed him as they'd left their rooms that morning. Peekay had been at Oxford a month and his life had settled into the usual student routine: lectures, tutorials and rather a lot of time spent both in the Radcliffe Camera and the Bodleian Library.

To this had been added a fairly heavy training schedule. Hymie had found a gym on the outskirts of Oxford near the Nuffield car works, where Peekay could work out with two apprentices from the Morris plant, known simply as Bobby and Eddy. Both boxed professionally. One was a middleweight, the other, like Peekay, a welter. They were country-bred, likely lads, fast enough, handy in the ring and very strong. Peekay had sharpened up, getting his timing right by boxing them both together, each taking alternate rounds. Wearing protective headgear, he'd go flat-out for six rounds four times a week.

The two Oxfordshire lads were contracted to spar for five bob a round. To keep them from becoming discouraged, Hymie secretly added a pound bonus if they could put Peekay on the canvas.

After only two weeks of intensive training, despite the heavy protective headgear they wore, Bobby and Eddy quite often found themselves on the seat of their pants in the middle of the ring. Peekay was getting back his form and by the day the appointment with Dutch Holland came around his speed was back; his punches had their old crispness and were probably landing harder. The year he had worked in the mines to build up his strength was beginning to pay off.

Neither Hymie nor Peekay was silly enough to think that a good showing against two straight-up-and-down Saturday night club fighters meant they'd get the nod from Dutch Holland, Britain's foremost fight trainer. The great man only worked with amateurs destined for the professional ring and he didn't seem over-anxious to accept the task of turning Peekay into a professional.

For his first appointment with Dutch Holland almost a year ago, Hymie had carefully prepared a portfolio of Peekay's amateur career. Holland had thumbed through this absently and stopped at the last page, which showed a ten-by-eight black-and-white photograph of Peekay in the traditional boxing pose.

'Not a bleedin' mark on him. How many fights did you say he's had, then?'

'One hundred and sixteen. He's hard to hit,' Hymie replied.

A small smile, more a smirk, appeared on Dutch Holland's face. 'Either that or he's been fightin' schoolgirls. I know a coupla lads will be happy to put a dent in that pretty-boy hooter,' he'd said, jabbing a small, pudgy finger at the photograph.

'They won't be the first to try, Mr Holland.'

'We'll see soon enough, lad,' Holland replied, but he'd reluctantly agreed to put Peekay through his paces when he eventually arrived in England.

The Thomas à Becket gym, situated above a pub from which it took its name, was on the south bank of the Thames near Bermondsey docks. Neither the pub nor the gym was open when they arrived half an hour early. A guy wearing a worn cloth cap and a woollen scarf wrapped around his neck and chin was sitting on the third from bottom step leading up to the gym. He was hunched against the cold with his hands under his armpits and looked up as Hymie and Peekay approached.

'You the two toffs the guv's been expectin' then?' It wasn't hard to see he was a pug. He possessed the best pair of cauliflower ears Peekay had ever seen and his nose had been flattened so many times it spread across his face in an arc almost as wide as his mouth. 'Which one of you gents is Mr Levy then?'

Hymie nodded. 'You the caretaker?'

The pug nodded and stood up. 'I hang about for the guv'nor. Don't expect you'll see him till half nine, though. Them two others neither.'

'Two others? The two boxers?' Peekay asked.

'Yeah, them two. I'll open the gym, but I'm warnin' you, freeze the knackers off of a brass monkey up there. By the way, me name's Fred.'

Peekay smiled. 'Nice to meet you, Fred.'

They climbed the outside stairs where Fred fumbled with a set of keys, his hands shaking badly. 'It was the war see, if it hadn't been for the flamin' war I'd a been British champ an' all.' He stopped fumbling with the keys and looked at them. 'Adolf put the kibosh on all that.' He found the key he'd been looking for and, holding it in both hands to steady it, inserted it into the lock. 'Done much fightin' then?' he asked, holding the door for them.

'A fair bit,' Hymie answered. Fred led them past two glass-partitioned offices and into the main area of the gym.

'Shit! This place smells like a wrestler's jockstrap! Can we open the windows please, Fred?'

Fred tapped what remained of his nose with his forefinger. 'That's the one good thing about me hooter, can't smell nothin'! Sorry, guv, them windows is screwed down for the winter.'

'Jesus, Fred, I'm expecting a lady! Can't you get *any* fresh air into this place?'

Fred looked surprised. 'This ain't much of a place for a lady, guv. Not too many ladies come by. Togger's sister sometimes and some of her friends. I'll fetch a chair for her from the guv'nor's office.'

Peekay looked at Hymie. 'What lady?'

'Harriet, she wants to meet you. Remember? I told you she's a sculptor . . . well, training to be one anyway. She's interested in boxing,' Hymie grinned. 'You know, the human body in its purest form.'

'Jesus, Hymie!'

'You'll like her, Peekay, I promise.'

Peekay sighed. 'I'm shitting myself with the prospect of two of Britain's best welterweights who've been instructed to knock my bloody head off and you decide it's time to show off your girl!'

'Them two welters, one ain't,' Fred interjected

suddenly. Both of them turned, having forgotten he was still standing beside them.

'What was that?'

'Them two welters, guv, one's a middle. Turned pro this season.'

Peekay looked at Hymie. 'I thought I was being matched against a couple of welters.'

'Ja, me too,' Hymie said, a mystified look on his face. 'Better wait and see.' He turned to the ex pug. 'Fred, did a parcel come for me? It should have been addressed to the pub downstairs.'

'Yes, Mr Levy, it come yesterday, I put it in the guv'nor's office. Will I fetch it then?'

'Hello! Anyone home?' a female voice called from the door.

'Shit!' Peekay exclaimed, suddenly anxious.

Hymie patted him on the shoulder. 'Cool it,' he whispered, then he raised his voice cheerily. 'Come in Harriet!'

Hymie moved towards the door and Fred followed him, presumably to fetch the parcel or the chairs, but at the same time he removed his cloth cap. The three words spoken by Harriet told him the person at the door was a lady.

In fact, Harriet Clive wouldn't have noticed either way. Her clipped accent, the unconscious product of a good English boarding school, belied a personality in which there was no place for even the slightest pretension. As she walked towards him Peekay saw an attractive girl who wore a brilliant green polo-neck sweater under the ubiquitous blue duffel of the time. Her faded jeans disappeared into a pair of scuffed brown riding boots. She was about three inches shorter than Peekay and by the way she moved towards him Peekay could imagine a nice shape under all that heavy stuff.

Peekay smiled as Harriet approached. She threw her head back slightly and, bringing her right hand up, she brushed her fingers through a mane of chestnut hair. Then she took his hand. 'Hello, I'm Harriet Clive, I've been dying to meet you.'

Peekay's heart pounded against his will. She wasn't beautiful, not even pretty in the conventional sense, but she was unusual looking. Her perfectly ordinary brown eyes were set high above angular cheekbones. Her skin was a very light olive with both her nose and mouth seeming a lttle too big for an otherwise dainty, heart-shaped face.

'Hello, Harriet. Hymie tells me you're interested in boxing?'

Harriet laughed. 'The human form, rather more. I'm hoping to be a sculptor. I don't know anything about boxing.'

Peekay grinned. 'Why don't you quit while you're ahead?' He pointed to Fred who had returned carrying two bentwood chairs, one stacked on top of the other. 'As Fred says, not too many ladies come here.'

Harriet looked suddenly concerned. 'Oh? I hope you don't mind my coming?'

It wasn't what Peekay had meant and he blushed. 'No, that's not what I meant, it's nice of you to come.'

'I'll be terribly quiet.'

Harriet hadn't quite known what to expect in Peekay. Hymie had spoken of him so often she had conjured up someone she wasn't quite sure she'd like. Rather too handsome and too good at everything, particularly games. She was beastly at games. In her experience, the strong, good-looking types usually turned out to be about as interesting as boiled cabbage.

Taking Hymie's descriptions of Peekay alone, she'd decided she wasn't looking for that much perfection in a man. In fact she simply wasn't looking. Hymie came down to London reasonably infrequently, so she wasn't obliged to turn it into a grimly serious affair. He was nice to occasionally think about when he wasn't there and nice to be with when he was. Actually, she thought of Hymie as a sort of male protection device. If another man badgered her or became too persistent she could put them off with chat about her brilliant Oxford boy-friend. Brilliant Oxford boyfriends always seemed to do the trick.

Meeting Peekay at last, her preconceptions were confirmed. The lightly tanned skin, the shock of hair just beginning to grow across the forehead, the deep blue eyes, the perfectly straight nose: he looked like he'd been created from a police identification kit. It was a superior face, she decided; not quite pretty, but still the sort of idealised looks which belonged in a Rupert Brooke poem. Peekay looked like the sort who went to Harrow, flew a Spitfire, and secretly harboured a desire to be beaten by someone dressed as his childhood nanny. Finally, she decided, he was much too dull-looking to sculpt.

Harriet had been hoping for a somewhat battered face, interesting because it was still young, yet showed the premature wear and tear of a hundred hard fights. If she were to sculpt him she'd have to concentrate on his body and rearrange his face. While her mind was working on these modifications she looked up, directly into his eyes.

Peekay actually felt as though he had been pushed backwards. Her look was so open, so cool and appraising, it was like the slap of a wet towel. Suddenly his defences, so carefully developed and so easily brought into play, seemed useless. He felt vulnerable and hoped like hell it wasn't showing.

Harriet, having decided her assumptions were correct, now saw something in Peekay's eyes which told her they were not. It was as though she'd walked into a soundless place, for about him was a stillness as if she was standing in the eye of a storm. She felt the need to resist him. She must avoid being alone with him.

Fred placed the two chairs beside the ring. 'Thanks, Fred.' Hymie reached into the change pocket of his trousers. 'Do us a favour, nick down to the caf and get us a couple of bacon-and-egg sandwiches?' He handed the old man a florin and then added another shilling, 'For your trouble.'

'Thanks, Mr Levy. Wait on, I'll get your parcel.' He returned a few moments later and handed Hymie a large soft-looking parcel wrapped in brown paper and tied with string. 'I'll be off. Be all right on your own then, Mr Levy?' he asked.

'Yes, thanks, Fred.' Hymie turned to Peekay. 'It's cold in here. Wear a tracksuit when you warm up.'

'What for? I didn't bring one, just a sweatshirt and my old bottoms, like always.'

'Here, catch!' Hymie tossed the parcel to Peekay, who caught it in one hand, bringing it into his chest.

'What's this?'

'Open it. No don't! Open it in the change room. As my mom would say, health to wear!'

Peekay excused himself and, picking up his bag, walked towards a door at the far end of the gym. On the left-hand side of the door was written the word 'Change'; on the right, the word 'Room' hadn't been added. It was as though the signwriter had taken himself off for a drink in the pub downstairs and never returned to complete the job.

The room contained a single shower, a toilet with the door removed, sundry benches along the walls and one which ran down the centre. Peekay was assailed by the damp smell of soap, stale sweat and dirty wet towels. He sat on the centre bench and tore open Hymie's parcel. The label on the outside read 'Lillywhites'. Inside was a bright blue tracksuit.

He unfolded the tracksuit top and what he saw took a moment to sink in. Embroidered in yellow silk thread on the back of the tracksuit were the words, 'The Tadpole Angel'.

Levy, you bastard!, he thought. You can't be serious! All that stuff was over, left behind in South Africa. They'd not even discussed it since his arrival in England. Hymie couldn't possibly want him to fight as the Tadpole Angel again.

Suddenly angry, Peekay hurled the tracksuit top against the wall and made for the door. Then he realised he'd be making a scene in front of Harriet. He retrieved the top and started to undress. He'd sort it out with Hymie later; now it was time that he started to concentrate on the business they'd come for. The tracksuit and the girl had left him distracted; he must get his mind on the bout.

Hymie and Harriet were devouring Harry's bacon-and-egg sandwiches when Peekay returned to the gym. It wasn't like Hymie to eat before noon, and the sandwiches were a sure sign he was nervous.

Peekay could feel the tension in his stomach which always came before a fight. It meant his concentration was back with him, although his stomach was tighter than usual and he knew he was a little scared. It had been more than a year since he'd stepped into a ring, other than with a sparring partner, and his whole boxing future was riding on this one work-out.

Peekay lifted his arms up high and, displaying the tracksuit, said through clenched teeth, 'Thanks, Hymie, a perfect fit!' Hymie had gone to his usual trouble but Peekay wasn't at all comfortable in it. He felt a bit ungrateful, knowing he was going to have to sort the name business out later. That is, until he suddenly realised Hymie was probably counting on him to feel rotten about making a fuss. He walked over to where the two of them sat. 'We're going to have to talk about the embroidery.'

Hymie spoke with a mouthful of egg-and-bacon sandwich. 'Sure, sure, turn round, let's have a deck.' Peekay turned to show his back. The yellow embroidery on the blue background was typical of Hymie, who loved continuity and tradition. Yellow and blue were the colours of the Barberton Blues, the prison boxing squad in the small bushveld town where Peekay had started as a boxer at the age of eight, and where he had been trained by his first and best boxing coach, the wily old coloured lag, Geel Piet.

'The Tadpole Angel! What a lovely name,' Harriet exclaimed.

'Now don't you start!' Peekay growled.

'Oh, but it is! There must be a story. Do tell, Peekay.'

'I think you'd better go and warm up,' Hymie said quickly, avoiding Peekay's eyes. 'Dutch Holland will be here any minute.'

Peekay could see the puzzled look on Harriet's face. 'Ask shit-face to tell you,' he said, jerking his thumb in Hymie's direction and, walking over to the wall directly behind them, he selected a skipping rope.

76

Peekay skipped lightly for a few minutes and then moved over to the small platform where the speedball hung. Soon a sound like the throbbing of jungle drums came from the blurred red ball and he knew his co-ordination was perfect.

A voice cut through Peekay's concentration. 'Well, that's one good thing, we won't have to worry too much about your coordination then will we, son?'

Ducking to avoid the flying ball, Peekay stepped off the platform. A light sweat had formed over his face and, pulling the tracksuit top over his head, he tossed it to Hymie. Then he looked directly at the man standing beside Hymie.

'Dutch, let me introduce you to Peekay,' Hymie said. His voice was calm enough, but Peekay knew he was as nervous as he was in front of the famous English trainer.

'Pleased to meet you, Mr Holland,' said Peekay.

Dutch Holland took his hand and shook it almost absently. 'Likewise, Peekay.' He nodded his head towards Hymie. 'We've heard a lot about you from your manager.' He looked Peekay up and down as a jockey might examine an unfamiliar horse. ''Ere, let me see your 'ands, son.'

Peekay extended both his hands. Holland took his right hand and turned it palm upwards, then back again, testing the flexibility of Peekay's wrist. Then he pushed Peekay's fingers apart, scrutinising them for past breaks or possible weakness. Folding Peekay's hand into a fist he slapped the exposed knuckles with the flat of his hand. He then repeated the process with the left hand before taking up the right again. He opened up Peekay's hand and placed his own over it. His was wider, though his fingers were shaped like small, fat, cocktail sausages and Peekay's extended well beyond them. Next he took a good look at Peekay's eyes, poking and stretching the soft tissue around them with the ball of his thumb.

Dutch Holland had the reputation for being the best cutman in Europe and Peekay wondered how those small, pudgy, clumsy-looking fingers could be so deft with a cotton bud stick, adrenalin, and a jar of vaseline.

Peekay, who'd had very few cuts in his career, was pretty confident that Holland would find nothing wrong with his eyes. He was equally sure of his hands, though they bore several permanent scars from working in the mines. They were strong, not only from working out daily with his bare knuckles on the coarse canvas punching bag in his hut, but also from a childhood spent at Doc's piano doing five-finger exercises. They were already the hands of a pro; the scar tissue built up around his knuckles from working the big punching bag with his bare fists gave them an extra layer of protection.

'Them's grafter's 'ands, son. You supposed to be a toff from Oxford University. How'd you end up with 'ands like a bleedin' navvy?'

Hymie, standing slightly behind Dutch Holland, winked. It was obvious he'd told the famous trainer about Peekay's stint in the mines. Borrowing from the idiom, Peekay replied, 'I've done my share, Mr Holland.'

'That's good, my son. I like a grafter. All boxing is about work and boxing as a pro is about more work than you've done in your whole bleedin' life.' He placed a cocktail sausage hand absently onto Peekay's shoulder. 'Might as well understand each other from the start. I do the shouting and you do the grafting, know what I mean?'

78

Peekay nodded as Hymie spoke up. 'Does that mean you'll take us on?'

Dutch Holland, a little smile on his face, jerked his head in Hymie's direction. 'Hang about! First your boy here is going to 'ave to show me if he can sort a couple lads out in a right and proper manner.'

He pointed in the direction of the change room. Peekay turned to see two boxers wearing their sweats, with their hands already taped, walking towards them. One of them was heavily set around the shoulders as though he worked with weights, obviously a middleweight; the other, like Peekay, was probably only just a welter.

'Hang on a mo! You said two good welterweights, Dutch,' Hymie protested.

Peekay knew Hymie was protesting as a matter of course. There wasn't a great deal he could do about the situation other than call the session off, and he wasn't about to do that. 'I changed my mind,' Dutch Holland replied, but made no attempt to explain any further.

'Peekay, this is Peter Best,' Holland said. 'He's had only six fights as a pro, five KOs and a decision in his favour. He's good and he's fast and as you can see he's a middle. Peter's come along so I can see what sort of punch you carry as a fighter.'

Hymie grimaced. 'Boxer, please, Dutch. Peekay isn't some country-bumpkin fighter, a one-punch Johnny who leads with his head.'

Peekay wished Hymie hadn't interjected. He felt small next to the much larger middleweight.

'Peter, Peter, bumpkin eater!' Dutch quipped, pleased with the pun. 'We'll see about that soon enough. If your lad's a poncey little boxer and can't put a man on the canvas with both 'ands he ain't no bleedin' good to me.'

'Hello, Peter,' Peekay said. He offered his hand to Best who grunted, barely touching it. Best was dark-eyed, square-jawed with a swarthy complexion, the type of looks known in Britain as black Irish. It was a face which just naturally looked unfriendly and it was obvious Best didn't do a lot to offset this initial impression. Peekay had already noted that Best's nose had been broken more than once and that he carried the pink wedge of a recently cut right eye. It was a sign of a stand-up fighter. He calculated the length of Best's arms. Best had a reach advantage of perhaps two inches; it would be difficult to hold him off so he could throw his punches from a safe distance.

'Not a man of too many words are you then, Peter?' Dutch said slapping Best lightly on the shoulder. 'You're in first against Jock of the Bushveld here, lad. Warm up and then get Togger to lace you. Wear your headgear.' He grinned. 'I don't want Peekay here to mark your pretty face.'

Dutch turned to the smaller of the two boxers. 'This is Togger Brown. He's here to test your speed. He's as good a young welter as you'll find in this or any other manor.'

Togger Brown was a ginger-haired, freckled-faced chap with a happy, open smile and friendly enough eyes. He stepped forward and shot his hand out. 'Nice to meetcha, Peekay. I don't mind admittin', you looked a tad fast yerself on the speedball an' all.'

'Hi, Togger,' Peekay smiled, relieved that Togger Brown seemed like a nice sort of guy. Togger, without waiting for Dutch Holland, stepped over, hand outstretched to Hymie. 'Nice to know you, Mr Levy.'

'Howzit!' Hymie said, greeting Togger perhaps not as warmly as he might have done. He liked to keep a small distance between himself and the boxers. Trainers and other managers didn't respect you if you acted like one of the lads.

'Righto, Togger! Get warmed up and *stay* warm. Your turn after Peter, lad.' Togger hadn't been able to take his eyes off Harriet since he'd entered.

Dutch Holland pointed to a box of bandages and three pairs of gloves which Fred had earlier put in the ring: two six-ounce gloves and a pair of twelves for Peter Best. At least Holland had seen to it that the bigger boxer should wear heavier gloves to cushion his punches.

Peekay sat down beside Harriet so Hymie could bandage his hands. Harriet was silent, though her eyes were excited. She'd opened up her sketch pad and she watched carefully now as Hymie fixed the bandages, noting how the tape passed high over the wrist and covered the palm while stopping short just before the first joint of the thumb and fingers. Hymie completed Peekay's left hand and Harriet lifted it carefully from Peekay's knee, feeling the texture and the tension of the binding with the ball of her thumb. She watched as it fell back naturally into his thigh, with the palm uppermost, fingers slightly curled inwards. Then she began to sketch.

Hymie held the left glove open for Peekay to insert his hand. Peekay made a fist inside the glove and pushed it against Hymie's chest so that Hymie could lace it up. He repeated the process with the right hand. Peekay got up, banging the gloves together to seat his hands firmly. This was the moment when a fight started for him, the moment his hands slipped into a pair of padded leather gloves.

The routine had always been the same from the very

first time when he'd been six years old, travelling alone in the train on a two-day journey to his grandpa's new home in Barberton. Hoppie Groenewald, the train guard and Northern Transvaal Railway boxing champion, had befriended the lonely little boy. He'd brought a pair of boxing gloves into the compartment. 'With boxing, small can beat big,' he'd said, pushing the frightened child's fists into the giant gloves. It was the moment boxing came to Peekay. He'd felt the huge gloves over his hands and instinctively knew they felt right. First the left then the right, that was Hoppie's instruction that first time, and this was the order he'd insisted on ever since.

'Righto! Make it snappy, lads, let's have the two of you up 'ere then,' Dutch Holland called from inside the ring. Best and Peekay climbed up into the ring from opposite sides and moved to the centre to stand beside the trainer.

Dutch Holland was a nuggety, square-jawed sort of chap with oiled dark hair combed directly back from his brow. His hairline receded to midway down his scalp and his black, almost bushy, eyebrows swept back to give his face a slightly owlish look of reproof. A narrow vertical crease ran permanently down the centre of his brow. It added to the impression of a man who grew quickly impatient when things didn't happen the way he wanted them to.

'Three rounds, one minute between rounds, you both know the drill.' Holland looked down at Hymie seated beside Harriet, who was sketching fast, her eyes darting up and back to the paper in furious concentration. 'Mr Levy 'ere will act as timekeeper,' he said, touching the stopwatch which hung around his neck. 'At the end of three rounds Peter steps down and Togger takes over.'

He lowered his voice slightly, addressing the two fighters. 'Now lads, I want a nice workout, no clinching, no unnecessary aggro. Now, Peter, we're here to see what the lad's got an' all. I want you to go hard, but no roughing up in the clinches, break clean and fast!' Best nodded and brought his right glove up to touch his nose. He sniffed noisily, looking at Peekay for the first time. Dutch Holland climbed down from the ring and, taking the stopwatch from around his neck, handed it to Hymie.

The two boxers moved over to their corners and waited for Hymie's signal. Peekay was nervous as hell. He'd waited a long time for this moment.

'Okay, ready?' Hymie looked down at the stopwatch, 'Box on!'

Peekay moved out of his corner towards a determined-looking Best. 'This guy only knows one way,' he decided. Best came straight towards him, trying to cut him off, gloves held fairly wide and low, affecting the more open stance of the professional, confident of his extra reach. If he couldn't trap Peekay in a corner he would expect Peekay to dance a little, moving him around the ring, a smaller man naturally wary of his bigger opponent, leading with a left, feeling him out.

In boxing you can quickly learn to take opportunities as they're presented to you, and the wide-open stance affected by the middleweight was a blatant show of arrogance. Peekay moved in fast and hit Best hard with a left lead to the jaw, followed by a vicious straight right, a one-two combination which set the bigger man back on his heels. Peekay was well out of harm's way as Best attempted the retaliatory right hook.

The surprise showed in his opponent's eyes. Peekay had hit him cleanly and hard with the back of the knuckles and Best was going to make the smaller man pay. But now Peekay started to box off the back foot, using the whole of the ring to stay out of trouble. It was simply a tactic to make the bigger man look bad as he threw punches and missed time and time again. If you can get a boxer to mistime his punches from the start, it can take a couple of rounds before he gets his combinations right. But Peekay knew that sooner or later Best would get him against the ropes or in a corner where he could do some real damage.

Peekay was a consummate boxer with a mind which quickly developed his opponent's faults into the pattern the fight might take if they were allowed to dictate it. Once he knew the plan he knew how to combat it. Halfway through the first round he thought he had Best set. He knew the kind of a fighter he was and what to expect. The middleweight was good with both hands. Peekay was to learn that this was a characteristic of all the Dutch Holland boxers. Best was also pretty fast, though much too dependent on a left upper-cut, a deadly punch when it connected, but when used too often, it was like sending a message via carrier pigeon: you could see it coming from a long way off. Besides, it opened him up for a right cross.

Peekay started to get inside Best, cutting off any advantage he might enjoy with his superior reach. This sudden change from boxing defensively confused the other boxer. Getting inside his opponent had two advantages: his body was exposed to a series of short, sharp, rapid-fire punches which sapped his stamina. When he attempted to retaliate, his punches had first to travel around the outside of the infighter's arms and elbows, losing a lot of sting on the way. Peekay was forcing him to shorten his punches, most of which he took on the back of his arms. In return Peekay was scoring with hard, clean shots to the body. Best's willingness to lead with his chin was to no avail. Peekay largely ignored his head. He knew that constant punishment to the body from a boxer, as fast as he was, could wear a big man down in a hurry. If the blows were set just under the heart they soon began to make their presence felt.

By the time Hymie called for the second round Peekay's breathing was even, but he noticed that Best's chest was still heaving. The fighter was gulping air in an attempt to settle himself down. Maybe the bastard isn't totally in shape, thought Peekay. This time he'll come out more carefully for sure. But Best, who must have suffered from a short memory, came at Peekay in exactly the same manner as he'd done in the opening round.

Peekay feinted with his left then hit Best hard with a right cross, pulling the blow inwards to tear at the recent cut to the fighter's eye. He'd resisted the left-right combination he'd used in the opening round in case Best set a trap for him. He pulled back out of harm's way, ducking and feinting and working the ropes as he watched the blood start to pump into Best's eye.

A boxer less intelligent than Peekay would have started to work on the eye, hoping to close it and so cut down his opponent's field of vision. Peekay knew that this would suit Best perfectly, offering his head as a target so he could land a couple of big punches which would put a lighter fighter like Peekay away.

Best's eye wasn't badly cut and Dutch would stop the bleeding between rounds, but Peekay wanted him to think he could hit him wherever and whenever it pleased him. Boxing is all about psychological control, and Peekay was working on Best's mind.

The two boxers were no longer sparring. Best was trying his hardest, with increasing frustration, to nail Peekay. The smaller boxer went back to working on the body, seating a number of good punches under the heart. Late in the second round Peekay moved Best onto the ropes and got him with an eight-punch combination which hurt him. He heard Best grunt as the middle-weight pulled him into a clinch. Despite his size Best was taking a lot of punishment to the body and plainly was not liking it. 'Come 'ere you, fuckin' bastard!' he'd invited Peekay more than once.

The two boxers were locked in a clinch when Hymie called the end of the round. Peekay released his hold of Best and stepped back, dropping his guard. Best caught him with a beautiful right upper-cut to the jaw. Peekay felt his head snap back and his knees start to buckle, but somehow he managed to stay upright 'That's for you, lad!' Best snarled.

Despite the lightness in his head, Peekay managed to smile. 'That's the only way you're going to hit me, shit-head!' he called after Best, who'd moved back to his corner.

The blow had been a deliberate foul. 'You bastard!' Peekay heard Hymie shout up at Best.

Dutch Holland stepped quickly into the ring and moved over to Best. 'You stupid git! Next time you do that, lad, you're out of my stable! I told you, no aggro!' He looked over at Peekay who was standing in his corner. 'You all right, son?' Peekay nodded, his head clearing from the blow. Hymie tried to enter the ring but Peekay waved him back. The punch had hurt him, but the advantage lay in remaining cool and showing no visible signs of distress.

'Do you want to continue, Peekay?' Holland asked.

Peekay smiled. 'Sure, Mr Holland, why not?'

Dutch Holland grinned. 'Cheeky young sod!' He turned to Best and started to attend to his eye, speaking to him in an undertone. 'Now I've warned you, ain't I? Get in there and do some work, Little Lord Fauntleroy here is making you look dead ordinary, my son.'

The final round was Peekay's best. He started off working close to the bigger fighter's body and by the middle of the round the middleweight had dropped his arms to protect himself, an obvious sign that he was hurting as well as tiring. With his guard down, Peekay was able to stand back a little and punch to the head. To taunt Best he hit him everywhere except on the eye, and soon the parts of his face exposed by the headgear carried bright red patches where he'd been nailed. A thin trickle of blood ran from his nose.

The big fighter's body looked untouched except for a sharp patch of red about the size of a large grapefruit under his heart where Peekay had hit him perhaps fifty times or more.

Best once again ignored Dutch Holland's caution to stay the aggro. His eyes clearly showed his fury as Peekay took the fight to him, making him miss badly. Every boxer dreams his opponent will lose his cool in the ring; nothing makes a good boxer look better than an opponent who throws caution to the winds and rushes in for the kill.

But in the end Best had enough class to last, even hitting Peekay hard twice when he moved in a little too close. They were two good punches, though he'd lost some of his speed and the blows did no more than remind Peekay in no uncertain manner to stay out of his reach. He was also grateful for the heavy gloves Best was wearing. Hymie called the end of the round just as Peekay landed another hard straight left right on the button.

Best didn't wait to touch gloves. Turning his back on Peekay, he climbed out of the ring.

Peekay looked over at Hymie and shrugged. Hymie raised his thumb without moving his hand from his lap. 'Nice one!' he mimed. Peekay's concentration had been such that he'd entirely forgotten Harriet's presence. Now, as Fred moved over to his corner handing him up a water bottle, he looked down at her, rinsing his mouth. She was still sketching, her eyes downcast onto the paper so that the lights from above the ring caught her chestnut hair, turning it into a blaze of deep coppery brown. 'She's Hymie's,' Peekay reminded himself, mentally slapping himself on the wrist. He was still a little high from the fight, delighted it had gone so well. He'd really expected Best to rough him up somewhat and counted himself lucky. He spat into the bucket Fred held up for him.

''Ere, more water, guv,' Fred said, handing Peekay the water bottle.

Togger Brown jumped into the ring, game as a fox terrier. He bounced around in his corner, throwing punches into the air and blowing hard, working at his aggression as Peekay took the remaining seconds to recover.

When Hymie called the start of the fourth round, what with one thing and another, there had been an almost two-minute break in between rounds. Peekay was feeling fresh, even exhilarated. He knew he'd performed better than well against the recalcitrant Best, and he was anxious to do the same in his sparring session with Togger Brown. To his opponent's surprise, Peekay faced him as a southpaw. It was an ability he'd gained as a small child under the direction of Geel Piet. The battered little coloured man believed a boxer should be as capable of leading with his right as with his left hand and Peekay had been trained this way from the very beginning. To the uninitiated, in boxing terms, it's the equivalent of being ambidextrous. A boxer who stands with his right hand and right leg forward is known as a southpaw.

Like every intelligent boxer who has watched his opponent box, Togger Brown had worked out the way he hoped to shape the fight. Now he found himself all at sea and it soon became apparent that he'd been mismatched. Towards the end of the round Peekay changed back to an orthodox stance and almost immediately put Togger onto the seat of his pants with a left-right combination.

Togger lay sprawled on the canvas and Peekay rushed over to help him up. The two punches had been so beautifully timed that he'd been almost unaware of how hard they'd been. Peekay started to lift Togger Brown to his feet, grabbing him under the armpits. Suddenly Dutch Holland was in the ring waving his arms above his head, stopping the sparring session.

Peekay held Togger around the shoulders. 'You okay?'

Togger's head was beginning to clear and he nodded, grinning. 'Jesus, Peekay! What a corker of a right hand!' He brought his glove up and sniffed, wiping his nose on the surface of the black leather.

Dutch Holland shouted to Fred to bring a bucket and sponge. Togger nudged Peekay. 'Still an' all, you gave that big bastard a good hiding,' he giggled, and whispered, 'Dutch thinks he's the big white hope. Big white dope, more like. Blimey! You didn't 'arf make him look ordinary!'

They climbed through the ropes together, though on the side opposite to where Hymie and Harriet sat. Togger Brown put his hand on Peekay's shoulder and looked serious. 'Can I box with you some more? I could learn a lot from you, I could.'

'Shit, Togger, it's all there in you. You move well, you're fast with a bloody good left lead.' Peekay shrugged and indicated the ring. 'It's just that I've been up there maybe fifty times more than you have,' he grinned. 'I've been knocked around a bit more.'

Peekay couldn't quite believe Togger Brown. His accent was straight out of a *Hotspur* comic. At first he'd thought the little freckle-faced fighter with the big smile was sending him up. He'd become accustomed to the well-varnished accents of the college proctors as well as a great many of his fellow students, but he hadn't yet attuned his ear to a broad London accent.

Fred arrived with the bucket and sponge and Dutch Holland called down to Togger to return to the ring so he could take off his headgear and gloves and check his reflexes. Peekay walked over to the side of the ring where Hymie and Harriet sat.

Hymie helped him out of the ring. 'Nice one, Peekay!' Harriet, not wanting to intrude, busied herself putting her sketch pad into her satchel. Peekay, observing her, could see that the hint of a smile played around her mouth. As Hymie lifted the protective leather headgear from his friend's head she turned towards him and looking up, fixed her eyes on Peekay. 'You were marvellous,' she said quietly.

Peekay felt suddenly light-headed. His instincts told him he was stepping into very dangerous territory. How the hell was he going to explain to Hymie he was in love with his girl?

'Can we go into my office, then, Mr Levy?' Dutch Holland said, climbing down from the ring. Hymie looked at Peekay and gave him a furtive thumbs-up sign. 'Here goes,' he whispered and then in a louder voice, 'Better have a shower, Peekay, be back in a mo.'

Peekay let himself smile at Harriet. Hymie hadn't removed his bandages and he sat down and began to pull at the tape. 'Oh! Please let me do that,' Harriet said. She unwound the bandage, winding it up carefully again as she removed it from his hand. 'What you're watching is four years of VAD training paying off at last.' She had a throaty, infectious laugh and Peekay found himself grinning stupidly. 'During the war as a kid in Norfolk I used to imagine a German flier parachuting down into the fields behind our house. I'd be the first there running across the fields in my VAD uniform and little brown bakelite first-aid suitcase banging against my knees. The Jerry would be lying there stunned and before you could say Jack Robinson I'd have bandaged him up like an Egyptian mummy. By the time the village folk would appear with their pitch forks and clubs I'd be standing between them and my captured flier. Then I'd imperiously order four of them to make a stretcher from his parachute silk. I'd be a terrific hero, of course, and have to go up to Buckingham Palace and get a medal for bravery ... perhaps two medals, one for bravery and the other for bandaging.'

Peekay laughed. 'I used to imagine I was the Spitfire pilot who shot him down. I had no idea you were waiting below to rescue the bugger!' They laughed together. 'Thanks, Harriet, you get eleven out of ten for de-bandaging,' Peekay said happily.

Harriet sighed melodramatically, then threw back her

head and laughed. 'I suppose I'm going to have to get used to hanging around dirty gyms waiting for a certain sweaty boxer and his manager.' She sniffed, squiffing up her nose. 'What a pong! Do they all smell like this?'

Peekay grinned. 'Only the better ones. Excuse me please, Harriet, I must pong rather myself. I'll warm down and take a shower.' On his way to the change room he felt as though he was walking on air. She's not yours! She's *not* yours, you fool! he insisted to himself, but it didn't help. Harriet Clive suddenly filled every nook and cranny in his mind.

Peekay entered the change room just as Peter Best was leaving. Peekay smiled and extended his hand. 'No hard feelings, Peter? Thanks for the opportunity to work out with you.'

Best did not accept Peekay's hand. Instead he jabbed his forefinger into his face and snarled, 'Listen lad! No fuckin' welterweight makes a fuckin' monkey out of me and hopes to stay fuckin' healthy. You'll get yours, mark my fuckin' words!' He brushed past Peekay and was gone.

'That's fuckin' wonderful!' Togger yelled after him, mimicking his accent. 'Remind me to nominate you for fuckin' sportsman of the fuckin' year, my son!'

'Shut up, Togger!' Peekay said, grinning broadly, bringing his finger to his lips. 'We don't want a fookin' shower-room brawl. He'll kill us! Besides, I think Hymie's about to convince your Mr Holland to take me on.' A look of mock seriousness crossed his face. 'You screw it up for me, Togger, and you're a dead welterweight!'

Togger stood nude in the middle of the room with a small tin of Johnson's Baby Powder in his hand. 'Oh, mate! From the opening bell you was never in the slightest doubt. Dutch thinks all 'is fuckin' birthdays 'ave come at once!'

'I hope you're right. Shower's cold, I suppose?' Peekay asked, attempting to make light of the compliment.

'Yeah, I suppose,' Togger said absently, then swung around. ''Ere! It's the middle of bleedin' winter. I mean, you 'ardly got a sweat up! Them showers is colder than fuckin' charity!'

Peekay laughed. He instinctively liked the little Londoner. He shrugged his shoulders. 'It's a nasty colonial habit, Togger.'

'Oi! I've heard about you lot, washin' all the bleedin' natural oils off of your skin with all them showers. 'Ere, lemme show you.' He lifted his left arm and upended the tin of baby powder. A cloud of powder exploded in the region of his underarm. He changed hands and repeated the process under his right arm. Then he shook the tin vigorously, rubbing the powder into his ginger-coloured short and curlies until they looked as white as Santa's beard. 'That's a British version of the winter shower,' he announced. 'You stay warm, smell like a rose and you don't 'arm your natural supply of precious body oils which stop you from aging prematurely and being all 'orrible and wrinkled up like a boardin' 'ouse prune!'

Peekay laughed, his ribs hurting where Best had landed a brace of good punches. 'No thanks, Togger, I guess I'm doomed to premature loss of my precious body oils.'

Fred entered with the bucket and sponge from the ring and observed the two young boxers. 'Makin' friends, that's good that is,' he glanced back at the door, as though Best had only just left. 'No point in bein' like

93

that afterwards, it don't make you no better.'

Hymie and Harriet were standing with Dutch Holland when the two young boxers emerged from the change room. Hymie was smoking a dark-brown Russian sobranie and the acrid smell of the Turkish tobacco filled the small gymnasium. It was mixed with the sweeter aroma of Dutch Holland's Cuban cigar.

'Dutch here says okay,' Hymie grinned.

Peekay whooped like a schoolboy, totally elated. 'Thank you, Mr Holland. I won't let you down, sir, I've never been surer of anything in my life.'

Dutch Holland turned to Peekay. 'If you're prepared to graft, son, I think I can promise you a crack at the British Empire title in two years, or I'm not the Flying Dutchman.'

'Sooner,' Peekay said softly.

Dutch looked surprised. 'What? What did you say, son?'

'Sooner, please, Mr Holland. I can't wait two years.'

Dutch Holland smiled. 'Sorry, lad, you can't hold a major British title until you're twenty-one, that's the law in this country.'

'Well, Mr Holland, we'll just have to miss out on it and go higher. It's not the law in America.'

Peekay was aware of the sudden silence around him. Hymie knew of course, but they'd agreed he'd say nothing about it to Dutch Holland, afraid it would frighten him away. Peekay had only spoken up now because he'd suddenly become afraid the British trainer might aim too low, content to take less than Peekay wanted.

'World?' Dutch Holland smiled, then seemed almost to chortle, which seemed a thoroughly inappropriate sound coming from his owlish face. He took a pull at his big cigar and, shaking his head incredulously, blew his cigar smoke towards the ceiling. 'The welterweight title is owned by Jake "Spoonbill" Jackson, a black boy from Louisville, Kentucky ...' He tapped the corona with a cocktail-sausage finger. 'Now, mind, I haven't seen this lad fight, but I'm not about to quibble with the latest *Ring* magazine who rate him the best boxer, pound for pound, in the bleedin' world! And he's only twenty-three, my son!'

'It's just that we're in a hurry, Dutch,' Hymie replied quietly.

'Hurry? You've got a jet-propelled rocket up your bums, the pair of you!'

Peekay's heart was beating fast. He'd probably acted stupidly but he couldn't help himself. He had eighteen months, at the outside two years, to get a crack at the title. He'd waited long enough; by the time he'd finished at Oxford he wanted it over. Holland simply had to try to understand that, now, at the very beginning of their relationship.

Harriet had wanted to go to the Tate to see the new Jacob Epstein sculpture as well as a recently acquired Degas bronze study of a child ballet dancer. Then she and Hymie were going to drive to Berkshire to a school-friend's twenty-first. Peekay was taking the evening train back from Paddington to Oxford. Togger listened as they discussed which train would be best; it was a Friday night and Harriet suggested Peekay catch an early train to avoid the commuters and people going up to the country for the weekend.

Togger followed Peekay to the toilet. 'Oi, how about letting me show you the bleedin' metropolis tonight? Stay over, mate, you can doss at my place. It ain't fancy but me sister's not home, you can have her bed. Wad-dayasay, Peekay? We'll 'ave a few jugs, see a bit 'a the West End, 'ave a few laughs?'

Peekay immediately agreed. He was still elated by the outcome of the morning but now he was beginning to realise just how much the prospect of the session with Dutch Holland had played on his mind. The idea of relaxing and seeing London with Togger appealed to him enormously. Togger agreed to meet him later at a pub down the Old Kent Road with the improbable name of the World Upside Down.

'Main bar could be a titch crowded. I'll wait in the saloon bar.' Togger glanced down at Peekay's shoes, his eyes travelling upwards until they reached his face. ''Ere, I'll bring you some clobber. I'll be the bleedin' laughing stock if I'm seen with you lookin' like that. What size clod'oppers you take?'

Peekay looked down at his duffel coat, brown corduroys and finally at his crepe-soled brown shoes known as brothel creepers. 'Seven,' he said.

'Do the best I can. See you later then, don't be late.' Togger left them at the steps of the Tate and ran to catch a bus.

Five

The clock on the charge office wall showed a quarter to two when Tandia finally lifted the large basin to her head and started to walk out of the Cato Manor Police Station. She kept her eyes downcast and followed Geldenhuis out into the dark street. As she passed through the door the black constable whispered, '*Hamba khashle, inikhosatana*, go well, young lady.'

'C'mon! I haven't got all bladdy night!' Geldenhuis called. Tandia walked slowly towards the police car. He stood beside the open boot and indicated she should put the basin in and then slammed it shut. 'Climb in the back, be quick!' he snapped, the authority now back in his voice.

Tandia's relief at leaving was so great that she hardly noticed which way Geldenhuis drove. They seemed to drive for some time through the dark streets of the township and then onto a tarred road with street lights. It was not until they reached the lighted street that he spoke to her again.

'I can't take you to the place where this woman is, so I'm taking you to the train station. There are no more trains tonight but you must wait there.' He offered no further explanation and shortly afterwards they drove up to the Cato Manor railway station. 'Wait in the car,' he said and then walked up the steps into the stationmaster's office.

He returned quite soon with a sleepy looking railway official and told Tandia to get out of the car. The man from the railway was the first person other than policemen Tandia had seen in what seemed to her like a lifetime. To Tandia he represented the normal world she had once known and she immediately felt more secure. The official wasn't wearing the coat of his blue serge uniform; his waistcoat was unbuttoned and his tie knot pulled down, which made him look friendlier. A bluish rash of stubble covered his jowls and he scratched at his crotch absently as though he was not yet properly awake.

In a manner common to South African whites, Geldenhuis spoke to the railway official as though Tandia wasn't present. 'Look, man, I want you to let this girl sit on a bench until the first train.' He paused. 'By the way, when is that?'

The railway official automatically reached for his pocket watch. Forgetting that his waistcoat was unbuttoned he dug his thumb and forefinger into the roll of fat where his fob pocket ought to have been. 'Ten minutes to five,' he said automatically, looking down into his empty hand.

'Ja, okay, she will be gone before then.'

The railway official looked at Tandia for the first time. 'Has she got a pass?' He pointed at her and turned to Geldenhuis. 'She looks like she's been in a fight. She's not a *tsotsi*'s girl is she?' The idea of her being a street hooligan's woman seemed to wake him up and he wagged the finger at Tandia. 'I don't want any trouble from a bladdy coloured or kaffir gang, you hear?'

'No, man, no trouble,' Geldenhuis said impatiently, 'Jus' let her sit on a bench, okay, hey?'

The railway man shrugged. 'Ja, if she's got a pass it's okay by me.'

Geldenhuis clicked his tongue. 'No, man, she hasn't got a pass! I just want her to sit on a bench until some people come.'

'You better give me your name and your phone number in case some other police come,' said the stationmaster.

Geldenhuis wrote down his phone number and name and, tearing the page from a small spiral notepad, handed it to the official who turned and walked away without bidding him goodnight.

Geldenhuis turned to Tandia. 'Don't try and leave here; you haven't got a night pass, and if some other police pick you up you'll be charged and go to the lock-up for six days. Just stay here on a bench, okay?'

Tandia nodded; the thought of being apprehended again terrified her. Geldenhuis opened the boot and she lifted the basin to her head. Very little strength remained in her beaten body and she rose slowly to an upright position. 'Can I go now please, sir?' she whispered.

'Ja, go!'

Tandia walked up the station steps into the building. 'Hey!' Geldenhuis called. The heavy basin on her head caused Tandia to turn slowly to face him. If he called her back again she knew she would surely faint. He stood with his elbow resting on the top of the open driver's door.

'Yes, sir?' it was hardly a whisper and the white policeman would have had difficulty even detecting the movement of her lips.

Geldenhuis patted the breast pocket of his uniform and grinned. 'Jus' remember, jong, in the eyes of the law you nothing but a whore!'

Tandia turned and walked into the station building where she found a bench on the platform stencilled 'Non-Whites'. She pushed the basin under the bench and sat down on the deserted platform. She was unutterably tired but the joy of having finally escaped Geldenhuis overcame her weariness for a moment and she impulsively rose from the bench and pulled the basin out from under it.

The two cotton shirts into which Apple Sammy, Tandia's kewpie doll, had been wrapped hadn't come undone when the basin had toppled to the road. Now she removed the doll and examined it. Apple Sammy had large, ingenuous dark-blue eyes which had faded somewhat and the once bright rose rouge on his cheeks was now only faintly discernible, but he seemed no worse for wear. Tandia adjusted the doll's legs and pulled at his tiny pink organza skirt.

Tandia sat with the small doll clutched tightly to her chest and started to rock. She was too tired to try to think about what might happen next. Weariness overcame her and despite her fear of being accosted on the lonely platform, she fell asleep.

Tandia wakened slowly. Her body ached terribly but her head, which also hurt, rested against a warm, wonderful softness. She felt herself cradled, as though she was being held in a comforting embrace. The experience was so unfamiliar that, at first, she believed herself to be dreaming. To add to the dreaming quality, a sweet-smelling perfume reached her nostrils. Slowly, tentatively, she opened her eyes.

'Shhh, *skatterbol*,' she heard a woman's voice say softly.

Tandia looked down. She still clutched Apple Sammy to her chest. She tried to sit up but the arm around her held her firmly. Frightened, she looked up into the caramel-coloured face of a very big and smiling woman with the longest false eyelashes she had ever seen.

The woman wore an outrageously large purple hat decorated with pink ostrich feathers. Her pink satin dress stretched tightly over her enormous bosom, at the same time allowing a large amount of warm caramel flesh to spill out of its deeply plunging neckline so that her breasts looked as though they were trying to escape. The effect the woman created was of richness, and the strong, sweet-smelling perfume which Tandia now realised belonged to her, added to the opulent effect.

'Don't be frightened, baby, I ain't going to hurt you none.' The words were clipped and staccato and sounded American. 'Name's Mama Tequila, pleased ter . . . meet'cha.' She offered her right hand for Tandia to shake.

'Hi,' Tandia whispered, barely touching the hand with its long, shiny red nails.

'What's your name, honey?'

'Tandia,' she cleared her throat, 'Tandia Patel.'

'Tandia, that's a real swell name. You got no place to go? That's it, huh? You little orphan Annie sittin' on your fanny?' Mama Tequila had the raspy voice of a heavy smoker and now she laughed uproariously at her own joke, interjecting her laughter with a fit of coughing. She stopped laughing abruptly and reached into her handbag, a large purple leather affair that matched her hat. From it she withdrew a silver cigarette case. 'Smoke, honey?'

Tandia, who was completely overwhelmed by the presence of this large woman, shook her head.

Mama Tequila helped herself to a cigarette, closed the case and tapped the tobacco end on its silver lid. She returned the case to her bag and then dug around in it to produce a regulation American army Zippo lighter. She flicked it alight and held it to the end of the cigarette, squinting through the smoke as she drew in and then exhaled. Then she slipped the cover back over the Zippo and returned it to her handbag. She spoke with the cigarette between her lips. 'It ain't pretty like everything else, but it sure lights every time. I kind of like pretty things, but a pretty lighter that don't work is like a pretty woman that don't work.' She withdrew the cork tip from her lips. 'Ain't no good to nobody, leastways herself!' She chuckled, 'I bet you like pretty things too, hey honey?'

Tandia didn't answer. She wanted to pinch herself to make sure she wasn't dreaming; nothing like this monstrous pink creature had ever happened to her before.

'Sure you do, you a very pretty girl, pretty girls got to have pretty things, or they die!' She shook her head slowly as though talking to herself. 'There is plenty of time to be ugly.' She turned and looked directly at Tandia. 'You got to use pretty, while you got pretty, honey, that the rule of womankind!'

Mama Tequila started to chuckle again, her breasts heaving. 'You see this big, hip-pie-pot-to-mass, honey? Well, once upon a time, I was just as pretty and dainty as you, baby.' She seemed to find this particularly funny, her laughter disappearing finally into a wheeze until she grew quite red in the face and started to cough. She threw the cigarette to the ground and bending forward brought both her hands up to cover her mouth. Tandia knew she ought to pat her on the back but she hesitated. She had never deliberately touched an adult female person before and now the idea frightened her.

Mama Tequila glanced at her briefly between a spasm of coughing. Her eyes were teary from the coughing and her mascara had started to run; she seemed to be appealing for her help. Tandia took a deep breath and started to slap the large woman on her back. To her surprise Mama Tequila ceased coughing almost immediately. In a voice drawn thin after the paroxysm of coughing she said, 'Ain't nutting but coffin nails, them damned cigarillos!'

She straightened up, dug into her handbag and produced an absurdly small lace handkerchief with which she wiped her eyes; then she held it to her nose and blew. She found a compact in her bag and proceeded to repair her make-up. Returning the make-up to her bag, she turned to Tandia, her face serious for a moment. 'This ain't no place for a couple of high-class ladies, honey,' she rasped.

Tandia instinctively liked the big woman. She wanted to go with her but her escape from Geldenhuis was still too recent. The idea of being tied to another human being she didn't know and whose motives she couldn't begin to discern, frightened her. 'Where we going to?' Instinctively she picked up Apple Sammy from her lap and clutched the doll to her chest.

Mama Tequila didn't answer her directly. Instead she looked hard into Tandia's eyes. 'Look, kid, you a mess. You been beat up bad.' She touched Tandia's face gently. 'Look what them mothers did to you!' She reached out and removed Apple Sammy from Tandia's grasp and placed the kewpie doll on her lap. Then she took both Tandia's arms, and drew them gently towards her. When she spoke again the toughness had gone from her voice.

'You poor baby, them wrists, they are bad. We got to clean you up, honey. We leave you like this you going to have yourself a pair of permanent bracelets.'

Mama Tequila placed Tandia's hands back on her lap one on either side of Apple Sammy. Then she rose slowly from the bench and began to tug at her skirt, pulling the tight satin back down to her knees. She adjusted her hat in an imaginary mirror, her hands fluttering around its rim, a small tug here and a little pat there, like two busy brown spiders, the ends of their fat legs dipped in brilliant scarlet.

She took a few steps towards the entrance of the station, and pushing two fingers into her mouth she let go a piercing whistle. She turned to Tandia. 'C'mon, kid, let's kick the dust, we're going home to Bluey Jay.'

In what seemed like a matter of moments a tall, very black man appeared. His head was completely shaved and a jagged scar ran diagonally across the top of his shiny scalp to just above his left eyebrow. It looked as though the skull had been cracked open and then clamped until it grew back together again. The eye directly under the scar was only half open, a condition which seemed permanent as the skin around the eye was puckered like the top of a leather drawstring purse. The tall black man smiled as he approached Mama Tequila and Tandia noticed that his two front teeth were missing but the incisors on either side had each been filed to a point and were made of gold.

'This is Edward, King George, Juicey Fruit Mambo, honey. He is my driver. Just call him Juicey Fruit Mambo. Never mind your basin, he'll bring it.' Mama

Tequila started to walk away. 'Now you just follow me, baby,' she called; she seemed to alternate the two endearments 'honey' and 'baby' as though she hadn't quite decided which suited Tandia best, though 'baby' seemed to be winning.

Juicey Fruit Mambo grinned at Tandia. He reminded Tandia of a horror story she'd read as a small girl in a book she'd borrowed from the school library. It had been entitled 'Doctor Weirdwolfe's Tales of the Super-natural'. The scariest story in the book was about a monster named the Master of Evil who lived in the *under-world* with a huge and grotesque wet nurse who cared for the monster children of his victims. They all lived in a giant tent made from the membraned wings of vampire bats, surrounded by a garden of carnivorous plants that fed on birds and bats and flying insects, reaching up on coiled stems to snatch them from the very air itself. The Master of Evil would come up into the *above-world* through the foul-smelling city sewers, into the dark, cold, misty streets where he would waylay young women returning from the tavern at night, biting them on the right breast with his two gold incisors so that nine months later they gave birth to boy monsters.

Juicey Fruit Mambo bent from the waist and scooped up Tandia's basin. He held it in front of him as though it was a tray filled with precious things charged especially to his care. Tandia thanked him softly and, picking up Apple Sammy from the bench, she followed the large, pink woman out of the station building.

Directly below the steps, where Geldenhuis had parked the police car, now stood a large black motor with its engine running and its back door open. Mama Tequila stood at the car door and waited for Tandia to reach her before she got in. She patted the seat beside her. 'Come, baby, you're safe in Mama's big, black, shiny Packard limousine. Come sit here with Mama, honey.'

The back of the car smelt of expensive leather, not unlike Patel's boots when they were new. Tandia sat wide-eyed and nervous on the edge of the back seat with her hands tightly gripping the seat in front of her. Mama Tequila took Apple Sammy from Tandia's lap and placed the doll between the two of them. 'She a proper lady riding in a limousine now, honey,' she said and then, as though to demonstrate how a proper lady sat, she closed her eyes and fell back into the soft leather, exhausted.

Tandia heard the slam of the boot closing and moments later Juicey Fruit opened the driver's door and slid behind the wheel. 'Home to Bluey Jay,' Mama Tequila instructed wearily without opening her eyes, 'We gonna take Miss Tandia here into our everlovin' care.'

The big car climbed away from the flats of Cato Manor station towards the Berea, away from the poorer parts of the city into the heights above Durban where the posh white people lived, a part of town where Africans, Indians or coloureds weren't allowed to live even if they had all the money in the world.

Soon they left the big walled houses and leafy streets of the Berea behind and drove down dark avenues of gum trees. The white bark on their perfectly straight trunks ghosted as the headlights caught and then lost them again. Once in a while they'd pass the shadowy outline of a house set back from the road and then they left the bluegums and for a short while they drove along the open highway on the road to Pietermaritzburg.

Juicey Fruit Mambo finally slowed the Packard and turned into a small dirt road.

The way was no more than a farm road, rutted and uneven in places so that Juicey Fruit Mambo seldom took the Packard out of low gear. Half a mile or so up this road he stopped at an imposing set of double wrought-iron gates set between two large white painted cement pillars. It was bright moonlight and it was easy to see that not even a wire strand fence was attached to either side of the brilliant white gateposts. In fact, these posts were not white at all, but a violent pink in the light of day; now, caught in the bright headlights of the car they looked dazzling white.

Juicey Fruit Mambo tapped the horn once sharply, even though a small boy of about eight years old holding a hurricane lamp was hurrying down the long curved driveway towards the gate. The boy was almost immediately followed by an old Zulu running on spindly buckled legs who carried a *knopkierie* and a short *asegai* in one hand and with the other held up his ragged khaki shorts to prevent them from falling down.

The boy placed the hurricane lamp on the side of the driveway and swung the gates open just as the Zulu came to a panting halt and stood to attention at the side of the driveway. Still clutching his pants he gave Juicey Fruit Mambo and his passengers a toothless smile and saluted, touching the large wooden knob of his fighting stick and the blade of his spear lightly to his grizzled head.

Juicey Fruit Mambo laughed. 'Go back to sleep, old man. Go back and dream of a hundred cattle and five fat-buttocked wives all of dem young with sweet milk in their breasts.' Pointing to the small boy, he added, 'Dis brave warrior will guard us well tonight, see, it is a miracle, his pants stay up on their own. So he has both hands free to fight de evil *skokiaan*.' He reached out and patted the small boy on the head and then pointed to the full moon which frosted the surrounding trees and silvered the surrounding landscape with a light almost as clear as day. 'Tonight, God has supplied de light. Do not insult him with your little lantern. If I had a newspaper and, if I could read, I would read by the light. Dere are no shadows in such a night to conceal danger. Is it too much to ask that you can walk by it?' He slipped the car into gear and moved into the long driveway leading to the house.

Around a curve the lights of the Packard revealed a large mansion resting amongst several very big trees. The house was in darkness except for a solitary light which burned a dim welcome inside the arched doorway. The driveway led directly past the front of the house and Juicey Fruit Mambo continued past the front door and around the far side of the house. Caught in the headlights, Tandia observed what appeared to be a row of outhouses. Juicey Fruit Mambo drove past these to the very end and turned the Packard into a lean-to garage.

Mama Tequila, who had remained with her eyes closed even at the gate, now opened them as Juicey Fruit Mambo switched off the ignition. 'Welcome to Bluey Jay, honey,' she said wearily.

Juicey Fruit Mambo opened the rear door on Tandia's side. The very first sounds she heard as she stepped from the car were the croaking of a frog and the electric singing of crickets. Holding Apple Sammy tightly she stood waiting, sensing the alien space around her. The air was cool and she could smell the slightly damp earth at her feet and the cudlike odour of the grass. It made her think of Patel in his cold grave and she shuddered involuntarily. A sudden breeze arose and sent the leaves of the large trees around the house roaring. Just as suddenly the breeze stopped and after barely a moment of silence the frog and the crickets took up again. The sky, almost pewter in the moonlight, showed a few of the brighter stars and through the branches of a giant old wild fig tree she could see the speckled light of the moon. Tandia had never been in the country before and she found it frightening and very strange. Never mind the Master of Evil lurking in the city sewers, some very strange things could happen in all this space and loneliness, she thought.

'Come, baby, it's late, we got to clean you up some and put you to bed.' Mama Tequila took Tandia by the elbow and they followed Juicey Fruit Mambo, who'd raced ahead to open the door and turn on a light in the small scullery which served as the back entrance to the house and which led directly through to a large kitchen.

Tandia walked slightly ahead of Mama Tequila as they entered the door, which was only just large enough for the big woman to fit through. She went into the room, brightly lit by four lights which ran down the centre of the ceiling. Taking up the middle part of the room was a huge, scrubbed-pine table above which, from a large circle of iron suspended on heavy chains, hung all manner of pots and pans. A huge cream AGA cooker with two giant covered hotplates sat in a whitewashed alcove. The walls of the kitchen consisted of wooden shiplapped cupboards of a soft yellow wood which stretched up from the floor to a ceiling turned a deep honey colour from a couple of generations of cooking vapours. The room was scrubbed and spotless and smelt of a mixture of blue carbolic soap, floor wax and linseed oil, with just a hint of ground coffee and yesterday's stock-pot added. Its red painted cement floor was waxed and shining. To one side, though commanding a clear view of the entire room, stood a very large leather club chair with a coffee table beside it, on which stood a black bakelite telephone.

Juicey Fruit Mambo pulled a chair from the table and indicated to Tandia that she should sit. Tandia lowered her aching and exhausted body into the chair. She gave a small sigh and rested her arms on the table and, still clutching Apple Sammy in one hand, she placed her head in the crease of her right arm. Within seconds she was asleep. Apple Sammy fell from her grasp and clattered to the floor. Juicey Fruit Mambo, without bending his knees, scooped up the little doll and placed it back on the table. Then he lifted Tandia carefully into an upright sitting position, placed his ear to her chest and pulled one of her eyelids up to examine her eye.

'I do not think she will wake up tonight,' he said as he rearranged Tandia's arms carefully on the table, making sure that her wrists were not pressured. Then he lowered her head to rest on the upper part of her right arm once again.

Mama Tequila came over to the table to look at Tandia. She spoke quietly in Zulu to the tall African. 'This one is a great prize; you must take good care of her.' She turned and walked slowly towards the large armchair.

'I hear you, Mama Tequila,' Juicey Fruit Mambo replied softly, his expression serious. 'She is like a young tsamma melon ready to be picked. I think, for the white man, this one, she is very beautiful?'

Mama Tequila gave a soft sigh, but made no reply as she shifted her huge weight down onto the leather armchair. A slow protesting 'pffft' of air escaped from the leather upholstery.

'I will make coffee and bring you some Cape brandy?'

'No, first you must wash the girl and bandage her. Put her in Hester's room for tonight. She's gone to the Drakensberg with her Boer from the Free State.' Mama Tequila fanned herself absently with a Japanese fan. The design on the fan showed a demure little geisha girl peeping from behind a fan of her own. 'Also, the way she walked, I think she been raped. Make sure she's clean at the back and is not hurt in the front.'

Juicey Fruit Mambo lifted Tandia's limp form from the chair and carried her from the room. Mama Tequila reached into her bag and found a cork-tip, but after taking only a couple of puffs she ground it impatiently in the ashtray beside her and reached for the telephone, which she placed on her lap. She dialed a number and sighed heavily as she waited for someone to pick up at the other end. 'Cato Manor *Polise Stasie*,' a sleepy voice answered.

'Sergeant, you the best, you hear! This little baby, she the greatest po-ten-shal I ever did see!' Mama Tequila gushed.

Geldenhuis switched to English. 'Ag, it's you, Mama Tequila. Everything is all right then?'

'You done me a good turn, Sergeant,' Mama Tequila paused for effect. 'My mama always told me, "Child, one good turn deserve another."' She waited for the policeman to make his demand.

'Not now. Some other time. I'll let you know,' Geldenhuis said.

Mama Tequila grimaced in annoyance. She liked things clean-cut, that way you knew where you stood. She chuckled. 'Your pleasure is my pleasure, Sergeant. You come any time, you hear?'

'Ja, okay, so long, Mama Tequila.'

She heard the click as he replaced the receiver. A lot of cops came to Bluey Jay. The law of the one-eyed snake was stronger than the Immorality Act forbidding sex between whites and coloured or black people, but she always felt uncomfortable when Geldenhuis arrived. He would sit in the small parlour bar and sip a beer and talk to the girls but he'd never partake, never leave the bar and slip quietly upstairs with one of them to return, in the timeless brothel tradition, half an hour later to slip into his seat unseen and unseeing as if nothing had happened.

There was something wrong with that one. By this she didn't mean that Geldenhuis was a corrupt young cop. Mama Tequila was completely resigned to that. After all, if there were no bad cops she wouldn't be in business, or at the very least, business would be a damn sight harder. It was more than that, and she wondered if it had been him who had raped the girl. She made a mental note to get to know Geldenhuis better. Until you knew a man's special weakness, that thing which would indict him in his own eyes, you were vulnerable. She was smart enough to know that the old-fashioned type of policeman, the good old guys who came for an occasional quickie and who you paid with a fiver every week and threw in a few quid as an annual donation to the Police Boys' Boxing Club, were on the way out. The Geldenhuis era had arrived.

Six

Peekay got off the Old Kent Road one bus stop too soon for the strangely named pub where he was to meet Togger, but a group of women crowding around a vegetable barrow sent him on his way. 'You got off too soon for the World, love, just keep walking.'

Togger was the only man in the saloon bar; there were several older women. He had an almost empty half pint of bitter in front of him and was yacking away to the old biddies. He seemed relieved when Peekay entered nearly ten minutes late. 'Found it okay, then?' Peekay nodded. Togger turned to the ladies in the bar. 'It's been fascinating meetin' you, ladies, but I'm afraid me an' me partner here 'as got to move on to warmer climes. Don't do nothing I wouldn't do now, will yer.' Togger downed what remained of his drink, picked up a large shopping bag and took Peekay by the arm. ''Ere, we'll just nick into the toilet. I got your *schmutter* for tonight.'

Togger was dressed in a black suit with a three-button jacket cut very long so that it hung below his knees. The lapels and cuffs were made of black velvet and the stovepipe pants were so narrow they took the shape of his legs. From the cuffs protruded a highly shone pair of winklepicker black shoes which came to a sharp point. With his white shirt he wore a black silk tie no more than half an inch wide. 'I hope it fits, it's me mate, Tim's. He works Friday night at the docks, same as me old man. It's good clobber, tailor made an' all.'

'It's good of you, Togger.'

'Naa! Think nothing of it, mate, least I could do.'

Togger waited while Peekay changed. Tim's suit turned out to be an amazingly good fit, even the shoes felt comfortable. 'Very suave. Very bloody suave,' Togger marvelled as Peekay opened the toilet door. 'You look smashin', mate.' Togger put his hand into his pocket and produced a small green bottle. ''Ere, 'ave a go at this, you'll smell like a bleedin' ponce, but the girls love it!'

Peekay cupped his hands and Togger shook three or four drops of the green cologne into them. He capped the bottle as Peekay patted the aftershave onto his jowls. 'Tim got it off a queer who bought it in Paris.' Togger read the small silver label: 'Pinaud eau de toilette.' He pronounced it 'Pinord ewe de toilet. It's the genuine froggie leg-opener stuff, mate, no messing about! A bird gets a whiff of this she's practically begging for it, right off!'

Peekay laughed. 'You know something, Togger, except for Harriet today and some of the girls on the boat coming over – but they were too stuck up and only went with the ship's officers – I haven't been near a chick since the last school dance which was . . . Christ, maybe two years ago.'

Togger looked genuinely shocked. He rubbed his hand through his ginger mop. 'You're kiddin' me now, ain't you, Peekay? You mean you just been wanking on your own?'

Peekay blushed, but nodded. There seemed no point in denying it. Togger laughed. 'Me grandad, he was a randy old sod, he used to say, "Ain't nothin' wrong with wankin', matter of fact, with masturbation you meets a much better class of woman!"'

Peekay laughed. 'All I meant was, it would be nice to meet a few girls for a change. The ones you see at Oxford seem to be trying their hardest to be neuter. They're not women, they're brains riding bicycles!'

'Say no more, my son. Leave it to your old mate, Togger. We'll 'ave a pint here and then we'll drop in home and stow yer clobber. After that we'll have a feed of fish 'n chips at a caf I know near the Elephant and Castle and then it's straight to the Streatham Locarno!' He paused for effect. 'It's Friday night, pay day, place will be wall-to-wall with top crumpet. Then, if we are not rewarded for leadin' blameless lives with a couple of first-class tarts, we'll take the tube uptown. Whaddaya reckon?'

'Lead on, MacDuff!' Peekay said happily. The teddy-boy outfit he was wearing made him feel different.

Togger picked up the shopping bag which now contained Peekay's clothes. 'You dance?' he asked. Peekay nodded. He'd learned to jive on the boat over.

'It's just round the corner.'

The house had a doorway set directly onto the street, part of a double-storey terrace. The door opened into a small parlour; the air was stale and smelt slightly sour as they stepped inside. An overweight woman who looked in her fifties – it was difficult to tell – wearing a dirty housecoat and slippers, lay dozing on a couch drawn up in front of a coal fire. She opened her eyes as they entered, though her expression didn't change. It seemed to take several moments for her to focus on them. 'Sh'you, Togger?'

'Yes, mum.' He turned to Peekay. 'She's on the sauce early, no use trying to talk. Me old man musta gone off early, she usually waits till he's off before she hits the bottle. Still an' all, that means the bedroom's free.'

Peekay saw how small the house was. 'Look, Togger, I'm not intruding am I?'

'No, Peekay, you're welcome. It ain't Buck House, but there's a bed for you.'

Togger picked up the carrier bag with Peekay's clothes. 'Hang on, I'll stow this stuff upstairs, won't be a tic!'

'A minute later Togger bounced down the stairs. 'Righto!' Togger glanced at his watch. 'It's half six, let's be off then, place is crawlin' with crumpet by now, you mark me words.'

They arrived at the Streatham Locarno about eight. The dance hall was already packed. All the girls were dressed up to the nines and stood around in groups watching the dancers and mostly giggling. Peekay and Togger stood on the edge of the large dance floor eyeing the talent. 'May I suggest a modis opa-randy,' Togger asked.

Peekay nodded happily. 'As you say, Togger. There are some bloody nice-looking girls here.'

'Now that's just it, yer see. Getting a good sort and not a scrubber takes a fair amount of cunning. If you watch carefully you'll notice most birds go around in pairs, a pretty one and an ugly one. I dunno why this is, must have something to do with nature. But a good-looking bird always has a proper turn-off with her. A fat pimple-picker with hairy legs. Take my word for it, go fer the scrubber. Do a coupl'a turns with her on the floor, then ask her mate for a dance. Works every time. The scrubber's happy 'cause she 'asn't been ignored, an' the good sort don't feel guilty no more for 'aving a good time, know what I mean?'

'Ja, I see what you mean,' Peekay said, looking about him. He soon spied a nice-looking blonde wearing a tight pink angora sweater, wide white skirt and black patent-leather high-heeled courts. Her hair was swept back into a ponytail. Beside her, dressed in a bright red, off-the-shoulder dress, which fitted her pudgy form rather too well, was her red-headed, big-breasted friend. 'Hey, Togger, see the dame in the white skirt, the one with the marvellous tits?' Peekay said urgently. He frowned suddenly. 'Are you certain about this theory of yours?'

Togger patted Peekay on the shoulder. 'Trust me, my son. Follow your old uncle Togger's instructions and you'll be in like bleedin' Flynn, I promise!'

Peekay moved towards the fat girl in the undersized red dress. 'May I have this dance?' he asked politely.

'Eh?' The fat girl, chewing gum, cocked her head and closed one eye to look at Peekay.

'May I have this dance?' Peekay repeated.

The girl giggled. 'Oo! Ain't you the polite one!' She turned to the girl beside her and giggled again. 'No thanks, we don't dance with toffs.'

'Hey! Who you callin' a toff, slut? This is me mate, Peekay, from South Africa. You gonna dance with him or not? Make up yer bleedin' mind, you slack tart!'

The fat girl looked surprised and then grinned at Togger. 'Oo! lovely!' She grabbed his arm. 'I bet you're a smashin' dancer an' all!' Togger was almost jerked off his feet onto the dance floor.

117

Peekay turned to the blonde in the angora. 'I'm a toff from Oxford University. Would you care to dance with me?'

'Don't mind if I do. I'm partial to a bit of class. I'm Doris. What's your name, then? Peekay, is it?'

Doris was a top dancer and Peekay had learned enough on the boat over to cope about as well as any of the other guys on the floor. Togger was lost amongst the whirling bodies, and after twenty minutes or so, Doris pulled Peekay away from the floor. 'What'll it be, Doris?' Peekay asked.

'Ooh! Don't mind if I do. I'll 'ave a Babycham,' Doris pushed herself closely against him, and Peekay felt the curve of her left breast against his chest. His heart began to pound. They found a table and Doris sat down while a somewhat agitated Peekay went over to the bar, fighting to calm his imagination so he could take his hand out of his pocket.

Peekay had a coke while Doris toyed with her Babycham served up in a cheap champagne glass with a short straw. She smoked, using a holder, and her nails were long and painted a shiny red. Try as he might, Peekay couldn't keep his eyes off her breasts. Doris didn't seem to mind. 'If you're such a toff, how come you wearing that suit, then? That's a Ted's clobber, that is,' she laughed.

Peekay grinned. 'It belongs to Togger's mate.' He reverted back to his usual accent. 'I'm not really a toff, Doris. Togger and I are boxers and I'm a student.'

'And you're from South Africa then? What the girls like in South Africa? They all black? What's it like goin' with a black girl?'

'Jeez, so many questions. Yes, pretty; no, I don't know.'

'Come again?'

'I've never been out with a black girl.'

'Why's that, then?'

'Well in South Africa,' Peekay paused, not sure how to answer. 'Well, whites don't go out with blacks, I mean girls.'

'Why not? What's wrong with black women?'

Peekay glanced up to see whether Doris was having him on, but her question seemed perfectly innocent. 'Ja, well nothing, I suppose, it's just, well it's not the thing to do.'

'You're barmy. If you ask me, I'd like to go with a black man. I got a girlfriend who goes out with a Jamaican, he's smashin'.'

Just then Togger emerged, held firmly by the arm. He was sweating and looked somewhat nonplussed. 'Oi, Peekay!' he called.

Peekay rose as they reached the table. 'What'll it be?' he asked Togger, who was standing slightly behind the big girl. Togger shook his head violently; his eyes cast heavenwards, he ran his finger across his throat. But it was too late. The big girl was already beginning to sit down. 'Ooh, Babycham!' She seemed to have forgotten that she'd earlier rejected Peekay and looked up at him, beaming.

'With a dash, please!' Peekay looked puzzled. 'My Babycham, with a little drop of brandy,' she repeated.

'Half a bitter,' Togger added wearily, borrowing a chair from an adjacent table and sitting down.

'Another Babycham, Doris?'

'Ta very much, Peekay.'

'With a dash?'

Doris giggled, giving Peekay a saucy look. Peekay was waiting at the bar when Togger appeared at his side. The barman was pulling Togger's half pint. 'Christ, Peekay, we got to scarper!' He pointed to the two Babychams on the counter. 'Know what they are? They're leg-openers, dead set!'

Peekay looked pleased. 'I thought that was the general idea?'

'Oh, mate! Have a heart! Two or three of them and that Gladys is gonna rape me! She dances like a bleedin' hippo. I think me shoulder's dislocated an' all.' He took a hurried gulp from the half pint on the counter, wiping his mouth with the back of his hand. 'Plenty more where them two come from uptown.'

'Not with tits like Doris!' Peekay said, reaching for the two glasses.

'Better! I know this strip joint, I know the birds an' all. You think she's got tits!' Togger rolled his eyes. 'One girl, Geraldine, she's got bristols you can see comin' round the corner ten seconds before the rest of her arrives.'

'Jesus, Togger, I reckon a few more dances and a few more of these, I could put the hard word on Doris.'

'No doubt about it, Peekay, but I reckon our friendship couldn't stand the bleedin' strain.'

Half an hour later, after Togger had sworn on a stack of imaginary bibles that he'd call Gladys and Peekay had written down Doris's number at the Dolls' Hospital where she worked in Hammersmith, they were back on a bus headed for the West End.

'I'm telling you, Togger, this better be bloody good,' Peekay chaffed. 'By the way, I want to congratulate you. That theory of yours, it works amazingly well!'

Togger threw Peekay a sour look; then he giggled. 'Jesus, Peekay, when she grabbed me and hauled me onto the bleedin' dance floor I nearly shit meself!'

'This strip joint, what's it like?' Peekay asked.

'About the same as any other, I suppose, only I know the birds at this one, so we won't have to pay a pound a drink.'

'How much?' He was aghast.

'Well that's it, you see, it's a private club like. You pay three quid to be a member and then you buy drinks for the girls at a quid a time; that's how the management makes a crust. There's hundreds of them clubs accounting for every taste.'

Peekay's mind boggled. This was the big time all right. 'I've only got about four quid left, Togger.'

'Blimey, Peekay, we're the bleedin' cog-nos-centee. Paying's for mugs 'n perverts. Besides, me sister works there, don't she?'

'Your sister's a stripper!' The words were out before Peekay realised what he'd said, or rather, how he'd said it.

Togger looked at Peekay with a hurt expression. Peekay grabbed his shoulder. 'I apologise, Togger. I didn't mean it to sound like that. It's just that I've never been to a strip club. I've never seen a stripper!'

'And you think a stripper's on the game, is that it?'

Peekay coloured violently. 'Togger, honest, I don't know what to say. This, it's all new to me. I was brought up in Pentecostal church, the Apostolic Faith Mission. Pastor Mulvery used to say that a girl who wears lipstick and paints her nails is a fallen woman, and as for a stripper? Shit, I don't think his imagination could stretch that far! But I'm telling you, it would simply have been another name for a whore!'

Togger grinned. 'Say no more, Peekay. It ain't unheard of for a stripper to forsake her art for the easy life on her back. You'll like me sister, she's a model

121

really, and a doo-wap-de-wally-wally girl. Strippin's only Friday and Saturday nights. Times are hard, she's moved out from home.'

'Doo-wap-de-what?'

'A doo-wap-de-wally-wally girl! You know when the singer's beltin' out a song, the three girls who stand behind him with their 'ands out making little circles and their hips swingin', going, '*Doo-wap-de-wally-wally, doo-wap-de-wally-wally*!'

Peekay laughed. 'That's bloody marvellous, doo-wap-de-wally-wally. Wait until I tell Hymie.'

Togger was suddenly serious. 'That's the problem with me whole family. They're all *nearly* but not quite. Carmen, that's me sister, she always wanted to be a jazz singer; she *nearly* made it ... but not quite.'

Peekay rested his hand on Togger's shoulder. 'Listen to me. I know what you're going to say, about this morning when I put you on the seat of your pants ...'

'You're right, Peekay. Here we go again! I thought. Till this morning I reckoned I was just about the best bleedin' amateur welterweight in Britain. I ain't been beat in three years; then you come along and give me a bleedin' boxing lesson!' Togger looked up at Peekay, his eyes tearful. 'Shit, not me also? Not another member of the *nearly-but-not-fucking-quite* family of fucking Browns!' Togger tried to smile. 'Me old man was *nearly* light heavyweight champion of the Merchant Navy, but 'e got knocked out in the final round when he was light years ahead on points.'

'Togger! Stop talking like this! We're in this together, you hear? You train with me, we're going to the top together.' Peekay shook Togger's shoulder. 'You want to know something?' Togger looked at him querulously.

'Take me, I'm so fucking scared I have to win or I'll shit myself.'

'What the hell are you talkin' about?'

Peekay paused. 'Take you, you're not scared of who you are. You're Togger Brown and proud of it. You're known around your manor, people like you, you're open to life and you let it in.' Peekay paused again. 'Even your mum, you're loving and kind to her. Let me tell you about my mum. She's a dressmaker, she worked all her life behind a Singer sewing machine. When she wasn't praying to the Lord she was working for the rich people in town, making their clothes. I had no old man and she kept us, me and my grandpa. But we didn't love her. At six I wrote her off. Ever since, I've felt guilty for not loving her, for not being a real son. You see, for reasons I'll tell you about someday, I was scared when I was a kid. Scared shitless. So I decided to hide, run away from life.'

'You're crackers, Peekay. You! Run away from life? You're going to Oxford and you just might end up world welterweight champion. Do me a favour, son!'

'No, Togger, listen to me, it's true. You can hide in two places, you can be a nobody and simply disappear into the crowd, or you can hide up front, way ahead of anybody else. But that means you can never lose. You've got to fight harder, punch better, get better marks, win, win, win! Sometimes, inside me, I feel fifty years old and always scared. Scared that they – I don't know who "they" is – that *they* will find out who I really am. They'll see the yellow streak under the winning streak, see what's really under all the camouflage.'

Togger's mouth fell open. 'Blimey, Peekay!'

'All I'm trying to say, Togger, is that you seem to be

the furthermost from a *nearly-but-not-quite* personality as it is possible to get.'

Togger, his face serious, looked at Peekay. 'Thanks, Peekay. No, I mean it. Thanks for that, I appreciate your sayin' that a lot.'

'Next stop Piccadilly!' the conductor shouted.

Peekay, following Togger, was soon helplessly lost in the maze of little streets that networked London's Soho district. He was amazed at being accosted by the pros. They stood with unlit cigarettes virtually on every corner. 'Wanna a good time, darling?' It was the universal opening and, to his surprise, some of them were really very sexy. Togger appeared not to notice them, stopping at last outside a building which resembled hundreds they'd passed and which fronted, apart from four or five steps to the door and a small railed fence, directly onto the street. An outside stairway led down to a basement door about ten feet below street level, above which burned a single tiny blue globe set into a socket on the lintel of the doorway. The window beside the doorway was blacked out, though the light from the street lamp reached halfway down the steps.

They descended the steps and Togger pressed the doorbell. Almost immediately the door opened and bright light spilled over them from the interior passageway. A very large, dark-haired guy with thick brows and bad acne scars, dressed in black pants, a white tuxedo top and a red bow tie, greeted them.

'Hello there, young Togger. How's tricks?' He asked in a friendly but surprisingly light voice for such a big man. 'Comin' in then?' He stepped aside, pushing his back to the wall so they could squeeze past him. 'Be a love and sign your guest in,' he said to Togger, without any affectation in his voice.

'Les, this is me mate, Peekay . . . from South Africa. He's a boxer, very handy an' all.'

Les smiled. He was missing three teeth on the left of his lower jaw so his smile looked lop-sided. 'How do, Peekay. We ain't expectin' no trouble, but you never can tell, nice to know we got a coupla likely lads on the premises.' He threw a punch at Togger, hitting him lightly on the shoulder. 'Take care now, Tiger!'

Togger wrote their names in a ledger which stood on a small table at the end of the passageway. Beside it stood a wooden plant stand from which an aspidistra sprouted. On the walls lining the passageway were several hunting prints; the wallpaper was in an art deco design and looked vaguely thirties in appearance. The effect was as though they'd entered the home of a middle-class, middle-aged couple who hadn't bothered to redecorate since their marriage. Only a small modern spotlight, which shone directly at the doorway to bring anyone entering into sharp relief, gave the game away.

The passageway led into a large room filled with a soft orangey red light from two spotlights set into the furthermost corners on either side of a small stage and bar which occupied the front wall area. The walls seemed to be painted in a gloss black and a red velvet upholstered bench ran around them. The remainder of the room was filled with small round tables, none of which seemed to take more than two people. The room was almost full, with about thirty men and a dozen women at the tables. On the bench surrounding the room sat almost as many men holding drinks, though no women. Several girls were serving, dressed in skimpy black satin dresses, the skirts not quite covering their bottoms and the fronts cut low. With this outfit they wore tiny white lace aprons and waitress caps, fishnet stockings and high heels. When they bent over the tables to serve they revealed a generous amount of panty bottom, and written across the panties in some sort of luminous paint were their names. The girl nearest to the entrance where Togger and Peekay stood appeared to be called Gerald, the 'ine' having slipped around the corner of her right buttock.

There appeared to be no band; instead a pair of speakers on either side of the small stage pumped out Dixieland.

'The red lights, they're for the skin tones, see,' Togger explained. 'Strippers always like to work under red lights, it gives 'em a sort of tanned look. You don't see all their bumps an' bruises.'

Peekay followed Togger over to the small bar which sported four chairs, all of which were empty. 'Patrons can't use the bar,' Togger explained. A small neat man in evening dress who appeared to be in his forties, his thinning blond hair greased and combed flat against his scalp, greeted them. 'Gawd, look what the cat's brought in. Who's your pretty friend, Toggalogs?' Without asking, he poured them each a brown ale, half filling the glass and placing the bottles with the remaining beer beside the glasses on the bar.

'Hello, Tony, glad to see you're your cheery self. Tony, this is Peekay, Peekay, Tony. Tony owns this cesspit.'

'Cheeky sod! Welcome to Fleshpot, Peekay,' Tony said, turning to take an order from one of the girls.

'Hello there, Togger, long time no see. Where you been then, darling?' It was the girl with Gerald on her bum.

'Here, there and everywhere, kom-see, kom-sar! You know me, Geraldine, keepin' me nose clean.' Togger turned to include Peekay. 'This is Peekay, from South Africa, he's a mate of mine.'

'Pleased to meetcha, Peekay. You a boxer then?'

Peekay rose slightly awkwardly. Geraldine was pretty and she had a great bosom. 'Hello, Geraldine, nice to know you.' He looked around awkwardly, trying to keep his eyes from her spendid décolletage. 'Wow! What a place. It's all a bit much for a country boy.'

'Keep your hands off that boy, you slack tart.' Tony handed Geraldine her tray of drinks.

'Look who's talkin'!' Geraldine shot back. 'See you both later then, I'll have my numbers by half eleven, I'll buy you a drink.'

'Better get ready, darling, show time!' Tony called after her.

Togger looked surprised. 'You going on, then?'

Geraldine laughed, though a little nervously. 'It's me debut; wish me luck.'

'Break a leg,' Togger said as Geraldine left with the tray. He turned to Peekay. 'She's a nice bird, is Geraldine, very tasty. She comes down with Carmen to the gym sometimes.'

Peekay was too polite to enquire about Togger's sister and Togger didn't seem to be looking around for her. He filled his glass with the remaining brown ale from the bottle. Just then the music stopped. Togger nudged him and indicated with a nod and a look in the direction of Tony behind the bar. Peekay turned to see Tony putting a record on a gramophone. He was wearing a top hat and white gloves; a black malacca cane with a silver top rested at the side of the gramophone. Tony saw Peekay looking at him and pursed his lips in an imaginary kiss. 'You really are a very pretty boy,' he said. Then he pulled at the lapels of his coat and picked up his cane.

Tony let himself out from behind the bar and skipped up towards the small stage just as a single blues note sounded from a trumpet. He did a small dance routine on stage, no more than a dozen steps, with a tapped finale, which brought him to a halt with his arms wide. Holding his cane in one hand and his top hat in the other, the microphone adjusted exactly to his height he said, 'It's show time, boys and girls! Show time at Tony del Grado's Fleshpot! London's hot-to-trot spot, where the spirit is willing and the flesh is sleek!'

Togger spoke quietly out of the corner of his mouth. 'His real name's Arthur Higgins. His dad's a bleedin' costermonger, got a barrow down Shepherd Market!'

The trumpet sounded low and sweet as it worked the blues number and Tony, in tune with it, allowed his voice to take on a sincere note. 'In the immortal tradition of the great Gypsy Rose Lee and in the name of all the artistes from the Folies Bergères and the Lido in gay Paree we bring you, for the first time tonight at the Fleshpot, the sensational Fifi la Tombo!'

The drums cut suddenly and a new, langorously slow blues number started. The house spots dimmed and a single spot opened on the stage as the curtain opened to reveal Geraldine in a black evening gown and long black velvet gloves, the gown hugging her body and slashed to the thighs. Her routine wasn't exactly Rita Hayworth; it was mostly easy stuff, the timing not critical, but nevertheless the audience seemed to like it. Peekay found his chest feeling constricted and the tight stove-pants held his erection painfully. He pulled at his collar, trying to stay calm. Lifting his glass to his lips, his eyes fixed on Geraldine, he poured brown ale down his chin, missing his mouth by half an inch.

Geraldine finally stripped down to a small red G-string and the lights cut, leaving the room in darkness. As the curtain closed, the house spots came on to tremendous applause, even the hostesses standing up to cheer.

'I've seen a lot worse in me time,' Togger exclaimed. 'Blimey, Peekay, her bristols must be made out of bleedin' marble. Didya see how they stood straight out?'

'I didn't notice,' Peekay said, sotto voce.

Togger looked up in surprise. 'You lying bastard!'

They both broke up in laughter. 'Christ, Togger, I'd throw a world title for a night with her.'

'Oi! Steady on, lad, when you've got the world title, just imagine the birds you'll pull an' all!' Togger stood up on the crossbars of the bar stool and reached over and under the bar counter for another couple of bottles of brown ale.

Peekay laughed. 'Don't think I haven't thought about that!'

The house lights dimmed and the spot returned to rest on Tony at the microphone. The record began to play a soft continuous timpany, more a feathering of the drums than a beat, the drummer tickling the skins, making them scratch and pant. To Peekay's surprise Tony addressed the microphone quietly, his voice hardly raised. 'Ladies and Gentlemen, I bring you ... Carmen Brown!' He reached into an inside pocket of his tails and produced a harmonica. The spot dimmed, though it remained on him, and a second spot opened up onto centre stage as the curtains lifted. Peekay could feel Togger go rigid beside him. Standing completely still, her arms raised high, wearing a white evening gown cut not very differently from the one Geraldine had worn, stood a beautiful coloured girl. Her dark hair fell to her shoulders and her skin was the colour of mimosa honey. The drum started to pick out a syncopation and Tony's harmonica blew a sharp, clean note as Carmen began to move, her slim body jerking to every drum beat and sliding to the soft roll of the harmonica. She couldn't possibly be Togger's sister. Ginger, freckled Togger. No bloody way! Her routine was the most sensuous thing Peekay had ever seen, a whipped cream experienced way beyond anything he'd ever fantasised, but out of respect for Togger he desperately willed himself not to become aroused. But he might as well have tried to stop his heart beating. By the time her routine was complete her honey-brown body was bathed in sweat as she bumped and smoothed to the drum beat and the harmonica. The harmonica rose high and held, the drum spat a series of sharp rat-tat-tat-tats and cut dead as Carmen raised her hands and spread her feet wide in the same position she'd opened with, though this time she stood only in a diamante G-string and high heels. The lights went to black just as she brought her arms down and hooked her thumbs into the silver G-string, pulling downwards. The place went wild. Carmen was something else all together: erotic, wild, she easily broke every demarcation the Apostolic Faith Mission could in their wildest imaginings have laid down for penultimate sinnership.

Peekay wanted to say all sorts of things. His heart was pumping and his mouth was dry. He placed his hand on Togger's shoulder, which was still rigid, but relaxed as soon as he felt Peekay grip it, as though his friend had somehow released the tension. 'Your sister, how can she be your sister, Togger?'

'Half sister, me old man's from Haiti. He jumped ship in Bristol when he was seventeen. Me mum is Irish and 'ad a bun in the oven, which was me without a known daddy, so she hitched him to give him citizenship and make her respectable. A quid pro quo.'

'Put it there, partner,' Peekay stuck his hand out.

'What for?' Togger took his hand.

'Well, I don't know who my daddy was either!'

'Honest?' Togger laughed, 'Funny that, ain't it? I mean not knowing who your old man was. Mind, I can't explain, old Doug, that's me old man, could'na been better, he gets a bit mad sometimes when he's had a few snorts. But he's never put an 'and on Carmen or me mum, not ever, not even once. And I soon bleedin' learned to stay out the way when he'd had a few.'

'So your sister, I mean Carmen, she's younger than you?'

'Yeah, I musta been just about ready to pop outa the oven when me mum got hitched to Doug, a year and two months. We went to school together, we was like twins. That's how come I learned to box. I was always fightin' some bastard because he called Carmen a nigger, like.'

'So who's the good lookin' friend, Togger?' A female voice said suddenly behind Peekay.

'Hello, Carmo!' Togger said, smiling broadly. Togger's sister moved to stand between them, bending down she gave Togger a peck on the side of his face. 'Peekay, this is me little sister, Carmen Brown.' It was obvious from the formal way he named her and the tone of his voice that Togger was proud of the beautiful young woman who stood beside him.

'You were marvellous, Carmen. I've never seen anything as wonderful in my life,' Peekay said.

Carmen laughed. She had a big mouth and her teeth were even and white and her dark eyes danced. 'I hope you mean sexy, Peekay? I'm paid to be sexy, not wonderful! Tony del Grado's Fleshpot don't want no class acts.' She looked up at Tony, who was back behind the bar. 'Ain't that right, Tony, baby?'

'Art doesn't pay the rent, darling. We're peddling pussy not Picasso!'

'No honestly, Carmen, I'm not an expert, this is the first time I've ever seen a strip show, but you were the best by far!'

Carmen looked at Peekay in surprise. 'First time?'

'Where've you been, lovey, under a rock? I don't suppose you're still a virgin, are you?' Tony said archly.

Peekay went beetroot, unable to respond. 'Only in the sense that he hasn't been sodomised by a berk like you!' Togger shot back angrily.

'Now, now you two!' Carmen said firmly. 'Nice to know you, Peekay, we'll have a drink afterwards.' She jerked a thumb in Tony's direction, 'I've got to go and hustle drinks for the fairy with the top hat and wand.'

Just then three sharp rings sounded from a buzzer under the bar. 'Shit! Trouble! It's Les. At the door!' Tony said in alarm.

'C'mon, Peekay!' Togger flew off the stool and was heading for the passageway. Peekay followed quickly.

The door stood ajar and Les sat in the doorway, his arms covering his head. Three men were bent over him, two holding him down while one kicked him in the ribs. Togger let fly with a right which sent the kicker backwards just as Peekay caught him in a rugby tackle. The big man was forced backwards, knocking the back of his head against the wall on the far side of the steps. Peekay was up in a flash as a second man's boot landed, just missing his groin but sending him backwards into the arms of the man he'd just tackled. Fortunately the impact where he'd hit his head against the wall had dazed him and Peekay was able to leap up again towards his attacker. There wasn't room to throw a punch so, grabbing the man by the lapels of his coat, he gave him a Liverpool kiss, his forehead smashing into his assailant's face connecting with the edge of his brow and the base of his nose. The man dropped to his knees clutching at his face.

Togger was on the ground with the third man on top of him. Both the man's hands were around Togger's neck, and he was bringing his head back to kiss Togger in the face with his forehead. With Togger's head already on the ground the 'kiss' to his forehead would damn near kill him. Les got to his feet just as Peekay dived onto Togger's attacker, grabbing him in a neck-lock and pulling his head back. Les threw an upper-cut at Togger's attacker at precisely the same time as Peekay jerked the man's head away, his own head twist-ing sideways to take the punch from Les directly on the nose. Peekay thought he'd run into a train. Everything went black and red, but somehow he managed to hold onto the man's neck as they both went sprawling.

Peekay was too dazed to hang on much longer and the man forced his arm from his neck and stood up. Through a daze of red and black lightning, his head spinning, Peekay grabbed frantically at the villain's legs, hugging them into his chest just as Togger, who'd climbed to his feet, hit the guy with a right upper-cut that came at him from the floor. Les's arm shot out, grabbed the man by the hair and jerked his head down, bringing his knee up at the same time, smashing the man's face into his knee.

'Let him fall, Peekay!' Togger shouted. Peekay released the man, who seemed to fall in slow motion, unconscious before he slumped to the floor.

Peekay crawled from out under Togger's attacker, his head clearing. He was laughing, blood pouring from his nose. Togger began to laugh and then Les. The first two attackers struggled to their feet, shaky and somewhat dazed, not sure where they were. Togger grabbed hold of the second one, and Les grabbed the bigger one, turning him around and wrenching his arm behind his back.

'Who fuckin' sent you?' demanded Les. 'Answer or I'll snap your soddin' arm off!' Behind him, Peekay giggled and Les started to laugh again. Somehow it wasn't the threat but the laughter which seemed to terrify the man.

'Nick Poultos, he paid us to do the place over,' the man panted.

'The Soho wine importer?'

'That's right.' It was the second guy who spoke. He had his hands in the air, blood pouring from his nose, down his chin and onto his white shirt front.

'G'warn, piss off you two!' Les managed a fierce expression at last. 'Take yer mate and fuck off outta here before I call the fuzz! Tell Poultos we'll be comin' for him.'

The two men lifted the third man up and between them they dragged him up the steps.

Les looked up at the people who'd gathered at street level and were watching them over the railing. 'Okay, show's over. Hoppit, ladies and gentlemen, it's all quiet on the West End front.'

Peekay covered his nose, using both hands. It hurt like hell, but he looked up at Togger and started to laugh again. The passageway was crowded with girls and some of the patrons pushed forward to see what had happened. Carmen was suddenly beside Togger, holding him fiercely by the shoulders. Togger grinned. 'I'm orright, luv.'

Carmen dropped to her knees beside the still laughing Peekay; blood from his nose running through his fingers. At her touch he stopped and moved his hands away. He saw the alarmed look on her face. 'Jesus, Peekay, the bastards have hurt you!'

Peekay grinned. 'Hi, Carmen. One hundred and sixteen fights, if you count today, one hundred and eighteen, all of them defending my dumb nose. Thank Christ it's broken at last!' He attempted to get up but Carmen held him. She pulled his head gently into her bosom, her fingers running through his hair. 'You're beautiful, Peekay, you're a beautiful man, broken nose 'an all.' She kissed him lightly on the forehead. 'Tonight you're coming home with me. It's time you broke something else as well.'

Seven

Tandia, who had never spent a day of her life in bed, woke very late on the Saturday after she'd been rescued by Mama Tequila. She felt too weak to move; her whole body seemed to be burning and her mouth was dry. She ran her tongue over her lips which were cracked and swollen. Her eyes had difficulty adjusting to her surroundings; the room hummed and seemed to spin slowly above her head, and the air around her had a fractured luminosity, like used cellophane paper. Slowly the humming ceased and the room grew steady but the cellophane nature of the air persisted so she could not very clearly make out the tall, dark shape standing quietly beside her bed.

Juicey Fruit Mambo smiled his sharp, golden-toothed smile and Tandia, feverish and disorientated, screamed and then began to sob. It was the Master of Evil from the underworld and he was going to bite her with his golden teeth. 'Don't bite me! Please don't bite me! Please, please! I don't want to have your baby!'

Juicey Fruit Mambo bent over her and placed his hand on her shoulder and Tandia became hysterical and tried to beat him off with her fists. The shock of finding herself confronted by the Master of Evil lent her strength. She rose up and, standing on the bed, beat frantically at the black man's chest. He brought his arms around her and held her tightly until what little strength she had gained from the sudden shock had spent itself. Exhausted, Tandia wept against his chest, blood running from her lip where she'd bitten it. Finally she lost even the strength to weep.

'Shhhh! Missy Tandia, no more now, you hear? I am not bite you. Shhhh! You very sick but not to die, I tink. No more for you cry, Missy Tandia.' After a while he laid her head gently back onto her pillow where Tandia, her eyes red from weeping but still bright with fever, stared up at him in catatonic terror.

Mama Tequila heard Tandia screaming but her progress up the stairs was painfully slow, although she was hurrying and was panting fiercely as she came through the door. 'Jesus! What happened?'

Juicey Fruit Mambo shook his head slowly, then he brought the palm of his hand against his forehead and wiped across it, flicking the imaginary sweat from his brow. 'She has the hot sickness, madam,' he explained.

'Go get some ice from the bar fridge. Also a towel. Quick, man!' Mama Tequila lowered her body onto the side of the bed and lifted Tandia's unresisting form from the pillow and held her tightly to her bosom.

To Tandia, in her state of confusion, Mama Tequila was almost as great a shock as finding the Master of Evil hovering over her. She was wearing a huge pale pink silk kimono which was embroidered in the elaborate oriental fashion with brilliantly coloured roses, peonies, humming-birds and butterflies. To Tandia in her state of confusion she looked like a garden dancing in the air with a grotesque disembodied head floating above it.

Tandia believed that she was beyond help. She had been carried to the underworld by the Master of Evil who had bitten her, not only on the chest but all over, so that now her body hurt terribly. Too weak to resist or even to sob, she lay helpless against Mama Tequila's heaving breasts as the huge woman rocked her, making soft 'shhhing' sounds.

After a while, when Tandia's breathing had grown more steady, Mama Tequila laid her back on the bed. Tandia felt sure she was about to die. Horrible as this seemed, it was strangely painless and an end which she welcomed. Patel would never forgive her if she had the Master of Evil's baby. She must die! It was very important! He wouldn't love her if she didn't die to save his fragile ego from destruction. A man like him who was known in the best white circus.

Juicey Fruit Mambo returned with a small enamel basin filled with water into which he had placed a couple of trays of ice cubes; a small towel was also draped over one arm. He placed the basin beside the bed and dug into his trouser pockets to produce a bottle of pills. Then he rinsed the towel, wrung it out to make a small square parcel of it, and placed it against Tandia's fevered brow.

'Hold her head up,' Mama Tequila said, shaking two small pink pills from the bottle. Juicey Fruit Mambo lifted Tandia's head from the cushion and Mama Tequila slipped two tablets into her mouth. The pills tasted bitter and Tandia swallowed eagerly from the glass of water Juicey Fruit handed her, drinking its contents down completely. 'She is thirsty, I will bring some more,' he said, and left the room.

The effect of the barbiturate soon sent Tandia to sleep and it was late in the evening when she wakened again. The fever in her still raged and she could hear someone singing, 'Lay that pistol down, babe . . . lay that pistol down!' It seemed to be coming from a long way away and she opened her eyes slowly. 'Pistol packin' Mama . . .' The electric light was on in the room and this time Dr Louis Rabin was at her side. Tandia knew then that Patel knew. Knew for sure!

'I'll give her a shot of Pen-G to fight the infection. Her pulse is very slow, which is probably from the shock; she is undoubtedly somewhat traumatised.' He didn't speak again for some time, his finger touching her lightly in various parts of her burning body. 'Hmm, from the contusions this little lady has been through a bad time.'

Then what seemed like ages later she heard his voice again, as though he was speaking in an echo chamber. 'Now Tandia, I'm going to roll you over, I'm going to give you an injection in your bottom. It's not very nice, I know. But it will fix you. So you be a brave girl now, you hear?'

She felt his cool, strong hands on her hot skin as he rolled her onto her side, then a sudden jab of pain from the needle, followed almost immediately by a slow, welling, almost unbearable pain as Dr Louis Rabin pressed down on the plunger and ran the dose of penicillin into her system.

Tandia started to cry again. The injection seemed to exacerbate all the other pains in her body. Patel knew about the monster baby, that's why he had called Dr Louis Rabin. 'I don't want to have the baby!' she sobbed, 'Please, Patel, it wasn't my fault! Please, please, I didn't do it!'

Dr Louis looked at Mama Tequila. 'What's this about a baby?'

Mama shrugged her shoulders. 'I think she was raped, doctor.' She turned to Juicey Fruit Mambo who nodded his head to verify her opinion.

Doctor Rabin spun round to look at the tall black man. 'You? You raped her?'

A look of astonishment crossed Juicey Fruit Mambo's face, then he shook his head and laughed grimly. 'No, doctor, I cannot do dis ting.'

'He's impotent,' Mama Tequila said quietly. 'We got a tipoff from the police and found her on a bench on the railway station very early this moming.' She pointed to Tandia's bandaged wrists. 'Han'cuffs done that. I think the police probably raped her.'

'Did she tell you that?'

Mama Tequila sighed, 'No, doctor.'

Doctor Louis started to unwind the bandage on Tandia's right wrist. 'Then let's not go around accusing people before we know, hey.' He removed the last of the bandage and gently lifted the boracic lint Juicey Fruit had placed around her wrist. What he saw caused him to give a low, spontaneous whistle. 'Not good. You're right, these lacerations could have been made by handcuffs.'

Juicey Fruit Mambo spoke quietly, 'I am sure, doctor.' He held both his arms together, wrists upwards, both his hands balled into a fist which he held out for Dr Louis to see. A deep welt of shiny scar tissue slightly less than a quarter of an inch thick made a complete bangle around both wrists. It was almost as though the scar had been carefully and deliberately fashioned. He laughed bitterly, 'I know dis ting, doctor. Same like me, she has the bracelets. I tink dis is a *bansella* for the black people from de policeman.'

Mama Tequila could smell trouble. Dr Louis wasn't afraid to take on the police on behalf of any of his patients. He wasn't scared of anyone; a man like that could make a lot of trouble for a person.

The doctor had removed the bandage and liniment from Tandia's other wrist and was probing the deep wound softly with the pad of his forefinger. 'You are right, doctor,' Mama Tequila offered, 'we don't know for sure, do we? Maybe a rope could have done this also? There are many, many bad people around these days.' She looked up at Juicey Fruit Mambo and shook her head almost imperceptibly, indicating that he shouldn't interfere again. He sniffed and pulled at the top of his nose with his forefinger and thumb and then rubbed his hand twice across his mouth as though trying to remove from his lips any further chance of spontaneous comment.

'There is too much police brutality these days. Mama Tequila, if you want to press charges I'll testify that, in my opinion, these lacerations were as a direct result of the over-zealous use of a pair of police handcuffs.'

Mama Tequila brought her hand up to her breast, trying hard to conceal her shock at the suggestion. 'No charges, doctor! You must understand, we want no trouble with the police in this place. Juicey Fruit Mambo will take good care of her wrists.'

'Oh yes, of course, it was the police who told you where to find her,' Dr Louis said.

He turned to Juicey Fruit Mambo. 'You've done a good job, the wounds are nice and clean.' He liked to explain things. 'She has good skin, I don't think she will scar too badly.' He brought out his bag and producing a small pad started to write. He wrote for some time, filling several pages.

The coloured woman and the black man waited silently until Mama Tequila could no longer contain herself. 'That is a very long prescription, doctor?'

Doctor Louis, 'Ag, man, just notes, you never know when such notes can come in handy.' He resumed writing but shortly afterwards came to an end. He flipped back to the first page. 'Mama Tequila, do you know who this young girl is?'

Mama Tequila shook her head, 'Only her name, doctor. Her name is Tandia Patel.' She was annoyed that Dr Louis had chosen to make notes but she could think of no way of preventing him.

Dr Louis wrote Tandia's name and surname on the top of the pad. 'Ja, I thought so. Her father was a patient of mine. He dropped dead three days ago of a sudden heart attack in the middle of refereeing a boxing match.' He smiled, 'She is his love child, you know.'

Mama Tequila sniffed. Was there no end to this man's naivety? She was still annoyed that he'd made the notes and she answered testily, 'I too am such a love child, doctor. South Africa is full of these love children. A white man grabs a black woman and for a few shillings they do it in the bushes because she is too afraid to say "no baas" or she needs the money so her children can eat. You call this a *love* child? What must I say, doctor?'

'Ja, I know, it's easy for me to talk, but Patel was different. He didn't throw her away, he brought her up and gave her a proper education. Only the other day he was telling me she's got one more year to matric. I'm telling you, Mama Tequila, this is a very bright girl.' He paused and rubbed his chin, 'I'm damn sure she doesn't belong in a place like this.'

Behind the doctor Mama Tequila could see Juicey

Fruit Mambo shaking his head sadly. 'You mean just the stupid ones belong in a whorehouse, doctor?' she said.

Dr Louis Rabin kept his head lowered and looked into his cupped hands. 'If I sounded patronising you must forgive me. But please, listen to me for just a moment. How many bastard children created between black and white manage to get a proper education? Tell me, Mama Tequila, when did you leave school? Standard five perhaps? Just before high school?'

'Standard two,' Mama Tequila said defiantly. 'I learned to read and write and do some sums.' It was enough.

The doctor turned to Juicey Fruit Mambo, 'And you, boy?'

Juicey Fruit Mambo's head shot up. 'I am not boy, doctor, I am a man, same like you!' Then, just as quickly, he looked down contritely, adopting the practised mendacity that the African learns to use before authority. The defiance was absent from his voice. 'I am not go to the school, doctor.'

Dr Louis flushed deeply but chose to ignore Juicey Fruit Mambo's admonishment. 'There you are! You see now what I mean?' He turned to look at the large woman. 'Standard two only and you are even more lucky than some. Here you've got one of your own kind, a young coloured girl who has not even a year to go for her matric. Someone who, I'm telling you, could go far. How can you put her on her back to work for you? I'm asking you truly now, explain to me how could you do a thing like that?'

Mama Tequila started to giggle, then stopped abruptly when she realised, following Juicey Fruit Mambo's outburst, that her laughter would be seen by

Dr Louis as a further put-down. 'Doctor, you a good man and I respec' you, you know that. All the coloured people respec' you. But now you got to lissen to me, you hear? You sit in your consulting rooms and the black people come and the coloured people come and even some white people, they come also. And the black man and the coloured look at the whites and think, "See, we also, we can have the best doctor, just like the white man!" When you give them medicine they pay just like the white man. But you know something, doctor? In the township hospital there are two black doctors and three coloured, also some Indian doctors. For much less money, sometimes even for nothing, they can see these doctors. Why do they come to you?'

Dr Louis Rabin opened his mouth to attempt to answer but Mama Tequila held up her hand. 'No, please, doctor, I'm telling you, you don't know the answer. I will tell you. You see, you a white man, no matter how clever the coloured doctor or the black doctor, even if they just as clever as you, they not.' She dug her finger in under her left breast to indicate her heart and made a twisting motion. 'They know in here, in their hearts, the white doctor is better. When my girls get sick and I call you, they know Mama Tequila loves them.'

'That's not true, Mama Tequila, a medical degree is the same for everyone!'

'Ja, but it doesn't work like that. The coloured doctor can take out your appendix just the same as you, but he can't take out a building licence to live in a big house in the Berea just like you. No, man! Who does he think he is? All of a sudden the cheeky kaffir thinks just because he a doctor, he also a white man!' She paused. 'And us too! The coloured and the black people, we also believe he is just a bladdy kaffir in a white coat,

144

or just a dirty coloured or bladdy coolie who is trying to be something he can't ever be. Tell me, doctor. Except now he gets maybe more money, how does all that white education help a coloured doctor or lawyer or teacher?'

Dr Louis sighed. 'Look, Mama Tequila, I'm a Jew. The Jews have been persecuted for hundreds of years. My family fled from Poland; my father, even today, hardly speaks English. Believe me, when we came here we had nothing, we were poor, poor as black people.' Dr Louis lowered his voice for emphasis and wagged a finger. 'But always! Always the Jews have understood one thing,' he smacked his fist into the open palm of his left hand. 'Education! Education is everything! But it takes money to be educated.' He smiled, pleased with himself. 'So to answer your question, to make money is very important.'

Mama Tequila threw back her head and laughed uproariously. 'You dead right about that, doctor.' She cleared her throat suddenly. 'Only one thing is different. If you had left Poland and you come here and you had a black face, what would have happened then?'

Dr Louis winced. 'I think I'm beginning to under-stand, Mama Tequila,' he said quietly.

The big woman laughed. Then she changed the subject abruptly. 'So tell me, to become a doctor takes how long, please?'

Dr Louis was still smarting from her rebuke. 'Six years, then two years' internship. Why do you ask?'

Mama Tequila looked down at Tandia, who from time to time still tossed feverishly, though she appeared to be asleep again. Juicey Fruit Mambo was holding a cold towel to her head.

'You see this little girl, doctor? You right about her,

this one, she's special, number one.' Mama Tequila paused for emphasis. 'Doctor, I've got people who come here to Bluey Jay, important, high-up people, white men, some even politicians, lawyers and magistrates, one is even a judge. These people will pay very, very, well for this one if I train her right. On her back this clever little skatterbol can make more money in the next eight years than your kaffir doctor or coloured lawyer will make in his lifetime!'

She pointed a long varnished nail at the doctor. 'I don't want to talk dirty in front of a doctor, but we coloured ladies, we got a saying: "The best brains a pretty coloured lady got is between her legs!"'

Dr Louis laughed in spite of himself. 'You don't leave me with too many answers,' he said finally.

'Come, we have some coffee, hey? Sarah made some *koeksisters* this morning before she went to Mass. If I tell her you came and didn't eat some she will be very unhappy.'

Juicey Fruit Mambo had remained behind with Tandia. He didn't know what had gotten into him. Almost from the moment he had set eyes on her he had felt differently about the young girl who lay tossing and turning in Hester's bed. It wasn't love. He felt a kind of kinetic energy in her presence as though he was connected to her by some form of invisible cord. He could feel the burning of her fever on his own flesh and sense the little girl's despair as though it was his own. Juicey Fruit didn't bother to examine these feelings. In such things his African culture, depending on your viewpoint, was either too primitive or too sophisticated. He simply decided that it was henceforth his job to care for Tandia, that the rest of his life would be taken up with this task.

146

Juicey Fruit Mambo had been with Mama Tequila for three years. He too had been a gift from the police. They'd stuck a cattle prod up his arse and burned him, so that he was no longer a man, whereupon they'd dropped him head first down a stairwell so that when he landed two floors below his brains had bubbled through his broken skull for all to see.

He had refused to die in the wretched cell into which they'd thrown him. In the two days of delirium which followed, the deep cuts to his handcuffed wrists were created, which were to earn him his permanent brace-lets. Reluctantly the police were forced to cart him off to a black hospital. For, while his broken skull could easily be explained as attempted suicide, the terrible lac-erations to his wrists were plainly the result of police brutality, something the coroner would be obliged to include in his report. When, five months later, he was released from hospital, the so-called terrorist gang of which Juicey Fruit Mambo was supposed to have been a member had been acquitted by the courts for lack of any reasonable evidence.

The police had made a real botch-up of the whole affair and the newspapers had been quick to point this out. Anxious not to attract any further publicity they'd taken Juicey Fruit Mambo to Mama Tequila so that if he tried to make a fuss, he would be immediately com-promised by reason of working in a brothel.

But Juicey Fruit Mambo hadn't made a fuss. He had the rest of his life to get even. The hate in him for the white man was a hot, palpable thing he carried with him every day of his life.

Mama Tequila poured a large cup of black coffee for Dr Louis and, without asking, she added four teaspoons of sugar and stirred. It wasn't the way he usually drank his coffee, but it was the way she believed he did and afer a few times it was pointless to bring it up. She handed him the cup. 'Okay, doctor, what must I do to get those notes you made, hey?'

Dr Louis looked into his coffee. 'You already know that.'

Mama Tequila said nothing. How could a man be so smart and so stupid at the same time? 'The price, it is too high, doctor.'

'Just one year, until she matriculates. Then she can make up her own mind. Let her finish her education, Mama Tequila.'

'What must I do with an educated whore? Who's going to pay?' Mama Tequila asked roughly, but she could feel the better part of her nature beginning to win. This worried her somewhat; in her experience conscience made a lousy book-keeper. 'I run a good house, doctor, this isn't a bladdy boarding school!'

'I tell you what. I'll throw in twelve visits free of charge to you or any of your girls for the remainder of the year if you promise not to put her to your kind of work until she matriculates. How's that?'

It was a generous offer; coming out to Bluey Jay in the middle of the night was a big sacrifice for any doctor, let alone a white one, to make for a sick whore. Mama Tequila lifted her coffee cup to her lips and blew the steam from the top; then she took a tiny ladylike sip and looked at Dr Louis out of the corner of her eye. 'Twelve visits, no time limit, maybe it takes two years, maybe even more.'

'Ja, that's okay by me.'

'Starting tonight?'

Dr Louis grinned, 'Ja, what's the difference?'

'Just one more thing, doctor. Tandia is going to this

148

big school to learn how to be clever, but there is things she got to learn here also.'

'What kind of things?' Dr Louis asked suspiciously.

'Ag, I can't explain, tricks of the trade. She got to make herself useful. There is all sorts of things a person on the game has to know.'

'A person on the game? I thought we decided she wasn't going to do that?'

'Ja, of course, but she like an apprentice. I got a big establishment to run, doctor.'

'Can she learn these things standing up?' Dr Louis asked.

Mama Tequila laughed, but looked hurt. 'We already shook hands, doctor. You got my word, the girl is safe with me until she finish her school, then she can decide what part of her body her brain is in.' Mama Tequila raised an eyebrow. 'If she got any brains left from all that education, she not going to need too many to work that out, also!'

Dr Louis pushed his chair back from the table and extended his hand. 'I'm proud of you, Mama Tequila.'

Taking the doctor's hand, Mama Tequila grinned. 'I'm telling you, doctor, I'm getting too soft in my old age. C'mon, hand over, where's the bladdy notes?'

Mama Tequila was as good as her word. With Tandia standing by, she called the headmistress of Durban Indian Girls' High School posing as Tandia's auntie. The headmistress declared herself annoyed at Tandia's absence. 'I know there have been extenuating circumstances and we do commiserate, but Tandia has been away for nearly three weeks. I'm sure I don't need to point out to you that a small note from her aunt dropped in the mail with an explanation was all that was required.'

'Her daddy, you know, Patel the famous boxing coach, he dropped dead all of a sudden, it made her very sad, Mrs . . .?'

'Miss Naidoo!' Tandia said in a loud whisper.

'. . . Miss Naidoo. You see, it made her sick and everything,' Mama Tequila continued.

'I'm sorry the child has not been well, but we do expect common courtesy, Mrs . . .'

'Mama Tequila!' To Mama Tequila she didn't sound sorry at all.

'Will she be sitting for the end-of-year exams, Mrs Tekella?'

'Yes, I suppose, the doctor says one more week, is that orrght?' Mama Tequila was not often intimidated, but she didn't seem to be able to get the hang of this stuck-up individual who was Tandia's headmistress. One thing was for sure, this one wouldn't know how to run a brothel if her bladdy life depended on it. All the clients would leave their trousers behind and run for the hills!

She had thought about adopting her Mae West persona, but as she generally used it only on her clients, she was glad now that she'd kept it straight. An American auntie from the deep South would have seemed an improbable relation for a schoolgirl who was the love child of an Indian and a Bantu.

'We begin exams in a week. Tandia will have missed all her preparation classes.'

'That's orright, Miss, don't worry, she's clever as anything. If you want her Monday she'll be there for sure, I guarantee it!' Mama Tequila was beginning to regain her usual composure and now she adopted what she considered was a snooty voice. 'My chauffeur will drop her off in a Packard personal.'

If Miss Naidoo had felt herself put in her place her voice gave no sign that this was so. 'She will need to bring a doctor's note when she returns. Goodbye, Mrs Tekella!'

Mama Tequila felt the receiver go dead in her ear. She turned to see Tandia with her fist in her mouth in an attempt to stifle her giggles. She had been able to hear the headmistress's shrill voice almost as clearly as if she had the receiver to her ear and, as far as she was concerned, Mama Tequila had come out quits, even ahead if you counted the bit about the car. Nobody in the history of the world had ever done that with Miss Naidoo before.

'Humph! This Miss Naidoo, she needs a man real bad, Tandy. I'm telling you, she one mixed-up lady, that one. What kind of car she got?'

Tandia looked at her in surprise. 'She hasn't got a car, Mama T.'

Mama Tequila clicked her tongue. 'She hasn't got a car and she hasn't got a man, tell me, has she got lots of pretty dresses and rings and things?'

Tandia laughed. Laughter was happening to her a lot lately. 'I think she's only got four dresses, they all nearly the same, not pretty at all and she never wears any jewellery, only a watch.'

'So tell me, why is she so stuck up, then?'

'Ag, headmistresses are like that, Mama T. She hasn't got time for a man or for riding around in a big car or looking pretty and wearing jewels. A person has got to work very hard and be very clever to have her job.'

'I see, if you very clever and you get a big education and you work very hard, you get this job?'

Tandia nodded. 'Ja, but also, you got to be lucky. There's not so many jobs high up like that for women.'

Mama Tequila put her arm around Tandia's shoulder and drew her into her bosom. 'Okay, skatterbol, if you want you can go back to this school. But I'm telling you something for nothing, this woman can't teach you anything that's going to help you, man, I think maybe it's all a big waste of brains!'

Tandia could hear Hester coming down the upstairs corridor. Hester wore scuffs which slapped against the back of her heel and then hard against the polished yellowwood floor boards. 'Hey, Tandia, guess what!'

Tandia raised her pen from her work. It was simply amazing how Hester could get noise, even a sort of rhythm, out of wearing a pair of scuffs. All the girls wore them when they were not working but Hester's scuffs went 'slap, schliptt, slap, schliptt, slap, schliptt!' 'How does she do that?' she thought. Though she had to admit it was typical of Hester, who did everything loudly and with drama. Hester was a noise factory. She just couldn't help herself. She even slept loudly, for she suffered from nasal polyps and snored so badly that Mama Tequila had given her the room at the end of the corridor with the bathroom in between it and the others.

Mama Tequila had also stopped booking her out on dirty forty-eights. Too many customers were returning her to Bluey Jay after one night demanding their money back. None of her clients ever complained that Hester didn't deliver. She delivered all right! That was part of the problem. Hester was so good at her job that she quickly exhausted even the most virile of her mostly middle-aged clients, who, attempting to renew their vigour with a couple of hours' shut-eye, would find themselves trapped in a room where the very walls seemed to vibrate with Hester's bronchial sonority.

Only the big Boer from the Free State didn't seem to mind. He'd get completely blotto on VSOP Cape brandy and then he'd giggle and take Hester into his arms, arms which were burnt a deep bronze from where the line of his short sleeves ended. 'Come, my little beauty, let me grow some grass between your two beautiful dark hills,' he would say, burying his great ginger beard between Hester's big brown boobs. 'Together we'll snore the night into little pieces smaller than matchsticks.'

With a sigh Tandia replaced the cap on her Croxley fountain pen. Hester's arrival always demanded her full attention. It was the end of her school work for the moment.

Hester's long pink fingernails appeared around the door. They were followed almost immediately by her head. Hester was a back-slidden Pentecostal and she would explain that the Lord didn't mind pink nails, pink nails were all right, almost natural; it was the long, shiny red ones like Sarah's that He was very against.

'Hey, Tandia, listen to this!' She walked over to where Tandia sat at the little table that served as desk. 'You going to get some new school uniforms, man. It's true! Only just now I heard Mama T calling on the telephone to Sonny Vindoo.'

'Sonny who?' Tandia was delighted at the prospect of the uniforms.

'Vindoo, he's the Indian tailor who makes us special things sometimes, when Mama T wants to put on a bit of a show for an important new client.' Hester brought the tips of the fingers of both hands to her lips and her eyes grew large. 'They pink!'

'What's pink?'

'The school uniforms, they going to be pink, God's honour!'

Tandia buried her face in her hands as Hester continued, 'You know how she's mad about pink? I'm telling you, jong, Mama T is having pink gym frocks made. I heard her tell Sonny Vindoo to find three pairs of pink stockings and a pink beret also.' Hester put her hand on Tandia's shoulder. 'I swear on my mother's grave, it's true!'

'She can't do that! They won't allow it. The colour is brown. The colour for Durban Indian Girls' High School is dark brown!'

'I dunno about that, jong. All I can say is I heard her clear as anything.' Hester put her fist up to her ear and brought her hand onto her ample dark bosom the way Mama Tequila did when she made a phone call; then she started to mimic Mama Tequila. 'Listen, Mr Dine-o-mite, I want you should go to John Orrs. Tell them Mama Tequila she want seven yards pink gabardine. Okay, lover? Also four yards pink cotton poplin. Nice, you hear? Pretty rose pink.'

Sonny Vindoo liked to be paid in kind, so Mama Tequila maintained her customer persona when she talked to him. The little Indian tailor looked a little like Mahatma Gandhi and affected a dhoti and round steel-rimmed glasses to emphasise the likeness. The very first time he had done any work for Mama Tequila he'd handed her an invoice on which he had written in his neat, clerical hand:

For services rendered please render the services of:
1 only Blonde Bombshell.

Which is how Sonny Vindoo got his name, Mr Dine-o-Mite, and at the same time got Sarah chosen for him, the frizzy, ginger-headed Sarah being the closest the Bluey Jay establishment could get to a blonde at the time.

Hester could mimic Mama Tequila down pat and despite her concern, Tandia was forced to laugh. But then she looked worried again. 'Oh no! What am I going to do?'

The pink school outfit was Mama Tequila's idea of sticking it right up Miss Naidoo. When she returned, Tandia was going to be the best-dressed, prettiest girl in the whole school.

Every time she thought about the pink gymfrock Tandia nearly died of embarrassment. How was she possibly going to tell Mama T? She'd begged Hester to tell her, but there was a darker side of Mama Tequila's nature and she took it badly when one of her projects was thwarted. Hester wasn't game to incur Mama Tequila's wrath on her behalf. In her world you looked after yourself first. It wasn't unkindness, it was instinct, like breathing, and her instincts had served her well in the past.

Tandia also now understood why Juicey Fruit Mambo had been grinning his head off for the last couple of days. He was happy for the surprise coming her way.

The next day was the Saturday before her return to school on Monday. At six o'clock sharp Mama Tequila reached into her small sequinned evening bag and produced a large brass key to unlock the door to her private salon. She was dressed to the nines; Saturday night was a big night at Bluey Jay, not as posh as a

Friday, but bigger and much, much noisier.

Saturday night at Bluey Jay was fun for one and all. The pianola in the guest salon ran hot with honky-tonk and *tickie-draai*. A girl could expect to turn a dozen tricks before the boys, their pockets lighter and with three months of wildly imagined promiscuity tapped and emptied in almost as many minutes, were shooed off the premises into taxis waiting to take them back to their cheap billets in town.

Now, an hour before the first of the Saturday night crowd would begin to appear, Mama Tequila entered her private salon and gazed with deep satisfaction at the magnificent room that never failed to convince her that God was on the side of the honest brothel-keeper. She wore a full-length pink crushed-velvet gown, pink high-heel shoes studded with rhinestones with a pink taffeta turban on her head. To top it all off she carried a large pink ostrich feather fan. She crossed the room as regally as the queen she was and sat on a high-backed Victorian chair of monstrous proportions which was covered in a watered taffeta of deep purple.

The salon and the shining yellowwood floors were Mama Tequila's special joy. She had come upon the mansion when, in a post-war return to Christian values, Durban's police commissioner, Kommandant Vermaak, had decided that the waterside brothels, which had done such a sterling job of rest and recreation for troops and sailors during the war, had to go. Mama Tequila, who owned two of these BB-TM ('Biff! Bang! Thank you, ma'am!') sex emporiums, was not displeased with the Kommandant's zeal.

She'd made a fortune during the war but now the quick-sex business had fallen on hard times. All her life as a working girl and later as a madam, Mama Tequila had dreamed of owning a brothel like one she had once seen in a movie set in turn-of-the-century New Orleans. She wanted a brothel that catered for the carriage trade, people with money and manners and political clout. A house with nice girls who knew their trade and didn't smoke *boom* or drink neat Cape brandy.

Mama Tequila had been raised in the slums of Cape Town's District Six and she'd learned, very early in life, that a man's snake wasn't like everybody said, colourblind. The white snakes liked to creep into black holes and the black ones into white. She'd also learned that coloured girls were the perfect compromise; they could pass, in most instances, for white with black snakes and for black with white ones. For it was the minds of the snakes that got a vicarious pleasure out of colour; the snakes themselves with their single blind eye, seldom stopped to compare skin tones.

When she found Bluey Jay on thirty acres of rolling green hills within half an hour's drive of Durban she'd known at once that there was a God in heaven. For the outside of the house, somewhat in need of repair, was almost a direct replica of the one in the movie. Inside nothing had been touched since the time of Bluey Jay himself. Whilst the drapes were faded and worn and the upholstery on the Edwardian couches and formal chairs and the Persian carpets were almost threadbare and some of the furniture was badly in need of french polishing and restoration, it was all there. Mama Tequila could hardly believe her eyes.

All it needed was money to restore it and Mama Tequila had plenty of that. She had found a Mr Leonard Polkinghorne, a highbrow Englishman who wore detachable starched collars and who had once worked as an assistant curator at the Victoria and

Albert in London, and was now head curator of the Pietermaritzburg museum. Leonard Polkinghorne was an expert on Victorian and Edwardian decor and she assigned him the task of returning the formal rooms in Bluey Jay to their former glory.

'Nothing changed, you understand, Mr Lennie, just exactly the same as before, only everything pink.' Mama Tequila couldn't bring herself to pronounce his surname, which seemed to her amazingly apt for the restoration of a house intended as a brothel and was yet another sign from God that she was doing the right thing.

'Mr Lennie, do you know what kind of place is this?' Mama Tequila asked when she took him out to show him the property. Leonard Polkinghorne looked at the scaffolded Bluey Jay and then back at Mama Tequila who sighed and said carefully, 'Mr Lennie, this is going to be a place where you come when you are tired of your wife.'

'Ah, I see, a rest home! That's perfectlay splendid, I'm perfectlay happy to be associated with a rest home.' Leonard Polkinghorne was very big on the word 'perfectly' which he pronounced in this funny way.

Mama Tequila sighed again; this was one dumb person orright. 'Ja, but more like an *excitement* than a rest, Mr Lennie.'

A slow grin spread over Leonard Polkinghorne's face and his eyes grew wide. 'I say! You don't mean?' Mama Tequila nodded her head. 'Yes you do! By jove, a brothel! How perfectlay marvellous!'

The one-eyed snake strikes again! Mama Tequila thought happily. 'The best, Mr Lennie, the best whore-house in the world and also, when you and I finish with it, the prettiest.'

The restoration of Bluey Jay outside and inside, and including electricity and new plumbing, had taken a sizeable bite out of Mama Tequila's wartime fortune, but Mr Lennie's fee wasn't one of her expenses. He elected to take his retainer in what he referred to as 'dalliance time'. Mama Tequila, happy to oblige, carefully worked out the total amount owed to him in hours. It was an agreement which Mr Lennie said suited him 'absolutely perfectlay', and which eventually took a great deal of the starch out of his collar. At Bluey Jay he was known to the girls as 'Mr Perfect Lay'.

All the girls had been told to appear at a quarter past six in the salon and they now stood around Mama Tequila's chair 'oohing' and 'aahing' her dress.

'Jesus, Mary, Mother of God! Have mercy on a poor working girl, Mama T! How much time am I going to have to give to Mr Dine-o-mite for this beautiful creation!' Sarah cupped her hands over her face and groaned in mock agony.

'Talking of Mr Dine-o-mite, he gonna be here soon,' Mama Tequila chuckled, 'but he just come to make a delivery.'

Juicey Fruit Mambo, dressed in a white tuxedo jacket, black stovepipe trousers, white shirt and pink bow tie, walked into the salon carrying a small scalloped silver tray on which rested nine tiny glasses of sherry and one of green chartreuse. There were eight working girls at Bluey Jay, not counting Tandia, and Juicey Fruit now dispensed a glass to each of them as well as to Mama Tequila. Finally he placed the glass of green chartreuse on an occasional table to await the arrival of Sonny Vindoo. He returned moments later with a glass of lemonade, which he handed to Tandia.

Mama Tequila, who had missed the fact that Tandia

hadn't been served a glass of sherry, now noticed the lemonade. 'Juicey Fruit Mambo, I do declare! You go back now and bring Miss Tandia a glass sweet sherry like everybody else! She a working girl too, you know.' She fanned herself lazily with the ostrich feather fan.

Juicey Fruit was not happy as he accepted the glass of lemonade back from Tandia and left the room. He returned in a few minutes with a single glass of sherry in the centre of the tray. Tandia took up the tiny glass. She had never tasted alcohol and she was actually quite frightened at the prospect; she imagined all sorts of things happening to her which would be quite beyond her control.

This was the first time she had been in this magnificent room with its rich cedar panelling and beautiful pink velvet curtains which fell from scalloped velvet pelmets above two large windows, to the floor sixteen feet below. The break-front covered an entire wall and was filled with dark green morocco leather volumes, the titles embossed in gold on the spine of each book. On the three remaining walls were four large portraits of pretty ladies dresed in the silks and satins of Edwardian England, the décolletage of each allowing a provocative display of creamy bosom. Several pink chaise longues and formal chairs, small tables and pink Persian carpets seemed to be arranged or scattered haphazardly around the room, and the beautiful yellowwood floor, where it showed in places not covered by carpets, kicked back the light from a huge crystal chandelier that cascaded from the centre of an ornate plaster-moulded ceiling composed of garlands of fruit and flowers, onto which clung a heavenly host of fat cherubs. Above the pink marble fireplace was a huge pink ceramic bowl of peonies. To give the beautiful room a final touch of distinction, to the side of the window furthermost from where Mama Tequila sat was a pink grand piano. (It was in fact a pianola but Tandia had no way of knowing this.) The room had a warm, flushed presence and Tandia had never seen anything as breathtakingly beautiful in her life.

Mama Tequila raised her glass, which looked like a topaz-coloured bauble in her enormous hand. 'Welcome, Tandia, to Mama Tequila's salon. You is now one of us, a working girl, only perhaps your work is a bit different. Tonight and from now on you only got one name, you hear? You Miss Tandy, jes' like Miss Hester, Miss Sarah, Miss Jasmine.' As Mama Tequila spoke a girl's name, the girl in question would empty the glass of sherry in her hand. 'Miss Colleen, Miss Hettie, Miss Doreen, Miss Johanna and Miss Marie. Now it your turn, Miss Tandy, you and me, we drink to your success, to Bluey Jay and to old Mama Tequila.' She lifted the glass above her head.

'Welcome to Bluey Jay, Miss Tandy!' all the girls chorussed as Tandia threw back her head and screwed her eyes up tightly in anticipation of a foul-tasting liquid. To her surprise she tasted only the slightly bitter taste of cold tea. She opened her eyes, her surprise showing.

'Hey, man, we got to watch this one, she likes it!' Hester squealed and the large room filled with the laughter of the Bluey Jay girls. It was the first time in her life Tandia had ever belonged to anything or anyone other than Patel. Despite the fact that Juicey Fruit Mambo had substituted cold tea for her sherry she felt a warm glow inside her. A thing which glowed between the chest and the pit of her stomach but also seemed to include her heart, it was a feeling which made her want to cry and laugh at the same time.

Juicey Fruit Mambo entered the room to collect the glasses. When he reached Tandia he grinned and as he took her glass he whispered, 'Dis skokiaan not for you, Miss Tandy, you must be very, very strong for the learning.'

The girls crowded around Tandia offering their congratulations and welcoming her to their society. In a few moments Juicey Fruit Mambo was back and he whispered into Mama Tequila's ear. She nodded and he left the salon again. Mama Tequila clapped her hands for silence and pointed to the door. All eyes turned as in walked Sonny Vindoo, carrying a large flat brown paper parcel on outstretched hands. 'Greetings and felicitations to the Madam Mama Tequila and her very, very beautiful girls and double greetings to Miss Tandy!'

He turned and bowed to Tandia, jerking his head forward in an almost military fashion, whereupon his glasses slid off his nose and landed on the parcel. The effect on Mr Dine-o-mite of losing his eyes was instant. Still holding the parcel he turned completely around twice and then headed blindly off in the direction of the grand piano. Without his spectacles Sonny Vindoo seemed unable to speak, and it was the light of the setting sun coming through the window beside the piano that attracted him. Tandia ran quickly ahead of him and grabbing his glasses from where they had landed on top of the parcel she slipped them onto the bridge of his nose and around his ears. The effect was equally instant. Mr Vindoo stopped on the spot and his voice returned, 'My goodness gracious me, you are a very, very kind young lady, Miss Tandy.' He turned to face Mama Tequila again. 'Your instructions, Madam, obeyed to the very last letter, everything in order, shipshape and Bristol style.'

'Honey, you got da verbal diarrhoea tonight, that for sure! Come now, give Mama Tequila that parcel. If you gone and done like I say,' she winked at Sarah, 'Miss Sarah, she in big trouble next Wednesday!'

Sonny Vindoo giggled and shook his head. 'You are talking about naughty-naughty time! That Sonny Vindoo is not this Sonny Vindoo. This Indian gentleman of very excellent morals who is standing here and who has even met the great Mahatma Gandhi himself, is very, very pure in his thoughts. It is the other one, the one who is coming up with a very excellent transcendental meditation plan!'

'Come again, Mr Dine-o-mite, what this transilmeddle jazz?' Mama Tequila asked.

'This is a very clever idea invented by an Indian holy man. You are closing your eyes and you thinking only very pure and excellent thoughts and next thing, by golly, you are travelling anywhere you want to go, sitting even in Buckingham Palace taking cha with Her Majesty Queen Elizabeth!'

He smiled and looked around at the girls, who were giggling politely behind their hands. Only Hester laughed aloud. To emphasise his point the little Indian tailor removed one hand from the parcel and wagged his finger at Mama Tequila. 'Only, I am not using it like this to have cha with the Queen. I am sitting in the back of the Chevrolet like a proper nabob and I am saying to Abdulla, "Abdulla, it is Wednesday". Then I am closing my eyes and thinking very hard with all my might about this very beautiful establishment,' he stepped forward and placed the brown parcel on Mama Tequila's lap and then, stepping back, spread his hand wide. 'That is why, when I am here, I am not here!'

'My God, I'm being fucked by a ghost!' Sarah yelled in mock consternation.

The room rocked with laughter and Tandia had never enjoyed herself so much. She'd forgotten for a moment about the gym frock, but now Mama Tequila, still giggling, began to open the parcel on her lap. 'Tandia, come here, baby,' she beckoned. The girls all crowded round to look. Only Hester remained slightly to one side, silent for once in her life. The crackle of the paper seemed to take an eternity and then Mama Tequila withdrew a bright pink gymslip. She held it up and the slip fell over her knees. 'My, that pretty? What you say, baby?' The girls all oohed and aahed and Tandia, despite her dismay, managed to smile. Mama Tequila handed the gym frock to her and delved back into the parcel. 'That ain't all, baby!' She produced a blouse and a pair of pink woollen stockings and a bright pink beret. You gonna be the prettiest li'l girl that school did ever see!'

Tandia burst into tears. Despite the terrible embarrassment the pink garments represented for her, she was loved. They cared, all of them, they cared about her, Tandia Patel. She wouldn't think of Monday, only about now, about the warmth and the love surrounding her. She handed the clothes to Hester and embraced Mama Tequila, her tears making dark, wet stains on the woman's pink gown. Then she turned to confront a grinning Sonny Vindoo. She hugged him as well. 'Thank you, Mr Vindoo, my clothes are very lovely,' she said tearfully.

'Miss Tandy, I am hearing you are going to Durban Indian Girls' High School, a very excellent institution. My daughter, she is married now, she went to this school, where she is getting first-class honours in her matriculation!'

Mama Tequila once again clapped her hands to gain attention, for Juicey Fruit had entered and nodded to her from the door. 'Hey-ho! Party time, darlings! The fine young men from them boats they here already in the other salon! Oh, ho! Let the business of Bluey Jay begin! Them honky-tonk fisherman boys they gonna die 'less they get their snake medicine tonight!'

She turned to Tandia. 'Miss Tandy, you be nice now and show Mr Dine-o-mite out the back door.' She turned to Sonny Vindoo, her eyes wide. 'Unless of course, he want to tran-sil-meddle-tate hisself back into the loving arms of Mrs Vindoo!'

Tandia woke early on Monday morning. Outside her window the bush doves were cooing in the wild fig trees, and although it was only a few minutes past five, the sun was already up. In the distance she could hear a couple of cockerels crowing. A soft breeze billowed the terylene curtains in her bedroom, carrying with it just a hint of wood smoke from the African *kraal* down by the river. It was a perfect early November morning and it had all the makings of a perfectly ghastly day for Tandia.

She had slept fitfully, the matter of Mama Tequila's pink school uniform never quite leaving even her sub-conscious. In the month since Patel's death much had changed for her. She found herself increasingly gregarious in the company of the girls and a special friendship with Juicey Fruit Mambo was rapidly developing. She felt entirely safe with him around her, a new feeling for her, and one which she found simply wonderful. With Juicey Fruit Mambo it was the way she had always believed it might become with Patel. But she was still a shy, frightened little girl and today the best friend in the world couldn't help her, she was on her own. Juicey Fruit Mambo would drive her to the school gates and from that moment on she was alone. She cringed inwardly as she thought about it. She was going to be the laughing stock of the whole school and she had no doubt she would be held up to ridicule in assembly by Miss Naidoo.

Tandia went down the hall to the bathroom to shower and to clean her teeth. After she'd completed her toilet she returned down the quiet passage, the smooth, polished yellowwood floors cool on her bare feet. Her own room was on the furthest end of the long corridor and she had to pass the rooms of all the sleeping girls except Hester. As she walked past the door to Sarah's room she noticed that it was slightly ajar and she moved over to close it. Mama Tequila, for reasons she had never explained, insisted that the girls sleep with their bedroom doors closed. Tandia's hand was on the door knob and, on a sudden impulse, she opened Sarah's door a little further. The room smelled of cigarettes and slightly stale perfume; on the dresser beside the bed was an empty half-jack of brandy and a used glass. Sarah was naked, lying on her side facing the door, her sheet kicked into a crumpled heap at the end of the divan bed. Tandia started to withdraw in embarrassment but then held still. There was something vulnerable about the way Sarah lay, she had her knees tucked up and she sucked on her thumb like a child. In repose her scrubbed face, small round breasts and slender shoulders made her look younger than she was.

Sarah suddenly opened her eyes, seemingly from a deep sleep. She showed no surprise whatsoever at Tandia's presence in the room. She turned over and reached for the Wesclock which rested on the floor beside the bed. 'Christ, Tandy, it's only a quarter to six, go back to bed, it's still night time.' She sat up and reached for the sheet, pulled it up over her body and rolled over in bed, turning her back to Tandia.

'I couldn't sleep, I'm used to getting up early.' She turned to go but suddenly blurted out, 'Sarah, what am I going to do!'

Sarah groaned and turned back to face her, 'What's the matter with you kid, can't a person get some sleep around here?' Tandy flushed and started to apologise, backing out of the door. 'I'm only playing, jong. Come and sit here,' Sarah said, patting the divan beside her.

Tandia walked over and sat down on the edge of the bed as Sarah propped herself up onto one elbow. 'C'mon, kid, you better tell me, are you in trouble or something?'

'It's Monday, Sarah, I've got to go back to school today!'

'So? You got new everything, you should be very excited, you a very lucky girl, what Mama T did was nice.'

'Sarah, the school colours are brown! A brown gymslip and white blouse. Mama Tequila has made everything in pink!

'You mean you the only one in the whole school with a pink uniform? Why didn't you tell Mama T?'

Tandia shook her head. 'I wasn't supposed to know, it was a surprise, remember? Sarah, what am I going to do?'

Sarah looked at Tandia. School carried no cherished memories for her, she had left at eleven and her impression of her time there was one of constant harassment, punishment and humiliation. 'Simple, man, don't go. Wait till Juicey Fruit drives away and then don't go in.

Go to the bioscope, there's a good picture at the Odeon, Fred Astaire and Ginger Rogers, they got a ten o'clock matinée.' She reached for her bag on the dresser beside the bed. 'Here I'll give you some money.'

'But Sarah, I want to finish school. Mama T said I could do that. They all going to laugh their heads off, all the girls and the teachers too. Miss Naidoo is going to send me home, and then what?'

Sarah sat up in the bed and took Tandia into her arms. 'Come now, Tandy, it's not so bad, sticks and stones can break your bones but words can never harm you.' Tandia had wrapped a towel around her when she'd come from the bathroom and her shoulders were bare. 'Sometimes it's good to be different, Tandy.' Sarah kissed Tandia gently on the top of the shoulder and then as gently on the neck. 'When you on the game, being different is normal.' Her hand pulled at the folded towel between Tandia's small, firm breasts and opened it up. Tandia's heart was pounding. Sarah's hands seemed to be melting her body as though years of tension were being run through her caressing hands. Tandia had never felt like this before, it was as though her body had grown another dimension, had become another place. Sarah's tongue was caressing her neck and then moved downwards to her breast, 'Sshhh! don't say anything, Tandy, everything will be orright.'

For a long time aferwards Tandia lay in Sarah's arms, her body filled with the warmth of loving. Even after her breathing had quietened down she wanted to lie there long enough to be able to fold her feeling into an emotional envelope she could store in her subconscious against hard times.

Sarah stirred. 'Go now, Tandy, when they laugh at you in school, jus' remember, you a proper woman now, you know things they don't know, they can't do nothing to hurt you, they all stupid girls in their brown gymslips, you hear?'

Juicey Fruit was waiting for her in the kitchen and when she arrived he sat her down at the head of the table and placed a plate of steaming mealiemeal porridge in front of her, pushing the milk jug and the sugar closer to it, fussing like an old umFazi. Next he brought Tandia two pieces of already buttered toast.

'Thank you, Juicey Fruit Mambo.' Tandia was not used to being waited upon.

'You very beautiful today, Missy Tandy.'

Tandia was unable to look Juicey Fruit Mambo in the eye lest she betray her feeling about the bright pink gymslip. 'You too, Juicey Fruit Mambo.'

Juicey Fruit had on a pink shirt and a red bow tie and he wore two gold sleeve bands just above the elbows. The creases in his black trousers were perfect and his black shoes were highly polished. He was obviously pleased that Tandia had noticed his careful colour coordination and his gold incisor teeth shone as he smiled at her. 'Mama T she give to me dis shirt, long, long time ago, it is very beautiful I tink.'

They left Bluey Jay at half past seven. Tandia was very quiet sitting next to Juicey Fruit Mambo in the front of the Packard. He had tried to make her sit in the back but she had protested which, in the end, seemed to please him. As they were coming down from the Berea towards the port Juicey Fruit Mambo glanced at her. 'Missy Tandy, why for you are not happy for going to school?'

Tandia bit her lip, but a tear ran down her cheek as she stared resolutely through the windscreen. 'Juicey Fruit Mambo, he also very sad when you not happy

169

today.' He glanced at her. 'Why you cry, Missy Tandy?'

Tandia could contain herself no longer. 'Ag, Juicey Fruit Mambo, you can't understand this thing. In the school the clothes the girls must wear is brown,' she plucked at her gymfrock. 'Like this but only brown.'

'But pink more pretty than brown?'

'Ja, I know, but they don't allow it. I'm going to get into terrible trouble and everyone will laugh at me!' She covered her face with her hands.

Juicey Fruit Mambo drew the car to a halt at the kerb. 'Missy Tandy, Mama Tequila she spend much, much money for dis clothes for your school. Dey not laugh for dis clothes, Missy Tandy. Dis clothes is for new!'

Tandia realised that he was deeply worried by her distress but was quite unable to comprehend the significance the colour of her gymslip and blouse had. 'You are right,' she said. 'Come now, we must go or I'll be late.'

Juicey Fruit Mambo pulled away from the kerb; he knew the matter remained unresolved, there were some things about women which he could never hope to understand and it was better not to try. He guided the big Packard smoothly through the narrow back streets and finally turned into Prichard Street, drawing up outside the school gates. He suddenly saw what Tandia had meant. Hundreds of girls were milling around the playground and moving through the gates; all wore identical clothes, a brown gymslip, white blouse, short white socks, brown shoes and a brown beret. He put the car into gear and started to turn the steering wheel so when a gap in the traffic arrived he could move off. He had no idea what to do except he knew he couldn't leave Tandia to go in alone in her pink uniform.

'What you doing, Juicey Fruit Mambo? I must get out here.'

'No, Missy Tandy . . .' His voice was cut short by an urgent banging on the window on Tandia's side of the car. They both turned to see Sonny Vindoo looking at them. He carried a big brown package under his arm and indicated that Tandia should roll down the window.

'Nearly I am missing you! Let me get in the back.' He opened the back door of the Packard and jumped in. 'My very clever son, University of Bombay, B.A. Degree honours, businessman and also photographer, his business is in Pickering Street, it is two minutes, no more, we must go there now.' He passed the parcel over the back of the front seat to Tandia, 'Open please!' he said happily, leaning forward to look over her shoulder.

Juicey Fruit swung into the traffic as Tandia pulled the string which held the large flat parcel together. The parcel contained a new brown gymslip, white blouse and a slightly worn brown beret. Sonny Vindoo giggled. 'I make these for you, Miss Tandy and also, the beret, which I am not making, it is left over from my daughter when she attended this excellent school.'

Tandia burst into tears. 'Please, please, no time for tears now, must change blinking, jolly quick!' He turned to Juicey Fruit Mambo. 'You must turn here, see the shop, "Singer & Necchi Sewing Centre".'

'I know this place, baas,' Juicey Fruit Mambo said. He had a huge grin on his face and his gold incisors flashed as he shared in Tandia's happiness.

The car drew to a halt outside a small shop. On either side of the doorway were display windows; on the one appeared the Singer Sewing Machine logo and on the other the Necchi. Painted under each imprimatur were the words, 'Sole Agency'. Several sewing machines of each brand were displayed in their respective windows. In the centre of each window set on a small easel was a large photograph. On one rested a portrait of a prosperous-looking Indian man hand-tinted in the old-fashioned manner, while on the other was a full-length colour photograph of a bridal couple. Above the door was a third sign which read: Jamal Vindoo – Photographer, Wedding and Family Portraits. Colour or Hand-Tinted. Apply Rear of Building.' An arrow pointed away from the door to a small lane running down the side of the building. It was a nice tidy little shop.

Sonny Vindoo jumped from the back of the car and hoisted up his dhoti. 'Come, Miss Tandy, hurry please!'

Tandia gathered up the parcel on her lap, got out of the car and followed Sonny Vindoo up the front steps of the shop. A young man appeared at the doorway but the little Indian pushed him aside. 'Good mornings later, Jamal!' Sonny Vindoo shouted. 'To the change room!' Tandia smiled through her tears at Jamal, whom she took to be Sonny Vindoo's Bombay-educated son, and who stood aside as she followed Sonny Vindoo into a shop which was filled with the whirring of sewing machines. At their entrance, several woman seated at the machines ceased sewing and looked up from their work. Sonny Vindoo crossed the room making for a bright orange floral curtain which hung across one corner. As he reached the curtain he held it apart. 'In here, Miss Tandy, I am waiting outside, doing guard duty.' He scowled through his steel-rimmed spectacles at the grinning seamstresses as though to indicate to them that he would not tolerate any interference or even comment.

Tandia found herself in a small store room filled with bolts of men's suiting and bright lengths of dress material. There was just enough room for her to stand.

'Thank you, thank you, Mr Vindoo!'

'No time for thank yous! You must hurry now, please. Any minute the school bell is clanking, then, my goodness, where shall we be then? We shall be up the bloomin Khyber Pass!' Sonny Vindoo fussed and drew the curtain back across the doorway.

Tandia changed quickly. There were no white socks included in the parcel, but she regarded this as a small matter. She couldn't take the grin off her face, she was saved! Mr Dine-o-mite had ridden to the rescue and at the same time had allowed Mama Tequila to save face.

She emerged from behind the curtains looking just like any other Durban Indian High School girl. Over her arm she carried her pink outfit. Even her socks looked no worse than as if they'd been accidently left to soak in a bucket with some red garment which had run.

Sonny Vindoo looked her up and down admiringly and silently congratulated himself. 'Not so pretty as before, but I think you are feeling much better, hey, Miss Tandy? It is a very great pity we do not have time for Jamal to take your photograph!'

Tandia bent down impulsively and kissed the little man. He'd come out without shaving and the white stubble on his cheek felt like sandpaper against her lips. Kissing anyone was something she could not previously have imagined herself capable of doing, but after Sarah's room this morning everything was changed; she was loved and a woman now, and different.

Like Sonny Vindoo on a Wednesday evening, Miss Tandy was a different Tandia Patel. 'Mr Vindoo, I will pay you back, I swear it!' She sighed and grinned and wanted to hug him again and again.

'It is my great personal pleasure,' Sonny Vindoo said and then, glancing at his watch, added in a panic, 'Come, come, we must hurry like blazes!' as he made for the door of the shop. 'Farewells later!' he yelled at Jamal as he disappeared into the bright sunlight outside.

Juicey Fruit Mambo was seated behind the wheel of the Packard, the engine of the big car running and the door on Tandia's side open for her to jump in for a quick getaway. Parked directly behind him was Abdulla in Sonny Vindoo's Chevrolet, who had tran-sil-meddle-tated from nowhere.

Eight

Peekay was fortunate in having E. W. White as his tutor at Oxford. White, a fellow of Magdalen, was considered one of the great tutors at law and Peekay was more than a little apprehensive when, on his second day at Oxford, he received a polite note inviting him to take tea in E. W. White's rooms the following afternoon.

The door opened to reveal a tall, angular man with dark brown eyes which belied his obviously English complexion. His hair was almost completely white, but because his eyebrows were blond, his eyes seemed incongruous, as though a hidden bloodline were surfacing. He wore grey flannels rather in need of a crease, heavy brown brogues, a light-blue cotton shirt with a slightly disarranged soft collar and a carelessly knotted club or college tie. From his bony frame hung a grey tweed jacket from which the side pockets permanently bulged, as though he was accustomed to jamming his fists into them for extended periods. He was, Peekay thought, the sort of man who would make Hymie's mum run to the kitchen for the skillet, memorising the contents of the fridge.

His eyes welcomed Peekay but he said not a word,

sweeping his right hand in the general direction of one of two large leather armchairs facing a friendly-looking, but unlit fireplace.

It was a curiously mute welcome and Peekay, nervous as hell, didn't quite know how to take his tutor. He'd memorised a little speech saying how pleased he was to be taken under E. W. White's tutorial wing, but now confronting him, it didn't seem quite appropriate. His tutor radiated a calmness which an over-hasty or mumbled introduction would have disrupted.

At this point, and still without speaking, E. W. White left the study and some moments later returned wheeling a rather battered-looking tea trolley. One of the wheels of the trolley squeaked as he pushed it across the worn Persian carpet which covered most of the floor.

Peekay liked the room immediately. It was predictable and contained no disappointments. The room of a tutor at Oxford, he thought, ought to look just like this one. On two walls were a number of antique black-and-white sketches of fishing scenes – lonely, flat landscapes of willow-banked rivers at which tiny figures sat with fishing rods etched against a lowering sky. An almost equal number of pale watercolours of not dissimilar scenes in faded gold stucco frames made up the remainder of the pictures on the walls. They were uniform in size and so similar they'd probably been sold in a job lot. To Peekay's delight, mounted on the wall above the fireplace, was a glass case containing a large brown trout. Its tail curled slightly upward almost touching the top of the glass box; its jaw was set open as if about to take the angler's fly. The taxidermist's brush marks showed clearly where he had applied the lacquer too generously just below the dorsal fin. Otherwise the

176

walls were entirely covered with books. Peekay liked the idea of a wall of books, though he *was* slightly disappointed that they weren't all matching tomes bound in morocco and embossed in gold. In fact, the cases were rather untidy, with books of every size and description filling every available space, some jammed sideways into the spaces left between the books and the shelf above. Small piles of books littered the floor beside the fireplace and near the door. Against the far wall was a Georgian rosewood desk and fronting it was a slightly lopsided-looking captain's chair of the swivel variety. The remainder of the room was taken up by the two large armchairs facing the fireplace, in one of which Peekay now sat. On the floor beside the other was a large hand-beaten copper ashtray, which was empty but smudged grey with powdered ash.

E. W. White brought the trolley to a halt between the two chairs and poured tea from an enormous brown enamel teapot, its spout protruding from a bright orange knitted tea cosy. Neither milk nor sugar was in evidence and Peekay was not asked if he took either. Instead E. W. White forked a wedge of lemon into Peekay's cup.

'Peekay? Just Peekay? Am I to understand that this single duosyllabic name is all that you are known by? Is this correct?'

'Yes, sir, that's right, only one name,' Peekay replied, hoping he wasn't going to probe any further.

E. W. White looked to see if Peekay was being flippant but decided he was not. 'Splendid! You may call me E. W., which puts us on equal terms. I must say I never much believed in the English tradition whereby a child is saddled with a veritable cartouche of names. One name, if it serves to identify plainly, is quite enough, don't you think?' He continued without waiting for Peekay's reply. 'After all, there are only two parts of the human condition which matter and both of these are singular. We only have one heart and one brain. They, in the end, decide whether we are worthwhile or otherwise. The rest is simply a mixture of affectation and progenital garbage upon which we English place far too much importance. Most Frenchmen are hard put to trace their grandparents on either side.'

'Would you say that continuity and tradition are unimportant then, sir?' Peekay asked, trying out the thought.

'Only when they are the continuity of learning and concern. If a person or a nation has both a good heart and a sound head, they or it can be forgiven shortcomings. Alas, England seems, for the time being at least, to have neither.'

Peekay wasn't sure he understood. He hadn't been in England very long and wasn't much chop on British politics. 'You see, simplicity is the key to almost everything. If something can be simply stated and simply understood, it will generally translate into a working concept. Law has chosen to neglect this fundamental truth and as a result has allowed itself to become reactionary, complicated and, for the most part, unjust. Why have you chosen to study law?'

Peekay wanted desperately to impress this rather intimidating Englishman. E. W. probably saw him as just another colonial: the South African, Australian, New Zealander and Canadian – all the same, bright enough, but bred in a cultural desert – England's rather tiresome obligation to the sons and daughters of the second-rate people she'd sent abroad to tame the natives. Peekay needed to let him know he was different, his reason for being at Oxford special.

'Well, sir, my country has problems which I believe can only, in the end, be resolved through the rule of law.' It sounded rather pompous and Peekay coloured slightly.

But E. W. chuckled. 'Ha! An optimist. I expect the opposite will happen. The law will be used to prevent a solution.'

'How do you mean the opposite? Surely when a problem is solved it ought to become the law?' Peekay's mouth was dry and he was having difficulty affecting the maturity he wanted to display.

E. W.'s reply, when it came seemed a little terse, though Peekay may have imagined this. 'The common law, as I have indicated, is no longer simple or straight-forward. Instead it is complicated, often obscure and usually costly, so it can be utilised for the most part only by rapacious men who have devised it to keep title to wealth and property and to maintain power. Poor men cannot afford it and so find themselves condemned by it. Rich men, on the other hand, cannot afford to be without it and, indeed, use the law to avoid justice. If this is true of property and individual power then it is also true of societies. The haves will fashion the law to serve themselves and to keep the have-nots from getting their share. You will know much more about this than I, Peekay, but the ideology the world is coming to know as "apartheid" is, I believe, essentially about one section of the population sustaining a lifestyle and maintaining privileges which are not available to another. Call it rich against poor, black against white. The law creates poverty for some and riches for others, slavery for the have-nots and freedom only for the rich. If you agree with me, Peekay, then explain how your precious rule of law will put such a situation to right?'

Peekay was overwhelmed. E. W. had demolished his prime reason for being at Oxford. Despite his humiliation, he admired the somewhat caustic Englishman who'd just done a complete demolition job on him. Peekay, who had thought himself on the side of the angels, was suddenly aware that in E. W.'s eyes he must seem not much better than any of his South African contemporaries.

Peekay had received a liberal education by South African standards and in the months he'd been on his own on the Copperbelt he'd grown distant from the ideas and values of most of his white South African peers. Theirs was thinking within a defined circle, with very little encouragement to step beyond its circumference. It was not that they were actively conspiring against the black people; there was simply no apparent context in which they could become aware of the need to question the concept of apartheid. Their lives were on track and the dichotomy based on colour was precise. Everyone knew where they stood. Thinking inevitably led to discomfort and perhaps even guilt. And guilt spoilt everything.

Peekay recalled a conversation he'd had with Gideon Mandoma, the young Zulu heir to a chiefdom, the man he'd fought in Sophiatown. After the fight they'd become firm friends and Peekay had arranged for the young Zulu boxer to train in Solly Goldman's gym in Doomfontein, where he himself worked out. The young Zulu had found a job as a furnace boy in a foundry which changed shifts at three in the afternoon so he could work out as a sparring partner with Peekay three days a week. Feeding a blast furnace with a shovel is hard work and the white foreman was a cruel, relentless bastard who was fond of taking his fists to the workers.

On the day the conversation took place Gideon had arrived at the gym with a split above his eye which, though dried and caked on the peripherals, showed a pink streak of bloody flesh running through its centre. The cut had obviously required stitches. Peekay had asked him how it happened. The young Zulu had tried to laugh it off but Peekay had persisted, until Gideon had shrugged and said, 'It was my turn to be beaten by the baas, Peekay.'

'How can you stand it, Gideon? Surely you must want to kill the bastard?' he had asked.

They had been gloved up, ready for a sparring session, waiting for two boxers ahead of them to relinquish the ring. Peekay was speaking in Zulu and since whites, as a general rule, do not speak an African language, there had been little fear of their being overheard.

Gideon had laughed. 'Let me tell you a story, Peekay. Once, when I was a small boy, a white farmer came to our kraal looking for women to pick beans. He carried a big basket and said that he would pay so much for every basket picked. The basket was nearly as tall as a woman, but a day begins at half-light and ends when the light is the same again; to the women it did not seem too big. The money was generous and the women agreed. He arranged to return at dawn the following day with his lorry.

'The stars still pricked the sky when the women rose. Even the herd boys still slept and the women pulled their cotton wraps tightly about the babies they carried on their backs. After whispering to the old women to rise in a short while to make the fires for the morning meal they left. They were all very happy because the drought was bad and the spring rains were late and now this unexpected good fortune had come their way and they were going to make some money.

'They worked hard all day in the hot sun, stopping only to take water or to comfort a child. The baskets were big and the beans were small and hid behind the leaves. The work was very hard, but they were happy and sang songs about the cooking pots and dress lengths they hoped one day to buy if more of this work should come their way. By sunset the beans were all picked and each took her basket to the white farmer to be paid. "I cannot pay you," he said. "Look, your baskets are not full, I agreed to pay only by the basketful." It was true,' Gideon had said, opening his forefinger and thumb, indicating about five inches. 'The beans were so far from the top in the best baskets and even a little lower in the others.'

Peekay had shaken his head; he had known in his heart that Gideon's story was not unusual, that it happened every day a thousand times over.

'We took the matter to the headman of our village and he took it to the next *indaba* with the chief,' Gideon had said. 'The chief listened. It was not an unusual story and I suppose there wasn't very much he could do. But it so happened that Inkosi-Inkosikazi, the greatest medicine man in all Africa, was from the chief's kraal. He was very old and it was thought he would soon die. It was a bit of an insult really, taking a trivial matter to such a great man, but the chief, who was wise, knew that a woman's anger makes the hut an unhappy place. He promised he would ask Inkosi-lnkosikazi if he would consider the matter of the beans. The women were contented; to have this affair of the beans looked into by the great medicine man connected them all with a great honour.

'That very night the rains came to Zululand and the women knew the spirits were on their side in the great bean affair. Even if the mighty Inkosi-lnkosikazi did no more, it was already sufficient.' Gideon Mandoma had laughed and lifted his hand about eighteen inches from the gymnasium floor. 'The young corn stood this high when a message arrived to say that Inkosi-lnkosikazi would pronounce on the matter of the beans and that the women concerned should be at the chief's kraal in two days' time. There was a great deal of excitement, women are not generally invited to attend even a small indaba.

'The news of the great indaba spread like a fire when the bush is dry. People from all over Zululand came to hear the great wizard. They brought newly fermented beer and dried tobacco and some of the precious seed *mealies* they'd been hoarding until the new season's corn was safely inside the seed baskets. Even the very old women, their backs bent double, tall sticks thumping the ground as they walked, set out for the chief's kraal.'

'Orright then, you two, stop nattering like a couple of old *yentas* and hop in the bleedin' ring,' Solly Goldman had called suddenly.

'Afterwards! You've got to promise to finish the story!' Peekay had said urgently.

Gideon had laughed, placing his hand on Peekay's shoulder. 'I do not think you are a white man, Peekay, just a white Zulu.' Then he had looked serious for a moment. 'That's why you are the Tadpole Angel.'

Peekay had spun around. 'Stop that, Gideon Mandoma! You call me that again and I'll drop you for the count, you hear?'

'Drop me? Your best punch is like a fly landing on my nose, white man!'

'Cheeky bloody kaffir!' Peekay had said in English. And they had both laughed as they moved towards Solly Goldman standing in the centre of the ring.

In South African society, the boxing ring was the only place Peekay and Gideon could meet on equal terms. Gideon, intellectually bright, with all the character and determination of a Peekay, was working in a foundry and living in a tin shanty; while Peekay sat sipping tea with his Oxford tutor.

'I know that, looking in from the outside, the rule of the law in my country makes a mockery of justice, E. W. But, equally I can't run from trying to find a solution by using the law. Without law there would be chaos in South Africa.'

'Ah, yes, chaos! How often men seem to initiate the greatest injustices and repression in the name of preventing chaos. The prevention of chaos was what brought the German people under Hitler and led to millions of Jews being crushed.'

Peekay knew that to pursue the argument would only lead to further humiliation. E. W. had probed his intellect and found him wanting. But Peekay neither knew how, nor did he want to back down gracefully, defeat meant relinquishing the central intellectual position he held for his future life.

'I'm afraid you're right, though being right doesn't help much. People such as Hymie Levy and myself have to return to South Africa to fight apartheid and, paradoxically, our only weapon is the law. The unjust, unfair and often ruthless instrument of the law is all we have.' Peekay hesitated. 'That is, short of violence, guns and bombs.'

E. W. became really interested in his new student for the first time. 'Ah, violence and guns. They are invoked as often in the name of law as they are in opposition to it. The trigger is a poor debater but the bleeding-heart liberal, filled with dogma and cant, is equally ineffective.'

Peekay wasn't sure what a bleeding-heart liberal was, but E. W.'s use of the expression suggested it was derogatory. 'I don't think I know what you mean.'

'Most revolutions, no matter how quiet, are not served well by the sympathetic intellectual who carps at the injustice of the culture but seems to live quite happily off the resultant lifestyle it affords him. The well-fed and housed white protest, lending its mouth to the black cause,' E. W. explained.

'And you see me as such?' Peekay felt hurt and humiliated. Somehow he had to make the tall man seated beside him see he wasn't the usual colonial apologist.

E. W., aware of his student's indignation sighed. 'The fuel of any revolution is injustice and heaven knows there has been enough in your country to stoke the revolutionary fires. But, as yet, I perceive *your* revolution as merely an intellectual idea. A few indignant members of the intelligentsia exorcising their guilt by plotting, usually without permission, on behalf of the oppressed. While this is both commendable and altruistic, it is not usually a successful ploy. The new leaders soon adopt the ways of their old masters. Witness India and Pakistan.'

E. W. looked at Peekay for a moment. 'You are not the first revolutionary to have sat in that chair. The last young chap who argued passionately about freedom from tyranny and equality of opportunity for his people, is today the tyrannical leader of a desperately oppressed nation on the same continent as your own. He has invited me on several occasions to be a guest at the presidential palace and seems genuinely surprised at my refusal. What evidence do you have that the black people in your country are ready to rise against the regime? A true revolution begins from the soil, from the grass roots. It is the final cry of despair from the ground up. Have you heard the cry "freedom"?'

E. W. was asking for hard evidence where there was none. Well, none of the sort which would satisfy a mind such as his. Africa was as unpredictable as a bomb lying in a field for years; one day it would explode, who knew when? But there were signs. Perhaps not the sort E. W. needed to become convinced, but signs nevertheless.

When Peekay had been very young his black nanny told him the story of *Igama sina kathathu*, the stork with three dances. The first dance, or starting dance, is slow and measured, done to a careful set of rules. The second dance is still measured, though somewhat faster and more inventive. The final dance is a flurry and a flutter, a wildly erratic affair in which the male stork often kills itself by breaking its own legs.

Peekay thought of the uprising of the black people in the same way. The analogy wasn't all that strange – dancing and singing were very much a part of black protest. The first dance, the dance which Peekay believed had already begun, was the muted struggle between black and white, a struggle being conducted largely through the courts. There would be trials followed by judicial sentences. The litany of justice would always be present, mostly meaningless to the recipient but painstakingly played out in form and function, precise and according to the book, the white man's book of laws.

The second dance was born of the conditions of the first, where more and more black people were driven from their homes. Already Minister Vorster was talking of separate bantustans, independent states which he referred to as 'tribal homelands', as if they represented some kind of homecoming for black refugees.

The third dance was bloody revolution, the final frenzied cry of pain, the atrocious day of reckoning, the river of blood.

Peekay saw his return to Africa as the beginning of the end of the first dance. It was still a time when the law could be challenged, where the etiquette of justice was intact and treason could still be proved. It was still a time when there was hope that some sanity might prevail.

'Yes, I think I've heard the cry "freedom". But I have to tell you in the African way, E. W. The greatest of the African medicine men told this story to the people. He was an incredibly old man, Inkosi-Inkosikazi, whose name simply means Man-Woman, denoting that he was above gender in even the male-dominated African society. His wisdom was for all the people and altogether pure.'

Peekay resumed Gideon's story, as his Zulu friend had done in the shower room in Solly Goldman's gym. 'Everyone was gathered for the great indaba. The old man began to speak in a thin piping voice which carried surprisingly to all the people present. This is what he told them.

'Once a small army of ants out foraging came across a dung beetle pushing a large ball of dung up a steep hill and making heavy work of the process. It was a time of drought and the ants were hungry. One of the ants walked politely up the to dung beetle and asked him if they could help in return for some more of this delicious dung for themselves.

'The beetle agreed readily and leisurely followed as the ants, singing happily, pushed the great ball of dung to the top of the hill.

' "We have completed the task and the sun is low in the sky, tell us where we can find some dung so that we can return with it to our homes before dark," the ants asked.

'"Hayi, hayi, hayi," the dung beetle shook his head sadly. "The dung is very far away, in a place which you cannot reach before sundown. Here, take this little bit, it will stop your hunger. Tomorrow, be at the same place just before sun-up and I will show you," the beetle promised.

'It wasn't much, but it was enough to feed their families for one night. "What an excellent beetle," the ants agreed.' Peekay paused, embarrassed. 'I'm afraid African stories are a bit long-winded, I'll try to make it short.'

'No, no, please, Peekay. I'm fascinated. Detail is colour and colour is essential to most good argument.'

'Well, the following day the ants were up early, even before sun-up, and together they hurried to meet the dung beetle. They waited and waited and the sun rose and they grew very thirsty. They had almost given up when they saw the beetle approaching, rolling another very large ball of dung before him. "Where have you been?" they cried.

'The beetle stopped pushing and looked very angry. "You are lazy. I came to this place early and you were not here. It's a good thing I am patient and am willing to give you a second chance. If you push this ball of dung up the hill again I will forgive you."

'So the ants apologised and, forming themselves into work gangs, they pushed the ball up the hill once more.

They were rewarded with the same amount of dung as the previous evening, enough only for one night. Once again, the beetle promised to show them the place of the dung if they weren't too lazy to rise and meet him the next day.

'Now this beetle was a very clever *skelm* and, try as they might, they always missed him in the morning. They were then obliged to push the ball of dung up the hill in return for just enough to keep their families alive.

'Soon the ants forgot how to forage for themselves and the only way they could feed their families was to push the dung ball up the hill and receive a small portion each night.

'Time went by and they no longer questioned the beetle's authority. He owned all the dung and they accepted that they worked for him and that he could beat them if he wished or starve their children or make laws telling them where they could go or even live. The old laws and customs of the ants were destroyed and the ants were forced to live by the laws and the customs of the beetle.

'Now the ants grew very unhappy but the beetle was strong and they were weak; and besides, they now depended entirely on the beetle for their livelihood.' Peekay laughed, looking up at E. W. 'We're close to the end and I promise not to be this longwinded again.'

'Don't give up while you're ahead. I haven't listened this long to a student for years. I am suitably impressed.'

Peekay flushed at the compliment. 'Like all good stories this one has a hero. One day a young male ant was born in the ant tribe. Right from the beginning he was different. "Why can't we forage for dung ourselves? Why must we work only for the dung beetle? It is well known that the ant was here before the beetle. Why does the beetle own all the dung?" he asked.

'"Shhh!" the elders among the ants cautioned, "the beetle will hear you and come and take you away and beat you and throw you into prison." But the young ant was brave and clever and very determined and soon all the young ants gathered around him and they made a plan to get the dung, which they believed belonged to them just as much as it did to the beetle.

'That day when the beetle arrived at the spot where the worker ants would push his dung up the hill they were nowhere to be seen. He shouted and threatened and stamped his feet on the ground but nothing he did or said helped. The ants had disappeared.

'Now the beetle had a problem. If he left the dung at the bottom of the hill the ants might come in the middle of the night and steal it. He started to push the ball of dung up the hill. But he wasn't used to working hard in the hot sun and the ball was very heavy. He would push it up part of the way and then his strength would fail him and the ball would roll down the hill again.

'But the beetle was not a fool and he was also very determined. He rested for a while and gathered his strength and finally, in the cool of the evening, he began to push. All the young ants watched from the top of the hill as he pushed and pushed and this time he managed to get it almost to the brow of the hill.

'"Now!" shouted the fierce young leader and they rushed at the ball of dung and began to push it back down the hill. The beetle was exhausted but he resisted stoutly. The other ants, observing this, rushed to help the young ants. The beetle could hold the ball on the brow of the hill no longer. Inch by inch the ball began to slide backwards but the beetle would not move away.

He was stubborn and he was selfish and he could not bring himself to believe that the ants were capable of overcoming him.

'"Share the dung with us equally and we will stop pushing on this side and help you on your side," the young ant cried.

'But the beetle was so used to being the baas and owning all the dung that he didn't want to share. "No!" he shouted defiantly. "Beetles are better than ants, ants are meant to work and dung beetles are expected to own dung!"

'So the ants pushed harder and the ball of dung began to roll backwards. The beetle, unwilling to jump out of the way and to lose his precious ball of dung, hung on. The ball rolled over and over with him clinging on for dear life so that his shell was cracked and he was bruised and bleeding; but still he clung to the ball of dung. When the ball of dung reached the bottom of the hill it was travelling at great speed, heading for a huge rock. The ball crashed against a rock and broke up, burying the beetle deep inside a heap of dung. The beetle was too weak and injured to crawl out of the dung. He suffocated and died, buried in shit!'

'Bravo, Peekay, a lovely allegory,' E. W. was obviously amused. 'But how does it tell us that an uprising is at hand? Is this not simply a folk story? The history of every nation is told with allegorical stories of good triumphing over evil.'

Peekay sighed inwardly. He was doing too much talking but it was too late now. He had to go on. 'Well firstly the message, or story if you like, came from the most important wizard of them all, a man who was accepted, not only by the Zulu people, but by all the tribes as the greatest of the medicine men. The story was his last; he died some weeks later. Therefore it was a message to all of the black people to take action and to do so with the absolute conviction that, in the end, they would prevail.

'But, if you understand Zulu, the message was not of a sudden uprising. What it carried was a plan. A course of action and a result. Inkosi-Inkosikazi foretold great suffering; the ball rolling down the hill with the beetle hanging on could go on for years, perhaps even decades. It also tells of the white men's determination, *their* willingness to suffer to hold on to their heritage. To the African, suffering is a familiar experience. The African people have always suffered and did so long before the advent of the white man. Suffering is an expected component of life. Shaka, the first great warrior king who forged the Zulu nation into the greatest war machine Africa has ever seen, could make an entire regiment march over a three-hundred foot cliff to demonstrate their obedience and their loyalty. The Zulu people expect that they'll have to fight, expect that they will suffer, expect that the Boer will not capitulate easily. Nevertheless the story of the dung beetle and the ants is a blueprint, a foretelling of a future with a certainty that, in the end, the people will prevail. It is the certainty of victory which will make them fight long and hard until they win. Victory is no longer an "if"; with Inkosi-Inkosikazi's prophecy, it has become a "when".'

Peekay was conscious of how melodramatic his words must sound to this rational and totally civilised man. He looked about the slightly untidy room. He was in a perfectly ordinary study in a great seat of learning in a country where the fundamental belief was that a combination of God, Queen, good manners and a fair-minded attitude to your fellow man was a perfectly valid prescription for life and one which the rest of the world shouldn't find too difficult to grasp. Witchcraft, superstition and any of the other tenets of a primitive culture played no part in this perception.

Some fucking Oxford undergraduate he'd turned out to be! He wasn't clever at all. This place was filled with people who were light years ahead of him. Not simply the dons, most of the students as well. They spoke better, thought better and certainly argued better. Peekay felt a sudden panic. E. W. wasn't obliged to take him. 'Christ! If he rejects me, what the hell will I do?'

E. W. was silent for a long time. Finally he said slowly, 'We are all believers in magic. Very few things are wrought by logic alone. Man has always fought for improbable causes, often against impossible odds, enduring incredible hardship in the name of some truth or other. In my own way, I too succumbed to the power of a just idea, when a moment's reflection and an ounce of common sense would have shown the futility of the struggle into which I threw my puny weight.' E. W. looked a trifle embarrassed. 'I spent six months as a true believer, among other things winding bandages in Spain.'

A sudden vision of E. W's gaunt frame in an ill-fitting republican uniform in the Spanish Civil War brought a smile to Peekay's lips.

E. W. grinned. 'Well you may laugh, I readily confess to having been a ridiculous soldier, too much Quixote and not enough Hemingway. Like the peripatetic Don Quixote on his horse, I was moved from one ordnance job to another in an attempt to find something I couldn't effectively mess up. Bandages were my last stop and then our side lost. I came home just in time to be recruited into Hitler's war. On the strength of my bandage-winding experience, which obviously, in the eyes of the War Office, counted for a great deal more than a degree in jurisprudence, I spent the entire Second World War in Plymouth lecturing to young ladies in the WRNS on contraception and sexually transmitted diseases gained as an indirect result of accepting gifts of silk stockings and candy from randy American marines.'

Peekay laughed as E. W. hoped he might. He'd watched the young South African carefully. Peekay's student details, submitted to Magdalen College by his headmaster, St John Burnham, indicated that he was a champion boxer and a good all-round sportsman as well as an outstanding student, who had been short-listed as a Rhodes scholar pending completion of his first degree. As a rule Rhodes scholars didn't impress E. W. who found them, more often than not, too busy with cricket or rugby to manage much more than a lower second.

E. W. was a man who exalted in the human mind and thought of the body as a rather clumsy method of carrying it about. Boxing, a sport which was known to damage the brain, he found both repulsive and primitive and he'd had serious reservations about accepting Peekay.

'And you? You believe in the er ... witch doctor's prophecy, Peekay?'

'Well, yes, I suppose I do. I'm African myself. The fact that a man of Inkosi-Inkosikazi's power and intelligence, who lived his life in peace as the spirits of the dead decreed he should, would turn around and instruct the people to rise against the white man, could mean only one thing. These same spirits, the great kings, elders and the shadows of his ancestors, Shaka, Dingane and Cetewayo, had joined to ensure the outcome. By allowing the wizard of peace to carry the message of war, the ancestral shadows had cast the bones and read the smoke. The people have no choice but to respond.'

E. W. brought his hands together, the tips of his fingers touching his lips. He appeared to be deep in thought. 'I'm sure we're on the same side, Peekay. But in terms of your time at Oxford perhaps we ought to use a different term of reference. The situation in South Africa is undeniably racist, but this is by no means unique. Almost every culture practises covert racism to a greater or lesser degree. The real enemy is the denial of personal integrity for the white South African, and that of social dignity and opportunity for the black South African.

'That one tribe is thought to be superior to another is once again, common enough. In this country for centuries we've used the class system to the same effect. What makes the situation in South Africa extraordinary from the point of view of jurisprudence, is the existence of actual legislation which decrees that a person of one colour is *born* superior to a person of another colour.

'This single element of the law is the linchpin which holds everything else together. While legislation of this kind exists, corruption of the spirit is inevitable. In the next three years together you and I will *not* discuss this problem in terms of black or white, but in terms of morality, integrity and how the law, used wisely, can indeed be the universally accepted instrument of truth and become accountable for justice in a civilised society.'

This was it, a true analysis of South Africa's plight. One that cut through the bombast and the dogma and the special circumstances. Peekay was overwhelmed with admiration. This was finally what he had come for, to learn to think clearly without sentiment.

'I wish I could have said that,' Peekay said softly.

E. W. brushed away the compliment. 'And you have come to Oxford. Why?'

Peekay answered as simply as he could, 'To do what you suggest. I have come to learn how to make the law honest.'

Looking directly at his young student, E. W. said, 'I'm not sure Oxford can give you what you want, Peekay. It is not the law which keeps a people safe, but the hearts and minds of some few good men and women who are its custodians. Conventional justice, when it is not in the hearts and minds of men, has only the power to corrupt. The letter of law may be upheld but its spirit is withheld. Isn't this what you are talking about?'

Peekay laughed. 'I'm not sure. You see South Africa doesn't have *honest* racial laws which can be corrupted by dishonest and venal men. We have no custodians to see that justice is done, because justice, in racial terms, is *never* done, almost by definition cannot be done! The good guys have no precedent, no fundamentally just law upon which to anchor their arguments.' Peekay frowned, looking for another way of putting his argument. 'Because racial injustice is perfectly legal, it is like shadow boxing. When you throw a punch there is nothing to hit.'

'And making the law honest? Do you have a vision, a picture in your mind, of what this means?'

'Well, yes, it seems to me that justice should be easy to understand, a natural outcome. The prisoner, sitting alone in his cell, confronted with what he has done, should be able to admit his guilt to himself and accept the verdict because he understands he has broken his contract with a society whose laws he agreed to honour.' Peekay paused, searching for the right words. 'The law should be based on the concept of natural justice. Too often the black prisoner doesn't consider himself guilty, doesn't even understand why he is being sentenced. Too often the law itself is a denial of natural justice!'

E.W's eyebrows shot up. 'Good! That's good, we can use that.' When he smiled his teeth were slightly uneven and stained yellow from years of smoking a pipe. The young man seated opposite him was vulnerable and gauche, certainly an idealist, but his convictions were not entirely based on the dreary tenets of social injustice every nineteen-year-old undergraduate who pretended to think carried around like a big stick. Nor did he think he knew the answer to everything.

'Will you take me then, E.W?' Peekay asked, concerned.

'I thought I'd indicated that earlier, my boy?'

'Well, it's just that . . . well, I wanted to make sure we get it right from the beginning.'

'What on earth do you mean, Peekay?'

'Well, you see, we white South Africans tend to have an enormous chip on our shoulders, mostly because we feel guilty, are guilty. I simply cannot afford to waste my time at Oxford trying to justify my guilt. I'd like you to accept that I'm guilty, but that I intend to do something about it.'

'My dear fellow, that will hardly do. You may be guilty wherever else you desire, the exception being in this study. Discussion is the basis of the college system; two or more inquiring minds in a small room is what Oxford is all about. The personal tutorship you receive here is essentially why you would choose to come to

Oxford. You are a boxer I believe? Here you will learn to attack and defend, the punch and counter-punch of discussion. You will win by using your intellect, it will be your only means of defeating an opponent. In this room there is no guilt. I simply won't have it!'

E. W. looked steadily at Peekay. 'We shall spend the remainder of your first term discussing natural justice.' He fumbled in the pockets of his tweed coat and produced a pipe from one pocket and a tobacco pouch and large box of Swan Vesta matches from the other. 'We may well spend the remainder of your time at Oxford discussing it. The rest of what you need to pass your examinations you can pick up in lectures and from the books I shall let you have.' He tapped the bowl of his pipe against the edge of the large copper ashtray, which gave off a loud ringing sound, and prepared to light it.

Peekay's grandfather smoked a pipe and the elaborate ritual about to take place was familiar. Finally the small study was filled with blue, molasses-flavoured smoke. Peekay knew that this was temporary, that pipes go out as a matter of ritual soon after they're lit, when they're put down, allowed to cool slightly and then taken up again. The second smoking is the meaningful one.

He sat patiently and watched his tutor, reflecting on what he had learned. Now that he was actually here, Peekay understood that he would be judged by the quality of his mind. No more sporting hero, nice guy, natural leader, the stuff of which schoolboy legends are made; here only the intellect counted.

It would be like being back with Doc. When things got tough, Doc used to say, 'Listen always on the inside, Peekay. Inside of your head, in a quiet place, is sitting waiting the answer.' He was going to enjoy E. W. White's Oxford.

E. W. removed his pipe from his mouth and placed it in the copper ashtray. Then he took one last gulp of tea and, rising, said, 'I say, what do you think of this tea?'

Peekay was somewhat taken aback. He'd just undergone an afternoon which consisted almost entirely of verbal spankings and in almost the same breath E. W. White was asking him whether he approved of his thoroughly shitty tea.

He rose, preparing to go. 'Well, it was a bit strong,' Peekay ventured.

'A chap named Goonesena whom I tutored in '47 sends it to me from Ceylon. It comes in a ten-pound plywood box beautifully sealed in tin foil, regular as clockwork every two months.' E. W. looked up at Peekay despairingly. 'I'm rather forced, as you can see, to make it in very large quantities or I should never use it up. Alas, (he pronounced it 'A-laas') what you see is a Darjeeling man, condemned forever to drink Ceylon.' He seemed genuinely upset.

Peekay had never thought very much about tea. He generally took it with milk and two sugars about midbrown. The idea that tea should come in more than one flavour had never occurred to him.

'Ceylon is seeking independence from Great Britain. Why don't you do the same thing to them?' Peekay said, hoping he didn't sound too flippant.

E. W. White threw back his head and laughed loudly. 'I say! Well done, Peekay. Hoist with my own petard, what!' He found his pipe on the trolley and paused to re-light it. 'I think you and I are going to get along splendidly. Next week I shall require two thousand words. Please write clearly. I'd like your thoughts on the concept of natural justice and how it affects the law.'

'English law, sir?'

E. W. looked slightly taken aback. 'Why, all law, of course! I am not aware that the English are any different from any other people when they are at the receiving end of things. Natural justice is the beginning of all true justice; we shall see where it leads. I think you might profitably spend a little time in the Bodleian consulting the work of John Fawcett, though, of course, I am more anxious to read your *own* thoughts on the subject.'

E. W., skilfully moving both of them towards the door, continued his instructions. 'So, please, dear boy, not too many notations in your essay on the thoughts of men long dead. Profundity is seldom achieved by misquoting the opinions of those who cannot return to defend themselves. It is an unfortunate habit cultivated by the more modest minds at Oxford who can only impress their peers by building a bulwark of old ideas. It disguises, of course, the absence of any new ones of their own. By all means use the quotes of the dead to clear the known ground, then dare to walk the wildest unknown path. In this way we can look forward to some intellectual progress.'

At the door they shook hands formally. 'Goodbye, Peekay.' He rubbed his hands together, as though he had suddenly made up his mind about something. 'By Jove! Next time you come I shall serve you Darjeeling. I believe you have given me the courage to liberate myself!'

Nine

Living in a brothel soon became a normal way of life for Tandia. Bluey Jay represented a grand step up for her; the dark little shed with its earth floor and constant smell of paraffin from the lamp which had been her only source of light at night was replaced by her own brightly-lit room with its divan bed and chenille bedspread, dresser, wardrobe and small painted table and chair where she did her homework. From her window she looked out into the branches of a huge old wild fig tree which had stood for a hundred years before Bluey Jay was built. One branch grew so close she could have climbed out onto it, and looking through its leaves seen the glint of the river bordering Mama Tequila's property and the five grass huts of the small African village resting beside it.

Mama Tequila, despite her seemingly benign exterior, ran a strictly ordered establishment where the rules were disobeyed at one's own risk. As she well knew, girls who make their living on their backs have a tendency towards indulgence in food, wine, pills and Mary Jane, which was her name for *boom* or marijuana. Mama Tequila needed her girls alive and kicking when they turned a trick and the 'trick zombies' who worked the dockside BB-TMs were not a part of Bluey Jay. To work for Mama Tequila a girl had to be able to please a man, not simply with her body, but with her entire presence.

At eleven o'clock every Sunday morning all the girls would meet in the kitchen for brunch. It was Josie the cook's day off, and Mama Tequila took pride in serving the repast herself.

She would be up quite early on a Sunday morning baking bread and scones so that Bluey Jay on the sabbath always smelled of furniture polish, fresh-baked bread and brewed coffee. Her speciality was the omelette, and she would prepare her mixture in advance, thickening it with fresh cream and dusting it with finely chopped parsley. Then she'd carefully remove the rind and cut out the white strips of fat from the crispy bacon which she served with her eggs.

Mama Tequila might have been fat herself, but she knew that a good brothel can afford only one fat ride. In the case of Bluey Jay this was Hester, who, anyway, was more plump than fat and whose diet Mama Tequila watched like a hawk.

Mama Tequila called these Sunday morning meetings, 'chew the fat chats', an expression which might have spilled over from her Mae West pose into her everyday language. Chew the fat chats were as close to democracy as Bluey Jay came. It was at these times that the girls could discuss the house with Mama Tequila, bring out any problems they might have with a regular client, or ask her considerable advice on the ways of mice and men.

On Sunday mornings Tandia often rose early to help Mama Tequila in the kitchen. At Bluey Jay everyone worked for their living and this included Tandia. Mama Tequila kept her promise to Dr Louis and Tandia was kept on her feet at all times doing her share to keep the house running smoothly.

Juicey Fruit picked Tandia up from school at three o'clock and they were back at Bluey Jay by a quarter to four. She was then allowed an hour or so for homework. At five o'clock she took over from Josie the cook or one of the girls as room maid. She would replace the bottom sheet and clean the wash basin, placing fresh towels beside it after each client. Tandia would work from five in the evening until half past nine, when she was packed off to bed and the other girls took over as room maids again until one in the morning, when the house closed.

On Saturdays, Bluey Jay only opened at half past six in the evening and Tandia was required to work through until closing. With the boys from the boats invading Bluey Jay, the joint would be jumping from early evening, and every hand was needed. Two coloured women also came out from Durban around five and worked with Tandia to keep the linen changed and the rooms clean. After Bluey Jay had closed down for the night, the two ladies would sleep in the servants' quarters at the back of the house and Juicey Fruit Mambo would take them back to town on Sunday morning when he drove Sarah to early Mass.

The chew the fat chats had made Tandia an expert in the theory of how to make a man happy, and Mama Tequila referred to her as the 'wise young virgin'. Mama Tequila saw no point in not exposing her to the finer details of the game. Tandia was a coloured girl, though a very clever one, and the more she knew about life, the better she might be at surviving it. The life of a high-class whore for a girl with a coloured skin was a damn sight better than most and Tandia had the looks and brains to go right to the top. Mama Tequila had very little time for dumb, lazy women and she demanded the highest standards from the eight she employed at Bluey Jay. 'Whores with a future' was how she described them.

Hester liked the idea of being a whore with a future. She was a back-slidden Pentecostal and it worried her a lot. It was an evangelical chorus much favoured by Pastor Mulvery, the new preacher at the Assembly of God mission hall she attended that finally decided her destiny.

Working in a fish factory with Jesus Christ as the foreman wasn't Hester's idea of heaven and so she'd become a whore, which seemed much the more intelligent option when you had enormous boobs which even the pastor couldn't take his eyes off during prayer meetings. She'd open her eyes in the middle of all the 'Hallelujahs' and 'Praise the Lords' and see him looking straight at them, his eyes almost standing out on stalks! So when Mama Tequila described Hester as a whore with a future, she liked it a lot.

Sometimes the chew the fat chats would get quite specific. One Sunday morning, a month or so after Tandia arrived at Bluey Jay and after she had started school again, Sarah asked a question about fellatio. 'Mama T, last week old Coetzee, you know, the magistrate from Pinetown? He couldn't get it up, too much brandy, so I tried to give him a number three, but it was hopeless. It just keeps hanging there like a old piece of *biltong*!'

Even though the girls had all laughed, this was serious business. Mama Tequila guaranteed satisfaction and it meant Sarah would have to give him a free session next time he came.

Mama Tequila rose slowly and waddled over to one of the shiplapped kitchen cupboards. From her apron she took the large bunch of keys which she carried about her person at all times. Selecting a small key, she unlocked the cupboard and withdrew the chamois leather drawstring bag which contained Herman the Hottentot.

Herman the Hottentot was an eight-inch, beautifully carved, wooden penis standing at full erection. The carving, complete with testicles, was of sneezewood, a handsome finely grained rose-red wood darkening to golden brown with a beautiful satin lustre. The detail was meticulous and the piece was much, much better than a simple pornographic curio. It also looked to be fairly old and someone, not Mama Tequila, had bored a hole into its flattened back and glued into it a one-inch piece of pine dowelling to act as a hand grip.

In fact, Herman the Hottentot, so purposefully carved, would have made an awkward dildo. But for Mama Tequila's purposes it was ideal.

The girls were all seated at the breakfast table with Mama Tequila at the top in her specially reinforced bentwood chair. Now she held Herman the Hottentot up and demonstrated with the tips of her fingers how to begin the massage and then, bringing the carving to her lips, she showed how the stimulation was completed with the lips and the mouth.

She placed Herman the Hottentot back on the table in front of her. 'You can do it perfect, but sometimes you going nowhere, man, the one-eyed snake is fast asleep. You can feel and kiss and stroke and suck, but you won't make that old one-eyed snake stand up. So you got to tell it a story where it is the hero.' Mama Tequila paused. 'You see, the mind makes the best erections. If you can get the mind on your side, then nearly always, the one-eyed snake will open his eye and stand to attention. In a case like magistrate Coetzee, you have to talk dirty, but not filthy, you hear? For Coetzee, who is Dutch Reformed Church, dirty is okay, he can understand dirty, but filthy reminds him you a whore. He a magistrate, he don't like that!'

'Mama T, how do you know the difference between dirty and filthy?' Hester asked. 'I always thought they the same thing? With the Pentecostals, the bad words they all banned, even saying "hell" and "dammit", they not allowed.'

Mama Tequila shook her head. 'Ag, never mind that, Hester, language is a wonderful thing, you can play with it, get it just right, like a acrobat on the high wire in the circus, balanced just perfect. If you got the right words, I'm telling you, you can get a man like old Coetzee to stand up every time!'

The girls all stopped eating. This was always the best part of a chew the fat chat. When Mama T got going there was nobody on the game who was better. Now looking over at Tandia she said, 'Make some more coffee please, skatterbol.' Tandia rose from the table as Mama Tequila took a cork-tip out of her silver cigarette case and lit it with her Zippo. 'Here the words you going to say,' she drew on her cigarette and the lighted end glowed brightly as she inhaled deeply; then with her head thrown back she exhaled a surprising amount of the smoke up towards the ceiling where the big fan caught it and dispersed it over the room.

'When you begin, you speak very slow, you hear? Like you a clairvoyant or something. Coetzee, you a naughty boy! I seen you, I seen you looking at her, the little kaffir girl. You hiding behind this big rock, I seen you, man, hiding there where the kaffir women come to wash themselves. This little kaffir girl, she maybe thirteen, fourteen, the same age as you, but she very mature, a woman already. The water on her, it makes her black skin shine and her bottom is nice and tight and round and firm, hey? Her legs is long and her little boobies, they perfect, turned up and big enough for only one handful. She is washing herself and the soap and her hands as they go all over her body, they your hands, man! You can feel they your hands. Her hands go between her legs. Her bottom, it moves round slowly as she washes there. She is a kaffir, a dirty kaffir, who you not allowed to touch. But your snake inside your pants, this snake doesn't know this. No, man! No way this snake knows. It wants to touch, there is a place it wants to go.' Mama Tequila picked up Herman the Hottentot and allowed her fingers to do wondrous things to it, demonstrating what they should be doing while the words were weaving their way into the mind of Coetzee the magistrate. The girls watched, completely fascinated as Mama Tequila continued her verbal titillation. 'Now all the other women, they go away, only the one your snake wants, she stays, the forbidden fruit is alone in the hot sun and cool water. The water she splashes over her body rinses away the soap. Then she sits down in the river and goes under and then stands up, her beautiful black body shining with the water running off her. She begins to come out, her feet are splashing in the shallow water now. She walks towards the big rock, her hips slow, nice, to where you are hiding. She lies down, right there on the warm river sand next to the rock. She lies there with her wet, shining black body and she closes her eyes. You take off your short pants and your snake is free, strong, standing up, a white man's big strong ...' Mama Tequila laughed suddenly and almost simultaneously the girls around the table let out a surprised sigh.

'Ag, damn!' Hester cried, dismayed that she wasn't going to hear the end.

Mama Tequila chuckled, 'Then, Sarah, if old Coetzee is not the most *upstanding* citizen you ever seen, then you better call the ambulance, you hear? Because for damn sure, he's dead!'

The girls all laughed and clapped. 'That was a good one, Mama T,' Sarah said, and they all nodded agreement. Mama Tequila was the best teacher; they all felt warm and needed and very superior. They were whores with a future.

Mama Tequila turned to see what Tandia was doing with the coffee. She was nowhere to be seen and Sarah jumped up and ran towards the big AGA stove. Tandia was pressed up against her corner of the alcove biting her hand, the tears running down the cheeks, her shoulders heaving with the effort to contain her emotion. Blood ran from the corner of her mouth where she had bitten into her hand.

'Oh my God!' Sarah stretched out her arms and bent down to embrace Tandia. She took the little girl in her arms and started to rock her. 'Shhh! Don't cry, Tandy. It's only pretend, don't cry, skatterbol, no one can hurt you, you hear? You safe here.'

The girls had all risen from the table and crowded around the cooking alcove. 'Let her go!' It was Mama Tequila's voice. Confused, Sarah looked up first at Mama Tequila and then back to Tandia. 'Leave her, you hear!' She turned to the girls. 'Out! Go to your rooms! You too Sarah, go now, jong, before I lose my temper.'

Sarah released Tandia, propping her up against the split logs stacked against the rear wall of the alcove. '*Maak gou*,' Mama Tequila said in Afrikaans, a language she rarely spoke and only when she was upset. Sarah rose quickly and left the room, following the other girls out.

Mama Tequila remained standing for perhaps fifteen minutes until Tandia began to calm down. 'Go to the table, Miss Tandy!' she ordered, turning slowly and moving across the room to the big club chair.

Tandia rose and, sniffing, sat at the table. Mama Tequila held a cork-tip in her hand which she now fed slowly into her mouth and lit with the Zippo. She withdrew the cigarette and pushed the smoke out lazily. 'Why you crying, Miss Tandy?'

'You, you know why, M ... mama T,' Tandia sobbed.

When Mama Tequila spoke again her voice was sharp. 'Now you listen to me, you little shit!' She lowered her voice as Tandia looked up at her in tearful alarm. 'You listen good, you hear? You can leave today, take your basin and pack your things.' She reached for her bag on the small table and started to rummage through it until she found her purse. She opened the clip and removed five crumpled one-pound notes which she flung down onto the floor in front of her. 'Take it, it's the five pounds we took out of your pants when you came here. Before tonight you out, gone from this place, you understand!'

Tandia's world collapsed about her. She'd only heard half of Mama Tequila's titillation talk to the girls when she found herself back in the cemetery talking to the dead Patel and then it all happened again, the handcuffs and the marble cross and the big, hard white man inside her. 'Please Mama T, let me stay! Please! I will do anything. Anything you want, jus' let me stay here, I beg you Mama T!'

Mama Tequila looked at Tandia and began to talk softly. 'You not special, Miss Tandy, you dirt. You nothing. You know why? Because you a coloured person who is sorry for herself. Inside you like a white person, inside you rotten white meat, you got a white heart. You think something bad happened to you? *Wragtig*, I'm telling you, you don't know what bad is! Rape! Rape is nothing, you hear? When Sarah was six her daddy raped her, when she was eleven he threw her out the house because he was putting his *slang* into her baby sister. At thirteen she a whore already, already working on the streets. But she's not sorry for herself, all the others is the same, some of my girls are worse even than that!'

'Please forgive me, Mama T, I swear on my mother's grave, it will never happen again. Please, I won't feel sorry for myself ever again, just let me stay!'

'Miss Tandy, this a whorehouse! The business we got here is to fuck men.' She pointed at Herman the Hottentot. 'Around here that is the boss. Hester and Sarah and Jasmine and Colleen and Hettie, Doreen, Johanna an' Marie, they all got one job, to make him happy. But they my whores, you hear? What happened before is over, finish and klaar, a white person can cry about yesterday, they got that luxury; for a coloured person there is no yesterday, you got to use all your courage and your strength to stay alive for today. You waste it on yesterday, you a dead kaffir. You understan' what I'm saying, girl?'

Tandia nodded, then sniffed and wiped her nostrils with the back of her hand. There was blood on her hand where she'd bitten herself and now the blood smeared over her face. She was just like the woman, the black shebeen whore at the police station. 'Yes, I will try, Mama T.'

'Try is not enough, Miss Tandy. If you going to be a whore, you going be a whore with a future. If you going to be a lawyer they going to try to kill you. And they not going to rest until they got you on the slab, the mortuary, a dead kaffir lawyer! You got to make yourself so when they stick the knife into your heart the blade break. When they get another one, it break also! And another and another. Then maybe you can have a future too!'

Tandia's voice was hardly a whisper. 'Please Mama T, let me stay.'

'Miss Tandy, this the first and last time, you hear?'

Tandia rose from her chair and rushed over to Mama Tequila and hugged her. 'Thank you, Mama T, I will not let you down.'

Mama Tequila patted Tandia on the back and then pushed her away, but she did so gently and Tandia knew she'd been saved. 'Go now, you can tell everyone they can come out of their rooms.'

Tandia was walking towards the kitchen door to leave when Mama Tequila called her back. 'No more what you doing with Sarah. No more, you hear?'

'Yes, Mama T,' Tandia whispered.

The hot coastal summer passed for Tandia as she entered her final year at high school. Except for Sundays, when she and Juicey Fruit Mambo would head for the high mountains, her time was taken up with work at Bluey Jay or school work.

Tandia had been brought down to solid ground with a terrible thump after the Herman the Hottentot incident. She was smart enough to realise that she would be required to adapt absolutely to the environment of Bluey Jay, that Mama Tequila would tolerate nothing less. Her quiet, shy ways would have to go. At sixteen Tandia had spent the larger part of her waking hours by herself, if not always physically, certainly in her head. The habit of going for long periods without talking was inappropriate at Bluey Jay, which was a rowdy, aggressive place, loud with vulgar laughter and sudden melodramatic tears.

To Tandia's astonishment the girls all seemed to cry for the wrong reasons. Never for the past which had been steeped with misery, but over such dumb things as a quarrel about whose turn it was to do something in the kitchen or simply because two of them were wearing the same colour gown or stayed too long in the bathroom, silly stuff which Tandia couldn't imagine even getting upset about.

Mama Tequila worked her hard but Tandia didn't mind; she'd always worked hard and now she learned to do with less sleep. She'd never been a big sleeper; her early childhood terror as she lay alone in the shed at the house in Booth Road had conditioned her. She began to find ways to be indispensable at Bluey Jay, not simply as a room maid but in a number of other chores as well. At first she had to practise laughing when one of the girls said something funny, but after a while she found that buried all these years inside her was lots of bubbling laughter. Driven at first, by the circumstances surrounding her, to seem gregarious and happy rather than naturally quiet and timid, Tandia now found that she was posing less and that laughter and involvement was coming naturally to her. At sixteen her body had suddenly shaped into its female lines. Curves which had been threatening to arrive seemed to wait almost precisely for her sixteenth birthday. Then they shaped her torso and rounded her hips into a tight lithe woman's shape. Her legs, always unusually long, now seemed to fit her body naturally. Each day she seemed to grow more beautiful. The girls at Bluey Jay had all been picked by Mama Tequila because of their looks. But they all understood that Tandia wasn't of the same clay. With her green eyes and perfect skin, she was destined to be a beautiful woman. They cherished this thought among themselves; Tandia was going to be too beautiful to ignore, even in South Africa.

For her part, Tandia carried her beauty with a naturalness and lack of affectation that endeared her to them all. She simply saw it as a contribution to the atmosphere at Bluey Jay, an abstracted thing which she could use to full effect in her new environment.

From Juicey Fruit Mambo she learned to run the bar and from Mama Tequila she learned how to hustle customers. A shilling glass of Scotch was five shillings at Bluey Jay and Tandia could convert it into a double and look abject at her mistake, making such a beautiful mess of trying to pour the extra Scotch back into the bottle that a customer would beg her to stop and be happy to pay ten shillings for his drink. She could water drinks perfectly for drunks and, if they were sufficiently drunk, get them onto cold tea without them knowing the difference. While the kaffir with the gold teeth had to be watched like a hawk, no customer ever thought of Tandia cheating them. At first Tandia was simply the late afternoon barmaid relief for Juicey Fruit Mambo, but after just a few weeks Mama Tequila announced at a chew the fat chat that Tandia had achieved solo status in the saloon bar.

It happened one Sunday morning when Tandia, like all the other girls, had appeared in her chenille dressing-gown in the kitchen. It was unusual for Tandia to be dressed this way, but Mama Tequila hadn't remarked on it. Tandia was usually up hours before the rest of them, dressed and doing her homework and already in the kitchen to help when she appeared to cook breakfast. Mama Tequila made a mental note to take her temperature after the session. Tandia up this late and still not dressed was obviously not well and she knew, since the day of the Herman the Hottentot affair, Tandia would rather die than complain of not being well.

Her announcement that Tandia was to be allowed the third billet in the bar was a singular honour. The girls showed their delight by getting up from their chairs and crowding around her.

Tandia flushed with pleasure. She loved the important feeling working behind the bar counter gave her, and to be put on an even footing with Juicey Fruit Mambo and Mama Tequila as custodian of the saloon bar was an unexpected honour. She'd been up and about since dawn, and now she stood up. Closing her eyes briefly and taking a deep breath to contain her terror she allowed the dressing-gown to slip from her shoulders. She stood before them in her pink gymslip and stockings, standing on her toes to simulate the effect high heels would give her. She had taken eight inches off the skirt of her gymslip and the tops of her stockings could just be seen held with the pink ribbons of her suspenders. Her blouse was unbuttoned to show the curve of her breasts

214

and she held herself in a provocative pose, her body slightly turned with her hands on her hips and her left shoulder thrust forward. Six months previously she might have looked like a young girl playing at being a femme fatale, but now she was provocatively sexy. Mama Tequila who seldom showed surprise at anything drew back and then burst into applause. Unthinking, she slipped into her American vernacular, 'Baby, you just the sexiest thing I ever did see!' she said, with obvious admiration. The girls all clapped and laughed and Marie ran from the room and appeared a few minutes later with a new pair of white high heeled shoes which she made Tandia put on. It was the biggest move Tandia had ever made on her own and it felt good.

Mama Tequila made Tandia practise walking in the pumps. She was stiff for days afterwards but Tandia knew the effect was worth it and she could hardly wait to return from school the next day and to appear in her new guise in the saloon bar.

Tandia had such a natural sweet innocence about her that the effect she had on customers was doubled. She was totally desirable and totally unattainable at the same time. The combination made her a formidable attraction behind the bar. For Mama Tequila made it known that, under no circumstances, was Tandia for sale. If anything this increased her desirability to the Bluey Jay regulars.

With Tandia at the bar, customers not only increased but stayed longer and spent more. Just in case a customer lost the urge to use the upstairs services of the house or was drinking too slowly, Mama Tequila would give Tandia a signal by placing her hand over her glass. Tandia would wait until the customer was ready to order again.

'Same again, Miss Tandy.'

Tandia would pretend not to understand the request and her eyes would grow big. She'd put her hands on her waist and lean back slightly with her left shoulder thrown forward, the way Mama Tequila had taught her. 'Oh, sir, not the same again! Last week was good, Jasmine says you were so very good and very nice to her also. But you can't have the same again!' Tandia would take a deep breath and giggle, 'So! This week we have a special treat for you! Doreen is going to take you today and she has some lovely, lovely surprises for you.'

Tandia was never explicit nor did she talk dirty. She was becoming an actress who worked with body language and with her eyes. Words could only have cheapened the merchandise she had for sale at Bluey Jay. Tandia understood when Mama Tequila said that a whorehouse was a theatre of the mind, and she intended to be the perfect understudy to the leading lady.

The client would laugh. 'That's not what I meant, Miss Tandy. Give me another drink.'

'Certainly, sir, what will it be? Another lager? It will be waiting for you, a big cold glass with the foam running down the side, just how you like it. Because you going to need a long, cold beer when Miss Doreen is finished with you, believe me!'

'That child, ain't she the limit!' Mama Tequila would shake her head and chuckle. 'Mister you take no notice dat little hustler! Miss Tandy you give the gentleman guest another beer before I take the strap to you, you heah?' The customers would wince at the sudden vision of someone taking the strap to Tandia. Mama Tequila would turn to the customer. 'I ain't saying she's not right, that Miss Doreen, she special, she the best, but she expensive.' Mama Tequila would lean over and whisper into his ear, 'For five pound she do anything, you hear? Anything you want!'

At that moment Doreen would walk into the bar, signalled by a buzzer under the bar counter. Mama Tequila would say, 'Miss Doreen I want you to be nice to our gentleman guest.' She would roll her eyes. 'Real nice. He deserve the best you got, Miss Doreen, the best he ever had, you hear?'

Ten

At the conclusion of her final year at Chelsea Arts School Harriet had applied for a grant to the National Arts Foundation, submitting two small maquettes of work she hoped to complete. The first was to be a three-quarter size study of two horses, while the other was a life-size sculpture of a boxer. Her application was successful and the grant enabled her to take a small cottage attached to an old stable with a lofted ceiling, which she hoped to convert into a studio.

The cottage, which went by the unprepossessing name of Cow Cottage, lay about five miles out of Oxford in a setting beside a small brook and amongst tall old oak trees which now stood bare and bleak against the December landscape. The doorway to the cottage was partly overgrown by a climbing white rose Peekay identified as Francis Eileste, while the garden was overgrown with sweetbriar roses and camellia fighting for a space in the pale sun with the weeds and bramble. Harriet, trudging happily around it in a pair of wellington boots, claimed to discover all manner of lovely things cowering under the onslaught of weed, winter and neglect.

Harriet, like Peekay, had grown up in the country. She had spent her childhood in Norfolk and was familiar with gardens. 'I shall have a lovely cottage garden. It's all here waiting for spring and a little love,' she exclaimed happily.

Hymie, on the other hand, was not reassured so easily. He would pass through the three acres of rolling lawns, talking about watering devices for carefully planted beds like the ones in the Levy family garden in Pretoria. He looked at it all as dispassionately as he might a small public park. 'Sure,' he said, looking disapprovingly at the stone cottage buried in weed and neglect, 'I hope you don't expect any of this love you're talking about to come from me? God made my arm to drive a gold Parker 51. Why else would He have given me thirteen of them for my barmitzvah?'

Peekay, on the other hand, was delighted. He longed to get his hands onto a bit of dark, wet earth again and, like Harriet, he could sense that the two-hundred-year-old cottage garden, given a little encouragement, would stage a magnificent comeback in the spring. He also loved the cottage, with its ancient shingle roof, green with moss and lichen, and its Headington stone walls – none too straight, so that the front door leaned decidedly to the left, as did all the windows. He pointed to the south wall of the cottage. 'It looks as though the big bad wolf stood on that side of the house and huffed and puffed and damn nearly blew it down!'

'Christ! What a mess!' Hymie snorted. 'Who are we supposed to be? The three little pigs?'

The interior of the cottage consisted of one large room with a hearth forming the centre of the northern wall which was blackened by a century or two of smoke from the open fire. The early afternoon light strained through the dirty windows, making the interior almost dark. The room hadn't been used for several years and, though dusty, was surprisingly dry and very cold. The floor was of heavy slabs of blue slate, although it was hard to tell in the semi-dark; they could equally have been brown or grey. There was no electricity and no evidence of plumbing. Water was obviously carted in from the brook.

'Jesus! Talk about cosy!' Hymie said in disgust, flicking his cigarette lighter to examine the hearth. 'Shit, Harriet, there's no bloody stove!'

The toilet, a small wooden construction, stood at the bottom of the kitchen garden beside the stream. It too leaned, though from the weight of a very old clematis, its winter-bare vine hugging the entire edifice and pushing it to the right, as if in stubborn defiance of the direction the cottage had decided to take.

The stable, which was more like a barn, was actually larger than the cottage, and the hayloft had been removed, leaving a vaulted ceiling. 'When I can get two large windows set into either side of the roof it will make a perfect studio,' Harriet explained. 'It's the only real expense actually, except for a coat of limewash inside the cottage and here and there a few tiny repairs. Otherwise the place is perfect, don't you think?'

Hymie lit a sobranie before answering. 'My grandmother on my mother's side, with only a large black frying pan on her back, fled from a shtetl in Russia where every house was a Taj Mahal compared to this dump!' He looked appealingly at Harriet. 'Do me a favour, come and live in Oxford? I tell you what. I'll buy you a bicycle so you can pedal out to this dump every day to work.'

'Oh, Hymie, can't you see how romantic it is?' Harriet exclaimed.

'Romantic? No stove! No plumbing! No bathroom! No bloody toilet! The only mod con you're going to enjoy around here is a hot and cold running nose!'

Harriet smiled. 'With a birch-log fire in the hearth, winter will soon pass and when spring comes you'll think it's a miracle, just you wait and see, Hymie Solomon Levy.'

'A miracle is right! A miracle if you're not dead in this cow of a cottage!'

Peekay was secretly glad. Harriet had asked him to pose for the boxer sculpture and he liked the idea of coming out into the country to do so. He'd known Harriet for fourteen months and had been careful to keep the relationship strictly kosher, always making sure that the three of them were together. She belonged to Hymie; but in his mind at night in bed, she belonged to him. At first he'd tried to dismiss her from his thoughts, telling himself how futile it was to allow his imagination to own her. But it didn't work. The famous Peekay mind control collapsed in a whimpering heap at the thought of Harriet in bed with him.

Peekay was not even sure, given the opportunity, that he'd have the courage anyway. His experience of women was one fantastic night with Carmen. He was hopelessly short of experience in the preliminaries. He'd been totally indulged by Carmen but in the process had received very little useful information in the preliminary kissing and feelup department. His mind was filled with schoolboy stuff, breasts which pumped up like rocks when you felt them and nipples that stood up so you could practically roll one around in your mouth like a large plump raisin. But the practicalities of, for instance, unhooking a brassière, were beyond him. However hard he tried to imagine it, he knew he couldn't do it.

The trouble was that Harriet was so nice. Peekay felt guilty about making love to her in his imagination. She wasn't just a stunning-looking girl you wanted to do it to. She was someone you wanted to like anyway. She was intelligent, independent and fun. She could be formidable in argument and she would kiss them both spontaneously, hug and touch and be loving, as though it was a perfectly natural thing to do. Which it was, of course; but which it also wasn't, of course.

After over a year together Peekay wasn't so sure Harriet was Hymie's girl. Harriet seemed to treat him no differently to the way she treated Peekay, and Hymie didn't seem to mind this in the least. They were seldom together alone and Hymie made no deliberate attempts to make this happen. If Hymie was sleeping with Harriet, they were going to great pains to conceal it from him.

The trouble was that he and Hymie never talked about it. It was the only thing they hadn't shared. This was mainly Peekay's fault. Because he felt the way he did about Harriet he was afraid Hymie would find out if they talked about her. Peekay wasn't sure he could hide his true feelings from his friend. So he'd gone along with the platonic bit, the two brothers and a sister thing they'd developed between them. It was infinitely better than having no Harriet in his life and Hymie seemed more than happy, even gratified by the arrangement.

Sex was the weakest link in the relationship between the two friends. Hymie had always seemed rather ambivalent about the subject. At school, when puberty had struck like lightning to keep their right hands cupped and guilty and where loud-mouthed fantasy had kept them all from going mad, Hymie had always remained cool. The contagious delirium caused by the

222

overheating of the group's collective sexual imagination seemed to pass him by. It wasn't as though he drew apart, he simply didn't contribute. This was unusual for Hymie. In most other things his opinion played a leading role. Peekay had once bounced his fist against someone's head for suggesting Hymie was a queer. But he had to admit that when the boys woke in the morning and carried their towels to the showers draped over their rigid tent poles, Hymie always sauntered in, slack as a wind sock on a still morning, his towel slung casually over his shoulder.

If Hymie didn't take much of a physical role in the restoration of Cow Cottage, as usual he made things happen. He sent Bobby and Eddy, Peekay's two former sparring partners from the Morris Works, scrounging around builders' yards until they'd found two huge Gothic arched windows. The two boxers arrived at Cow Cottage in a Morris van 'borrowed' from the works on a Saturday morning and before mid afternoon, when the light was beginning to fade, they'd shaped two large holes in the stable roof and edged them in plywood covered with copper sheeting. The following day they'd hoisted the windows up onto the roof and fixed them neatly into place. Hymie had paid for the windows; they were Harriet's Christmas present from him. But when he'd gone to pay the lads they wouldn't hear of it.

Both boxers had become friends, particularly of Peekay. They'd become infinitely better boxers after working out with the young South African who was generous with his knowledge and was often in their corner on a Saturday night calling the tactics. They'd also met Harriet on several occasions and it was clear they approved of her thoroughly, urging Peekay in a good natured way to wrest her away from Hymie, whom they referred to as, 'the Management'.

Bobby would shake his head. 'She's a fighter's lass, lad. 'Taint no good wastin' a good sort like 'er on the Management!'

They were both originally farm lads and seemed to be able to turn their hands to most things. They'd returned the following Saturday, having again 'borrowed' a works van, and spent most of the day loading up the furniture Harriet had found in a number of second-hand locations around Oxford. They'd even been reluctant to stop for lunch, a couple of bottles of Morrell's brown ale and hunks of bread and cheese with thick wedges of freshly dug onion.

The onion was a self-sown distant relative of an antecedent onion patch and had revealed itself when Peekay turned the soil in the kitchen garden, binding it with lime and manure in preparation for the new planting they planned for spring. Peekay had also repaired the garden beds and fixed the drainage, leaving a generous clump of mint and aromatic bronze fennel and another of cotton lavender and Jerusalem sage which seemed to have thrived on the harsh times. He also left several smaller clumps of lily-of-the-valley and bright yellow winter aconite to add a spot of cheer. Against the wall of the stable forming the southern side of the kitchen garden and only a hop, step and jump from the back door of the cottage, grew damson and quince, while along the northern edge ran a badly neglected hedge of rosemary which he trimmed and weeded so that the gaps would grow back in the summer. The brook, a sprightly little stream, formed the bottom border to the garden.

By nightfall on the fourth Sunday, three weeks and a

day after Harriet had told a slightly bemused farmer she'd pay him the fifty pounds a year rent in advance, she'd moved into Cow Cottage. The interior of the cottage smelt of fresh calcium and paraffin from the four hurricane lamps suspended on chains from the blackened beam which ran down the centre of the room. Two large second-hand kilims lay on the scrubbed slate floor, which had turned out to be a rich brown colour. At the end of the room, furthermost from the hearth, stood a large imitation Queen-Anne bed of oak veneer, purchased for three pounds from a dealer in Aylesbury, while in the centre rested an enormous chesterfield with broad curved arms of flat wood which looked straight out of a Noel Coward play. Two matching armchairs made up the rest of the centre of the room. The chesterfield and armchairs were covered in a red moquette edged with brass studs in the style of the thirties. The arms of the suite were badly scratched with several dark cigarette burns in the wood, but Eddy promised he'd cut the varnish back, clean it all up and re-lacquer them over the Christmas break. Further along the room near the hearth stood a fairly large scrubbed-pine kitchen table with six bentwood chairs and a kitchen dresser. Finally, sitting squat and happy in the corner to the right of the hearth was 'Bobby's Bounty', a black pot-belly stove Bobby had discovered in a gatekeeper's lodge at an entrance to the Nuffield works.

Eddy had fitted the stove with a new chimney and fixed the flue, and Bobby had set to work on it with stove black, finally buffing it up until it glowed a deep, contented black. On the door of the small stove, in raised cast-iron lettering, read the words 'Rocky Mountain Cooker' and in smaller letters below, 'Made in

British Columbia: home of the Canadian Mounties'.

With the little stove had come four bags of washed coal, sufficient to last the winter, which Bobby and Eddy explained had been mysteriously placed in the back of the Morris van when they'd left it parked beside a coal truck outside a pub close to the single men's hostel where they lived.

While the handsome little cooker boasted only one plate it worked a treat and when its fat, round belly was fired up it kept the room nice and warm, even without a fire in the hearth.

Harriet had yet to add such things as bookshelves and posters and the general clutter of things that come to stay in a home, but when the hurricane lamps were lit at night, the room had a bright yellow warmth. Even in daylight, with the windows now clean, the light in the room was soft. Harriet's only initial concession to her femininity was a brilliant patchwork eiderdown on the double bed and lace curtains which framed the small cottage windows. Also, there were two huge damask pillows plumped against the bedhead in a most inviting manner.

It was eight days before Christmas when Hymie got a telegram from his father. It stated that his grandmother was dying and asked him to return home. Hymie wasn't overly fond of his Russian grandmother, which was yet another of the things he felt secretly guilty about. In a Russian Jewish family it's practically compulsory to adore your *buba* and when he'd been little his mother had scolded him for his indifference. 'Go kiss your poor buba, Hymie! God forbid, when you come back from the bioscope, who knows? Maybe she has been taken already away.'

When he'd been younger and before he'd realised that

the old harridan was indestructible, he'd race home from the cinema, his heart pounding, convinced he'd see a black hearse parked in the driveway with men in long black coats and top hats carrying his dead grandmother, dressed in her full-length silver fox coat, depositing her into a coffin in the glass-sided hearse. Then, just as the hearse was about to pull away, she'd sit up suddenly and look directly at him, wagging a bony dead finger. 'Shame, boy! You didn't kiss your poor old *babushka* goodbye! Such a small thing! And me who carried already a big black frying pan on my back all the way across Roosha so you could have always nice fried fish!'

'Shit! My grandma's dying again!' Hymie announced in disgust as he read the telegram that their scout Bennett had just delivered to his rooms.

'Oh, I'm sorry to hear that, sir,' Bennett said. 'Shall I pack your bags for the tropics then?' In his mind he could see a big, fat ten-bob tip coming his way. News of a death at home always brought out the best in the undergraduates.

'Yes, thanks, Bennett, only one small suitcase.' Hymie watched as Bennett shuffled into the bedroom before he moved over to the cupboard above the fireplace and took out a bottle of sherry and two small glasses. Moving over to the window, he poured the sherry and, handing one to Peekay, he sat himself in the remaining club chair, holding the stem of the small glass in both hands. 'What a bugger! I was really looking forward to Christmas at Cow Cottage.' The disappointment was clear in his voice as he said, 'By the way, I've ordered a hamper and a Norfolk ham from Fortnum & Mason ... and a goose!'

Peekay looked up, astounded. 'A goose!'

Hymie laughed. 'Ever since I was a kid and read *A Christmas Carol*, where Scrooge finally comes good with a fat goose for Tiny Tim's family, I've wondered what goose at Christmas tasted like. I thought we'd cook it on that terrific rotating spit Eddy made for Harriet's hearth.' Hymie was talking faster than usual to conceal his dismay.

Peekay looked at his friend. 'Christ I'm sorry, Hymie. It won't be the same without you, but maybe your grandma is, you know, on her deathbed?' Harriet had invited Bobby, Eddy, E.W. and her mother, who was divorced from her father, a marine engineer who'd gone to live in America.

'Fat bloody hope! The old cow gets ill unto death every bloody Christmas.' Hymie paused to explain. 'I think I've told you before, my old man throws this big party in our garden for all his workers. He always dresses up as Father Christmas, the only Santa in the world who says, "Oi Vey!" The moment the old witch sees his Father Christmas suit going to the dry cleaners, in late November, she starts to complain about pains in her chest. "Oh, oh, I should die already in a house where is going on a Christian feast!"

'Of course, my dad doesn't believe her. But it's bloody hopeless. My grandma goes on clutching her heart and moaning and refusing to eat. When this happens my old man has to contend with my mother. I can hear her now, "So, what you waiting for? Mama should die and where is my son? Her only grandson? She should die and then it's too late to call the air force on the phone to bring him home? Shame on you, Solomon!"'

Hymie rose from the chair and moved over to the window to re-fill his glass, waving the bottle at Peekay, who declined. Then he returned to his chair. 'It's really a cryptic message you see.' Hymie dug into the pocket of his tweed jacket and produced the scrunched-up telegram. 'Here listen! I'll read it to you the way my old man wrote it. You have to understand, for two weeks now the old harlot's been dying on him and my mum's been nagging him to the point where he can't get it up when he visits his mistress in Johannesburg.' Hymie held the piece of paper in front of him and in a deadpan voice read, '"Babushka is dying."' Then raising his voice suddenly, '"PLEEEASE COME!" You see, it's a plea for help. That's why I can't ignore it. I can't let the poor old bastard down. His Christmas party for the staff is the single most important thing in his life.'

When Peekay had stopped laughing he asked, 'But how's you being there going to help?'

'Well, at least it will get my ma off his back. With me there grandma will be happy. She likes a tidy death, everything tidy and in its place, especially the only grandson.'

Peekay drove Hymie to Gatwick early the following morning to catch the BOAC Comet to Johannesburg. Hymie handed him his camel-hair overcoat as they entered the airport passenger terminal. 'Wear it if you like, you've been through an English January.'

It felt strange to Peekay seeing Hymie off, holding the soft coat over his arms and knowing that in less than twenty-four hours Hymie would be stepping out into bright sunshine, walking through a garden where tiny hummingbirds hovered like jewels above the flowers, their long beaks competing with the bees for their share of the nectar.

It had been fourteen months since Peekay had been

home, a fleeting trip of only three days to say goodbye to his friends on the way to Durban to board the boat. Knowing he'd be away at least three years he wanted to see his mum and grandpa, Mrs Boxall the librarian, Miss Bornstein his teacher, Captain Smit and Gert of the prison boxing squad, and above all, his adoring Dee and Dum, the two black twin house servants who'd grown up with him and who loved him passionately. Doc, the old German professor of music and Peekay's beloved childhood mentor, was dead, but he'd walked up to his small cottage which stood alone on a *koppie* overlooking the town. Peekay had sat in Doc's marvellous cactus garden and, speaking to the giant *Pachypodium namaquanum* which now stood almost eight feet high, had told it all that had transpired and that he was finally on his way to Oxford.

Peekay wrote home often and Mrs Boxall and Miss Bornstein replied regularly. His grandfather wrote only once, a letter which named twenty-nine varieties of roses in the garden and reported precisely on the condition of each, until Peekay could smell the soft dawn fragrance of roses in a tropical garden before the heat rises and burns away the perfumed air. The old man had ended the letter as he would a conversation. Peekay could almost see his pipe going, puff, puff and the blue cloud of smoke swirling about his head. 'There's a good lad,' the last words in his letter said.

His mother too had written once for his birthday, a letter which mostly consisted of an admonishment in the name of the Lord, chastising him for his stubborn refusal to be 'born again' and ending with the words: *I am not mocked, saith the Lord.*

Dee and Dum had also written once, in Shangaan, big, crude capitals with only three lines in pencil on the page, each of them doing a line, with the last line shared. Peekay had held the page to his lips and the tears had rolled down his cheeks.

Peekay had been so anxious and preoccupied with Hymie's unexpected departure, sharing in the acute disappointment of his friend at not spending Christmas at Cow Cottage, that he was halfway back to Oxford when it struck him that he'd be alone with Harriet for the next month.

His heart began to thump. 'Oh, God! What am I going to do?' he wailed aloud to himself. He immediately began to talk himself out of all the things which raced through his head. Peekay winced as he thought of the two large pillows propped against the headboard on the big Queen-Anne bed. 'She's not interested. If she was, I'd know. She thinks of me as a brother. That's it! We're like brother and sister. Bullshit! *You* don't feel that way about her. Yes, but that doesn't count. It's how she feels about me! I'm her brother. She feels safe with me. Don't change that. If Hymie comes back and I've split with Harriet because, well, something went wrong what's he going to think. It's like a trust, isn't it? I mean, if I tried something and was repulsed? What would he think? He'd have every right to think I'm a bastard!'

A lump had developed in his throat and he found it hard to swallow. He lifted his bum from the car seat and, with one hand, pulled at the crotch of his pants to make more room for the severe lump which had suddenly grown there. 'Oh, God! Stop it!' Peekay begged himself.

Christmas Day wasn't quite perfect without Hymie, but it came damn close. It had started to snow early on Christmas Eve and had continued until mid morning on

Christmas Day so that the Oxfordshire countryside was suddenly transformed. To Peekay it was like a miracle, a white Christmas spent in an English cottage in the English countryside. Hymie would have moaned and pointed to the wet, slushy roads, secretly sharing in his delight.

With snow covering the ground and the roof of Cow Cottage and clinging to the Francis Eileste, the white rose, now pruned neatly back to surround the doorway, the scene indeed resembled the cover on a chocolate box. It was a scene such as might quite easily have appeared on a four-pound box Hymie's father's salesmen presented as a free gift to a customer when they'd signed up for new Wilton in the lounge.

Mrs Clive, Harriet's mother, had arrived on Christmas Eve from Norfolk in a small green Austin estate wagon which boasted wood panels on the rear section to give it a country look. The small car was loaded with stuff for the cottage: towels and linen, pots and pans, even a hessian sack of yew logs for the hearth on Christmas Day and, of course, loads of good things to eat. Together with Hymie's hamper there was enough food to feed an army, and the Christmas table was positively groaning with food as Mrs Clive fussed around it, arranging crackers and nuts. At one end of the table was a space for the goose; its rich, delicious aroma now filled the cottage and kept the hearth fire spitting, splatting and hissing.

Eddy had arrived early to supervise the roasting. The plump goose had already begun to brown on the outside by the time Harriet's mother returned from Oxford where she'd gone to matins and stayed to attend the Christmas service at Christ Church Cathedral. And by the time Peekay, Bobby and E.W. arrived in the Ford

Prefect, Hymie's goose, under Eddy's expert attention, was positively Dickensian in its perfection. It was a goose Tiny Tim's father would have been proud to serve to the Queen.

Hymie's hamper included two bottles of Chateau Margaux and a Chateau Palmer, both excellent vintages. They'd begun Christmas lunch with a bottle of Möet et Chandon. By the time Harriet's mother served the Christmas pudding everyone was pleasantly sozzled. The exceptional wine might well have been wasted on the three young boxers but E.W., who was a bit of a wine buff, held his glass up to the lamplight. 'In a great year there is a delicacy about a good Margaux and a sweet haunting perfume, which makes it undoubtedly the most exquisite claret of all.'

'There's brown ale brewed in the village I come from that I feel the same about,' Bobby declared.

They all toasted Hymie's excellent taste, the speedy recovery of his grandmother and finally, full to bursting, the four younger people staggered from the table to the chesterfield and the two welcoming armchairs. Made of sterner stuff, E.W. and Mrs Clive remained at the table and shared a bottle of excellent port that E.W. had brought with him. Harriet and Peekay sat on either side of the chesterfield and Eddy sank deeply into one of the armchairs, while Bobby occupied the other. Too satisfied and happy to talk, they dozed.

Peekay, unaccustomed to so much wine, rose to empty his bladder. It had started snowing again and the kitchen garden was blanketed in fresh snow; the world around him was white and clean. To his delight he saw a white owl sitting on a bare branch of one of the oak trees. It sat so still, it seemed a part of the mute, ordered winterness of tree and landscape. If only

Hymie was with us it would be perfect, Peekay thought. He returned to the warmth of the cottage, going first to the studio to gather up an armload of yew logs. He placed several logs on the hearth which immediately began to crackle and spit and, smiling at E.W. and Mrs Clive, who seemed remarkably happy in each other's company, he trimmed a hurricane lamp which had begun to smoke, before returning to the chesterfield.

The sharpness of the cold outside had cleared his head and heightened his senses. Peekay felt himself examining Harriet closely at the other end of the old chesterfield. She lay curled up in one corner of the large couch, her head snuggled into a bright green cushion. The light from the lamps caught her beautiful hair and gave her skin a soft, warm glow. Her eyes, closed in sleep, revealed her thick eyelashes which lay like tiny crescent moons on the brow of her cheekbones. She was achingly lovely and he felt a sudden pain just below the heart, right on the spot where you hit another boxer when you want to soften him up, so that later you can bring him slowly to his knees. Peekay had a sudden vision of an unclothed Harriet on her knees in front of him. He almost winced in an effort to rid the image from his head. 'Stop it!' he screamed in silence. 'Stop it! She's Hymie's!'

Thinking about his friend calmed Peekay down some-what. Hymie would have arrived back in Pretoria on the day prior to the Levy's Carpet Emporium Christmas party. Peekay wondered how it had all gone, chuckling inwardly at the thought of Hymie's grandma moaning and clutching at her failing heart as the great Christian party took place in the garden outside. No doubt he'd hear all the lurid detail when Hymie returned at the beginning of the new term.

Hymie's dad's Christmas party grew more spectacular each year. Every year the Pretoria police warned that it created traffic congestion and would probably not be allowed to take place the following year. What they were really saying was that the people in the rich and influential suburb in which Hymie's parents lived had complained again that Africans had been arriving by the truckload with their families since early morning and the area wasn't safe. The police referred to the event among themselves as 'the Jew's kaffir party', but they knew it had been sanctioned 'at the very top' and that they were powerless to do anything about it unless trouble started.

Anywhere else in the world the party would have seemed a curious affair, but in South Africa it was normal enough. A fence was constructed more or less down the centre of the garden with a huge marquee on one side and a smaller one on the other, the former to serve the four thousand blacks and coloureds and the latter to accommodate the ninety white families who worked for Hymie's father. Two complete fair grounds with ferris wheel, rides and sideshows were set up, one on each side of the fence.

The only exception to the black and white dichotomy strictly observed in the Levy garden was a miniature railway track which ran around the periphery of the entire garden. Here the station was set up to cross over onto either side of the fence so children of both colours were forced to board the train together, mixing freely in the open carriages. Hymie's dad called it 'The Freedom Train'. Dressed in his Father Christmas outfit he would get into the quarter-sized replica steam engine and drive it around the ground himself, toot-tooting happily as he passed through the white side of the garden, hugely amused at the faces of parents as they saw their children holding hands with black kids and having a high old time.

The tables in the marquees on both sides positively groaned with good things to eat, the only difference being the drinks. Only soft drink was served on the African side, as black people were not allowed to drink hard liquor outside a township beer hall. Huge turkeys and hams and roast suckling pig with potatoes and corn and all manner of other delicacies were served. The dessert tables were piled with trifles, cakes, jellies, custards, confections and dried fruits. Chefs in aprons and tall white caps served food all day long. On the black side several oxen were roasted on an open-air spit over a pit of hot coals, while on the white there was a *braai* with *boere wors*, steak and chops in a never-ending barbecue.

Solomon Levy spared no expense on presents for the kids; there were tricycles for the tots and dolls for the smaller girls and bicycles for the older boys and girls. All the expensive makes, like Raleigh and Hercules and Philips. These were a precious possession a black child could never possibly hope to buy. At the age of fifteen, childhood ended with the last of Solomon Levy's Christmas bounty, when every boy received a size twenty-eight adult bicycle and every girl a Singer sewing machine. For the black and coloured kids and for many of the poorer white ones, when they finally climbed into the lorries to be taken back to their homes in the various townships or suburbs, it was the happiest day of the whole year. For Solomon Levy it was the day every year when he paid his respects and gave thanks to Jehovah for sending him to the promised land.

It was also a day the *Broederbond*, 'bond of brothers', noted. The white supremacist, Afrikaner secret society ruled by religious fanatics, whom some said were the true power within South Africa, resolved to do something about the Jew's kaffir party. A brilliant young police lieutenant, named Geldenhuis, a member of the *Broederbond*, who had made his reputation as head of SAT in Durban and who had recently been promoted and moved to Pretoria, had been given the task of compiling a dossier on the carpet king. The day would come when his Jew money would no longer protect him: *I am not mocked, saith the Lord.*

Eleven

Shortly after its win in the 1953 elections, the Nationalist government formed a covert police squad in all major cities whose job it was to track down the subversive elements in the urban black, coloured and Indian communities. To cover their activity, but also because the government saw a connection beween the two, they were given the public brief of enforcing the Immorality Act. Both these aims, covert and otherwise, suited the career aspirations of Geldenhuis perfectly. He applied and was accepted into the special police unit known simply as the Special Branch, though the unit was popularly referred to as the Spy and Thigh Squad, which later became abbreviated to its acronym, SAT.

The appointment of Geldenhuis to SAT was his biggest career move yet. Meanwhile Tandia, the black *slimmetjie* whom, as a type, Geldenhuis so despised, had all but completed her secondary school education and aspired to enter university to read law. Geldenhuis too had been busy during the year, learning the Zulu language – a facility which in the years to come would make him a formidable interrogator.

He knew instinctively that future personal power lay

in exploiting the Immorality Act, that the sexual apartheid of South Africa contained all the ingredients for achieving that power. Geldenhuis saw a situation where a white official – in his imagination this was always a magistrate or person capable of influencing the affairs of apartheid – was sexually compromised by ruthless black activists seeking to subvert the system. He was convinced that sex would become the major weapon the terrorists would use to undermine the infrastructure of apartheid, and he set about building a reputation for himself as the guardian of white morality. He made frequent arrests, mostly on the waterfront where the hapless 'trick zombies' worked, bagging a mixture of customers: foreign sailors, white kids drunk and derring-do on a Saturday night out, fishermen and whalers and the general human flotsam of port life together with an occasional solid citizen, a minor public servant or a small shopkeeper. It was these *respectable* arrests which soon earned Geldenhuis a big reputation. The newspapers played them up and in the process destroyed the lives of a lot of little people and their families, while at the same time pandering to the righteous indignation of the 'thou shalt not commit adultery' segment of the white, Calvinist public, who saw adultery committed with a black or coloured person as the most venal of all possible crimes: a triple whammy which, in some minds, transcended even murder.

Durban became one of the first cities openly to establish an Immorality Squad, and in less than a year it was being led by Detective Sergeant Geldenhuis. His appointment was a popular one; not only was he a diligent and persistent law officer but he had also recently gained some public notoriety by beating a black fighter named Gideon Mandoma. The twelve-round championship fight had resulted in a bitterly disputed verdict and Geldenhuis had taken the South African welterweight boxing title.

Then Jamal Singh had been arrested. The Singh case had attracted widespread publicity, doing more to damage South Africa in the eyes of the world than anything previously perpetrated in the name of apartheid. The government and the Dutch Reformed Church saw it as the price to be paid for moral rectitude in a world which was clearly controlled outside of South Africa by the Jews and the Communists. Geldenhuis had hidden in the boot of Singh's car as the Indian businessman had driven off to keep an assignation with a white prostitute and had photographed Jamal Singh and his sex partner *in flagrante delicto* in the back seat of Singh's olive-brown Chevrolet. The barrister appearing for Singh had asked how Detective Sergeant Geldenhuis had known his client's designation. Geldenhuis had replied that it had been a matter of diligent detective work. Asked to explain this further, he had admitted to concealing himself in the boot of the car on several occasions. At the conclusion of the trial, which became known as the 'Cop in the Boot' trial, Jamal Singh had been sentenced to five years in prison. Geldenhuis had received a letter from the Minister for Justice, commending him for his diligence as an officer of the law and for his outstanding example as a member of the Afrikaner race.

It was this letter which, seated at the bar counter at Bluey Jay, he now showed to Mama Tequila, with Tandia in attendance behind the bar. Tandia remained terrified of Geldenhuis who had been coming to Bluey Jay fairly regularly over the period she had been with

Mama Tequila. She had told her about Geldenhuis wanting her to spy for him and, to her surprise, Mama Tequila had laughed.

'Rule number one, Tandy, nobody has a name in a brothel. If a customer says his name is Pinocchio, next time he comes in you say, "Good evening Mr Pinocchio". If the police show you a picture of this guy you shake your head, you never seen him in your life before. That the one rule cannot be broken in a place like this.'

Geldenhuis had tried on several occasions to get information from Tandia but she had simply invoked rule number one and smiled, though she'd quaked in her boots, saying she didn't know the identity of any of the people who came. After a while he stopped asking.

Tandia was quite unable to explain to herself why she felt guilty when Geldenhuis appeared; guilty at having been raped. The totally irrational response that she was at fault, that somehow she had done something to have caused it to happen, refused to go away. Sometimes the memory of it struck her like a blow to the head, a physical thing she could feel. Then she would crawl up into a ball and try to think it away, wash it out of her system with tears that squeezed to the surface like shards of glass. Rape was not only a thing of the mind, an imagined hand which held her heart like an unforgiving sponge and squeezed until she felt the muscle and the sinew and the blood vessels popping out between her fingers as though, at any moment, it would split from the pressure and allow the life to explode out of her. It was also a great heaviness in her gut as though her stomach contained two large round river stones submerged in black bile which made her feel nauseous and too weary to rise from her bed. This second feeling was her fear, the never-ending malignant fear. It would come upon her the moment she set eyes on Geldenhuis.

While some of the policemen were still regular customers, this was less and less true as the Immorality Act took effect. A police officer in the Transvaal had been given a four-year prison sentence on a morals charge and now, with the formation of SAT Squad, the code of honour which existed between policemen had been largely eliminated. No officer in the force was safe any longer.

Mama Tequila didn't use her American persona with the police, for they were strictly about business: the business of survival. She'd been in business long before the Immorality Act and her connections with the Durban police force and judiciary went back a long way to friendlier times when a policeman could remove his khaki uniform and have a little bit of fun for a change.

Mama Tequila wasn't silly enough to trust the police, even in the good old days, and the huge old safe at Bluey Jay contained at least one ten-by-eight, black-and-white photograph of each of her customers caught in a compromising position. Some of these photographs had turned brown with age and were mostly of policemen who had used her services when she ran her dockside BB-TMs. There was only one exception: Geldenhuis. Much as Mama Tequila had tried to suggest to him that a bounty of golden flesh was available to him at no charge, Geldenhuis had never used the services at Bluey Jay.

'That's a very nice letter, you can't get more high up than that.' Mama Tequila proffered the letter to Tandia but Geldenhuis snatched it from her hands.

'Ag, it's nothing, I jus' got lucky.' He folded the letter and returned it to his wallet. He laughed suddenly. 'You know what I told Jamal Singh, I said to him, "You

242

stupid bastard, if you want a stray fuck why didn't you call me!" But then I looked in his eyes and I knew all of a sudden that what he wanted was a white woman, it had to be a white woman. Sies, man! What a disgusting bastard! What could I do? I had to arrest him.'

'You mean you was lying in that car boot just to warn him and then give him my address?' The sarcasm was apparent in Mama Tequila's voice.

Geldenhuis flushed and picked up his beer and took a sip to regain his composure. 'Of course not, man. We knew he was doing it, that was one thing we knew for sure, but catching him, that was another thing! Always he would slip the police tail. I had to do something, man. You never know how many white women a bastard like that will do it to if you don't catch him and put him in gaol.'

'Detective Sergeant, I been a whore a long time. I been a owner of a whorehouse also a long time. A black whore, a coloured whore, a white whore, they all the same. A whore is a whore! What make you think a white one is better than a black one? Their pussy, it work just the same.'

'Ja, I see what you mean, Mama Tequila,' Geldenhuis said politely, 'but you got to understand, when a Indian wants to do it to a white person it's a political thing. "Look!" he's saying, "I'm just as bladdy good as you, I can screw your woman just like you."'

Mama Tequila kept the smile on her face, though Tandia could see that the back of her neck had gone a crimson colour, a sure sign she was very angry. 'I jus' got one word to say, Detective Sergeant. Bullshit!'

For a moment Tandia thought she'd heard Mama Tequila incorrectly. Geldenhuis's blue eyes had assumed the dreamy, faraway quality she recalled from the interrogation room and she knew she'd heard correctly. It made her fear rise up and threaten to choke her. Her hand shot up involuntarily and gripped her throat in alarm. She was afraid to look at Geldenhuis, for she knew instinctively he would never forgive Mama Tequila's insult. But when he spoke his voice was perfectly controlled. 'You a coloured person, I don't expect you to understand.' Then he took up his beer. Holding the glass up in front of him as though he were about to propose a toast, he threw back his head and drained it, wiping the flecked foam from his mouth with the back of his hand. 'I need to see you privately, Mama Tequila.' He looked momentarily at Tandia and then turned back to Mama Tequila. 'Is there somewhere else we can go?'

Mama Tequila returned to the bar about half an hour later. 'Give me a double brandy, Tandy.' Tandia reached for the VSOP bottle and measured the brandy into a small balloon glass. It was unusual for Mama Tequila to drink during the afternoon; she usually had her first snort around six.

Mama Tequila took the glass and raised it to her lips, taking a slug straight down so that half the brandy in the balloon disappeared. She grimaced as she placed the glass back on the bar. 'Miss Tandy, we got troubles!' she said.

'What sort of troubles, Mama T?'

Mama Tequila looked up at Tandia, her eyes slits of polished anthracite buried in a bed of mascara and false eyelashes. 'Whores' troubles, Miss Tandy. Geldenhuis wants you!'

It was Wednesday in the longest week of Tandia's life. Wednesday afternoons, from after lunch until five,

Mama Tequila called 'Pay and Lay Day'. It was the time at Bluey Jay she kept for the cops, all of whom were required to arrive strictly by appointment and on time.

The procedure was simple. One cop in and one cop out. The first police officer at Bluey Jay would drive his car to the back of the big old house, the next to the front. When the second arrived the first was already waiting in his car and when the second had been taken indoors the first drove off. This way Mama Tequila could pay off and if necessary accommodate six dishonest policemen in one afternoon.

On this Wednesday there would be only Geldenhuis. Much to Mama Tequila's annoyance he had insisted he be the only person at Bluey Jay that day. All the girls had been given the afternoon off to do their Christmas shopping in Durban and had left before lunch in the Packard. Packed like herrings in a tin, with a scrunch of skidding back tyres on the gravel and squeals of laughter, Juicey Fruit Mambo roared off with Mama Tequila's entire sex inventory. By half past one he had returned and waited at the cattle gate for Geldenhuis to arrive.

Geldenhuis arrived at Bluey Jay a little after two and apologised to Mama Tequila who met him at the door. 'Sorry, Mama Tequila, but that cheeky bladdy kaffir of yours stopped me at the cattle gate and had a look in the boot! I don't know what he expects to find there.'

Mama Tequila laughed. 'A policeman, maybe?' Despite himself, Geldenhuis grinned. Then he abruptly cleared his throat. 'We alone here, hey?'

She nodded. 'Josie, she's the cook, I told her not to come today. The black servants all gone home to their kraal and the girls in Durban doing Christmas shopping. Only you and me and Miss Tandy, ja and of course, Juicey Fruit Mambo, who will stay at the gate until you come out again.'

Geldenhuis pushed past Mama Tequila further into the hall. 'I think I'll jus' take a look myself. Do you mind?'

Mama Tequila spread her hands. 'Help yourself, we got nothing to hide here, Sergeant.'

'*Detective* Sergeant,' Geldenhuis corrected, grinning. 'You don't get it for nothing, you know. Stay in the bar, okay? I just want to have a quick deck for myself.'

'Miss Tandy will also be in the bar when you get back,' Mama Tequila called after him. In her eight years at Bluey Jay her authority had been absolute and now, for the first time, she felt like an alien. It was like being back in a BB-TM during wartime when the military or naval police would just walk in and open doors and walk out again without even giving her the time of day. People like that had no respect.

Mama Tequila wasn't a woman who put a lot of trust in life; she knew that in the process of living it you did more picking yourself up and dusting yourself off than tapdancing. She had long since discovered it didn't do to harbour grudges. The world was full of bastards and hating them was a time-consuming and poorly paid business. But there had to be exceptions, and Geldenhuis was developing in her mind as one of them. The spoiling of Tandia by him upset her greatly, although she wasn't prepared to admit this, even to herself.

The moment Mama Tequila had mentioned Geldenhuis's desire for her, Tandia had begun to shake. She had placed the glass she'd been polishing onto the counter where it rattled momentarily as its base landed imprecisely, her shaking hand misjudging its surface. 'Please Mama Tequila, don't make me do it, not to him!

Anyone, even old Coetzee or Mr Perfect Lay! Please! I beg you!' A darkness had formed inside her head and around her eyes and she had gripped the edge of the bar counter so her knees wouldn't collapse under her.

Mama Tequila had taken the bottle of Cape brandy from the counter and, picking up the glass, she had poured a dash of brandy into it. 'Here, drink. Drink all of it.' Tandia had taken the glass and swallowed the brandy. The shock to her system had been enormous as the fiery liquor hit her throat. 'Come sit here, Miss Tandy,' Mama Tequila had said, patting the bar stool next to her. Tandia, her eyes watering from the effect of the brandy, had lifted the bar counter and come to sit beside Mama Tequila.

The large woman had lifted her brandy balloon. 'Time's come, baby. Them's the breaks. I kept my word to Dr Louis. Now you finished school you owe me, you hear?'

Tandia hadn't tried to protest as she fought to conceal her fear. Mama Tequila had taken her hand. 'Tandy, sometimes we got to do things we don't like. That goes for everyone, but most all for women and even more, most of all, for coloured women. When you live in the white man's world that the rules. It's no use crying, no use saying it's unfair, because you wasting your time. Okay, so you got to learn the rules better, you got to be more clever than they are. You got to be better than the white man at being a bastard. You hear what I say, child?'

Tandia had nodded. The burning sensation of the brandy had left a warm glow in her stomach. 'Mama T, I'd rather fuck a dog!' she said fiercely.

Mama Tequila's head had jerked back in astonishment. She had never heard Tandia use a coarse word.

She had stared at her in amazement; then her face had broken into a huge smile. 'Miss Tandy, so would I, baby! But sometimes you got to fuck the dog shit instead!'

Mama Tequila had kept Tandia busy in the bar until late the previous night. Mr Dine-o-mite and the Singh brothers, cousins of the famous Jamal Singh, and a friend were the other regulars that night. With them they had brought two Indian businessmen from the Transvaal who, apart from going upstairs for a while, spent the evening marvelling at the beautiful old house and happily paying for double Scotches. Around eleven, when the two Transvaal wallahs were too drunk to make much sense and one of them complained of having his Scotch watered, Mama Tequila looked suitably shocked and used this as an excuse to send them all packing. The Singh brothers apologised profusely, insisting on paying for four extra Scotches to make up for the bad form of their Transvaal friends and leaving a ten-bob tip for Tandia. A little after eleven o'clock that night Mama Tequila closed Bluey Jay down for the night and Tandia was free to go to her own room.

Tandia found herself running down the corridor as she drew closer to her room. The panic, kept at bay all evening, was rising up in her like a dark presence. There was no escaping, she would have to sleep with Geldenhuis, and she was about to drown in the misery of this thing inside her. She closed the door behind her and rushed to the window, sure that she was about to suffocate. At the window she took great gulps of night air until after a while the feeling in her settled down to the old heaviness, the great big round stones in her belly.

Tandia stood by the window. Outside the night was silver, like the first night she'd arrived at Bluey Jay; and once again the moon was full and she could see it through the leaves of the wild fig tree. The room in the early December heat was warm and a mosquito buzzed around her head. She let it be; mosquitoes, for some reason, never bit her. The ache inside her was so intense it seemed to swell outwards, filling the room. A wave of panic swept over her and she found herself on the window sill and in a single step outwards into space she had climbed onto the huge old branch that grew right up to it. The moment she found herself in the tree she felt a strange relief overcome her. She was alone in a secret place, and with the leaves concealing her from the rest of the world the moonlight turned the space around her into a cocoon of silver. Tandia sat there in her own space unable to cry. In the early hours of the morning she crept back into her small room and collapsed on the bed where she rolled herself up into a ball and clutched Apple Sammy to her breast, sleeping fitfully until she was wakened by a wood pigeon calling in the branches of the fig tree.

Geldenhuis came back into the bar and sat on a stool at the far end of the bar, nearest the door. 'Howzit, Tandia?' he said casually. Then he turned his attention to Mama Tequila. 'I never realised it was such a big house and also so posh. I never been in a nicer place than this. I reckon B. J. Vorster himself wouldn't have a better house. A beer please, Tandia.'

'Detective Sergeant, you know better. It's Miss Tandy, that how all the girls is addressed in this place.' Tandia froze. Mama Tequila was treating her exactly like one of the girls, like a whore.

'Ag, man, with us it's different. We know each other from old times, hey Tandia?'

Tandia placed a glass of lager on the bar in front of him, not responding to his question.

'All the same, that the way we do it here. If you want to use this house you got to understand the rules.'

Geldenhuis laughed. 'Okay, you win.' He reached for the beer in front of him and, lifting it up, downed the entire glass in one go.

'Would you like another beer, Detective Sergeant Geldenhuis?' Tandia asked softly.

'No, man, I'm in training. One beer a day, that's all I'm allowed.'

Mama Tequila clapped her hands. 'We got a special treat for you, Detective Sergeant, you and Miss Tandy. You've got the Jade Room, a very beautiful room, all green, everything in it is green to go with Miss Tandy's dress and also her eyes.'

Tandia was dressed in one of Marie's green satin dresses that went to just below the knees. The thin shoulder straps set off her shoulders and the curve of her breasts. Mama Tequila had made her wear lipstick and a little eyeshadow, and it made her look more grown up. Tandia was utterly desirable and Mama Tequila had never seen her look more beautiful. 'May God forgive me,' she thought.

'Not the green room. I don't like green!' Geldenhuis said suddenly.

'But we made it ready.' Mama Tequila smiled. 'This is my house, Detective Sergeant Geldenhuis. We like to give our guests the best. I insist you take the Jade Room.'

Geldenhuis turned on Mama Tequila. His eyes narrowed. 'I wasn't born yesterday, you know! Not the bladdy Jade Room, you hear?'

Mama Tequila looked contrite as she fanned herself. 'I'm sorry, Detective Sergeant, we like things to be nice. Perhaps the Pink? The Pink Room, it's very nice also.'

'Ja, okay, the Pink is orright.' To conceal his anger he turned to Tandia and attempted a smile. 'Come, show me where is the Pink Room, Tandia.'

Mama Tequila raised her glass to her lips. '*Miss Tandy*,' she said softly, as though speaking to herself.

Geldenhuis followed Tandia up the wide sweeping staircase which led to the client wing of the big old house. Her heart was beating furiously, but somehow the fact that Geldenhuis seemed to be making no attempt to be nice made it easier. She would just lie still and think about being up in the branches of the wild fig tree in the moonlight, floating inside the silver cocoon, hidden even from herself. Mama Tequila had given her a tube of lubricant gel. 'You use this, Tandy, and breathe hard you hear, hard as anything!' She had demonstrated, bringing her voice up to a series of sobbing gasps. 'Then they think you liking it and it's over quickly.'

They entered the Pink Room, the pride of the brothel. It was a room designed for dalliance but not one in which to spend too much time. The pinkness over-whelmed a person as an aphid might feel finding itself suddenly thrust deep into the petals of an overblown rose. To compound the incarnadine feel of the room, a strip of mirror about three feet wide and six long was fixed to the ceiling so that the entire room was repro-duced in its reflection. In the very centre of the mirror was a small circle of clear glass no more than three inches in diameter. Looking directly into the mirror with the myriad details of the room reflected into it made it impossible to see the circle, but fixed neatly into it was the lens of a reflex camera.

'This a very nice room, better than the green one, I think,' Geldenhuis said, standing in the centre of the room with his hands on his hips and looking about him in a proprietorial manner. 'Why did the old cow want us to have the green one?'

'The Jade Room, it is also nice,' Tandia said, starting to remove the satin bedspread. She folded the spread neatly and looked down at the pink satin sheets which fitted perfectly without a wrinkle, precisely turned over at the top. Geldenhuis crossed the room and entered the small shower recess. She could hear him pull back the pink plastic shower curtain. When he entered again he'd removed his tie, and unclipped his Sam Browne belt and police revolver, which he now placed on the vanity table beside the bed.

Tandia kicked off her high heels. She wasn't wearing stockings and only wore a pair of panties under Marie's dress. She moved over to where Geldenhuis stood and started to undo the brass buttons on his tunic.

The sequence of a seduction was familiar to Tandia, as it had been discussed often enough at the chew-the-fat chats. Tandia removed Geldenhuis's khaki tunic and placed it on a hanger in the wardrobe; then she returned and unbuttoned his shirt. Geldenhuis had started by putting his hands around her tiny waist but now he put both his hands on her bottom, one on each buttock, and began to massage. Tandia knew she was supposed to gyrate her hips and move in closer to him, pretending to be sexy, but she couldn't do it. She peeled his shirt over his shoulders and waited for him to remove his hands from her bottom so that she could slip the sleeves away from his arms. But he let the shirt hang from his waist and continued to pummel her bottom. 'C'mon, Tandia, be a little responsive, man. I like you, I want you to like me also.'

'Let me take your shirt off, Detective Sergeant.'

Geldenhuis removed his hands and pulled the sleeves away from his arms. He quickly moved towards the wardrobe to hang his shirt up. 'You can call me Jannie when we like this, you hear?' Tandia nodded her head. Geldenhuis stood in his pants and boots with his torso bare. He was a medium-sized man and he carried no fat. The muscles on his stomach were clearly defined above a trim waist, and his torso widened out into big, well-muscled shoulders. In boxer's terms he looked like a puncher, as though he might carry a knockout in both hands, a left-right combination which could put an opponent flat on his seat with a look of surprise on his face.

'So far so good,' Tandia thought to herself, knowing that the hard part was yet to come. She moved back to stand in front of Geldenhuis and, as his hands went out to hold her, she knelt down on the carpet in front of him and started to undo his bootlaces. She worked the laces very loose so that the boots would come away easily. Then she removed his boots and socks and placed them beside the bed the way she had been shown.

Still on her knees Tandia undid the flybuttons on Geldenhuis's trousers and then unclipped the waistband. Hooking her thumbs into each side of the waistband she pulled downwards until her thumbs included the elastic band of his underpants. Then in a single movement she pulled both garments down to his ankles. She waited, her eyes downcast, while he stepped out of them. Tandia was terrified of raising her eyes, as she knew she eventually must do. She had never seen an erection other than the one represented by Herman the Hottentot. Mama Tequila had explained that the next bit was essential. 'Tandy, some men, they not clean, they got things, maybe a little sore or something, even very small it dangerous, you hear.' She had picked up Herman the Hottentot and showed Tandia where to look. Then she had placed her forefinger and thumb around the base and run them firmly along the satin-smooth length of sneezewood to the carved bulbous tip. 'You do like this, you milk it and watch. If a drop comes out that clear like water you okay, but if it milky, even a little bit cloudy, you finish and klaar with this man, you hear?' Tandia was now aware that to make this examination she must pretend to 'fondle' Geldenhuis, to pretend she was indulging in foreplay, and she knew suddenly that this was something she simply couldn't do.

Instead, averting her gaze, she half-turned as she rose, so that by the time she stood erect she had her back to Geldenhuis. She brought her hands around and unhooked her dress at the back and pulled down the zipper to reveal the curve of her beautiful back. Then she pulled her dress down over her thighs and, taking her panties with her, she stepped out of Marie's dress.

Tandia now stood completely nude with her back to Geldenhuis, terrified to turn around. She could sense him moving towards her and her heart beat furiously.

'*Magtig*! You're beautiful!' she heard him say and then, almost in slow motion, the nightmare of the cemetery started all over again. Geldenhuis reached out and grabbed his tie from the vanity table. With his free hand he gripped her by the back of the neck and pushed her hard so that she fell sprawling across the bed on her stomach. Then he grabbed her arms and brought them behind her back, tying them together at the wrists using his necktie.

'Don't shout, you hear! If you shout or scream, I promise I'll kill you!' Tandia's hands were securely tied and she felt his hand press down into the small of her back as it pinned her down. She turned her head to see him again reach towards the vanity table beside the bed and withdraw his service revolver from its holster. 'Lie very still or you a dead kaffir, you hear?' Tandia was close to fainting with terror when she felt the sudden cold of the barrel between the crease of her buttocks. She jerked involuntarily. 'Lie still, dammit!' The cold steel worked closer in, then she felt a terrible searing pain as the barrel was pushed into her anus. She gasped and then screamed. But Geldenhuis anticipated her and slammed his cupped hand across her mouth, cutting the scream short. He jerked her head back and held her. 'You scream just once more and I pull the trigger you black bitch!' He held her head pulled back until she was forced to relax and then he took his hand from her mouth and allowed her head to collapse back onto the bed. The barrel hadn't moved and, apart from the pain, she felt as though she was about to become incontinent.

When Geldenhuis spoke again his voice was calm. It was the same reasonable tone she remembered from the interrogation room of the Cato Manor police station. 'What's this I hear about going to the university, hey? I thought we talked about that? Remember? When I told you we don't like *swart slimmetjies*. Clever kaffirs just make trouble. Why do you want to make trouble for me, Tandia? Why, hey? I told you I was your friend. But now, all of a sudden, now you want to go to the university to study law? That's a very dangerous precedent. I don't think we can allow such a dangerous precedent.' He was exerting a steady downward pressure on the revolver so, as he talked, the barrel moved further and further inwards. 'In fact, I can definitely say, we not going to allow this precedent.' She heard Geldenhuis sigh heavily. 'Tandia, you make me sad, you hear? First you break your promise to me. I ask you to tell me the names of people who come here, but you never did that. Now you want to go to the university, when already I told you I don't like *swart slimmetjies*!' She felt the downward pressure of the barrel; the pain was making it hard for her to concentrate. 'I think maybe I wasting my time on you, I should just pull the trigger now and shoot the shit out of you.' He laughed, 'What you say, hey? What's another dead kaffir anyway?'

Tandia lay very still. She never doubted for a moment that he would kill her if he chose to do so. The pain had now become a deep throb and she knew she must be bleeding. Her fear completely enveloped her, like a soldier on the battlefield pretending to be dead as the enemy passed by. The rhythm of his legs against her increased and, rather than hear him, she sensed that he was breathing harder. She gasped as the revolver was painfully and suddenly withdrawn and she heard the soft clunk as it landed on the carpet. 'Turn over!' Geldenhuis demanded. Terrified, Tandia turned onto her back. Geldenhuis stood over her. His blue eyes, sharp and angry, seemed to pierce directly into her like the pin-sharp pain of a sunspot focussed on skin through a magnifying glass. His left hand held his erection arrogantly and his right rested on his waist. Suddenly his mouth shaped into a snarl and his hand shot out and grabbed her hair, jerking her into an upright position.

'Suck!'

Somewhere, deep down in a long, dark corridor of her soul, Tandia heard a silent scream. Her mouth opened and took him in and her teeth bit down as hard as she possibly could.

Tandia heard a scream and felt a stunning blow to the side of her head. The scream and the blow mixed so that the man's scream and the pain to her head became one, a misted crimson thing that rang sharply like the sing of electricity through wire. As Geldenhuis struck her she must have released her grip on him, for, clutching at his scrotum, he reeled backwards, tripped and fell, hitting his head against the side of the vanity table. This undoubtedly saved Tandia's life. Geldenhuis was a boxer who was used to taking a punch and the blow to the back of his head was only sufficient to slow him down for the few seconds it took Juicey Fruit Mambo to cross the room. Geldenhuis, intent on killing Tandia, didn't see him coming. His hands closed around the gun just as the African loomed over him. He heard the sudden snarl of an animal coming in for the kill and saw a glint of gold teeth as he felt himself being lifted above the black man's head. He fired at precisely the same moment as his body smashed against the wall.

Juicey Fruit Mambo, tears streaming down his big, ugly face, bent over the bed, lifted the unconscious Tandia into his arms and carried her from the room. 'It all right, Missy Tandy, I come for you, Edward King George Juicey Fruit Mambo, he look after you now, he be warrior for you, always.' The huge black man wasn't even aware of the blood dripping from his ear where the bullet from Geldenhuis's gun had sliced off the lobe neat as anything.

Twelve

As the year progressed Peekay became concerned about his life at Oxford. Though the principles which the great institution of learning attempted to imbue in him were noble in themselves, he sensed they were not enough for what lay ahead of him. Oxford was largely about the *game* of life and he knew the life which lay ahead of him couldn't under any circumstances be thought of as a game. He felt almost guilty thinking this way, but his instincts told him that Africa was different, that he should not be too quick to discard the ways of his childhood and the instinctive caution which is part of the survival mechanism of the continent.

The physical side of Peekay's new life was less complicated. Holland decided to take Peekay into the professional ranks immediately, though Peekay had delayed this a couple of months to meet a university obligation. Holland was certain that no amateur welterweight in Britain could go two rounds with Peekay, and he wanted to iron out several of the fighting habits amateurs acquire which do not serve them well in the professional ranks.

Peekay's stance in the ring was rather too peek-a-boo,

that is to say, he held his gloves too high in the amateur way, where scoring more points than your opponent is the sole objective. Dutch Holland wanted more power in both hands, which meant Peekay had to open up his gloves in order to punch with more authority. Holland liked his boxers to know that both their hands could be relied upon to put an opponent onto the deck. A sprained or broken hand is a common enough occurrence in the ring and, after a good defence, a 'sleepmaker' in either hand is the best insurance a boxer can have. Peekay also had to learn to pace himself over ten rounds of boxing, a far more arduous task than fighting a three-rounder.

There wasn't a lot Holland could teach Peekay about the art or the skill of boxing and so he concentrated on adding power to his punch as well as teaching him other techniques he would need if he was to survive in the professional ring. This included the basic psychology of fighting, such things as how to look at the referee if your opponent is using his head to rough you up in a clinch or even, if the referee seems blind or determined to ignore this basic form of fouling an opponent, how to return the compliment in a number of subtle ways.

Despite E. W.'s tutorials, as his second year at Oxford went by, Peekay might well have taken Oxford too seriously. He loved the long periods of study, the lively debate and intense argument. Given half a chance he could happily have settled into a dogged routine of study and training, the business of getting his money's worth. But Hymie saw things differently.

One summer evening, after returning from a training session in London, they decided to cut through St Hilda's College so Peekay could see the Chinoiserie bridge over the Cherwell. Standing on the beautiful oriental bridge watching the slow, dreamlike flow of the river in the late twilight, Hymie remarked casually to Peekay, 'You know, this place is an investment opportunity we'll never again come across.'

Peekay laughed, taking in the tranquil river scene. 'You're a true romantic, Hymie. Do you realise, Percy Shelley may well have stood with Byron on this bridge?'

'Sure. Did you know Shelley was expelled from Oxford for lying?' Hymie replied. He turned, so that he was leaning with his back pushed against the rail of the bridge, squinting into the distance, looking downriver in the opposite direction to Peekay. 'No, man, I mean it. If we use this place properly it's money in the bank.'

'You mean the Oxford myth, exploiting the cultural cringe when we get back home?'

'That too, but that's only worth a passing lick at the icing on the cake. If anything, the bloody Boers will try to cut us down to size once we get home. Make no mistake, the Nats are in power for a long time. The brilliant hairy-back bigots from Stellenbosch University will be running the show from now on. A couple of smart-arse Anglophile Oxford graduates conducting a law practice that helps kaffirs get off won't impress them one little bit.' As usual Hymie was thinking ahead.

'The way you talk, Oxford doesn't sound like much of an investment. In what way, an opportunity?'

'Our friends. We must choose them for the future.'

Peekay turned to look at Hymie in surprise. 'You're not serious? Shit, Hymie, isn't that just a tad dry-eyed?'

Hymie laughed. 'My mom has a saying: "If a nice Jewish girl is sitting at the bus stop waiting and a Rolls Royce should happen to pass and also to stop and the back door should open, where does it say in the good book it is a sin to save a little time and take a little ride?"'

'You don't mean friends, do you? That's simply an euphemism for contacts, isn't it? We might as well have business cards printed!'

'Jesus, Peekay! You can be a bloody boring Protestant prick sometimes! You can pick up a law degree anywhere.' Hymie slapped Peekay on the arm with the back of his hand. 'Look at us! I mean, we're a couple of cultural country bumpkins who have learned enough to scale the school wall into the orchard on the other side. Only it so happens it's the Garden of fucking Eden! What are we going to do, sit cross-legged under the tree of fucking knowledge in the hope that an apple will fall into our lap?'

'As usual my learned friend makes his point forcibly, but do we have to shake every bloody apple off the tree?' Peekay replied.

Hymie was getting excited, the way he sometimes would when he wasn't getting through to Peekay. 'Let me tell you about Cecil bloody Rhodes! Okay, he's a big name around here, right? You even sat and, in my opinion, got rooked out of his scholarship. Remember?'

Peekay grinned. 'I was too young.'

Hymie ignored him. 'Cecil bloody Rhodes was a dumbdumb! The full mahogany sideboard. When he applied for entry to Oriel the Provost lamented, "All the colleges send me their failures!" Believe me, Peekay, Cecil Rhodes didn't come here for the education. He came for the introductions, and look where they got him!'

Peekay turned back to lean against the beautiful wooden rail of the Chinese bridge. 'Just for once, Hymie, do me a favour and leave out the historical precedent. How do you propose to suck up to every half-decent brain in Oxford so they'll be beholden to us for the rest of their lives?'

'Easy, man!' Hymie said, grinning. 'Start a society!'

'Oh, great,' Peekay imitated Togger Brown, 'that's a smashin' idea, that is!' He turned to face Hymie, his expression serious. 'Do you know how many societies there are already at Oxford? If you can fart in tune you'll find a choral society celebrating its bicentennial who are prepared to cherish your skill!'

'Peekay, don't you see? This university is filled with people who don't fit in. The odd bods. Guys who've always been a pain in the arse because they're very bright in one thing and a walking disaster in everything else. They can't catch a ball, count change, kiss a girl without losing their spectacles. They disagree with everyone about everything and the idea of joining any-thing whatsoever is utterly repugnant to them. But, and this is my point, if you follow their later careers you discover some emerge as powerful people, while others retire into back rooms and split the fucking atom! Either way, most of them rise to the top of the milk.'

'A society for those people who positively, under no circumstances, join societies? The theory's okay, but how do you get them to join?'

'Well, they need a cause they can believe in.'

'A cause? But those guys are the original cynics.'

'Or the true believers ... that is, if you can get through to them.'

'And just how do you propose to do that?'

'I'm working on it. Something ridiculously simple. Something they wouldn't dream of supporting in a million years!'

'You mean, something so alien to their personalities

that they'd have this one thing in common with each other?'

'Yes, that's it! That's it precisely. We have to find that something! It doesn't have to be a universal truth, or last forever . . .'

Peekay turned suddenly and grabbed Hymie by the shirt front. 'No you fucking don't, Hymie! I won't do it. No bugger you, that's not fair! Piss off, you machiavellian little Hebrew.'

'Leggo my shirt!' Hymie yowled. 'You know I abhor physical violence!'

Peekay released him. 'It's not on, Hymie! You can go to hell!'

'Why not? It fits. It's no skin off your nose. And it's not as if I'm asking you to do anything you're not already doing.'

A slightly hurt expression crossed Hymie's face. 'Why are you being so unreasonable, Peekay?'

'Because it's too hard-arsed. Too bloody deliberate. It's a set-up. It's using people!'

'So? That's a sin all of a sudden?'

'Morally, yes! It's . . . it's manipulative. It's essentially vainglorious and conniving!'

'Bullshit, Peekay, it's simply filling a need. A need exists, we fill it, we benefit. There's no morality involved.'

'It's just another way of picking up the tab, Hymie.'

'Sure, I don't deny that. Give a little, take a little. But, as my dad says: "Always leave a little salt on the bread!"'

'Christ, Hymie, no more folksy aphorisms. This isn't just another scam, like at school.'

Hymie grabbed Peekay's arm and continued in an urgent voice. 'Look, I've thought it all out and honestly it's kosher. Just hear me out, will you? Your boxing supplies a much-needed outlet for the aggression of these odd bods.' Hymie held his hand up. 'Okay! Don't tell me they don't need an outlet, because they do. Did you know that of the fifty or so nervous breakdowns in this place every year, most occur among the so-called brilliant loners. Those guys who get their jollies spending all day Saturday in the Bodleian pouring over old vellum!'

'I've been known to do that! And these Odd Bodleians? I'm supposed to be the saviour of these intellectual ragbags?'

'Christ, Peekay, that's fucking brilliant! "The Odd Bodleian Society!"'

Peekay ignored Hymie's compliment, though if there was to be such a society formed, the name wasn't half bad. 'You haven't answered my question. I'm the guru?'

'No, you're the cause, I'm the guru. You give them a reason, the welterweight championship of the world. I'll give them the philosophical crap and they'll give us the smartest fan club in the history of professional boxing.' Hymie shrugged and smiled. 'See! Simple! Now everyone's rewarded!'

'And that's where the problem exists,' Peekay interrupted. 'This place is the citadel of amateurism. You know as well as I do, my being a professional boxer is the standing joke around here. The colonial oaf who brought his streetfighting past with him to Oxford. Remember, when I knocked out the guy from Cambridge they all booed!'

'Precisely, man! It's perfect! Don't you see? This is the very thing to attract the odd bods. It's in contradiction of everything their snotty-nosed cricket and rugger contemporaries stand for. Believe me, Peekay, they'll lap it up!'

'Says who?'

'You just leave it to me, my son.'

Hymie was a master in the use of haphazard time, that is: time spent apparently relaxing. He saw people in an abstract sense as time savers. To him a person was a repository of knowledge who, unlike a library, had the virtue of being available at the end of a telephone or could drop in on one. Cross-examination came naturally to him and even before he'd instituted the Odd Bodleian Society he had gathered an extraordinary collection of people around him, all of whom regarded him as a friend.

Hymie used people in an unabashed way, but never shamefully. And he was generous with his gifts, thoughtful of their needs; he never used people. To Hymie, who wouldn't accept Peekay's explanation that basically, down deep in the forgotten corner of the garden where the tall weeds grow, he was a rather nice chap, this would have been a clear indication of poor judgement and wasted human resources.

Within a month, Hymie had recruited fifty-seven members to the Odd Bodleian Society. Its first meeting took place at the Marlborough Arms in St Thomas Street just across the Isis.

The venue had been selected by Hymie for three reasons. Pubs were out of bounds to students, so the idea of a pub was immediately attractive to his members. The Marlborough Arms contained a back room large enough to accommodate the society, with a small door leading from it into a back lane should a don come snooping. Finally, Morrell's brewery was just two doors down, so the pints were guaranteed to be good.

At this first meeting Hymie had himself appointed president for life. This was less a matter of ego than of necessity, as he was the only person in the room with whom each member of the new society believed he had something in common.

The rules were simple. The cause they all stood for was the world welterweight title to an Oxford man by 1955. Attendance at Peekay's fights was the honourable intention of every member, and black tie and starched bib was mandatory on these occasions.

Peekay had pointed out to Hymie that, despite Hymie's personal charisma and the controversial nature of the society, these were probably insufficient to hold their common interest, given that they shared very few others. What was needed was some sort of mystique. In fact, a creed. It was Peekay who, searching through his own conscience for a good reason to become involved in Hymie's permanent and useful friend programme, had come up with the solution. This was to be the cornerstone of President Hymie's inaugural address.

'It gives me great pleasure to address this first gathering of the Odd Bodleian Society for the very first time,' Hymie began. He seemed unusually nervous. Hands immediately thumped on tables and someone shouted, 'Tautology!' The room immediately filled with laughter.

'Just checking to see who's not drunk,' Hymie quipped to loud boos from the audience. 'I don't need to explain why we're here. You're all here because you are about to become the brains trust of the loathsome and repugnant sport of professional boxing.' More thumping and cheering followed and Hymie waited for it to die down. 'Or so you thought!' He enunciated each word as the room became silent.

Hymie started to pace across the small space at the front of the room. He was in full control and knew he had the interest of his audience. 'The people in this room are the most brilliant at Oxford.' (More thumping.) 'The crème de la crème! Whichever country we come from, it is we who will blossom into the future.' He stopped pacing and leaned over slightly, lowering his voice. 'But! Our ultimate success will not come from our brains or our gifts.' Hymie paused, appearing to look at each of them. 'It will come from our belief in ourselves. It will come from what Peekay here calls "The Power of One!"'

'The Power of One,' Hymie repeated. He had his audience eating out of his hand. Peekay was witnessing the style which was to make Hymie famous in the courtroom, the ability to lift a jury, even one composed essentially of white bigots.

'The power of one determination! The power never to compromise your beliefs or your art or your science, to believe that you are capable of anything if you listen to the small voice, to the single truth. If you have the fortitude . . . the guts! If you have the stamina for the long haul. The power to triumph over the odds you will have to face!'

Hymie's rhetoric was effortless. 'And there will be odds!' he continued. 'Politicians and powermongers will want to buy you and direct you. They will bend and twist the universal truths and they will try to swaddle your conscience with hyperbole and rationalisation!'

As Peekay looked about the room he could see that the members' eyes were almost glazed. Talk about politicians and powermongers! Hymie was going a bit far, manipulating them, doing to them precisely what he was warning them against. What a rotten, conniving shit! But it was going down a treat.

'. . . Only a sustained and invincible belief in yourself will allow you to maintain your integrity and achieve the goals you have set for yourself. You must be utterly determined to believe in your ability to prevail no matter what!' Hymie paused to catch his breath and the room suddenly erupted. It was powerful stuff all right. It was Hymie focusing precisely, getting to the parts of them which lauded the reason why they were different.

Christ, he's getting a bit didactic, Peekay thought. He's said enough, perhaps too much . . . the last bit, the sustained and invincible belief in yourself and the importance of your own integrity, were the things in which Peekay believed implicitly but he'd always seen them as beliefs which owned a private voice. These were quiet, determined, essential things a man might confide to a friend, a philosophical direction you have to find for yourself; they were not cheap tricks performed in public so that they might achieve gratuitous emotional rewards from an audience. Please, Hymie, stop! You've said enough! Peekay begged silently.

'You may well ask what the hell the world welter-weight championship for an Oxford man has to do with all of this?' Hymie asked, dropping his voice. 'At the age of five Peekay was sent to a boarding school. He was the youngest child and the only English-speaking boy in this small, viciously racist backwoods Afrikaans school. The Boer children beat him every day and bullied him mercilessly.'

Peekay closed his eyes and winced. None of this had been a part of what they'd discussed. He had never expected to witness his beloved friend being so blatantly opportunist.

'Peekay was befriended by a train conductor, who convinced the little boy that if he could learn to box, that big could beat small, that he would never again be beaten up, that he could even become the welterweight champion of the world if he believed hard enough, if he never gave up!'

Peekay had had enough.

'I say, Hymie, that's not quite fair!' He was pale with anger and his voice, though low, carried around the room.

Hymie looked at Peekay surprised. The power of his anger was palpable. His voice had been a growl, the sound of a wounded animal. Hymie's heart missed a beat. Jesus! He'd gone too far! Peekay was the most fiercely proud person he'd ever known and he'd used him. He'd done this to the person he loved the most in the world.

The room grew strangely quiet. They too had been brought up with a jolt, the spell of Hymie's rhetoric broken.

Some of them looked at Peekay, their eyes showing sympathy, whether for the story they'd just heard or for the invasion of his privacy was impossible to say. These were mostly young men who knew what it was like to be a loner, to be the odd man out at school, to be the swot, the sap, the drip and the school misfit. Either way they could identify. They knew what it was like to dream privately, never daring to reveal your dream lest you be ridiculed by your peers.

The first to stand up was a smallish man with big hornrimmed glasses named Elmer Milstein, an American from New York. He was simply known as Milstein; at Oxford, people even refused to use a name as silly as Elmer.

Milstein spoke directly to Peekay. 'Say! This thing is ... well, it's between the two of you.' He looked around the room. 'Whaddaya say, you guys? We retire to the saloon bar until they've sorted it out?'

There was a scraping of chairs as the members of the newly formed Odd Bodleian Society rose and silently left the room, taking their half-downed pints with them.

Hymie looked up at his friend. There was nothing he could say. He had seated himself on the edge of a table and now he shrugged his shoulders. The look in Peekay's eyes was unbearable. 'Jesus! What a fuck-up,' he said helplessly.

'Why? Why, Hymie?' Peekay asked.

'Peekay, I swear to God, I'm sorry. You're right, it was vainglorious and contemptible.' Tears welled in Hymie's eyes.

'It's not that easy, Hymie. Your apology, even your tears are not enough. You were contemptuous of the people in this room. You betrayed the trust between us!' Peekay was still angry but his voice had become very calm.

Hymie looked slowly up at Peekay. His friend's eyes were cold. He could think of nothing to do but to attack. When he spoke his voice was bitter. 'It's because I'm a Jew, isn't it? Secretly you despise me. A fucking Judas! That's it, isn't it, Peekay?' The tears in Hymie's eyes brimmed, but he held his gaze steady. 'You're the only one who's allowed to lead. You with your blue eyes and the glorious two-fisted attack of the master fucking race!'

Peekay remained silent. He loved Hymie more than anyone in the world. He loved his quick mind, his generosity and even his cynicism. He knew Hymie loved him and he hated the thing he now saw in him, the fear, insecurity and guilt which made him say what he'd just said. Peekay could identify with it all and he knew how it could corrupt the soul.

They were both refugees but he was the stronger of the two. He had already been corrupted. He knew how the war had turned out. At the age of five he'd been beaten and tortured, even made to eat shit.

Hymie had never stood to fight, stood with his back to the wall. He'd always run. His fear was for the unknown and his guilt was for all the Jews who'd stayed behind to be rounded up and forced into the cattle trucks. It was time Hymie stopped running.

'Listen to me, you contemptible little bastard!' said Peekay. 'I'm going to go into that saloon bar and I'm going to call all those guys back in. Then you're going to tell them how we designed this scam. How we intended to ingratiate ourselves with the long-term plan to exploit their friendship. To use them!'

Hymie looked up alarmed. 'I couldn't do that. You can't make me do that!'

'No, that's true, I can't. You're going to have to do it for yourself!'

Hymie sniffed then reached for his handkerchief and wiped his eyes, then blew his nose. 'That's easy then, I *can't* do it.' He looked up at Peekay. 'Okay, I admit it, I'm a moral coward.' He looked down again, between his legs at the floor. 'It's all right for you, all I am is smart. I can't settle things with a pair of boxing gloves. I can't even remain silent the way you can. My silence means nothing. A silent Jew? What's that? That's an anachronism. It doesn't make me smart. It doesn't make me wise.' He looked up again, the pain showing in his eyes. 'It makes me nothing! I exist because of my fucking mouth and my head and my wit. Now you

271

want to take the only defence I've got away from me. I'm sorry, you're asking too much, Peekay, I can't, I simply can't do it!'

Peekay shook his head. 'Hymie, none of the things you've just said about yourself are true. I wish to Christ you didn't have to carry around all this fucking emotional baggage. But if you can't face the mob, you'd better leave.'

Hymie rose. 'What are you going to do?'

'Apologise.'

Hymie grinned weakly. 'Well that's different! I can do that with you.'

Peekay sighed. 'No way, Hymie, it's on your own or not at all.'

'Fuck you, Peekay!' Hymie grabbed up his duffel coat and student's gown which lay on a chair. Crossing the room, he unlatched the doorway leading to the lane and stormed out.

Peekay sat very quietly, not even noticing the tears which ran down his cheeks. Christ, it wasn't such a bad thing. No worse than many of their scams at school. Hymie probably didn't even mean it. It had simply seemed like a good idea at the time!

But Peekay knew that somehow they'd come to a crossroads. They'd soon be returning to a country where the blacks were beginning to despair, one in which the dung beetle was demanding too much and returning too little to the worker ants. They were going to be severely tested, their integrity constantly challenged by both sides. Moral cowardice was the easiest way there was to destroy themselves.

Peekay was even beginning to have second thoughts about Oxford. He wasn't at all sure that the law he was being taught, the neat, concise rules laid out for the behaviour of a society was the intellectual ammunition he was going to need when he returned home. He sensed that to win in South Africa, even if it meant alienating both sides, the truth could not be compromised. It was going to require a strength and wisdom well beyond the careful intellectual paths of law taught at this venerable institution.

Oxford was giving him, and he felt sure would continue to give him, a great deal. But what it couldn't give him was what he'd come for. It couldn't teach him a set of rules which he could impose on his alienated society in the hope that it would make things better, like a suddenly discovered cure for a hitherto incurable disease. But he did know that the sort of compromise represented by the Odd Bodleian fiasco, their scam, was just the way their ideals could be undermined and the aggression it would take to be a spiritual terrorist sapped and eventually dissipated.

The news from South Africa was bad. He'd already heard recently that Sophiatown, together with Cape Town's District Six, the two best-known examples of South Africa's many racially integrated communities, was going to be pulled down in the guise of slum clearance. District Six, which boasted more than a hundred years of mixed-race living, was to be converted into a whites-only community.

The words 'terrorist' and 'treason' were increasingly being used by government spokesmen to prepare the whites for the police brutality and white supremacist legislation to come. Government propaganda, carried mainly through the Afrikaner press, was growing increasingly hysterical. The second dance had begun.

They were returning to this. The law he was learning, the sweetly practised ways of civilised men, were going to be useless. Here at Oxford he was learning to play a game, and what he needed to learn was how to wage a war. It was strawberry mousse, not the diamond-hard intellectual and spiritual training they were going to need to stay alive and help to bring about change in South Africa.

It was this last point which caused Peekay to question his motives in helping to form the Odd Bodleian Society. If Hymie and he were to establish a law practice in which they hoped to win the trust of black people, they would need absolute integrity. The way in which they had gone about planning the Odd Bodleian Society demonstrated clearly that they were not yet to be trusted; it showed that they too had been infected by the virus of contempt, the white disease which was endemic in their homeland.

Peekay wiped his eyes with the back of his hand and walked towards the saloon bar. Pausing at the door he looked for Milstein. Finally he caught the American's eye. He indicated with a jerk of his head that they should all return and then went down the passage way back to the room to await their arrival.

Peekay entered the back room to find Hymie waiting. He was wearing his duffel coat and over it, his gown. He stood slightly hunched up, small and vulnerable. His unmistakably Hebraic nose, strong features and dark, swept-back hair made him look like the Rabbi in Marc Chagall's painting. Peekay's heart went out to his friend. Hymie hadn't looked up as he entered. Peekay remained silent, walking over and standing beside his friend. He nudged Hymie in the ribs. 'Welcome back, shithead!' he said, out of the corner of his mouth.

Hymie waited until they were all seated and then indicated to Peekay that he too should sit. Peekay seated himself at a table in the front of the room opposite him. The room fell silent and Hymie, clearing this throat, began.

'I owe you an apology. I have deceived you and, I believe, used you ungraciously.' Several of the students looked at each other and shrugged, their lips pursed, faces questioning. 'Ja, I can see you don't believe me,' Hymie said quickly. 'But it's true. I haven't harmed you or your reputations. Not yet anyway. But nevertheless you were being set up.' Hymie ventured a look at Peekay, but his friend had his eyes fixed on the table in front of him and was unaware of his glance.

For once in his life Hymie didn't quite know how to continue. If he told them about their intention to open a law practice designed to fight apartheid and explained how he'd hoped to manipulate them through the Odd Bodleian Society to establish a basis whereby they could be called upon in the name of friendship to help in the years to come it would make him look honourable. They might even conclude that the end justified the means.

If he revealed the second reason, the marvellous 'brains trust' publicity campaign he'd devised for Peekay's world-title bid, they might equally conclude that it sounded like fun and once again he'd be off the hook. Hymie knew that he could probably talk his way out of the predicament he found himself in. But that would be running. He was tired of running. He'd been halfway down the lane when the utter weariness of running from himself had overtaken him. Peekay was right. He had to come clean. He had to stop being scared of the grey shadows which haunted his life.

'The point is, I couldn't give a fuck about any of you! I simply wanted to bind you all into a fraternity so in the years to come I could lean on you in the name of Oxford, the Odd Bodleian Society and the successful outcome of Peekay's world-title fight. What you see in me is a supreme opportunist, a user!'

It was almost as though an electric shock had passed through the room. Suddenly they all understood. A chap named Jamie Jardine whose great grandfather had helped pioneer the China opium trade, stood up, holding his pint high, almost under his chin, his stomach pushed out. He was a fat, ginger sort of chap practically custom designed to be persecuted at any boarding school he might have attended. He was reputed to be a brilliant mathematician and a superb violinist but looked as thick as an ox and at the moment appeared somewhat inebriated.

'I say, that's a bit sniffy, old chap! A bit on the nose!' He possessed a slight lisp and his remark was delivered in a plummy public-school accent which would have been comic anywhere else.

'You're quite right, Jardine. It was contemptible,' Hymie said softly.

Jardine, who had probably never in his life been allowed to be right, stuck his premature paunch out even further at the same time lifting his chin. 'You ought to be ffrashed!' he said pompously.

There was a murmur around the room, even some laughter. 'I say, steady on, Jam Jar!' somebody called. 'You're pissed again. Sit down old chap!'

Peekay rose and turned to face the others in the room. 'We apologise to all of you. I am as much to blame as Hymie.' Peekay lowered his head. 'It was a cynical thing to do. I am deeply ashamed.'

There was the scrape of a chair as Jardine sat heavily. The room became totally, embarrassingly still. Peekay looked up again. 'May I make a suggestion?' Several heads nodded, grateful that he had broken the silence. 'That you carry on with the idea of the Odd Bodleian Society?' He paused and grinned wryly. 'I guess we're all misfits. I want to become a barrister and the world welterweight boxing champion. Frankly, I don't blame people for thinking I'm a bit strange, a bit potty.' Peekay moved over and stood beside Hymie. 'Hymie and I will, of course, resign immediately and you will naturally choose some other cause.'

Milstein jumped up and walked over to where Hymie and Peekay were standing. He turned to address the room. 'Listen you guys, I don't know how you feel, but what I've been listening to is a crock of shit!' Several of the chaps in the room grinned, relieved that the tension had been eased.

'Peekay's right, it's a damn good idea and I, for one, don't want it modified. Friendship isn't something you buy! It's not an obligation obtained through a fraternal past. It's something you feel, something you give willingly, or not at all. I've known Hymie more than a year. If he doesn't give a shit about me then he's made a damn good job of hiding this fact. He's been kind, considerate and generous to me on a number of occasions.' He turned to Peekay. 'With the greatest respect, Peekay, I joined the Odd Bodleians because of him. Personally I find boxing repugnant. On the other hand, I find your determination to prevail an inspiration. I'm sure there are others here who feel the same way.' He paused to take a breath. 'I even think I understand why Hymie acted the way he did.'

He looked about the room. 'I don't suppose I'm the only other Jew here, but I do know what it's like. You can never quite believe a Gentile can possibly like and respect you for who you are. You spend your whole goddamn life compensating. What others seem to be given willingly in comradeship and trust you have to earn, sometimes even by scheming.'

Milstein turned to Peekay. 'You're absolutely right. I've been a misfit all my life, the clever kid nobody liked. A smart-ass with all the answers. In my high-school class book, under my name it said cryptically: "Will go far!" Somebody wrote on my personal copy: "Yes please!"'

The room broke into sudden laughter and Milstein grinned. 'Anyways, I reckon we change nothing. This is the best chance I've had in my whole life to make a few good friends.' Grinning suddenly, he added, 'Whom, by the way, I intend to exploit shamelessly in years to come!' He turned back to Hymie and Peekay, 'And included among my friends is the dynamic duo, The Tadpole Angel and Attila the Rabbi!'

The room erupted into laughter and applause, with a dozen or so enthusiastic 'Hear, hears!' added. Milstein waited until the applause had died before turning to Hymie. 'Well, Mr President, aren't you going to buy your fellow Odd Bodleians an inaugural pint?'

Jam Jar rose unsteadily to his feet. 'Bloody poor show! Ought to be flogged! I'll have a pint of Morrell's special please, Mr President.'

Thirteen

Detective Sergeant Geldenhuis had been admitted to the exclusive Bayview Private Clinic built on the heights of the Berea overlooking the wide sweep of the bay and the city below. Mama Tequila had paid for a private room for him and, despite all the windows being open, the oppressive humidity beat the best efforts of the electric fan, which swung in a wide arc above the policeman's bed. Small beads of sweat showed on her upper lip as she fanned herself. It was going to be another stinker, and she yearned for the cooler months of July and August when the air was light and clear and the sun was warm on a person's back.

It was six in the morning and Mama Tequila was bored. She'd been waiting since dawn. Now she looked around for the hundredth time at the details of the room. Why always white? she asked herself. Why not pink? Pink would cheer a person up, make them feel better when they just had a big op. If she ever built a hospital it would be pink and then everyone in it would be a lot happier.

But she was forced to admit it was unlikely, whatever the colours of the wall or the sheets, that Geldenhuis

279

was going to be happy when he regained consciousness. Lying there with a tube up his nose he looked a proper mess. His head was bandaged, his shoulder strapped and his arm was in a sling, the arm fractured and the collarbone broken when Juicey Fruit Mambo had smashed the policeman's body against the bedroom wall. But, of course, the real damage was the secret concealed below the starched sheet covering him from the waist down.

The cover-up was simple enough and it would hold up well if Geldenhuis agreed to cooperate, which Mama Tequila felt confident he would do. Juicey Fruit Mambo had been a different matter. He had pronounced himself anxious to see that the policeman bastard bled until he croaked. At first there was no way he was about to leave Tandia and drive Geldenhuis to where Dr Louis could operate. He only agreed to go after Mama Tequila had convinced him that the bleeding from her anus was reasonably superficial and that her face, though badly swollen, was not permanently damaged; and that besides, if she didn't get Geldenhuis to the hospital, Tandia was as good as dead anyway. But he went only on the condition that Dr Louis came back to Bluey Jay to look at Tandia.

Mama Tequila, afraid, with some justification, that the big Zulu might kill the police officer on the way to the hospital had gone with him. She also needed to get Dr Louis to cooperate with the motor accident story. Half a mile or so from Bluey Jay, she had picked the spot for the accident to be faked. Juicey Fruit Mambo had driven a hundred yards or so further on to where the road took a sudden turn around a stand of tall old blue gum trees and announced it as perfect. The police car would appear to have missed the turn and skidded off the road into one of the big trees.

Before they left, Mama Tequila had inserted a small sterile sea sponge into Tandia's rear and, despite the hot afternoon, wrapped her in a warm eiderdown. Then she had given Tandia an Amatyl tablet, hoping to calm her down sufficiently to make her sleep. She'd previously given her a stiff brandy and the combination of brandy and bromide had made Tandia groggy even before Mama Tequila left with Juicey Fruit Mambo for the hospital.

Jamal Vindoo, who had been concealed in the attic with his Leica, was the only other person left at Bluey Jay that afternoon, but Mama Tequila ruled out the possibility of his staying with Tandia. She had immediately sent him back to Durban on his motorbike with his precious spools of film and a set of instructions on what she wanted done with them. His role as photographer might just prove to be the salvation of the whole situation. She'd heard Jamal roar off on his BSA and had prayed silently, '*Please* God don't let there be a fuck-up with them photos!'

Tandia would be alone at Bluey Jay for the next two and a bit hours until either they returned from the hospital or the girls arrived by taxi from town. Juicey Fruit Mambo had suggested they take Tandia to the hospital, but Mama Tequila had also vetoed this idea. Tandia was coloured and would not be admitted, so that Dr Louis would have to examine her in the Packard. Besides, it would look far too suspicious and raise needless questions.

In her own mind, Mama Tequila had no choice. The police officer automatically qualified over Tandia for treatment. It was a matter of common sense and she wasn't about to let her heart rule her head in such a fundamental and important matter. Even if Tandia's injuries had been worse than those of the police officer, so that by leaving her behind it may have meant that Tandia would die, Mama Tequila's options remained the same. In the end Tandia was just another kaffir girl. On the other hand, the death of a white police officer in a brothel, in particular the leader of SAT, would destroy them all. Mama Tequila was prepared to sacrifice a dozen Tandias rather than to have that happen.

After Juicey Fruit Mambo had dropped Geldenhuis and Mama Tequila off at the hospital and returned to stage the accident, she confessed the entire story to Dr Louis. 'Doctor, I should have listened to you,' she said in conclusion. 'God is punishing me. I promised you I wouldn't put the child to work on her back until she finish school. I done that, Doctor. I kept my word to you! But when Detective Sergeant Geldenhuis came along, what could I do? It was blackmail, doctor. What could I have done? You tell me.'

Dr Louis patted the big woman on the shoulder. 'Mama Tequila, I'm a doctor not a priest. You did what you had to do. I'm not saying it's nice, but then who am I to say? Just the other day a patient of mine, a Jew who was in Treblinka concentration camp during the war, told me how the guilt is eating him up alive, how in the concentration camp he was what they called a Kapo, a Jew who was a policeman of his own people. He told me how he had condemned hundreds of his fellow Jews to death just so he could stay alive himself.' Dr Louis sighed. 'We are all guilty, we all do things that destroy others.'

Mama Tequila was greatly heartened by Dr Louis's observations. Her conscience wasn't in the least bit concerned nor was her soul tainted with the slightest sense of guilt.

Whores are whores and life wasn't meant to be easy. If you played on the street sooner or later you got run over by the garbage truck. But the nice, safe, white Jewish conscience of Dr Louis meant he was going to cover for her. He'd as much as said so. All she had to do was push the advantage home.

Her eyes were downcast, her false eyelashes brushing her cheeks. 'I give you my word, doctor, God's honour, on my mother's grave, Tandia will never work in my house again! Never, you hear?' Mama Tequila raised her eyes slowly. It seemed to Dr Louis that the wetness of a tear made her coal-black eyes shine between the two broad strips of mascara, but he couldn't be absolutely sure.

'That's good, Mama Tequila. I am very fond of Tandia and she is going to be in a great deal of pain. I will go out to see her just as soon as I have finished with the barbarian policeman.'

'How long will that be, doctor?' Mama Tequila asked.

Dr Louis shook his head. 'It will be late, I'm afraid. You see, it's a big operation. He needs a general anaesthetic, maybe three hours. What has happened is very serious. I only hope I can patch him up.' His face was serious. 'The chances, well, I've got to tell you right now, they're not good.'

'You mean he could, you know, lose it?'

'Ja, that's possible, but I don't think so. A human bite is notoriously poisonous. Sepsis will undoubtedly occur. He will be in a great deal of pain for a very long time, but the bite is quite near the top, so we'll hope for the best, hey?' Dr Louis was off again explaining everything in detail. 'If I can stem the arterial bleeding and if the urethra is not badly crushed, that's the pipe where he urinates, we may still end up with something that dangles.' He shook his head. 'But I don't think it will give him much pleasure to look at again or even to use.'

Mama Tequila was genuinely shocked. 'What do you mean, doctor? You mean, he can't make love no more ... ever?'

'Well, ja, perhaps even that. It's not so much the scar tissue and the damaged arteries that will inhibit some of the blood from getting through, the psychological damage to his self-esteem will be enormous. This, on its own, is capable of causing erectile failure.'

Despite her anxiety, a slow smile spread over Mama Tequila's face and she clapped her hands in delight. '*Wragtig*! There is a God in heaven! You mean you can fix him up so he can do it, but really he can't, because he too ashamed of his one-eyed snake?' She giggled gleefully. 'Just wait till Juicey Fruit Mambo hears about this!'

A nurse came over and told Dr Louis it was time to scrub up. Mama Tequila held onto his arm. 'Please, doctor, you must let me see him first when he wakes up. I beg you, I must be the first to see him, even before the police. It is very important.'

'I understand, Mama Tequila. I'll drop out to Bluey Jay to take a look at Tandia Patel after I've finished here. I'll let you know then when it will be okay to see the patient. You might as well go home now, it won't be tonight, that's for sure.'

Juicey Fruit Mambo returned to fetch Mama Tequila and he drove her to Pickering Street. They pulled up outside the sewing-machine shop and he helped Mama Tequila out of the back of the car. 'Don't wait here, come back for me in half an hour, you hear?' He watched as she walked slowly down the side passage to the back of the shop, and when a strip of light appeared as the door was opened, he drove off.

Jamal Vindoo was a handsome young man with a complexion the colour of crystallised honey. He appeared to be in his mid twenties and had grown a Clark Gable moustache, perhaps to give his boyish good looks a little more maturity or because he thought it would make him more attractive to the girls. Clark Gable moustaches were all the rage with the young guys at Bombay University where he had studied, to his father's immense pride.

He ushered Mama Tequila into a small reception area which contained two wicker chairs and a small wicker couch, on which were fitted cushions of bright Indian cotton. A matching wicker coffee table, draped with an elaborately embroidered shawl, took up the remainder of the space. Standing in the centre of the table was a brass vase which contained a dozen or so brightly coloured yellow, pink and red paper roses and a round brass ashtray. On a small shelf on the wall furthermost from the door burned the *Deepam*, or God lamp; placed beside it, in a miniature brass vase, burned a single stick of incense.

To anyone entering the room there was no hint that it was a photography studio. The only picture on the wall was a large oval walnut frame which contained an old-fashioned hand tinted photograph of a much younger Mr Dine-o-Mite, who looked sternly out into the world through his pebble, steel-rimmed glasses, wearing his best Mahatma Gandhi lookalike expression.

'Sit, please.' Jamal Vindoo casually indicated a chair and then, realising Mama Tequila's size, moved his hand to denote the wicker couch. 'May I bring you some refreshment, some cha perhaps, Pepsi?'

Mama Tequila shook her head and got straight down to business. 'Sit, Mr Vindoo. Look, I want to thank you again for coming. The man who does it other times is in hospital with pneumonia.' It seemed appropriate to exaggerate the previous photographer's bout of 'flu. 'You did me a big favour; you came, no questions asked, I liked that!' She looked at him, her face grim. 'What you saw today is very serious. If it got out what happened, I'm telling you, man, they throw us into jail and they throw away the bladdy key!' With a groan she eased herself down into the wicker couch and, opening her handbag, produced her silver cigarette case and Zippo, which she placed on the coffee table beside the ashtray.

Jamal Vindoo looked hurt. 'You can trust me implicitly in this matter. I am a very discreet person, Madam Tequila.'

'Not Madam! In my profession that mean something else. Mama, Mama Tequila.' The words 'discreet' and 'implicitly' grated on Mama Tequila; so did the young Indian's carefully modulated stuck-up accent. She sighed heavily. 'In my experience, *trust* is always a matter of how much money. *Discreet*, that a question of how much more.' She dug into her handbag and produced an envelope which she held out to him. 'In here is fifty pounds.'

Jamal Vindoo took the envelope, and as he did so he bowed his head. 'You are very generous, Mama Tequila. I will fetch the prints.' He started to walk towards the door leading to the interior of the studio, and stepped through a curtained doorway leading to an interior room. A few moments later Jamal Vindoo returned with a large manila envelope which he handed to Mama Tequila.

Mama Tequila looked up at the young man. 'In here is everything I asked for?'

Jamal Vindoo nodded. He stood over her with both hands in his trouser pockets, jiggling his goolies. 'Sure, two ten-by-eights and three five-by-four prints of everything, just as you asked.'

Mama Tequila withdrew a fat pile of photographs. The young Indian photographer had been away from Bluey Jay less than four hours and he must have worked hard to get the prints ready. She was pleased with what she saw. The photographs were well contrasted and perfectly in focus. In some he had used a zoom lens with devastating effect. Mama Tequila's heart thumped as she looked at his work. For the first time she understood clearly what had happened, from the moment Tandia had stepped out of her dress with her back turned to Geldenhuis to the arrival of Juicey Fruit Mambo.

She halted momentarily when she came to the first shot where Tandia stood naked. The photograph framed Tandia's body perfectly, with only Geldenhuis's hand and part of his arm reaching out into the picture. To Mama Tequila, Tandia was simply and utterly exquisite.

Mama Tequila's voice was businesslike. 'Your pictures are good, man. I can use you. Ten pounds with the negative. That for every client.' She drew on her cigarette, then exhaled. 'What do you say, Mr Photographer?'

Jamal Vindoo suddenly burst into laughter. Turning to her he extended his hand. 'You got a deal, Mama Tequila!'

Mama Tequila and Juicey Fruit Mambo returned to Bluey Jay to find that Dr Louis had just arrived and was attending to Tandia. He had given her a local anaesthetic and was making a proctoscopic examination. The area was badly swollen and while the muscle hadn't been torn she required quite a bit of sewing up. The effects of the barbiturate had largely worn off and Tandia was awake and in a lot of pain when he arrived. The needle he used for the anaesthetic needed to be inserted in several places and Tandia, biting into the soft part of her thumb, drew blood trying to refrain from screaming. Now, as he stitched her, Dr Louis said, 'Tandia, you're going to be extremely sore for the next couple of weeks and must go on a diet of soft food only. I will treat the infection with sulphur drugs and you must rest for at least a week. You can't go to school until you can sit down again.'

Tears ran down Tandia's cheeks as she spoke. 'When will that be, Dr Louis?'

Dr Louis stroked her brow. 'No use going for a couple of weeks, I'd say.' He touched the cheekbone just below her left eye. 'Anyway, my girl, you're going to have a doosey of a black eye, you don't want to go to school wearing a shiner like this, do you?'

'We're doing our matriculation trials, I can't miss them!' Tandia's consternation was obvious.

'Look, I'll come every day and help you with your Latin and science. I think I'm still good for those. Maybe maths also. The rest is just silly stuff you can study on your own.' Dr Louis withdrew two small bottles. He held up the first. 'These, they're called Amatyl, you take one at night before you go to sleep for the next week.' He held up the second bottle. 'These are painkillers, you take two every four hours.' He was about to put the pills on the table beside her when Juicey Fruit Mambo's hand appeared and took the bottles from him.

Dr Louis turned in surprise. He had been aware that Mama Tequila had entered the room while he had been examining Tandia but he hadn't seen the black man enter and stand quietly beside the window directly behind him.

Juicey Fruit Mambo sensed what Dr Louis was thinking. 'I been nurse aide one time, I will look after Missy Tandy, doctor.' He grinned. 'I hear also for de food, only soft, very soft. I will make for her.'

Dr Louis turned back to Mama Tequila. 'I will come every day for the next week or so.' He saw Mama Tequila's expression and put his hand up. 'Don't worry, no fee. You pay for the barbarian in hospital, I'll take care of Tandia.' He placed his hand on Tandia's shoulder. 'It's going to be a bit painful when the anaesthetic wears off but Juicey Fruit Mambo will give you a pill. You've had a hard time, but you're going to be all right. I'll come and see you tomorrow. Goodbye, Tandia.' He rose and gathered his stethoscope and other belongings from the bed and placed them in his bag.

'Is he, you know, is he going to die, doctor?' Tandia asked fearfully.

Dr Louis laughed. 'No fear! But he's going to be a very sick policeman for a while.'

'I'm sorry, I didn't mean it! I tried to do what Mama Tequila said. I don't know how it happened. Will they throw me in jail?' she sobbed.

Dr Louis took Tandia into his arms. 'Sssh! Tandia, take it easy, hey? Nothing is going to happen to you. You go to sleep now. In the morning it will be all right, you'll see.' He lowered Tandia onto the bed and pulled the eiderdown over her. 'You poor little bugger,' he said softly as he rose and moved to the door.

'Thank you, doctor, thank you for coming to see me.'

Dr Louis stood at the door. 'You couldn't do me a favour could you, Tandia?' He didn't wait for her to reply. 'You couldn't get a first-class matric and then study law and then take on the barbarians in Pretoria and beat the bastards hollow, could you?'

Tandia nodded through her tears. 'Ja, doctor, I promise,' she said, her voice barely above a whisper.

Dr Louis waited for Mama Tequila to pass through the door before he shut it quietly behind him, leaving Juicey Fruit Mambo with Tandia.

'Is she going to be truly orright, doctor?' Mama Tequila asked as they walked down the yellowwood corridor.

'Ja, physically, yes, the revolver did surprisingly little damage. It is more the shock than the physical aspect which concerns me. The body can heal but the mind takes a lot longer. That's why I will come every day for the next week. She will be very depressed. It is important to keep her mind on other things.'

Mama Tequila felt reassured by his words. Mental anxiety was the prostitute's lot in life. You learned to cope, to bury the hurt and the fear so deep that you sometimes found it difficult to find. It was better to be hard. It was best to get that over with when you were young.

At the top of the stairs they found Jasmine waiting. 'How is she, doctor?' she asked shyly. Jasmine was a Cape Malay and a favourite among the girls, quiet as a mouse.

'You can go in, sit with her if you like. She's a bit upset now, but she's going to be all right,' Dr Louis said.

Mama Tequila glanced at her watch. The little prostitute reacted immediately. 'Sarah said it was okay, Mama Tequila? We only got five clients, she said I could come?'

'Ja, okay, but not too long, you hear.' She looked at her watch again. 'It could get busy before midnight. Juicey Fruit Mambo is also with Tandia. Tell him he must go and help Sarah in the bar.'

'Yes, Mama T. Goodnight, doctor,' Jasmine said, hurrying away.

Jasmine opened the door to Tandia's room quietly. Tandia was lying on her side with her back to the door and Juicey Fruit Mambo stood to attention at the foot of her bed. The huge black man held his hands clasped in front of him and slow tears rolled down his cheeks. There was absolute silence in the room and he seemed not to notice Jasmine's entrance until she walked over to him and took his arm.

Standing on tiptoe, she whispered Mama Tequila's instructions. Juicey Fruit Mambo nodded and walked from the room, making no attempt to stem his tears.

Jasmine let herself down carefully onto the bed and placed her hand on Tandia's shoulder. After a while she began to hum an old slave lullaby her grandmother had sung to her as a child. The words finally broke free from the hum, sad and sweet and low and comforting . . .

> Slaap Piccaninny
> Die vee's in die krual
> Almal my skapies
> en bokkies . . .
> More vroeg kry jy
> van soet pap en maal

291

en'n paar spier-wit sokkies . . .
Doo Doo . . .!
Doo Doo . . .!

Although it was only a song about a small herd boy who, having put the sheep and goats away for the night, could dream of a breakfast of sweet porridge and a pair of snowy white socks, it carried with it a great yearning for freedom and a cry for the beloved country. A silly little lullaby that contained all the love of the coloured people for their land and their place in it. A song of the twilight people, the words washed in the tears of the forgotten tribe.

Geldenhuis stirred. Even before he sensed the pain in his groin he felt the rawness in his throat and then, as though it was moving up slowly from somewhere deep inside of him, the pain arrived. It pushed remorselessly to the forefront of his consciousness until he could feel the sweat of it break out on his forehead and the sharp singing of it in his head as the pain buzzed him, roaring through his body. A glass of water was held to his mouth and he gulped at it greedily. 'Not too much, you'll vomit.' The glass was pulled away and the cool water down his throat seemed to evaporate in seconds as the furnace of pain burned through every nerve and muscle and sinew in his body. He thought he could hear himself crying, but he wasn't sure. Maybe it was someone else, someone in another room. The pain was beyond crying. Crying wouldn't help it. It was beyond the simple business of anguish or the false hope of a scream. It ate at him, it had huge jaws which tore at his flesh, like a pack of hyenas tearing at a carcass in the dark. A dark night. No moon. Just the tearing of flesh and the crunching of bones somewhere out there in the darkness. He felt a stab of cold on his arm, a small square of ice that burned, not like the other, but a pain no less, then a stab, everything exaggerated, everything bigger than him, bigger than he could possibly bear. A mountain of pain sat between his legs; then the relief as the morphine struck his brain and took hold of his body and blanketed down his pain, patting it into place, leaving him gasping with sweat-soaked relief.

'The kaffir! The fokking kaffir with the gold teeth! I'll kill the black bastard!' These were the first words that came from his mouth. Then he lay still for a long time, panting, his chest heaving. Outside, in the tropical garden, the birds filled the air with morning sound.

'Water, someone give me some water,' Geldenhuis croaked. The nurse had left with the hypodermic needle in a small, kidney-shaped metal dish covered with a white napkin. Mama Tequila rose from her chair and held the glass to his lips. Geldenhuis drank deeply and she took a chance and let him drink the glass down. This seemed to make him feel a little better and he opened his eyes. At first they remained blank, then the sense appeared in them, like a pebble plopped into still water. 'Mama Tequila? Where am I?'

'Lie still, you a very sick person, Detective Sergeant.' Geldenhuis tried to move his head but the pain cut through the effects of the morphine. He stared helplessly at Mama Tequila.

'What happened? Where is this place?' He seemed overcome by the effort to talk and closed his eyes again.

'You had a bad accident, Detective Sergeant. Listen very carefully, don't say nothing, you hear? Jus' listen. You were going to see a farmer by the name of Van

Jaarsveld, remember? He lives about two miles before Bluey Jay.' After the long wait for him to regain consciousness, when she had rehearsed the story a hundred times, Mama Tequila was now only too anxious to get the story out. 'His wife, she phoned you, her husband been having it off with the kaffir girl servant.' Mama Tequila dug into her handbag and produced a note, 'I wrote it all down here, everything, just like it happened. She held it open in front of Geldenhuis. 'Open your eyes, man, you got to read it!'

Geldenhuis hadn't indicated that he'd heard a word but now he opened his eyes and started to read the note reading a few lines then closing his eyes and then having another go, until he nodded his head imperceptibly. 'Read it again, sergeant! It very important. You have to tell this to the police when they come!'

'More water!' Geldenhuis croaked. Mama Tequila poured a fresh glass from the water jug beside his bed and again he drank the whole glass down. His eyes were bright, almost as though he was in a fever. 'You lying, you hear, I remember everything, now! You fokked, you hear? You finish and klaar!' The anger showed clearly in the policeman's face as his mind started to rebuild the incident at Bluey Jay.

'Please, Detective Sergeant, I beg you!' Mama Tequila held the piece of paper in front of him again. 'Read it, this is what happened, I'm telling you, it's the only way! I'm begging you, on my bended knees, Detective Sergeant Geldenhuis!'

Geldenhuis closed his eyes when Mama Tequila placed the note in front of him. Now he opened them again. 'I swear it, I'm going to kill you and that black bitch who bit me . . . and the kaffir! The kaffir with the gold teeth! You all dead, you all fokking dead kaffirs, you hear!' He closed his eyes again and lay still, panting from the effort of his outburst.

'Open you eyes, Detective Sergeant Geldenhuis,' Mama Tequila said softly. Geldenhuis opened his eyes and the shock of what he saw pulled his body rigid. The pain cut through the effects of the morphine and he nearly passed out Mama Tequila held a ten-by-eight print of him standing behind Tandia, the snout of his police revolver pushed deeply into her while his left hand held his erection. In the photograph he was grinning, and every detail, the blood running down the inside of Tandia's thigh, even the chamber of the revolver showed clearly in the picture. Geldenhuis closed his eyes and two large tears ran down his cheeks.

'Okay! Now fok off you black bitch!'

'No, sergeant, not before you read the note one more time!' Mama Tequila held it open again in front of him. Then, when he'd nodded, she folded it and put it into her handbag. 'I will pay for you while you here. You got a broken pelvis also, that what Dr Louis Rabin going to say,' she pointed to the sheet covering his waist, 'to explain what happened down there. You can't be moved, you hear? Not for a long time. The doctor, he will see the police when they come. You can't have no visitors today, you too sick.' The big woman rose stiffly from the chair beside him and gave a big sigh as she moved from the room. She wasn't stupid and she knew enough about men like Geldenhuis to know that the nightmare had only just begun.

On her way out she stopped to see the night sister. 'Please, sister, you have got perhaps a favourite charity?' She opened her purse and took from it two five-pound notes. 'I want to show my very sincere appreciation. As you can see I am a very small person who is not possible to see in a place like this so early in the morning?'

The sister smiled. 'You don't need to do this. Dr Rabin already told us you weren't here this morning.'

'No, take it, please!' Mama Tequila pressed the notes into the woman's hand.

'Thank you! I will use this money for the African baby clinic I run in Clairwood every Saturday.'

Mama Tequila laughed. 'Ag, babies! In my line of work, sister, that a dirty word!' She turned and walked slowly down the corridor and into the sunlight where Juicey Fruit Mambo, polishing the bonnet of the Packard, waited for her.

'Edward King George Juicey Fruit Mambo, I think we going to be okay.' She paused and sank back into the soft leather of the Packard's rear seat, closing her eyes. 'For the time being, anyway.'

'I think you very, very clever madam, madam!' Juicey Fruit Mambo announced as he switched on the ignition and turned the big car into the hospital driveway. The Packard's tyres scrunched on the gravel as they drove past a long bed of scarlet canna under a blaze of flamboyant trees. Sitting opposite the road as they turned out of the gate were two grey rhesus monkeys. 'I think that policeman he got friends who come to visit,' Juicey Fruit Mambo giggled. But Mama Tequila didn't hear him, she was already asleep.

Any half-decent police enquiry would have shot holes through the accident staged to explain Geldenhuis's injuries. After all, most arrangements contrived in a crisis fall apart on closer examination. But it wasn't in the interests of the SAT Squad to dig too deeply. Geldenhuis had corroborated the evidence Mama Tequila and Juicey Fruit Mambo had given the investigating sergeant, who wasn't trying to be Sherlock Holmes anyway,

Old Coetzee, who was the magistrate appointed to preside at the routine enquiry, saw no reason to ask a whole bunch of awkward questions. He ruled that the accident was due to the driver's failure to correct his steering while attempting to avoid an animal crossing the road.

Of course there were rumours, but these were dismissed by most solid burghers as too bizarre and silly to entertain. The 'cop in the boot' was a hero as well as a clean-cut, upright boxing type. Geldenhuis's 'broken pelvis' mended in about three months, which meant his return fight with Gideon Mandoma had to be cancelled. It wouldn't take place for twelve months or so now, the time it would take his bones to knit properly and for him to get back into fighting trim.

In mid January, when Geldenhuis was only halfway through his recovery, the matriculation results came out. Tandia achieved a first-class matric with distinctions in four subjects and a high distinction in Latin.

Tandia called Dr Louis Rabin and Sonny Vindoo when she obtained her results and, in her mind, there now remained only one more thing to do. After lunch that afternoon she persuaded Juicey Fruit Mambo to drive her in the Packard to the Christian Indian cemetery where Patel was buried. Going back was a difficult thing for her to do and for a while she simply sat in the car outside the little graveyard, trying to summon up enough courage to enter.

From where she sat she could see over the wrought-iron fence; the tall marble cross to which she had been handcuffed still stood there. Strangely, she could barely remember the policeman who had raped her. It was the dark spectre of Geldenhuis who lurked in the shadows of her consciousness. This was where it had all started, where the nightmare had begun. Her fear of Geldenhuis had never really left her; it would come out of the blue like a punch in the belly, or lurk like a grey shadow at the edge of her mind. Sometimes it was the first thing to happen when she awakened. At other times it arrived suddenly, striking at her when she was reading a book. Then again, it came like a slap in the face when she was cooking or making a bed or warming a brandy glass for a client in the bar. It was always with her, a little bit or a lot. The only place it didn't seem to come was when she climbed out onto the branch of the old wild fig tree at night and sat in her silver cocoon. The fearful presence of Geldenhuis hadn't found her there, didn't seem to know about this place or couldn't come through her bedroom window.

Juicey Fruit Mambo, sensing Tandia's melancholy, climbed from behind the wheel and went to sit in the back of the car. 'I am very tired today, Miss Tandy. Last night de frogs dey make many, many noise outside my house by the river!' Juicey Fruit Mambo had his own room in the outbuildings behind Bluey Jay but preferred to live in the kraal with his adoring gang of kids. Now he crossed his arms and with a deep sigh closed his eyes. In a matter of seconds he commenced to perform an exaggerated pantomime of feigned sleep, so much so that his pretend snores softened the edge of Tandia's anxiety and gave her the courage to leave the safety of the car and enter the gates of the cemetery.

In the fifteen months since Tandia had left him, Patel's grave had changed. The rounded mound had been flattened and a carpet of untidy grass and dandelion weed now covered the red clay. An ostentatious polished black basalt tombstone had replaced the wooden cross. To Tandia the makeshift wooden cross had seemed more appropriate to the business of death. There seemed to be something slightly obscene about a squared-off block of hard polished granite planted above the slow and natural decay of dust to dust.

Tandia read the inscription on the black tombstone.

Natkin Patel.
Born 6th Ianuary 1898,
died 14th October 1952.
Boxing promoter and businessman,
beloved daddy of Billy and Teddy,
husband of Injira Patel.

'And father of Tandia Patel, who just got a first-class matric, hooray!' Tandia was suddenly no longer afraid. 'We did it, Patel! Four distinctions and a high distinction in Latin! What do you think of that, Mr Boxing Promoter! Mr Well Known in White Circus!' She laughed happily. 'What do you think of that, hey, Dad, Daddy, Pa, Pop?' She used all the pronouns together and they fitted perfectly, natural as anything. Patel had come back to her, he loved her again, that was for sure!

Fourteen

Harriet seldom talked to others about her work although Hymie assured Peekay that it was considered very good. She'd had an exhibition of her drawings at a small contemporary art gallery in Cambridge, and a critic from the *Manchester Guardian* had declared 'Miss Clive's charcoal sketches are both impressive and heroic with a surprising strength, which gives promise of good work to come.'

Extrovert in so many things, Harriet considered it slightly vulgar to discuss her work. But on one occasion, late in the spring term, when Peekay had agreed to model for her as the rider of the larger of the two horses, she'd talked freely about sculpture and what it meant to her. It was almost as though she was prepared to state her philosophy once only, after which the evidence would either speak for itself or remain mute.

'My father builds bridges,' she explained. 'Bridges have to be structurally sound but they can also be beautiful. People don't need to be told when a bridge is beautiful. They don't gradually acquire a taste for the way a bridge looks. They simply know it's beautiful by the way it's a part of the river or ocean landscape, a part of the early morning light and the sunset, the mist and the rain and the water which flows beneath it. Bridges are pieces of sculpture with a purpose, but nonetheless sculpture – and, like bridges, all sculpture should have a purpose.'

Peekay was sitting astride a carpenter's horse over which Harriet had folded the patchwork quilt from her bed to simulate the rounded back of a horse. She'd worked from first light until it grew too dark to see for three weeks in her stable studio and she'd almost completed the shaping of the first horse in the setting of her two horses and a rider. Now she was working on the armature of the rider, bending and shaping the thin steel rods and threading them together with wire to make the beginnings of the torso. She worked with a small pair of bolt cutters and a pair of pliers and her movements were confident and skilful.

'What do you mean by a sculpture having a purpose? Do you mean to celebrate an event, such as a great battle or a general on his horse in the park, or Lord Nelson standing on that dirty great big doric column in Trafalgar Square, that sort of thing?' Peekay asked.

'Heavens no! That's almost exactly what sculpture shouldn't be made to do. Good sculpture should please the eye because it is a part of the landscape, whether it happens to be the urban landscape or park land.' Harriet pointed to the near completed shape of the horse she'd been working on. 'See how it's standing?'

Peekay looked at the plaster-of-Paris shape of the horse standing in the centre of a tarpaulin in the middle of the studio. To the side of it was the beginning of the second slightly smaller horse. Its shape was roughly formed by an armature of steel rods covered with chicken wire; this was how the nearly completed horse beside it had started its life. Harriet had bangaged the chicken wire with strips of coarse hessian dipped in plaster-of-Paris, building up layer after layer and allowing it to dry. When it was completely built up she'd commenced to shape the plaster-of-Paris as though it was a solid medium. The effect gave the horse's appearance a solidarity and astonishing strength. It stood with its neck craned and ears swept back, its forelegs wide and firmly positioned on the ground, its rump pushed slightly backwards as though it was baulking at someone or something unseen.

'See the way it's so animated? It isn't a heroic horse on a plinth, it's a horse suddenly anxious about its forward progress. Something has arrested its attention and made it tentative. The rider will try to exert this will on the horse, make it move forward and overcome its anxiety. The drama is between the rider and the horse. It's an intensely private thing.'

'I can see that!' Peekay said, excited by the explanation. 'You're right, your horse isn't an exact down-to-the-last-tiny detail replica of how a horse looks; it's simply a wonderful expression of how a horse feels.'

Harriet seemed pleased. 'It's the sort of horse which should be naturally set into a park among the trees with its hooves on the grass, where to the eye, it seems to belong; and where, at any distance at all, it seems to be quite real.'

'That's what you mean about a piece of sculpture having a purpose?'

Harriet nodded, her expression serious. 'The second horse, following slightly behind, will enhance the feeling, as though the bareback rider has taken the horses down to a stream to drink and they've all had a swim and now they're going home. If someone were suddenly to look up, say a little girl playing on a swing in a housing estate, and she saw my horses and rider through the trees, she'd know exactly what it would feel like if they were real, because, you see, in a sense they are real. Horses and people riding have always been a natural part of the dreaming landscape. Do you know when I first knew I wanted to become a sculptor?' Harriet asked suddenly. She stopped working on the torso and sat on an upturned tea chest. 'I was twelve and on holiday with my parents in Italy a year after the war. We'd driven into a small village in Tuscany which was reputed to have a beautiful church. My father's potty about churches. As usual the church was the main building in the piazza but this one was surrounded by huge trees, wonderful big old fig trees. It was the local saint's day, I forget which saint, and the village people were all out, playing bola, gossiping in small groups, mothers wet-nursing their babies, people seated at tables under the trees drinking wine, the men smoking. Under several of the trees stood a man playing a piano accordion, each musician taking turns to play a few chords before the others joined in so they all played the same melody.

'I can remember how hot it was, how the women sat on chairs with their skirts hauled up to their knees, fanning themselves with small paddle fans dyed pink and green, which seemed to be made of plaited bamboo and carried the name of a brand of tinned tomatoes.' Harriet laughed. 'I know I'm telling it in detail, but that's how I remember it. The people seemed so natural, so easy with themselves and, although I was only twelve, I sensed, despite the war, I mean them losing it, that nothing much had changed in their lives. There was a sort of internal combustion that worked for them collectively as though the mass was greater than the individual and time had been previously arranged and there seemed no good reason to tamper with it.

'We hadn't been long in the piazza when the bells sounded and the people started to flock towards the church. To my astonishment I realised that many of the people were pushing wheelchairs, while others hobbled towards the church on crutches. A boy of about my own age passed me pushing a man who had no legs in a wheelbarrow. They gathered around a huge stone statue of the virgin mounted on a plinth which stood outside the church. The plinth was stepped to hold hundreds of lighted candles. The enormous statue showed the virgin aloof, towering above the women, many of whom were ululating while others had thrown themselves at the base of the stepped plinth and seemed to be imploring the mother of Christ to heal their sick and cause their lame to walk again. In a few moments the piazza had changed from a natural and eternal village scene to one of frantic and frenetic people playing out an arcane ritual to the rigid, cold and unforgiving mother of God.

'It wasn't love I felt emanating from the blessed virgin. It was fear, deeply atavistic pagan fear. The church which taught love had mastered only fear. The Mother of God, who represented the warmth and continuity of motherhood, had become a monstrous apparition of power. In the piazza, with the washed-blue Italian sky above the warm cobblestones and dark shade under the giant fig trees, where moments before there had been music and laughter and soft afternoon drowsiness, now there was hysteria and madness. The hands and minds which had fashioned this virgin mother of God had been corrupted. New hands were needed, hands which would fashion a virgin to walk amongst the village people, one who nodded and smiled and stopped to listen to a bit of gossip, exchange a recipe, run her hand through a small boy's hair or comfort a mother whose child had been stillborn. A virgin mother of God with her feet on the ground.' Harriet bent down and picked up the maquette of two horses and a rider. She placed it on her lap, absently running her hands across the back of the smaller, rider-less horse. 'It was at that moment, I think, that in my mind anyway, I became a sculptor.'

Peekay was silent for some time, obviously thinking about what she'd said. 'Harriet, in Africa we would call you a visionary and the people would make songs up about you and as the women shucked corn or stamped meal or fed their infants they would sing them, sing about the woman who took the feet of the mother of God and placed them on the ground.'

Harriet blushed, 'You are sweet, Peekay. The truth is, I'm fearfully retarded. While the other kids in kinder-garten went on to better things, I never quite got over playing with plasticine.'

Harriet rose from the tea chest and, walking over to him, she sat astride the wooden saw horse facing him. There was only just enough room for them both and the inside of her thighs and knees touched his own. Pee-kay's heart began to pound furiously as Harriet rested her arms on either side of his shoulders. She leaned forward, her breasts not quite touching his chest, and, closing her eyes, she kissed him. Then she pulled back, her face only inches from his. 'Peekay, how much longer must I wait for you to ask me to make love?'

Peekay blushed furiously. A lump had grown in his throat which made it almost impossible for him to speak. 'But . . . but, you belong to Hymie,' he croaked.

Harriet looked shocked. 'I belong to me, Peekay. I love you but I'll always belong to me.' She didn't wait for Peekay's reply, aware that her response would embarrass him even further. Instead she kissed him again, slightly opening her mouth, allowing her kiss to melt softly, lovingly over his lips, opening his own so that their lips fused.

Peekay's whole body was a confusion. His mind reeled with the shame of his presumption, his heart thumped like Modjaji's drums and his maleness rose within him, the very heat of it like nothing his wildest, most erotic fantasies had ever conjured up. Mickey Spillane hadn't mentioned this part, this sudden overwhelming paralysis, when only one part of you seemed to work, draining the strength and heat from all the other parts so that the sum of everything became an urgent, blinding desire.

Harriet pulled her head away slowly, breaking the contact carefully, as though too sudden a movement might shatter something; the air around them, time, movement, distance, the kiss itself. 'When you said, "That's the only way you're going to hit me, shithead!" that was the moment . . . that was the moment I fell in love with you,' she said.

Peekay looked confused. 'Huh?'

'When Peter Best fouled you after Hymie had called the end of the round, the first day we met, that's what you said after he'd hit you. That was the moment!' Harriet began to unbutton the cardigan Peekay was wearing. It was cold in the studio and she'd made him put it on after he'd posed for a while with his torso bare. 'This old cardigan of Daddy's, it doesn't suit you at all,' she said, slipping it over his shoulders.

Peekay's arms came up to her, pulling her against him and holding her. 'Oh, oh, Harriet you're so beautiful, please, please can we make love?' His face was buried in her hair, which smelt clean and slightly perfumed.

Harriet pushed him away gently and rose, her legs still straddling the saw horse. Then she smiled a wicked little smile and lifted her arms so that Peekay could remove her sweater. Peekay stood up, oblivious of his erection, and pulled the sweater over Harriet's head, whereupon Harriet swivelled her torso so that her back was facing Peekay, her bra strap firmly clipped in the centre of a flawless, elegant back.

Peekay's hands suddenly trembled. 'Oh fuck! Push to the right . . . pull to the left! Shit no! That was when you worked from the front! Pull to the right, push to the left! Jesus!' The bra came away into Peekay's hands. For a moment he looked at either end of the bra strap, not quite believing his eyes. Then he let the bra fall from his fingers. He was in control. Harriet had turned back to face him, planting tiny kisses on his face, her fingers working at his belt buckle. Peekay's hands rose and cupped her wondrous breasts, 'Oh, oh, Jesus!' They both stepped over the saw horse together and Peekay, removing one hand, dragged the large, colourful eider-down from it to the floor.

Fifteen

Prior to her brutalisation by Geldenhuis, Tandia had accepted Mama Tequila's right to work her on her back after she had completed high school. She had even thought of it as a perfectly legitimate way to earn sufficient money to pay her way through university. But after her experience with Geldenhuis she knew that, come what may, she could not be turned into a working girl. Not by anyone, not for anything. Tandia knew that the instinct which had made her bite Geldenhuis would assert itself again. It was the first time she had tasted hate and she now knew she could live with it. She understood fear and she now understood hate. She could exercise charm and power over those around her; this would have to be enough to survive in the hostile grown-up world she found herself in.

Dr Louis sought Tandia out whenever he visited Bluey Jay. He had become very attached to her and would encourage her by talking dreamily of her prospects. 'Tandia, you're the first of a new breed, the new Africa. The brain hasn't been called grey matter for nothing, you know! It has no colour bar. When your kind have shown the barbarians in Pretoria that you are intellectually just as sound, just as good as they are, they can no longer call you savages. One day we will have a new class system in South Africa, like the rest of the civilised world! A system based on a person's ability. You, my dear, will be one of the beautiful new South Africans.'

But one of the barbarians in Pretoria, the Minister, among other things, of Bantu Education, Doctor Hendrik Verwoerd, was taking no such chances. Not too long after Dr Louis had his dream, Verwoerd invented a new little kink in the Bantu educational system: 'The Bantu is inferior. Science has proved his brain size is smaller than the whites. Therefore they cannot hope to compete with the white man!' To prove this, the all-white parliament passed the Bantu Education Act. It forbade the Bantu people from learning the same subjects at the same level as the white student and set up a separate curriculum which educated the blacks and the coloureds to virtual serfdom.

'Nice one, Verwoerd!' the white part of the nation cried in appreciation and tucked him into their minds as a future prime minister.

Girls were taught Domestic Science, a euphemism for washing and ironing, cooking and other domestic chores. They were taught arithmetic, but only sufficient to count the change when the missus sent them to the shops. Boys became carpenters and builders and all the other manual labour niceties which involve dirt, sweat and broken bones and which allow an overclass to be supported by an underclass of skilful hewers of wood and careful wielders of water.

In one hit, Doctor Verwoerd, one day to be the chief white honcho, the Prime Minister of South Africa, had smashed the Aristotelian concept that the mind shall decide the priorities for mankind and be the arena in which equality is decided.

The black people, trying to reach for the stars, were being educated with their faces pushed into the dirt. Skin tone was winning over grey matter. Dr Louis's barbarians were in full cry.

Dr Louis would hold Tandia's hand, as though she was a person he liked a lot. He was so genuine in his enthusiasm for his lovely dream that Tandia began to believe it too, if only for the hour he would spend with her going over her essays and cluck-clucking over her Latin tenses.

He was a Latin nut and was probably responsible for Tandia's high distinction in the subject. Over the months of her final year at high school he had often visited Tandia to work with her on her Latin and maths, and over the cramming weeks before her matriculation he would come almost every day. He was the first person she had called after receiving her matriculation results. Sonny Vindoo was second. 'Jolly, very good show, Miss Tandy, we are having a very big celebration and I am awarding you a new dress, any colour, any style, any material your very superior mind desires!'

Sonny Vindoo would often speak to her of Mahatma Gandhi, how he had come to South Africa to challenge the precepts of apartheid with the absolute logic of a fine legal mind; how, with ruthless authority and undeniable credentials, he presented to his opponents in the South African government under Jan Christiaan Smuts the absurdity of the concept of racial inferiority based on colour or creed. 'Miss Tandy, evil can withstand truth for a very, very long time. Evil is a very clever bugger, but in the end, truth, you can be sure, will prevail.' He would look directly at her through his pebble glasses: 'British Justice, my dear, it will win the day.' He said this in such a way that Tandia imagined British Justice as a troop of cavalry, a cloud of dust on the horizon, riding to the rescue of the coloureds and blacks of Africa. The fact that British Justice had hitherto shown very little truth and almost no equality for the black man, nor had it shown any inclination to lead the race relations of South Africa from darkness into the light, didn't seem to concern Sonny Vindoo in the least. He and Dr Louis were on the same side against the overwhelming forces of evil. They were both soft men in the hard fight which lay ahead. Tandia loved them dearly, but she knew, in the end, South Africa would need the hard-as-diamonds Juicey Fruit Mambos to rise up and crush the oppressor more than it would need the strawberry mousse of white liberalism. Truth and justice had failed to appear when needed and so had no further part to play in the settlement of the scores. She had felt the cold, remorseless steel and the ripping, cutting, sliding of a gun barrel inside her. She knew what it was going to take to win.

It was a long way to have travelled in fifteen months, and as Tandia left Patel's grave with its obscene new headstone, she wondered when she would return again. On a sudden impulse she tried to close the cast-iron gate that led into the cemetery but it sagged on its hinges; weed and grass had grown around its base, holding it firmly in place. Patel's influence was not over yet.

When Tandia reached the Packard, Juicey Fruit Mambo was now genuinely asleep in the back seat. She shook him awake. 'Come on, Juicey Fruit Mambo, we have to get the pies and sausage rolls for tonight.'

That night at Bluey Jay there was to be a party. From the end of the second week in January to the first Monday in February Mama Tequila closed Bluey Jay. With lots of money in their pockets, the working girls all went on holiday.

The party was held on the Friday prior to the Sunday when they left, and always began in the same way. Juicey Fruit Mambo would serve them all a glass of champagne, French no less, and Mama Tequila would make her speech.

This year her evening dress hugged her figure so tightly that it looked like a series of undulations laminated in scarlet velvet. The hemline and the plunging breastline were trimmed with pink ostrich feathers and she wore an elaborate Indian-style turban of the same material, with three pink ostrich feathers pluming towards the ceiling. From toe to top of ostrich feathers she stood seven feet tall and was undoubtedly the most imposing presence in the salon – which included the grand piano with its tummy open, festooned with pink-and-white balloons. Mama Tequila's fingers were encrusted with diamonds and a two-inch diamond choker around her neck flashed a distress beacon every time she moved her head.

The girls all gathered around her holding their champagne glasses. They too wore evening dresses. Tandia wore a simple peacock-blue shantung sheaf which fitted her figure closely and was cut high in the Chinese cheongsam style to reveal almost the full length of her left leg as she walked. It had been a Christmas gift from Sonny Vindoo, who had been back twice to make sure it fitted perfectly. Sarah and Hester, in a rare collaboration between Catholic and Pentecostal, had paid for her high heels, which they'd had covered with the same shantung so as to match her gown. Standing in the circle with the other girls, waiting for Mama Tequila to start the pre-holiday proceedings, she looked simply ravishing.

The painters, carpenters and plumbers, under the supervision of Mr Perfect Lay, who drove down from Pietermaritzburg twice a week to supervise them, were due to start work on the following Monday, after the drapes and the carpets had been removed for cleaning and the upholsterer had checked the couches and chairs for repairs. Mama Tequila liked Bluey Jay to commence business each year looking and feeling brand new, a house refreshed. The night when the girls kissed the working year goodbye was known as Frog Friday.

The rules for Frog Friday were simple: the girls could drink as much as they liked, get as drunk as they liked and, in the morning, sleep as long as they liked. All day Sunday, taxis would arrive from town to take them to Durban Central to catch their trains to wherever they were going. It was a day of kissing and crying, of sudden panics, things packed, unpacked, decided upon, decided against, outfits changed, changed again and then returned to the original. The best part of the working girl's holiday might well have been the excitement of getting ready to leave.

Mama Tequila held her glass above her head. 'Okay, man, let us begin. A toast to us all and also to Bluey Jay!'

'Us and Bluey Jay!' the girls all chorused.

'And Juicey Fruit Mambo!' Tandia added.

They all turned to see Juicey Fruit standing behind them in his tuxedo and pink bow tie. He was shaking his head, suddenly embarrassed by the attention.

'Juicey Fruit, where's your glass?' Jasmine said.

Putting down her own, she hurried over and, taking up a champagne glass, filled it. When she handed it to Juicey Fruit Mambo, he shuffled his feet and smiled and looked acutely ill at ease.

'A toast to Edward King George Juicey Fruit Mambo, the pride of Zululand!' Mama Tequila shouted.

'The pride of Zululand!' they all joined in.

Juicey Fruit Mambo lifted the wide-rimmed glass and, opening his huge mouth like Bluto in a Popeye cartoon, managed to empty the entire glass down his throat without it ever touching his lips. The girls all clapped and Juicey Fruit grinned, his two gold incisors shining.

'So now, we here again to begin another Frog Friday. One more year has passed and we still here, we still the best whorehouse in the world!' Mama Tequila appeared to glance behind her to the entrance to her salon, as though she expected someone to appear. 'You hear that, Mr Minister for Injustice! We still here and we going strong, man, like the bladdy blue train!'

'I'll drink to that!' Sarah shouted, and upended her glass.

'Me also!' Hester echoed, and did the same thing.

'Yeah!' the girls all shouted, throwing their heads back and emptying their glasses.

'Keep the champagne coming, Juicey Fruit Mambo,' Mama Tequila ordered. 'But seriously, my dears, let me say a few things I got on my mind before you's all get sozzled, hey?'

They all quietened down and Mama Tequila waited until Juicey Fruit Mambo had refilled her glass before continuing. 'Firstly I got to say you all good whores. The best! I couldn't ask for better. Except for Tandy. Jesus! She never going to make a whore, I'm telling you that, for sure!' They all laughed, and Tandia blushed violently.

'She got too much brains to be a whore, Mama T!' Doreen laughed. 'You can't have no whore speaking Latin and algebra!'

'Ag man, you mad! Algebra is not a language!' Marie said.

'It's like doing sums, only harder, stuff like A plus B equals something else you never heard of to the square root, jong!'

'A plus B equals Tandia never going to be a square root!' Mama Tequila cackled and the room broke up again. 'Now shurrup everybody! I haven't said nothing of what I'm going to say to you yet!' She emptied her glass again and turned, waving it. 'Where's that cheeky bladdy kaffir?' she said, joking, 'Juicey Fruit Mambo, a person could die of thirst around here. Keep the champagne coming, you hear!' The big black man, laughing at the insult, hurried over and filled Mama Tequila's glass. Mama Tequila took the bottle from his hands. 'You see what it says on this bottle? Veuve Clicquot. You know what means that in frog language? It means the Widow Clicquot. I'm telling you, man, that Mrs Veuve Clicquot that some dame! Her husband passes away (God rest his soul), next thing you know she's having a party with her own name on the champagne. Now that class, you hear! In any book, that first class! That the kind of woman whose champagne we like to drink.'

Mama Tequila was getting pretty tipsy, which meant she'd been toasting the Widow Clicquot all afternoon. 'Okay, okay, listen, ladies! On Sunday you all going far and wide to have a damn good holiday. You got a handbag full of money and you all got a good time to give away for free,' she burped. 'Now, that the first thing I want to talk about. Don't give no free pussy to no one, you hear! You want to know why? Okay, I'll tell you why. A whore got to have some respect for herself.' She looked around the room, her glance seeming to take in each of the girls. 'And don't give it to a bright boy or a jazz man and also no coloured who wear a big fedora and drive a convertible because, man, you know where they been and it isn't where you want to go which is straight to Dr "VD" Suluman when you get back.' Mama Tequila stretched her forefinger and thumb wide. 'Which is a needle this long in your bum every day for a week! That all I want to say on the question of loving. So now you can have some more champagne and . . .' She turned to Juicey Fruit Mambo. 'Go see if the big surprise arrive yet.'

The girls were surprised. Mama Tequila's Frog Friday wasn't a party in the traditional sense with proper men. If a person wasn't one of the girls at Bluey Jay and didn't get drunk it could be pretty boring really. But, for the eight working girls at Bluey Jay, it was an occasion buoyed up by the prospect of going on holidays and this, along with the French champagne, was enough to get the party going. But this year things had been different.

The Geldenhuis incident with Tandia had left them all fearful in the weeks leading up to Frog Friday and had dampened down much of the anticipation the girls felt about the end of the working year. It wasn't something they spoke about much, even to each other. It was something they felt, a dark, private shadow which hung over their future. Bluey Jay was a way of life, but also it was a tenure which promised to lead to a normal life with a man and kids and a home of their own. Each of them had a dream and Tandia because of what she'd done to Geldenhuis, had put this dream in jeopardy. They felt angry and betrayed, not really as much by Tandia but more by Mama Tequila herself. Mama Tequila had seen the opportunity to compromise Geldenhuis, which was fine and all right, but she'd risked them all in the process by using a person any of the girls could have told her was not up to the task.

For her part Mama Tequila was aware of this. She accepted that she'd played it the wrong way. She'd been too anxious to compromise the policeman, to get enough dirt on him to ensure her own survival. There were other ways open to her. A quiet word in the Detective Sergeant's ear by Dr Louis, for she still had his examination notes from when Tandia had come to Bluey Jay, would probably have discouraged him, for a while anyway.

Geldenhuis had too much to lose. He was a local hero, a national sporting identity and a police officer who had been brought to the favourable attention of the Minister of Justice. His career was on the up and up; all he had to do was keep his nose clean and, sooner rather than later, he'd find himself in Pretoria hitting the big time.

It wouldn't have taken a lot of pressure to keep him at arm's length. But Mama Tequila couldn't resist nailing him once and for all. She didn't like him and had stupidly allowed this to be a factor in her decision to sacrifice Tandia. Now she'd have to be very careful with the girls or her mistake could destroy her. With the amended Immorality Act three years in existence prostitution had been driven underground; the girls in it were mostly black crud or lazy white sluts who were badly trained with a booze problem or a pill or hashish habit, or all three. She knew her chances of recruiting a new line-up such as the present one at Bluey Jay was virtually impossible.

Every year at Christmas Mama Tequila handed them their post office books with the money they'd made for the year. Every year on their return from holidays she started a new book for each of them. Now she had nothing with which to hold them; they were all fully paid up. Whores are naturally superstitious, and, if they thought their luck had run out at Bluey Jay, they might just call it a day and stay away. Sarah would come back, of course, because she was being trained to run the house. But then, on the other hand, if she felt there might be no house to run, she too might not return.

Johanna, a girl from a small country town in the Northern Transvaal, who normally didn't say very much and just got on with her job, brought all their fears into the open. 'Maybe I'm stupid, jong, but I'm not so stupid I don't know that what happened to Geldenhuis isn't finish! That bastard is a Boer and a policeman; that's the worst combo there is! I'm telling you, man, our troubles, they just beginning!'

Mama Tequila knew she was going to have to turn on one hell of a party to win back her authority so they would trust her sufficiently to return after the holidays.

'Sarah done a poem!' Doreen shouted. She was a girl who had started life, like Jasmine, in the slums of Cape Town's District Six, and she was notorious at Bluey Jay for the fact that she couldn't hold her liquor. She was already quite tipsy.

'On the peeano!' Doreen added, and Hettie and Colleen rushed over to the grand piano. Removing the balloons from its interior, they gave each of the girls several balloons to hold and closed the lid. Sarah sat down on the piano stool, removed her high heels and then, helped by Hettie and Colleen, climbed onto the top of the grand. She fumbled in the bodice of her gown for a moment and produced a small sheet of folded paper from her bra.

'Juicey Fruit Mambo! More frog juice for the poet!' Mama Tequila demanded. But the huge black man appeared to have left the room. Hester picked up the bottle of champagne.

'Hey! Where's my glass?' Sarah asked.

Jasmine handed Sarah's glass to Hester who filled it and passed it up to her. Sarah held the glass out in front of her slightly above her eyeline.

'I dedicate this noble poem to Mama Tequila and all the working girls and also Juicey Fruit Mambo!' She smiled, 'And, oh yes! To the best lover in South Africa, the one and only, transil-meddle-tated, Mr Dine-o-Mite!' They all cheered and sipped from their glasses.

Sarah took a generous gulp of champagne and handed her glass to Jasmine. 'But the main person I dedicate my poem to is Tandy.' She looked around at all the girls and at Mama Tequila.

That one will one day make a bladdy good madam, Mama Tequila thought to herself.

Sarah continued. 'We very proud today with what you done, Tandy, being in the paper and all with top marks in everything, Latin and algebra and hard stuff like that. I'm telling you, to know a person like you, with so much brains a person's head could burst, is a very big honour.'

Tandia buried her head in Jasmine's shoulder, totally embarrassed by the sudden attention. 'But being clever an' all, that's one thing, but being brave that a altogether different thing.' Sarah paused and looked around at them all again in a melodramatic fashion. She was a little tipsy, but so were they all and her longish pauses didn't seem to worry them. 'Tandy done the bravest thing I ever heard of in my whole life as a working girl. Something we all thought about lots of times before, when some bastard is giving a person a bad time. So here is my poem,' she said finally. Holding the scrap of paper almost at arm's length, Sarah cleared her throat and commenced to read.

> *Roses are red*
> *Violets is blue*
> *Geldenhuis was bit*
> *So now he can't screw!*

The laughter started slowly in Mama Tequila and built like a rumbling volcano, shaking her to the foundation, gushing from her, a veritable explosion of mirth. 'Ho ... ho ... ho ... hee ... hee ... hee, snort-snort, hee-hee-hee ... Oh my God! Ho ... ho ... hee-hee-hee ...' Juicey Fruit rushed to support her as her knees gave way, but still she laughed, a massive scarlet chortling blancmange of heaving mirth. The girls came to help her as Tandia pushed the piano stool under Mama Tequila's bottom to take her sagging weight.

It was the sort of laughter they all needed. And Tandia knew that she too was expected to laugh. Sarah had, after all, done it for her. Tandia was not unaware of the unspoken disapproval of the working girls, and Sarah's poem had been a gift of generosity. The Geldenhuis incident had been with them all. Now, at last, it was out, brought to the surface by a silly, childish little poem which had somehow made it all warm and safe again.

Mama Tequila knew that she couldn't have asked for anything better, and she now realised how much strain she herself had been under. It was good to laugh and she let it all roll out of her. At last she was sufficiently in possession of herself to talk, but she was afraid that if she spoke in her natural voice her emotion might show, so she slipped into client vernacular. 'Sarah, honey, you the best, you hear? You da poet lorrikeet!' She started to chuckle softly. 'Say it again, Sarah, do it one more time, baby!'

Sarah held the poem out and started to read again, but before she had completed the first line Mama Tequila was off again. The poem was a trigger all right! She raised her arms above her head to clap her hands together and suddenly her red velvet gown split from under the armpit down to her thighs. This caused fresh gales of laughter. 'Ho . . . ho . . . ho . . . hee . . . hee-hee, I think I going to wet my pants! Sarah, Mr Dine-o-mite, he ain't going to get no pussy for this dress, you hear?'

Frog Friday, despite the anxiety they had felt leading up to it, was showing all the signs of being an all-time success. Hester and Marie, each taking an arm, led Mama Tequila across the room towards the door. As they reached the entrance to the salon Juicey Fruit Mambo appeared. 'It is all ready, madam,' he said.

Mama Tequila fumed back into the room and addressed the girls. 'Go now into the other salon, everyone! In there is my big going-away surprise!' Turning to Hester and Marie she said, 'You too, darlings! Juicey Fruit Mambo will help me to my room. Go on, go now, enjoy your party. Hurry, jong. If you get there fast you can take first pick!'

Hester's scream of delight as she entered the client salon made all the other girls come running. Standing around the room were eight of the best built hunks of super manhood she'd ever laid her eyes on. Their arms bulged and their pectoral muscles smashed aside the buttons on their shirts to reveal chests and stomach muscles a girl could die for. Hester, with four or five of Madam Veuve Clicquot's special thigh-warming tonics under her belt, was willing to commit suicide on the spot. She grabbed at the biggest, horniest man she could see. Doreen did the same and soon every man in the room had a girl draped on his arm. This was Mama Tequila's special treat: beautiful, taut, young coloured men who looked like Adonis to make up for all the wheezing and burping, the pot bellies and the limp little willies they'd had to coax to life during the year. Or, as Hester had once said, 'Some, they an insult to a one-eyed snake, man! They just blind worms with a swollen head!'

Tandia, for whom no man had been allocated, walked over to the pianola and, sitting down, started to pedal it. Most of the tunes were well-known *boere musiek* numbers, old favourites that caused the feet to tap and the blood to rise. In about five minutes flat the place was jumping.

Juicey Fruit Mambo dispensed beer from bottles buried in tin tubs of crushed ice, and the two coloured women from Durban appeared from the kitchen carrying pies and sausage rolls and an assortment of good things men like to eat: sausages and chops and big, juicy steaks. The girls were swung and danced and picked up and fussed over until the shirts of the men clung to their massive chests. Sarah removed the shirt of her partner and the other girls soon followed suit. It was a sweating, laughing, dancing, hugging, swinging, lifting party and Marie told Hettie she thought she'd passed away and woken up in heaven.

And then Johanna got the gramophone going and the lights dimmed and the night softened to Nat King Cole's 'Mona Lisa' and the couples drew closer, chest and breast and breathing heavier as Frank Sinatra stroked them with 'Bewitched, Bothered and Bewildered' and 'The Lady is a Tramp'. One by one, they danced off the floor and up the blackwood stairway, each girl with a man in tow and a lot of loving mischief on her mind. The beautiful young man carrying Jasmine up the stairs stopped halfway and said:

'Man, if I die now, I'll kill myself!'

As parties go, there have been bigger parties, louder and more colourful ones with live music and more spectacular entertainment, certainly more drunken parties or parties for more important people, but Frog Friday 1954 was, in its own small way, one of which the human race had a right to be proud. No one threw up or grew violent or felt left out or unrequited. At two a.m., Juicey Fruit Mambo knocked on the various doors to tell the boys their taxis were waiting. They appeared soon afterwards and each wore a smile and a stunned look in his eyes.

As for the girls? The widow Clicquot could not have done a better job. Everything the French sailor had told Mama Tequila about her champagne proved to be true. Mama Tequila's eight working girls had been transil-meddle-tated right into heaven.

But all this happened long after Tandia had been replaced at the piano pedal by one of the coloured ladies from Durban. Halfway through the evening, after the men had all eaten, Juicey Fruit Mambo handed over the task of serving drinks to the other one and left the party. Some twenty minutes later he returned to tell Tandia she was required in Mama Tequila's salon.

'What is it, Juicey Fruit Mambo?'

He grinned, his gold incisors gleaming. 'I think you be very, very happy, Missy Tandy, big *indaba* for you!' he giggled, but would say no more.

Tandia stopped in the girls' waiting room and patted her face with a towel and added a touch of lipstick. She couldn't imagine what Mama Tequila might want. Frog Friday had been the biggest day of her life, the day she matriculated with honours and, in her mind, started her life properly and truly. From now on she was beautiful and brand new, no longer the daughter of Natkin Patel, known in the best white circus, but Tandia Patel, a black *slimmetjie* who was her very own person. And for just a moment, as she opened the door to Mama Tequila's salon, she wasn't scared at all.

She was surprised and delighted to see Dr Louis and Sonny Vindoo. Her surprise was even greater when she recognized the round, squat shape of Old Coetzee with his puffy eyes and whisky nose, his untidy suit jacket open as usual, showing his waistcoat with his gold watch chain looped across his big belly. With him stood a very tall, thin man in a dark suit with perfectly round glasses which sat halfway down his long, sharp nose. His steel-grey hair, plastered down with hair oil, was parted down the centre just the way Patel had worn his. His narrow face had a disappearing chin and it looked as though he didn't laugh a lot. In his dark grey serge suit and white shirt he needed only to stand on one leg and he would have been Icabod Crane.

Sonny Vindoo rushed to welcome her. 'My dear, dear, Tandia, how very beautiful you are looking!' He giggled, 'I must be having the name of your dressmaker at once, my goodness, yes!'

Old Coetzee pulled himself up to his full height which

wasn't much bigger than five foot six inches. '*Magtig*! You are a pretty girl, man!' he said, to Mama Tequila's surprise. He was an important, upstanding Afrikaner and she couldn't remember ever hearing a Boer paying a compliment such as this to a coloured person. What a waste, Mama Tequila sighed; she would be worth a king's ransom if she worked on her back.

'Please, everybody sit!' Mama Tequila indicated the comfortable high-backed Victorian armchairs which had been drawn into a semicircle round a low coffee table with ball-and-claw legs. 'Juicey Fruit Mambo will bring drinks.'

'You must come and meet Professor Ryder, the head of the Law School at Natal University,' Sonny Vindoo said. 'And, of course already you are knowing Magistrate Coetzee.'

'Howzit, Tandia,' Dr Louis called, using the casual slang expression to ease her nerves.

'Good evening, Magistrate Coetzee, good evening, Dr Louis,' Tandia said politely, trying hard not to sound nervous. Her heart was thumping. The thin man, who looked like one of the marabou storks Juicey Fruit Mambo had once identified for her on a walk along the river, was from the university.

In her pink gymslip behind the bar it was easy to know the role she was required to play. She was Miss Tandy with the beautiful smile who kept the drinks coming, the shy, ingenuous part of a double act with Mama Tequila. But what was she here? What was expected of her? She knew instinctively that she was required to impress Professor Ryder, who didn't look like the sort of man who was going to be a pushover charmwise. There could only be one reason why Sonny Vindoo and Dr Louis were here, though how Old

Coetzee fitted in she couldn't imagine. He'd paid her a compliment, which was a very strange thing for a man like him to do.

In her mind she saw him standing to rigid attention, the top part of him fully dressed right down to his watch chain, but with his trousers around his ankles. Across his left shoulder was the old Boer Mauser that usually hung on the wall directly above the blackwood stairs. Sarah knelt on the floor in front of him.

Sarah had accidentally come upon the solution to Old Coetzee's erectile problem when he'd taken down the old rifle and, with tears in his brandy-bright eyes, stroked it lovingly. 'Miss Sarah, this is a Mauser 8mm carbine, it's what nearly beat the *verdoemde rooinekke* in the Boer War! This is the rifle that defended the *republiek!* I worship this rifle! With five thousand more Boers on horseback and this carbine, I'm telling you man, Queen Victoria would be crying tears in her English teapot and *Oom Paul* would still be president of the *republiek!*'

Sarah couldn't be sure about Queen Victoria but she knew for sure Oom Paul, the first president of the Transvaal Republic, had been dead for more than fifty years. 'That's very nice, Magistrate Coetzee, if you want you can bring it with you,' Sarah suggested, in an attempt to coax the old bugger into the pink room so that she could begin the arduous task of bringing him to gratification. Old Coetzee lumbered after Sarah, following her into the room like an excited schoolboy.

Thinking only to amuse him Sarah had commanded, 'General Coetzee, Commander of the Boer Republican Army, friend of President Oom Paul Kruger himself, stand to attention!' To Sarah's surprise Coetzee had immediately shouldered the old German rifle and stood to rigid attention beside the bed. Sarah was not one to miss an opportunity and she'd quickly slipped her hands under his waistcoat and undone his belt and trousers, pulling them down to his ankles. 'Watch careful as anything, you hear? The British are everywhere, jong!' she commanded him. Old Coetzee's eyes darted around the room as Sarah went to work on him. Occasionally, he'd remove the Mauser from his shoulder and fire an imaginary shot. 'Got him, got the *verdoemde rooinek* right between the eyes!' he shouted quickly, working the bolt action of the old rifle to eject the imaginary cartridge case before placing it back over his shoulder. In a surprisingly short time, Old Coetzee had risen to the occasion and before you could say, 'God save the Boer Republic!', she'd finished him off with French.

As Mama Tequila and the other three men sat down, Tandia extended her hand to Professor Ryder. 'How do you do, sir.' It was a brave thing to do; coloured girls don't shake hands with important white people who might think they were cheeky or trying to be the same as a white or something. Immediately he'd released her hand she began to worry.

But Professor Ryder didn't seem to mind. He sat down and crossed his long legs and looked at Tandia over the top of his glasses, which appeared to have slipped halfway down his long nose. 'Dr Rabin tells me you know your Latin, Tandia. Certainly a high distinction in your matriculation exam is very commendable.' He cleared his throat, reached up and brought his glasses back to rest on the bridge of his nose. 'We'll begin with something simple, okay? I want you to conjugate a few curly irregular verbs. The future perfect tense of the verb "to use", if you please?'

Ah! thought Tandia, he's like Dr Louis, always a puzzle trying to trick me with a deponent verb, passive in form but active in meaning. She had learned from Mama Tequila the value of a little drama, and now she gave the lanky professor a dazzling smile where he might have expected a serious schoolgirl demeanour. '*Usus ero, usus eris, usus erit. Usi erimus, usi eritis, usi erunt,*' she said, to Dr Louis's obvious relief.

'Very good Tandia.' The professor appeared to be thinking. 'What about the perfect tense in the subjunctive?'

Tandia completed this request as effortlessly as the first. '*Usus sim, usus sis, usus sit. Usi simus, Usi sitis, usi sint.*'

Professor Ryder grinned. 'That's the easy bit over. Now let's try you on Virgil's *Aeneid*, the fourth part.'

Tandia could feel the blood rising into her face and her mouth was suddenly dry. She regretted her previous aplomb. Virgil's Aeneid IV was Dr Louis's territory and, to please him, she'd studied the Latin poet more diligently than she was required to do at school, even after a while getting to quite like him. But she wasn't sure what the professor would expect from her.

'*Dulces exuviae, dum fata deusque sinebant, accipite hanc animam, meque his exsolvite curs;* "sweet relics, sweet so long as God and Destiny allowed, now receive my soul and free me from this suffering",' Professor Ryder recited, making each word sound as though it was delivered from a lectern.

The relief Tandia felt was palpable. She knew this passage was part of the Queen of Carthage's death soliloquy. She knew the two lines that followed, and quoted them in a quiet but firm voice which belied the terror she felt. '*Vixi, et, quem dederat cursum fortuna, peregi;*

et nunc magna mei sub terras ibit imago. "I have lived the life and finished the course Fortune has allotted me. Now my wraith shall pass in state to the world below."'

The professor followed with another passage from Aeneid IV. It was one of Dr Louis's favourites and she had no trouble completing it.

'Very good! "*Hunc ego Diti sacrum iussa fero, teque isto corpore solvo,*"' Ryder quoted, his voice deep and over-projected; he seemed to be enjoying himself and Tandia was beginning to feel embarrassed. It was gobbledy-gook to Sonny Vindoo and Mama Tequila, and probably to Old Coetzee as well.

Tandia knew that these were the last lines of Book IV but she didn't know them nearly as well as the other two passages. Her mind went blank. It was a four-line stanza and the last lines had simply disappeared from her memory. 'Ah ... ah ...' She looked at Dr Louis, who seemed to be urging her on with his eyes, the fingers of both his hands spread wide.

'It is my favourite, man! Don't finish it, Tandia, let me please. *Omnis et una dilapsus calor, atque in ventos vita recessit;* "At once all the warmth fell away and the life passed into the moving air."'

'My goodness me, that was very well done!' Sonny Vindoo said, clapping his hands in applause. 'Miss Tandy could perhaps complete it prettier, but I'm telling you, no better!'

Professor Ryder laughed. 'We shall never know! You have some very good friends, Tandia Patel. Did you know that?'

'No, sir ... yes, sir! I mean, I don't know, sir.' Tandia looked up at Professor Ryder and he could see she was very close to tears, the strain of his examination clearly showing. 'Please, sir, I mean, Professor, please let me go to your university? I will work hard, I will do anything!'

'Ja, I can tell you that true, Professor. Tandy can cook and clean and you can ask her anything, she knows it right off, anything you want to know. The hardest stuff you can think, she knows it already,' Mama Tequila tapped her head, 'it right here inside her *kop*!'

'Ja, she's very clever, the most clever you can find anywhere, but I think there are some other problems, hey, Professor?' Sonny Vindoo had sensed that Ryder was troubled and that he had hoped to gain a slight advantage by compromising Tandia with his impromptu examination.

'No problems! She will pay, we don't want no charity, you hear!' Mama Tequila's voice was indignant.

'That's not the question, Madam Tequila,' Professor Ryder said. 'The girl's marks are sufficient to get her a scholarship to our university college for non-whites, I'm sure I can help her there, though I regret there is no law faculty. Perhaps Fort Hare?' He paused and clasped his hands together in front of him. 'It's ... well frankly, it's just damned awkward in my own faculty!'

'You mean because Tandia's a coloured?' Doctor Louis asked quietly.

Ryder looked uncomfortable and glanced at Tandia. 'Perhaps Tandia should leave the room?'

'No, Professor, she a big girl, leaving this room not going to change her colour!' Mama Tequila said.

'I wasn't simply referring to the student's colour. There are other complications. She's a female, and well, er ... law for a woman?' Mama Tequila's outburst had added to his obvious discomfort. Tandia could sense he was beginning to wonder how he'd been persuaded to come to Bluey Jay in the first place.

'Okay, let me say something!' It was Old Coetzee who spoke. 'In this room is Mr Vindoo, he's an Indian and Mama Tequila who is a coloured person and Dr Louis who is a Jew and you, Professor, who are a Britisher and me, I am a Boer, an Afrikaner, but, in the end, we are all South Africans, you hear.'

Just then Juicey Fruit Mambo entered carrying a tray with ice water and two decanters, one of Scotch and the other brandy. He'd also opened a bottle of cocacola and added it with a glass to the tray for Tandia. He placed the tray down on a small coffee table and, as quietly as he'd entered he turned and walked back towards the door, giving Tandia a quick, encouraging flash of the gold incisors as he left. Old Coetzee pointed to the departing black man, 'And the Bantu, we like to forget the Bantu, who are also South African, not just Zulu or N'debele, Sotho or Shangaan or Pondo, but just as much, maybe even more, South Africans than us.'

Tandia moved over to the tray and started to pour drinks for everyone. She knew all their preferences, except that of Professor Ryder. She placed her hand on the Scotch bottle and he nodded, then on the water jug and he shook his head and pointed to the ice tray. Hiding behind the bottle of coke she found the tiny glass containing green chartreuse which Juicey Fruit Mambo had poured ready for Sonny Vindoo.

As Tandia brought him a second Scotch, Professor Ryder rose from his chair. He took the glass from her absently. 'Magistrate Coetzee, I am, I must say, enormously impressed by your perspicacity.' He paused, preparing to make his point. 'But I must insist, you have missed the central point, the simple question of biology. My people have been in Natal for a hundred and ten years, ever since the 1840 settlers. We, the British South Africans, realised just like the Boer South Africans that miscegenation was not the way to go forward, that the mix of black and white didn't advance the noble savage or appreciate the white man. In fact the opposite was true . . .' He stopped suddenly and coloured violently, turning to look at Mama Tequila. 'I do apologise, Mama Tequila, what I have just said must seem unforgivable to you. I beg your forgiveness, I apologise.'

Mama Tequila laughed. 'What are you apologising for, Professor? Embarrassing me? Or for telling what you think is the truth?'

'Well, er . . .'

But Mama Tequila continued. 'I am a coloured person, that not a person in South Africa. A black is a person, and a white is a person. But I am a non-person. For the Afrikaner I am his guilt. He calls me a *Hotnot*, because he says I'm from the Bushman and the Hottentot, or a Cape Malay or even round here in Durban, a Mauritian coloured or a *Maasbieker*, who is a coloured person who supposed to come from Mozambique. Always I am something else from somewhere else, not what happened when his daddy or his *oupa* lay down with a black kaffir girl when the *ounooi* has gone to visit her sister in another *dorp*.

'For the Englishman I am an inferior non-person, a mistake for which he thinks only the Afrikaner is responsible, a *boere* bastard! How come there are four million non-people like me in this country, answer for me that, hey? I'm telling you something, Professor, I am the result of the hate and the fear and the greed Magistrate Coetzee just talked about. Three hundred years of hate and fear. So what am I? I'm going to tell you now! You the Britisher! You the Afrikaner! You the Jew! You the Indian! You know what I am. I am the child of South Africa. Not the non-person, the *real* person! You hear, I, me, this person who is sitting in this big chair, Sophie Van der Merwe, born in District Six on August 28, 1889, in Cape Town. I am the only *real* South African!' Mama Tequila was crying quietly. Her tears, gathering mascara on the way, ran black down her rouged cheeks. Professor Ryder sat down abruptly, as though he had been filled with air and now was suddenly and unexpectedly deflated.

Sonny Vindoo got up from his chair and moved over to join Tandia, who ran over to comfort Mama Tequila. 'Please, take no notice, I am just a stupid old woman, a *hout kop*,' she sniffed. 'Tandia, more brandy for Magistrate Coetzee, also Scotch for the doctor and the professor.'

'No, no I'm fine,' Dr Louis said, placing his hand over his glass.

'Go sit, Sonny,' Mama Tequila said, pushing the little Indian gently from her. She smiled through her tears. 'I don't know from where comes these stupid words, I am jus' a old coloured woman who doesn't know no better, man! Now it my turn to apologise, Professor.'

Old Coetzee rose from his chair a little unsteady on his feet, but when he spoke his voice was quiet and reasoned. 'What we have just heard, maybe it will not change any of us. I am a Boer, an Afrikaner, my mind says one thing, my heart says altogether another thing. We, *die volk,* we a stubborn people, a stupid people of the heart. I don't think we will ever learn this simple lesson.'

He polished off the remainder of the brandy and

handed his glass to Tandia, indicating with his open palms that he did not require a refill.

Mama Tequila, who had recovered from her lapse, hoped to hell he would remember Sarah was not available tonight and would go home quietly.

The magistrate removed his gold hunter from his fob pocket and glanced down at it. 'Professor, it is getting late and you are our guest, so I will spare you further rhetoric. It is a strange little fraternity here tonight, very unexpected, hey? I'm sure you will appreciate that what has been said in this room is private. How is it that a man can go his whole life and never sit down and talk in a group such as this one? The true terror of apartheid is that it separates our minds, we do not know each other's thoughts. We all have too much to lose by loose talk. But I just got this one more thing to say. It concerns Tandia Patel, who as you can see is a coloured person. A non-person just like Mama Tequila. She is also a *real* child of South Africa and I must add, as an old man of course, if all our children were as beautiful we would be the best-looking race of people on earth.'

Tandia felt herself blushing violently. Old Coetzee continued. 'Today, out of a possible five hundred marks in five subjects in her matriculation exams, Tandia Patel obtained four hundred and eighty-one! Is this a non-mind in a non-person? Is this the inferior result of miscegenation? Or do you have a place in the Law faculty of your university for a beautiful, intelligent, real child of South Africa?'

Tandia could feel her heart pounding and her head seemed to fill with blood. She burned fiercely; then she grew as suddenly cold. She tried to hold herself rigid, but she seemed to have no control, and her entire body trembled as the professor spoke.

'Tandia Patel will be the first coloured female student to read Law at Natal University, that is my promise,' Professor Ryder said quietly.

Tandia brought her hands up to her face and burst into tears. She wasn't prepared for this moment. Her upbringing contained nothing in it which told her how to react. She panicked and turning on her heels rushed for the doorway. Pushing blindly through the door, she found herself in Juicey Fruit Mambo's arms. 'Oh, oh, Patel, daddy! I been accepted in the best white circus!' she wept.

The huge black man picked her up, his gold incisors flashing, and his smile seemed to disappear past his shot-away earlobe. 'Edward King George Juicey Fruit Mambo, we very happy for going to the university, Miss Tandy! We very smart combo, for sure!' He laughed, swinging her around again. 'Me, myself, I am cleaning for dat classroom and you, you learning to be big, big lawyer for de people so de white policeman he be very, very afraid!'

Sixteen

Peekay's first professional fight took place at the end of April. There had been a last-minute cancellation by an English boxer named Terry Cousins who was scheduled to fight Jacques Habib, a French Algerian welterweight, in a non-title major preliminary bout at Earl's Court. Cousins's trainer, Charlie Perkins, had called Dutch Holland to say that his fighter had come down with the 'flu and had asked him if he had a welter in his stable who could fill the bill. Dutch had seen the French Algerian fight on four previous occasions and felt that Peekay, despite his lack of experience in the professional ring, could take him – or at least make a damn good fight of it.

Holland was of the school who believed it wasn't such a bad thing if a boxer lost his first professional fight, providing always that he wasn't badly hurt in a mix-match. He wanted to see Peekay blooded; he'd never had a boxer near as good, but he needed to know just how good Peekay really was.

'A young boxer can have everything in the book, dance like Fred Astaire, fast as a bleedin' rat up a drainpipe, punch like Joe Louis, Einstein's flippin' brains, but it's what he does when he's too tired for fancy foot-work, too buggered to lift his arms and he's got one round to go with his opponent ahead on points. That's when you know if you've got a champ or a chump.'

Dutch had already taken Peekay into the professional ranks. Now he needed someone to put real pressure on the young South African and he felt that Jacques Habib, a tough and experienced professional once ranked number one in Europe and now a little past his prime, might be just the man to sort his lad out. If Peekay looked like taking a bad hiding he would throw in the towel. The press would lambast him for creating a mix-match and the British Boxing Commission would prob-ably hold an inquiry. But if Peekay survived it would be worth it. Even if he took a bad hiding from the Arab, provided he showed he had heart, he would still be good enough to get a crack at the British Empire title in a couple of years.

Hymie was concerned, but he trusted Holland's judgement and, as Peekay pointed out, by going higher up the ladder so early it would be that much quicker to get a shot at the world title.

Peekay had resolved to tell Hymie about Harriet and him after the fight. Apart from telling Harriet that he would confess to Hymie almost immediately, they hadn't discussed it. Peekay was anxious to avoid another blast from Harriet on the subject of her emo-tional independence. The mere use of the word 'confess' had raised her ire. 'You have nothing to confess! I don't belong to Hymie. You haven't stolen me. I belong to myself!' She'd stormed off in a huff, leaving Peekay scratching his head.

Harriet had called him a pompous ass and he sup-posed he was in a way. But he couldn't help feeling guilty and he knew he had to tell his friend. His reason for waiting until the fight was over was based on his knowledge of Hymie. Hymie would be anxious not to upset him before his first professional fight and so might too easily dismiss the affair. This would allow Peekay to get off lightly and perhaps, as a consequence, allow the issue to remain dormant and unresolved between them.

While Peekay hated the idea of hurting his friend, he felt himself morally obliged to take whatever scorn Hymie cared to dish out. He'd pinched his girl, and he was expecting Hymie to fire both barrels at him simultaneously.

Peekay knew he'd been a bit of a prick over the Odd Bodleian affair. After all, what Hymie had done wasn't so bad. He'd merely tried to make a point by using Peekay's childhood rather cleverly in an attempt to knit a hopelessly disparate bunch of chaps into a group of boxing supporters. It was a tall order even for Hymie, but by challenging him, Peekay had completely destroyed any chances he'd had of pulling it off.

Peekay was also aware that some people saw him as too perfect, too good at everything; now with Harriet, he'd be seen as the guy who got the girl. But he didn't see himself the way others did. Rather he knew he was the one person amongst them who had been soiled, who had been corrupted. Since he'd been a small child he'd spent his life trying to get the taste of shit out of his mouth.

Peekay was beginning to understand how powerful sex was as a weapon and how, if he wasn't terribly careful, it could come between him and his beloved friend, even if Hymie accepted his affair with Harriet. He loved Harriet with a passion, but a fair part of the passion began with his loins, whereas his feelings for

Hymie were born out of a steadfast friendship which had lasted longer than anything else in his life except his relationship with Doc. Not to have Hymie as his closest friend was unthinkable.

Peekay's final preliminary was at seven, an hour before the main event, a ten round light-heavyweight contest which, by coincidence, featured Peter Best's brother and a Nigerian boxer. Both were unbeaten and it promised to be a good fight, although Best, the British Empire title holder was expected to win.

Peekay's opponent, Habib, with thirty-two fights to his name, was a tough and respected welterweight who had won twenty-five of his fights, lost six and drawn one, though eighteen of his wins had been by knock-out. In his last fight he'd been narrowly beaten by an American negro stationed in Germany with the US Occupation Forces. The French Algerian, who at twenty-nine was a little past his prime as a fighter, was nevertheless still rated third in Europe and had to be considered very much the favourite against the unknown student from Oxford.

Such was Dutch Holland's reputation in the fight game, that Frank Mitchell, the boxing writer for the *Daily Express*, cautioned his readers to watch the young South African carefully. He commented:

> *Normally I'd be asking myself why the*
> *British Boxing Commisson was allowing a*
> *match-up between the experienced and still*
> *highly rated welterweight French Algerian*
> *Jacques Habib and an unknown young*
> *South African boxer who goes by the*
> *unlikely name of the Tadpole Angel. But*
> *with over twenty years' experience of the*

fight game, I have learned to respect the
judgement of the incomparable Dutch
Holland, who is handling the South
African boy. Holland would not have
brought the young fighter who, by the
way, is reading law at Oxford, against the
vastly more experienced French Algerian if
he wasn't expecting big things from him.
Holland is a trainer known for his caution
and has the reputation for bringing his
fighters along carefully.

Make no mistake, my money remains
firmly on the Frenchman from Algiers, who
may be a little past his prime but still
carries the best left hook in Europe – when
it connects. But I'll be watching the
Tadpole Angel very carefully too, and I
suggest fight fans do the same. You may
find it worthwhile catching an earlier tube
to Earl's Court to witness this six-rounder.

Hymie and Peekay arrived at Earl's Court just after six
to find Dutch Holland and Togger waiting for them.
Harriet and E.W. were there to meet them too.

'Dutch, we haven't mix-matched Peekay this time,
have we?' Hymie voiced the fears they all felt.

Dutch shrugged. 'I hope not, my son. I got a reputation to keep as well, you know.' He turned to Peekay,
speaking quietly. 'You and your manager better be off
to the dressing room. The fight's on in half an hour.
Togger wants to handle the bucket and sponge. That
orright with you?'

Peekay nodded and smiled at Togger who, with
Harriet and E.W., had moved closer, conscious of the

tension between the three men and relieved by Hymie's sudden laughter. Togger looked gratified. 'You won't regret the decision, Peekay. I learned me spongin' technique in a bleedin' Turkish Bath in a Soho club. I can bring a dead member to life with a soapy sponge.'

Peekay laughed at Togger's crudeness. He knew, though, that Togger was worried for him. Habib was a big name to be fighting first off. Peekay could feel the familiar tightening of his stomach, but this time the tension was worse than usual. He wasn't kidding himself, he was scared and suddenly he wasn't at all sure they hadn't made a terrible mistake going in at Habib's level.

After Peekay had changed into his boxing gear, Hymie bandaged his hands and slipped on his gloves, leaving them unlaced. They were waiting for a fight steward to call them to the ring. Then Hymie fished into the pocket of his sports jacket. 'Here, I've got something for you.' Peekay looked up as Hymie continued. 'A friend of yours gave it to me with specific instructions. I saw him last Christmas in Johannesburg.' Hymie imitated the soft tones of an African speaking English. 'Tell for my brother, always when he sits on the pot, he is so still, at this time when he waiting for the fight, he must wear for this, it will make him strong. It will make him the grandson of Shaka Zulu and the son of Dingane.'

Peekay, despite his pre-fight tension, laughed. 'Gideon! How is the cheeky bugger?'

Hymie handed him a single lion's tooth on a gold chain. 'It's one of the two he wears around his neck. He's given you half his own talisman.'

Peekay looked at Hymie, his eyes wide. 'It's an incisor tooth from the lion he killed as his initiation into manhood,' he said astonished. Then Peekay frowned, suddenly dismayed. 'He's put himself in terrible danger, breaking the spell of his own protection by halving it.'

Hymie looked sharply up at Peekay. Christ, Peekay believes it, he thought to himself.

Peekay slipped the chain with the lion's tooth over his head. He was very close to tears. 'Hymie, what a wonderful thing to do!'

'Mandoma loves you, Peekay, he's your Zulu brother.'

'And the chain? It's heavy, it's gold isn't it?'

'It's from your Polish brother,' Hymie said, attempting to sound flippant. 'Your Zulu brother's also got one.' He laughed suddenly. 'We're all linked you see. I'm the big mouth and you two are the teeth!'

Just then a ring steward entered to tell them that the previous fight had one round to go. Then Togger appeared. 'Oi, I just seen the Arab! Mean-looking geezer, he's bouncin' up and down, frowin' punches like he's trying to get out the dressin' room by punchin' down the bleedin' wall!'

Hymie draped the electric-blue silk dressing gown, with the words 'The Tadpole Angel' embroidered on the back, over Peekay's shoulders. He also draped a small white hand towel around Peekay's neck as they left.

The lightweight contest before Peekay's fight was coming to an end and the crowd was excited. The two boxers, a young Irishman named Terry O'Grady, whose nose was bleeding badly, and a Cuban who called himself Sugar Boy Romero were going at each other hammer and tongs, each hoping the final round would give them the decision. The bell went and the referee, taking the judges' cards, announced the Cuban the winner. It was a result half the crowd agreed with, the other half, most of them seemingly Irish, booed loudly and stamped their feet.

Peekay could feel the tension in his stomach building further. He felt slightly nauseous and the voices around him were beginning to blur as he started to concentrate, turning inwards, his ears tuned into Hymie and Dutch, as though they were on a special frequency band in his head. He climbed into the ring. He was an unknown and not an Englishman, but as a colonial the crowd gave him a good cheer. You could sense they expected the outcome in favour of the tough and seasoned Habib. Peekay raised his right hand briefly in acknowledgement and, moving over to his corner stool, sat on the pot.

Habib had fought four times in England before and was known to the crowd as a fighter who went hard all the way. Many of them had seen him knock out his four British opponents and he'd earned their respect. A big cheer went up as he entered the ring. He raised his gloves, touching them above his head, and walked around the ring acknowledging their support. As he passed the seated Peekay he lowered a glove and clubbed him harmlessly, though somewhat arrogantly, over the ear, hoping to intimidate the young fighter. Almost without thinking Peekay stuck his leg out so the French Algerian tripped, stumbling clumsily, regaining his balance only by grabbing onto the ropes.

A roar went up from the crowd as Habib turned angrily, squaring up to Peekay and urging him to get up and fight. Except for his foot, Peekay hadn't moved and his eyes remained downcast. A buzz of excitement ran through the crowd as Habib reached his corner and stood with his back to Peekay, talking excitedly to his seconds and gesticulating towards his opponent's corner.

'Nice one,' Hymie grinned.

'You've got him angry, my son. That can't do no 'arm.' Dutch Holland walked over to the Algerian's corner to inspect his gloves, making his second take his gloves off and feeling the bandages. Then he kneaded both gloves carefully, examining them closely so that the excitable Habib became infuriated, waving his arms about indignantly.

Habib's manager had walked over to Peekay's corner to examine his gloves. He had his back to his own corner and was unaware of his fighter's pique. 'You are a very brave man,' he said to Peekay in a heavy French accent as he massaged his gloves. 'Perhaps too brave and too young, no?'

Just then there was a murmur from the crowd as fifty or so young men, dressed immaculately in starched bib and dinner suits arrived at the ringside. Hymie had observed earlier that a block of ringside seats were unoccupied and had assumed they were a group booking for fight fans who chose to arrive in time for the main light-heavyweight event.

The Odd Bodleians had gathered from all over England, interrupting the university vacation to be at the fight. Peekay's concentration was so complete that he was barely conscious of their arrival until Hymie whispered, 'The Odd Bods have arrived! It's absolutely fantastic, almost all of them are here. They're waving!' Hymie said excitedly.

Dutch was smearing vaseline over Peekay's eyebrows and ears. ''Ere, your toffee-nosed cheer squad's arrived,' he said morosely. Peekay looked up and, lifting his glove, he smiled and waved. The crowd had begun to whistle and boo and the Odd Bods sat down laughing, pleased by the attention they were getting.

Dutch turned to Peekay, speaking quietly. 'Take it easy now, my son. Don't let them take your mind off what you're doing. Let him come to you. Let him do the work. Bide your time, hold him with your left, but watch his left hook, it's how he does most of his damage.'

Just then the strains of a violin cut through the pre-fight hubbub, quietening the area immediately around the ring side. The silence spread around the stadium. Peekay couldn't believe his ears. The large form of Jam Jar was standing up in the front row with a violin, playing the overture to Doc's *Concerto for the Great Southland*. The overture was hauntingly African and picked up the feeling of a vast, sad land. Doc had written it in prison (where he was interned during the war as an enemy alien) using the five tribes who, for the most part, made up the prisoners. Each tribe took a part, the poignancy of their singing unbearably beautiful as they sang of their love for Africa. The Concerto climaxed with the Zulus singing the great song to Shaka Zulu, the mightiest of all the warriors.

The crowd had hushed as the beautiful strains of Jam Jar's violin moved to complete the overture and then picked up the opening notes of the Zulu part. The Odd Bodleians rose and came in as one, their voices rising like thunder in the hills. The rest of the audience hushed as the beauty of the male voices rose, singing of the great Zulu impi that came as wind waving in the tall grass, sweeping all before him. It ended again with the roll of thunder as the male voices in the stadium rose in triumph and then started to die down slowly until the deep hum seemed to vibrate the air about the ring.

Suddenly Jam Jar's violin cut in again, picking up the refrain and bringing it to a conclusion, the male voices behind it holding the deep, humming sound and allowing it finally to die.

The audience went wild as the Odd Bodleians sat down. Peekay was not conscious that he'd risen to his feet and now the tears rolled down his cheek. He'd been scared, feeling a little overwhelmed by the fight with the highly rated Habib. *The Concerto for the Great Southland* performed by the Odd Bodleians was the strength he needed. He turned to Hymie, removing the gold chain with the lion's tooth from his neck and handing it to him. 'This fight's for Gideon,' he said softly.

Hymie had tears in his eyes as he took the talisman. 'I had no idea this was going to happen!' He withdrew a handkerchief from his pocket and wiped his eyes, '*Months ago* I'd talked about the composition and Milstein had asked me if I had the music and lyrics. I got my sister to send them over.'

Peekay sat down on the pot again, closing his eyes, regaining his concentration so that he didn't see the referee enter the ring. Dutch tapped him on the shoulder and Peekay opened his eyes, he was ready. He looked up at Habib but saw instead a black man, Jake 'Spoonbill' Jackson, welterweight champion of the world, the fastest two fisted puncher in the world. Peekay was going in after him.

The referee called the two boxers into centre ring and Habib jumped forward, throwing punches into the air, eager to get going, his anger showing. Peekay wasn't buying the showmanship and waited a moment before moving quickly and quietly to stand beside the referee.

Both boxers waited as the Scottish referee introduced them to the crowd, using a microphone which dropped down from the ceiling. The French Algerian held his gloves high and did a little shuffle as his name was called, while Peekay briefly raised his left glove. The referee allowed the microphone to retract and spoke to the two boxers, spelling out the rules of the fight. Neither listened, they'd heard it a hundred times before. The Algerian, jerking his shoulders up and down in a relaxed manner, fixed Peekay with a grin, but Peekay made no attempt to look at him, staring instead at his feet, his hands hanging calmly at his side. As the referee told them to touch gloves Peekay looked at his opponent for the first time, his eyes giving nothing away. They returned to their respective corners to wait for the opening bell.

The crowd sensed a good fight coming up, though there must have been a great many experienced fans present who, like Mitchell of the *Daily Express*, were wondering how a young, unknown South African boxer could stand up to the tough, two-fisted attack of the experienced Arab fighter.

Peekay resumed to sit on the pot, while the slightly taller Habib stood waiting in his corner. The bell sounded for the first round and the dark-eyed fighter moved like a blur towards the young blond boxer trying to force him into the neutral corner.

Peekay was fast enough to step through the gap, taking a left and a right on his gloves, fuming Habib and moving backwards towards centre ring. He knew Habib wanted him on the ropes where he could rough him up early and perhaps put a few hard punches into the body. The Algerian came hard at him again, throwing a lot of leather, and Peekay was hard put to keep him out. Habib was strong and his aim was to unsettle the less experienced boxer quickly.

Habib broke away suddenly, dropping both his hands, a sign of contempt intended to throw Peekay. Perhaps he hadn't met a boxer with Peekay's speed and anticipation before. Peekay sensed the gesture coming, read the other man's thoughts through his eyes. He hit him with a straight left followed by a lightning right cross which sent the French Algerian sprawling, hitting the canvas hard.

Peekay moved quickly to a neutral corner as the ref started to count. The Algerian fighter had risen to his haunches, using the count to clear his head. At eight he stood, nodding to the ref that he was all right. The respect was back in the fight; he'd underestimated his opponent and he now knew he had a fight on his hands.

Peekay moved in quickly, but with caution. He'd hurt his opponent but his eyes were clear. It would take more than an early knock-down to intimidate the other fighter. The Algerian pushed him away with a couple of short rights, but Peekay stepped around the left that followed and caught his opponent a good blow under the heart. Habib went into a clinch, holding Peekay until the ref ordered them to break.

The first round began to take shape, Habib still the more aggressive, chasing Peekay around the ring, both boxers scoring well, neither doing any real damage. Towards the end of the round Habib caught Peekay with a right cross which sent the younger boxer several paces backwards and brought a roar from the crowd. It was a beautiful punch and Peekay felt it in his toes.

The knock-down probably gave the round to Peekay but the other boxer had seemed more aggressive. He was beginning to look impressive, as though in control, the way an experienced boxer can, often without doing a lot more than his opponent. He'd caught Peekay several times on the ropes and done some damage. He was faster than he'd looked on film and Peekay knew he had the capacity to put him away with either hand.

The second round saw Peekay staying away from the Frenchman, counter-punching and moving Habib around the ring. Peekay was a back-foot fighter who allowed his opponent to come to him so he could work out the other man's idiosyncrasies. Neither Hymie or Dutch could pick anything about Habib's style which Peekay could use. After the knock-down the Arab boxer wasn't being careless and was putting his punches together well. He seemed to be breathing a little heavily after the first round but this could have come from the effects of the knock-down. Nevertheless Peekay determined to move him around as much as possible, making his opponent miss, keeping himself away from the ropes. Peekay managed a couple of hard hooks to Habib's body, one of which made him grunt. But it was a reasonably tame round which the Frenchman probably took with his extra aggression. Almost at the end of the round he seemed to gain confidence and was starting to be a tad liberal with his left hook; all Peekay had really managed to do was to confirm to his opponent that the novice wasn't going to be a pushover.

The third round in a six-rounder is the one in which a boxer tries to assert his authority. Peekay was clearly the faster of the two fighters with a slightly longer reach. But the French Algerian was bigger about the shoulders, stronger in the legs; he was a stand-up fighter and needed to get Peekay on the ropes where he would work on him. His tactics had been right when he'd come out for the first round; it was only his arrogance which had been his undoing.

'He's going to come out hard, lad, try to work you in close. Keep him walking, dance him, he's beginning to work a little flat-footed. If he gets a little slower, in the second half of the round take the fight to him, surprise him,' Dutch said.

Peekay had already decided Habib was a good fighter but lacked imagination. Dutch was right. If he was certain the Algerian had lost some of his speed then turning the tables on him might work.

The bell for the third round went and, as predicted, Habib came out fast and aggressive. Peekay danced him, slipping his punches, occasionally tying him up. Habib was strong and he tried to pull himself out of the clinches but Peekay held him, allowing the other fighter to waste his energy whenever possible. The older fighter was throwing so many punches that some of them were landing and hurting Peekay; but Peekay was doing enough to frustrate Habib's aggressive stand-up style and the Algerian was getting angry, which was affecting his timing. Peekay was also hitting him on the break and tying him up whenever he got in close. It wasn't what Habib expected and his frustration was making him careless. Using both hands to get at Peekay's head, Habib was leaving his torso open, whereas Peekay was laying down a pattern of punches which would begin to tell later in the fight.

Towards the end of the round, Habib decided to go for Peekay's body and brought his left hook into play, missing on several occasions. Peekay waited until he tried it just once too often. The younger fighter was perfectly balanced and positioned for the right cross. It came as though in slow motion, exploding to the side of the French Algerian's jaw. The older man staggered backwards and, moving in fast, Peekay hit him with a left to the head and another right cross; then closing in he belted him hard to the body with a left hook, following through with a hard driving right under the heart. The Algerian backed into the ropes, where he tried to grab Peekay and hold on. But the younger boxer was too fast and he hit him again with a straight left. The punch was hard, but going away so that some of the sting was missing. It was enough for Habib to grab onto the ropes and stop himself going down. Peekay moved in just as the bell went for the end of the round. He'd left his run ten seconds too late to knock Habib down, a timing mishap which could cost him the fight.

The crowd, sensing a big upset, were solidly behind Peekay, hoping for a fourth round knock-out. But in the fourth round, Habib managed to tie Peekay up, even hitting him with a left-right combination which had Peekay going for a few seconds as he back-pedalled frantically out of trouble. Yet Habib simply wasn't fast enough to capitalise on the two great punches, and Peekay was able to escape. The round came to an end and, while the crowd were now plainly on Peekay's side, the honours probably went to the French Algerian who had grown stronger and stronger as the round progressed. Peekay's inexperience showed; he'd let his quarry off the hook and, coming up for the fifth round, he seemed likely to walk into a whole heap of trouble.

In the fifth round, the Algerian had worked out Peekay's hit-and-run tactics and he began to stalk the young South African, moving him into a corner whenever he could. Peekay was mostly able to fight his way out but, towards the middle of the round, the big-shoul-dered Algerian nailed him with a beautiful left-right combination which put Peekay down.

Peekay had seen the punch coming but his head somehow wouldn't move. The left smashed into his mouth and the right that followed felt as though his head had been taken off. He went down fast, his bum bouncing on the surface of the ring. 'Jesus, he's nailed me. Get up! Get up!' his mind screamed. 'Christ, I've been knocked out! Get up! Get up!' But the voice in his mind came back clean and far away, as though it was an echo travelling up a long glass funnel. 'No count? There's no count! It's over, I didn't hear the count!' Peekay tried to stand but it was as though he had no legs.

Habib, elated and angry, certain that he'd hit Peekay hard enough so he wouldn't get up again, didn't move immediately to a neutral corner. Standing over Peekay he swore at him in a mixture of French and Arabic. The referee screamed at him to get into a neutral corner but the Arab remained standing over Peekay's fallen body.

The seconds gained were critical. Peekay felt the pain rush back into his legs as the count commenced at last. He still couldn't see properly but his strength was returning. 'The count! Listen for the count! Take all the time you've got! Get up at eight!' he told himself.

At the count of eight he was on his feet with enough strength in his legs to move, his eyes clear. The referee gave him a few precious seconds more as he examined him. 'Box on!' he commanded.

Habib came in fast but missed, first with a straight left and then badly with the right that followed. Peekay moved in and held him, buying the precious seconds until the referee shouted for them to break. Then

Peekay switched to southpaw as he came out of the break and hit Habib with a beautiful right lead, stopping the French Algerian momentarily. Peekay was back in the fight again, and the crowd was loving his courage as he managed to weave and dance through the remainder of the round, staying out of trouble.

'Jesus, Peekay, we thought you were gone! Nice one!' Hymie said as Peekay, breathing heavily, sat down.

Dutch Holland examined his right eye, which had started to swell. 'Not much harm done,' he said, smearing fresh vaseline over the eyelid. 'At least it's not cut. How's your sight?'

Togger was sponging Peekay down, trying unsuccessfully not to look worried as Peekay sucked on the water bottle and rinsed his mouth and then spat into the bucket at his feet. 'Fine, Dutch, I can see fine. Christ, he hits hard!'

'You can't leave it to chance, my son. We reckon he's taken three. You're going to have to look very convincing in this one, lad.'

Hymie pointed to Habib, who was standing, punching his gloves together, waiting for the bell. He was still breathing hard but trying to conceal it, glaring over at Peekay. 'Look! His heart!' Hymie exclaimed. 'He's taken a lot of punishment.'

'You've marked him, lad. That's nice close work. He's hurting. Work it, work it hard, keep going under the heart,' Dutch instructed.

'As always, you'll wear him down and finish him on the ropes,' Hymie added lamely. There is a time in a close fight when there is nothing to say. Hymie was simply covering his concern with words.

Peekay understood what they were saying. He had to do more than win the round convincingly to be sure of the fight. 'He's bloody strong. I don't know whether I've got time,' Peekay replied.

'So are you, my son, fitter and stronger. The punch that put you down would have finished off any other welter in Britain.' Dutch said. He was concerned. Peekay had let the fight slip away. All Habib had to do was hang in and he could win. Dutch was no longer concerned with Peekay making a good showing; he'd seen enough already to know he had the makings of a champion, one with the skill to take him to the top. Peekay was now into the part of the fight which requires character, where the men are sorted from the boys, the would be's if they could be's. Whatever happened in the next three minutes, Dutch would have all his questions answered.

The bell went for the final round and Peekay moved into the centre of the ring. He knew he had to knock Habib out to win but the Algerian was crowding him, working up too close for a big punch. Peekay was hurting a lot, the blows from the French Algerian were remorseless. He was taking most of them on the back of the arms, and he could feel his arms starting to weaken. He needed to dig deep, deeper than he'd ever been before. Hoppie Groenewald's voice came to him suddenly. It was clean, unhurried. 'Always Peekay, remember, first with the head and then with the heart. A fighter must have himself a plan. Always a plan!'

At precisely that moment, as though Peekay and Hymie were synergised, Hymie turned to Dutch Holland, his dark eyes shining fiercely. 'Peekay will take him out, Dutch! I'm telling you, man . . . no way he's going to lose this fight!'

Dutch shook his head. 'Our lad's spent, 'e 'asn't got the punch no more to put Habib on the deck.'

Peekay switched suddenly to southpaw, as Habib moved in again. Habib expected him to back away and he held his gloves a little low, confident Peekay wasn't going to come after him. The switch in style caught him by surprise as Peekay moved forward and hit him with a left cross, followed through with a hard right.

Peekay needed those two punches to slow Habib down, to move him backwards onto the ropes. There he had to open him up, where he could work him to the body, to the spot under his heart. There was only one way. He must offer the Arab his head as a target, hope he could ride the punch, and force the Algerian to open up. He was gambling that he could read Habib, that the other fighter would follow his big punch with a left hook, miss and leave himself wide open for a hard left to the head. Habib would bring his gloves up to protect his head from the expected right hand and in doing so, he'd leave his torso open, where Peekay could hit him with everything he had under the heart. Peekay needed an eight-punch combination, a Geel Piet eight solidly into the spot to slow the other fighter right down, allow Peekay to box him, and wait for the big punch that might put him out. It was a plan which depended on Peekay reading the Algerian perfectly; but he couldn't think of a better one. If he'd underestimated the power still left in Habib's straight right, his opponent would knock him out. He had no choice; winning the round was not enough. He had to take the chance.

Peekay opened his gloves, closing them again, opening again, signalling, offering his head. Habib saw his chance as Peekay opened just a little wider, and the right smashed into Peekay's swollen eye. Perfect. The eye socket, the strongest part of the face, absorbed the power of the punch as Peekay rolled with it. Habib's left hook followed but Peekay wasn't in line for the punch. Instead his own left smashed into Habib's nose. It was the hardest punch Peekay could ever remember having thrown. Habib staggered back against the ropes, his nose broken, his good eye filling with tears. He was blinded, and his gloves came up instinctively to cover his face as Peekay knew they would. Then Peekay's right hook came from low down, with all the follow-through from his shoulder to catch the French Algerian under the heart. The left had been a spectacular punch, but it was the right hook that did the terrible damage. It was the best punch thrown all night and he could feel Habib's ribcage give as the blow ripped into his body. In went the Geel Piet eight, so fast that Habib's agonised grunt from the deadly right hook was still coming out of him when Peekay pulled back.

Habib sank to the canvas as though in slow motion. He was unconscious before his knees hit the surface of the ring. But even so, his right arm hooked around the centre rope and his left glove pushed against the canvas propping him up. He may have been out but he wasn't going to lie down.

The blood ran into Peekay's eye where Habib had hit him earlier. The eye was closing rapidly and even his good eye was less than fifty per cent effective, as though he was looking through a red haze. If Habib managed to get up from the canvas and landed half a good punch into the eye, Peekay was history; you can't fight if you can't see. Peekay felt no elation as Habib's arm dropped from the rope and he sank to the floor. For the first time in the fight he was really scared. He had nothing left.

Peekay moved quickly to a neutral corner, conscious that every second delayed gave the French Algerian time to recover. For the first time he heard the roar of the crowd. At the count of seven Habib managed to stand, using the ropes to pull himself upright. Peekay couldn't believe his eyes. He'd hit the Algerian harder than he'd ever hit anyone in his life. The punches under the heart, coming as they did, after fifty or more well-timed blows to the same spot should have taken him out for a twenty count. But the bastard was up, facing Peekay, a blood-smeared grin on his swollen face.

The referee seemed in two minds. He wasn't fooled; it was a fighter's grin. He knew Habib was hurt bad. For a moment it looked as though he was going to stop the fight. Oh God, please call it! Peekay begged silently. Please let me win! But the ref wiped Habib's gloves and signalled for the fight to continue.

Peekay closed in and pushed Habib into the ropes with two barely effective straight rights to the face. He came in so his left eye was closest to his opponent, allowing him maximum vision. Habib tried to pull Peekay into a clinch but failed, and brought his gloves up to protect his broken nose.

Peekay dug deep. He was fighting from memory, the years and years of doing it right, putting all his punches together for the maximum effect. The orthodox right hook under the heart from Peekay was almost polite it was so businesslike. Earlier in the fight it may just have stopped Habib momentarily; but now it was enough. The French Algerian grunted softly, it was almost a moan as he toppled onto the canvas. He was out cold before he hit the deck. One minute and forty-five seconds into the last round, Habib had fallen over like a sack of potatoes. The referee stood over him counting, but it was a mere formality. Habib still hadn't moved as he was counted out.

The crowd exploded with excitement and the stadium was in an uproar. They'd found a new champion. 'Angel! Angel! Angel!' they chanted.

Hymie turned to Dutch. 'What did I tell you!' he screamed. He was climbing into the ring when he felt Togger brush past him. Togger rushed over to Peekay and, grabbing him about the thighs, hoisted him off the deck.

'You was bleedin' sensational. The best, the best! The world champ!' Togger yelled. He swung Peekay around to where the Odd Bodleians were seated before putting him down. They were all on their feet yelling 'Angel! Angel! Angel!' with the crowd, their arms held high above their heads.

Hymie pointed to them, then grabbed Peekay and hugged him. 'Christ, when the Arab got up again, I think I shat my pants!'

'Me too!' Peekay gasped.

Dutch Holland remained in his corner, all his questions about Peekay answered. 'You'll do, my son, you'll do very nicely,' he said quietly to himself.

Peekay, flanked by an excited Hymie and Togger, resumed to the corner. Dutch Holland looked at Peekay angrily. ''Ere, lad, that's living too fuckin' dangerously! Next time you offer your bleedin' noggin as a trade for a chance to knock your opponent out you better find yourself another trainer!'

In fact, it was the courage and critical judgement that showed in this very decision which made Dutch Holland finally sure he had a world champ on his hands. Dutch hoped that Peekay would never again have to repeat the tactic. Peekay had been mismatched. It was the French Algerian's arrogance and tempera-ment which had cost him the fight. That wouldn't happen again. The next time Peekay stepped into the ring his opponent would treat him with the utmost respect. In future his skills as a boxer would decide the outcome of his fights. Nevertheless, Holland was deeply gratified that the young man in his charge had come through his baptism of fire with nothing more than a couple of black eyes and a bruised rib or two. It was a small enough price to pay to find out he had a lad on his hands who had the courage to kiss the knife. Dutch knew that from such raw material world champions are made.

Peekay held out his right hand for Hymie to remove his glove. He was stunned by Dutch Holland's reaction. His body was covered with red blotches where Habib had hit him and his right eye was closed. He winced, trying to smile. 'Shit! Nobody told me it was this hard!' he said, trying not to seem upset by his trainer's remark.

'Welcome to the professional ranks, my son. You're going to have to learn to put 'em away sooner. Saves a lot of wear 'n tear on the old carcass,' Dutch said without smiling.

Peekay fought back his tears. Christ what do I have to do? What does the bastard want? he thought. He kept his head down so that Hymie couldn't see how upset he was and held out his left glove for his friend to remove.

'Oi! Fair go, Mr 'Olland! Peekay done marvellous! He knocked 'im bleedin' out didn't 'e? 'E's never been put down before, never!' Togger yelled, defiant and plainly upset for his friend.

Dutch Holland looked down at Togger. 'You're right son,' he said quietly. 'He's done bleedin' wonderful, but he's a toffee nose, these intellectuals can't take too much praise all at once.'

'Try starting with just a little bit, then, Dutch,' Hymie shot back at the trainer, his sarcasm plain.

'There's plenty of time for that later, Mr Levy! If the lad had ten per cent more going for him in both 'ands he'd have been enjoying an early shower. We got lots of work to do if we gonna take your man anywhere special. I haven't got no time to stand around throwin' bleedin' bouquets.'

Not wanting to show his feelings, Peekay excused himself and walked over to Habib's corner. '*Merci*,' he said, smiling, nodding his head to Habib's manager and seconds. One of them held an ice pack against Habib's face so that the Algerian fighter hadn't seen Peekay approach. '*Merci, mon ami, j'espère que je ne rencontre jamais un pugiliste qui me bat si fort que vous*,' Peekay said, in halting schoolboy French.

The second withdrew the ice pack. The French Algerian's nose was badly swollen. The bleeding from his left eye had been stemmed but the eye itself was competely closed and raised well above his cheekbone, and he could barely see out of the other eye. Habib was surprised to see Peekay, but took only a moment to smile. Sniffing back a trickle of blood which had begun again from his nose, he rose from his stool and, taking Peekay's arm, he held it aloft to cheers from the crowd.

'One day you will be world champion, Tadpole Angel,' he said, speaking in French. 'Then I will say, "*Eh bien*! He's not so great, one time I nearly knocked him out!'

Jam Jar had invited Hymie and Peekay to the Savoy with the Odd Bodleian crowd for a champagne supper, calling Hymie from across the ring as they were leaving for the dressing room. 'Wonderful fight, brought out positively the worst in me! Loved it!'

Hymie nodded, acknowledging his invitation, 'The singing . . . it was marvellous!' He imitated playing a violin, 'You were terrific!'

Seventeen

Maybe there is some connection between repressive regimes and good roads? The road from Johannesburg to Durban is claimed to be equal to any in the world, including the autobahns built by Adolf Hitler and the autostrade constructed in Italy by Mussolini. As roads go, this one is wide, fast and well made, with long perfectly flat grey stretches. There is a popular notion that parts of it are designed so that Sabre jets can land on it when the black revolution comes.

The journey in the big Packard promised to take just over five hours of fairly sedate Juicey Fruit Mambo driving. Mama Tequila with Tandia in tow was headed for Sophiatown to visit her sister Flo, or Madam Flame Flo as she was known by the *majietas* and the bright boys of Kofifi, the other name by which this rag-tag, multiracial community was known. Madam Flame Flo was the biggest shebeen queen in Sophiatown, a well-known figure who had resided there since the mid thirties.

In this little Chicago with its unpaved, dirty alleys and roadways delineated by leaning fences, ruts and puddles, the good mixed in almost equal proportions with the bad. There were some rich people, but they were overwhelmed by the poor; and as for the middle class, they were simply those families who ate three times a day.

In Sophiatown there were stone walls topped with glass built by the wealthy to keep out the marauding poor, but these most often acted as the one sturdy wall to the shanties of beaten tin and scraps of timber which were abutted to them. In this thoroughly mixed community there were no nature strips or carefully manicured lawns to create a no-man's-land separating the haves from the have nots. No municipal laws called for segregation by colour, income or status, so Sophiatown became more a conglomeration of ways to live than the result of town planning.

The township paid almost no taxes and in return received very little help. The utilities were almost nonexistent, and electricity was a status symbol. Most families lived and died by lamp and candlelight. A toilet was usually a pit in the ground topped with a small moveable outhouse of corrugated iron with a crude seat built into it. In the summer the sides were too hot to touch and hundreds of bluebottles filled the interior. You could hear and smell the presence of a *kakhuis* long before you arrived at it.

The sprawling 'Blackopolis', as the newspapermen called it, was also the biggest pain in the arse the Nationalist government had on its racist agenda. There were also other, smaller pimples on the backside of apartheid: Alexandra to the north, Orlando township to the south-west and, of course, Cape Town's ancient and venerable District Six, a slum which had existed for nearly two hundred years. But none was thought quite as important to cauterise from the body of the Nationalist state than was Sophiatown. Blacks from every tribe, as well as those who had been Kofifi-born and claimed no tribe at all, coloureds, Indians, Chinese and whites, lived together and had done so for well over thirty years. Racial harmony was not what the government were about and they had no intention of allowing an example of it to continue.

In fairness, the word 'harmony' was a description ill suited to the goings-on in Kofifi. Sophiatown was an untidy drawer which had jammed and refused to close in the neatly arranged filing cabinets of Johannesburg, where every class and colour knew its proper place. But Sophiatown was also the last living demonstration of the thing Old Coetzee had spoken about in Mama Tequila's salon, where people put aside their differences and had a shot at living together as human beings. Another name for it was hope.

Madam Flame Flo had started making her fortune almost immediately after arriving in Sophiatown from the Cape. She had been a good-looking woman of twenty-five, with an almost pure white, blue-eyed bastard baby and no real prospects ahead of her.

Fortune had smiled on Flo Van der Merwe from the very beginning. At the bus station on her way to Sophiatown she had sat down beside a diminutive coloured man who took a shine to her blue-eyed baby daughter and who introduced himself as Geel Piet, which simply meant Yellow Peter. Flo was to learn that names were important in Sophiatown; but only the very rich and the law abiding, both of whom were in limited supply, called themselves by their real names.

Geel Piet, who claimed to have been a professional boxer and from the look of his face must have been a very bad one, turned out to have made a vocation of having his bones broken in just about every prison in South Africa. It was difficult to tell his age. His body seemed to bear witness to a series of unfortunate happenings more than to an aging process. It was as though he'd been poorly constructed in the first place, had been broken regularly over his adult years and on each occasion been badly mended.

Geel Piet had tagged along with the slim woman with the flaming henna-dyed hair and her chubby fair-skinned baby, promising to help her find accommodation. True to his word, he found her a place to live. A friend of a friend had a small, dark room for rent with a communal tap and a pit-toilet shared by several houses in the vicinity. The room was at the top end of Good Street, Sophiatown's major and most notorious thoroughfare. It had seemed to Flo an exciting and rather frightening place to live after the quieter streets of Cape Town's District Six.

After settling her in, Geel Piet had stolen five pounds from her handbag, her entire stake for a new life in the big city. He had returned just after eleven o'clock curfew that night with an armful of groceries, handing the destitute and distressed young mother twenty pounds. Geel Piet was a racing man extraordinaire and had brought home two winners at Turffontein racetrack that afternoon.

Geel Piet didn't stay in Sophiatown long. Over the ten years that followed, he used to visit Madam Flame Flo occasionally, always between bouts in prison. Even after she had become rich and a famous figure in Sophiatown, she never turned him away. Perhaps the only clean sheets and soft bed Geel Piet ever knew were in the spare bedroom of her large house. In her mind he'd laid the foundation for her fortune and Madam

Flame Flo wasn't a fair-weather friend, the sort of person to forget a thing like that.

On the morning following her arrival in Sophiatown, Geel Piet had shown Flo how to brew a concoction which he'd learned to make in Barberton Gaol, a small but notoriously brutal and greatly feared prison in the Eastern Transvaal. The homemade liquor consisted of yeast, a quantity of the small-seeded brown maize known as kaffir-corn, brown sugar and the coarse brown bread the natives ate. It was all mixed together in a four-gallon paraffin tin filled with water and allowed to stand overnight. The result was a pungent brew with a real wallop! Flo had named it Barberton and dispensed it in jam tins at a nice profit to the Saturday-night Good Street crowd.

Over the years many shebeen queens had produced their own liquor, but Flo's special brand of Barberton was never seriously challenged. Some people said that her secret ingredient was arsenic, others claimed it was cyanide pinched from the gold refinery at Modderfontein, others that it was the rainwater she used from her big round tank. Madam Flame Flo never told, and in a country where liquor was forbidden to blacks (except for the sour, fermented porridge-like kaffir beer served in government drinking compounds), she became a very rich and even, in her own way, powerful woman.

In 1945 Madam Flame Flo had heard of Geel Piet's death at the hands of a warder named Kronkie in the very same Barberton prison from which her famous concoction was derived. She had ordered a polished granite tombstone on which she'd inscribed:

GEEL PIET
We drink to
his
sacred memory.
DIED 1945

She'd loaded the headstone onto the back of a bakkie, driven the three hundred and forty miles to the tiny mountain town of Barberton, and arrived at the notorious prison. There she had demanded to see where Geel Piet had been buried.

At first the Kommandant had refused to take her seriously. 'Hey, jong, he was just a *boesman* who died. We just dug a hole and put him in. *Dood vlies is dood vlies!* Dead meat is dead meat. Who you think he was, Jesus Christ in disguise?'

But Madam Flame Flo had persisted, and eventually she had been shown the plot where the prisoners who hadn't made it through their sentences lay buried: a large bare piece of ground where two or three hundred round boulders no bigger than a man's head were arranged in rows approximately five feet apart. The prisoners called it *amaTshe* and the warders simply translated this into *die Klippe*, the Stones. The boulders were all approximately the same size and of a whitish stone cut from a local quarry. Prisoners working in the quarry, when given the task of making a headstone, would shape it into a rough approximation and size of a human skull. At first glance, laid out in rows, the stones looked like a neatly organised killing field, which was a fairly accurate description of the state of affairs. Barberton wasn't a big prison, but it had more prisoner deaths than any in the country. The institutional joke among the Boer warders was that when a magistrate sentenced a black man to Barberton, he turned white. The Stones testified to the grim reality of this puerile joke.

The warder had waved his hand expansively over the stone-studded plot. 'Take you pick!' he had said, amused.

Madam Flame Flo had paid the man a pound to get three prisoners to unload the headstone from the bakkie and transport it by wheelbarrow to the Stones. Word had gotten around, and by the time the prisoners arrived, several more warders had gathered to witness the weird stone-laying ceremony for a beaten-up little boesman who wasn't worth a pinch of shit.

'*Was die Hotnot jou soetman?* Was the Hottentot your sweetheart?' one of them shouted, and the others all joined in the laughter. There was no doubt about it, kaffirs were funny buggers, but these boesmen were fucked in the head spending good money on a tombstone for a worthless piece of shit like that.

Just then a tall, fair-haired warder arrived on the scene. 'Are you the woman looking for Geel Piet's grave?' he asked, more or less politely, in Afrikaans.

'*Ja, baasie,*' Madam Flame Flo answered, not knowing what to expect from the white man.

'*Kom!*' he instructed, and started to walk to the very centre of the plot where Madam Flame Flo noticed a white boulder perhaps one-and-a-half times larger than the others, and quite nicely carved into an almost completely round ball. The warder waited for her to arrive. 'Put it here,' he said, and, turning, whistled to the prisoners who had reached the edge of the graveyard. To Madam Flame Flo's surprise the young warder dropped to his haunches and rolled the whitewashed stone away.

The headstone must have been very heavy, for the

metal wheel of the barrow cut a clear rut into the hard red clay. With great difficulty the three men lifted it from the barrow and placed it where the boulder had been. It sat in the centre of the bare plot, an obscenely new and extravagant symbol set amongst the humble skull stones. There seemed nothing more to say. '*Dankie, baasie.* Can you tell me please when he died, do you know the date?'

The sergeant smiled. He had a pleasant, open face and his expression wasn't in the least condescending. 'That's easy, man. It was the night the Germans surrendered.'

Madam Flame Flo thanked the warder again as the three prisoners, laughing among themselves, left, one of them wheeling the barrow containing the rock which had now been replaced by the ludicrous tombstone.

The warder looked directly at Madam Flame Flo for the first time and offered her his hand. Surprised, she accepted it. 'My name's Gert. I'm not saying the boesman was a good man,' he grinned at the memory, 'he was a proper *skelm*, but he was also a real man. Geel Piet was the best boxing coach I ever saw.' He turned abruptly and walked away.

Madam Flame Flo turned back to the polished headstone. Behind it the green hills rose up and rolled back and tumbled into mountains blued and smudged in the high distance. It was a beautiful place for an old lag to die. '*Slaap lekker ou maut!* Sleep well, old friend,' she said quietly, and then added, 'Thanks, you hear? Thanks for everything you done for me.' Then she began to weep quietly, less for her friend than for the hopelessness of her kind, the twilight people who didn't belong, the new children of Africa spawned from the ugly, guilty lust of white for black and unwanted by

369

both. She thought of her daughter with her fair skin and blue eyes who had escaped the tyranny of colour but who could never have a child lest it throw back and condemn her for the fraud she was.

On her return to Sophiatown Madam Flame Flo tried to re-name her liquor. She wanted to call it Geel Piet, but the name never caught on. The original name, Barberton, stood for something, and that sort of thing is not lightly put aside. Tradition in a daily start-from-scratch town like Kofifi, with few routines and even fewer laws, is important for continuity, a powerful emotional glue which holds people together. A person can't just go around changing things willy-nilly, even if the sentiment is a good one.

Barberton, and for that matter its many imitators, produced an affliction known as 'liquor flame' amongst its often poorly nourished drinkers. Liquor flame was a skin disease which resulted in the top layer of the skin peeling away. It was this affliction which gained Flo her nickname. Far from being ashamed of it, Madam Flame Flo regarded the appellation with a great deal of pride.

Madam Flame Flo had never moved from the spot Geel Piet had found for her to live. First she'd bought the room, then the house, and then the three small houses surrounding it. She had dug a septic tank and constructed a four-bedroom red-brick home with two bathrooms, where visitors would bring their children to inspect the indoor toilet. Behind the house was a large shed where the forty-four gallon drums of Barberton were brewed. Directly under the floor of this outhouse were several large tanks into which the fermented drink was strained and poured. Beside the shed, resting on its own concrete platform, was a huge round corrugated-iron rainwater tank which used the roof of the main house as its catchment area. This was the water used to make Barberton, and the whole set-up became Madam Flame Flo's brewery. Buried in the yard was a forty-four gallon drum into which the slops were emptied. This drum existed essentially as a decoy for police raids. While Madam Flame Flo paid police protection as a matter of routine, as an equal matter of routine she was regularly raided. She was too big an operator to go unnoticed; any policeman with a nose on his face could detect the slightly sour smell of the fermenting kaffir-corn and yeast simply by walking past the house.

In the strange game of corruption which existed in Sophiatown between the white police officers and the inhabitants, several unspoken rules applied. In Madam Flame Flo's case raids took place without warning so that she was obliged to pay protection to half-a-dozen street gangs. These comprised mostly teenage boys, no less vicious for their youth, and responsible for a great deal of mayhem and quite often even murder in the township. A police presence in numbers in the vicinity of Madam Flame Flo's end of Good Street would always be reported in time for her to empty the above-the-ground brewing vats into the below-the-ground tanks, and to appear innocent but for the single forty-four gallon drum conspicuously buried in the back yard. There was a second implicit law which applied in Sophiatown, this being that what is in the ground belongs to the ground. The police, after a lot of pretentious looking around, would eventually come upon the buried drum. It would be dug up and confiscated and Madam Flame Flo would be duly charged with allowing persons unknown to conceal liquor on her premises. This offence carried a biggish fine which she duly paid, though not without vehemently protesting her innocence.

The big Packard arrived in Good Street followed by a pack of yelling urchins curious to inspect the new arrivals. Madam Flame Flo, impatient to greet her sister, couldn't wait for Mama Tequila to get out of the car. She opened the back door and climbed into the rear seat as the Packard came to a halt outside her house. The two sisters embraced loudly and with copious tears.

Madam Flame Flo was already chatting as she entered the car, so that her words came out punctuated by sobs of welcome. 'The white bastards are going to take my beautiful home away! Come, my sister, your room is ready, at least you can enjoy it one last time. How are you, *liefling*? I have food, you must eat, we can still eat, though God knows how much longer before those Boer bastards take the food from out our mouths!'

Tandia, not wishing to be a part of the emotional sistering taking place in the back seat, got out of the car and was immediately surrounded by more than a dozen ragged black children who seemed to range from about seven to ten years old. Juicey Fruit Mambo was attempting to shoo them away, but these kids were city bred and they stood their ground, prepared to run only when they felt real danger which, in the way slum kids know these things, they sensed wasn't coming from Juicey Fruit Mambo's fierce-looking scowl.

'Oh my, I am so heppy you have come! We must talk plans, you hear?' Madam Flame Flo cried to Mama Tequila. 'In Sophiatown it's finish and klaar. God, I can't tell you what I been through! I'm telling you, any day now they going to come and fetch me and take me to Sterkfontein Mental Hospital. God's truth!'

'And the business? How is the business, Flo?' Mama Tequila laughed, patting her scrawny sister on the back with a heavily jewelled hand.

'That, God be thanked, is first class. With so much trouble and people losing their houses and going to Diepfontein and Meadowlands there is a lot of need. Business is good, that I got to say! But soon, no more! When they move the coloured folk out, that the end. The police already told me, no Barberton in the resettlement area. "What are the people going to drink, skokiaan?" I ask that big Dutchman, Potgieter, who is the crown sergeant at the Newlands police station. You know what he say, ousie? He says, "The government is trying to make a place for decent boesmen to live, no more blerrie shebeens, you hear, no more Barberton, no more skokiaan, we going to build a big beer hall!" That's what the dumb bugger says. So I look at him all solcastic. Since when does a coloured person drink kaffir beer? I ask him. "Here!" he says and scratches his big *dom kop*, "Maybe the authorities forgot we not mixing boesmen with black kaffirs no more. I seen it on the plans, they got a big soccer stadium and a beer hall in all the drawings!" So maybe there's a chance, hey? I ask him. That Potgieter he's the biggest crook, no way he going to run a clean show, no way, man! He looks at me sideways and his piggy blue eyes is all small in his fat face and his mouth goes like he's sucking a lemon, "Maybe you should start a brothel, hey?" he says. "Maybe that would be not such a bad thing for the boesman in the new place?" He laughs and then he says, "I seen a beer hall, but I didn't see a brothel in those plans." He picks his nose then and looks at me and then down at what he took out his nose. Sies, man!

What a disgusting type, hey? "Ja, I think a brothel, that better than selling Barberton and we only charge a fixed sum every week for police protection and no fines," that's what he says to me.'

Mama Tequila laughed. 'We talk inside, Flo, I been sitting in this lousy car seat since seven this morning.'

Flo clambered out of the rear of the car backwards and Juicey Fruit Mambo began the complicated process of extracting Mama Tequila from the Packard. In the last year or so she'd put on nearly forty pounds and while getting into the car wasn't too difficult, extracting her had become somewhat of a traumatic experience for them both. First he moved Mama Tequila's legs so they protruded out of the door; then he moved around to the other side of the car. Climbing into the back, he pushed her further along the seat until her legs could reach the ground. He then moved back to Mama Tequila's side of the car and while she propped the soles of her shoes against the uppers of his boots to prevent her slipping forward, Juicey Fruit Mambo began to rock her, slowly increasing the rhythm until with a final jerk he pulled her up out of the seat. The crowd around the car applauded as Mama Tequila arrived in a vertical position Juicey Fruit Mambo's brow was covered with beads of perspiration from the effort.

Mama Tequila acknowledged their tribute by beaming into the crowd, which now consisted of even more kids and quite a few adults as well. The original gang, the discoverers of this diversion, had a proprietorial look about them, as though they expected to be congratulated for finding so curious a spectacle on an otherwise dull Monday.

Still panting from the effort of getting out of the Packard, Mama Tequila started to walk slowly towards the house. 'Howdy folks, I do declare, it sure nice to be in this fine town of yours! Yessiree!' She looked at the shacks and shanties, leaning fences and dusty trees in the dirty street. 'It just the nicest place I ever did see!' she declared; then looking around, beamed again at the crowd. 'And I can tell, it gonna be real friendly, just like being home!'

A small gasp of appreciation went up from the crowd. In Sophiatown anything American was a very big deal. The small crowd welcoming her with their eyes decided that the enormous woman with the big, shiny American car was a celebrity, and that the beautiful young girl with her was probably also one. Someone whispered the words, 'Fillim stars!' An excited murmur swept through the crowd.

Mama Tequila, her timing as usual immaculate, took her sister by one arm and Tandia by the other and moved towards the house. 'I so excited to be here, honey!' she said in a voice loud enough for the onlookers to hear. 'My, my, now ain't that something else?' she indicated the red brick house as though she'd suddenly stepped around a corner and seen the Taj Mahal. Madam Flame Flo grinned. Mama Tequila had visited her a dozen times before at this same house, but she liked the showmanship; it couldn't do no harm anyway. Mama Tequila, still beaming, climbed the steps onto the front stoep, insisting that her sister and Tandia enter the house first. She turned at the door to face the crowd, and bringing both heavily bejewelled sets of fingers to her lips, she blew them a kiss. A spontaneous cheer broke out. Mama Tequila knew that her arrival would be the big news in town that night.

Madam Flame Flo seemed to Tandia to be everything Mama Tequila wasn't. She was thin as a wisp of morning smoke. Her voice was pitched high and she spoke rapidly. Her every movement was quick and impatient as though she was spring-loaded and would go off at the merest touch. She had prepared a huge lunch, mostly of cold meats: beef and mutton, silverside, salami, polony and cold pork sausages. Mama Tequila lost no time tucking in. She hadn't eaten since just after five that morning and declared herself to be starving. To her delight, the kitchen maid entered with a large bowl of roasted corn cobs. Sinking her fork into one end of the cob so it acted as a handle, Mama Tequila ripped the hot golden seeds of corn from the husk with her teeth. Yellow butter ran down the corners of her mouth onto the napkin she had carefully folded around her neck.

Tandia was too excited to eat. Johannesburg with its yellow mine-dump mountains and the tall buildings reaching up into the sky made Durban seem like a small *dorp*. This was the big time all right! From the moment she'd been accepted by Natal University, Tandia knew where she was headed. Nothing was going to stop her. If a person made a name for herself in a place like this, she would be known in the best white circus all right! And she wanted that, though not the way Patel had craved it. Tandia would be known as the black woman who fought on even terms with the white oppressors of her people. A black who would spit in the face of apartheid. When she thought like this she would develop a glow, a burning deep within her. She wasn't even sure she understood what it was, whether love for her kind or hate for the whites, but it came increasingly and it gave her a strength which transcended even her fear of Geldenhuis.

Even Sophiatown was a surprise to Tandia. She'd

never before witnessed a multiracial society and while poverty was evident everywhere, this place on the fringe of the big time had a non-interfered-with look about it. By contrast, Cato Manor, where she had been born and brought up, was an orderly urban slum kept under the heel of authority, which bred a passive resignation in its inhabitants. Cato Manor had none of the dynamism of this place on the high veld where the air seemed lighter and where the sky, a washed-out blue, seemed higher.

She'd warmed to the dusty-ankled, bright-eyed ragamuffins who'd run behind the car, yelling and cheering their progress. Some rolled hoops made from the spokeless rim of a bicycle wheel, guiding them with short sticks held into the grooved rim; others pushing skeletal motor cars shaped entirely out of bits of wire and driven by long sticks, each attached to a small wire steering wheel with which the driver turned the wheels. Catapults dangled around the necks of the kids, bouncing on their chests as they ran. Juicey Fruit Mambo had slowed right down to navigate the ruts and the puddles of dirty rainwater and the kids were thumping the back of the car with the flat of their hands as they cried a good-natured welcome.

Tandia sensed that the people, the crowd who had gathered around them when they'd stopped outside Madam Flame Flo's home, were different. For the first time she felt she belonged to something larger and more important than herself, that she was to be given a reason why her life was turning out so well. It was silly she told herself; how could she feel so much about this place? She hadn't walked more than fifty feet, the distance from the street into the dark cool house. And yet she sensed all of these things clearly. It was as though

Sophiatown was the first place that made perfect sense to her in her life, this dirty little township where the spirit of her people rose above the squalor, the thuggery and the exploitation.

'So what do you think, ousie?' Madam Flame Flo leaned with her elbows on the dining-room table, her chin resting on her hands. 'What do you think about a brothel for coloured folk in the new township they calling Coronationville they making for us? Give us your honest answer. Not what you think you'd like me to hear! No soft pedalling you hear? What do you say, hey?'

Mama Tequila had settled herself down to some serious eating. 'Sshhh! Flo, not so much talk! You like a blerrie machine gun!' She had reverted to the Transvaal pronunciation of the word 'bloody', switching automatically from the more anglicised Natal 'bladdy'. She wiped her mouth with the butter-stained napkin around her neck and brought her coffee cup to her lips. She took a lingering sip from the cup. 'It all depends, Flo, what kind of whorehouse you want,' she said finally.

'The kind that makes lots of money! That the kind I want! What other kind is there?'

'Ja, of course, but in this new place you got only coloured trade. That means trouble, because you can't run a good whorehouse with only coloured people. You most likely got to run a BB-TM!'

'So, what's so wrong with that? In a BB-TM the money comes fast. No fancy overheads. Like *you* in the war. Jesus! You was raking in cash like it was going out of style!'

'Ja, jong, but soldiers and coloured people, they not the same thing. A soldier comes to a BB-TM because

378

he's away from his home and his girl or his wife, or because his platoon they all also going. He needs a woman, he got dirty water on his chest and he want to get it off. A coloured *kerel* goes to a BB-TM when he's drunk because if he not drunk he's a natural freelancer who thinks he can get it for nothing. And when he's drunk he likes to fight and to gamble. So now what you got? You got trouble, you hear? You too old for that, Flo. Too rich also. Look! You can't open a house like Bluey Jay no more. You know how many coloureds come to Bluey Jay?' She held up three fingers. 'Three, they all rich. If I had to depend on coloureds there would be no bums bobbing in the beds, I can tell you that for sure, jong. It would be a no-go show, I'm telling you!' Mama Tequila paused and held up her hand. 'I know what you going to say and ja, I agree, here there is more coloureds than Durban. But all the same, to run a nice house you got to have rich. And also, without white you going nowhere, man! The white man is the one who likes to have black pussy! With him you can run a nice quiet house and make him pay. And you can't have no white whores for the coloured people, not because there not plenty around, but because the authorities say they can't live in this new place you going, what its name, this Coronation place? Also white whores they trouble, man, they poor whites who got no hygiene and they big friends with doctor brandy and Mary Jane!'

'Ja, okay, but what say we get only very pretty coloured girls? Just like you got at Bluey Jay. A pretty girl, no matter what colour, men always want?'

Mama Tequila arched an eyebrow. 'Flo, you know it already, a coloured man always wants what he can't get. He can get a coloured girl, he married to one! He want white pussy which is *verboten*. Even if your girls they real pretty, they still just like his wife.'

Mama Tequila took another sip from her cup before continuing. 'Flo, darling, you seen it yourself on a Saturday night! Good Street, that a damn funny name, it a good street orright! It good for pretty coloured girls and black girls who are dancing the *marabi* dance and selling freelance pussy at cut rates! Darling, in a whorehouse you got overheads. First you got to buy yourself a nice place, because if you rent, the landlord is always putting up the rent. Then you got to pay the police, not just one kind of police, you hear? You got to pay the SAPS, the Black Jacks, the Ghost Squad, the Homicide Squad, the Robbery Squad and even the Special Branch. Then the gangs; killers like Kort Boy who runs the Americans, even the tsotsi gangs so you got protection from themselves. Then you got maybe fifty people who all got their hand out. The council and the health department, you name it. In a whorehouse pay-out day is every day!'

Mama Tequila was warming to her subject. 'But all that's nothing, man! Because it's not so long before you get your first murder. Some drunk *hout kop*, wooden head, puts a knife in a girl because he think she looks like his sister or men fight over gambling and the guns come out.

'Now you got blood. When a whorehouse got blood it got trouble. No more police protection. The police, the Homicide Squad takes over and the next thing you in the *Rand Daily Mail* and the *Star* and you got to close down. When you start again somewhere else, every time it becomes harder 'cause now you got a rep. Soon you only get scum, only the crud comes and then it only a matter of time before someone pull the trigger and the gun is pointing at you. Bang! You dead! You a rich, dead nice-time girl!'

'Jesus!' Madam Flame Flo exclaimed. 'And I thought the shebeen business is bad! How come you never told me this before?'

'You never wanted to run a whorehouse before, my darling.' Mama Tequila leaned forward, 'Flo, you rich! Go buy yourself a nice place, get somewhere where your daughter can come sometimes to see you, somewhere where nobody can see it's happening.'

Flo sighed heavily. 'Ja, I dunno about that.'

'Ag, man, you can find a place. What about Newtown or Fordsburg, they got coloured and whites living there a long time already?'

'No, man, that all finish and klaar now! They kicking the coloureds out of Newtown and Fordsburg also, the same time they going to bulldoze Sophiatown. We all going to our own place. Indians one place, coloureds to Coronationville and the blacks going to Meadowlands and Diepkloof. That leaves the whites anywhere they want except not the places where the black and the coloured and the Indian folks been forced to live.' She laughed bitterly.

Tandia, who had been listening to the conversation, for the first time really understood what Mama Tequila had been through to get to the point where she owned and operated Bluey Jay. Maybe she wasn't a good person, but Mama Tequila was strong and resilient and a fighter. Tandia knew she too had to be all of those things if she was going to succeed. She knew that the burning inside of her was about being these things. 'Excuse me, Mama T, and also Madam Flame Flo?' she said suddenly. Mama Tequila looked up in surprise. While she had accepted Tandia as being present in the room, in terms of her conversation with her sister, Tandia had been mentally screened out. She was there to have lunch but not to be a part of the discussion. Her look of surprise turned to annoyance when Tandia added, 'I have an idea.'

Mama Tequila smiled. It was the smile the wolf gave to Red Riding Hood. The girls at Bluey Jay knew it and knew also it didn't augur well for the recipient. 'Maybe you could go take a nice walk in the sunshine, Tandy?' she said, her lips pursed.

Tandia opened her mouth and then thought better of it and began to rise from her chair. Some resilience hey? Just one Red Riding Hood smile from Mama Tequila and you weak as piss! No, bugger it! She sat down again and smiled prettily at both women. 'Swaziland! Why doesn't Madam Flame Flo open a whorehouse and a gambling place in Swaziland?' Tandia asked.

Mama Tequila and Madam Flame Flo had both stayed alive and prospered because they could think fast and on their feet. The coffee cup in Madam Flame Flo's hand dropped to the table, spilling coffee everywhere as a look of astonishment crossed her face. 'Jesus Mary and Joseph!' She turned to her sister. 'You said she was a *slimmetjie!* Jesus! That the best idea! That the best idea I ever heard in my whole life!'

Mama Tequila chuckled. Her scorn of a moment ago turned to approbation for the young girl who sat with them. 'This one is going to go a long, long way, I'm telling you, little sister, one day she going to be a somebody white people going to take a big notice of.'

Swaziland was a British Protectorate, a small mountainous country coloured red on the map which looked as though someone had taken a polite bite out of the eastern side of South Africa. It lay some four and a half hours' drive from Johannesburg and was just beginning the tedious process of being handed back by Britain to its rightful owners. The independence of Swaziland didn't trouble South Africa much, for the tiny country was and would continue to be largely dependent on South Africa for its daily bread.

Apart from forest products, sugar, iron ore and asbestos, the Swazi people had little to offer the Union of South Africa except the sweat of their backs. A part of the black labour which dug the gold in tunnels a mile below the streets of Johannesburg was Swazi. These indentured labourers were recruited to work in the mines on the Witwatersrand by the Native Recruiting Corporation for a minimum period of one hundred and eighty shifts. The Swaziland economy depended heavily on the repatriation of the money they earned. The mine labourers were paid almost no money while they worked and lived on the mine compounds. When they'd served their time – for life in the all-male dormitories where the men slept one above the other on concrete shelves and were fed like animals from giant cauldrons and who carried a copper bracelet with a number and not a name was a perfect simulation of prison – they were repatriated by overnight train to the Swaziland border, where they were paid the full amount of their six months' wages at a de-recruitment centre. The economy of this small, unimportant and very beautiful corner of Africa was based entirely on the export of sweated labour.

While there was some speculation that an independent Swaziland would be a training ground for black terrorists, the Boers consoled themselves with the knowledge that they could choke off the livelihood of the Swazi people in a matter of days should they threaten trouble or become uncooperative.

Tandia's suggestion was a stroke of genius, though it was early times yet. It might be ten years before Swaziland would be released from the paternal guidance and moral stricture of the British Colonial Service, it was time to buy land and start the business of making friends with the royal family. The King of the Swazi, King Sobhuza II, would, they felt sure, see no virtue in the South African Immorality Act and with the establishment of a brothel and casino would see an opportunity too good for his small country to miss. Mama Tequila and Madam Flame Flo instantly believed themselves to be the two people who knew just how to put this proposition to the middle-aged black monarch who preferred a leopardskin to a suit and who had been absolute tribal ruler of his people for thirty-three years.

The two women were excited, Mama Tequila just as much as Madam Flame Flo. Mama Tequila wasn't stupid; she knew that events were catching up with her at Bluey Jay. She'd be lucky if she had another ten years. The Geldenhuis affair, the biggest and most dangerous threat to Bluey Jay's existence so far, was bound to have serious repercussions as Geldenhuis set about reaping his revenge. Bluey Jay was, she knew, an anachronism, a small island of defiance in a sea of defeat. Even this was an exaggeration. Mama Tequila knew you couldn't stay open without the tacit approval of some pretty high-up officials in the government, and now they were under increasing pressure and sooner or later would have to capitulate.

In Swaziland there was a place for both sisters to start again. Mbabane, the country's mountain capital, was an ideal location for people coming from the Transvaal and Natal. All Mama Tequila's old clients would still be available to her on an occasional dirty twenty-four and the rest of the white male population could now get legit black weekend pussy no more than four hours' drive from their front door. The Van der Merwe sisters would be united at last. Flo would handle the casino and she, the one and only Mama Tequila, would run the whorehouse.

Mama Tequila wanted more time to think, and she didn't want Flo to overwork her praise for Tandia's suggestion. Tandia was after all beholden to Mama Tequila, and the big woman wasn't about to let her off the hook too easily. She intended to build up a burden of indebtedness in Tandia before the little *slimmetje* became a lawyer. A person never knew when a lawyer might be needed. Mama Tequila wanted a good, solid debt she could cash in if the time came and the need arose.

'Ja, it is a good idea, but also it's got some problems,' Mama Tequila said in a flat voice. Flo was about to protest, but her sister raised her hand. 'Later! Later, you hear? Tonight maybe we can talk. One thing is good, with something like this you could have Stephanie with you?'

'Ag, man, I was going to tell you before about that. She wants to get married.'

Mama Tequila spread her arms out towards her sister, a look of resignation on her face. To anyone observing, as Tandia did, it would have seemed a curiously inappropriate reaction. Delight and congratulations might have been expected.

Tandia was filled with curiosity at the prospect of Madam Flame Flo's daughter being married, but the expression on Mama Tequila's face told her not to become involved. Quite suddenly, Madam Flame Flo began to cry.

'Flo, no tears, you hear!' Mama Tequila snapped.

Madam Flame Flo sniffed and blew into her napkin. 'It's so hard, ousie!' she said in a tiny voice.

'I know, but crying not going to help!'

'She's, she's going to marry a Boer!' Madam Flame Flo blurted out. 'My baby is going to marry a fucking Boer!'

'It's better than a fucking kaffir!' Mama Tequila shouted at her.

'It isn't, ousie! I rather she married a tsotsi or a gangster than a verdoemde hairy back!'

'Flo, lissen! When you gave her to the nuns to bring up like a nice little white girl, when you kissed her goodbye at that convent boarding school, it was all over between you and Stephanie. It was all over, you hear? You gave her to the white world! You can't go blubbing to have her back now she wants to marry a Afrikaner!'

Madam Flame Flo avoided her sister's eye and fumed suddenly to Tandia. 'How old are you, Miss Tandy?'

'Seventeen, eighteen this year,' Tandia replied.

'Nearly the same. My daughter is nineteen, this year twenty.' She smiled at Tandia. 'She's not nearly as beautiful as you, but she has white skin, blonde hair and blue eyes, dark blue like the winter sky.'

Tandia flushed. 'I'm sorry,' she stammered, 'I know how you must feel.'

Madam Flame Flo sniffed again and wiped her nose. 'Ag, it's my own fault. I deserve this,' she started to cry softly again. 'My beautiful Stephanie, she going to marry a white Boer bastard who's just like her fucking daddy!'

'Flo! You want I should call Juicey Fruit Mambo and get back in that big Packard and go home? Because if that what you want you got to just keep on like this!

You want to run a brothel? Ha! You couldn't run a ring-a-ring-a-rosie contest! With Stephanie it's finish and klaar. We decided that long, long ago! You cry one more time, I'm going home, that for blerrie sure!' Mama Tequila dipped into her handbag and produced a tiny lace handkerchief. 'Here!' she snorted, holding it out to her sister.

Madam Flame Flo took the hanky and dabbed at her eyes. She was embarrassed by her outburst and at the reprimand from her older sister.

Tandia rose from her chair. 'I think I'll go for a walk,' she said quietly, in an attempt to extricate herself gracefully from the situation.

'No, please, Miss Tandy, you stay,' Madam Flame Flo sniffed, pulling her head right back. 'I'm orright now, really, it's okay, all over.' She smiled through the last of her tears. 'You can be my daughter, you hear?'

Tandia smiled back. 'What about being my Aunty? I'd like to have you as my Aunty Flo. But only if you call me Tandy.'

'That's true,' Mama Tequila chuckled. 'No more Miss Tandy, this not the right place; just Tandy from now on.'

'You got it!' Madam Flame Flo said smiling broadly. 'From now on I'm your Aunty Flo and you just plain Tandy who is beautiful and clever and has nice manners also.'

The crisis was over and Mama Tequila flipped open her cigarette case and removed a cork-tip, lit it and blew a cloud of smoke towards the ceiling. 'Ja, okay, Tandy, you go for a walk, but just be careful, you hear, all the bright boys and the tsotsis will want to make your acquaintance.'

'Juicey Fruit Mambo will want to come,' Tandia

replied. She would have preferred to venture up the street alone, to feel the strange sense of freedom she'd experienced the moment they'd entered the ramshackle do-it-yourself township, but she knew Mama Tequila would expect the big black man to tag along.

'Ja, that's a damn good idea,' Mama Tequila said.

'Goodbye, Aunty Flo,' Tandia called softly to Madam Flame Flo.

Madam Flame Flo smiled. She seemed to have recovered, and she watched Tandia leave the room. 'So beautiful and so clever!' She handed the balled, wet hanky back to her sister.

Mama Tequila returned the handkerchief to her bag. 'Ja, I never seen Tandy like this before. Usually the cat got her tongue. She's a very quiet type person. I think maybe being up here on the Rand and in Sophiatown is making her different.' She turned to her sister. 'Flo, I must go lie down for my beauty sleep, you hear? I going to take three Aspro, I got a terrible headache from the drive. Is there water in my room?'

'Oh my God! I forgot the pudding!' Flo said, alarmed. 'Some pudding! Wait, you must have some. It's jelly and custard with peaches, just how you like it always!'

'No, jong, *ek is heeltemal versadig, liefling*. I don't like to eat much at lunchtime. Tonight maybe, hey?' Mama Tequila pushed her plate away, made a clearing on the table directly in front of her, and placed her handbag onto it. Then she put both her hands flat on the tablecloth and, pushing down, slowly rose from her chair. She smiled at her sister. 'We made a good start today, Flo. Here, man! This Swaziland thing, it a blerrie wonderful idea! We talk some more tonight, hey?'

'There is water for washing in your room. I'll send

the kitchen girl with some nice cold ice for your sore head,' Flo said, grateful that she was back in her sister's good books.

'Flo, *moenie worry nie, alles sal reg kom, liefling*!' Mama Tequila comforted her. 'Lots can happen in young love between the diamond ring and the band of gold. And don't worry about yourself, you hear? When they going to bulldoze your house?'

'When the winter comes, June, July, maybe August. We won't have another summer in Sophiatown. This the last.'

Mama Tequila killed her cigarette in the ashtray. 'Little sister, we seen a lot of things in our time. We seen hard times and some good. But one thing I know, as long as a white policeman can be bribed – and that a long, long, time, baby – and as long as men like to get drunk and their one-eyed snake want pussy, we got no problems, only we got opportunities.' She glanced towards the door, which was something most coloured and black people seemed to do when they were about to mention the Boer government. 'Even if that bastard Strijdom tries to close us down, like he trying to close down Sophiatown! Maybe with Sophiatown he can do it. He can come in and smash everything with a big bulldozer so people's houses are just bricks and their past lies in the dust. But if he thinks he can come here and bulldoze the Van der Merwe sisters, that will be the day! He got to get up very early in the morning to do that!'

Flo was dishing out a small helping of jelly for herself. 'Maybe just a little pudding, to take with me in my room,' Mama Tequila said, and then continued. 'You know who we like, little sister? We like when you put a drop of that mercury stuff. You know, what they

389

call it, man? Quicksilver! Remember when we was young *oubaas* we would pour some quicksilver on the linoleum and then we'd try to pick it up with our two fingers. Remember that? Well, that what we like, you and me!' Mama Tequila suddenly burst out laughing. 'As long as a man got a mouth so he can open it to drink and a one-eyed snake trying to wake up in his trousers, you and me, darling, we in business!' She took the bowl of jelly, custard and big halves of golden tinned peaches which Flo had now heaped almost to overflowing into a soup plate and, chuckling, waddled from the room.

'*Slaap leiker, ousie,*' Madam Flame Flo called after her.

'Ja, I will sleep like a baby,' Mama Tequila called back.

Tandia found herself outside in the bright sunshine. January is hot on the high veld, but at nearly six thousand feet, Johannesburg has no humidity and the air is almost always crisp and clear. Sometimes when the wind blows it raises a fine curtain of dust from the mine dumps that settles over the city and causes the skin to itch and the eyes to inflame. But these occasions are infrequent and generally the high veld climate is delightful. So at half past one on a cloudless day, despite the dirt and the piles of rubbish burning on the side of the road, the ruts and the puddles left from last night's rain in the roadway, Good Street looked bright and inviting to Tandia.

Juicey Fruit Mambo was outside beside the Packard. He'd washed it down and now it was surrounded by street urchins helping him to polish the big brown machine. They were laughing and shouting and having a high old time. Almost all the kids had a sucker stick poking from the corner of their mouths. Juicey Fruit Mambo's small-boy magic evidently worked just as well with these tough little urban kids as it did with the kids from the kraal down beside the river. He was a master of small-boy psychology, which was generally heavily slanted towards unabashed and blatant bribery.

'Have you eaten?' Tandia asked as she approached.

'Yes, Missy Tandy, plenty scoff in dis place,' Juicey Fruit Mambo answered. 'Madam Flo, she very nice madam.'

'I see you have made friends already, hey?' Tandia indicated the kids who had come to stand around the big black man and now stared shyly at her. She lifted her hand in a signal of friendship, waggling her fingers. 'Hi, everyone!'

'Good afternoon, miss!' they chorussed. It was a class-room routine which neither they nor she had expected and both parties seemed surprised at the spontaneous reaction.

Juicey Fruit Mambo grinned. 'Eh, eh, eh! Dis boys dey big skelms, but I tink dey my friend, also.' He suddenly looked serious. 'You want to go somewhere, Missy Tandy?'

'Just for a walk. You can stay if you like, I'll be all right on my own.'

Juicey Fruit Mambo looked shocked. 'Dis very bad place, Missy Tandy. You not walk by yourself, plenty tsotsi boys in dis place!'

Tandia loved Juicey Fruit Mambo too much to protest, and they set off down the street followed by at least a dozen urchins of various shades, the darkest of them seemingly a full African while the lightest, despite the dirt that seemed to cover him from head to toe, was unmistakably a tousle-headed blond with blue eyes.

'Dis skelms, dey ask for me, is dis young missus a fillim star? Ja, for sure! I say. Ja, ja, dey tell to me also, we know dis, we hear dat big fat mama how she talk Americano language!'

'Juicey Fruit Mambo! You shouldn't say such things, they'll tell grown-up people and then we'll get into trouble!'

Juicey Fruit Mambo began to laugh uproariously and all the kids joined in, not knowing why he was laughing but prepared to share in the merriment of their new friend. After all, he had bought them suckers all round at the coolies' and told them about his magic gold teeth. Which of course, they knew was a heap of crap, but a person couldn't let a good story like that go past when it came from someone who looked after a Packard and also a big, fat American fillim star and a very pretty young one who could possibly be just about anyone a person could see on the fillims.

'Maybe she's Snow White!' Flyspeck Mendoza, a dark-eyed, dark-skinned, curly-haired kid said gravely.

Dog Poep Ismali, whose father had a bicycle shop in Annadale Street, objected, 'Ag, man! Snow White wasn't a real person! She was just pitchers *drawn* with a pencil and coloured in! You can ask my sister, if you like? You mad if you think there is real people who is dwarves like Grumpy and Dopey?'

Too Many Fingers Bembi, the small black boy who looked like a pure African, giggled. 'Your stupid brother who is gezonked in the head looks like one of them dwarves and he is dopey!'

The kids all laughed, but Dog Poep Ismali, who was the cleverest in the class, ignored them. 'I think she definitely the one riding the black horse in *National Velvet*.

That for sure, man!' To emphasise his certainty, he added, 'Only she was much younger then, now she's grown up some more.' Dog Poep offered this observation as though he was fitting the last piece of absolute proof into place.

They all instantly agreed with him, even those of them who hadn't seen the picture. Dog Poep had a sister who worked as an usherette at the Odin bioscope and so he was considered a bit of an authority on the fillims. Besides, they all very much wanted to believe him.

'Why you laughing, Juicey Fruit Mambo? You told them something you shouldn't have, didn't you?'

'Dis boys, dey want for you to marry,' Juicey Fruit Mambo giggled. Then he beckoned to one of the older boys. 'You tell for Missy Tandy, who you want for her to marry, okay?'

'What's your name?' Tandia asked the small boy who had stepped forward. He was too dark to pass for white. His matted hair was brown and curly and his eyes a lighter coloured brown than Bantu. His shirt was dirty and it missed two buttons and the pocket of his equally dirty shorts was torn.

Taking a raspberry sucker from his mouth the boy smiled as he answered, 'Johnny Tambourine, miss!' Then, resting his head on his shoulder, he looked up at her cheekily and asked, 'Have you come from Hollywood to marry Gideon Mandoma, miss?'

The kids must have seen how she instinctively reacted to the boxer's name, for they all started to laugh. Of course, that was it! Mandoma, the welterweight who had lost a disputed title-fight decision to Geldenhuis, must live in Sophiatown. The brown-eyed kid was talking about one of the two boxers Patel had rated higher than any other amateurs he'd seen in the ring.

'Mandoma, the welterweight? He lives here?' Tandia asked.

'Ja, miss, he's the best in the world! Welterweight champion of black Africa and also really the white champion because he was rooked!' Johnny Tambourine said this vehemently. 'It's God's truth! They *verneuked* him, miss. My uncle was there, he saw the whole fight. Mandoma won every round!'

Several of the other kids chorussed, 'It's true, miss, they rooked him!'

'They gave the title to the policeman whose name is Geldenhuis,' Dog Poep Ismali explained gravely, bringing a little sensible consideration into the emotional outburst. 'It was because Gideon Mandoma is a kaffir they wouldn't give it to him. The whites don't want a kaffir who could beat a white man, miss.'

At the mention of Geldenhuis's name Tandia had gone cold. He was still there, the dark shadow that never went away. She shook her head and skipped down the road ahead of the kids. She hadn't skipped like this since she'd been a little kid herself and it helped to erase the policeman's footprints in her mind.

'I don't even know Gideon Mandoma! How can I marry him if I don't know him?' she called back, covering her sudden apprehension with laughter.

'Easy, miss! You can meet him any time you want, he's a big friend of ours!' Johnny Tambourine, who seemed to assume the mantle as leader, called after her. Then all the kids, pushing their hoop-and-wire contraptions, took off after her yelling and laughing.

'Ja, he's our friend!' they shouted happily.

Tandia started to run down the road, her arms spread wide. 'Not today, thank you. Today I want you to show me all around the place, okay?'

Johnny Tambourine was the first to catch up with her. 'You can join our gang if you like, miss?' he offered.

Tandia stopped and turned. 'Thank you, I'd like that, that's very nice of you, Johnny!'

'Johnny Tambourine, miss, that's my name. You see my pa plays in the Harlem Swingsters with Gwigwi the clarinet player at Balanski's Picture Palace, that's how I got my name.' He was certain that Tandia would be impressed.

'Oh, I'm sorry Mr Tambourine whose first name is Johnny. I promise on my word of honour it won't happen again.'

'You can be our *nooi*!' Flyspeck Mendoza suggested, giggling.

'Of course!' Tandia replied. She looked serious for a moment. 'Unless of course you've got some other girls for sweethearts?'

'No, miss!' they all shouted.

'No, miss, only you, we only like you!' Dog Poep replied hurriedly, anxious to assure her that she was the only woman they cared sufficiently about to invite into their gang.

'Good! What must I do to be your nooi and also be in your gang?'

This seemed to bemuse them somewhat, until a small blond boy named Kaas Kop, looking down at his feet and making a circle in the earth with his dusty big toe, spoke up. 'Ag, man, nothing hard, just easy stuff like being pretty an' all that?' They all nodded their heads in rapid agreement.

'Ja, miss, that's all!' they chorussed.

Johnny Tambourine waited until the noise had died down. 'Ja, just stuff like that, you don't have to, you know, do things.'

'What sort of things, Johnny Tambourine?' Tandia asked.

He looked awkward. 'Well, like you married to us or anything. You don't have to do that, you know what married people do?'

'There's too much talk about marriage around here!' Tandia laughed. 'I'll just be your nooi, but not like we married, okay?'

They all looked serious and nodded their heads in agreement. 'And you don't have to spill blood also!' Johnny Tambourine said. 'Girls don't have to do it to belong,' he added, inventing this new rule for female membership.

'I jolly well hope not!' Tandia winced, 'I'm not at all the brave type!'

'That's okay, miss,' Dog Poep Ismali said. 'That's what we for, we can be brave for you any time you like.'

'Okay, I'll try and be the best nooi you ever had,' Tandia said graciously. 'You must call me Tandy. No other name, just Tandy! Now you got to show me around the place, you hear? Juicey Fruit Mambo and me, we want to see everything in Sophiatown, okay?'

Some of the kids raced ahead and then turned to watch Tandia and Juicey Fruit Mambo walking up Good Street towards the Odin, the largest cinema in the whole of Africa. Outside the large cinema was a poster which displayed a picture of a smiling young boxer, gloved and stripped to the waist in the classic boxing pose. The poster announced the coming Saturday night fight between Gideon Mandoma and an Irish welter-weight named Terence 'Iron Jaw' McGraw. Tandia's heart began to beat faster and she knew that somehow she had to persuade Mama Tequila to take her to see the fight.

Eighteen

The following morning when Peekay awoke he hurt. His bones hurt, his muscles and joints hurt and his head hurt. But his head hurt the most, from a combination of Habib's fists and too much champagne. Both his eyes were pumped up, mere slits, the eyelids stretched and swollen, purple as aubergine.

The three young men had returned to Harriet's aunt's flat in Knightsbridge well after midnight. To Harriet's surprise it was Peekay, looking as though he'd been in a bad accident, who was supporting Hymie and Togger. As it turned out, Peekay's sobriety was only a matter of degree. She'd bathed his eyes with boracic powder and tried to persuade him to go to bed. But Peekay was too tired and too drunk to listen. Much singing and exaggerated replaying of the fight had taken place before she'd finally coaxed Togger onto a couch in the sitting-room and Hymie and Peekay onto the two beds in the second bedroom. E.W., who'd been enormously disturbed by what he'd witnesed in the ring, had taken a little pink pill and didn't stir from the safety of the tiny bedroom study. Harriet had the run of the whole flat, since her aunt was abroad – she spent her winters every year in the south of France.

In winning against Habib, Peekay had received the worst beating in his life. Despite his protests, Hymie insisted he check in to Guy's Hospital for a thorough examination. Apart from bruised ribs and bruising to the back of his arms, where he'd taken a lot of Habib's punches, the examination showed him to be in a sound condition. The young Australian intern summed up. 'We've given you a neurological examination; your reactions seem okay, the X-ray shows no broken ribs. You won, I believe? Bloody hell, I'd hate to see the other bloke. Okay, mate, if you start getting headaches, throwing up, that sort of thing, get back here fast. Blood in your urine is nothing, you can expect it for a few days, but if it persists, come back. You'll have a couple of beaut eyes for a week or two, but other than that, if you take it easy for a few days, I reckon you'll be right as rain.'

They returned to the flat and Harriet spent the latter part of the morning sketching Peekay's battered face. 'This is marvellous stuff, darling. I may never get the chance to see you like this again.'

'Christ, I hope not,' Peekay cried.

Harriet laughed. 'You're too pretty. From a sculptor's point of view you've definitely changed for the better.' She grew suddenly serious. Leaning over, she gently kissed both purple, swollen eyelids. 'Please, Peekay, darling, don't ever get hurt this badly again!'

Peekay brought his hands up to hold Harriet's head, then brought her face towards his swollen lips and kissed her deeply on the mouth. When at last they pulled away from each other they observed Hymie, propped against the door jamb, watching them from the doorway.

'Kissing it all better, are we?' He seemed to hesitate for a split second. 'Is the mouth-to-mouth resuscitation only for the boxer? There's a manager over here who's fading fast, about to expire from a terminal hangover.'

Harriet threw her head back, grinning. She didn't appear in the least embarrassed. She crossed to Hymie and kissed him on the mouth, lingering long enough for the kiss to be intimate, before drawing away. 'How about some coffee for everyone?'

She turned and walked from the room without looking back. She was wearing trousers as usual and a green cashmere sweater which showed the swell of her breasts. Despite his hangover, Peekay found himself wanting her.

'Hymie, we must talk,' he said the moment Harriet had left the room.

'Later, Peekay.' Hymie flopped into a chair. 'What we both need is a glass of champagne ... hair of the dog.'

'Not for me!' Peekay said quickly. 'Hymie, I really need to talk to you. It's important!'

Hymie shrugged absently. 'I know you do, Peekay. We'll talk in the car on the way back to Oxford this afternoon. Last night was a mis-match. I've never seen you fight better, you were bloody marvellous. But we won't do a stupid thing like that again, will we?'

Peekay nodded silently. He knew Hymie understood why he'd agreed to fight Habib. A win against such a fighter automatically eliminated about seven opponents. These were fighters Peekay would normally have to box to get to the professional level represented by Habib. It could possibly mean getting a crack at the world title a year earlier. On the other hand, had Habib beaten him, say played with him and then knocked him out in an early round, it would have set them back disastrously, perhaps forever.

'Ja, you're perfectly right,' Peekay said finally and then added, 'for once I've got a saying, it comes from Geel Piet. I once asked him how he managed to stay alive in prison. 'Ag man, *klein* baas,' he said. 'When you're skating on thin ice you may as well tap dance.' Peekay shrugged. 'We got lucky last night.'

Hymie sprang from his chair and grabbed Peekay fiercely by the shoulders. 'For Christ's sake, Peekay! That French bastard nearly took you out. You took a hiding into the bargain and finally you had to offer him a clean shot at your jaw so you could gamble on a Geel Piet eight to take him out of the fight. That's not winning tactics! That's fucking suicide!' He paused, catching his breath. 'You're probably the most intelligent boxer in the world and certainly amongst the most skilful. If we can't win using your wit and your skill, then let's get the fuck out of the game before you suffer brain damage!' He drew back, releasing Peekay's shoulders. 'You know something, man? Dutch was right to blast you!'

Peekay didn't speak. There was nothing to say. Hymie was right. But he was also wrong. Peekay knew that he hadn't just got lucky. He'd picked his way through no-man's-land before. Sometimes you're only saved because you are prepared to die, prepared to negotiate the minefield. Sometimes danger is your friend and only ally. How could he explain, even to Hymie, that he knew with absolute certainty when he'd offered Habib his jaw, that the best punch the French Algerian was capable of throwing wouldn't knock him out. In his head Peekay was fighting for the welterweight championship of the world, whereas Habib was fighting for a purse. They are not the same thing; a dream is often lonely, but providing you're prepared to prevail, it's invincible.

It was also why Peekay knew Oxford wasn't going to give him what he was going to need in South Africa. They were going into a fight in which you had to be willing to put your life on the line every time. There could be nothing but a total commitment. He was going to go against people who wouldn't play by the tidy rules of jurisprudence, the laws set down like markings on a football field. They would change the playing field to suit themselves and the only way to beat them was to venture everything you were and everything you had to offer every time you stepped into the arena. He would always have to offer his jaw, take an instinctive risk. South Africa was going to be the final round against Habib all of the time and there was nothing at Oxford that could prepare him for that.

Hymie and Peekay set out for the return to Oxford about mid afternoon when the effects of the fight and their hangovers were less severe. The snow of Christmas had long disappeared. The countryside on the way to Oxford was ploughed and looked winter worn, with birch and elm lining the horizon like upturned witches' broomsticks against a steely sky. Peekay thought of it as 'a crow-lonely landscape'; every once in a while the only sign of life would be a lone black crow resting high in the filigreed branches of an elm or birch, its raucous caw the one sound above the wind and engine noise.

It's funny that, he thought to himself. Africa too has its crow-lonely landscape, but instead, it is hot and harsh, with the midday sun beating the bush into silent submission, blackening the shade so that where it throws, under a tree or rock, it looks like a deep, cool hole in the sun-leached landscape. Only the anthracite crow is game enough to caw into the squinting African stillness.

'Hymie, I think you know what I'm going to say. It's about Harriet.'

'But you are going to say it anyway?'

'I can't even say it happened by mistake. That we were thrown together.'

'I'm glad you're not trying to blame it on the irresistible forces of nature.' Hymie glanced quickly at Peekay. 'Jesus, we're lucky.'

It seemed a curious remark and Peekay didn't know quite how to respond. 'Lucky?'

'Ja, for Harriet to deflower you.' He paused momentarily. 'At least we have that in common.'

Peekay sensed that Hymie wasn't angry. There was no sarcasm in his voice. 'Hymie, I know she's yours but I can't help it. I can't keep my hands off her. I can't say I'm sorry. I'd be lying. I don't know what to do.'

Hymie kept his eyes fixed on the road ahead. 'You don't understand. I'm bloody glad she accepted you and that, unlike me, you were able to make love to her.'

'Shit, Hymie, what are you saying?'

Hymie gave a wry little snort. 'I'm a phoney, Peekay. In the sex department I'm two sandwiches short of a picnic.'

Peekay was too shocked to respond. Hymie seemed to read his thoughts. 'You needn't worry, I'm not a homo!' He glanced quickly at Peekay, who despite himself, was unable to conceal his relief. 'Even that would be something. Alexander the Great was a homosexual, Michelangelo . . . the list of the greats who preferred their own sex is ten miles long. I wouldn't mind being included on it one day. You can live with knowing what you are. That's the trouble. I'm nothing. I'm fucking nothing!' He slammed down hard on the brakes and the little Ford skidded crazily for a moment, its back tyres bumping before it stopped.

Hymie cut the engine and pulled on the handbrake. 'I can't get it up! I have absolutely no desire whatsoever to fuck. Not a male or a female or even a bloody duck! Not you, whom I love more than anything in my life, not Harriet, whom I adore. Not anyone . . .' His voice trailed off. He paused, then gave a bitter little laugh. 'How does my world end? Not with a bang but with a wimp.' Even in his pain Hymie couldn't help joking.

'But you said, Harriet . . . you know, had taken your virginity?' the expression seemed old-fashioned.

'Yeah, she did. No matter how bizarre the experience, you can only lose your virginity once, thank God. We were both blotto and somehow, Christ knows, I managed to get an erection.'

'Jesus, Hymie! That means something, surely?'

Hymie shook his head. 'I don't recall what it was like. I was too pissed. Shortly after we'd done it, or at least I *think* we'd done it, I threw up all over the sheets. Being sick was the more memorable of the two incidents. At least I remember that part. I guess I can technically claim I'm no longer a virgin, but to be honest Harriet might as well have been a knothole in the ironing board.'

'Hymie, I'm sorry. I'm sorry on two fronts, for your predicament and for blowing your cover. It goes without saying . . .'

'Well then, don't say it! The truth is, I'm glad. I'm glad you know. It's worried me since school that you've never questioned my obvious lack of libido. Now you know the truth,' Hymie looked up at Peekay and shrugged his shoulders. 'For what it's worth.'

'A doctor? There must be something?'

'Ja, sure, one day maybe.'

That seemed to be the end of it. In all the time Peekay had known him, this was only the second time Hymie had admitted a weakness. The business with the Odd Bodleians and now this. He knew there was no point in persisting with his sympathy, Hymie didn't operate that way. He was the most clear-eyed, clear-minded person Peekay had ever known, even more so than Doc. He would put this thing aside and get on with his mercurial life.

Hymie turned on the ignition and they pulled away, saying nothing for a while. They passed through a small village of thatched cottages just like the ones on the lids of Hymie's father's chocolate boxes. The air smelt vaguely of wood smoke and wet hay and the gardens were clothed in sombre winter greenery. In one garden, where they'd stopped at an intersection, the dry spines of summer's hollyhocks stood stark against a grey cottage wall.

'What about Harriet?' Peekay asked at last. 'We haven't resolved anything.'

Hymie grinned. 'On the Richter scale of sensitivity you haven't even made the graph-line waver. What do you mean, what about Harriet? You sleeping with her? I thought we'd discussed that?'

'Well no, not really, not our mutual relationship.'

'Ours? You mean mine? Do you want it to change?'

'No! I'd hoped things would, you know, continue,' Peekay hesitated. 'But I couldn't see how.'

Hymie grinned. 'And now you can?'

Peekay flinched inwardly. 'Yes, and now I can,' he echoed softly.

'Peekay, you have to get rid of the male notion that you own a woman. Harriet can't be owned. When sex isn't a big deal you get to see things a bit differently. You don't think with your cock all the time.'

'I say, that's a bit unfair!'

'Not at all,' Hymie contradicted. 'Consider the hours you've spent thinking about losing your virginity. About having your famous whipped cream experience.'

Peekay was becoming distressed. While neither of them were raising their voices, they were plainly quarrelling. Harriet was squarely positioned between them. How nearly Hymie could have been right.

'Hymie, you're wrong, I didn't lose my virginity to Harriet.'

Hymie's foot involuntarily came off the accelerator and the car veered momentarily towards the wrong side of the road before he hastily corrected his steering and pushed down on the accelerator again. 'Shit, Peekay, what are you saying?'

Peekay told Hymie about the night with Togger, retelling it in some detail, taking the time to move away from the quarrel, including the funny bits, forcing Hymie to laugh.

It was a vastly expanded version of the story he'd told when he'd arrived back at Oxford with a broken nose. Then he'd simply recounted to Hymie how he and Togger had been involved in a fight in a nightclub. It had been the truth as far as it went. Peekay couldn't explain exactly, even to himself, why he'd kept the full story from Hymie. It had been so wonderful with Carmen, he instinctively didn't want to debase it. He knew Hymie would want every detail and that, in the retelling, the components of the evening would be reduced to what they probably were: a sleazy nightclub for perverts serviced by a bunch of hard-faced female drink hustlers who were willing to take off their clothes to a taped sound track so they could make the rather sad claim of being in showbiz. It hadn't been like that at all. To Peekay it had been a magical evening which could never happen again. In losing his virginity to Carmen he had also lost his innocence. Henceforth he would see the peeling paint and the purple bruises on fleshy thighs, the greasy satin skirts and shark-tooth lines of black thread where the fishnet stocking had been drawn together in hasty repair.

Finally Peekay got to the part in the story where he told Hymie of his seduction by Carmen. He had kept her relationship to Togger out of the story, sensing that Togger would want this. He painted the scene of her strip-tease, hoping that Hymie might isolate it in his imagination, the one contrast to the surrounding sleaze. But he knew, in reality, that this was unlikely. He retold the fight briefly and concluded with Carmen's offer to take him home.

'And so you see, I never got what I wanted. I might as well have lost my virginity to one of the whores in the mines. I got laid by a stripper in a cheap nightclub for drunks and perverts.' Peekay felt the sudden sting of shame as he denigrated Carmen's status and generosity in an attempt to mend Hymie's hurt.

Hymie glanced over at Peekay. In the darkness of the car cabin Peekay could only guess at his expression, but when he spoke his voice was relaxed. 'You bastard, Peekay! You kept all this from me?'

'Ja, well, you know ...' Peekay knew Hymie wouldn't pursue it. He'd conclude Peekay was ashamed of the manner in which he'd been deflowered. 'Which brings us back to Harriet,' Peekay said, knowing he must force the discussion to some conclusion.

'I'm sorry, Peekay. I was wrong. I guess I was hurt. I wanted to think that your motive was simple penis blunder, the cock erect, blind to reason.' Then he added lamely, 'It helped explain my own inadequacy.'

'You're in love with her, aren't you, Hymie?'

Hymie was silent for a moment. 'Yes,' he paused. 'That must be hard for you to understand.'

Peekay put his hand on Hymie's shoulder. 'It would almost help if it was. But no, it isn't. I feel like a proper bastard.'

'Peekay, you are a proper bastard. Not because you stole my woman. Harriet makes up her own mind about her sleeping partner. Besides, as you now know, I was never a contender and never owned her. You're a proper bastard because you didn't see the possibility of my friendship with her outside of sex. What about all the other sensibilities? Sex doesn't make Harriet unique. Though I can't vouch for it, she's probably pretty interchangeable with a thousand women in that respect. Sex is the least unique aspect of a woman. Her uniqueness lies in dozens of other ways which attracted her to me, made me love her. You're a bastard for not understanding this fully.'

He grinned suddenly. 'Forgive me, Peekay, but when you've got an inactive dick you begin to realise that love has more to it than coitus. I hope you'll not spoil the relationship I have with Harriet by getting your aggressive cock in the way.'

Hymie had spoken without raising his voice and with his eyes mostly on the road. The afternoon had closed in and he now turned on the car lights. The darkness within the car and the throb of the engine seemed to lock them together in time.

'Pull over, Hymie. Stop the car,' Peekay asked.

Hymie braked and pulled the car over to the edge of the road. They were close to the outskirts of Oxford. Peekay embraced Hymie silently, then pulled away smiling.

Hymie laughed suddenly. 'Shit you look terrible!'

'But I feel great!' Peekay replied. 'Bloody woman, she's got us both by the short and curlies.'

Hymie laughed. 'She's only a woman. If we combine our resources and work together we may just get the better of her.'

Life as a professional boxer as well as a student had to be carefully managed. While Hymie took care of all the contracts and gathered the analytical information on Peekay's opponents, Dutch required that Peekay work out three times a week in the London gym as well as fight once every month somewhere in Britain. On two occasions, Peekay had fought in Brussels and once in Paris. It meant a tight weekly schedule for Peekay, who had no intention of letting up on his studies. Despite his reappraisal of Oxford he wanted a first and this meant planning his routine very carefully. Mostly he'd drive down to London in the Ford Prefect, where he'd do a three-hour work-out, which included a sparring session, usually with Togger, but sometimes with any of the middleweights who, aware of the lesson Peekay had given Peter Best, were always anxious to get into the ring with him. Then he'd drive back to Oxford, getting back to Magdalen just before midnight.

While he had almost no time for leisure in his second year at Oxford, Togger and Peekay had formed the habit of having a pint of bitter and a game of darts in the Thomas à Becket downstairs after training.

Hymie had arranged a non-title fight with the British Empire Champion, Iron Bar Barunda, a welterweight from Ghana who now lived in the British Isles. Peekay couldn't fight for the British title because he was not twenty-one, but he could enter for the British Empire title. Both were held by Iron Bar Barunda. Barunda wouldn't put the bigger of his two titles on the line which meant Peekay couldn't get past him in the line-up for fighters he had to beat eventually to get to Spoonbill Jackson. Hymie had managed to negotiate a non-title event with virtually the whole purse going to the black boxer. If Peekay beat him, Hymie's contract stipulated that they'd get a crack at the title in December. Only three continental welterweights were rated higher than Barunda; if Peekay could get past them he was in line for a top North American fighter as well as Soap Dish Jurez, the Cuban, and Manuel Ortez, the Mexican; both of these were welters who were rated contenders for a future world title fight. The fight was to take place during the Oxford summer vacation. Peekay and Hymie had managed to stay at Harriet's aunt's flat in Knightsbridge while Peekay prepared for the fight. Harriet herself had been invited to the University at Aix-en-Provence to teach for five weeks and would miss the bout.

Harriet's Aunt Tom had grown very fond of both young men and since her return to England had become an avid boxing fan. Dressed in an immaculate dinner suit she'd attended all Peekay's fights. Her brilliant henna-coloured Eton crop could be picked out in the centre of the Odd Bodleians where she sat with a set of bongo drums between her knees and a thin black Spanish cheroot dangling from her lips. Bongo drums are not exactly African, but Aunt Tom was a skilled and versatile drummer and used it to beat out the rhythm for the *Concerto for the Southland*, which had by now, along with the Odd Bodleians, become a famous feature of all of Peekay's fights.

Togger and Peekay were in the Thomas à Becket after a training session when Fred, the ex-pug they'd met on their first day, approached Peekay with Dutch Holland.

'This letter come when you was away. Nice lookin' young lady bring it around.'

'Oh yes! Very ris-kay!' Togger said. ''Ere, you gunna open it, ain't ya?'

Peekay assumed a haughty look, mimicking Togger's accent. 'Do yer mind? This is private mail, this is.'

Togger looked crestfallen and Peekay laughed. 'Here, you open it,' he said, handing Togger the envelope.

'You serious then?'

'Ja, sure, go on, read it, man.'

Togger peeled the back flap open very carefully, opening the letter inside he sniffed at it, 'Cor, it don't half pong!'

'C'mon, Togger, what's it say,' Peekay laughed.

Togger began to read.

> *Dear Peekay,*
>
> *How are you? My brother saw you at Earls Court and says you're awfully good. You never did phone me. Maybe you did and I was out? Anyway, I remember you well. Have you got a girlfriend?*
>
> *If you want you can call me at the Dolls' Hospital HAM 7295 on Wednesday we close early, 3.15. We could go for a drink or something. My mum thinks you're smashing, even if you are a toff. My dad*

says there's no future going with a boxer,
but I told him to mind his own business!
   Ta, ta, then, I must get my beauty sleep.
   Love and kisses,

Doris

P.S. My best part is still in the front!
P.P.S. Now you'll think I'm being saucey!!!

'I reckon you're in like bleedin' Flynn, my son.' Togger paused, flapping his pale eyelids, 'Oh yes, very ris-kay!'

'Christ, Togger! Quit that dumb expression, will you? I know exactly what to do, I'll call her, say can she get hold of Gladys, Togger wants to know.'

'Don't you bleedin' dare! Some of me mates saw me that day we went dancin', I only just got me reputation back. Seriously, Peekay, wot'cha gunna do? I mean, 'Arriet's away, ain't she? She's been gone how long, four weeks?' Togger stroked his chin, 'But I suppose you gotta stay faithful like. Mind, she has got a lovely pair 'e tits.'

'Peekay reached over and took the letter from Togger's hands. 'I don't know, we'll see, I've got to go. Aunt Tom's taking me to the Festival Hall. Yehudi Menuhin is playing the Brahms Violin Concerto amongst other musical niceties a peasant like you wouldn't appreciate.'

Peekay arrived back at the flat in Knightsbridge just in time to change for the concert. Aunt Tom handed him a letter from Harriet, the second he'd received since she'd left for the South of France. He didn't have time to read it until he climbed into bed.

Harriet wrote well, but in snatches of thought. She'd been asked to stay another month and felt it was too

411

good an opportunity to miss. What did Peekay think? She'd come under the influence of a sculptor named Claude Shonneborg, who'd studied under Giacometti. Shonneborg's name seemed to crop up much too often in the letter and Peekay hoped that Harriet's preoccupation with her work would as usual have reduced her libido to a barely flickering flame. Although by the end of the letter he'd convinced himself this was not the case and promised himself rather smugly that he'd call Doris in the morning.

'Hello, Hammersmith Dolls' 'ospital, who is it?' a young woman's voice answered.

'Howzit, Doris? It's Peekay. You know, Babychams with a dash? I got your letter.'

'Hello, Peekay.'

Peekay cleared his throat, 'Hurrph, it just happens to be Wednesday, what say we have a drink after your work?'

'Why, that's smashin', Peeekey, I'd like that very much. There's a little club just round the corner what's very nice, very quiet an' all.'

Peekay took down the address. It was too late to turn back now, he told himself. He decided to run around the perimeter of Hyde Park. It would take his mind off Harriet and the Giacometti apprentice, Claude Shitbag. His pulse actually quickened as he thought of the possibility of being unfaithful to Harriet. Peekay decided he'd run further, to include Kensington Garden; and to run past the round pond again. He didn't quite know why, he'd always imagined the round pond in *Peter Pan* was set amongst trees, big old oak trees and birch and Elm, so that you came upon it suddenly, unexpectedly, glimpsing slivers of silver through low hanging branches. He'd been terribly disappointed to find it was

412

simply a round pond with cement edges set into a stretch of grass, not a bit romantic, in fact as ponds go it was rather bleak and had absolutely no character and wasn't even on the Serpentine.

He wondered briefly whether Doris's tits would disappoint him the second time around. After all, he'd been a virgin when they'd seemed wonderful. Perhaps, like the round pond, his imagination had overworked them.

Peekay arrived at the Dolls' Hospital at precisely three o'clock. The window of the shop was filled with broken dolls. Separate dolls' limbs, torsos, heads, arms and legs, a doll's graveyard. There were dolls with no eyes, hollow sockets in broken and cracked heads. Dolls with scarred and broken cheeks, dolls with only one blue eye, half open. Headless dolls and armless trunks, bits of elastic sticking out of holed armpits. They filled the window to a height of about two feet, legs and arms and faces, bodies piled together like victims of a massacre, pushed into a heap by a tyrant bulldozer.

Directly above the pile of broken bodies hung several swings made with green silk tassels suspended above the eyelevel behind a scalloped, dark green painted pelmet, its edges trimmed with gold. Across the length of the pelmet, painted in old-fashioned gold script, were the words *Dolls' Hospital*, and directly underneath in smaller, neat type, *H. Rubens, prop.* On each of the swings sat a beautifully restored doll.

Peekay went into the shop.

The interior was about thirty feet wide with an old-fashioned wooden mahogany counter that ran the width of the shop. Directly behind the counter were six carpenter's work benches, an old-fashioned Singer industrial sewing machine and an equally old wood working lathe.

The large room was bathed in brilliant bluish light from light boxes above each work bench. The effect was of a place with too much light, it was as though the owner of the shop could abide no shadows about him.

The shop appeared empty and the work benches deserted when a small man struggling into a navy overcoat which seemed to reach almost to the floor walked from the doorway of a small partitioned office at the furthermost point in the room. He looked up and hurried towards Peekay, doing up the top buttons of his overcoat.

'Please sir, we are closing now the shop.' He spread his hands in a gesture which seemed to suggest that, should Peekay make an objection, he regretted there was nothing he could do. He wore a homburg hat and round, old fashioned gold-rimmed glasses, a white shirt with celluloid collar and a black silk tie.

The total appearance was of a small, neat, clean-shaven man who was being dragged down by the weight of his overcoat. The cuffs of his neatly pressed blue serge trousers showed no more than three inches below the hem of the coat.

'Good afternoon, sir, I've come to pick up Miss ... er, Doris.' Peekay suddenly realised that he'd either forgotten or had never known Doris's surname.

The little man visibly relaxed and he dug into his overcoat pocket and triumphantly produced a pair of leather gloves, much as a conjuror might produce a live rabbit. He held the gloves up for Peekay to see and, turning, flapped them in the direction of a door at the back of the room. 'Doris? So you want Doris.' He seemed to be thinking. 'Ah yes, that is nice! Miss

Mobbs! Is here a young man!' He called in a voice that carried surprisingly, even though he didn't appear to have raised it.

'Coming, Mr Rubens!' Peekay heard Doris answer back.

Mr Rubens turned back to Peekay, as though only he could possibly have heard her reply. 'She is coming,' he said reassuringly, 'you must wait now, please.' He dug his right hand into his coat pocket again. This time he produced a large bunch of keys, holding them up for Peekay to see. Peekay wasn't quite sure whether he ought to applaud.

'Thank you, sir.'

Mr Rubens nodded. 'Excuse me, young man,' and he moved over to the far end of the counter and punched the cash register open and removed a small wad of one-pound notes. He licked his thumb absently and counted the notes, aloud in German, to thirty-six.

'Thirty-six,' Peekay said suddenly. He'd been counting with the old man and surprised himself when he too declared the final tally out loud.

Mr Rubens' eyebrows shot up, 'So! You are German?' He pronounced the word *Chermin*.

Peekay was embarrassed. 'I'm sorry, sir, I didn't mean to intrude. When I was young I had a friend who taught me to count in German. It was during the war. I was just seeing if I,' he smiled, 'remembered.'

Mr Rubens looked up at Peekay sternly. Bending over the cash register his glasses had slipped halfway down the bridge of his nose and he now looked over the top of them. 'This Germin, he was a Jew?'

'No, sir, he wasn't.'

'A Germin who is not a Jew is teaching you in the war?'

Peekay didn't know why, but he felt compelled to explain to Mr Rubens that Doc hadn't been a Nazi, was the furthermost thing you could get from being a Nazi. 'He was a musician, a professor of pianoforte. It was in Africa.'

'Humph! Who played also maybe Wagner?' Mr Rubens snorted, obviously unconvinced.

'No sir, Beethoven and Mozart, he wasn't at all fond of Wagner, he found him too Teutonic. I don't think my friend was much of a German.'

'Humph!' Mr Rubens undid the top button on his overcoat and, sliding his hand into the lefthand side, withdrew a leather pocket book. He unzipped the wallet and flattening out the wad of notes slipped them full length into the pocket book, completing the task and re-zipping the wallet just as Doris appeared.

'Hello, Peekay, you two met then?'

'Well no, not officially,' Peekay said.

'Mr Rubens, this is my friend, Peekay. Peekay, this is my boss, Mr Rubens!'

'Ha! He is learning to count from Germans!' Mr Rubens said abruptly.

Doris looked from Peekay to the little man and back to Peekay, her expression bemused. Peekay shrugged almost imperceptibly. 'You better be goin' then, Mr Rubens, or you'll get to Ladbrokes too late to place a bet on the four o'clock at Epsom.'

The effect of this announcement brought a look of panic onto the little man's face. He grabbed at the region of his chest where he'd recently stowed his wallet.

'Here, give us the keys, I'll lock up. Where's your brolly, then?' Doris sighed. 'Stay here, I'll bring that too.'

416

Doris returned and handed Mr Rubens back the keys. "'Ere, hold your wrist out, you've forgotten your watch again.'

Mr Rubens pushed back the sleeve of his coat, taking with it the starched cuff of his shirt. Doris strapped a watch on to his wrist; about three inches above it Peekay observed a dark tattoo number on his arm.

Mr Rubens looked up at precisely that moment and saw the expression on Peekay's face. 'Already I have been counted in German, young man,' he said softly.

Doris glanced at his wristwatch before releasing his arm. 'Blimey, it's twenty-past, I'm workin' in me own time!' Turning, she approached the front doors and opening a large fuse box at the side of a door she rapidly killed half a dozen switches with the ball of her thumb, plunging the shop into darkness. She unlatched the two doors as Mr Rubens preceded them down the steps. The old man locked up the shop.

'Good night, Miss Mobbs, thank you.' He turned to Peekay and gave him a slight nod, 'Good night, young man, I think it is better that you count in English.' He walked away.

'C'mon then, Peekay!' Doris linked her arm into his and clung to him as they crossed the street. He imagined he could feel the pressure of her marvellous left tit right through his duffel coat.

Nineteen

Tandia need not have worried about attending the Gideon Mandoma bout. Madam Flame Flo was a well-known Sophiatown ringside figure who never missed a fight. She knew her fighters and she knew her boxing.

She'd been taken to her first few fights by Geel Piet. She'd loved the brash boxing world, the dressing up and the American slang, the cigarette smoke, the excitement, the sweat, and of course the parties afterwards. But in the process she'd learned to love the game itself. She also saw clearly how it was a way for a coloured or black man to achieve fame and even some fortune, and the idea that black could meet white in the ring on equal terms where the best man won enchanted her. Madam Flame Flo took her boxing very seriously and the boxer she loved with a fierce pride and inner joy was Gideon Mandoma.

'I only seen him lose once, because the last fight he lost don't count. Man, he was rooked! But that first time. Magtig! What a fight. I don't think I will ever see a better one than that, even if I live to be one hundred years!'

Tandia was aware that she was talking about the

same fight Patel had so often described, the fight between Gideon Mandoma and the Tadpole Angel where he had acted as referee. From Patel's countless re-tellings she knew every blow, every nuance of the contest. But now she wanted to hear it all again, hear it from fresh lips, see it with new eyes. So she said nothing and waited for Madam Flame Flo to continue.

'The Bantu, the black people, they had this thing about the white boy, the one they called the Tadpole Angel. In all his fights he always fought Boers and always he won. It was the blacks who give him this name, *Onoshobishobi Ingelosi.*

'That mean Tadpole Angel in Zulu. There was some other things also about this white boy. You know how superstitious the kaffirs are? I never heard the whole story but they thought, maybe because he always fought Boers and won, but I think it was something else also, they thought he was a great chief who would save them. Crazy, hey? A white kid, only about fifteen years old, a rooinek also, who was going to save *them* from the hated Boer.'

'That the first time I ever heard of a white man who is going to save the coons, not even a man, just a boy. What happened to him? Where's he now, man?' Mama Tequila asked.

'That the best part, I was coming to that,' replied Madam Flame Flo. 'He in England at the university in Oxford but he also now the British Empire Welterweight Champion and they say he going to go to America to fight for the world title later this year. That why everyone here so angry because Gideon Mandoma was rooked in his fight with the Boer Geldenhuis. You see, when the Tadpole Angel come back Mandoma or Geldenhuis is going to fight him. All the black people

and the coloureds we want a re-match, we want Gideon Mandoma to fight the Tadpole Angel again.'

'For the same reason as before?' Tandia asked.

'Ja, for the blacks it's the same reason. Gideon Mandoma is a very big hero for the blacks, he is a chief, already he is very involved in the ANC freedom campaign. If he can win against the white man, then he will be *Onoshobishobi Ingelosi*, the chosen leader. For me and the other coloured people, we would like him to be leader, but also it would be the best fight possible. Last time when the white boy won, it was very close. The fight could easily have gone Mandoma's way. I'm telling you, man, it would be a fight and a half!'

Tandia wanted Madam Flame Flo to go back to the original fight. 'Aunty Flo, in the beginning, in the first fight wasn't it to decide who would be the *Onoshobishobi Ingelosi*?'

She looked at Tandia in surprise. 'You right. I forgot that. How come you know this?'

Mama Tequila laughed. 'Tandia's daddy was the ref who did that fight.'

'Jesus! Your daddy was the Indian referee, Natkin Patel? You that Patel! Then you know all about the fight between Gideon Mandoma and the Tadpole Angel!'

'Ja, but only from my father, I never heard it told by anybody else. I want to hear it from you, Aunty Flo. My father, he said the Tadpole Angel and Gideon Mandoma, they were the best amateur prospects he ever saw in his whole life. He was also training Geldenhuis for the fight with Mandoma when he died.'

It was Madam Flame Flo's turn to be amazed. 'Jesus, Mary and Joseph! It's a small world, hey? No wonder you want to meet Gideon Mandoma, it like he a part

of your family and everything! Your daddy was training Geldenhuis?'

'Ja, but he thought Mandoma would win. He said, "Geldenhuis is a bladdy good welterweight, world class, if it wasn't for the Tadpole Angel and Mandoma he'd be South African champion, maybe even more, the champion of the British Empire. But the other two, they better!" He said that only a few days before he died.'

'Wragtig! He said that?' She turned to Mama Tequila. 'Jesus! What a small world, hey, ousie? Tandy who is now with you was Patel's daughter!' Her eyes shone with genuine excitement.

Tandia repeated her previous plea. 'Please, Aunty Flo, tell us about the first fight.'

'Ja, okay.' Madam Flame Flo smoothed her dress with the flat of her hands, stroking the top of her legs. 'Who knows how a kaffir's mind works? Don't ask me! The black people, they followed this white kid from when he was very young and then all of a sudden this witch doctor throws the bones and reads the smoke and she says, okay now the *Onoshobishobi Ingelosi* is a man. You know, fifteen years old, now he must prove to the people he is still the Tadpole Angel. Crazy kaffir stuff like that. So they choose Gideon Mandoma, who is a real Zulu chief and also a boxer. If the white boy wins, fair enough, he still the Tadpole Angel. If Gideon Mandoma wins he the new one and he has the power to lead the black people.'

'Gideon Mandoma,' Mama Tequila asked, 'did he also believe all this stuff?'

'Ja, of course! But not just him, everyone. Even me, a little bit. They had the fight over at the school, in the soccer field. Ten thousand people came. God's truth, two kids ... the white one was still at school and

421

Gideon was only sixteen years old and ten thousand people turned up for that fight.' Madam Flame Flo smiled at the memory. 'That night we sold one hundred and fifty gallons of Barberton! But only afterwards. The black people didn't drink at the fight. I'm telling you, man, it was deadly serious.'

'Maybe Gideon Mandoma will get this fight with the white guy. When you say he is coming back?' Mama Tequila asked.

'They say first he's going to fight for the world title in America, then he's coming home. August, September maybe.'

'I don't think Geldenhuis will be ready to fight by then,' she winked at Tandia. 'He had a bad car accident.' Tandia was grateful that Madam Flame Flo's concentration was on her sister so that the shrewd little woman wouldn't note her anxiety at the mention of the policeman's name.

'Ja, it was a great shame, why couldn't the bastard have died?' Madam Flame Flo rejoined. 'They say he'll be better by the end of the year. That's when he would fight the Tadpole Angel for the British Empire Welterweight title. It would be Gideon's fight if he hadn't been rooked. I admit it was a close fight, but everyone, even the *Rand Daily Mail* said it, everyone knew Mandoma won except two of the judges. Those two Boers gave it to Geldenhuis by one lousy point.'

Mama Tequila sighed. 'Ja, my little sister, if what should have been had happened, it would be a different world. The best way to win, no arguments, is to put your opponent down for a ten count. That the only way for the black man and the coloured. If it's going to be a "maybe" then it going to be the white man's maybe not the black man's maybe, that for blerrie sure!'

Saturday night on Good Street was something else, a magic six or eight hours when the people of Sophiatown forgot the trauma and the struggle of the past week, bottled and corked their tiredness and set out to celebrate the business of being alive. The Mandoma fight was on at the Odin; afterwards there would be a short political rally; and then the dance halls and the streets would fill with the jazz and jive of people having a good time. Saturday night in Sophiatown was get drunk, get laid and get dancin' time! Sunday, repenting time, was a long, long way away as the rhythm thumped into Good Street from the shacks and shebeens and good-time places.

Madam Flame Flo's house was no more than a hundred and fifty yards from the Odin, but, naturally, the Packard, which shone to within an inch of its life, was used to deliver the three women to the cinema entrance. Juicey Fruit Mambo, in his tuxedo and red bow tie, hurried round first to open the nearside door facing the cinema for Madam Flame Flo. Then he opened the door facing the street for Mama Tequila to be rocked out of the rear seat of the big car as inconspicuously as possible.

Tandia was dressed in the brilliant green cheongsam which Sonny Vindoo had made for her. With it she wore the matching high heels Hettie and Sarah had given her for Christmas. Her dark springy hair, no more than an inch long, was cut evenly over her scalp so that it looked like a sophisticated cap. From her ears two large gold hoops hung, borrowed from Madam Flame Flo. Her lips were painted a shiny, Rita-Hayworth red, and her magnificent green eyes were heightened with a touch of eyeshadow which started quite dark in the corners of her eyes and went to the palest green over the broad arch of her eyelids.

Tandia was stunningly, ravishingly beautiful, caught at the precise moment when she had become a woman. No awkward gesture or even faint trace of childhood remained. A sudden silence fell on the crowd as she stepped from the car. Then there was a gasp of appreciation as the men entering the cinema for the fight whistled and cheered loudly.

Tandia had learned a great deal about men working the bar at Bluey Jay and now she instinctively reacted to please them, dropping her gaze in a gesture suggesting a hint of shyness and tilting her head slightly as she smiled. The crowd was delighted by the glamour she added to the occasion. There were several young women in the crowd, all dressed up to the nines, but Tandia outshone them all.

The crowd parted as Mama Tequila, dressed in a peacock-blue satin evening dress and turban with matching everything and Madam Flame Flo in a halterneck, red organza dress with matching red satin high heels, walking on either side of Tandia, entered the building.

'It's showtime ladies, we all ritz, glitz and tits tonight!' Mama Tequila said happily as they were ushered by a pretty young Indian girl to the ringside seats that Madam Flame Flo had obtained from her friend and Gideon Mandoma's manager, Mr Nguni. The Indian leaned over Tandia as she was seated.

'My little brother,' she giggled, 'the one they call Dog Poep, he said you were pretty, but I didn't believe him, little brats has got some funny ideas. But I was wrong, you the most beautiful woman I ever seen in my whole life even on the movies.'

Tandia loved the compliment but was quick to repay it. 'You too, you a very pretty girl, what's your name?'

The little usherette smiled. 'Esmeralda,' she replied.

'Esmeralda Ismali, it sounds like a song, like a love song,' Tandia said smiling. The Indian girl's eyes were wide with pleasure as she left.

Tandia found herself enjoying the atmosphere enormously as the crowd shouted, whistled and catcalled instructions and insults at the two fighters in the ring. With the main bout approaching they were impatient for the preliminary bout to end.

Johnny Tambourine, wearing a clean white cotton jacket several sizes too big for him and with a large tray of peanuts and chocolate bars held by a strap around his neck, appeared suddenly at her side. 'Hi, Tandy, everybody is saying you the most beautiful person they ever seen. I think they hundred per cent right!' he announced, and at the same time unloaded a packet of peanuts and a chocolate bar into her lap. 'It's for you, for nothing, because you our nooi and in the gang an' all,' he explained.

'Thank you, Johnny Tambourine, but you can't do this, *you'll* have to pay!'

Johnny Tambourine looked shocked at the suggestion. 'No man, never! I pinched it off another kid's tray, *he'll* have to pay.' Johnny Tambourine must have seen the look on Tandia's face and now he frowned, slightly annoyed. 'It's orright, Tandy, he isn't a member of our gang or anything like that! They done it to me lots of times when I was little.' Then he grinned, deciding to forgive her stupidity as a gang member. 'So long, I got to go now, see ya later, you hear?'

'No wait a minute! Johnny Tambourine, come back here, give me your arm.' He returned and stuck the sleeve of his white coat at her. 'Hold your arm stiff,' Tandia instructed and began to roll the sleeve neatly to just above his wrist. 'Now the other one.' She repeated the performance on the other sleeve. 'Okay, that's better now, hey?'

Johnny Tambourine grinned. 'How am I supposed to pinch stuff off other guys' trays if my hands is showing?' But he was obviously pleased at the attention and aware that men from all over couldn't take their eyes off Tandia. 'Thanks, Tandy, see you after the fight. If I can pinch an eskimo pie I'll bring it!'

Tandia raised her hands in alarm. 'No! No ice cream, Johnny Tambourine!' But the small boy was already several rows away shouting, 'Peeee-nuts! Chocooo-litz! Peeee-nuts', his oversized white jacket reaching to well below his knees.

The final preliminary came to an end in a flurry of exhausted ineffectual blows and the crowd booed both fighters good-naturedly out of the ring.

A young black man with a big smile and a beautifully fitted black evening suit with a white carnation leapt into the ring. He seemed to vibrate, several parts of his body moving at the same time as though he was headed in several directions at once. He moved over to lift the microphone up into the ring, giving Tandia a pearly-white smile as he did so.

'Good evening my brothers and sisters, majietas and girls! Please give a warm welcome to the sensational Dorothy "Dotty" Masuka, the sizzling hepcat, Africa's own soul lady, the one and only yippy-woo-biddy-hi-de-ho lady, the singing sensation from Bulawayo! To accompany the first African lady of song I give you the Harlem Swingsters with the immortal clarinet of Mister Funny-face himself, the great Gwigwi!'

The crowd started to stomp and whistle and yell their heads off as half-a-dozen musicians climbed into the

426

ring. A small, smiling man moved to the microphone as the compere hopped out of the ring. He held a clarinet in his hands, putting it to his lips as the bass started to beat out the rhythm and the alto sax pumped out a blues number slow and mournfully. He appeared to blow, but no sound came from the clarinet. He withdrew it, looked at it, tapped it with his finger as though remonstrating with it, all the while pulling funny faces. He tried and failed again as the rhythm in the background increased and the alto wailed plaintively. Finally, he moved over to the edge of the ring and, using the clarinet, pointed at Tandia, beckoning to her with his index finger to come to the edge of the stage.

Tandia was almost paralysed with fear but Mama Tequila, nudging her, whispered, 'Tandy, this your big chance, baby, go-go!' Shaking, Tandia rose and walked to the edge of the stage, to the thunderous applause and whistles of the crowd. Gwigwi brought the clarinet sideways to his lips and kissed it and then pointed to Tandia and kissed it again, whereupon he handed the instrument to her. Tandia, smiling despite her terror, brought the clarinet to her lips and kissed it lightly, handing it back to the little man. Gwigwi, smiling and miming his ecstasy, walked backwards towards the mic and, bringing the clarinet up to his lips, he blew a long, sweet, absolutely pure note that reached up, cutting through the smoke and the hubbub of the crowd, holding its distance and clarity until the cinema was completely hushed and the lone clarinet became the spirit of them all, and then fading down, slowly, perfectly controlled until it warped into a whisper hardly heard at all.

The cinema broke into wild applause and the band picked up the beat, quickened the pace and swung into Dixieland. The lights came down low until a single spot held onto the musicians in the ring; then they brightened again to show a smiling black woman in a red satin evening dress, who walked over to the microphone and began to sing with only Gwigwi's clarinet and the bass to accompany her.

> *I love my thing*
> *'cause my man's my thing*
> *Call him drink, drank, drunk . . .*
> *he's still my thing!*
> *He jobs for me . . .*
> *that you wouldn't have thunk.*
> *So I love my thing . . .*
> *Eee . . . Ma . . . Ye . . . Mo . . . Wunk!*

> *I love my thing*
> *'cause my man's my thing . . .*
> *He wins for me,*
> *and he makes me drunk,*
> *drunk with the love*
> *I've fallen in!*
> *So I love my thing . . .*
> *Eee . . . Ma . . . Ye . . . Mo . . . Wunk!*

The crowd waited half a beat after the song had ended before going wild. Tandia found her pulse racing and she could hear her heart pounding in her breast. Stop it! You don't even know him! she admonished herself. She knew Dorothy Masuka had been singing about Mandoma. Her voice was smooth and hot and suggestive and her eyes told a story of sinuous, slow, beautiful lovemaking. Tandia felt a warm stirring in her thighs and breasts that she'd never experienced before. 'Stop it! Stop it!' she demanded to herself. She brought her

428

arms up and hugged herself and discovered she was trembling. The lights went down and in the dimness she could see the singer and the musicians climb down from the ring, but the heat within her remained, curled up inside of her like a dangerous, illicit, delicious thing.

Slowly the lights returned and the applause died down and then there was a stirring in the crowd and some spasmodic whistling and clapping as Terence 'Iron Jaw' McGraw, a pale, red-headed Irishman climbed into the ring followed by his manager and one of his seconds.

The Irish fighter wore a green silk dressing gown on the back of which was embroidered a shamrock and the initials T. McG. He walked to each side of the ring, bowing at the crowd and putting his gloves together and raising them above his head. He caught sight of Tandia in her brilliant green dress, and mistaking the colour as the sign of a fan he blew her several kisses, much to the delight of Mama Tequila and Madam Flame Flo.

'That Irish should be so lucky!' Mama Tequila boomed. 'Iron Jaw' McGraw's manager walked over and slipped the boxer's satin gown from his shoulders, whereupon the Irishman began to shadow box, throwing short left and right jabs, bobbing and weaving from an imaginary opponent and hooking into the air, grunting as each punch was thrown. He was nicely built for a welter and his pale pink shoulders were covered with fat ginger freckles, a strangely incongruous sight in the cinema filled mostly with blacks and coloureds – although there were a few white faces in the ringside seats.

Tandia could see a coloured man, a black man and a white come to sit at the judges' table. The timekeeper and referee were having an earnest conversation at the time-keeper's table. There was a sudden roar from the crowd and Tandia turned to see a huge man in evening dress coming down the aisle on her left. Behind him was Gideon Mandoma in a white satin gown down to his ankles, the satin hood almost completely covering his face.

Mandoma was looking down at his feet so that it was impossible to see him. He seemed to be oblivious of the crowd as he walked behind the huge black man whom Tandia guessed must be Mr Nguni, Madam Flame Flo's friend and Gideon Mandoma's manager. Her heart beat wildly. She had heard so much for so long about the Zulu welterweight and she could hardly believe that she was going to see him fight, see the man whom Patel had called maybe the best raw talent he had ever seen in the ring.

Mandoma had his back to her as he climbed into the ring, and as she was seated almost directly behind his corner the white satin hood continued to obscure his face from her view. The crowd had begun to chant, 'Mandoma! Mandoma! Mandoma!' 'Iron Jaw' McGraw finally went to his corner and sat down as Mr Nguni walked over, watching as his seconds taped his hands and fitted the gloves. His own manager was over in Mandoma's corner checking the same ritual on the black man.

To Tandia's surprise it was Mr Nguni who walked over to the microphone and introduced the two fighters. Madam Flame Flo leaned over and explained, 'He not just Mandoma's manager, he also the promoter.'

Mr Nguni tapped the microphone with the tips of his fingers to see whether it was alive and then, satisfied, leaned over it. 'Ladies and gentlemen,' he said in carefully enunciated English, 'tonight is an international non-title fight between the welterweight champion of Ireland, Terry "Iron Jaw" McGraw – thirty-eight professional fights, twenty-two knockouts, thirty wins, one draw, seven losses – and Sophiatown's very own black welterweight champion of Africa, Gideon Mandoma!' He paused for the applause to die down. 'Twenty-seven professional fights, twenty-six wins, twenty knockouts, no draws.' The big man paused long enough for it to have the desired effect, 'one loss.'

At the mention of Mandoma's recent defeat the crowd booed and stamped their feet. Mr Nguni was first and foremost a promoter and he was beginning to build towards the second Mandoma vs Geldenhuis fight which he knew would be a big attraction. He also felt that the better man had lost, but consoled himself with the fact that the return fight was going to be a big earner for all and sundry. Which, the way he had black boxing tied up, meant that the 'all' was him and the 'sundry' was everyone else. He passed the microphone through the ropes and climbed down from the ring without glancing back at Gideon Mandoma.

The referee stepped from the neutral corner, signalling the seconds out of the ring and the two boxers to the centre. Mandoma rose from his corner stool and his white satin gown was removed. Tandia gasped involuntarily. The black boxer was beautiful. His body shone like well-tooled leather and his muscle definition was perfect. Strong shoulders tapered to a slim, superbly muscled abdomen and waist. He had the light, well-developed legs of a true welterweight: strong in the quadriceps, lean, almost thin calves and slim ankles. Tandia was well used to the round, flattish face that distinguishes the Zulu tribe and she was surprised therefore to see that Mandoma's nose was straight and narrow and his brow and jawline were clearly pronounced in an open, handsome face. Tandia saw a flash of perfect teeth as he fitted the mouth guard into his mouth. Gideon Mandoma looked like a young chief. There was a quiet authority about the way he stood beside the referee while the Irishman danced up and down on his toes smacking one glove into the other, eyeing the black man as the two boxers listened to the pre-fight instructions.

Tandia was almost choking with excitement and her heart thumped in her breast as the two boxers resumed to their corners and waited for the bell. Mandoma sat quietly on his stool while McGraw preferred to stand, appearing to be anxious to get underway. The bell went for the first round and the young Irishman rushed towards the black man, leading with three or four lefts which Mandoma took on the gloves and then attempting a rather predictable right upper-cut which missed by several inches.

The Irishman stood high with his gloves held wide and fairly low in a stance which usually denotes aggression in a fighter. Mandoma was also a fighter, but by contrast he held his gloves high, almost in front of his face, his left shoulder protecting his chin. He fought in a slightly hunched-over positon.

Mandoma moved to the centre of the ring, inviting the Irish boxer to come after him. The red-headed boxer moved in surprisingly fast. Feinting with the left, he hit Mandoma hard on the nose with a right. The black boxer had been waiting for the left lead that he had every right to expect, and the blow landed straight and true, a very classy straight right. A thin trickle of blood started from Mandoma's nose. He sniffed and brought his glove up to his nose as though he were trying to use the glove to wipe it. The Irishman closed in fast, thinking he'd hurt Mandoma. He led with a left which Mandoma took on the gloves and followed with a right cross which he threw too hard, pushing him slightly off balance so that he raised his chin a fraction. To a good fighter a quarter of an inch can often be enough, and Mandoma's right upper-cut seemed to come in slow motion. Moving under the Irishman's elbow, it caught him flush on the underside of the chin, rocking him on his heels and then seating him hard on the ground.

Pandemonium broke loose. So much for McGraw's iron jaw! At the count of ten, McGraw still hadn't moved. Two minutes and thirty seconds into the first round the fight was over, and Mandoma raised his gloves from where he was standing in a neutral corner to acknowledge the roar of the crowd, who had risen in their seats and were applauding wildly. A chant began in one corner of the cinema and soon it was taken up by all. Without realising it, Tandia also found herself standing and yelling the boxer's name, 'Mandoma! Mandoma! Mandoma!' She had never felt anything like it before. She wanted to laugh and cry at the same time, to hug the person beside her, to rush up into the ring and to embrace the black man, to wipe the small trickle of blood from his nose as he stood, his gloves raised high, his chest heaving and his hard brown body burnished with sweat. Mandoma was everything Patel had said he was and he was also very, very beautiful. The most beautiful human being Tandia had ever seen.

And then suddenly her perception changed. Instead of the Irishman on the canvas she saw Geldenhuis lying at Mandoma's feet. The white policeman she feared more than anyone in the world lying at the feet of the black man, bleeding and battered, the black man triumphant at last. The burning deep inside her began and welled up, the fire of it threatening to consume her. The roar of the crowd receded in her ears as though she was standing alone in the giant theatre. A stillness fixed upon her, and from the stillness she heard two words, two words that she'd never before spoken or even thought to speak, but now they sounded clear and clean like the touch of cool water on parched lips. '*Mayibuye Afrika*! Come back Africa!' Her clenched fist rose high above her head as though of its own accord as the words left her lips and danced and echoed around the giant theatre. '*Mayibuye Afrika*! *Mayibuye Afrika*! *Mayibuye Afrika*!'

Tandia's life as a terrorist had begun, born under the ring lights in the heat and sweat of a boxer's win in a palace of dreams where a black man stood over the body of a white one, his arms raised in victory. She could feel her fear for Geldenhuis turn to heat, begin to glow, first red, then white hot. Then slowly, infinitely, remorselessly, it began to cool down, to grow cold slowly over years and centuries and finally aeons and as it cooled it grew into hard, cold, bitter hate and it was all the more dangerous because it was forged out of her fear.

'Come, darling, we must go.' It was Madam Flame Flo taking her by the elbow. 'You liked that, hey? Ja, I can see you liked that. You will be a fan also.' She winked and squeezed Tandia's arm. 'Maybe even more than a fan, hey? Magtig! What a boxer! Come, we must go. Later you will meet him, you can even dance with him if you want. Mr Nguni has invited us to a party at the Taj Mahal.' She turned and waited for Mama Tequila to raise herself from her seat. 'But first we go to the ANC rally, to the protest meeting at St Peter's, to Father Huddleston's.'

When the three women reached St Peter's church hall it was already crowded. The people at the protest meeting were somewhat older than the boxing crowd and a fair proportion of them were women. Some wore the green, black and yellow uniform of the ANC and carried banners protesting against the eviction notices and the demolition of Sophiatown. Most of the women were dressed in their glad rags, though even those dressed to the nines could not compare with the sheer glimmering bulk of Mama Tequila.

Madam Flame Flo was, of course, well known as one of Sophiatown's most notorious shebeen queens and in this particular company perhaps not as well liked as with the boxing crowd. Her shebeen had often enough seen the money these women worked so hard to get used by their men for the liquor which drove them crazy and chased them into the arms of the good-time girls. Many of them believed that Madam Flame Flo was letting the community down. Some, though, did call their greetings; they were the ones who knew that Madam Flame Flo gave generously to the ANC and helped in unorthodox but useful ways.

Madam Flame Flo and her party were led to the front row by a buxom woman wearing the colours of the ANC. The mood in the hall was optimistic and there was a great deal of laughter as people recognised friends and warmed to the business of the protest. Soon all the seats were taken and only standing room remained.

Father Huddleston, Sophiatown's much loved Anglican priest, standing on the slight platform at the front of the hall, looked tall and frail. The priest stood to one side of a slightly battered-looking kitchen table, his long arms clasped below his waist. He wore a priest's cassock fastened by a wide leather belt. His head was remarkable, with its pronounced jaw, thin hawk-like nose and piercing blue eyes. He had a crew cut; the barbers impatient clippers seemed to have shaved him clean to the skin from the top of his large ears to the curve beginning at the crown of his head. At the very top of his head grew a tuft of evenly clipped, thick, steel-grey hair which seemed well adapted to survive in the harsh, rarefied climate of his six foot five inch frame.

Everything about Father Huddleston suggested self-denial. He was the Model T Ford of the priesthood, a stripped-down sort of a man at the extreme opposite end of the pompous, vainglorious posturing of the clerical order. Had he been in the church of Rome he would have been a serious candidate for sainthood, an idea he would have found unnecessarily mawkish and unseemly. There was nothing saintlike in the general behaviour of Father Huddleston. He was an ordinary and often impatient man who stood his ground and had his say, fearing no one, never slow to debunk the sophistry of apartheid or to challenge the actions of the police or the authorities. In fact, his character was best summed up by Madam Flame Flo when she pointed him out to Tandia. 'That's Father Huddleston. I'm telling you, man, he's one sonofabitch of a priest.'

It was not Father Huddleston's meeting. He was simply lending the venue and opening the evening with a short prayer. The chairman of the protest meeting was a young African seated alone at the table. His name was Robert Resha and he was well known to most of the audience in his role as an ANC executive as well as sportswriter for *Drum* magazine, the urban African magazine delighted in by the blacks and held in great suspicion by the white authorities.

At the conclusion of a short prayer the entire audience sang in perfect harmony 'Aaaahmen!' Then they moved on to sing '*Nkosi Sikelela i'Afrika*', the one-time Presbyterian hymn which has become the black national anthem of South Africa. The protest meeting had begun, and the audience waited eagerly for Robert Resha, who was known for his bold and fiery speeches.

Father Huddleston left the stage and took his place in the front row of the audience, where an empty seat awaited him. Now alone on the platform, the young black man rose quietly from where he now sat alone at the table on the platform. He lifted his right arm high, fist clenched, thumb extended. '*Mayibuye Afrika!*' he cried.

The crowd, their own arms extended in salute, returned the cry. '*Mayibuye Afrika!*'

'My brothers and my sisters,' he began, 'tonight you will not hear from me, or Father Huddleston. Tonight we have a new speaker who is known to you all, but who is also not known to you.' He smiled. 'Because this man is a very quiet cat, this man is a man of action who has not before used words for the cause.'

There was a sigh of disappointment in the crowd. They had come to hear a fiery speech by Resha himself; now they were going to be subjected to a novice. They had put away their tiredness and dressed up for nothing.

Robert Resha raised his hand. 'Be not disappointed,' he proclaimed, using the biblical style. 'This man, he is a Zulu, with the golden voice of his people. You will remember tonight. This is my promise to you.' He turned, walked to a doorway leading from the back of the stage, and nodded at someone the crowd was unable to see.

To the sudden delight of the audience Gideon Mandoma, dressed impeccably in a navy serge suit, white shirt and red tie, stepped through the doorway. As though he was announcing a boxing match, Robert Resha threw up his arms. 'Ladies and Gentlemen, citizens of Sophiatown and all who live in Western Native, I give you my friend and all-Africa boxing champion, Chief Gideon Mandoma!'

Gideon walked towards the table to the warm applause of the audience. Even the mums of Sophiatown, who couldn't have cared less about boxing, knew of Gideon Mandoma, the quiet, smiling Zulu who was black champion.

'My friends,' Gideon began slowly, his English carefully enunciated. Madam Flame Flo had told Tandia how Gideon Mandoma had educated himself by going to night school and doing a correspondence course and how, in just five years, he too had sat for and passed his matriculation examination last November, the very same examination that Tandia had passed so brilliantly.

The English that the young chief spoke was less the language of Sophiatown and more the one he'd learned from his school books. Gideon now told of his coming to Sophiatown from Zululand via Durban, where at the age of twelve he had left his kraal because of a severe drought to seek work and where, by joining the YMCA, he'd been introduced to boxing, finally coming to Johannesburg at the invitation of Mr Nguni.

'I am telling this for you, because you see I am two things in my life. I am a Zulu who was born in a kraal, who herded my father's cattle and who respected the laws of my chief. But also I am someone else,' he smiled,

'I am a majieta!' The audience laughed as he identified with the tough, cynical, street-smart young men of Sophiatown. 'Now I cannot return to my father's house, even if I am a chief and those people need me. Because now I am much more, I belong to a new tribe of Africa.' He smiled again. 'We who live in Sophiatown, Alexandra, Orlando and all the other townships, in Jo'burg, Durban, Port Elizabeth, Cape Town, even Pretoria, we are the new people. We are the new South Africans. We are not Zulus, or Pondo, Swazi, Sotho, Basuto, we are not coloured or Indian and even yes, we are not white! These things are past, they cannot be brought back. This is the new Afrika and this place ...' He paused and looked about him as though he were looking beyond the tin walls of the church hall. 'This place is the birthplace of the new Afrika, the new South African.' He paused again and looked about the room at the serious faces looking up at him, his own face serious. Tandia could feel her heart pounding. She could see that the people around her felt the same way; not a stirring or a cough broke the silence.

'Let me tell you the ways we are different. The language we talk, it is not English, it is not Afrikaans, or Zulu, or any of the languages of the tribes. It is the language of all! Here English, there Afrikaans, here Zulu or Sotho or Fanagalo. The music we play, we call it jazz, but it is not American, it is not English or the *tickie-draai* or *boere musiek* of the Afrikaans, it is Township, township jazz. It is our music. Our ways are our ways and our thoughts are our thoughts. New ways, new thoughts. New people.

'Let me tell you why we must fight to keep these new ways. Our ways are not the ways of the Boer. This man, this white Afrikaner tribe, they do not want to be a new people. They wish always to be an old people. They believe in white superiority, this is an old way. They say the white race, the Afrikaner race is God's race and they are God's servants and we, the black people and the coloured people, we must be the servants of God's servants! It is God's will, it is God's purpose, it is so because everybody knows, God is a white man and he is on their side!'

Gideon smiled and then laughed, his brilliant smile lightening his face so that the audience found themselves chuckling with him. 'But we must not grow angry at the white, racist God-fearing government of South Africa. Because you see, what they want for themselves, they also want for us. When Dr Verwoerd and Mr Strijdom speak of apartheid, they think in their hearts they are giving us what we want! They think the Zulu is like the Afrikaner and wants only to be with the Zulu, his own tribe, and the Sotho and the Shangaan and the Pondo and the Basuto they also, they want only to be with their own kind, to talk their own language and sing their own songs and marry their own women and grow their own crops and tend their own cattle!'

Mandoma leaned forward over the table, his eyes travelling once more over the crowd. His pauses were precise. He knew how to feel the crowd and manipulate it, massage it with his voice which rose and fell, grew harsh then soft again, shot forward in a rapid spate of words and then rested until the audience silently begged for him to continue. Now he spoke quietly again. 'These Boers who believe in white superiority and race purity, they have made a fundamental error in believing that the black people also believe in this racist nonsense. They do not see that in Sophiatown and Cato Manor and Jacobs in Durban, in District Six and Windermere in Cape Town and the townships of Port Elizabeth and everywhere else where the black people huddle, we have become a new people, the new people of South Africa! We do not ask is a man coloured, or Indian or black, we do not ask his tribe, we ask only one thing!' Gideon Mandoma's voice grew low so that the audience strained to hear him. 'We ask only, is this a good man or a bad man? Is this a good woman or a bad woman? Is this a good child or a bad child?' His voice rose and grew harsh. 'Not black! Not coloured! Indian! Chinese! Not even white! We do not look at the colour of a skin, we look at the heart which beats inside the skin.'

Gideon Mandoma's voice began suddenly to tremble. He was plainly upset. 'It is this which the white man wants to kill. It is this love, it is this understanding, it is this beginning. These old white men and these old white ways want to kill the new South Africa before it becomes real. And that is why they want to destroy Sophiatown and send us all to separate places which they have built to match our colour. This township, this dirty, ugly place of tin shanties and cardboard houses, this place where a black child is already old when he is ten years old, this drunken place of whores and she-beens, of dirty streets and hungry children, of sickness and murder. This is the place where freedom has decided to make its home, where the brotherhood of man can emerge, where his colour is the colour of his heart and not his skin. This is the place the white racists must destroy before it destroys them. They will show no mercy. They will come in the night and in the early morning and they will load us onto lorries, our mattresses and our beds and our children and our cooking pots and take us to our new places. To Diepfontein and Soweto, to Coronationville. Why cannot these new places with the new soccer stadiums and the schools and the health centres be used for all the people? Clean places where a man can rest and a family can grow up without fear. But this will not be. They will not be denied the inglorious, stupid, absurd concept of separation and superiority.' Mandoma paused, allowing his words to take effect, and then he began again, his voice low and steady, the voice of a leader bringing his people together, binding their wills and their determination to his own. 'We must fight. Not because we are servants and they are masters, not because we are black and they are white. But because the human race cannot progress backwards. They are trying to return us to a time and a place that cannot exist for us. We are a new tribe, the South African tribe, and we cannot go backwards, we cannot be undone, we cannot be ignored and, in the end, we cannot be defeated!'

'*Mayibuye Afrika!*' someone shouted from the back of the hall, and soon the audience was standing, their fists in the air, shouting their defiance. Small groups of women rose and, pushing the chairs aside, began to sing and dance. Soon everybody was dancing and singing with their arms raised in the traditional salute. Gideon Mandoma was a new star in the firmament of black politics. First a chief of the Zulu tribe, now a chief of the people tribe. They had heard his power. He had the lion's breath. He had the lion's roar. He had the lion's courage and the gift of moving the people. This one was a new leader who would fight for them. From this point on he would no longer be a black boxing champion fighting to beat a white in the boxing ring. From now on he was a black champion who carried in his fists and in his mouth the message of the underclass, of the people who wanted justice for themselves and for their children – the tired, exhausted people who pulled the plough of the white man's South Africa. Gideon Mandoma would lead them to the promised land.

Tandia felt the power in the black man, the power to move and to make things happen. She would follow him. She knew she was in love with him, a thing she had thought impossible. But she also knew that she had heard the breath of the future. It had passed over her and whispered to her. She was a part of the fight, she would march beside Mandoma, she too would be a part, a fighting part of the new South Africa to come and of the new South Africans. She was not stupid enough to think it would come about through rhetoric or even violence. Geldenhuis was not an isolated, sick human being; he was in many ways, in the ways that counted when you summed up an enemy, a typical Afrikaner. He would die rather than give an inch. She saw clearly that her love was not what was needed, she would need her hate. Her hate must be equal, it must surpass that of Geldenhuis. She sensed that Mandoma was not a man who could hate enough. He would need a woman beside him who could tear at the white man's flesh with her teeth. He would need her.

'Come, darling, we are going now to the Taj Mahal,' Madam Flame Flo chuckled. 'You will meet him there, I will introduce you.' Juicey Fruit Mambo had drawn up in the Packard and was waiting to help Mama Tequila into the back. They were surrounded by the dancing women who had left the hall and now were dancing in the street. Urchins crowded around the car and suddenly Tandia felt a warm hand in her own, as what felt like a small ball of paper was pushed into her hand. She looked to see Johnny Tambourine withdrawing his hand from her own; Dog Poep Ismali, Flyspeck Mendoza and Too

Many Fingers Bembi also surrounded her, and behind them stood the rest of the gang.

Tandia hardly had time to greet them when four Black Jacks, the township policemen, burst into the circle of people surrounding the car. A policeman grabbed Johnny Tambourine while the others each grabbed Dog Poep Ismali, Flyspeck Mendoza and Too Many Fingers Bembi and started to beat them with their night sticks. The four small boys began to scream as the heavy sticks beat at their shoulders and backs and a crowd gathered around. Tandia looked quickly down into her hand and saw that she was holding several crumpled pound notes. Without even thinking about what she was doing she slipped her hand through the slit of her cheongsam which came almost to the top of her thigh, and hooking her forefinger over the top of the waist elastic, she slipped the notes into her panties. In almost one movement she turned and slashed at the face of the nearest policeman with her nails. The black policeman who had been laying into Too Many Fingers Bembi backed away clutching at his face.

'Leave him, you bastard! Leave him, you hear!' Tandia screamed at the man and turned and slashed at a second policeman, missing him as he pulled back from her sharp talons just in time.

'Stop!' The voice was a roar and the crowd, including the Black Jacks, stopped, alarmed at the sound. Juicey Fruit Mambo stood in the centre of the circle, huge and menacing. In the few seconds before the black policeman could react he opened his huge mouth and smiled, his gold incisors gleaming. The crowd gasped and then Juicey Fruit Mambo turned to the black policeman. 'Why you want to beat dis boy with your stick?' he asked in a low, threatening voice.

'They have stolen money! They have stolen money from this woman!' the Black Jack sergeant pointed to a woman who stood on the edge of the crowd. Tandia turned to look at the woman who was large and wore lipstick and bright blue eye make-up painted over her eyelids. She was gross, and Tandia knew instantly she was a street whore. She had the same look of the drunken woman who had been thrown into the police cell with her the day she had been raped.

'That's the one!' the woman shrilled, pointing at Johnny Tambourine, 'and also him and him,' she shouted, jabbing her finger at Too Many Fingers Bembi and Flyspeck Mendoza.

'Hester, you drunk you hear!' It was Madam Flame Flo's voice. She had climbed out of the Packard and, breaking into the circle, she now stood in front of the large black woman.

'I am not drunk, these boys they attacked me and they took my money. Five pounds!'

'Five pounds you earned from lying on your back!' someone, a woman's voice, called from the crowd. There was sudden laughter.

'Hester, you owe me that much. You owe me five pounds. You are clean, you hear? The debt is wiped, but only if you say, only if you tell these policemen you made a mistake?'

The sergeant spoke up. 'We must search them.' He grabbed Johnny Tambourine and pulled him towards him. Juicey Fruit Mambo's hand came down hard on the policeman's shoulder, but he was smiling.

'The boy will show you,' he said. 'All boys they show you.' Johnny Tambourine removed his shirt and then pulled the lining of his shorts out. A single two-shilling piece landed on the dirt road together with three marbles, several lead washers, four screws and a length of string.

'I got it for selling peanuts at the fight, God's truth!' he said, stooping to pick up the coin. He stood there in his dirty khaki shorts held around his waist by an old leather belt.

'Take also the belt,' Juicey Fruit instructed. Johnny Tambourine removed his belt and held onto his shorts to prevent them from falling to the ground. Juicey Fruit stuck his thumbs into his own belt so that his trousers came away from his abdomen slightly; then he did a little wriggle, which brought laughter from the crowd. 'Make also so!' he instructed. Johnny Tambourine grinned and swivelled his hips dancing from one foot to another, playing to the crowd in a parody of a dance. Juicey Fruit Mambo turned to the police sergeant. 'You see, no money here,' he said, grinning. 'Now all boy make like same!' he declared, pointing to Flyspeck Mendoza and Too Many Fingers Bembi.

The two boys quickly followed suit, revealing pockets which contained very much the same sort of things that spilled from Johnny Tambourine's.

Madam Flame Flo brought her hands to rest on her hips. 'I open my big mouth, now I must pay, hey. These boys is innocent but still I will cancel the money you owe me, Hester. But first you must withdraw the charges, you hear?'

The big whore smiled. 'I made a mistake,' she said to the sergeant. 'All the boys in this township they look the same.'

The policeman who had been scratched by Tandia was standing directly beside the Packard, the palm of his hand covering his cheek. Mama Tequila's fat arm appeared out of the window and tugged at his sleeve.

She was holding a one-pound note. 'Medical expenses,' she said. The black policeman, glancing quickly to see if they were being watched, took the money and touched the peak of his helmet.

The sergeant lifted his night stick menacingly and pushed at Hester roughly. 'Go! Go, you fat whore, before I arrest you. You are wasting the time of the police!' He turned to Madam Flame Flo. 'Your driver, he is very lucky, next time he will not be so lucky, hey.'

'Come around to the shebeen tomorrow, I will have something for you,' Madam Flame Flo said quietly. If the Black Jack sergeant had heard her he didn't react. Scowling at her, he walked away, calling to the crowd to disperse.

'Come, Tandia, come, Juicey Fruit, we must go to the Taj Mahal. I think we have enough demonstration for one night, hey?' Madam Flame Flo climbed into the back of the car with Mama Tequila. 'Let's get the hell out of here, jong ... before the proper police come!'

'I'm sorry, Aunty Flo,' Tandia said from the front of the car. 'I didn't mean it, but they were hitting the kids!'

'You did right, Tandy, but not in Sophiatown. We just lucky they were Black Jacks and not SAP. If you attack a proper policeman like that he will shoot you, no problems!'

'Tandy! You a fucking arsehole, you hear!' Mama Tequila spat. 'You put our lives at risk, what for? For a bunch of fucking snotty-nosed kids! You must be crazy, you hear!'

'Dis boys, dey her friend, my friend also!' Juicey Fruit announced from behind the wheel.

'And you, you black bastard, you crazy also!' Mama Tequila screamed at the big black man.

Tandia remained silent and waited for more from the

angry woman. Instead, Juicey Fruit started to giggle and then to laugh and Madam Flame Flo followed. Mama Tequila was also laughing as they drew up outside a large corrugated iron shed that seemed to be vibrating from the hot jazz music coming from within. They had arrived at the Taj Mahal, the biggest and the most notorious shebeen in the township.

Mama Tequila had elected to be taken home, and Juicey Fruit Mambo let Madam Flame Flo and Tandia off, promising to return before midnight. The joint was jumping as the two women entered. It was a huge tin shed with a lofted open roof which had windows set into the roof thirty feet above the floor. The lighting was indifferent and the effect was of smoke and music, noise and pink strobe lights that cut across the dance-floor in the centre, pulling the jiving couples from darkness into light and back again.

The band sat on a platform structure built at the end of the room several feet above the heads of the dancers and the drinkers. Benjo 'Gwigwi' Mrwebi who had earlier played clarinet at the fight was leading the Three Jazzalomos with Jacob 'Mzala' Lepers on the bass and Sol 'Beegeepee' Klaaste at the piano. The sound was hot and sweet and the booze was moonshine, Barberton served in jam tins. An occasional half-jack of brandy was raised quickly, furtively to the mouth, a gulp and back into the pocket, guilty blood too good to share except with your nice-time girl.

Madam Flame Flo, with Tandia in tow, worked her way through the crowd of drinkers and dancers. The tables were full, overcrowded with the nice-time girls seated on the men's laps. Those who couldn't find a table stood against the walls. It was impossible to talk, and people drank and shook and grooved to the music or found a place on the dance floor, the jazz and the noise sealing them from each other. Those who had girls danced and used their hands to touch the parts that best expressed their thoughts and smiled for the time they would spend in a dark alley afterwards when the Barberton and the dancing and the jazz had left their thighs aching for release and a crumpled pound note had passed from hand to the safety of a brassiere wet from dancing.

Madam Flame Flo, signalling for Tandia to follow, stooped slightly and passed under the band floor, opening a half-sized door cut into the wall at the back of the large shed. They squeezed through the narrow doorway and Tandia found herself in a large room with half-a-dozen tables. The room was lined and painted and on the walls in neat frames all of one size were photographs of musicians and nightclub performers. From the ceiling two large fans rotated. About thirty people sat at the tables, smartly dressed men and five pretty women in evening dress. The tables were all furnished with good glasses and bottles of brandy, gin and whisky. Despite the fact that the bandstand was only separated by a wall, the music filtering through, though loud, allowed for talk.

Mr Nguni, the tall African boxing promoter from the fight, rose from a table nearest the small doorway at which five men sat. Tandia caught a glimpse of Gideon Mandoma before the bulk of Mr Nguni blocked the table from her view. Her heart began to pound and she felt weak at the knees, as though her legs were about to give way from under her. She wet her lipstick with her tongue and swallowed hard, trying to conceal her nervousness. 'Welcome, Madam Flame Flo,' Mr Nguni said, extending his huge hand. Then, turning slightly, while still holding Madam Flame Flo's hand, he greeted Tandia. 'Welcome to Sophiatown, Miss Patel, we are most happy to have you with us. Come, you must sit at our table. There is someone I would like you to meet.'

The big man moved aside so that Tandia and Madam Flame Flo could pass. Tandia found that she was standing almost directly in front of the table. The men, with the exception of Gideon Mandoma, half rose in their chairs before sitting back again. Gideon Mandoma rose fully from his chair.

Mr Nguni indicated the people at the table. 'You all know Madam Flame Flo?' They all nodded. Mandoma smiled and, extending his hand, shook Madam Flame Flo's.

'Nice one, Gideon, you made mincemeat of that Irishman tonight!' Madam Flame Flo said. He smiled and thanked her politely.

Mr Nguni held Tandia lightly by the elbow. 'Gentlemen, allow me to introduce Miss Tandia Patel from Durban.' Mr Nguni indicated the four men with a sweep of his hand, not bothering to introduce each individually. Tandia smiled and acknowledged the seated men, whereupon Nguni turned and placed his large hand on the boxer's shoulder. 'Miss Patel, may I introduce you to Gideon Mandoma?'

Tandia's eyes met those of Mandoma and she held his gaze. She knew she was being over-bold, that she should have glanced up at him and then away, pretended indifference, or shyness, played the shy-young-woman-meets-nice-young-man game. But she couldn't. She was held by the boxer's gaze as though mesmerised. She knew at once she had found what she wanted; she had found the antidote for Geldenhuis. She could love this man as much as she hated the other. At close quarters, Gideon Mandoma was even more beautiful than she could possibly have imagined.

Gideon Mandoma smiled, the brilliant white smile that she had seen earlier in the church hall. 'Welcome, Tandia.' He refrained from shaking Tandia's hand but instead indicated the chair beside him. 'Sit, please.' He watched as she lowered her eyes and seated herself. Then he sat back into his own chair. 'I saw you at the eviction protest meeting tonight. You are the most beautiful woman I have ever seen. Do you have courage to match your beauty?'

Tandia could feel his eyes on her as she raised her own to look at the boxer. Mandoma's expression was serious and showed no hint of condescension. He seemed to be asking a serious question and was not simply trying to humour her. 'I will take my courage from you, Gideon Mandoma,' she said quietly, 'but I will bring you something also.' Tandia paused and forced herself to look away and then lower her eyes. 'My daddy, Natkin Patel the boxing referee, he always said to win a world championship a boxer must have hate. Without hate the pain is too much and raw courage is not enough.' Tandia looked up again and her beautiful green eyes burned fiercely into those of the black boxer. 'To win this fight for our people . . .' Tandia paused. She spoke barely above a whisper, yet her voice carried to him clearly. 'I will bring with me the hate you will need, Gideon Mandoma.'

Twenty

Hymie took his finals at law in June of 1954. He'd made the decision to remain in Britain to prepare Peekay for his title fight in America towards the end of the following year. *Ring* magazine named Peekay fifth in the world rankings, but with a string of good wins to his credit it was getting close to the time when they could talk to Jake 'Spoonbill' Jackson's manager, a New York Irishman named O'Rourke, and notify the New York Boxing Commission and the World Boxing Council they intended to challenge for a title fight.

During the following year when Peekay would complete his degree, Hymie planned to travel to South Africa fairly frequently to prepare their entry into a law practice in Johannesburg. They hoped to work in practice for a year until they were admitted to the bar. When this happened they would either buy the practice outright or purchase the major share in a partnership arrangement.

Peekay had advanced up the boxing ladder and had taken the British Empire title from Iron Bar Barunda though the black man still retained his British title. Togger had also fought Iron Bar Barunda two months later and had been narrowly beaten. A return bout, this time with the British title at stake, was scheduled for September.

Trinity term at Oxford ends in June and the new university year begins with the Michaelmas term in October. In the four months between June and October Peekay had five fights, winning against all the top European welters as well as the highly rated Italian contender, Bruno Bisetti, whom he'd fought on the same bill as Togger's title fight at Harringay.

Both boxers won, Togger taking the coveted British Welterweight title from Iron Bar Barunda in a closely fought ten-rounder. It was a popular decision. Togger had developed into a very skilful boxer and was considered to be London's own. Peekay could barely contain his delight at his friend's win and later Hymie was to blame the fact that Peekay only won his fight against the Italian on points on this distraction.

Peekay's points win over the Italian in London had come after a string of knock-outs and the Italians took great heart by this. When Peekay fought Bisetti again, this time for the vacant European title, he faced a very partisan Turin crowd. It proved to be a damned good thing he knocked the Italian out in the ninth, for no matter how far ahead he may have been on points, the excitable Italians would never have stood for yet another points decision going to Peekay.

The win over Bisetti made Peekay the top welterweight outside of North America. Peekay became the darling of European boxing and the only boxer around who looked like bringing a world championship belt back from across the Atlantic.

The Odd Bodleians were present at every one of Peekay's fights including the one in Italy. If the Turin crowd had been somewhat partisan, this did not include the Odd Bodleians who received a standing ovation. Hymie had arranged for a record to be cut of *Concerto for the Great Southland* sung by the Odd Bodleians, which had done well in the UK and now became a great hit in Italy as well as Germany, but proved to be only a modest success in France.

In Germany it became known as a composition by the famous twenties concert pianist, Professor Karl Von Vollensteen, a romantic figure in the twenties who'd disappeared from the concert stages of Europe after a mysterious illness, never to be heard from again. The story of Doc and Peekay, much of it exaggerated, appeared in *Stern* magazine with a picture of Peekay on the cover. Doc's shadow had reached a long way from the crystal cave of Africa where he lay.

By the end of 1954, Peekay's name was beginning to appear regularly in *Ring* magazine where he was increasingly mentioned as a serious contender for the welterweight crown. Only the Cuban, 'Soap Dish' Jurez and the Mexican welter, Manuel Ortez, remained as the bridge to Madison Square Garden in New York, and the chance to get a crack at the world champ, Jake 'Spoonbill' Jackson.

Setting up and promoting these two bridging fights, and the elimination fight with an American welterweight, took up a lot of Hymie's time in the first months of 1955. He wanted at least two of the three fights in Britain. Peekay, doing his final year at law, hadn't the time to travel either to North America or Cuba. Nor could they yet afford to go.

The fight against 'Soap Dish' Jurez took place at Harringay Arena in North London and was a sell-out. Soap Dish proved to be well named; he was a slippery customer to handle, and like Peekay a consummate boxer. It was only Peekay's power in both hands which finally wore him out, knocking him down three times in the eleventh round, whereupon the referee stopped the fight, awarding it to Peekay on a TKO.

Manual Ortez, whom Peekay fought two months later, proved an entirely different kettle of fish. He was Habib all over again, but younger, faster and fitter. He'd gone the distance with Jake 'Spoonbill' Jackson three months earlier in an unexpected title bid and while he'd lost in the eyes of all three judges, the final points score separating the boxers had only added up to a three-round superiority for the champion.

His tearaway, non-stop fighting style was difficult to counter. A slum kid who'd fought his way out of the tin shanties of Mexico City, Ortez was as tough and determined a fighter as ever climbed into a ring. He fought as though his life depended on the outcome, which in a way, it did. Peekay had connected with half-a-dozen beautiful straight rights which should have slowed him down, but he just kept coming, forcing Peekay onto the back foot, careful to stay out of the corners where Ortez was devastatingly effective. He was a boxer who used everything he had, including his elbows and head whenever he could get away with it, which was often enough to be disconcerting, so Peekay had to be careful not to lose his cool.

But by the eleventh round Ortez had used up too many punches and taken too many hard blows to the body and he started to slow down. Midway through the final round Peekay caught him on the ropes and finished him off with a Solly Goldman thirteen. The Mexican boxer was out for the count before he hit the canvas.

Peekay was only one fight shy of a shot at the world title and *Ring* magazine recognised him as the number one contender. The following day his face appeared on the front cover of most of the Sunday papers in Britain and every Sunday paper in South Africa. He had become a national hero in both countries, the undisputed challenger for the world welterweight title.

On the *stoep* of Mr Nguni's home in Sophiatown, Gideon Mandoma held a copy of the Johannesburg *Sunday Times* up for Tandia to see. They'd both been invited to lunch and Gideon sat with Tandia on the veranda while Mr Nguni, his manager and also prominent African boxing promoter, held a business meeting with two Indians who had arrived unannounced from out of town. Juicey Fruit Mambo had the Packard parked outside the house no more than a few feet away and, as usual, was busy polishing it. He wasn't yet sure how he felt about Tandia's attraction to the Zulu boxer and if Gideon tried anything on he wanted to be around if he was needed.

'My brother will be the next world champion!' Gideon declared happily. The picture, which must have been taken at some earlier fight, showed Peekay with his arm up in a salute with the lion's tooth showing clearly around his neck. 'See, he has my luck, my brother wears my luck, he will be the next world champion, for sure, you will see!' He shook his head in admiration. 'Hayi, Hayi, Hayi, surely he is the leader of the people? He is the one, the Tadpole Angel.'

Tandia was shocked as Gideon Mandoma handed her the paper. Holding it up in front of her so he couldn't see her expression she stared angrily at the front page photograph of Peekay with his hands held high. She struggled to regain her composure so when she spoke her voice was soft, almost plaintive. 'He is a white man, Gideon. He will betray you. How can he be our leader?'

Gideon looked surprised. 'He is my brother, Tandia. His heart is not white, his heart is same like me,' he said softly.

Tandia's hand was shaking as she handed him back the paper, but Gideon didn't seem to notice. 'And you?' she asked. 'Are you not the Tadpole Angel? Patel said you were the best, even better than him, I swear it's true.'

Gideon laughed. 'This is not for me to say, Tandia. The people, they have decided. I have fought my brother and I have lost. Peekay, he is the Tadpole Angel, it is in the smoke and in the bones.'

Tandia brought her hands up and clasped her head. Despite her timidness she was a city girl and Gideon's superstition shocked her. 'My God, Gideon! You don't still believe the Sangoma?' She knew instantly she'd said the wrong thing.

Gideon Mandoma spun around. He'd known this beautiful young girl only a few months. Tomorrow she returned to Natal with Mama Tequila, where she would study law. He didn't want to fall in love with her. It wasn't convenient. It wasn't in his plans. There was too much to do. The ANC was too important, and so was his education and his boxing career. He didn't need a wife. He didn't even need a girlfriend. There were plenty of clean women he could sleep with. It was better to just send her away, forget about her. She was questioning his beliefs; the tribal blood in her had dried up, she was a city girl not afraid of the power of the spirits. Better to just send her away, to say nothing.

457

Gideon was a Zulu who did not allow a woman to speak to him like this, question him in these matters. He felt obliged to put her in her place. 'Shut your mouth, woman. There are things you don't understand, you hear? Peekay and me, we have suckled at the same woman's breast. Go now, I am tired of your talk!' He reached down and grabbed the newspaper from the floor. Hiding behind it, he pretended to read.

'See, already we fight over this white man. Please, Gideon, forgive me!'

Juicey Fruit Mambo was suddenly at her side. 'Go away!' she shouted at him in sudden childish frustration. Juicey Fruit backed away, stepping down the front steps slowly. He'd heard Gideon's rebuke. It was fair. Mandoma was heir to a chiefdom and a man; Tandia ought not to upset him. Nevertheless, the little Zulu had better not put a hand on her or he would break his bones.

Tandia was terrified. She loved Mandoma passionately and had done so from the first moment she'd set eyes on him in the darkened Odin cinema when he'd demolished the inept Irishman. She didn't want to lose him, although she knew she must, for the time being anyway. She would study law and come back to be at his side. She had worked it all out in her head. Please God, don't let it end like this, she thought. She *must* leave to return to Bluey Jay with her relationship with Mandoma intact, ready for the next time they met. Next to her hate, he was the most important thing in her life. She had joined the ANC, though Mandoma had insisted this be done secretly. 'You are a student, it must not be known,' he had said. 'Verwoerd's Bantu Education Act will soon remove all blacks from white education. Students who belong to the ANC will be the first to go.'

'I am sorry, Gideon. I didn't mean it, I take it back, all of it. You must forgive me, I am only a poor, stupid woman.'

Gideon lowered the paper slowly and looked sternly at Tandia. These city girls have a lot to learn about respect and the space where a man sits, he thought to himself. 'It is not right that you talk like this, Tandia. I am glad you take back your thoughts.'

Tandia broke into a brilliant smile, though she was afraid of the quiet, beautiful Zulu boxer who would one day be a chief. Despite her terror, her voice was calm and soft when she spoke. 'No, not all of them. One part I don't take back.' She took a deep breath. 'You must fight Peekay and you will win. Then *you* will be the Tadpole Angel.'

Despite himself, Gideon laughed. 'My right hand cannot fight my left hand, we are brothers.' He paused, his eyes grew soft as he looked at the beautiful young woman who stood in front of him. 'This thing will happen if it will happen, it is not for me to say. First I must fight Jannie Geldenhuis.' He grinned. 'This one, he is not my brother. I will wait until he is better, then I will fight him again. This time we shall see who is white and who is black.'

Tandia went cold. The spectre of Geldenhuis loomed up in her subconscious, almost paralysing her. Her fear of the white police captain was so great that she thought him invincible. 'Please, Gideon, he is evil, you must not fight him, he has too much hate, even more than me.'

Gideon grinned. 'I do not have to read the smoke and throw the bones to know this, Tandia. I must fight him because I am a man and a Zulu, and my turn has come.'

Hymie was worried about Peekay and he took his concern to Dutch Holland. They were nailbitingly close to challenging for the world title. 'Dutch, Peekay's won the last seven fights on a KO, except his first fight with Bisetti. Each time he's been behind on points coming into the ninth round. Christ man, Peekay is one of the most skilful boxers in the world and he's having to rely on a knock-out for a win?'

'There ain't nothin' much better than a knock-out, my son. How bleedin' else do you want the lad to win? He's had fifteen pro fights, he's won thirteen by knock-out. He's beaten the best fighters in the world bar the Yanks. This weight division ain't exactly filled with chumps neither; there's more good welterweights around at the moment than you can shake a stick at.' Dutch spread his cocktail-sausage hands. 'Blimey, what's got into you? There ain't been a contender, in any bleedin' weight division, in twenty years who done what our lad's done! Not even Joe soddin' Louis.'

Hymie was not convinced. 'Dutch, listen to me, man. Jackson is a boxer, a consummate boxer. They don't come any better. Like Peekay, he's got a punch in both hands but he can box just as well. I won't say he's a better boxer than Peekay, but *Ring* magazine says he is and Budd Shulberg says he is and Nat Fleischer in an editorial last month says he's the fastest and best exponent of the skill of boxing he's ever seen. You know what he calls him? "The Ghost with a hammer in each hand!" He reckons he was coasting against Ortez. We have to accept that in terms of boxing, Jackson's practically the immaculate conception!'

'Peekay's come in from behind in seven of his thirteen fights to win. And three of them have been his last four fights. With a guy like Spoonbill Jackson at the other end of your gloves that's bullshit boxing. Peekay's not going to wear him down then take him out in a late round! No bloody way!'

Dutch was reluctant to listen; he'd never taken kindly to Hymie's advice. Peekay's success had added greatly to his own prestige as a trainer, and he knew Hymie was right, but he couldn't yet bring himself to agree with his criticism. 'I'm only his trainer. You two talk all the time, why don't you talk to him, let me know what the lad says?'

Peekay was studying for his finals in June and Hymie was reluctant to talk to him about the problem. He knew Peekay wanted a first and he reasoned they'd have nearly four months after the exams with only two fights, a preliminary against a highly rated American welterweight. The likely boxer was a marine stationed in Florida, a negro fighter originally from Harlem who went by the unlikely name of Jasper 'King Coon' Sinder. If he beat Sinder, that left the title fight.

Peekay tried not to think about the title fight, which proved impossible. You can't think about something everyday, almost every hour of your life and then dismiss it while you study for your exams. He was studying hard, working with E.W. every day, his tutor anxious for his charge to do brilliantly in his final exams. Peekay was forced to fight Ortez during the last month of cramming and he'd found it hard to concentrate on his studies as well as the fight. He'd won against the Mexican, but tediously again with a knock-out in the final round. He knew Hymie was worried about him. It had been a torrid year with no easy opponents; every fight had sapped him, making it hard to recover fully for the next one. Nothing had changed, except his body was tired.

461

Peekay began to ready his head for Jackson, but his concentration was split. He had to get his exams out of the way first.

During Peekay's last year at Oxford Harriet increasingly drew away from him. Her study of the group of boxers, completed when Peekay had fought Bisetti, had received wide acclaim. It had been cast in bronze and purchased by the town fathers for the atrium of a new sports stadium to be built in Louisville, Kentucky.

Harriet's next commission proved to be the one on which her later international fame would be built. The same church in Dresden for whom she had created the altar piece commissioned her to do the piece she had dreamed of for so long, the Walking Madonna. The sculpture would stand nearly eight feet tall in the grounds of the new church and was by far the most important piece she had been commissioned to do.

As Harriet's creative juices rose so her libido fell. It was not that she consciously felt any differently about Peekay, but her preoccupation with the task ahead so completely filled her conscious thought and possessed her that Peekay was simply squeezed out. The Walking Madonna was the first major female piece she had done; it was also the fulfilment of a childhood dream, no different for her than the world welterweight title was for Peekay. She became almost completely introspective, the voice within her sufficient for her emotional needs.

Peekay's split with Harriet finally came halfway through March. One day, Peekay ran the five miles to Cow Cottage to find Harriet in one of her dark moods, almost unable to talk. He worked silently for an hour in the garden. It was spring and after two years of loving care the cottage garden was back to its best, though in the past weeks both of them had neglected it and it

462

needed weeding, which Peekay now set about doing. Peekay could never quite get over spring in England. The day before he'd driven from London back to Oxford in Hymie's little Prefect. The tulips had been out in the parks in a brilliant parade of red, yellow and white. Clumps of daffodils and crocuses were growing haphazardly out of the grass while bluebells spread an azure picnic cloth under dark old oaks. Peekay had thought of the snow three months earlier, and had imagined how the flowers had waited under a cold white blanket until a day such as this one, when they'd pushed with all their might and then shaken free their pretty heads to announce that spring had officially arrived.

A shadow fell over where Peekay squatted beside a patch of sweet basil. He was pinching the small white blossom from the stems so the plants wouldn't go to seed early. He looked up to see Harriet standing beside him.

'Dear, dear Peekay, you must understand it isn't you. I love you so very much, but you must wait until this thing is out of me. I can't go to your fights anymore. I can't include your fighting in my head at present.' She paused, waiting for Peekay to react, but Peekay was too old a hand at camouflage to reveal his feelings. He was silent, gathering his thoughts so that he would say the right thing, say it sotto voce, easily, without emotion, forgiving her, understanding, his hurt completely concealed.

Finally he stood, wiping his soiled hands down the sides of his rugby shorts, like a small boy caught making mud pies. 'Don't worry, Harriet, I do understand really.' He'd put his hand out towards her, but she'd withdrawn from it, taking a step backwards.

'Please, Peekay. Please don't.'

Peekay had called the Dolls' Hospital the following day and Mr Rubens had answered. 'Where you been, young man? Doris is waiting, one month, three days and you are not calling.'

Peekay laughed at the old man's chiding. 'Hello, Mr Rubens. May I speak to Doris, please?'

'Wait, I find her.' Peekay heard the clatter of the phone as he dropped the receiver onto his desk.

Peekay had enjoyed his first date with Doris. They'd had a good time and although she'd allowed him a bit of a feel-up, she wasn't going to be a pushover. At first it had been circumspect; he was in love with Harriet and although Doris did all the right things to him Peekay was able to resist the temptation. But Harriet blew hot and cold. Peekay, who was highly sexed, never quite knew how he'd find her; and finally his resolve crumbled. In his mind Harriet went to bed with him on her terms, when *she* felt like it. Doris, on the other hand, simply liked to accommodate him. Peekay was able to tell himself the meaning of the sex involved was not the same thing, that he was entitled to enjoy Doris and she him. Making love to Doris, he rationalised unfairly, was for the simple release of tension and not the sometimes almost mystical experience Harriet made of it, depending on her mood.

Besides, Peekay found he liked Doris a lot. She was funny, like Togger. She seemed to enjoy being with him, as though she was out on a special treat, though she found many of his mannerisms 'dead quaint', like taking her arm when they went up steps and holding her chair out when they went into a working man's caf for a cuppa.

In the background Peekay could hear Mr Rubens shouting for Doris to come to the phone. There was the sudden rattle of the receiver being picked up. 'Hello, lovely, the old man givin' you an 'ard time then?' Doris was her usual bright self.

Peekay laughed and made arrangements to pick Doris up at the shop.

'Smashin', it's about bleedin' time an' all! Too much work and not enough play makes Peekay a dull boy. Tell yer what? I'll wear me new Merry Widow, it don't do me no 'arm, even if I say so meself!'

The thought of Doris in a Merry Widow bra left Peekay feeling quite faint.

Twenty-one

Harriet had drawn deeper and deeper into herself. Her Walking Madonna had taken almost a year from the maquette to the point when it was ready to be cast in bronze. Carmen had kept her promise and had returned to pose for the work, giving Harriet two-and-a-half weeks of her three-week holiday at Cow Cottage.

Peekay and Togger saw very little of her and when they did she talked of little else but Harriet and the Madonna. Carmen had fallen under Harriet's spell and from all accounts seemed to have overcome Harriet's desire to be alone and claimed, without affectation, that they'd talked for hours on end while she'd posed.

'For the first time in me life I feel I've got a brain, not just a body but a noggin I can use and I reckon I know how I'm gonna use it an' all.'

They'd been sitting at the bar in a small Soho pub and now she drew herself up, throwing her head back as she looked disdainfully at them both. 'In Paris I'm learnin' how to put clothes on, not take 'em off. I gotta job in a fashion house on the Faubourg St-Honoré.' Carmen paused at the look of surprise on both their faces. 'Okay, I admit, it's not too flash, a bit of sewin'' and cuttin' and a bit of house modellin', but I'm learnin'.' She leaned forward grabbing Togger suddenly by the arm, her eyes shining. ''Ere, you remember how when I was a little nipper I used to sew all the clothes for Elizabeth Jane and later, when I was about eleven or twelve, I'd make all me own dresses? Well, now I'm learnin' to cut and design proper. I'm gonna save and save and nights I'll go to the *Polytechnique*; then I'm gonna make children's clothes, the most beautiful children's clothes in the whole bleedin' world!' Carmen was breathless with the excitement of telling them her plans, but she suddenly pulled herself upright on the stool again, afraid she'd said too much.

A large grin spread over Togger's face. 'I think we just come to the end of the nearly-but-not-quite Browns. When me boxing career's over I reckon I'm gonna invest me prize money with you, no risk!'

Carmen smiled, holding a beautifully manicured hand out to Togger. 'Put it there, partner!'

'Here's to Brown and Brown! If Hymie was here and not in New York he'd order champagne.' Peekay turned to the barman. 'Barman, a bottle of Bollinger, please!'

When the bottle was empty at last Carmen's eyes grew soft and her mood nostalgic. 'You staying in London overnight in Hymie's flat then?' she asked Peekay.

Peekay grinned. 'I reckon it's my turn to ask you home.'

On those occasions when Harriet needed someone to enter the circle of her self-imposed solitude, apart from her two-and-a-half weeks with Carmen, it was Hymie she chose. Hymie was the first person to see the completed Walking Madonna.

467

'Christ, Peekay,' he reported, 'it almost touches the central beam, that's bloody nearly fourteen foot from the ground. It's astonishing, a masterpiece.'

Peekay felt a little hurt that Harriet hadn't chosen him as the first to witness her triumph, but he'd more or less reconciled himself to losing her, at least while she was involved with the sculpture.

'And what of Harriet? Has the Walking Madonna changed her? Will she again be the Harriet we both know?'

'You mean will she return to you?'

Peekay didn't protest. 'Yes, I suppose I do mean that. Have I lost her, Hymie? Has she gone to you?' A new thought seemed to occur to him. 'Or have we both lost her?'

Hymie sat quietly thinking. They were in the small sitting room of Hymie's flat overlooking Sloane Square. Finally he spoke. 'I was hoping I could tell you she was mine, Peekay. That I'd won her back. I wouldn't have minded that. All's fair in . . . Do you find that strange?'

Peekay shook his head and Hymie continued. 'You had your turn, I'd like to think now it was mine.' He grinned, 'I admit it would have given me some satisfaction! But it's not true, old son. Harriet, as I said right at the beginning and she quite emphatically maintained herself, never belonged to either of us. Not even in the least sense. Sure she loves us both. But we lie a poor second, perhaps even lower on her list of emotional needs. From now on, you will see, she will take us only on *her* terms.' Hymie sighed. 'For me that's enough. I haven't any sexual ego to get in the way, to compete. For you, I sense it will not be enough. If I appear to have grown closer to Harriet it is because I've capitulated. Utterly!' Hymie looked up and grinned. 'It's just as well you're bedding Doris with the marvellous tits, Peekay, the next physical relationship Harriet has will not be with you. It will be with whoever she is pleased to have at her moment of need, which is rare enough, like a dry creek bed taken in sudden flood and then, as suddenly, empty again.'

Peekay gave Hymie a wry grin. 'I can't say I'm not disappointed, I am. Bitterly. Even though the past year's been pretty bloody, I guess I was lucky to get what I got, not just sex, but the time spent with Harriet. It was like being plugged into electricity. She was wonderful.'

'Will you tell her that, Peekay?'

'I'll try.'

'Peekay, it isn't over. Why don't you try falling in *like* with Harriet? If Harriet was a man, let's face it, we'd be awestruck, overwhelmed by the sheer talent brought to the friendship. Try forgetting she's a woman, someone you took to bed.'

Peekay laughed. 'I can't, Hymie. I have to try to get her back. I can't simply walk away and call it a day. It wasn't just a sex thing. I admit it, I started sleeping with Doris when Harriet and I were still together, still relatively happy. If it was a sex thing it would have died then. It was, it *is*, a lot more.'

Hymie was silent for a moment, pulling his lower lip into his mouth. 'Peekay, she's changed, she's different.'

'Changed how? You mean the new Harriet wants a different kind of man? Older?'

'Peekay! For Christ's sake, leave it alone. Harriet's changed, that's all. I didn't say anything about a man!'

Peekay felt himself go cold. 'Carmen?'

Hymie observed that Peekay had turned white. 'You don't supose she slept on the chesterfield for two-and-a-half weeks do you?'

'Christ! It never bloody entered my head. Harriet and Carmen sleeping together! Harriet a lesbian?'

'Hey, now! Wait a minute, Peekay, don't go jumping to conclusions! It doesn't have to be one thing or the other. I told you, the new Harriet takes what she wants when she wants it. She was modelling a female body so she got involved with it. It was simply an object of intense interest. Being intimate with Carmen, with Carmen's body, was perfectly natural for her. What I'm saying is that from now on you don't judge her, you simply accept her. Accept her as a friend. Gender has bugger-all to do with it.'

'And Carmen? Christ, I lost my virginity with Carmen.'

'Peekay, Carmen's been around. She's probably no more a lesbian than you are a homo. She's a big girl, you always knew that!'

'When did you know? Shit! Why didn't you tell me earlier?'

'Sitting on the sidelines you sometimes see the game more clearly than the players. What was I supposed to tell you? You and Harriet haven't been together for yonks.'

'Ja, Hymie, but you know how I felt! For fuck's sake, it would have helped to *know*!'

Hymie took out a cigarette. He'd given up the dark brown Russian sobranies and now smoked Benson & Hedges in a small square red tin. He tapped the end of the cigarette on the lid of the tin. He realised the extent of Peekay's hurt, the crushing blow to his pride. It had taken a lot of courage for Peekay to maintain his love for Harriet. He had to play things in a lighter vein, to allow Peekay to get out from under. 'Peekay, you know what your trouble is? You're a hopeless bloody romantic! What's more you're also a horny one! Women watch you a certain way. They bed you with their eyes. When you fall in *like*, as you have done with Doris with the marvellous tits, at least you're in control. You of all people should know that achieving the things you want is all about control. Our future success against the injustice of the system when we return to the bloody fatherland is dependent on control. We will survive only because we never lose control. Remember that! Forget the romantic part, the love part, the *falling in* part. The only thing you're likely to end up falling in is shit!'

Peekay watched as Hymie lit his cigarette. For the first time in his life Peekay found himself completely at odds with him. He could understand the logic, the intellectual truth of what Hymie was saying, but it was not sufficient to convince him.

Peekay, who had spent his life camouflaged, never allowing his emotions to show, knew suddenly, hopelessly and with not a little real fear, that in the matter of love his heart was capable of ruling his head. It was a weakness against which he sensed he had no protection. It was like finding you have an incurable disease when you feel no symptoms. It was there, lurking in the womb, snapped onto the sperm, invading the egg, a gene transferred to destroy him prematurely, waiting for just the right time to manifest itself in his body.

After leaving Oxford, Peekay moved into Hymie's flat in London. He was to fight the American, King Coon Sinders, just two weeks after the end of the Trinity term. Hymie had managed to arrange for the fight to take place at the US Marine base in Munich.

Hymie, through the company they'd set up to handle the financing and proceeds of the title fights, Angel

Sport, sold the fight to the US military in Germany, permitting them to buy the television rights to every US base in Europe. This money he used as expenses and for the boxers' purse money. In addition he contracted the US TV network crew to film the fight for a ridiculously small amount of money, which helped to gain additional publicity in the States for the Tadpole Angel.

At last Peekay was ready to challenge Jake 'Spoonbill' Jackson. The welterweight championship of the world had all the makings; the poor boy from the South with a ninth grade education and the brilliant young law student from Oxford. A.J. Liebling, writing for the *New York Times*, referred to it as 'The Catfish and Caviar Contest'. *Sports Illustrated* were smart enough to include a reaction from the champion in the feature they ran on Peekay.

Jake 'Spoonbill' Jackson's comment was quoted verbatim:

> *You know what is a Spoonbill, man? A Spoonbill, he got long legs and he walks in the water and when he sees a goddamn tadpole he gobbles it up! Tell him all that education he got, it ain't gonna help. All that tadpole gonna need is enough education to count to ten, after that he with the angels . . . permanent!*

Peekay had two and a half months to prepare for the world championship fight which was scheduled to take place on 27th October in Madison Square Garden. He would train initially in England and then they'd take the boat to New York to spend the final two months at a training camp in Colorado.

Jam Jar had come up with the idea of having Peekay train at the highest possible altitude. Most of the Odd Bodleians were by now experts at boxing and he reasoned that the fight might well go to the man with the most stamina. By training at the highest possible altitude and then coming down to sea level for the fight, Peekay would have extra capacity. It was a theory well worth exploiting. They'd hired the services of a small-town boxing promoter named Mike Graw to set up a camp and he'd managed to rent a small dude ranch high in the mountains near Pike's Peak in Colorado.

Dutch had been against the mountains at first. He'd brought a fighter to the States before and there was an accepted way of doing things if you were a serious contender. If you were fighting in 'The Garden' you selected a training camp not too far from the action, somewhere the more fanatical fans could visit you and – much more importantly – where the press could drop in for a story. 'The fight game in America's all about publicity, you gotta get the newspaper boys on your side. If they give you the thumbs up it's on for one an' all! The other way and you're history.'

'We'll move up to New York a week before the fight. That ought to be enough time for a press conference every day,' Hymie had suggested.

Dutch had continued to protest. 'Hymie, it ain't me. Personally I hate the bastards in the game in America. It's a dirty business and the less we have to do with them the better. But it's the lad I'm thinking of. If 'e don't know the score it's gonna throw him summink awful. All the carry-on the Yanks go in for, it gets a fighter pumped up, ready. Besides, the promoter, he's gonna insist on all the malarky, it builds up the gate.'

'Dutch, Peekay's a fast learner. A week will be

sufficient. As for building up the gate, that's not included in the contract. In fact, it's one of the few bloody concessions I managed to get. They didn't think Peekay's rep carried much weight in America. People will simply come to see the shit knocked out of the Limey!'

In fact Hymie had tied up the contract for the fight some months previously when he'd made the trip to sign up King Coon Sinders, stopping for a week in New York. The contract had been on condition that Peekay won against Sinders, but apart from this clause, which was now negated, the formalities were long over when the four of them, for Togger was now included, arrived at O'Hare a week after the fight in Munich and exactly nine weeks before the title fight.

Hymie knew he had a lousy contract. Jackson's manager was a big, red-nosed, morose Irishman who smoked large, foul-smelling Philippines cigars most of the time and drank Four Roses whiskey neat. Michael O'Rourke looked like a larger version of W.C. Fields, though he had none of the great comedian's acid humour or repartee. He was stubborn and not very bright, but he knew the fight game and he was accepted in New York boxing circles.

From the beginning he'd insisted the fight be pro-moted by another Irishman, a millionaire scrap-metal merchant from Philadelphia named Patrick O'Flynn. O'Flynn, with a consortium of New York Irish, had promoted most of Jackson's fights and O'Rourke wanted it no other way. Hymie was soon to discover why.

The deal they wanted from the start had been one-sided to say the least. The purse was set at one hundred thousand dollars with Jake 'Spoonbill' Jackson taking eighty-one thousand and Peekay, win, lose or draw, a flat nineteen thousand dollars. They would barely cover their costs. In addition, Hymie had to pay O'Flynn a further two thousand dollars for the seats occupied by the Odd Bodleians.

Hymie had little option but to go along with the deal. Jackson was established as a title holder who was expected to hang on and hang in and Hymie had to have the fight come what may.

The TV deal had been sewn up before Hymie had met with O'Rourke and O'Flynn. Both had been delighted when Hymie had capitulated with little more than a token fight except to ask for the TV rights to the fight worldwide. Both Irishmen knew they didn't have a snowball's hope in hell of interesting a major American network in the fight and they readily agreed.

Hymie wanted a second clause inserted into the contract. He wanted a return bout, win, draw or lose in the first fight, in which he guaranteed Jake 'Spoonbill' Jackson a purse of three hundred and fifty thousand US dollars in return for agreeing to contest the title in Johannesburg. There was no withdrawal clause and a three-month postponement clause which required the offending boxer to be examined by three medical practitioners from the other boxer's country before the postponement clause came into effect. The fight to take place no later than six months after the Madison Square Garden bout.

It was nearly double the largest purse for which Jackson had hitherto fought and the return bout clause was quickly drawn up by an attorney at law and inserted in the contract.

Elmer Milstein had booked the four of them in at the Plaza. He met them at Idlewild when the Pan American

Boeing Stratocruiser landed at seven o'clock in the morning.

Hymie stared in astonishment at the car Elmer had brought along. 'Jesus, my old man's identity crisis is over! Just wait until Solomon Levy hears about this Lincoln. It's in such appallingly bad taste he's going to love it to death!'

Twenty-two

Elmer Milstein had purchased a second-hand, twelve-seater Chevvy bus which was to take them the fifteen hundred mile journey through the centre of the United States to Colorado. Most of the trip would be over flat-land states: through cities like Indianapolis, St Louis and Kansas City. While this meant they'd make good time, Peekay wanted to see the south. It meant catching a Greyhound bus to Atlanta and then flying from Atlanta to Kansas City to join up with the others coming across in the bus. The trip, though an additional expense, had one other advantage: it meant Peekay would only miss two days of training rather than four or perhaps five.

They were running out of time and Peekay was anxious to settle into a training routine. He'd not fought in America and he had to learn the fight culture of the place quickly. He wanted as much going for him as possible. He told himself he had to be perfectly prepared if he had a chance against Jackson, that everything mattered. Though good sparring partners mattered the most. It wasn't simply their ability, although this was very important, but also their minds.

Jake 'Spoonbill' Jackson was black and from the South, Peekay could recite his boxing history in his sleep but he needed to know what made his opponent tick.

They'd met Hymie and the rest of the New York party in Kansas City. The only other addition to the troupe was an elderly fighter's manager who claimed his name was Daddy Kocklelovsky but who was known as the shortened version, Daddy Kockle. He was a negro with snowy-white hair. He'd been born in Texas during the presidency of James A. Garfield, which made him at the most sixty-six years old.

Daddy Kockle had seen Jake 'Spoonbill' Jackson fight on several occasions and he'd taken the job in Colorado, not at all sure that the unknown Peekay wouldn't be badly mismatched in the ring. Jackson at his best was a formidable opponent; most experts believed him to be unbeatable. But after watching Peekay, the speed and intelligence of the young South African had impressed him. As the fight drew closer he became more and more convinced that the man who needed the title the most would be the ultimate winner.

One afternoon he called Peekay aside. 'Tell me, son, how bad you want to win?'

'Bad, Daddy Kockle. *Real bad*!' Peekay replied, using the Americanism for emphasis.

'Real bad ain't enough. Jackson he want *real bad* also. Tell me, you hate Jackson some, a lot, you don't hate him at all; which is it?'

'I just want what he's got, it belongs to me, the title, it's mine. But I don't hate him, Daddy!'

'Son, you got two weeks. By the time you climb in that ring you gotta hate that nigger, you hear?'

Peekay was shocked at the expression. 'Christ! I don't think of him as a nigger! He's a fighter, the world champion! I want his title. I've thought about owning that title a hundred times every day since I was six years old. I don't give a fuck who owns it, it's mine, that's all!'

'I like that, son. You got heat. That a good start. But you ain't got hate. You gotta have hate! For some other title, maybe heat enough. In a world championship it ain't. Why you think Jackson been saying those things 'bout you in the newspaper and on the radio? You saw what he said in the newspaper yesterday. He says he's buildin' up his dislike. He said he got enough already built up to put you out in the fifth round but he's buildin' on it! Dis-like! That's jus' 'nother word foh hate, sonny boy!'

'Let me tell you something. I want that title so badly my teeth hurt just thinking about it. Every muscle, every sinew, every second of my day and night is involved with winning it. It's not getting rich that matters for me. The title isn't about getting rich and driving around in a big Cadillac with my name painted on the door. It's about being free to be myself, the person hiding behind the person. I'm trapped inside myself, Daddy. The title is the doorway to my escape! That's why I'm coming down the mountain to take Jake "Spoonbill" Jackson!'

Peekay had never talked to anyone like this before and he didn't understand why he was telling Daddy Kockle now, or even if he was making any sense to the old man.

'I can't reckon too much on that, son, what's inside a man is there for his own self. But I can reckon on knowin' how a fighter get ready foh fightin'. He got to know he superior, he better! Now you lissen to me, son. What I got to say now it ain't pretty and it ain't oughta be spoke by no black man. You gonna fight a nigger. That not the same thing as fightin' a white man. A nigger got some things in his head you use right, you can whup him. Inferiority things, things he can't help hisself 'cause they borned into him. Ain't so long ago we coloured people, we been slaves. Jackson, he's a southern boy, from Kentucky. That ain't no place a coloured boy ever grow'd up brave! That's Klan territory, that's mighty fearful country. Right now, in that boy's home town, there are white folk saying, "That Nigger, he's too sassy, he got a big mouth foh a nigger. Maybe that white boy he gonna whup him good, teach him his place!"'

'Jesus, Daddy Kockle, it's nice knowing you're on my side but this is racist stuff, it's everything that repulses me!'

'Never mind no racist! You think like that, Peekay, you gonna lose! Hear me, this ain't no boxing match, this is war! What kinda war you got when you gonna love thine enemy!'

'I don't *love* Jackson, I just don't hate him because he's black. Give me some other reason to hate him!'

'Ain't no other reason. That's the strongest. That's the one reason supersedes all the others. That's the one reason ain't got logic. It's the bes' kind of hate foh a fightin' man!'

The old man shook his head, 'My granpappy he tol' me a sad tale his granpappy tol' him concernin' the slaves. He told when the Arab captured him and his brothers in his village in Africa and marched them to the ships and sold them to the white man captain of a big ship. He told how they chained them in the hold below, but the young women they put in a big cage on the deck. Then come those sailor men with a bottle and the bottle it contained blood and they drank the blood and they done raped them black women in the cage. They were raped by cannibals! Blood drinkin' cannibals who killed their men below and drank their blood!' Daddy Kockle chuckled. 'Ain't that somethin'? All the time, it ain't the black people who are the cannibals, it's the white! That's the kind of fear that lies inside the black man. That's the kind of hate. It ain't logic hate. It ain't logic fear. My granpappy he prob'ly figured out what them sailor men bin' drinking from that bottle was rum or port wine. But what his granpappy tol' him is the truth accordin' to the way he want to feel. It ain't no logical truth. That make no difference. It's the emotional truth. The emotional truth got the fear and the hate contained in it!' Daddy Kockle paused. 'That's the hate Jackson got in him! That the hate you gonna come into the ring to fight, but also the fear. Now lissen, boy, the idea! The idea is you got to make the fear in that southern black boy more than the hate. Then Jackson, he gonna be whupped!'

'Daddy Kockle, I'm going to have to take this problem to the mountain, I just don't know what to say. I'm sorry, but I can't build up an emotional reaction to Jackson based on his colour. My life, my future life, is dedicated to the proposition that all men should be born equal. What happens to them after that is up to them. But they must be given equal social and intellectual opportunity based on their minds, their skills and their personalities. When you declare a man or woman inferior, second class, because of pigmentation, then you sin beyond any possibility of redemption. That's the very point of a boxing ring; it's twenty foot by twenty foot of equal opportunity. When you climb into the ring, all you've got is your brain and your fists.

If you win it's because you're the best man, not because you've been given a totally unfair advantage as a birthright!'

Daddy Kockle clucked and shook his head. 'Hallelujah! Praise the Lord! You're a good man, Peekay. But that ain't winnin' talk, that losin' talk if ever I heard it, son.'

In the bright crisp September and October afternoons in the Rockies when they'd completed training for the day Peekay would head for the mountains. Togger had accompanied him on one early occasion but they'd seen a rattlesnake on a rock catching the last of the afternoon sun and he'd decided the countryside was for the birds.

Peekay had been raised in the mountains with Doc and while the Rockies, iced with early snow, were somewhat different to the soft shouldered hills that rolled back into the high mountains which cradled the small lowveld town where he'd spent his boyhood, they nevertheless filled a deep need within him.

In the mines and during his Oxford years he'd been away from the high crags and terraces that leave a man free to think his mind clean and clear. From the dude camp he'd quickly climb through the ponderosa pine where the silvertailed squirrels darted from tree to tree, less scared at his approach than curious. Beyond the pine he'd climb through sparse clumps of sycamore and mountain ash on beyond the Alpine flora to the sharp outcrops of rock and cliff face. Twice he'd seen a lone coyote on a ridge and imagined it was the same one, an old loner who liked the privacy of the high ground where he could look at the Rockies climbing higher to the North West and the vast plains beneath him where the Sioux and the Cheyenne had once ruled and buffalo had once grazed in their tens of thousands.

Peekay would return at sunset from his mountain walks in time to take his turn chopping firewood, for it was logsawing in the early mornings and chopping at night. Invariably he'd mention a possible solution he'd found to a problem they'd come against during the day's work-out or when they'd been discussing tactics over lunch.

A golden eagle, the first Peekay had ever seen, hovered no more than a boy's kite flight above him, so close he could see the ribbed feathers in its wingspan tipped with backlight. The eagle seemed to symbolise all that was beautiful in this magnificent country which Peekay was beginning to love enormously. The people they'd met had, for the most part, been so open, kind and hospitable that Peekay had been able to put the Jackson campaign into perspective. What he hadn't reckoned with was the power of the media, who'd grabbed the catfish and caviar analogy and were milking it to death.

Jackson had abandoned his often clever invective of earlier weeks and lately had been building on his hate thing. It was the first time a black American boxer had used the black/white dichotomy in a determined way. In the America of the mid fifties, black sportsmen were still expected to behave in a modest and submissive manner, grateful for the opportunity sport provided them to rise above their peers. It was an unstated thing, built out of a century and a half of accepting the negro as the underclass. Jackson's aggression towards his white opponent was seen as unseemly and provocative, and it was beginning to polarise fight fans along racist lines. It even had the effect of turning many of Jackson's own fans in the white Southern States against him.

The point was, if Jackson was simply building up the

gate and his reputation with it, he was doing a remarkable job and the 'catfish and caviar' concept was working brilliantly. But in the last weeks he'd been pushing the concept of hate seemingly beyond the simple pyrotechnics of boxing promotion. If as Daddy Kockle insisted, rage and hate were indeed indispensable allies in the ring, then Peekay needed to do something to neutralise this advantage. Jackson's umbilical fear, passed on through generations of persecution and humiliation, was the way to do so. How to do this without being a white supremacist was the problem Peekay now faced.

The irony was, as a small boy who had himself been persecuted and humiliated, Peekay knew the kind of meaningless fear that gnaws at the lining of your gut. He had been taught by the great Inkosi-Inkosikazi, the greatest medicine man in all of Africa, to visit the night country where he could control his anxieties or solve the problems confronting him. And so, seated on a huge outcrop of rock just below the snowline in the Rocky Mountains, Peekay returned to Africa, to a primitive, deeply atavistic part of his mind, where he would seek the strength to confront Jackson's hate.

In Peekay's mind the night country was a very real place, the place of three waterfalls and ten stepping-stones in the Africa of his soul. He now prepared to enter it and closed his eyes, waiting for the stillness to come, the measured downward plunge into the night country, like the slowness of a man seen falling from a cliff at a great distance.

A sudden roar of water filled Peekay's head and he stood on a ledge above the first waterfall. Far below him the river rushed away, tumbling and boiling into a narrow gorge. Just before the water entered the gorge was the pool of the ten stepping-stones, ten anthracite teeth strung across its shimmering, gargling mouth. Inkosi-Inkosikazi spoke into the roar of the water, his voice quiet, almost gentle:

> *You are standing on a rock above the*
> *highest waterfall, a young warrior who has*
> *killed his first lion and is worthy now to*
> *fight in the legion of Dingane, the great*
> *impi that destroys all before it, worthy*
> *even to fight in the impi of Shaka, the*
> *greatest warrior king of all.*
>
> *You are wearing the skirt of lion tail as*
> *you face into the setting sun. Now the sun*
> *has passed beyond Zululand, even past the*
> *land of the Swazi, and now it leaves the*
> *Shangaun and the royal kraal of Mojaji,*
> *the rain queen, to be cooled in the great,*
> *dark water beyond.*
>
> *You can see the moon rising over Africa*
> *and you are at peace with the night,*
> *unafraid of the great demon Skokiaan who*
> *comes to feed on the dark night, tearing at*
> *its black flesh until, at last, it is finished*
> *and the new light comes to stir the herd*
> *boys and send them out to mind the*
> *lowing cattle.*

As Peekay stood on the rock above the highest water-fall, waiting to jump, he could see the moon rising, held huge in a star-pinned sky, a bright silver florin throwing its light down onto the ten black stepping-stones two hundred feet below, where the third waterfall crashed down.

485

Inkosi-Inkosikazi's voice came to him: *You must jump now, little warrior of the king.*

Peekay took a deep breath and launched himself into the night. The cool air, mixed with spray, rushed past his face. He hit the water below the first pool, sinking briefly before rising to the surface. With barely time to take a breath, he was swept over the lip of the second waterfall and then again down the third, plunging into the great roaring pool at its base. He swam strongly to the first of the great stones glistening wet and black in the moonlight. Jumping from stone to stone, he crossed the river, leaping to the pebbly beach on the far side.

Clear as an echo the great witchdoctor's voice cut through the roar of the falls. *We have crossed the dreamtime to the other side and it is done.*

Peekay opened his eyes, above him, over the far Rockies, huge cloud castles of light rose in a sky beginning to dim for the night. He picked his way down to the dark line of ponderosa pine, sending shale sliding and small rocks tumbling ahead of him. It had turned cold, the first hint of winter coming to the high mountains. This was the last time he would go up to the mountain. Tomorrow they would leave for New York. It was exactly one week before he would climb into the ring at Madison Square Garden. One week and sixteen years of waiting to become the welterweight champion of the world.

In his head Peekay carried the line he knew would undermine Jake 'Spoonbill' Jackson's hate.

Twenty-three

The weigh-in took place mid morning on the day of the fight at the offices of the New York boxing commission just up from Madison Square Garden. The auditorium with its high ceilings was crowded with people: reporters and photographers hoping for a confrontation between the two fighters, ex-fighters and hangers-on, people who hoped to be seen and who called hello loudly to others they hoped to impress.

Mrs Smith, the cook from their camp at the dude ranch, was there wearing a brilliant yellow dress with a pale blue picture hat and carrying a yellow silk parasol like a walking stick. Yellow and blue were Peekay's colours and she wore them with a huge smile as she walked with Dutch. O'Flynn the promoter was talking to Hymie waving his hands, obviously upset over something and Elmer Milstein was talking to the unit manager of ABC Wide World of Sports who was setting up a camera.

Jake 'Spoonbill' Jackson hadn't yet arrived. It was the champ's perogative to be late and to be weighed in first and Peekay stood quietly with Togger and Daddy Kockle. He'd made no concession to the event and wore the blue tracksuit Hymie had given him the first day they'd turned out for Dutch three years earlier. The yellow silk stitching proclaiming 'The Tadpole Angel' on the back had faded and where some of it had been worn away Mrs Smith had lovingly re-embroidered it, sitting by the fireplace in Colorado.

There was a sudden lifting of the noise level in the auditorium as Jake 'Spoonbill' Jackson entered. Jackson was a smooth-faced man with an elongated head which didn't seem in the least bit negroid. His head was completely shaved, but he'd grown a pencil-line moustache which hardly showed because his skin was so black. Now he wore a white satin dressing-gown with an American flag on the back and a plain pair of basketball boots, with the laces undone, flapping on the floor as he walked. The dirty sneaker-style boots contrasted strangely with the ritzy-looking robe. He untied and removed his robe, allowing it to fall into the hands of Michael O'Rourke, who stood directly behind him. Then he stepped out of his shoes and stood barefoot beside the scales in a pair of white satin boxing shorts. Around his waist hung his WBC World Championship Belt, a grotesque gold and enamelled affair which resembled an elaborate kidney belt. With a grin he stepped onto the machine expecting the official to commence weighing him in.

However, the small bald-headed man in charge of the scales simply waited. Jackson grinned a trifle awkwardly; unclipping the belt, he handed it to O'Rourke. He'd obviously worked up a little scene which had backfired and to cover his embarrassment he now turned to the crowd. Standing on the scales like an orchestral leader, he raised his arms.

'What a Spoonbill stork do to the Tadpole?' he yelled.

'He munch him!' the ten or so people in his retinue shouted.

'And then what he do?' Jackson shouted again.

'He crunch him!' they answered.

'And when he munch him and crunch him what he do then?'

'He swallow him down!' The group yelled at the top of their lungs, some of them punching the air above their heads like a group of cheerleaders.

Jackson turned to Peekay, acknowledging him for the first time. 'You call me Catfish, you damn right, I Catfish!' He turned to the group once again, 'What a Catfish gonna do to a tadpole?'

'He *munch* him and *crunch him* and *swallow him down*!' they yelled back gleefully.

Jackson pointed his finger at his opponent. 'You hear me now, white boy! You hear me good, Tadpole! I'm hungry, I'm hungry, man! Tonight I gonna *eat you*!'

Peekay regarded him silently for a long moment. Then he said, 'I have only this to say to Mr Jake Spoonbill Jackson,' he paused as the whole room waited to hear his response to the champion's goading. 'If he takes his hate with him into the ring tonight I will win for . . . *hate is a slow witted ally in the ring*.' They were the words he had been given in the night country.

The commission doctor examined them both, measuring their heartbeats and taking their blood pressure. They weighed in almost identically, Peekay just four ounces lighter than Jackson, who came in a pound under the welterweight limit. The whole procedure was all over in less than fifteen minutes. Now only waiting time remained and Peekay returned to the hotel to rest.

Dozens of telegrams had arrived from South Africa, notably from St John Burnham, Peekay's old headmaster, Gert and Captain Smith at the Barberton prison, the mayor and town council of Barberton, Miss Bornstein, Peekay's primary school teacher, Mrs Boxall and one from Gideon Mandoma which read:

> Hambari ngokunakekela bafowenu ma
> bulala ingonyama.
> *Go carefully my brother and kill the
> lion.*

Among the many telegrams were some from E. W., Harriet, and one from Doris which read: *Roses are red ... Violets are blue. Win or lose, I'll still love you! Doris xxx*

Doris with the wonderful tits, as usual, was about as subtle as a meat axe, but Peekay found he missed her rather more than Harriet.

Hymie came in and sat on Peekay's bed. 'I don't seem to have spent enough time with you, over these last eight weeks, old mate,' he grinned.

'All the time I needed, Hymie.' Peekay punched Hymie lightly on the shoulder. 'As long as you're in my corner tonight, that's all that matters.' Peekay could feel himself becoming sentimental and changed the subject quickly. 'Why were you and O'Flynn having a set-to this morning?'

Hymie explained how Aunt Tom wanted Mrs Smith in with the Odd Bodleians and O'Flynn had insisted they forfeit six seats for the space her piano would occupy or pay him two hundred and fifty dollars a seat. Mrs Smith, a ferocious pianist, wanted to join Aunt Tom in playing for the Odd Bodleians.

'Jesus, Peekay, I usually love dealing with the Americans, they're open, honest and they make decisions fast.

But the guys running American boxing are crud! It's full of hoods, hoodlums and rip-off merchants. I'll be bloody glad when you take that championship belt and piss off.'

Peekay realised what a strain it had all been for Hymie, who'd worked solidly for a year to bring the event off so that they'd end up with some money in the bank despite the lopsided purse they were getting for the fight. Peekay was going to need money to buy his share of a law practice and the often delicate negotiations had largely fallen to Hymie. 'Thank you, Hymie. I owe you a big one,' he said softly.

Hymie looked at his friend almost fiercely. 'Never! I could never begin to give you back what you've given me, Peekay. Without you I would have ended up just another rich Jew in carpet and underfelt.'

Hymie and Peekay left the hotel together, driven to the Garden in Elmer's family's Lincoln. Sensing they wished to be alone the chauffeur activated the electric window, sealing the back from the front of the car. It was a ritual the two of them had kept since the first fight they'd worked together at school. Just the two of them going through tactics, talking the fight into each other's heads. The driver was directed to a side entrance.

Daddy Kockle and Togger were waiting for them in the dressing room. It was a big and cold place about as welcoming as a public latrine. Against the left-hand wall stood a makeup bench above which was a mirror surrounded with small naked globes, most of them either smashed or not working. Peekay entered and threw his bag on the bench which was scarred with a thousand cigarette burns. The surface of the mirror, where the mercury had blistered into brown blobs, made his face look as though it was covered in liver spots. A bentwood chair, the rattan missing from the seat and replaced by a section of plywood, stood in front of the bench. A wooden bench ran down the centre of the room and another ran across the far wall where it was stopped short by a closed door. A rub-down table rested between the centre bench and the wall opposite the mirror. From the ceiling a naked bulb of very high wattage flared concentrated white light into the room. There was absolutely nothing comfort-able about the dressing room. It looked like it was; a place to leave and a place to come back to without making any impression. The door on the far wall, Togger discovered, led to a shower and toilet.

Dutch arrived, looking nervously at his watch. There was plenty of time. Togger held a small hand towel. It seemed to be a prop, to give his hands something to do for he was twisting it unknowingly into a length resem-bling a thick piece of rope. Only Daddy Kockle seemed relaxed and was seated on the rubbing table with his legs crossed.

Peekay started to undress. Togger, happy to find something to do, took Peekay's clothes and hung them up on a wire hanger like a valet. Peekay fitted the pro-tector harness on, a jockstrap device with a hard, leather-covered aluminium crotch box. Then he pulled on the light blue shorts with the yellow waistline which Hymie had ordered for the fight, after which he pulled on a pair of thick socks. Leaving off his boxing boots, he moved over to the rub-down table. Daddy Kockle jumped from the table and Peekay saw he'd brought his clarinet.

Dutch started to work on Peekay's shoulders, first rubbing him down with vaseline, then taking the towel from Togger and rubbing what vaseline remained off again before starting to massage his shoulders. 'Just a light one, lad, loosen you up a bit,' he spoke softly as though only the two of them were in the room. 'Take your time tonight, build it slowly, you've got fifteen rounds.' It was advice he'd offered a hundred times before.

With half an hour to go, O'Rourke arrived to supervise the taping of Peekay's hands. He was smoking a large cigar and looked cheap and ruddy, wearing a grey pin-striped suit, a green-striped shirt with a gold collar pin, a bright green tie and a real carnation in his buttonhole. They were surprised to see him. It was usual to send the fight manager along or even the trainer to supervise the bandaging. 'I've come to do the honours meself,' he announced, smiling. 'The Garden's sold out, standing room only. Mr O'Flynn's a very happy man.'

'He ought to be, he got a grand out of me for the piano,' Hymie said.

'Well now, a piano takes a lot of space, son! At two hundred and fifty bucks a ringside seat, I reckon you got off light, my boy!'

'I'd rather you didn't call me son or boy, Mr O'Rourke. Only your fighter is further from being of Irish descent than I am and I imagine we're both grateful to our antecedents for this fact.' Hymie turned to Dutch. 'Have you got the bandages, let's get this over! Daddy Kockle, you better go do the same and check out *Munch, Crunch and Swallow*'s hands.'

O'Rourke removed the cigar from his mouth, tapping ash onto the floor. 'Now, now, no hard feelings, Levy? We've come this far. It could have been worse for you, to be sure, we don't take too kindly to strangers playing on our turf.'

'Sure, Michael, you've been a perfect gentleman. Let's leave it there, shall we?'

But O'Rourke was clearly not finished yet. 'Be thankful you got a crack at the title, we could have held out, made things a lot more difficult, son.' O'Rourke stuck his chin out and pushed the cigar back into his mouth, holding it between his forefinger and thumb, waiting for Hymie to challenge him again on his use of the word 'son'.

'Hey! We're all a little tense,' Peekay exclaimed. 'Did you bring a pen, Mr O'Rourke?'

O'Rourke kept his eyes on Hymie, squinting down at him. Then he grinned, 'Sure thing, Peekay.' He removed his hand from the cigar and looking down at his left-side top pocket he withdrew a solid gold Parker, holding it up in triumph for all to see.

When Dutch had completed taping his hands, Peekay held them out for O'Rourke, who crisscrossed the bandages with his pen. He drew back. 'Okay, may the best man win, Peekay, and we all know who that is,' he said, attempting an enigmatic smile.

Hymie walked over with the Everlast gloves, offering them to the Irishman to inspect. O'Rourke shook his head, indicating that Hymie should go ahead and put them on. The gloves were a new bright red colour and soaked up the light where they curved around the fist. Hymie fitted the left glove on first, the way Hoppie Groenewald had done that first time on the train. *First with your head and then with your heart!* It was such a long time ago.

Peekay banged the two gloves together, feeling the fit. O'Rourke punched him lightly on the shoulder, then he turned and left the room.

Peekay slipped off the rub-down table and, crossing

the room, sat down on the bench against the wall. Togger knelt down, slipped the soft boots onto Peekay's feet and tied the laces, taping the ends to the boots so they didn't flap around during the fight.

Daddy Kockle entered with an official who stood just outside the door holding onto the lintel with both hands and leaned in as he spoke. 'Ten minutes! The champ wants to go last. Get ready to move when you hear the ring announcer declare the result of the last fight on the undercard.'

Daddy Kockle said, 'We got a police escort to the ring, now ain't that something?'

Peekay closed his eyes, emptying his head. Doc had been dead six years, lying in the crystal cave of Africa. 'You can be it, absoloodle!' he'd said when Peekay had announced he intended to be the welterweight champion of the world. 'Every day you must say, I am champion of za world! You will see, one day you will be it.'

'Son, this is for you,' Peekay heard Daddy Kockle say. 'This is the song my daddy played on his horn when something good happen.' He paused, holding the clarinet ready for his lips. 'It's called, "Crossin' over Jordan to the Other Side".'

Daddy Kockle, seated once again on the rub-down table, began to play. The sweet low sound of the clarinet climbed slowly, filling the room and calming the sharp light. The negro spiritual lifted Peekay, holding him, cradling him in its arms, rocking him, calming him, until at last it softened to an almost mute note then faded like a snowflake into nothing as it let him go.

Peekay opened his eyes and Daddy Kockle put down his instrument. 'Son, I got a whole heap of respect for you,' he said quietly.

The noise of the crowd lifted suddenly and they heard the ring announcer beginning to call the introductions. Though they'd not yet glimpsed the crowd they could feel the excitement in the Garden. The women at the ringside were wearing formal gowns and the men evening suits and tuxedos. The mink from the Bronx and Harlem mixed with the silver fox from Sutton Place, and diamonds in every configuration called it a draw between bandit and banker. Boston blue blood mixed happily with prominent figures from boxing, showbiz and the Italian, Irish and black underworld. Several of the better-known TV and sporting personalities drew an excited response from the crowd as they made their way to the ringside, the loudest applause perhaps being for Joe Di Maggio of the New York Yankees.

'Time to go,' Hymie called softly, holding out the blue-and-yellow silk robe with 'The Tadpole Angel' embroidered on the back.

Peekay held his arms out for Hymie to slip the sleeves of the silk robe over them. First tying the front of the robe, Peekay put his hand on Hymie's shoulder and they walked out together to the sudden and growing roar of the crowd. Hymie could feel the slightest tremble coming from Peekay's hand. It was a good sign. The adrenalin was beginning to pump; Peekay was ready to fight.

The roar of the crowd lifted as they came into sight. There wasn't any doubt Peekay was popular, the noise had a shrillness to it, pitched high. 'The women, they love you, Peekay,' Daddy Kockle shouted. Peekay entered the ring, the lights overhead at first blinding him, so he looked into blackness as he acknowledged the audience, one glove raised above his head.

The Odd Bodleians had risen as he entered. Each

wore a yellow rose in the lapel of his evening suit with a flash of blue ribbon laced through the buttonhole. Aunt Tom was dressed in a dinner suit, a brooch of canary yellow diamonds and blue sapphires clipped to her lapel.

Mrs Smith, seated at the piano, looked like an enormous party decoration in a full length, fitted evening dress made entirely of electric blue sequins. Pinned to her large bosom was a corsage of tiny yellow roses. Peekay, raising his glove, acknowledged them with a grin. Then he walked over to the rosin box in his corner and dusted the soles of his boots before sitting on the pot.

The applause as the champion entered was tumultuous; the home-grown boy was getting the acknowledgement he deserved as a great fighter. Jake 'Spoonbill' Jackson came down the aisle surrounded by his large entourage, led by half-a-dozen policemen. He climbed into the ring, jumping up and down with his arms held high above his head, twisting with each jump so that as he landed he faced a different section of the crowd. The tremendous noise hadn't stopped since he'd first appeared in the aisle.

Daddy Kockle began to massage Peekay's shoulder lightly.

'Righto, my son, let's concentrate on fightin' fifteen rounds,' Dutch said.

The ring announcer now stepped into centre ring and the microphone was lowered down to him. He was a small, bald man, dressed in a white tuxedo jacket and black evening pants. The bow tie to his white shirt was no more than half-an-inch wide but stuck out nearly six inches on either side of the tiny centre knot. The first quick impression he gave was of someone with an arrow through his epiglottis who'd had both ends sawn off for the sake of mobility and convenience.

'Ladies and gentlemen, be upstanding for the national anthem.' To everyone's surprise the usual scratched record didn't come wheezing on. Instead the opening chords of 'The Star-Spangled Banner'. came from Mrs Smith at the piano where one of several microphones was located. The Odd Bodleians picked up the beautiful anthem and carried it to the crowd. It was stirring stuff and Jake 'Spoonbill' Jackson stood at attention in the centre of the ring while Peekay stood quietly in his corner. The applause was tremendous as they came to the end, the crowd conscious of the compliment they were being paid.

The crowd returned to their seats and the Odd Bodleians remained standing. The noise in the huge place died down as the prelude to the *Concerto for the Great Southland* played, merging quickly to the start of the great Zulu chant. The voice of Mrs Smith called to the chanters in song urging them to declare for the great Shaka King of the Zulus. The male voices responded. At first like distant thunder, when the great clouds on the Drakensberg are still tipped with white, then louder as the storm clouds mulled and gathered swelling and building following the beautiful contralto voice as it called down in the valleys and up in the high mountains for the young men who had killed a lion and who had lain with a maiden to come and declare themselves for the great warrior king. Then Jam Jar, laying aside his violin, took up the calling. The voices rose in the great war cry, the blooding was coming, when the great Zulu impi would descend in waves, like wind in the grass, to crush the enemy.

Jam Jar's voice held high and then died slowly as he

mourned the Zulu dead. Then it rose again as he called the living to pay homage to their fallen comrades. Softly, tenderly the deep male voices rose, like far-off thunder rolling across the valley of a thousand hills, building the sunlight, wiping the sky clean; then again the thunder of their voices rolled louder and louder until it crashed into the valley of the dead and rose again in one sudden, stricken, terrible outcry and stopped. Only the single cry of Jam Jar's violin was left to bring the chant to a close. The enemy was vanquished and the dead returned to their shadows.

For a few moments there was no sound, the crowd stunned by the impact of the chant. Then they rose as one and applauded. They all knew suddenly that this was a challenger who had come to fight for a title, if necessary to die, rather than to walk away without it.

The ring announcer raised his right hand high and, holding onto the microphone with his left, intoned, 'Under the authority of the State of New York Boxing Commission and the New York Athletic Commission, the World Boxing Council, I declare the welterweight championship of the world open to contest!'

He paused, looking over at Peekay and indicating with a jerk of his head that he should rise. 'In the blue corner, weighing one hundred and forty-three pounds and twelve ounces and wearing blue shorts, with fourteen professional engagements for thirteen knock-outs and one decision on points, the British Empire Welterweight Champion and the Welterweight Champion of Europe, the contender, from Oxford University, England and South Africa, Peekay, the Tad-a-pole Ang-el!!'

Peekay lifted his arms to acknowledge the tremendous and sustained applause. He resumed his stool and the announcer waited for the cheering to die down before he turned to face Jake 'Spoonbill' Jackson. Jackson was pumped up, already standing, his gloves held above his head, running on the spot and jumping in small, excited jerks.

'In the red corner, wearing white shorts, weighing one hundred and forty-four pounds, with thirty-two professional fights for thirty-two wins and thirty knock-outs, the undefeated genius of the square ring and welterweight champion of the world, from Louisville, Kentucky, Jake "Spoonbill" Jack-son!!'

The crowd went wild and it was nearly two minutes before they could be stilled again.

'Your referee for tonight, from Mexico City, Mr Emmanuel Sanchez. Judges appointed by the State of New York Boxing Commission are Judge Joseph Tesoriero, Judge Mannie Mankerwitz and Judge Hoover J. Booker.'

'We got ourselves a I-talian, a Jew and a coloured man, no goddamn Irish; can't be no fairer than that!' Daddy Kockle announced, satisfied.

The referee called the two boxers into the ring and gave them the usual instructions to break at his command, to retire to a neutral corner in the event of a knock-down and not to hold in the clinches; finally, he described the deduction of points or disqualification for a foul. Peekay, as usual, looked down at his feet while Jackson stared directly at him, hoping to catch his eye and stare him down.

Sanchez directed them back to their corners: 'Come out fighteeng, boys!'

Peekay returned to his corner and Hymie removed the lion's tooth from about his neck. 'Gideon goes with you, Peekay,' he said quietly.

The warning bell sounded and then the bell and the two welterweights came out of their corners fast, Jackson covering more ground so that they met on Peekay's side of the ring. Jackson threw a left which Peekay parried and moved left, so that they now stood in the centre of the ring. Jackson threw another left and followed it with a right, Peekay taking both blows on his gloves. Jackson's stance was slightly stooped and he held his gloves wide. It was a sign of a very quick fighter who was confident he could close up in time from a left lead, no matter how fast it came. Peekay thought he might be bluffing, seeing if he could get away with the arrogance of the hit-me-if-you-can stance, at the same time trying to intimidate his opponent from the very start.

Peekay's left lead shot out so fast that Jackson had no time even to blink. It hit him square on the mouth, knocking his mouth-guard half out. It wasn't a bad punch but it was a brilliant insult. Jackson backed away fast and Peekay let him go. The referee called a stop, allowing Jackson to replace his mouth guard. 'Box on, boys!' Sanchez called.

Peekay's lightning left had been sufficient to tell the other fighter he was going to have to work for every point he scored. There had been absolutely no margin of error for the punch and it hadn't needed any. It carried the hallmark of a classic boxer. Jackson's gloves closed noticeably and Peekay realised he had earned the first psychological advantage.

Some fights take time to settle down, the boxers playing out a number of ploys, each probing for weaknesses, testing a theory; but Peekay's left had come so piston straight and so clean and fast that Jackson knew instantly how perfect his opponent's timing was. The games were over and the serious fighting had begun.

The two men traded punches in the centre of the ring for a moment, each scoring, Jackson with a nice right hook and Peekay with a right cross. Both were throwing a lot of leather, but their mutual defences were superb. It was hard to find a fault in either man's technique. It was beautiful boxing and Jackson managed a pay-back for the punch on the mouth when, towards the end of the round, he caught Peekay with a long, raking right flush on the jaw which spun him around. It was a lovely punch and if Peekay hadn't been going backwards it could have done a great deal of damage. The bell went for the end of the first round without either boxer seeming to have gained any advantage.

'Can you see any weaknesses?' Peekay asked Hymie and Dutch.

'It's early times yet, my son. But he's no faster than you. If anything you've got the edge. The left to the mouth, that was magic.'

'He lifts his left shoulder up a fraction, perhaps to protect his jaw,' Hymie said.

Peekay nodded. If Hymie was right, later on in the fight when Jackson had lost a bit of speed he might not see a left cross coming at him quite as quickly. It wasn't the deadliest punch in the book, but behind the right pair of gloves it could do a lot of harm to a fighter slowing down.

The bell went for the second round. Jackson came out hard and scored well with three good punches. He was very fast and put his punches together beautifully; Peekay was hard put to keep him out. Jackson came in a second time, but Peekay tied him up. The referee called for them to break and Peekay got in a beautiful hook under the heart. It was the best punch of the fight so far and he heard Jackson grunt as it landed.

Peekay was a body puncher, preferring gradually to weaken the structure rather than to try and knock it out with one blow. Jackson's inclination was to go for the head. His speed against previous opponents had generally been enough to get through their defence and, with a knock-out punch in both hands, he only needed a couple of good blows to the head to beat an opponent.

But Peekay was too fast and made him miss, which hadn't happened very often in his career. Both boxers were scoring but not doing much damage, although in the second round Jackson hit Peekay with a left jab in the eye and had the satisfaction of seeing it puff up towards the end of the round. It was a close round, but if anything it was Jackson's.

The third through to the seventh were much the same, both boxers learning quickly and punching accurately. Both were fighting at a furious pace. It was going to be a matter of who lasted the distance.

Dutch had doctored Peekay's eye and the swelling had receded. Jackson had tried getting back onto it, but each time he'd thrown a left jab, Peekay's right hook found its mark under the black fighter's heart. Jackson's skin was too dark for the familiar red blotch to show but Peekay knew it was there and Jackson too was aware of what was happening. He dropped his right just a fraction to keep Peekay out, leaving the way to his eye open. Peekay sent a good punch in, testing Jackson's eye.

They came out for the eighth round, meeting in centre ring, both fighters on their toes. Peekay opened up a cut above Jackson's eye; it wasn't big and he wasn't interested in working on it yet. The punch which had opened the eye hadn't been that hard, which meant Jackson had a weakness. Weaknesses are for exploiting later when some of the fight has gone out of your opponent. Jackson's eye would keep.

The black fighter tied Peekay up in a clinch, trying to swing him around on to the ropes. The referee called for them to break and Peekay stepped back. The left hook coming at him seemed to be in slow motion; it caught him flush on the jaw and dropped him sprawling to the canvas. Peekay felt nothing, except that his legs wouldn't work. Above him Sanchez was flicking his fingers into Peekay's face counting him out. At six the pain came into his legs and by eight he was standing, his head clear but his legs still heavy. Jackson came at him and Peekay tried to tie him up, but Jackson hit him with a right hook under the heart and down he went again. But, surprisingly, this time his legs seemed to be getting better and he rested until eight before getting up. Jackson came in hard, his hands wide again, the way he'd started out in the first round. Some guys never learn. This time the straight left from Peekay was right on the point of the chin with the full weight of his shoulder behind it, with Jackson moving into the punch. The black figure simply stopped coming forward and then seemed to be propelled backwards, losing his legs from under him he landed on the seat of his pants and lay sprawling on his back. Peekay turned to move to a neutral corner when the bell went for the end of the round.

Jackson's seconds rushed out, dragging the unconscious fighter back into his corner. Jackson's eyes had opened by the time they'd seated him onto his stool. The referee signalled for a doctor but by the time the doctor had climbed into the ring his eyes were clear and he stood, ready to come out fighting.

Peekay felt better. He'd taken two of Jackson's best shots and he was still on his feet. On the other hand, if Jackson hadn't been rescued by the bell the fight would have been over. Jackson wasn't invincible. He'd keep fighting the percentage way, wearing him down, *first with the head then with the heart*; it was familiar territory for Peekay. If he could stay away from Jackson's big punch, he could play in his paddock.

The ninth round was the sort of round good fighters use to pace themselves when they know they've got a long fight on their hands. But in the tenth Jackson caught Peekay on the ropes and put in nine beautiful punches to his opponent's torso, each one slamming into him as though a hole had been punched through his rib cage; the last, a vicious left hook, seemed to lift Peekay's heart up through his rib cage, into his lungs. A terrible pain rose up from his chest, a molten substance rushing up through his mouth and nostrils like a solid object bigger than the spaces through which it was trying to escape. He didn't even sense he'd fallen, only the sensation of rushing head-first down a narrow, stainless-steel tube at great speed with light bouncing off the inside surface of the tube, burning out his eyes, a caterwauling scream echoing down the luminous tube. He came out of the other side of the tunnel like a cork forced out of a bottle, to hear the referee count to seven. To his surprise he was on his haunches with one glove resting on the canvas. But his legs held; the punishing miles running up the mountains in the high altitude were paying off. He stood upright at nine and he could see the surprise, even consternation on Jackson's face as he came in to kill him off. Nobody had ever taken a nine-punch combination from Jackson and got up off the floor.

Somehow, by hanging on grimly, using everything he knew about ringcraft and clinching whenever he could, Peekay managed to get through the remainder of the round. Jackson too was near exhaustion, or Peekay would never have got away with it. Something had to happen; neither of them was capable of fighting another five rounds. The bell went for the end of the tenth round and Peekay moved wearily to his corner.

Hymie towelled him quickly while Togger squeezed a sponge over his head, repeating the process three times so that Hymie's towelling was to no avail. Dutch grabbed a towel and wiped Peekay's head and started to work on his eye which had begun to close again. Daddy Kockle standing behind Peekay was massaging his torso around the heart, the pain of his hands working almost unbearable.

Hymie looked at Dutch and Peekay caught the look in his eye. They were going to throw in the towel. 'Don't, don't do it! We haven't begun to fight yet.'

As though on cue, Mrs Smith's piano started, picking up the very last part of the Zulu chant; instantly Jam Jar's violin cut in and the male voices rose, deep and strong, rising to a crescendo as the bell went for the eleventh round.

Jackson came out as a southpaw, obviously hoping to open up Peekay with his left. Peekay immediately changed to fight him the same way. To his surprise, the shoulder Jackson had kept up high in an orthodox stance he now dropped too low. Jackson threw a left which missed Peekay, but the right cross with which Peekay countered hit Jackson flush on the jaw. The black fighter staggered, grabbing onto the ropes. Peekay moved in and hit him two good right hooks under his heart. Jackson grabbed Peekay into a clinch and they wrestled for a few moments before the referee managed to part them.

Both fighters were oblivious to the roar of the crowd which had continued almost non-stop through the fight. They were witnessing one of the greatest title fights ever seen at the Garden and for the most part they were an audience who knew their boxing. As Jackson and Peekay broke from the clinch Jackson reverted back to an orthodox stance. He'd come off worse in the change of stance and he could feel the tremendous pain building up under his heart. Towards the end of the round Peekay got him with another hook to the heart and Jackson went down. He was in luck again; Peekay had left the punch too late and when the black fighter rose to his feet at the count of nine he had only fifteen seconds to survive to the end of the round. Going into the twelfth round they had two knock-downs each and it was still anyone's fight.

Back in the corner Dutch worked frantically on Peekay's eye, which had now completely closed. Fortunately so had Jackson's, and Dutch realised that the difference in the result of the fight might just depend on which of the two boxers saw the more clearly. Blood from internal bleeding had filled the inside of Peekay's eyelid and Dutch was trying to work it out again before it began to clot too badly, with very little result.

'Cut it, Dutch!'

'No, son, you'll wear the scar all your life; it could be dangerous.'

'For Christ's sake, Dutch! He'll nail me with his left hand if I can't see! His left is better than mine, I'm not seeing it coming half the time. Cut the eye!'

Dutch hesitated, looking to Hymie for help. Time was running out.

'You fixin' to cut that eye? You heard the man!' It was Daddy Kockle. 'Man only get one chance foh immortality; he got to do the decidin' hisself. He say cut, you cut!'

Hymie nodded and Dutch reached into his pocket for a scalpel blade. He tore at the wrapping, but, as he pulled at the paper, the blade slipped from his hands and fell to the floor outside the ring.

'Jesus, Dutch!' Hymie yelled.

Dutch shook his head. 'I ain't got a spare, lad,' he said in dismay.

Togger's hand reached out and grabbed the lion's tooth hanging around Hymie's neck. It was an incisor from a young lion, still keen-edged. He pulled it over Hymie's head. 'Cut!' he yelled.

Dutch took the tooth and sliced into the eyelid; the sudden sharp tear made Peekay wince. The blood flowed quickly, releasing the pressure from the eyelid. Dutch quickly stemmed the wound with a match-head twirled with a tiny hood of cotton wool and laced with adrenalin. He was the best cut-man in Europe and when the bell went Peekay could see clearly through an eye which was no longer bleeding.

Jackson's left eye was still up, leaving him vulnerable. Peekay was running out of energy. He didn't know how much more he could take or even dish out, whether he could get Jackson with a single punch any more. If he wasted his energy going for Jackson's head, constantly having to batter through his defence, it could be too much. Jackson had been dropped with the heart punch and it hadn't been all that hard. The punching down-under was beginning to tell. Peekay would leave the black man's head alone; he was tough as nails and it would have to be a very big punch to the cranium to

508

put him down. Peekay knew the punch to do it just wasn't there, he'd spent it earlier in the fight. He would stick to his last, work away at the body, try to get Jackson in the fourteenth. But he'd keep the black man's eye closed, just in case.

Jackson's right eye was badly cut as well as closed, but clever boxer that he was, he kept his damaged eye on Peekay's far side. It was the intelligent thing to do but by doing so he made his first big mistake. He was certain that Peekay would use his left, swinging it round from beyond the peripheral of the closed eye where he couldn't see it coming. He knew Peekay had the punch in his left hand to put him down. Jackson was a head-hunter; he couldn't conceive of an advantage such as he was giving Peekay not being taken up. He was a superb boxer and now he made his right hand do the work, protecting his eye. Which was how Peekay figured he'd react. The straight right Jackson kept throwing to keep Peekay away from his damaged eye left the area under his heart exposed every time. Peekay was landing the left hook consistently, hitting Jackson on the spot, squeezing the juice out of him.

They fought this way for the next three rounds, both fighters concentrating on keeping the damage they'd done on the boil. Short punches, not hard, but hard enough to keep doing the work of weakening their opponent. Both were exhausted but the altitude training was beginning to pay off for Peekay; his legs were holding and he was using the breaks between the rounds well, storing up everything he had for the final two rounds.

While Jackson looked in slightly worse shape there was still nothing in the fight. Jackson had never gone fifteen rounds, his non-championship fights being fought over twelve. His title defences had always ended with a knockout inside ten rounds. Peekay too, was in no-man's-land; twelve was also his maximum. The last three rounds of a closely fought championship is all guts; the fighter with the most heart wins. The bell went for the fourteenth round and Jackson, already on his feet, came storming over to Peekay. There was little point in back-pedalling; staying out of harm's way could cost Peekay the fight. They slugged it out toe-to-toe. Jackson had worked out Peekay's tactic and was no longer protecting his eye, so Peekay hit him solidly with the left, opening up the eye badly, the blood covering Jackson's face. Should he go for a TKO? It was unlikely they'd stop the fight unless the eye looked in danger. As though reading his thoughts, Jackson changed back to protecting the eye and almost immediately caught Peekay with a beautiful right hand which put him down.

Peekay wanted an eight count; he was exhausted and the punch had made him groggy, but his head cleared quickly. He had to make the knock-down look slight, so at the count of three he was back up on his feet. He managed to tie Jackson up in a clinch until the strength returned to his legs. The referee called for them to break and Peekay moved out of trouble.

Jackson, sensing that he had Peekay, came at him with a long, raking right, but missed. Peekay hit him on the shoulder with a left, spinning him around. Jackson's right had been too hard and he'd left his torso exposed. Earlier in the fight Peekay would have put three, maybe six punches down, all of them hard, all of them within half an inch of the spot; now he put all his strength into the hook. He felt it land, enter and continue, as though Jackson's ribs had simply caved in.

Jackson grunted and then sighed, falling against the ropes, his arms slung over the top. Peekay hit him with a right cross on the nose, busting it. A white-hot pain shot up his arm as his hand broke. For the second time in the fight, the bell went. Jackson was out on the ropes. The fourteenth round had been enough to win the fight for Peekay though technically he hadn't knocked Jackson out. Jackson's seconds had dragged him into his corner and were bringing him round. A doctor had climbed into the ring and was examining him.

'Stop it! Stop the fight! Stop the fuckin' fight!!' Togger was yelling hysterically at the medico. He wanted it to be over, to be Peekay's. Daddy Kockle was weeping openly.

Dutch worked on Peekay's eye. 'Steady now, my son. You've got it. Just keep stickin' him, keeping him away.' He didn't think Jackson would come out for the final round, but Dutch, the consummate professional to the last, wasn't going to raise Peekay's hopes.

Peekay began to weep silently. He didn't know why; the pain was terrible, but it wasn't the pain. He knew if Jackson came out for the final round it was all over, he couldn't fight him with a broken hand. Hymie brought his mouth to Peekay's ear. The noise from the crowd was so terrific it was the only way he could be heard. 'One more, just one more, Peekay. I love you, Peekay. Just one more. Stay on your feet, just one more round!'

Peekay drew Hymie's head down so his ear was against his mouth. 'It's all over, old mate. I've broken my hand!' he sobbed, the tears running down his cheek.

Hymie's face crumbled. He choked back the tears, but they came anyway, his heart suddenly feeling the size of a pumpkin in his chest. He couldn't think, the shock

511

was too great. Tears streamed down his face. 'Oh, God, take my life! Take anything! But don't let Jackson get out of his corner!'

The ten-second bell went for the final round and Jackson stood up. The bell went and the two fighters went into the final round. Jackson's stamina was remarkable, and Peekay tried to keep him off with his left hand, prodding at him, holding him out.

Jackson knew with a sudden certainty what had happened. It lifted him, made him strong. The white boy's hand was broken, he was defenceless. He picked at Peekay, hitting him cleanly, playing with him; there was time, he had no strength, but there was time left. He had to make sure of the big punch, he only had one left in him, maybe not even that. Weaken him down, break the white boy. Break him to his knees! He worked his mind, gathering the strength he needed. Only one punch. One to finish the fight!

But he'd left it too late. And he was careless. Knowing Peekay couldn't hit him, his gloves were wide open. Peekay's broken hand came up and connected under his heart. He heard Peekay scream with pain as the punch landed. Jackson went backwards, bouncing on the ropes; if he went down he'd never get up again. He clung on desperately, a deep red fuzz, like scarlet cotton wool, in front of his eyes, closing him down, bringing him to an end. He waited blindly for the shock of the punch which would put him away. But it never came. Peekay, groggy with the pain from his hand, was disorientated. Finally he managed to hit Jackson with a left, but the punch had no power. Jackson's knees caved in momentarily, but miraculously he stayed up, his arms hooked around the ropes. Only his courage kept him on his feet. Then he could dimly see Peekay through the red haze. Peekay threw another punch, another left; his right hand was useless, he barely had the strength to hold it above his waist. Had Jackson spat on him he'd have knocked him down. Jackson grabbed Peekay, his arms raising in slow motion, pulling his opponent into a desperate, instinctive clinch. Both boxers crashed to the floor. Both, on all fours, struggled to get up first, Peekay not having the strength in his left hand to push himself up from the floor. Finally he made it, hardly a second before Jackson. Technically it wasn't a knock-down and the referee signalled for them to fight on. The crowd was screaming for the knock-out to be accepted. Peekay had won, they'd seen it clearly; it was the white boy's fight! Jackson was trying to keep his balance, swaying on his feet, the bright crimson blood from his eye splashing down onto his jet black shoulder. The two boxers faced each other a foot apart, unable to move, neither with the strength to throw another blow. The bell went and Jackson gave a small sigh and fell backwards to the floor, landing hard on the seat of his pants, eyes wide in sudden surprise, then backwards still further, hitting his head on the deck where he lay sprawled on his back, one arm stretched out the other at his side, motionless.

Peekay hadn't the strength to move and collapsed into Hymie's arms as his friend ran to embrace him, tears streaming. 'Never, never again,' Hymie wept.

The Garden was chaos; suddenly a chant started at the back, then grew: 'Pee Kay! Pee Kay! Pee Kay!' People battered the back of their seats with the palms of their hands and beat the soles of their feet on the boards, 'Pee Kay! Pee Kay! Pee Kay!' The chant grew louder; people at the ringside now stood up, throwing their fists into the air. 'Pee Kay! Pee Kay!' Society matrons and bankers shouted with good time girls, crooks, card sharps, con men, promoters and racketeers: 'Pee Kay! Pee Kay! Pee Kay!'

Jake 'Spoonbill' Jackson's people had brought him into his corner for the third time. Jackson had come round, but he was hurt badly, his nose broken, his eye badly cut and both eyes closed. He was coughing blood where his broken ribs had punctured the lung. Peekay wasn't a lot better, his eye closed, his hand, possibly his jaw and probably several ribs broken.

The ring was filled with people and the police worked frantically to clear it. It was ten minutes before the announcer was able to get to the microphone. The TV cameras were recording the chaos from their platform above and to the side of the ring.

'Ladies and gentlemen, I have the judge's decision!' The announcer was forced to repeat himself four times before the Garden grew sufficiently quiet for him to continue. 'Judge Joseph Tesoriero scores it forty-four points Jackson, forty-four points Peekay!' A roar of approval went up, though mixed with some booing. 'Judge Mannie Mankerwitz scores it forty-four Peekay, forty-four Jackson!' The roar from the crowd increased; most people would have settled for a drawn contest. The crowd hushed as the final judge's decision was announced. 'Judge Hoover J. Booker scores it forty-four Peekay, forty-five Jackson!'

There was a moment's stunned silence and then the booing began. It was clear that the crowd wasn't happy. 'The winner on points and still welterweight champion of the world, Jake "Spoonbill" Jack-a-son!' the announcer bellowed.

Chairs were being broken and the police moved in to stop the riot. Twenty police surrounded the ring holding back the crowd. Jackson rose to his feet, his hands in the air, one hand holding the elaborate championship belt. The ring was being pelted with objects and Jackson was hit by a small cushion as the boos increased. He looked about him confused; he could barely stand up and his seconds rushed to surround him. In a moment he was lost from sight in the ring.

Slowly the police gained control. The Odd Bodleians under Jam Jar's direction had stood firm. Now they started to sing, 'When the Saints go Marching in'; it was the music, perhaps more than anything, which calmed the crowd.

Peekay rose wearily; he too could barely stand. He moved over to the people surrounding Jackson, trying to get to the champion to congratulate him. Intent on protecting their man, Jackson's seconds wouldn't let him into the circle. Peekay turned to return to his corner. A TV commentator had managed to get into the ring and he now accosted Peekay.

'The crowd are obviously disappointed, they think you won, I think you won, do you think you won?' he yelled.

Peekay wanted to cry. He was empty. He'd hit bottom, there was nothing left. He felt dead inside.

'Jackson won. That was the judge's decision,' Peekay said into the microphone.

Inside him a voice cried out, protested that there was more to it than this! That he had a right to be hurt, to feel bitter, to allow himself the indulgence of suggesting it was a home-town decision. But in his mind he'd always won the title convincingly, not like this. Had he won, Jackson's side would feel as he did now. His camouflage was back.

'What will you do now, Peekay?' the man asked, disappointed, wanting the vitriol.

Peekay paused. The noise from the crowd was dying down, the police gaining control. The camera on the platform above the ring framed his face in the lens; the picture, in black and white, showed a young man with his right eye closed, deep lines of exhaustion etched down either side of his mouth, his good eye sharp, curiously untouched, incongruous, looking as it did out of a battered, broken face. But his face also registered a small, wan smile, which served to make the moment America witnessed more poignant. 'I'm going to find a quiet place where I can bawl my eyes out.' He paused and shrugged his shoulders, his mouth was close to the microphone and carried clearly, hardly above a whisper, like a small boy's. 'You see, I don't know what to do. I don't know how to fight any better than that.'

Back in the dressing room the doctor appointed by the New York Athletic Commission examined Peekay. He was a man in his fifties, wearing a cheap, baggy suit. He had a wild mop of steel-grey hair and a somewhat untidy, bushy moustache, stained yellow with cigar smoke. He looked well worn and comfortable, as though he was used to working around fighters. He handled Peekay expertly, knowing precisely what he was looking for. 'The hand is broken badly, in more than one place I should think; counting your wrist bones there are twenty-seven possibilities.' He grinned. 'It isn't possible to hit a man with a hand broken like this, hit him hard enough to lay him down. Nobody could take that much pain at once. But you did. I saw it myself. I've looked after boxers for thirty years. That was the best, the best fight I've ever seen!' He cleared his throat, embarrassed at his outburst, his voice brusque again. 'We'll need to X-ray immediately, then set it. If the broken bones are set incorrectly, your days as a fighter will be over, son.'

He put his stethoscope to Peekay's ribs, testing both sides. 'Breath in!' Peekay took a deep breath. 'Pain? Sharp, sudden, like a knife going in?'

'No sir, just straight pain.'

'That's good, looks like none of the breaks have punctured the lung. They're probably all broken any way, the X-ray will tell. I also want a brain scan. You took a lot of punishment about the head.' He started to pack his bag. 'Sorry I can't give you a shot of morphine to kill the pain, it will interfere with the anaesthetic. Jackson will be in hospital for several days, you'll have to join him there, at least overnight.' He walked to the door. 'He left in an ambulance, on his back. I guess you can walk out and leave in a limo . . . like the champ you are, son!'

Dutch had needed to cut the glove from Peekay's hand and now it was swollen to nearly twice its normal size. Peekay sat with the elbow cupped in his left hand, holding the hand upwards, above his heart so the blood would drain from it and relieve the pain a little. Togger was holding a towel packed with ice, making Peekay hold his broken hand in the ice as long as he could before bringing it up again. He too had cried unashamedly at the end of the fight and again when the decision had been announced. Now he stood quietly by, trying to pass on some of his love for his friend to use as emotional balm to soothe him. 'If I live ter be a hundred, I'll never see a better fight, never be more soddin' proud, Peekay.'

Daddy Kockle was standing quietly by the door,

holding a large cardboard box Hymie had given him to keep. The old man was exhausted.

Hymie had been talking quietly on the phone, now he walked over to Peekay. 'Come, old mate, we've got to take you to Cedars of Lebanon.' He grinned. 'I told Aunt Tom your hand was broken and now one of New York's foremost orthopaedic surgeons is standing by to operate on it.'

Peekay rose, he was physically exhausted and every bone in his body felt as though it was broken. He was forced to lean on Hymie as they walked towards the door. He saw Daddy Kockle looking at him. The old man's eyes were moist. 'What's in the box, Daddy Kockle? It's not big enough for my coffin.'

'Christ, I forgot!' Hymie said. 'It came on this morning's flight from London. Strict instructions from Doris, you're to open it after the fight.'

Peekay grinned. It was the Hans Kellerman doll; Mr Rubens had kept his word. 'It's for you, Togger. Open it when you get back to the hotel.'

Daddy Kockle handed Togger the box. 'For me?' Togger showed his surprise. 'Thanks, Peekay!' As Peekay didn't offer any further explanation he put the box under his arm and prepared to follow them out.

Peekay left the brightly lit room. Several people were standing in the corridor. Peekay removed his hand from around Hymie's shoulder. 'I want them to see me walking out.' He gave a wry grin, 'After all, my feet are the only bits of me which don't feel broken.' They walked down the passage followed by Dutch and with Togger carrying Carmen's Elizabeth Jane.

Daddy Kockle remained behind in the dressing room, seated on the rub-down table, shaking his head and clucking to himself. He glanced up into the mirror on the opposite wall, patting his snowy white hair. Only four of the twenty-four lights still shone around the perimeter. His face, blotched with the brown mercury discolouration on the mirror's surface, seemed to show every one of the sixty or more hard years of his life. He talked directly at the image in the mirror, the beginning of a smile on his face.

'Nossah! That boy, he ain't licked yet. Right now he fixin' to come back and, when he do . . . Why he gon' whup that sonofabitch! Whup him so good, he gonna lay down for a week 'foh he gets up!'

He picked up his clarinet, brought it to his mouth, and blew the sweet, clean opening notes to Crossing over Jordan to the Other Side.

Twenty-four

In early November 1955 Peekay and Hymie returned to Johannesburg directly from New York. Despite Peekay's loss, he returned a hero. The documentary, 'The Making of a Champion' with a quick title change to 'Fight for Your Life!' had preceded them; cut into a two-hour documentary, it had been released in every cinema in South Africa as a main attraction, and drew record crowds in both the black and white cinemas.

While Peekay held himself together in public, his camouflage intact, his defeat by Jake 'Spoonbill' Jackson was devastating for him. It ran so deep that he couldn't talk about it even to Hymie. The unthinkable had happened; he'd climbed the mountain, measured his spirit, allotting each step he took to the right amount of energy, never allowing himself to enjoy a win or even to savour a sense of triumph over an opponent. Only one thing mattered: getting to the top of the mountain, reaching the point where only the sky stretched away above him. Now he found that he'd been unsighted, that beyond the top stretched another peak; and he was completely spent.

For Peekay, welterweight champion of the world

wasn't a title, it was the meaning of his life, the very principle on which he'd based his entire personality. He was too intelligent not to know it wasn't the end of the world, but his emotional grief over-ruled his logic. From the age of six when he'd felt the huge boxing gloves slip over his small hands, he had committed himself to the single principle that the individual can move the mountain; that small can beat big; that hope and determination and singular purpose were the three powerful allies against all the odds. And now he felt betrayed. He needed something else to win and he didn't know what it was.

He'd been told a thousand times by well-meaning, sincere friends that in any other arena anywhere in the world he would have won the fight; and each time he heard this, he felt further defeated. To win by a disputed decision would have been worse for Peekay than losing. He hadn't dedicated his life to the vagary of a single judge's opinion, to luck. Winning or losing on a margin so frail that in a single pause, the time it took to take another breath, he might have come out the winner was not why he'd travelled this journey. He must win so that the thousand and the ten thousand and the million voices heard. Most of all he had to win so that *he* heard it clearly, cleanly, a clarion bell ringing in his mind. Small could beat big, good could triumph over evil.

And now he was defeated. But in Peekay's mind it wasn't Jackson who was evil. The black American boxer had simply been the peak on the mountain. When the mountain is conquered it is what it does to the climber that counts; the mountain itself doesn't change. Peekay was fighting the good and the evil in himself.

Suddenly he longed to die. To climb up into the high mountains, over Saddleback and higher still to the crystal cave of Africa, to lie beside Doc, his body held safely in the heart of the great mountain. Had his life been forfeited by his defeat he would have accepted it willingly. The effort required to get back off his knees was so great. It was a fear well beyond any he had ever experienced, for it was the first time in his life he'd reached down and come back with nothing. He had spent it all, there wasn't anything more. When he stepped into the ring with Jackson the second time he'd simply be blown away.

He went home to Barberton, where, for the first time in years the loneliness birds returned, the great pterodactyl-like creatures with their greasy feathered wings and long, chipping beaks, their sharp eyes the colour of anthracite. He could hear their membraned wings flapping inside him, like canvas in a high wind, flapping as they squatted, laying their huge stone eggs, then fracturing them into shards of flint that began to fill up every corner of his being.

He had just five months to prepare for the next fight and he had nothing to give it. He was a loser and he had been living a lie. But Peekay could show none of this. People were flocking to the film. He was surrounded by the hyperbole of a nation who felt they'd been cheated and had decided to accept him as a hero anyway. The anticipation being built up for the return bout was immediately at fever pitch. South Africa wanted its revenge and Peekay was going to deliver it for them.

From the moment they arrived back, Hymie began the process of organizing the return fight. He wanted to stage it at Ellis Park, the famous rugby and cricket ground in Johannesburg. While, in principle, the city council was only too happy to oblige, a major problem existed. Hymie and Peekay insisted that there must be the same number of seats allocated for blacks as there were for whites. Ellis Park was a white sports ground, with room for only two thousand black and coloured spectators and, for their use, a single toilet block with six urinals and three toilets. With a thirty thousand capacity crowd, half of them black, the existing toilet facilities for black people plainly weren't enough. The idea of allocating fifty per cent of the available 'Whites Only' toilet facilities to the blacks was unthinkable; and, in any case, it was against the law to do so.

The sitting member for Doornfontein, who included Ellis Park in his constituency, attempted to get a special act of parliament passed in which, for one day only, half the white toilets at Ellis Park changed colour. This was immediately thwarted by the minister representing the Department of Community Development who pointed out that this would only be constitutionally possible if half the white toilets all over South Africa became black for the same period of the fight, between four o'clock and nine o'clock in the afternoon on the 26 April. The speech, quoted directly from Hansard, was reported in all of the newspapers the following day:

> *If this iniquitous private members' bill is allowed to pass in this house then civilization as we know it will have come to an end in South Africa. Decent white people will be confronted with a dilemma when trying to go to a public toilet on the afternoon and evening of 26 April 1956. All of a sudden, toilets which yesterday were*

white are now black. But not only that!
Which toilets? Suddenly a black man will
be able to walk into any white toilet he
likes; when you apprehend him, all he will
have to say is, 'Sorry baas, I thought this
white toilet had turned into a black toilet.'
'No!' you say, 'Not this one, that one.' But
which one is that one? Who are you to say
which white toilet has turned black and
which one has stayed white? What we have
here, coming all of a sudden out of a clear
blue sky, is the potential for black people
to use white toilets just whenever they like!
I put it to you, how would you like your
daughter to use a toilet where a black
woman has just two minutes before sat?
Now I hear you saying it is only for one
time, a few hours, but you are wrong,
man. It is a precedent! Once a black man
has sat on the nice clean seat of a white
toilet he will think suddenly he is all high
and mighty. Next thing he will be sitting at
the table with his knife and fork in his
hands wanting to eat with your family!
One thing is for sure, there is no telling
where something like this will end. As it
says in the bible; 'Those who sow the wind
will reap the whirlwind!'

The solution, when it came, was simple. The pupils at
The Voortrekker High Technical School, an Afrikaans
institution in Pretoria famous for its boxing and rugby,
taking the initiative, did a crowd study during the Natal
versus Transvaal provincial rugby match held at Ellis

Park. They discovered the ratio of urinal users to toilet users was fifty-five to one. The major problem it seemed, therefore, was the dispersal of urine for a period of some four hours. They offered to build, in return for twenty tickets to the fight and cost of materials, three zinc temporary urinals one hundred foot in length. The city council quickly passed a by-law amending the Urban Sanitary Health Act to allow for the temporary structures to be built. The second largest problem was solved. The largest remained; permission for fifteen thousand black people to congregate in one place. The decision rested with the commissioner of police for Johannesburg and the East Rand, Major General Bul Van Breeden and the Minister of Native Affairs.

Unlike Bokkie Venter, the fifty-two-year-old Van Breeden, relatively young for the senior position he held in the police force, was a man with strong convictions who took a delight at thumbing his nose at Pretoria. He was also of the old school with very little time for the 'Hitler Youth' breed of policeman, as he referred to the young officers rising to positions of seniority in the new police force. He thought of himself as a good Afrikaner and a loyal member of the Nationalist Party but he was an exception; he was not a member of the *Broederbond* and didn't allow politics to interfere with his judgement as a policeman.

He'd also boxed at the 1924 Paris Olympics as a light heavyweight where he was defeated by an American negro named Barnstable Jones, nicknamed 'Barnstorm Jones' for his attacking style, in a memorable bout in the semi-finals.

Major General Van Breeden saw Peekay's loss to Jake 'Spoonbill' Jackson as not dissimilar to his own.

Barnstorm Jones had gone on to take the gold medal in a fight which wasn't anything like as hard as the semi they'd fought. All his life the police commissioner had imagined a return fight and, in his mind, Peekay's opportunity to fight a second time for the world title was the return fight he'd wanted so badly himself.

When Hymie had requested an interview with Van Breeden and asked if he could bring Gideon's manager Mr Nguni along, he'd welcomed the opportunity to meet the young Jew who'd played such an important part in Peekay's success. Nguni was known to him as a successful businessman who controlled boxing and soccer among the black people on the Rand. He'd run a check on his local record and, apart from a minor infringement concerning a stamp on his pass two years previously, his record showed that he was straight. It was a shrewd move to bring him along.

The three men got on well and, in principle, it was agreed that the fight with an equal number of black to white fans could take place at Ellis Park. A police captain named Clive McClymont was appointed as police liaison officer for the fight and Van Breeden introduced them to him in his office.

McClymont seemed a nice, quiet sort of chap in his mid thirties and was an expert in crowd and traffic control. He'd listened quietly and then asked several intelligent questions. Hymie found he liked him immediately. The general had grinned when he'd introduced them. 'Don't worry, Mr Levy, we didn't pick McClymont because he's a rooinek, but because he is the only police officer in the traffic division who knows nothing about boxing. There's going to be a lot of heat generated over this decision, might as well have a police officer with his mind on the job, what do you say, hey?'

Hymie asked if he could give Van Breeden four ring-side seats. The police general grinned broadly. 'Normally yes and thank you, Mr Levy, but we've got ourselves a hot potato issue here. Pretoria won't be happy; better make that a firm booking for four ringside seats and I'll pay for the tickets myself.' He turned to McClymont. 'Please make sure you get a personal cheque from me and deliver it to Mr Levy yourself.' Hymie grinned to himself. Major General Van Breeden was one helluva smart cop who wasn't going to let a careless detail trip him up. McClymont was his witness that his ringside seats were kosher.

Soon after they shook hands formally in the Afrikaner manner, symbolically sealing the deal. The policeman was careful to shake hands with Mr Nguni as well. He rose from his desk and walked with them to the door. 'It's a pity you couldn't have brought Peekay, I'd like to meet him,' he said as they stood waiting to depart.

'Of course! Some other time,' Hymie replied quickly. 'He's not in Johannesburg at the moment, sir. He's resting, away from it all, mending his body. Did you know he comes from Barberton?'

'Yes, I did. Yesterday he climbed to Saddleback. That's a hard climb; he's feeling a lot better, I think?'

Hymie's eyebrows shot up. The police major general seemed to know more about Peekay's whereabouts than he did.

'Ag, its not good police work, Mr Levy. Scratch an Afrikaner and you find a blood relation just below the surface of the skin. When I knew you were coming in to see me I called Captain Smit of the Barberton prison, he is my second cousin. You probably know that he gave Peekay his first formal boxing coaching when he was seven years old. Wragtig! He worships the ground that young man walks on.'

'It's kind of you to take an interest in Peekay, sir,' Hymie said to the general.

'Ag, Mr Levy, in my business it is sometimes better to know the people involved than to assess the evidence. It is people who make things right or wrong, who make things good or bad. Allowing fifteen thousand black people and fifteen thousand white people in a sports ground where a white man is fighting a black man, on the evidence available, is asking for trouble.'

He grinned. 'But I think not. This will be the first time that the black fans will be on the white man's side. It seems to me we have a remarkable young man here. Any person who can do this in South Africa we must allow to proceed. There is more involved here than boxing.'

The police general turned to Mr Nguni. 'I am told you were the leader of the black fan club who followed Peekay and turned him into the Tadpole Angel. Is this true?'

'It is not true, sir. I am a Zulu and also I am a boxing promoter. But the legend of the Tadpole Angel, I did not make this. This is written in the smoke and in the bones. I am just taking the people to see who is the *Onoshobishobi Ingelosi*, the Tadpole Angel.'

'You people believe in this thing then? You believe a white man will come to lead the black people?'

The huge Zulu spread his hands. 'It is told who has the power, it is this one,' he said simply.

'This power? It is forever?'

'Who can say this thing? Maybe the *sangoma*, they can change this, I do not know, I am not sangoma, sir.'

'So it will be all right. I mean when Peekay fights the

American negro, the blacks will behave themselves?'

'I think I can guarantee for you, it will be orright, sir, the people, they want the *Onoshobishobi Ingelosi* to win.'

'You manage the black fighter, Mandoma, don't you?' the general asked suddenly.

'Gideon Mandoma, the black Welterweight Champion of Africa, he is my fighter,' Mr Nguni said, suddenly proud.

'Black Africa!' Van Breeden answered with a slight edge to his voice. 'If I remember correctly, he was beaten by Jannie Geldenhuis, the South African Welterweight Champion.'

Mr Nguni shook his head, his grin spreading, 'Hayi, hayi, hayi! He is very clever this policeman, Geldenhuis. I don't think he wants to fight Mandoma again. Mandoma he wants to fight, but Geldenhuis will not fight I think.'

'Is that so?' Van Breeden said smiling. He pushed his chair away from his desk. 'Well Mr Levy, Mr Nguni, it's been nice to meet you both. I'm pretty sure we're in business. All you got to do now is go to the Boxing Control Board and ask them, as a formality, to get a permit from the Minister of Native Affairs.'

Two days later a letter arrived from the South African Boxing Control Board saying that their request for a mixed audience to take place at Ellis Park had been refused. No further explanation was added and a phone call to the board revealed little more, other than that they'd already sent in a letter appealing against the decision.

Hymie called Clive McClymont who arranged for a second interview with Major General Van Breeden. This time Hymie was instructed to attend alone.

The general lost no time in getting to the point. 'Look, man, I have called the minister, he is not willing to allow a mixed audience of this size.'

The general looked up at Hymie and spread his hands. 'I'm sorry, Mr Levy, my hands are tied.' He smiled. 'Things could be worse; whatever happens the fight will be a sellout, even with a white audience.'

'I guess it's a matter of conviction, general.'

'I appreciate your convictions in this matter, Mr Levy, but surely the compromise has been forced upon you? It's not of your own making. Your conscience is clear.'

Hymie laughed. 'Ha! Try telling that to Peekay.' He rose from his chair and extended his hand to the general. 'Thank you, sir, I appreciate that you did all you could to make it happen.'

Van Breeden took his hand. 'What will you do now, Mr Levy?'

'London! We'll fight in London. It will be a sell out at Wembley Stadium and the simultaneous TV hook-up will make us twice the money we can hope to make here, sir.'

The general was too wise to show surprise but he released Hymie's hand. 'That's a great pity. World championship fights don't come along every day.' He shrugged his shoulders, smacking his lips. 'It's a blerrie shame, but I don't know what else I can do.'

The general looked up suddenly, squinting slightly. He was a big man who'd more or less kept himself in shape; the grey was beginning to win in what was once jet-black hair and his dark eyebrows emphasized his intelligent, sharp brown eyes. Major General Van Breeden wore his uniform well. 'You know, maybe there is a way.' He indicated the chair. 'Sit! Let's think this out.' Hymie sat, saying nothing.

'Well, maybe we can make a deal here. Not me and you, you understand, you and me with the Special Branch.'

'How, sir?' Hymie asked, leaning forward.

'Jannie Geldenhuis, the South African Welterweight Champion, is a lieutenant in the Special Branch. Why don't we promise him a fight with Peekay after he's fought the American?'

Hymie laughed. 'Nice one, sir! Why didn't I think of that!' He frowned suddenly. 'If Peekay wins the world title from Jackson, he will only defend it *once* before retiring from the ring.'

'So let the fight with Geldenhuis be the once.'

'It's not quite that easy, general. Mandoma has met and beaten more fighters than Geldenhuis. Also a couple of higher-rated welterweights, for instance, the Mexican Manuel Ortez and the Italian Bruno Bisetti. Geldenhuis, you will remember, was involved in a car accident and couldn't fight for nearly fourteen months. *Ring* magazine rates him number twelve while Mandoma is rated equal ten. If Peekay become world champion, the World Boxing Council won't approve the fight.'

'What if Peekay loses to Jackson?'

'If Peekay loses to Jackson he won't fight again, no matter what.'

'I tell you what!' Van Breeden said suddenly. 'Let Geldenhuis fight Mandoma on the underbill! The winner to fight Peekay?'

Hymie stuck his hand out. 'You've got a deal, sir! If Peekay wins the title he puts it on the line against either Mandoma or Geldenhuis. Whatever happens, we still get to see who deserves to be the overall Welterweight

Champion of South Africa, Geldenhuis or Mandoma.'

Later, when Hymie phoned Mr Nguni in Meadow-lands where he'd built himself a rather grand new house, he said, 'Well the plan worked. Van Breeden figured it out, Gideon's got his fight with Geldenhuis.'

Nguni had thrown back his head and laughed, his big Zulu voice thundering down the phone.

He finally managed to say, 'You are very clever, Hymie. Gideon thanks you, and me also, I thank you.'

'Forget it, it wasn't clever at all. Just two businessmen who discovered they both had something to sell to each other. As my father would say, "For business like this, maybe is coming down an angel and kissing me!"'

Twenty-five

Peekay returned to Johannesburg at the end of January to prepare for the world title. He set up a training camp which he could share with Mandoma, each acting as sparring partner for the other while Gideon worked with Solly Goldman as his trainer and Peekay with Dutch Holland. Several local black, coloured and white sparring partners were selected on an ad hoc basis, though Togger was brought out from London to act as a principle sparring partner. Hymie had selected a small farm in Elandsfontein, some fifteen miles outside Johannesburg, as the training camp and Peekay, Gideon and Togger shared the same bunkhouse which caused some comment in the newspapers. Peekay when asked about this by a visiting reporter had replied, 'The closest you can get to a man is in a boxing ring. You share his sweat and his breath and his arms and his chest. You don't get much closer when you make love to a woman. He doesn't snore so why would I be concerned about sharing a room with him?'

The South African papers made much of this, the most blatant headline being: PEEKAY SAYS OKAY TO SLEEP WITH BLACK MAN! which appeared in a

Bloemfontein paper. But the ongoing quarrel was more the fact that Peekay had elected to train with Mandoma. Almost to a man, the sports pages cried foul! The Peekay camp, they maintained, was giving the Bantu fighter an unfair advantage over Geldenhuis, in that he came under the eye of the world-famous trainer, Dutch Holland, and also enjoyed the services of Solly Goldman, South Africa's foremost trainer.

It was even mooted in parliament that a law should be passed preventing people of mixed race sparring together. In fact, five years later, just such a law was passed.

Peekay was asked about this in an interview he'd given with the press just prior to going into training camp. 'It's perfectly true that Mandoma will benefit from working with Dutch Holland, though he's been under the training of the great Solly Goldman for several years already and Solly remains his trainer. It seems to me that a black fighter of Mandoma's class has none of the infrastructure and training facilities the South African Police College have made available to Jannie Geldenhuis. Mandoma has to work for a living and when he's in training camp he isn't earning. Working out with us means he'll be eating the right food and getting the right sort of rest and I get the best sparring partner I could possibly hope for. I'm delighted with the arrangement, wouldn't you be?'

Baasie Pienaar, South Africa's foremost sportswriter stood up. 'Good morning, Baasie,' said Peekay. 'I believe you attended the New York fight? I'm sorry I didn't see you to say hello.'

Baasie Pienaar grinned. 'You did better than that, Peekay, you gave me the best fight I will probably ever see.' He cleared his throat. 'I happen to think, like you in New York, Mandoma got a bum steer last time he fought Geldenhuis. There's been a lot in the paper about it being unfair that he's sharing your camp; I just want to say, personally I'm glad.' There was a murmur of surprise in the room. *Die Vaderland* was the leading Afrikaans newspaper and, politically speaking, the mouthpiece for the government. 'Because I'm a reporter, I also have a question,' Pienaar went on. 'Geldenhuis says he'll take Mandoma in the seventh. Do you have any comment?'

Peekay laughed. 'He's a brave man, Mandoma is the most under-rated welterweight in the world. But why don't you ask Mandoma yourself.' He pointed to the back of the room where Gideon was standing with Togger.

Gideon took a couple of steps towards the front of the room. 'Mr Pienaar for two years already we have been wanting for dis fight. Always Mr Nguni he asks, "Please Mr Geldenhuis, why you not want to fight the black champion of Africa?" But always he say, "No!".'

Peekay saw the look in Mandoma's eyes when he talked about Geldenhuis. It was the same thing he'd seen in Gert's. His eyes had gone blank, turned inward, focused on his hate; even his voice seemed to take on a menacing tone, giving a fierceness to his words which was not actually contained in what he said. 'I am very, very hungry for dis fight. I do not think I will lay down in round seven.' Gideon gave the white reporters a huge smile, but behind its humour Peekay could hear the snarl of the lion, his talisman. 'I am a Zulu, I am chief, I do not think in the ring I have to lay down for dis policeman. In the ring he has only got gloves on his hands same like me, there is no sjambok and there is no revolver.'

The room broke up in uproar and Peekay terminated the interview. The reporters left, they all had their afternoon headline. Pienaar walked over to Gideon. 'Nice one, Mandoma,' he said quietly.

The *Johannesburg Star* was first on the streets. MANDOMA ACCUSES GELDENHUIS OF POLICE BRUTALITY! Baasie Pienaar's paper, *Die Vaderland*, ran the headline, PEEKAY RATES MANDOMA WORLD BEATER. Hymie was delighted; things were hotting up, in terms of promoting the fight. Nothing they could have dreamed up as a publicity stunt could have had anywhere near the same impact on boxing fans. Geldenhuis had obligingly come back with a comment which, paraphrased, said that in or out of the ring, his hands, with or without gloves, were enough to give the black man a hiding.

Tickets for the fight had gone on sale the day before and in two days the thirty thousand reserved seats for the fight had been sold out. Hymie was assured of sufficient profit to pay Jackson the huge win-or-lose purse he'd promised him to fight in South Africa and sufficient to pay Mandoma and Geldenhuis the biggest purse either had ever earned.

On the morning of 26 April, an English-speaking announcer on Springbok breakfast radio called the thirty-thousand crowd expected at Ellis Park the largest gathering of blacks and whites in one place since the British fought the Zulu at the battle of Isandhlwana in 1879.

The remark had been intended flippantly, but, inasmuch as it was a fight which brought both sides together, the symbolism was there for all who wished to see it; and in South Africa that was just about everyone. The old fears were working overtime; the flames fanned by an eager media who imbued the event with the drama of a high-noon shoot-out. Make no mistake, this was no less a battle for race superiority than any other fought against the kaffirs.

At Ellis Park a white rope ran like a snake down the bleachers and cut across the rugby field to end in the centre of either side of the ring and, by doing so, dividing the entire park in half. This was dubbed 'the wall' by the press and was designed to separate the black fans from the white – no less a wall than one made of granite blocks.

The crowd control designed for the fight seemed to be the usual overkill. A black policeman would stand every ten feet on the African side of the white rope with his back to the white spectators looking directly into the black crowd for troublemakers and a white one would stand between him and the next black policeman with his back to the black fight fans. The white police officers all carried revolvers and police batons which hung from their Sam Browne belts, while the black constables were armed with riot sticks.

The fight had been sold out for nearly three months. Nevertheless African ticket-holders started to arrive at dawn and seemed content to sit on the pavement outside the grounds where there was much singing of the Chant as the good-humoured crowd waited for the gates to open at one o'clock.

The Mandoma versus Geldenhuis fight was scheduled for four o'clock in the afternoon, a ten-rounder followed at a quarter past six by the world-title fight.

It was late autumn in Johannesburg, a glorious time of crisp mornings and bright, cloudless days when it remains reasonably light until almost seven in the evening. Johannesburg, with its high altitude, grows quite chilly soon after sunset, and a great many of the Africans had brought blankets with them. Red is a favourite colour and by five o'clock the African side of the field was splashed with scarlet.

Closer to the time of the first major fight the African cognoscenti began to appear, most of them in evening suits and some even in tails. There were few women amongst them; even the gangsters and gamblers had decided to leave their molls behind, the importance of the fight and the prestige of owning a ringside ticket being too great to waste on a woman. Although some white women appeared on the opposite side of the ring, this too was made up largely of white men.

It was a surprise therefore when, half an hour before the first fight, three women appeared on their own and started to make their way across the short strip of no-man's land leading from one of the entrances under the stands to the ringside seats.

The excited black crowd, anxious to applaud any-thing on their side which seemed in the least bit worthy of attention, started to cheer at the perfectly splendid sight which appeared below them.

Thin as a rake in a glittering red diamanté fishtail gown, and wearing a short mink jacket to which was pinned an enormous corsage of purple orchids, was Madam Flame Flo, the famous shebeen queen from Sophiatown. Beside her, big as a circus tent, dressed in a pink satin dress with plunging neckline and wearing a pink fur stole as big as a small blanket, was Mama Tequila. On her head rested a satin turban shaped like a beehive and embroidered with a thousand tiny mirrors. From the centre of the turban, clipped down under a huge circular diamante brooch, were three pink ostrich feathers. It was a sight to make the seventeen thousand African men in the stadium positively drool with admiration.

Walking behind both women in a simple white crêpe evening dress and a satin stole came Tandia Patel. Her beauty had an immediate effect on the people watching.

The Bantu crowd began to clap, drumming their feet on the wooden floor of the stands so that the sound had the resonance of a hundred drum rolls. The white side rose to their feet, anxious to see what was happening, and thirty thousand eyes trained on the three women crossing towards the ringside seats.

'Jesus, *ousis*! We got the spotlight!' Madam Flame said in alarm.

Mama Tequila chuckled, her giant breasts rolling like twin mountains in an earthquake. 'Honey, jes keep yoh head high, what *we* got now we came here to get!' She stopped and turned, waiting for Tandia to catch up to her: 'You walk tall now, sugar, this your fight too, baby!' Mama Tequila was in her full American mode and loving every moment.

Tandia was quite certain she was about to die. She was terrified that Gideon Mandoma might be somewhere looking out at her and that he would not approve. Her fear of disobeying Mama Tequila fought with her natural modesty. She was Mandoma's woman now and a law student, but the huge old whore still completely dominated her. Though Gideon and she were an item, she saw almost nothing of him; during the university vacations she was expected to work at Bluey Jay and it was only when the brothel closed down after Christmas and she came with Mama Tequila up to the Rand to stay with Madam Flame Flo that they could be together. Madam Flame Flo had moved from Sophiatown to Meadowlands and Tandia had to rely on Juicey Fruit Mambo to drive her to see Gideon.

Their relationship was still very tentative and mostly based on politics. She hadn't even slept with him. Once when he'd brought up the subject she'd been terrified but had agreed, though there hadn't been a place they could do it. She knew she must, that to consolidate the relationship it was necessary, but she told herself they'd do it after she graduated at law, when she came to live in Johannesburg.

For the black crowd the three glittering women had added a dimension of class to the day's proceedings. They could savour in advance the pleasure they'd get from relating, perhaps twenty years hence, the story of how they'd been present at the two greatest fights in history. Now they could include in the long preliminary the two *abaFazi* who shone like the sun on water and the beautiful young one.

Hymie and Peekay, unseen by the crowd, were seated in the enclosed members' stand watching the crowd. Jackson had made a great fuss of being photographed entering through the gate for blacks only, pointing to the sign with one hand and pinching his nose in disgust with the other, the whites of his eyes showing in mock horror.

'Christ, Peekay, look at that!' Hymie exclaimed suddenly. He passed his binoculars to Peekay. 'Get a deck of the two women coming towards us on the black side!'

Peekay, looking through the glasses, started to grin immediately. 'She's wonderful! Oh, Hymie, they're sensational. I wonder who they are? You don't suppose they're Jackson supporters do you?'

Peekay suddenly let out a gasp followed by the short, sharp expletive. 'Shit!'

Hymie's grin changed to sudden alarm. 'What is it? Here, let me see,' he said, reaching for the glasses. He now saw the third woman who had caught Peekay's attention.

He focused on Tandia. She was absolutely ravishing. Her green eyes set into a classically proportioned honey-coloured face seemed to be looking directly at him through thick black lashes. Her slightly parted lips gave her a rather bewildered, totally ingenuous expression.

Hymie lowered the binoculars and turned to look at Peekay, who sat with his chin cupped in his hands, his elbows resting on his knees. He wore a slightly stunned expression. 'Shit no, Peekay!' he whispered. 'Not now, not ever! For Christ's sake, she's coloured!'

Peekay gave Hymie a wry grin. 'Maybe she's American? I could go and live in America.'

Hymie laughed. 'Forget it Peekay, we've got a fight on our hands. If she's Jackson's girl you're going to have to knock him over first. Come on, it's time to see Gideon. You promised him and I promised Mr Nguni, no matter how busy I was, I'd personally make sure you'd be there to wish Gideon good luck.'

In fact, Hymie had been as busy as a one-armed wallpaper hanger and had found himself doing just about everything leading up to the title fight. From the beginning when they'd had the kerfuffle about segregating Ellis Park and the debacle over the toilets, seating had been the major problem. Right up to the end, even though half the ringside seats had been sold to black people, the trustees of Ellis Park were still demanding that they be reserved exclusively for whites. When this wouldn't wash, they'd demanded an extra sixty seats for white patrons.

In a gesture of appeasement, Hymie had managed to get a travelling theatrical company to hire him a dozen wooden stage units, designed to build an outdoor stage. The trustee seats were placed on these, affording them a grand, if not intimate, ringside viewing platform. Hymie's gesture was lost on the furious trustees who, to a man, hated him for sticking up for the rights of the 'coons'.

One more seating problem occurred on the morning of the fight. O'Rourke, Jackson's manager, had approached Hymie, pointing out that his party hadn't been allocated seats together and demanding that something be done about it.

Jake 'Spoonbill' Jackson's entourage consisted of twelve people. Three of them would be in his corner but the remainder, five black Americans and four white, were not prepared to be separated along racial lines. Hymie pointed out that he had no choice, that the law required the separation, but that he'd placed them in the front row on the side of the ring divided by the rope. In effect, they were all in the same row with only a two-inch rope dividing the five blacks from the four white Americans.

'It's the principle, me boy!' O'Rourke demanded in a sanctimonious voice. 'It may be a bit of a rope to you, but it's a wall as high as Everest itself to me and the boys. We do come from the land of the free you know!'

O'Rourke had gone to some pains to avoid Hymie during the week the Jackson party had been in town. The snub had started at the airport where Hymie, caught up in an emergency, sent Solly Goldman to welcome him and transport the entourage from Jan Smuts airport to a magnificent old mansion set on fifteen acres of land which he'd staffed and provisioned fully as their training camp.

542

O'Rourke had refused to take Hymie's call when later he'd phoned to welcome him to South Africa. 'Tell him, if he can't come to the airport to welcome us, I can't come to the telephone to talk to him,' was the message carried back to Hymie by one of Jackson's people. Hymie grinned, recalling the non-existent welcome they'd received when they'd arrived in New York for the first title fight.

O'Rourke and Jackson had made themselves freely available to the press. Jackson, concentrating on Peekay, claiming there were no more surprises in the white man's limited attack, prophesied that the fight would end in a knock-out in the seventh, the same round Geldenhuis had forecast for Mandoma. He was unaware of the special relationship Peekay enjoyed with black fight fans and it was clear that most of his name calling was predictably meant to win the sympathy of South Africa's black people.

On the other hand, O'Rourke took every opportunity to be critical of just about everything. His first act had been to fire the entire black staff working at the training camp, claiming they were spies placed by Hymie. Now, on the final morning, he was making a fuss about the seating arrangements and, in the process, hugely enjoying Hymie's discomfort.

Hymie phoned General Van Breeden and requested permission for the Americans to be seated in any order they wished on either side of the rope. Van Breeden chuckled into the phone. 'You know something, Hymie? Sometimes I think we're all going crazy! Ja man, no problems. Wait, I'll get Captain McClymont to fix it with the senior police officer in charge of ringside crowd control.'

Hymie waited as the general summoned McClymont

on his office intercom and then came back on the phone. 'You can put a negro on either side of me if you like.' He chuckled again. 'Pretoria already think I've sold out to the kaffirs by allowing them to see the fight in the first place.'

Half an hour before the Geldenhuis versus Mandama fight the ringside seats were full. The huge ground was packed to the heavens and though it was still light, the ring lights had been turned on, casting a phosphorescent glow some twenty feet beyond the ring.

Mr Nguni's concern to have Peekay visit Gideon Mandama before the fight was a very real one. Two days before the fight, Gideon had suddenly insisted he must go to Zululand, to his home in one of the many hills behind the Tugela River. He wished to go alone, accompanied only by a driver from his own clan.

When Mr Nguni informed Solly Goldman of Gideon's departure he wasn't at all happy. He didn't like to have any fighter he was training out of his sight for the final forty-eight hours, a time which he regarded as psychologically the most important. Nguni had persuaded him that the visit was essential, but privately he was also worried. He knew that, surrounded by his extended family, Gideon might easily lose the razor-edge concentration he required as a fighter. He had offered to have Gideon's particular *umNgoma*, witch-doctor, driven up to Johannesburg to personally attend to him, or even to obtain the services of any of the famous sangoma who operated in Soweto.

Gideon's reply had been simple. 'He is too old to leave his fireplace, but he is the one who can see me with his heart.'

Mr Nguni understood perfectly. What Gideon was saying in effect was that not only was the *umNgoma* he wished to see able to cast the necessary spells, but there existed an intimate relationship between them as well.

Relationships and trust in a time of battle are enormously important to the Zulu warrior, who has less a fear of dying than of letting down his brother who fights valiantly at his side to protect him. In exactly the same way, it was crucial to Gideon to have Peekay with him just before he entered the ring against Geldenhuis.

Peekay entered Gideon's dressing room a quarter of an hour before the fight was due to start. 'I see you, Gideon,' he said quietly as he walked in.

Gideon looked up and smiled his brilliant white smile, extending his already bandaged hand and greeting Peekay in the double-fisted African handshake. 'I see you, Peekay,' he said shyly.

'The drought is not yet broken in the Tugela?' Peekay asked. He too spoke in a reserved way, as though it had been some time since they'd met, even though he'd seen Gideon just two days previously.

'It is very, very bad, Peekay, the cattle are dying, there is no more grass.'

'And the river? The river is holding?'

'Only pools. The cattle must walk far and they are weak.'

The reason for Peekay's formal greeting was simple enough. In Zulu terms Gideon had been away, not so much on a journey as on a transformation. In tribal eyes he was changed. He'd resumed a somewhat different person after being with his shadows and the shadows of his tribal ancestors. These were still with him, his guardian angels; they would protect him during the fight, and due respect must be shown to them. By greeting him traditionally Peekay was acknowledging

Gideon's changed state of being and was formally acknowledging and honouring the presence of his shadows.

After a while Gideon smiled, signalling his preparedness to get down to a normal conversation. Peekay resumed his smile and the two boxers reached out and touched hands shyly with the tips of their fingers, each lightly brushing the inside of the other's palm.

'I have brought you something, Gideon,' Peekay said softly. 'You must close your eyes.' Peekay took the gold chain with the lion's tooth from around his neck and looped it over the black boxer's head so that it joined its twin already around his neck. 'Your strength has served me well, my brother; now it must return to you and stay with you forever. It is your manhood and your destiny as foretold to you by your *umNgoma*.'

Immediately the chain with the lion's tooth fell over his neck, Gideon knew it was the other half of the charm which spelled his coming to manhood. The bandaged fingers of his right hand reached up to hold the tooth and when he opened his eyes they were filled with emotion.

'Haya, haya!' he said, shaking his head, bewildered at Peekay's generosity. He could say no more. Peekay had guessed correctly; the witchdoctor who had attended him had questioned the breaking of his strength, the dividing of his manhood spell. He would have cast spells and made potions to compensate for the missing charm. Now, moments before the fight with Geldenhuis, Peekay had made him whole by returning it to him and had used the correct words in his presentation and by doing so, made it possible for him to accept the return of a gift he had once given himself.

'I see you with my heart, Peekay,' he said at last, these

546

awesomely personal words sealing the acceptance.

'It has always been yours, Gideon. It was only *yayinto yernilingo*, a magical loan. I needed it for the strength it gave me to get to the world title; now it must return to make your strength complete.' Peekay hesitated for a moment before adding, 'My *okumiselwe khona*, my destiny, is foretold; I must go with the snake and not with the lion. The snake is my talisman as the lion is yours.'

Gideon looked into Peekay's eyes. 'This snake, it is *uMamba*, the black one?'

Peekay nodded and Gideon gave a low whistle. 'This *iNyoka*, it is very powerful. The lion rips and tears to make a kill but its death-making is not certain and often the prey will break free. But *uMamba* strikes near the heart; the poison works slowly but there is no escape, death is certain.'

Peekay could see that his new talisman made perfect sense to Gideon. Apart from his courage, Peekay was not the lion type in the ring. This new talisman his shadows had found for him was perfect and, like the return of his own, a wonderful omen for the fight.

'You will be very powerful tonight, Gideon,' Peekay grinned. 'The *iBhunu*, the Boer, will be in for a big surprise. You have doubled your power. Before was enough to beat Jannie Geldenhuis; now you are truly a man who goes with his shadows into the ring and is invincible!'

'Haya, haya, Peekay, I hear you. But Geldenhuis will not come easy, he has great hate.'

'And your hate?'

'It is different, it is an old hate passed on to me by my shadows; it cannot go away but it does not feed on raw meat like the *amaBhunu*.'

Geldenhuis had never trained harder for a fight. He was superbly fit and confident, and had every reason to be. On paper, the fights he'd had leading up to this contest were of a somewhat better quality to those fought by Mandoma. He knew this would hold him in good stead against the black man, whom he hoped had been lured into a false sense of his own ability by a string of comparatively easy wins against fairly mediocre opponents. It rankled him enormously that Gideon was placed above him in the world rankings on the basis of having defeated Soap Dish Jurez, the Cuban, the only really classy fight the kaffir had had in a year.

Once his injuries had fully healed, the Special Branch had given him three months on light duties, which, in effect, meant full-time training. Two of his sparring partners were young white fighters on their way up, both middleweights, so he could get used to a physically stronger, harder punching opponent like Gideon Mandoma. His third sparring partner was a young Zulu who fought a lot like Gideon. Of the three sparring partners the young Zulu was the least skilled but the toughest, a non-stop battler whose fighting name was the Black Tornado.

While Geldenhuis sparred in the normal way with the two white middleweights, the black fighter was used to sharpen the policeman's aggression. Geldenhuis would work him over as hard as he could, building up his hate. The young Zulu fighter, though tough as nails, was no match for the policeman's skill in the ring. Geldenhuis would often knock him down; though in the three months the Zulu had endured these hidings, the policeman had been unable to knock him out. Tom Majombi, the Black Tornado's real name, was too proud to simply lie down like any sensible pug when he'd taken enough punishment. Day after day, the black fighter took a terrible pounding at the police lieutenant's hands, and in the final week of training the white boxer's aggression and hate had sharpened to the point where he beat the young African so severely that he started to bleed from his ears. Geldenhuis was ready.

Now, with the entrance of the Afrikaner policeman into the ring, the band struck up *Die Stem*, the South African National anthem which means 'The Voice'. Geldenhuis stood in the centre of the ring as the fifteen thousand white people sang; the entire audience stood. He'd never fought in front of a crowd even one-fifth as big and he would remember the moment for the remainder of his life. The beautiful words of the anthem reached his soul; at that moment, Jannie Geldenhuis knew what it was to be an Afrikaner, and his pride and joy and love overwhelmed him so that he stood with tears running down his cheeks. He was fighting for more than just a chance to get to Peekay; he was fighting the same fight his ancestors had been fighting for three hundred years. He was fighting to keep his blood pure, he was fighting for the survival of his race. The Zulu would have to kill him to win.

Gideon entered the ring to a tremendous roar from the crowd. He too stood in the centre of the ring while the black anthem *NKosi Sikelela i'Afrika*, 'God Bless Africa', was played by the band, this time accompanied by fifteen thousand black voices. The white audience, who for the most part had remained seated, was awestruck by the sound. This was an Africa they didn't know, this was a voice they hadn't heard, and it was both chilling and beautiful.

Gideon stood with his gloves raised, turning to the crowd. He too had never boxed to a crowd like this before and he felt great pride in the black people who had come to see him fight. They were giving him a hero's welcome and they made him strong; the black champion of Africa wanted the white title as well. His mind flashed back to the prison cell where Geldenhuis had completely lost his cool when he thought Gideon had broken his hand and he would be denied the fight and thus the opportunity to get to Peekay. Tonight he would be denied that opportunity again; the judges were the same international panel selected to judge the world championship bout. There would be no pigment decisions, the best man would win. Gideon knew that the shadows were with him, even the great Shaka and Dingane. He was fighting for his people, for their dignity and honour and the greatness of their hearts.

The referee called them both into the centre of the ring and neither man looked at each other as they received instructions.

Tandia, seated directly below the ring in the front row, was overwrought before the fight began between the man she loved the most and the man she hated the most in the world. Of the two emotions, hate was the stronger and with it fear. In her mind Geldenhuis was invincible and she was terribly afraid for Gideon. She was close to tears, and by the time the bell went for the opening round she held Madam Flame Flo's hand in a fierce grip, her whole body shaking.

The first round was torrid enough, with both fighters standing toe to toe, both boxing well and keeping the other out. Geldenhuis hit Mandoma with a beautiful right hand towards the end of the round, sending him back several paces; then he'd come in fast, hoping to put another couple of good punches in, but Gideon tied him up and the bell went. If anything it was this single punch which separated the two fighters in the first round.

The second and third rounds were not dissimilar, both boxers trying to get on top, punching hard and accurately but seldom penetrating the other's defence. It was surprising that after three rounds no pattern seemed to be emerging. But the fans were getting their money's worth; neither man would back down and the pace of the fight was too fast to last.

The fourth round was Geldenhuis's best. He came out early and caught Gideon again with a right to the jaw. Gideon went down, though he was up at the count of four, not staying down, as Solly had advised him for an eight count. Geldenhuis was all over him and it wasn't until halfway through the round that he began to even things out. The fourth round ended with a definite advantage for Geldenhuis, although he'd thrown an awful lot of leather trying to nail the black man and he was showing the first signs of slowing down.

Five and six saw the fight beginning to change. Gideon was punching the more accurately of the two fighters, landing more often. Fought at a slightly slower pace, it was easier to see what was happening and the crowd began to sense that the black man was starting to get on top. It was the first time Tandia released Madam Flame Flo's hand; six rounds had ended and the seventh was the one when Geldenhuis had promised he'd put Gideon away. Now Gideon was starting to look the better boxer.

Forecasting your opponent's demise is good for pre-fight publicity but in boxing it comes back to haunt you too often. History will tell that by the seventh round Mandoma had Geldenhuis where he wanted him. Geldenhuis came out strong, determined to keep his promise, but seemed to almost run into a hard left to his jaw. It was a dumb punch but he was badly hurt and he dropped like a stone, a bewildered look on his face. He rose at the count of eight but he was very groggy on his feet, whereupon Mandoma set about the task of working his body, working the policeman onto the ropes and ripping punches into him just below the heart. Geldenhuis seemed to have no counter for these deadly short blows and he rapidly weakened. It almost looked as though he was only staying on his feet because Mandoma wanted to keep him upright.

The bell went and Mandoma was met at his corner by an excited Solly Goldman. 'You could have put him away, why, why? You could have put him away in the seventh, turned the books on him!'

'I want him for one more round, this next round is for Tandia,' Gideon said. He turned to Togger, who was acting as one of the seconds. He grinned, raising his glove as Togger was about to insert his mouthguard. 'Please, Togger, you go tell her this round is for her.'

'It's my pleasure, Gideon, a looker like that. She your girlfriend, then?'

Gideon nodded as Solly pushed him up. 'It's not over yet, my son. You get in there and box. It's not over until the man counts ten!' He was furious at Gideon's break in concentration.

But it was. Right at the start of the following round Mandoma hit Geldenhuis hard and put him down again. When Geldenhuis got up at eight he stumbled around the ring as Mandoma pushed him about with his left hand, though without following through with the right. The black fighter taunted the policeman, dropping his gloves and showing Geldenhuis his jaw, making the police lieutenant miss simply by bobbing and weaving around. Then, towards the end of the round he dropped him four times in quick succession. 'This one is for Shaka!' he said coming after Geldenhuis and putting him down. Geldenhuis stayed down for a count of seven, then rose. The referee examined him and let the fight continue. Ten seconds later Gideon put him down again; 'For Dingane!' he spat as he walked away to a neutral corner. The third time Geldenhuis went down, Gideon waited until he rose and let the white man pull him into a clinch. 'That was for my mother, white man!'

Geldenhuis grinned and spat out his mouthguard and spoke through his broken mouth. 'You better kill me now, jong. Because if you don't, you a dead kaffir!' Then he spat, sending a spray of blood and spittle into Gideon's face.

With fifteen seconds to go in the eighth Mandoma positioned Geldenhuis with his back to the front row of black ringside seats, working him onto the ropes. Then he hit the helpless policeman with a straight left, knocking him backwards hard into the ropes so that his shoulders and arse opened up the top and middle rung. Gideon followed with a looping right hand which caught Geldenhuis on the left underside of his jaw, knocking him completely through the ropes. 'That's for me!' he hissed.

Then Gideon did something for which he would never be forgiven by the whites; he spat at the sprawling Geldenhuis. For a split second there was complete disbelief in the crowd, both black and white; then the roar rose on the black side of the rope. They'd witnessed the impossible; black had openly shown its contempt for white. The ants had defied the dung beetle.

The policeman landed backwards on his arse, skidding with the momentum and coming to rest at

Tandia's feet in the front row. His head jerked violently and blood from his nose arched towards her in slow motion, splashing over the skirt of her white gown, like a Japanese brush-drawing of a sprig of cherry blossom. Though unconscious, his eyes were open and he appeared to be looking directly up at her.

Tandia screamed as a roaring panic filled her head. She didn't see Geldenhuis at her feet, instead her mind exploded into a vision of a pink room where she knelt naked, bent over the edge of a bed covered with pink satin. She fainted, slumping against Mama Tequila.

Both Captain Smit and Gert had witnessed Gideon Mandoma's head come back and move forward again in what was unmistakably a spitting action directed at the fallen Geldenhuis. Smit had to bring his mouth up to Gert's ear and shout to be heard above the roar of the black crowd 'That fokken kaffir has "the power". Somebody is going to have to kill him or he's going to be big trouble!' Gert nodded, hearing but not attempting to reply.

The black crowd was on its feet, their fists raised. '*Amandla! Amandla!* Power! Power!' they chanted. The white police drew their revolvers and the black constables, trained in crowd control, suddenly appeared holding riot shields, which had been resting all the while at their feet. They raised their fighting sticks in readiness to charge. '*Amandla! Amandla!*' the black crowd chanted, oblivious to the danger they faced from the police. Some of the white crowd had risen, ready to move out in a hurry.

Gideon stood in a neutral corner as the referee commenced to count Geldenhuis out, finally crossing his arms and scissoring the air with his open palms to indicate that the fight was over.

It was the traditional moment in boxing when the winner leaps into the air and holds his hands high in victory as he circles the ring, and all hell breaks loose in the crowd. But Gideon Mandoma did no such thing. Instead he took three steps to the centre of the ring where he stood at rigid attention with his head bowed, as if in sorrow, his gloves brought together over his scrotum.

The effect on the black crowd was instantaneous. By some sort of osmosis his will imposed itself on the crowd and they grew silent almost in the time it took to catch a breath. Then the young Zulu chief's voice rang out clear and sharp echoing through the giant stadium, 'ukuBekezela abakowethu! Patience my brothers!'

The crisis was over. Moments later, the referee from Cuba raised Gideon's right hand and the ecstatic black crowd acknowledged him with waves and waves of roared approval, their aggression of a moment before turned to a fierce and benign love for the new leader who had been revealed to them.

General Van Breeden leaned over to Captain Smit on his left. 'Wragtig! Did you see that, hey? Tonight a new Dingane is born, you mark my words!'

Geldenhuis was back on his feet, his arms around the necks of two of his seconds who helped him back into the ring. This brought a spontaneous cheer from the white crowd as well as steady applause from the black. He moved jerkily towards Mandoma, his legs clearly unsteady; they started to give way again just as he reached the black boxer. Gideon grabbed him, preventing him from going down. Flashlights popped everywhere as the black man held the white in a macabre embrace.

Twenty-six

After the Mandoma win, the preliminaries to the title bout were close to magical. The black crowd, buoyed by Gideon's brilliant victory, were in the mood for more. Jackson had come out first, carrying a huge American flag and followed by his entourage. This had caused terrific excitement and the crowd had been generous in their applause. Things American were popular in the African townships and, against any other white opponent, the American would undoubtedly have been the black favourite.

When Peekay, accompanied by Hymie, walked out onto the field from the entrance under the members' stand, the tension was almost unbearable. The huge black crowd, unwilling to wait for the opening wail of the great Gwigwi's clarinet to lead them, broke into spontaneous song. Seventeen thousand voices lifted in harmonious greeting as the Chant to the Tadpole Angel rose like thunder into the evening air.

It was spine-chilling stuff and many of the whites would later swear they'd felt the hair standing up on the back of their necks. The Chant continued until Peekay climbed into the ring and sat on the pot in his corner.

'Christ, Peekay, stop bawling,' Hymie said into the sudden silence as the voices rose one last time and then suddenly cut dead. It was obvious that he too was enormously moved.

Almost immediately the obese figure of Jam Jar rose up on the white side of the ringside audience. The opening strains of his violin carried over the loudspeakers and twenty-eight Odd Bodleians, led by the small, neat figure of Aunt Tom, stood over half-a-dozen microphones as they commenced to sing the *Concerto for the Great Southland*.

The beautiful voices of the Oxford men rose in chorus and almost immediately the blacks came in. First the Xhosa; the concerto rising higher and higher under the huge stadium seemed to expand with the sound. The same was true of the Sotho, Ndebele and Swazi as they picked up the theme and the audience went with it. Finally, when the great chorus of the Zulus came, the huge stadium filled with the fulminous sound as five thousand Zulu men rose to stamp their feet as they took the great tribal song into their chests and wound it upwards into the heavens itself. The thunder rolled over the stadium and surrounded the people, lifted them up, rose high and crashed down on them as the impi of Shaka and Dingane swept down from the hills like wind in the grass.

For one moment, all of South Africa stood together united in the storm of love, both black and white drenched until no colour or creed or worthwhile difference existed. All, for a few moments, felt *the possibility*, the possibility of one land and one purpose and the perfect harmony of one people.

General Van Breeden, seated beside Captain Smit, wept openly; and directly opposite them, on the black side of the rope, Mama Tequila, Madam Flame Flo and Tandia did the same. The bitter, sad land paused from the hating and reached up and touched the face of God who, for a few moments, stayed His vengeance and stilled His wrath.

When the opening chords of the Star-Spangled Banner played for Jackson and immediately after it, *Die Stem* for Peekay, they came almost as a relief to an emotion which, if it had been allowed to endure, would have burst the hearts of the huge crowd. Peekay seemed to be in a daze, even when the Mexican referee called the stats for both fighters and brought the fighters together into the centre of the ring, where Jackson, taking advantage of the ref's poor English, spat out, 'I'm gonna whup your ass, whitcy'. Peekay appeared not to hear him as he returned to his corner. With a huge roar from the crowd the bell sounded for the opening round and Peekay moved almost casually to meet a fiercely advancing Jackson.

Jackson came at him hard and Peekay prepared to snap his concentration into focus. There was a diamond-hard pin of light that seemed to move around his head as though spotlighting the next move, reading his opponent's mind. But this time all he could hear was his mother's voice, 'I am not mocked, saith the Lord'. Jackson hit him hard with a straight left, surprised that he'd made it through his opponent's defences so easily. He followed with a lightning right which connected high on Peekay's head but which nevertheless knocked him backwards. Peekay didn't seem able to focus; he was boxing blind, not reading Jackson. It was like lifting your hand and finding your fingers don't work any more. He moved frantically on the back foot, trying to stay out of trouble, his mind a blank, instinct alone defending him. The end of the round came and Jackson was clearly on top.

'What the hell's the matter?' Hymie shouted.

'I don't know, I'm not seeing it, it's not flowing.'

'For Christ's sake, Peekay, you know it backwards, every rhythm, every combination, they're pre-programmed in your head, they have to happen!'

'Stay on the back foot son, stay outta trouble till it starts to come,' Dutch said calmly, but he was worried. He'd never seen Peekay like this.

The next two rounds were the same. Jackson was clearly starting to move in on Peekay, getting through his defences. Peekay's timing was way out and it was all he could do to stay out of trouble.

In the fourth round the voice in his head started again. First it was Mrs Schoemann's voice speaking in tongues, the weird cacophony of words that made no sense. Jackson was beginning to hit him almost at will; it was only Peekay's instinctive skill that was minimizing the effect of the punches. He saw the right hand coming but there was nothing he could do about it; it landed on the point of his jaw and he went down, the voices reaching a crescendo. He lay there, the voices going faster and faster in his head like a tape recorder speeded up. At eight, the number was the only thing he could make out in the gabble of sound in his head. He stood. Somehow he managed to get through the round.

Hymie was shaking him. 'Peekay! What's the matter, what's happened?' Peekay didn't answer. 'Christ, he's out on his feet we better throw in the towel,' he heard Dutch say, 'The lad's going to get hurt bad.'

'No!' was all Peekay could manage. His head seemed to be clearing; the bell went and he went out to meet a Jackson who now wore a tight grin on his face.

The American stalked Peekay and put him down in the fifth round. The voices were back, this time his mother's. *The devil is black and has a tongue of fire and leaps to destroy the children of the lamb. His number is seven and with his hands he will destroy you, tearing at the flesh of our flesh and the bones of our bones.* Jackson was going to take him in the seventh. When was that? The next round. Peekay danced, trying to stay out of trouble. Jackson's glove kept coming. Like a steam shovel, like a piston, bang, bang, bang, but it wouldn't be until seven. *The Lord is not mocked ... With his right hand he will smite our firstborn and with his left also. His colour is black and his tongue is the fire of hate and he will triumph over the flesh of our flesh and he will vanquish him.* Jackson hit Peekay with a right, an insult; he hit him leading with a right and then followed with a left upper-cut, and as Peekay hit the floor the bell went for the end of the round. Hymie and Togger rushed to bring him back to his corner, but by the time they reached the corner Peekay's legs were beginning to return to him. He hadn't laid a decent punch on Jackson for three rounds, the fight was a fiasco. Dutch held the smelling salts under his nose and Peekay came to, shaking his head violently. There was a stillness in the crowd that was awesome; they were seeing their man demolished, destroyed by the furious black American.

Tandia couldn't watch any more and had her head buried in Mama Tequila's huge breasts. Peekay was Gideon's friend, Gideon idolized him and she was seeing the black American do to him what in her imagination she had seen Geldenhuis do to Gideon. Madam Flame Flo was shaking her head. 'He was so marvellous, that first time in Sophiatown, he was so marvellous!' there were tears in her eyes.

Now Peekay waited for the bell to go for the seventh. Dutch had worked hard to close a small cut above his eye. 'Son, what's on your mind? We're fighting for a world title! Wake up, you're taking a hiding, you have to lift your work rate! Watch his left, it's setting you up too often for a straight right; use your feet, don't let him set you up!' He was trying to stay calm and not show the edge of panic in his voice.

Peekay spat into the bucket Togger held out to him and handed the water bottle back to him. He was still breathing hard as he looked up at Hymie. His face, which so few boxers had ever managed to hit, was a mess, the flesh puffy and raw with the eye Dutch had worked on starting to close. 'I can't see it, I can't see the fight in my head, Hymie. I'm blacked out, just voices, my mother's voice, it's as though a light in my head has gone out.'

The bell sounded and Peekay rose to see the bull-like Jackson coming at him, his shoulder muscles polished with sweat, hunched to get the most power from the punches he was beginning to throw almost at will. The negro's face was virtually untouched and there was kill in his eyes, like a predator certain he has his quarry cornered.

Peekay managed to parry his left lead and move out of the way of the right which followed. He spent most of the round on the back foot trying to slip Jackson's punches and when the black boxer grew frustrated and attempted to move him onto the ropes he tied him up. Nevertheless the American managed to hurt him with two beautiful punches under the heart. Somehow, though both punches were capable of putting him down, Peekay stayed on his feet. But the voice was back. *'I am not mocked! His colour is black and his tongue is fire . . . flesh of our filesh . . . with his right hand he will smile . . . he will be utterly destroyed, utterly destroyed!'*

'The lad is finished, Hymie, he could take a terrible hiding, you *must* use the towel!'

'No, Dutch! No way! We're not stopping the fight, not unless he says so!' Hymie had never seen Peekay like this, he'd never before witnessed him humiliated in the ring, a feeling which he knew would be infinitely worse for Peekay than the physical damage he'd endured in the first fight with Jackson. The black boxer was making a fool of him and Hymie wanted to scream at him to stop, to take the title and go away and never come back again. He felt devastated, as though he found himself caught in a nightmare from which he couldn't wake and seemed helpless to control.

'He's fightin' like a zombie, Hymie,' Solly Goldman hissed. 'It's gotta stop, son!'

Hymie looked at Togger, who had no say in the matter anyway. 'Don't, Hymie, please don't!' The little fighter's blind trust in Peekay was still miraculously intact. 'He'll come out of it, just give him a chance!' Togger was crying.

'Peekay decides!' Hymie shouted again; it was as though by repeating his denial he could shout down an inner voice which urged him to throw in the towel. 'That is, if he makes it through this round!'

The bell went for the end of the round. Peekay dragged himself back and slumped wearily into his corner. Dutch massaged his shoulders as Togger handed him the water bottle. It was pointless offering Peekay advice, he was finished. He only hoped Jackson wasn't going to toy with him, make him eat crow. 'Easy now lad, Hymie wants to talk to you,' he said, knowing that he and Peekay had come to the end of the road, that Peekay would never fight again.

Hymie scowled, hating Dutch Holland. 'Peekay, how are you? What do you reckon?'

Peekay, spitting the water he'd taken from Togger into the bucket, shook his head. 'I can't ... get my mother's voice ... out of my head ... she ... she said things ... bad things about this fight.' His chest was heaving and the words came out between gasps like a small boy who's been running away from a bully and finds the safety of a grownup he knows.

Suddenly a black arm pushed Togger's bucket aside and Mandoma looked into Peekay's face. The Zulu's eyes blazed and he was shaking as he started to talk, spitting venom in Zulu. 'You white bastard! I shit in your mouth. You want to take it from me! You want to stop me from being *the one*! If *you* lose this fight, *I* lose my chance!' He grabbed Peekay by the throat. 'You coward, you are not *uMamba*, the great snake, you are a worm who feeds on dead flesh! I spit on your shadows!'

Togger and Dutch grabbed at Gideon and pulled the black fighter away. Peekay hadn't moved. Even when Mandoma grabbed at his throat his eyes remained fixed, as though he was in a trance. As if triggered by the word '*uMamba*' the giant black snake rose up in his vision, the flat wedgeshaped head so close he expected its darting, flicking tongue to touch the bridge of his nose, the tiny, flat, remorseless eyes looking into his own. The sudden highpitched cackle in Peekay's head was the voice of Inkosilnkosikazi. *The head, bring the head down slowly to the ground, release your left hand, you must take away his eyes, the poison is all in your right hand.*

As suddenly as it had appeared, the snake's head dipped below Peekay's line of sight. There was a sudden rush of wind through the leaves of the giant yellow-wood tree above the forest canopy and then the bell for the eighth round sounded. Peekay rose. He could see Jackson coming towards him, he could see the hate in his eyes. The light in Peekay's head went on and the shape of the fight yet to come was clearly etched in his mind. He could handle the hate. The fear had gone as he moved towards his dancing opponent, who was wearing a huge malicious smile.

Jackson held the smile, dancing round Pcekay, waiting to plant a combination that would put him down. He'd lost all respect for him but for one thing. Peekay should have stayed down long ago, he was a tough sonofabitch. And then Peekay's beautifully timed left hand came out like a jab of lightning, smashing through the smile on Jackson's face and sending his mouthguard flying, breaking three teeth. Peekay was back in the fight.

The ref stopped to retrieve Jackson's mouthguard and Jackson spat out the broken teeth into his hand. The crowd had come alive, not believing what they'd just seen. Jackson grinned; he'd been careless, a lucky shot. He hadn't expected a punch like that to still be in the white man, but he was pretty sure he'd sapped most of Peekay's strength and he could now take anything the white man could dish out. He was still strong, although he was beginning to feel the effects of the altitude and was taking a little longer to recover between rounds. There was plenty of time left, he told himself; Peekay couldn't go beyond ten. But Peekay continued to land hard, clean punches that snapped his head back. The white man was working to his head; that wasn't his style, he was a body man. Now they were coming; sharp, clean, hard, into the nose, into his mouth – and then, towards the end of the round, Peekay drew blood again as he caught him with a mercurial right cross which opened up the old wound above his right eye, tearing a gash almost completely across the soft tissue below his eyebrow. The round was Peekay's, the first he'd won.

The next round wasn't exactly fireworks. The American tried to finish Peekay off but Peekay tied him up and on the break managed to hit him consistently to the head, banging away at the tissue above the broken eye. Peekay was resting, regaining his strength. Jackson's cut-man had worked frantically with adrenalin between rounds to close the gash above his eye. Peekay was working it, ripping his punches across the eye so that now it was taking a lot of internal blood and closing fast. Peekay wasn't trying to put Jackson away, but he was slowly beginning to bring Jackson's head to the ground and the crowd sensed that, miraculously, the tide was beginning to turn in the fight.

By the end of the tenth round Peekay was on top and he'd opened Jackson's left eye as well. In the following, the eleventh, Peekay closed it almost completely and Jackson was left with no more than thirty per cent vision in both eyes as Peekay, growing stronger by the minute, began to put his punches together brilliantly.

Dutch couldn't believe what he'd seen. Hymie was grinning and Solly and Togger were falling over each other to sponge and water Peekay. Dutch was still cool. 'All you do is hold him for the next two, work him up. You're too far behind to win on points, lad. You got to take him out in the thirteenth or fourteenth. Save your strength, you've taken a fair bit of punishment, save it for the big one.'

When the bell went for the end of the eleventh round the crowd was screaming and hadn't let up between rounds. Peekay was taking the fight to the American and giving the rapidly tiring Jackson a boxing lesson. It was almost as though they'd been allocated six rounds each to beat the living daylights out of each other. Jackson was plainly weary when they reached the end of the round. Peekay had kept at his head, putting the punches in with his left hand.

'Shit, they're cutting Jackson's eyes,' Togger yelled.

'Good!' Dutch said. 'There's too much old scar tissue, they'll cut. But listen, lad, if you can bang them shut again, that's the end. They won't be able to open them up again!' He tried to keep his voice calm. 'Listen carefully, son. The American has to try and take you out in this next round, he has no bleedin' choice! If he can hang on he'll win on points but he knows he can't. Dance him lad, stay out of clinches, keep off the ropes. If you can put a couple good hard 'uns into the eyes to close them for good, that's all it'll take – then stay away, you hear me now. You're on top, you can get him in the next round. There's plenty of time, you've got three rounds up your sleeve.'

The twelfth round was perhaps the greatest in both men's careers. Jackson put Peekay on the canvas in the first fifteen seconds with a beautiful right cross. Peekay was on his feet at the count of six but shaky on his pins. Jackson came at him again and put him to the floor again with a sharp left which seemed to travel no more than eight inches but caught Peekay on the point of the jaw.

Peekay lay sprawled looking up at Jackson. Everything seemed fine except that he couldn't move. Inkosi-Inkosikazi's insane, high-pitched cackle filled his head ... *The poison is in your right hand!* Almost immediately the feeling returned to his legs and he was standing at the count of eight. Jackson took him onto the ropes where Peekay tied him up. The ref called for them to break and Peekay came out of the break as a southpaw, leading with his right hand instead of his left.

Jackson went down to a right-left combination moments later. It was the first of three knock-downs for Jackson in the twelfth. Later Baasie Pienaar would write in *Die Vaderland*:

> *Jackson, who'd fought brilliantly for the first ninety seconds of the twelfth, now seemed to have no counter for the southpaw switch of Peekay. The Tadpole Angel hit the black fighter one hunded and fifteen times in the remainder of the round, which included the three trips to the canvas. It was the most remorseless attack led with a right hand that I have ever witnessed. The Angel hits hard and clean and has a KO punch in both hands even this late in a fight, though the same punches earlier in the fight would have put the American away half a dozen times. Nevertheless they were still good punches and Jackson must have a head like Mount McKinley; how he managed to get back on his feet and see the round out this sportswriter will never know.*

The thirteenth round lasted only thirty-two seconds before Jackson took a perfect right cross on the nose, smashing it. The punch forced him backwards where he grabbed frantically at the ropes to stop himself going down. His entire body was exposed for a few moments and Peekay exploded a Solly Goldman thirteen-punch combination into the American which was so fast, perfect and complete that it would be talked about by boxing aficionados for years to come. Jackson simply pitched forward, sprawling on the canvas; then he rolled over once, his arms outstretched as though he'd been crucified. It was obvious, even from the furthermost row in the highest stand, that he wasn't going to get to his feet again for a long, long time.

Peekay moved to a neutral corner to wait for the Mexican referee to count Jackson out. It was all over. The small boy had conquered his fear. It had been enough to overcome the hate and the power that came with it. The long journey, begun at the age of six, was completed. Peekay was the undisputed welterweight champion of the world. 'Thank you, Hoppie Groenewald, wherever you may be,' Peekay said quietly to himself.

The crowd erupted and chaos reigned. Then, as suddenly, the hum of the Chant began to break through the tumult as fifteen thousand Africans rose up and danced in the stands, their arms raised in the victory salute. Suddenly the greater part of the white crowd joined them and turned and hugged each other and they too danced; white hands reached out past the police and over the rope to join hands with black. While the rope held and the policemen remained at the ready, it might as well not have been there at all; that is the peculiar thing about happiness, it comes from the heart and not

568

from the head and when it demands to be shared it can't be separated by ropes, walls or least of all, by guns and three-foot fighting sticks which shatter kneecaps.

Peekay's dressing room was mayhem as he lay on a massage table while Dutch worked on him. Hands reached out to touch him, shouting their good wishes, and the room seemed filled with the dinner suits of the Odd Bodleians, including Aunt Tom. Some of the Oxford men had only arrived the previous day in South Africa and now shared in the ecstasy of winning.

Jam Jar was playing his fiddle in between taking deep swigs from a bottle of Chivas Regal which he passed out to anyone who seemed inclined to partake. Van Breeden, Smit and Gert, grinning from ear to ear, were standing nearest to Peekay trying to make themselves heard.

'I've never seen anything like it! I never seen anything like it, you were dead, Peekay! *Wragtig!* I never seen anything like it!' Captain Smit repeated, his voice hoarse from shouting. Gert, as usual, said nothing, but his pride in Peekay showed in his eyes and you would have needed a charge of buckshot to blast the grin off his face.

Solly Goldman was walking around the room collaring anyone he could find to listen. 'Six years ago, I taught him. I never seen 'im use it, I never seen anyone use it, it was impossible they said, too difficult. Solly, they said, there's not enough time to seat thirteen good 'uns home! Then tonight I seen the Solly Goldman thirteen-punch combination win the championship of the whole world!'

It took Hymie almost half an hour to clear the room. He'd arranged for four buses to take the Odd Bodleians and other invited guests to Pretoria where a victory celebration for two hundred guests was arranged at

Solomon Levy's palatial home. The ever-efficient Captain McClymont had laid on a police escort to accompany the buses. As well, he arranged for four motorcycle cops to escort Peekay and Hymie when they were due to depart an hour or so later, after the police had dispersed the main part of the crowd.

The moment the room was clear Peekay told Dutch he felt better. Dutch lifted him gently to a sitting position. 'Peekay, I'm not much with words, son. I've handled a lot of lads, good 'uns too. I don't mind sayin' I thought you was gone in the seventh. That was the bravest comeback by a fighter I've ever seen and what's more, my son, five of the last seven rounds, well, I doubt I'll ever see better boxing.' He towelled Peekay's shoulders. 'I still don't believe I saw that thirteen-punch combo, it was the fucking immaculate conception. You was magic, son!'

Peekay grinned. 'Thank you, Dutch. There was a lot of work in those winning rounds. I shall always be grateful. One more fight to go. I know your contract is up but I hope you'll agree to train me?'

Dutch Holland cleared his throat. 'Now's a lousy time to tell you, Peekay.'

Peekay looked up quickly. The sudden jerk of his neck sent a stab of pain down his right shoulder. 'Tell me what, Dutch?'

'Son, I'm a professional trainer; win, lose or draw, the next fight with Mandoma is your last.'

'So?' Peekay was too tired to be polite.

'Mr Nguni has asked me to train Gideon Mandoma. If he wins against you he's going to have a big career in the ring. Even if he doesn't, the title will be vacant and I think he could take Jackson or any of the other top contenders.'

570

Only Hymie, had he been present, would have seen Peekay's reaction and known that Dutch Holland's announcement was like a sudden kick in the scrotum. 'Dutch, that's great! Solly Goldman has had a hard time playing second fiddle and I'll be happy to go back to him.' Peekay extended his hand. 'I shall miss you in my corner.'

'Peekay, you make me feel a right berk.'

'Dutch, I owe tonight to Mandoma. Had he not interfered in the break before the eighth, Christ knows what would have happened. Nothing was going for me.' Peekay rose from the massage table, wincing from the effort. 'I understand your decision, Dutch. It seems only right that Gideon should have the services of the best fight trainer in the world.'

Peekay wondered whether Hymie knew of Dutch's decision. He felt betrayed and his gut was taut with anger but he was buggered if he was going to let on to the Englishman. He wondered to himself why Holland couldn't have waited for just one more fight? Mr Nguni must have made him a terrific offer. Peekay made a note never to underestimate the black fight manager again, and smiled once more to conceal his thoughts. 'No hard feelings, Dutch.'

Holland smiled back, relieved. Then he draped the small towel he was carrying over Peekay's head and took his hand. 'Keep warm, son,' he said, 'I promised I'd make a champ outta you and I done that; not too many trainers part with their fighters when they're at the top.'

Togger entered the dressing room at that moment. Peekay beckoned him over and whispered in his ear. Togger nodded and left the room. Peekay removed his gown, boxing shorts and jockstrap and moved painfully into the shower cubicle.

The doctor who had examined him immediately after the fight pronounced his nose broken and also several suspected broken ribs. His face was swollen but seemed to have responded well to the ice packs Dutch had used on him immediately after the fight. Apart from a black eye where Jackson had cut him, his face was almost back to normal. If anything, despite the pounding Jackson had given him in the first six rounds, he was in a lot better shape physically than after the New York fight.

Peekay was out of the shower with a towel around his waist when Togger returned and closed the door behind him. 'He's waiting outside, Peekay,' he said.

Peekay walked to the door and opened it, pulling Gideon into the room. Dutch had left and Solly, together with Hymie and Togger, stood silent, not sure for a moment what was going to happen. Then Peekay hugged the black fighter and both of them started to laugh.

'Shit, Peekay! Don't do that to me!' Hymie yelled, holding his heart in mock consternation. 'I thought World War Three was about to start!'

Peekay grinned. 'You think I'm crazy? This black bastard had an easy fight, he could probably go another ten rounds!' He turned back to Gideon and put a hand on either shoulder, looking into the eyes of the black boxer. 'Thank you, my brother, it is your title, you broke the *isiBango*, the spell, so my shadows could come to my rescue; it is you who are *the one*.'

'Haya, haya, Peekay, this is nice but it is not the truth. You are still the *Onoshobishobi Ingelosi*; the people have seen you tonight. They are very, very happy.'

'Then you will come to the celebration in Pretoria? It is as much for you as it is for me.'

572

Gideon looked grave for a moment. 'Hymie has invited me, but I am with some other people.' He switched suddenly from Zulu to English. 'Me also, I must go home with them.'

'How many people? One hundred, two hundred, your whole *isigodi*? You are a very big hero tonight, Gideon Mandoma!'

Gideon laughed, his marvellous white teeth showing. 'Three *abaFazi* and a driver! They are all.'

'Three women! Haya, haya! They are the victory gifts to the chief, hey?'

Gideon brought both hands up and covered his mouth, laughing. 'Only one is *isiXebe*, my sweetheart, Peekay.'

'Bring them all along then, you hear? Mr Nguni will be there, you will not be alone with all the white people.' Gideon seemed pleased. 'Thank you, Hymie, we will come.'

Peekay touched Gideon lightly on the shoulder. 'The *iBhunu* was outclassed, you deserve a crack at the world title and I'm bloody glad it's you and not that shit Geldenhuis.' Peekay turned and reached for a clean, freshly laundered shirt which hung on a wire hanger from a hook on the wall.

Gideon seemed to hesitate for a moment. 'Peekay?'

'Ja?'

'I meant what I said, you know, in the ring?'

Everything hurt as Peekay turned slowly to face Gideon. He measured him with his eyes, just the suggestion of a smile at the corners of his mouth. 'Ja, I know, but you're going to have to fight a lot harder than you did against the policeman or you're going to end up with more than shit in *your* mouth, black man.'

Gideon grinned. 'Your testicles are two dead frogs, white man!'

'Already you have found three women to cower behind, kaffir!' Peekay shot back.

They broke into simultaneous laughter, Peekay holding his recently strapped ribs, wincing with pain between his laughter. It was obvious that Gideon knew nothing of the plan to have Dutch Holland train him for the title fight.

The party was well underway when Peekay and Hymie arrived, but someone must have seen them coming for the band struck up 'For he's a jolly good fellow!' the moment they entered. Peekay had to endure this embarrassment as the two hundred or more people present joined in song. He spent the first half an hour greeting people before he excused himself to go upstairs to Hymie's room to phone home.

Fifteen minutes later he came downstairs again, and it was nearly midnight before he finally found himself alone again. He was dog tired; the elation at being the new world champion was beginning to wear off and his body was growing stiff and sore as his metabolism slowed down. He waited until nobody seemed to be looking before opening a french window and slipping quietly into the garden.

Outside it was bright moonlight and he filled his lungs with the crisp autumn air. Peekay found himself standing in Solomon Levy's rose garden and he bent over a yellow rose, tipped with saffron. Cupping his hands on either side of the half-opened bloom he directed the exquisite perfume to his swollen nose, surprised and delighted that he could still capture the faint familiar perfume which reminded him of home and of his grandpa's rose garden. When earlier he'd called home his mother was unavailable to talk to him, but the old man had grunted his pleasure and told him, 'There's a good lad,' about six times, so Peekay knew that he was hugely delighted. Then his grandpa had said that Mrs Boxall and Miss Bornstein as well as old Mr Bornstein and old Mr McClymont, and Mr Andrews and Kommandant Kruger from the gaol – in fact everyone who was anyone and a lot of people who weren't – had called to say how delighted they were and how proud the town felt and that if he called, to tell him they wanted to be remembered to him. Peekay's grandpa chuckled. 'Georgie Hankin called to read me his front page in tomorrow's *Goldfields News*, it says: PEEKAY! MORE FAMOUS THAN JOCK OF THE BUSHVELD!'

'Mr Peekay?'

It was a young female voice and Peekay, surprised, straightened up, turning in the direction it came from. Standing in the soft moonlight stood the most beautiful creature he'd ever seen. He knew instantly it was the girl he'd seen crossing towards the ringside before Gideon's fight, though now she wore a green evening gown, her perfect shoulders, the colour of new honey, bare in the bright, cold moonlight.

'Roses, you like roses? The welterweight champion of the world likes roses!' There was laughter and real surprise in her voice.

Peekay pointed to the yellow rose. 'It's named Macreadie Sunset and is a variety bred by the Macreadie family who, for two hundred years, created some of England's most famous roses. This one is my grandpa's favourite, it's a very old variety and goes back to George the First.'

Peekay reached into his pocket and withdrew the small pocket knife which had once belonged to Doc. He opened the blade, which was worn from constant honing, and bending over the rosebush he carefully cut the rose from the main stem. It was autumn, and he left a bud point at the end of the stem so that it would grow another branch to replace the one he'd removed. Then he expertly worked the half-dozen thorns off the stem of the rose using the side of his thumb, rendering it smooth and harmless. 'I suppose we ought to introduce ourselves, although I guess you already know who I am.'

Tandia extended her hand. 'Tandia Patel, I'm a second year law student from Natal University and . . .' she smiled and added a little breathlessly, 'I'm also Gideon Mandoma's girlfriend.'

Peekay's heart missed several beats, though he managed to conceal his dismay. 'Would he mind very much if I gave you this rose, Miss Patel?' he asked, looking into her marvellous eyes.

Tandia laughed. There was an attractive shyness to her laughter, as though she was holding some of it back. 'Maybe he'll want to fight you, Mr Peekay?'

'Peekay, please!' he grinned at Tandia. 'I guess he'll be doing that soon enough anyway.' He handed her the rose. 'So, what say we give him a proper excuse, Tandia?'

She took the rose and brought it to her nose, closing her eyes as she inhaled its perfume. 'It has a beautiful smell. You seem to know a lot about roses.'

Peekay grinned. 'I know a lot about roses, boxing, a little about law and nothing about you.'

Tandia dropped her eyes, looking down at the rose she held. 'Me? There is nothing to tell.' She shivered involuntarily.

'You're cold, Tandia. Come, we'd better go inside.'

'Oh, but I've disturbed you!'

'I can't think of a nicer way to be disturbed. Have you eaten?'

'No, I've been too excited . . . well, nervous really.'

'Don't be. I haven't eaten either and I'm suddenly ravenous. C'mon, let's go before Gideon comes looking for us. I've had all the fighting I can handle for one night. What I don't need is an angry Zulu warrior!'

Tandia put her hand lightly on Peekay's shoulder. 'Peekay, you were wonderful! My father said you were the best. You and Gideon, the two best prospects he'd ever seen. He said you'd be world champion one day. I only wish he'd been there tonight.'

'Your father?'

'Ja, he was a referee, he handled your first fight with Gideon in Sophiatown, when you were just kids.'

'That Patel! The Durban referee? Why's that's absolutely amazing! You're Indian then?'

'No, half. My mother was a Zulu.' As though anticipating his next question she quickly added, 'Both my parents are dead.'

They'd reached the door and Peekay paused. 'I'm sorry to hear that, Tandia.'

'Ag no, please, it wasn't like that. My mother died when I was a baby and my father, well it was . . . a strange relationship.'

'If I may say so, they made a beautiful baby,' he paused, looking directly at Tandia. 'I mean that's strictly a professional observation, one lawyer to another, you understand.'

'Why, thank you, my learned colleague,' Tandia replied, dropping her gaze from his.

Christ, she's beautiful, Peekay thought.

577

Tandia was amazed at how relaxed she felt in Peekay's presence. She'd observed him slip through the french window into the garden and had decided suddenly to follow him. The decision set her heart pounding and she was conscious of the male eyes which followed her as she moved across the room. The eyes of the South African whites, slightly guarded, afraid to look at her openly and the looks of the Odd Bodleians, open and frank in their admiration. On the way to Pretoria they'd stopped at Madam Flame Flo's new house in the coloured suburb of Meadowlands so she could change out of her bloodstained evening gown into the green one. She knew she looked sexy.

As she went back into the house with Peekay, she found herself surprisingly at ease, even excited by being with him. She'd expected some sort of contest, the male thing trying to assert itself and dominate her immediately. She would naturally comply with it, stroke the ego presented to her by the white boxer, play on the aspect of forbidden fruit, both as a coloured and as Gideon's woman.

Peekay, she knew from Gideon, was liberated. Gideon said he simply didn't see colour. This made him vulnerable. He was the welterweight champion of the world as well as a brilliant young graduate from Oxford, Mr Nice Guy. He'd be bending over backwards not to show any skin bias and would also be over-anxious to appear modest and unassuming. But Tandia also knew that in the end the one-eyed snake in him would win. That would come later, that would be her ultimate weapon. Tandia knew it was important for her to make an impression on Peekay, and on the Jew also. Think ahead, she told herself. Think the bad things that can happen, because they will, for sure. Think them out and have a plan of action. You must know who to know long before you need to know them. It was more of Mama Tequila's advice; and it was what had given her the courage to follow Peekay through the french window to confront him in the rose garden.

She'd found him smelling a rose, standing in the moonlight, his face battered and his nose broken, smelling a rose, happy to be by himself. She didn't know quite what she'd expected, but smelling a rose wasn't an acceptable discovery. She'd watched him in the clear, bright, cold night. There was a quietness about him, a lack of tension, like being in a warm, clean place. Yet she could feel the power.

Tandia was an expert on power. Most power, she'd observed, was based on hating, though some was driven by ambition or triggered by wealth or arrogance or both. Power was about getting something, making people bend to your will, imagining something and then making it happen no matter what.

The power she sensed around the white man putting his broken nose into the petals of a yellow rose was different; it was infectious and seemed to swell and recede as though it was trying to include her within its spectrum. There seemed nothing complex about it; it was singular but simple, it made no demands on her and it made her feel safe.

Tandia could never remember feeling completely safe; maybe when she was very young on Patel's knee when he was boasting to someone about her green eyes. The closest she could get to the feeling she now experienced was when she sat in the branches of the big old fig tree which grew beside her upstairs window at Bluey Jay. The tree seemed to be the only place in the world which was her own. In all the time she'd been at Bluey Jay nobody had ever seen her seated within its leafy canopy or discovered her secret. She had become so obsessed with the idea of its importance to her life that she waited, often until two or three in the morning, before she climbed out onto the branch where she would sit and think until the dawn came up and put the shine back onto the surface of the sweeping river that formed one boundary of Bluey Jay. Then she would creep silently back to bed, her head filled with enough cleanness to see her through another day. The aura she now felt around Peekay made her feel the same way. This made her very suspicious and decidedly uncomfortable.

He was white and gifted, brilliantly educated and a sporting genius. The white rose of South Africa's European culture would open its petals to him. There would be nothing he couldn't have: wealth, beauty, position and power. Nothing was beyond his reach; his skin was white and his eyes were blue and he would wake up between crisp, clean sheets every morning for the remainder of his life.

Gideon said he was a white man who didn't see colour. In such things Gideon was a fool. White men like Peekay didn't need to see colour; truth and justice and understanding were abstract virtues for them and if, in the end, nothing changed, you sighed and laid your noble head down, satisfied you'd done your best. It was no less a crock of shit in the end than the policeman with a salivating alsatian at his side and a sjambok in his hand.

Tandia hated all white men except Magistrate Coetzee and Dr Rabin. And this white man for whom she felt such a strange attraction was possibly the worst of them all. She should have known all along. When Peekay was still a boy Patel had eulogized him. Patel always ended up admiring the biggest white bastard in the pack.

And so, seemingly in a matter of minutes, Tandia, having felt herself invaded, built her hate back up again, layering it with reminders, insights and the phantasmagoria of loathing until it regained its comfortable thickness. It had all been done by a white man who'd barely spoken to her, but who'd cut a yellow rose from a bush, removed the thorns from its slender stem with a practised flick of his thumb and quietly and politely handed it to her before inviting her to dine with him.

Peekay and Hymie were a part of Tandia's long-term plan. She would graduate at the end of the year and, from what Gideon had told her, the law practice the two Oxford men were about to open seemed just the sort of place she'd like to join, the first rung in the ladder she would have to climb so she could get even with the world.

Tandia was only just nineteen and she saw herself as a terrorist and a Communist, though she'd not yet effected any acts, even small ones, of terrorism or joined a secret cadre. This didn't stop her seeing herself as totally committed to the overthrow of the white South African regime and the implementation of a socialist state.

Unlike Gideon, who saw a South Africa where blacks shared power with the other racial groups on the basis of a universal franchise, which meant a black prime minister and a black majority, Tandia believed in the Africa for Africans movement with its uncompromising cry, 'Hurl the white man into the sea!' In fact, she would sometimes make Juicey Fruit Mambo drive her down to the harbour where she would stand on the sea wall built to contain the yacht basin, imagining a continuous line of whites being marched over the edge and into the sea. 'Good riddance bad rubbish!' she would shout into the crashing waves, her fist raised in the ANC salute.

There is a time in most thinking adolescent lives when we are granted the gift of absolute certainty, when all is known to us and a position on everything is willingly taken, with no possibility of compromise. Tandia, no less than Peekay, believed in truth and justice, but the difference between them was that her Africa included no whites and insisted on revenge before the Freedom Charter could become a reality.

When she first talked to Gideon about terrorism he'd been reluctant to discuss the topic. But after his arrest and interrogation by Geldenhuis on the night of the far-cical national raid in the name of the Suppression of Communism Act and with the subsequent Treason Trial at present underway, he'd started to think differently. He was one of the leaders of the ANC Youth League who now talked openly about an armed struggle against apartheid. 'We are not ready yet, but its time will come and then we will call it *Umkonto we Sizwe*, The Spear of the Nation,' he told her. Five years later, when in December 1961 the first acts of sabotage announced the formation of *Umkonto we Sizwe*, the young black acti-vist lawyer, Tandia Patel, was secretly sworn in as the first female member.

Twenty-seven

The lower end of Fox Street, just opposite the Johannesburg Magistrates Courts is a dingy part of town where at sunset the streets go suddenly empty. Newspapers blow across the pavements and the smell of garbage and the rancid fat of cheap cafes pervades the atmosphere. In the vacant blocks sow-thistle grows among the torn-down building debris. But it was handy for Africans coming into court and that's why Peekay chose it for their law chambers.

Hymie would have preferred more fashionable chambers, but Peekay insisted that although whites would come to scungy rooms for good legal advice, blacks would be intimidated by oak panelling, carpets on the floor and rows and rows of leather-bound tomes – all the plush and hush of the legal profession.

Nevertheless Solomon Levy insisted on carpeting the offices, as well as the long corridor leading to them, with his very best red British Axminster. In the end, the black people *were* intimidated. They would often remove their shoes before walking down the pontifical corridor, or if they wore no shoes, when they saw the brilliant red carpet they paused to wash the soles of their feet at the courtyard tap before entering the building.

The law firm of Levy, Peekay & Partners became known in African as '*inDawo ye cansi elibomvu*', the place of the red mat, and after a while it was shorted to 'Red'. By 1958, when Gideon and Tandia both joined the firm, it was not uncommon for an African plaintiff, asked by a magistrate whether he had counsel, to proclaim proudly, 'Yes, baas, I am standing on the red mat!'

An African arrested at a political rally or taken at home during a night raid would jam his feet against the buckboard of the kwela-kwela and resist being thrown into the back of the police van until he was sure someone within earshot had heard him scream, '*ukuBizwa Bomvu!* Call Red!'

Peekay's reputation as a defender of the black people had a spectacular beginning in a preliminary hearing before Magistrate Coetzee, the recently appointed chief magistrate of Johannesburg, in which he sought to indict two police officers on a charge of murder. Because of the high profiles ot the people involved, it was a hearing which kept the nation hurrying out to the front lawn for the morning newspaper and gave the black people their first tangible evidence that the *Onoshobishobi Ingelosi*, the Tadpole Angel, was their true defender now that he was grown to adulthood. As the case came to court and continued for nearly three years it established the Red Mat's reputation among the people and also saw Tandia Patel introduced as Peekay's junior counsel.

Two days after Peekay was crowned Welterweight Champion of the World he and Hymie were admitted to the South African Bar. The following day he received a call from Madam Flame Flo, whom he'd met briefly at the Levys' party.

'Peekay, I'm sorry to bother you, I suppose you very busy you and all?' she began.

Peekay laughed. 'Madam Flame Flo, I have a desk, a telephone and a law degree. Somehow I know they all go together but I'm not sure how. So far I haven't been given the opportunity to give even *free* advice. What can I do for you?'

'Well, I dunno, man, first let me tell you the story. Yesterday I got a call from a doctor at Baragwanath Hospital about a young black boxer who has been brought in with a bad ear infection. He was a young boy who used to help around the shebeen in Sophiatown, a tribal kid who became quite a good boxer under the name the Black Tornado. He doesn't have anyone here, you know, his own people, so when they asked for next of kin, he gave my name. Well, the doctor said the ear came from his having been badly beaten. Well, I mean, man, he's a boxer, so I didn't think much about it. The doctor told me the boy said he had some money in the Post Office, but they wanted me to guarantee his hospital fees.' Madam Flame Flo paused. 'Well, I mean, man, you can't just go guaranteeing people all over the place, so I said I'd come out and see him. Well, to cut a long story short, it turns out this boy, whose name is Tom Majombi, was the black sparring partner for Jannie Geldenhuis leading up to the fight with Gideon and the damage they done to his ears, it wasn't just an accident.'

'You mean there was malicious intent?' Peekay asked.

'I dunno what you call it, jong, but I'm telling you something for nothing, it was on purpose!'

Peekay agreed to go out and see Tom Majombi, taking a Nagra tape recorder with him.

Peekay drove over to the huge black hospital in Soweto. It turned out that Tom Majombi appeared to have lost the hearing in his left ear and complained of a ringing sensation in his head, with a great deal of pain. Peekay immediately agreed to pay for the X-rays needed to check whether permanent brain damage had occurred, and for any other medication Majombi might need.

Peekay spoke to the Zulu fighter in his own language. 'The *iBhunu* punches very hard, I think? With heavy sparring gloves and with your headgear on, he is still able to make your ears bleed?'

Tom Majombi laughed. 'The gloves I wore were heavy, but the ones he wore were for fighting; six-ounce gloves and there was no headgear for me, only for the *iBhuni.*'

The young black fighter went on to explain that when no outside witnesses were present he was not permitted to wear a headguard. The idea was to closely simulate the effect of a real fight, with the Zulu boxer wearing the heaviest possible sparring gloves, permitted to fight back as hard as he liked.

Majombi boasted quietly about how he had refused to go down, but admitted he was no match for the brilliant Geldenhuis. Day after day, he took a lot of punishment to the head with no protection. He recalled how Colonel Klaasens, Geldenhuis's trainer, called this aggressive sparing '*bloed krag*', blood power, and boasted it was designed to feed his fighter's hate for the kaffir boy, Mandoma.

Despite his apparent stupidity for not playing possum in the ring when he'd had enough, Tom Majombi proved to be an intelligent young man who would be able to handle himself in the witness box. Peekay felt sure he could bring either a legal indictment against

Geldenhuis or at the very least have him and his trainer up before the South African Boxing Board tribunal for disciplinary action and compensation to the young black fighter. Before he left Peekay gave instructions that Tom Majombi was to get the best possible treatment available. He signed a commitment to pay and he left.

The following morning Peekay called the hospital to enquire about the results of the X-ray and he was told that the Zulu boxer had been removed to Pretoria Prison Hospital for further observation. The young intern who'd originally called Madam Flame Flo came to the phone and told Peekay that a kwela-kwela had arrived to remove the young boxer less than two hours after Peekay's visit. He'd been powerless to prevent the removal or even to ask that the Zulu boxer be taken by ambulance, so he'd sent a request to the superintendent of the prison hospital for X-rays to be taken, though he was extremely doubtful that this would be done. Peekay told him to keep the duplicate paperwork of Tom's admission and to hide it.

'Haya, they are not stupid,' the African doctor replied laconically, then added 'these *amaBhunu* are from the Special Branch. The admission papers and medical notes have been confiscated; no record exists of Tom Majombi's stay at Baragwanath.'

'There must be something. Look for it, we may need it later, doctor.'

After he put the phone down, Peekay turned to Hymie.

'The bastards have got Tom Majombi. He was supposed to have been taken to the Pretoria Prison Hospital but I've checked and they have no admission for anyone of the name. Tom Majombi has been

587

abducted by the police, forcibly taken out of a hospital without being arrested. We've checked all the local police stations. In effect he's been kidnapped.'

'Can the police be charged with kidnapping?' Hymie asked.

'The point is he's disappeared and we know he was taken by the police. But I can't get any leads from that point. It can only be Special Branch and it can only be Klaasens and Geldenhuis.'

'But we have no proof.'

'We have his testimony on tape. That's not a bad start.'

'Look, I'll call Van Breeden. Moving against a police-man of Klaasen's rank could be bloody difficult; he may help, though I don't see why he should.'

'Jesus, Hymie, if it was a white boxer!'

'Okay, okay! I'll call him.'

The police major general listened and promised to call him back. He did so an hour later, suggesting Hymie drop round to de Villiers Square to see him.

Hymie was shown directly in to see Van Breeden and the policeman came straight to the point. 'Listen, Hymie, it's not so easy. I've got Colonel Klaasen's record, he's head of Special Branch in Pretoria, a member of the *Broederbond* and was *Ossewa brand-wag*. He's also on the executive board of the Police College and his record shows him to be an exemplary officer. I'm telling you now, I'm not prepared to move against him even if the evidence was better than it is. We've checked both Baragwanath and the Prison Hos-pital in Pretoria; nobody of the name of your Zulu boxer appears to have been admitted. My advice to you is to forget the whole thing; the boy is not charged with anything and will be safe if we just let the whole thing die down. If you stir things up, who knows? People disappear all the time.'

'Sir, Peekay won't buy that answer.'

'With the greatest respect, this incident with the black boxer, if it was reported to a local police station it is doubtful the sergeant would take it seriously enough to make even a phone call. Peekay has to grow up! This is South Africa, the Nationalist government has been in for nine years and looks like being in forever. Justice for a black man is not the same as for a white. Peekay would do well to understand this.'

'General, I appreciate your time and I hear what you say. I assure you Peekay isn't trying to prove anything or big-note himself, but in matters such as this he thinks with his heart. He'll march on Pretoria Prison personally unless I can give him some sort of assurance that Tom Majombi hasn't been abducted and is getting the best possible attention.'

'You mean he'll bring the matter up with the press, don't you?'

Hymie nodded. Van Breeden sighed. 'Okay, tell him I'll call Colonel Klaasens and drop a hint to him that we know there is a black person, a Zulu boxer by the name of ... Van Breeden looked down at the pad in front of him.

'Majombi, Tom Majombi,' Hymie said.

'Ja, okay, I have it here, Tom Majombi. This should be enough to keep him safe. I can almost personally guarantee it.'

'I am grateful to you, sir.' Hymie was genuinely appreciative of Van Breeden's help. He pushed his chair back ready to rise, conscious that Van Breeden had made time in his day for something so trivial it probably wouldn't normally even appear in the charge book of a district police station, but which nevertheless now involved the tedious business of the police investigating the police.

'Hymie, don't go for a moment.'

Hymie sat back in his chair again. 'Yes, sir?'

'I don't scare easily and I don't much like being threatened. In this country there are a million Tom Majombis and, depending on your viewpoint, each has a genuine grievance against the white man, the police, the system and the state. You would be well advised to stop tilting at windmills because, I'm telling you, you won't win!' Van Breeden smiled. 'I have a feeling that the law firm of Levy and Peekay is going to be a very big pain in the arse. Particularly the Peekay part. Will you do me a favour?'

'Well, that depends, sir.'

'Spoken like a true lawyer. But even good lawyers need friends and I'm beginning to feel you're going to need your share of contacts in the right places. Do you understand me, Hymie?'

'Well, it still depends, general.'

'Both you and that difficult little welterweight partner of yours seem destined not to make too many friends among the lower ranks of the police force or magistrates or even the higher echelons of the judiciary.' But Van Breeden smiled again. 'The two of you will make a lot of noise and get your names in the paper, but you won't change anything. Let me tell you something for nothing, man! In the end the black people will despise you and the Nationalists will ignore you. And if they can't ignore you they'll find a way to silence or eliminate you.' Van Breeden leaned forward over his desk, serious now. 'There are new laws being drafted right at this moment. One of them allows the government to retain anyone in custody for as long as it likes without trial. Another allows them to place a person under house arrest. He or she is confined to their own home and may not meet with more than three people at a time. It can happen to anyone for any reason at any time.'

'Sir, I'm a Jew. The last time that sort of law existed my people were damn near eliminated.'

'I want you to keep the line open between us, Hymie. I want to be able to pick up the phone and call you and have you do the same for me.' The policeman smiled. 'A special phone. Your office phone and your house phone will be tapped, that I can guarantee, not by my department, but by the Special Branch.'

Three weeks after Peekay first visited Majombi in hospital the Zulu boxer was found dead on the side of a lonely farm road midway between Johannesburg and Pretoria. The death of the black man had been reported to the Meadowlands police station who had sent out a police truck to pick up the body and remove it to the morgue. Tom Majombi was just another dead kaffir in a day that would usually produce four or five of the same.

A small crowd as usual gathered outside the township mortuary as the two Black Jacks pulled the corpse from the police van. A brown paper bag had been pulled over Tom Majombi's head and tied with a piece of string around his neck, so that faceless, he resembled a limp, dark, dusty scarecrow. A head bag was easier to use and cheaper than a body bag and served the same basic purpose, to avoid identification in the event that the dead man was someone of political importance whom the crowd might recognize.

Johnny Tambourine and Dog Poep Ismali pushed to the front of the crowd gathered around the police van.

Their families, along with the rest of the gang, had been forcibly moved from Sophiatown to Meadowlands and Moroka. Now the two boys stared at the body and Dog Poep Ismali jabbed Johnny Tambourine in the ribs. 'Hey look, it's Tom Majombi,' he announced in a loud whisper.

'How can you tell?' Johnny Tambourine whispered back.

'The tattoo, see the tattoo on his arm!'

Etched on the deep brown forearm of the young Zulu fighter in the familiar midnight blue of tattoo ink was the name Black Tornado, Tom Majombi's fighting name.

The news of the boxer's death was soon on the township streets and, as always, reached Madam Flame Flo by nightfall. She called Peekay and he went directly to the morgue. It was after five and the white man who was responsible for the morgue, a large Boer named Klopper, at first refused to admit him.

'It's after hours, man, tell him to come back tomorrow,' Klopper had told the black clerk who'd come to tell him a white man was making an enquiry. Occasionally a white would come to the mortuary looking for a black servant whom the family may have been fond of, but Klopper didn't like this. They were *kaffir boeties* and not to be encouraged. But then he'd glanced down at the card the black man had handed him and had seen Peekay's name. 'Here, man, why didn't you say so, this is the Welterweight Boxing Champion of the whole world!' He hurried out to meet Peekay.

Peekay identified Majombi's body. 'When does the doctor perform the autopsy, Meneer Klopper?' he asked.

'Ag, man, we don't worry too much.' Klopper waved his hands, indicating the fifteen or so bodies lying on the cement floor of the mortuary. 'When you seen one stab wound you seen them all. The doctor comes in for half an hour, maybe sometimes forty minutes, every day and writes out certificates for the coroner.'

'And if there isn't any stab wound?'

'Man, then it's only one of two things, a heart attack or the spoke.'

'Spoke?'

'Ja, man, a bicycle spoke is a major murder weapon. Come I'll show you.' He walked over to the body of a young male and turned him over onto his stomach. The man was naked and there appeared to be no marks on his body. Klopper went down on his haunches and pointed to a tiny red spot between the first and second vertebrae at the base of the neck. 'The victim is pushed forward and a sharpened bicycle spoke is pushed in. His spine is cut. He's dead in ten seconds, maybe less, and there's no mark, no noise. Here in Soweto, Advocate Peekay, the spokesman is the hired killer. A good spokesman is higher up than a gunman. He can kill a kaffir in a crowd and nobody will notice; they just think the man fell down or something.'

'Tom Majombi, how did he die?'

'Ag, man, I haven't looked. Tomorrow the doctor will say maybe.'

'Maybe is not sufficient, Meneer Klopper. I would like to bring my own doctor, two doctors.'

Klopper was visibly upset. 'We have a government doctor. We don't like other people sticking their nose in our business, Advocate.'

'Meneer Klopper I'd appreciate your cooperation in this matter. Tom Majombi was a boxer, I'm a boxer.

In the ring a boxer is just a boxer,' Peekay explained.

'But outside he's just a kaffir again,' Klopper added.

'Please, I don't want to bring a court order, it just makes more paperwork for you.'

Klopper scratched his chin. 'I don't know, man, it's highly irregular.'

'Perhaps they can come in, say, two hours before your pathologist comes, that way there is no confrontation?'

Klopper thought about this for a while. 'Okay, man, you must be here half past seven tomorrow morning.'

Peekay had challenged the coroner's finding in court. The government pathologist's report simply showed 'death by causes unknown'. However the evidence by the two independent specialists told a different story. Both indicated that the morgue examination was too superficial and, after the government pathologist had seen Majombi, they had caused the body to be moved to a private hospital where they'd performed an exhaustive autopsy.

Klopper hadn't mentioned the visit of the two private medical men prior to the government's pathologist's arrival, thinking not to upset him. Now the government found itself totally compromised as the evidence showed that Tom Majombi had died of a massive brain haemorrhage, the result of a middle-ear infection caused by a ruptured eardrum.

It was three weeks from the time Peekay had seen the boxer in hospital to the discovery of his body, and from the report it was also obvious that he hadn't been treated since his original hospital diagnosis.

Dr Dinkelman, the forensic surgeon who'd been present at the autopsy, was asked to explain in court at the preliminary hearing how massive brain damage,

594

sufficient to cause death, could occur as a result of middle-ear infection. The surgeon showed how repeated punching to the naked ear by a soft boxing glove would compress air inside the canal which, unable to escape outwards, would blow inwards into the eardrum which would eventually rupture. If the rupture wasn't attended to it would set up a middle-ear infection which would eventually lead to brain hae-morrhage and death.

It was this single point on which Peekay's potential right to have his case heard rested.

'This middle-ear infection, is it painful, Dr Dinkel-man?' he asked.

'Extremely, the man would be in a great deal of pain,' the doctor replied.

'So much pain that he would be likely to seek medical attention?'

'Almost undoubtedly.'

Peekay turned to Magistrate Coetzee. 'May I suggest, your honour, that the reason why Tom Majombi didn't seek medical attention at this stage was that he was incarcerated somewhere?'

The counsel for the government, a senior police pros-ecutor named Opperman, objected. 'This is conjecture, your honour; there is no evidence to say the deceased was incarcerated.'

Peekay sighed. 'Your honour, I am trying to establish the degree of pain suffered by the deceased. I will rephrase the question.' He turned to the doctor in the witness stand. 'Is it possible, doctor, that Mr Majombi would simply grin and bear his condition? A Zulu stoic, far braver than you or I?'

Dinkelman frowned. 'No, sir, even if he was able to stand the pain of an untreated middle-ear infection, what would follow the initial infection would be impossible for him to sustain in silence. The man would have been in the most dreadful agony.'

'Thank you, Dr Dinkelman. One or two more questions, please.'

'Is it one or two?' Opperman asked, laughing. 'In a South African court we like to be precise, Mr Peekay!' He was trying to take the mickey out of Peekay, pointing up his inexperience to the court.

Peekay brought his finger to his nose, rubbing the tip, but ignored Opperman's remark and continued. 'Apart from intense pain, what would be the outward signs of such a condition?'

'Night sweats at first, then a high fever and shivering; severe vomiting; finally delirium.'

'And you said that the infection eventually travels to the brain. How long would this process take?'

The coroner rubbed his chin. 'If the conditions in which the entire infection took place were unhygienic . . .'

'As in a prison cell?' Peekay said.

'Objection!' Opperman sighed.

'You were establishing the degree of pain, not the whereabouts of the deceased, Mr Peekay,' Magistrate Coetzee said. He was a big drowsy-looking man, recently transferred from Durban where he'd been Chief Magistrate to take the same position on the Rand. Peekay was quickly learning to respect him. 'Objection sustained,' the big man added in a tired voice.

'Please continue, doctor,' Peekay asked Dinkelman.

'Well, yes, where was I now . . .'

'You were talking about conditions, unhygienic conditions,' Peekay reminded him.

'Ja, okay, under unhygienic conditions we could

expect the prognosis to go from onset to termination in three weeks to a month.'

'The deceased appeared at the Baragwanath Outpatients a week after he claimed he'd first felt the pain. He was found dead nearly three weeks later. Does this fit with a typical prognosis, doctor?'

'If what you tell me is correct, then certainly,' Dinkelman answered.

Opperman laughed. He was enjoying himself. Not bothering to address himself through Magistrate Coetzee or even to rise, he pointed his pencil at Peekay: 'Mr Peekay, I must object. You are young and this is, I believe, your first case.' His tone was tinged with sarcasm. 'We are not in the habit of *planting* evidence, even if this clever technique is taught in England where, I believe, you received your legal training. *You* have alleged that the deceased turned up at the Baragwanath Outpatients. There is no evidence to prove this was ever so!'

Magistrate Coetzee looked up. 'Mr Peekay, are you trying to establish the time it took for the native boy to die, or is your point that someone deliberately interfered with his attempt to be treated in a hospital and that this interference was the direct cause of his death?'

'Your honour, my learned colleague may regard this case as one simply involving a dead black man. Or as Mr Klopper put it earlier in this preliminary hearing, "Listen, man, I can't be responsible for every dead kaffir now, can I?"' Peekay mimicked Klopper perfectly. 'Nevertheless, I intend to prove that Mr Majombi did register at the hospital and was diagnosed with an inner-ear complaint and that shortly thereafter he was forcibly removed by the Special Branch on the instructions of a senior police officer who I am prepared to name in this court.'

'That will not be necessary, Advocate,' Magistrate Coetzee said.

'I am asserting that people under the direction of this man caused the deceased to be taken in a police van to a place or places unknown, where he was unable to ask for, or was refused, treatment for his condition, and as a direct consequence died an agonizing and unnecessary death.'

Peekay paused, and appeared to be rubbing the point of his nose with the tip of his forefinger, a gesture for which he would become famous in the years to come. 'When the Red man touches his nose everybody watch out!' the Africans would say of him later, for they learned that the gesture always signalled an unexpected turn in events.

Now Peekay began again slowly. 'I admit I may be clumsy and lack the sagacity of my learned colleague, whom I note feels so much at ease in this court room that he considers himself free to confront me directly without addressing himself through the bench. However, must I conclude that where *he* was trained there is a distinction made between the sanctity of a black life and a white?'

Magistrate Coetzee sighed. 'We are not here to be lectured on the sanctity of life, Advocate. Will you kindly stick to the point.' Though the magistrate's expression didn't change, he liked the young lawyer who refused to be intimidated by Opperman, a notorious bully who took great delight in putting young counsel in their place. 'Would the counsel for the deceased now show the court any evidence he has to prove, or at least to strongly suggest beyond reasonable doubt, that the deceased, Tom Majombi, was a patient in Baragwanath Hospital,' the magistrate instructed.

Peekay turned to his law clerk, who was acting as his junior. The man handed him an envelope which Magistrate Coetzee instructed the clerk of the court to retrieve. 'Your honour, I submit a letter signed by myself on the day in question, in the presence of a doctor and nurse authorizing any extra medical attention Mr Majombi would require and for which I guaranteed payment.' He turned to his clerk again, who handed him a manila folder. 'The carbon copy, in other words, the hospital copy of the letter you have, is contained in this file which I now also submit to this court as further evidence. You will note that in this letter the patient's name and address appears and specific details are given of his prognosis and of the treatment required.'

Opperman jumped to his feet. It was obvious Peekay had caught him unawares. 'Counsel requests permission to study this document, your honour,' he said.

'Advocate Opperman, may I remind you that this is a preliminary hearing. The evidence will be assessed by me alone.' Opperman was suddenly aware that he'd underestimated his young adversary. This was the third and, most likely, the final day of the hearing and Opperman had relaxed, confident that if any evidence existed which would show that the kaffir boxer had been admitted to hospital the young, inexperienced lawyer would have revealed it long before now. On more than one occasion during the hearing he'd been neatly caught in a verbal trap of Peekay's making. In his mind he'd made light of this; without any real evidence, it would take more than a clever young tongue to outwit him. Now his expression showed real enmity towards the young advocate, a sure sign to Magistrate Coetzee that the ground had been taken from under his feet.

'I'd like to validate this document, your honour. As you know, it is relatively easy to reproduce material of this nature. What's in a receipt? A few hastily scribbled words, such a thing is easy to forge. Nobody knows this better than you, your honour!'

Magistrate Coetzee looked up over the top of his glasses at the government lawyer. 'Advocate Opperman, if I am such an expert on forgery, then I would also be in a position to know whether the document seems genuine. In which case, I take it you will be satisfied with the court's decision on this matter?'

Opperman sat down heavily. 'Certainly, your honour.'

Magistrate Coetzee had mixed feelings about the new evidence. He was now sufficiently convinced by Peekay's conduct during the hearing that some prima-facie evidence existed against the police for conspiracy and that there was also sufficient cause for charges to be laid against Geldenhuis and Klaasens for assault leading to the death of the young black boxer. On the other hand, cases against members of the police force usually ended up in a horrible shit fight and he hated the idea of ruling for the crown that the two senior policemen in the Special Branch of the South African police force had a case to answer.

Magistrate Coetzee knew nothing of the hate which Geldenhuis felt for Peekay, but he knew how difficult it would be for a young barrister's career if he earned the enmity of the police force at the outset. Peekay would almost certainly lose his case; but win or lose he could expect a rocky road ahead in his career.

The tired old magistrate hoped that it might be otherwise for the young lawyer; but he told himself that if he knew anything about men, Peekay wasn't going to give up easily. Momentarily he wished that he wasn't so old and cynical and that his gout didn't play up as much as it did. He would have liked to keep the hearing in the Magistrates Courts and preside over it himself. It would have given him the opportunity to match wits against the young advocate who carried a flaming sword and a fine mind into battle. He told himself he would also, in the process, have tried very hard to see that justice was done.

But Magistrate Coetzee had too much brandy under his belt and too many years on the bench to want to take on a trial which could last who knows how long? His transfer from Durban to Johannesburg was his last before he retired and he wanted his remaining few years to be as peaceful as possible. At his age he knew better than to be caught in the crossfire. He had fifty acres waiting for him in the Eastern Transvaal where his land formed part of a bend in the Crocodile River. There, small buck and guinea fowl and an occasional warthog came to drink at sunset and when you lay at night in bed you could hear the distant crash of the rapids as the water swept across the rocks in a bend in the river.

Magistrate Coetzee comforted himself that he could look forward with some anticipation to following the ensuing court case. He would take great pleasure in watching the way this upstart from Oxford would conduct it. On the other hand, the young advocate was about to make a lot of trouble for everyone, trouble which could be avoided if Magistrate Coetzee now ruled that insufficient evidence existed for the case to go on trial. The police would be happy and, in the long run, he'd be doing the young rooinek lawyer a real favour. Personally he wasn't under any illusions; a Bantu death, no matter how you looked at it, wasn't equal to a white one. Why then should he care? His duty in this matter was plain: he would serve Pretoria best by declaring that no proper evidence existed to justify a trial.

At the end of the third day's hearing, at two in the afternoon, immediately after the court had returned from luncheon recess, Magistrate Coetzee announced that, in the opinion of the court, a prima-facie case existed against the two members of the South African police force, Lieutenant J. Geldenhuis and Colonel N. J. P. Klaasens, together with persons unknown, for conspiring to abduct a patient from his hospital bed and, as a result, to cause him such grievous bodily harm as to lead to his death.

Peekay had won the right to go to trial.

For Jannie Geldenhuis the news was devastating. His defeat by Mandoma had left him severely depressed, to the point where he'd considered taking his own life. He knew he would never step into the ring with Peekay and to add to this, he would now have to appear for cross-examination before the man he hated the most in the world. He, Jannie Geldenhuis, a brilliant young lieutenant in the police force would have to stand in the dock, not as an officer of the law, but as someone whose reputation and career was on trial. And what for? For the death of a stinking black kaffir, a meat bag whom they'd tossed into a cell because he'd been stupid enough to talk to Peekay and Mandoma. What the fuck did the black bastard expect? They'd paid him good money to be a sparring partner. In his sick head, Geldenhuis told himself that Tom Majombi had been a plant. How else would Peekay have known about him? He had gone directly to Baragwanath the day Majombi had been admitted. It was too bloody neat. It was a conspiracy, a conspiracy to make sure that he never got a chance to fight Peekay. Majombi was a deliberate plant, he'd been feeding Mandoma information prior to the fight. The reason he'd lost was because Tom Majombi had told Gideon about his weaknesses. The rooinek and the Jew had framed him. Jesus! He and Klaasens had played right into Peekay's hands! By stupidly allowing the Zulu fighter to die in an isolated police cell, there was now no possibility of proving that such a conspiracy had existed. Geldenhuis felt sick at the stupidity he had shown.

The more Geldenhuis thought about it, the more convinced he became that *he* was the victim and not Tom Majombi. What did they care about another shit black fighter? It had to be a set-up! Otherwise why would Peekay agree to pay Majombi's hospital expenses? Since when do white guys go around paying the hospital fees for kaffirs they don't even know?

Geldenhuis shook his head, disgusted with himself. If only he'd realized sooner, he would have made the black bastard confess. He was suddenly angry again. It was fucking Klaasens! He'd assumed control of the abduction and in the process he'd totally fucked things up.

Geldenhuis told himself that had he been in charge he'd have thought it out. He'd have discovered the plot. Klaasens hadn't even talked to Majombi. Christ! That was fundamental police stuff, routine, the sort of information you fall over without even trying when you're conducting an interrogation. He would have kept Majombi alive to confess in court and then later quietly killed the black bastard.

Geldenhuis winced at the stupidity of the whole thing. The rooinek and the Jew had played him for a sucker. Now Peekay had him crucified. He, Jannie

Geldenhuis, was indicted on a fucking murder charge!

When the young policeman had fitted all the pieces together his physical reaction to his total dismay was a compulsion to throw up. The vomiting and retching continued for an hour until he was so weak he sank to his knees in front of the toilet with his head hanging into the bowl. Every time he threw up he swore to God that, come what may, he would spend the remainder of his life dedicated to the destruction of Peekay. The kaffir didn't matter; he'd get Mandoma anyway; but it was Peekay and the Jew – above all, Peekay. He wouldn't rest until he'd killed him, but before he did that he would humiliate him. He would find a way to discredit him in the eyes of everyone, to totally destroy him.

Finally someone found Geldenhuis unconscious, with his head resting in the toilet basin, his hair swimming in his own sick.

Magistrate Coetzee set a date for the trial to come before a judge six months ahead. Peekay immediately filed for a further three-month postponement so that he could defend his welterweight title against Gideon Mandoma. His request was rejected by the chief magistrate and Peekay faced the prospect of going into court three days after the first defence of his title.

Twenty-eight

Peekay's title defence proved to be as big an affair as the fight with Jake 'Spoonbill' Jackson, though this time the home crowd was torn between the Tadpole Angel and the charismatic young chief, Gideon Mandoma.

Gideon had meanwhile fought Togger Brown in Orlando Stadium for the British Empire title. Peekay and Solly Goldman were in Togger's corner; Dutch Holland, who'd moved over to train Gideon after Peekay's world title fight, handled the black boxer with Mr Nguni. Mandoma's aggressive punching, especially with the left hand, proved too strong for the mercurial Togger; Gideon defeated him fairly convincingly by knocking him out in the thirteenth round of the scheduled fifteen-round fight.

Dutch Holland now owned fifteen per cent of Gideon which, if Gideon made it to the world title, would prove to be a nice little earner for him. Peekay had persuaded Gideon to allow Hymie to draw up his new contract; when all was said and done, Hymie had managed by a combination of implied threats and cajoling to get Mr Nguni to agree to a maximum of twenty per cent for himself with all out-of-pocket expenses exceeding twenty per cent of the gate coming from his cut.

At the outset Mr Nguni had opposed the new arrangement although, properly handled, it was a decent enough cut. Peekay was hugely surprised when he discovered that Gideon's manager had previously owned seventy-five per cent of the black boxer.

Peekay confronted Gideon when he'd heard of Mr Nguni's cut. 'Gideon, how did you get this insane contract? You're not stupid.'

Gideon laughed. 'It was a long time ago. I was sixteen years old and hungry. Nguni, he told me to touch the pencil and he would feed and clothe me and put money in my pocket. It is the same with all his fighters and soccer players also.' He looked at Peekay. 'Nguni is a chief, but he is also *namandla* and he has many, many cattle. He is very powerful; these boys they come from his *isigodi*, they must do what he says.'

'And you?'

Gideon drew back, puffing up. 'No, Bra! I am same like him, I am chief, I am not from his *isigodi*. That paper, it was because I was hungry and still *umfana*, but I am not a boy now, now it will be okay, you will see.'

Hymie asked Peekay not to make a fuss about the other black sportsmen until they'd sorted out Gideon's contract with Mr Nguni. He patiently persuaded the black boxing manager that, should Gideon become world champion, Mr Nguni stood to be infinitely better off. Furthermore, Gideon could well defend his title as many as a dozen times. The profit opportunity represented was a hundred times greater than seventy-five per cent of a good undercard fighter.

Hymie felt a little foolish explaining all this to the huge black man. Mr Nguni was a shrewd and resourceful businessman and Hymie told himself he would have seen the advantages immediately. Why was he making him spell things out so laboriously in front of Peekay and Gideon? What was Nguni up to? Mr Nguni seemed reluctant at first to agree. What he seemed to be baulking at was the principle that his fighter would receive the bigger share of the prize money. It was essentially a matter of face.

Peekay was aware that it wasn't the money but the percentages which concerned Mr Nguni. They made Gideon of greater importance than himself in the partnership. Peekay pointed out to Mr Nguni that Gideon was a chief in his own right, that the contract in the tribal sense was between two equals and that therefore a precedent existed for the uneven split.

Although nothing had been said, Peekay was certain Mr Nguni would be aware he was prepared to hold up the contract for the title fight indefinitely unless he agreed to Hymie's proposed contract. Nevertheless, he was surprised when Mr Nguni seemed suddenly to capitulate and accept his argument of the equality of two chiefs and also, without equivocation, all the clauses that Hymie had drawn up to protect Gideon's principle sum.

Nr Nguni was no fool. He knew Peekay held the better hand. His only concern was not to lose face in front of Gideon. Zulus talk and if it got out that Gideon's *isigodi* had got the better of his, he would be shamed. This he prevented by making Hymie spell out the deal in Gideon's presence and also by forcing Peekay to use the precedent of the two equal chiefs. The huge Zulu was an ambitious man with long-term plans for himself, most of which relied heavily on the possibility of Gideon becoming the world champ. Hymie was right, he'd end up making more money anyway, even though he controlled a smaller share of Gideon. But, for the time being anyway, money alone wasn't at the root of his ambition.

To be the manager of a world champion was a position Mr Nguni wanted more than anything. It would put him on a par with the black American fight promoters, which in the eyes of South Africa's black people, would earn him enormous kudos. But it would do something else as well. Mr Nguni's secret political ambitions had very little to do with the ANC's struggle for freedom, which he basically saw as a waste of time. He wanted to be seen as a black man among important white people in the capitals of the world. This would do a great deal for his future status in the white political arena.

Mr Nguni was a hard-eyed realist. Come the black revolution, he was confident that he could buy the political leverage he needed. Revolutions always need money and when the time came he would trade it for power, which in turn would earn him more money. It was all very simple. Keep your nose clean and don't confront either side, the ANC or the white government. But what about the other consideration? What if the revolution didn't come? What if the *amaBhunu*, the Boers, won the fight again, as seemed more than likely? Already they were talking in Pretoria of creating separate bantustans, separate independent countries for the various black tribes. The Zulu tribe was three million strong, nearly one quarter of the total black population. When the time came for the independent state of the Zulu people, they would need a president. This president would have to be carefully chosen. He would need to be a chief in his own right, a man of impeccable credentials who outwardly seemed to be his own man, acceptable to his own people, both the migrants from the townships and the peasants on the land. It would also help if he appeared independently wealthy, a man of the world who believed in the capitalist system and was respected by the white political leaders of other countries. But, above all, he would need to be someone the white government in Pretoria could trust. President Nguni had a nice ring to it.

In the meantime Mr Nguni appeared to eschew politics. The ever-smiling black promoter appeared essentially as a sporting man who, through the promotion of boxing and soccer, was beginning to be favourably noticed by the Pretoria government. In fact, a dossier already existed on him in Pretoria.

> *Zulu Nguni – Mathew. Born: Masinga,*
> *Zululand, 1920. Tribal Chief (Minor)*
> *Pass No: ZU 00 73152 T/N.*
> *Occupation: Sports Promoter – Boxing,*
> *Soccer. Also manager, Zulu Mandoma –*
> *Gideon, South African Welterweight*
> *Champion, British Empire Champion*
> *(ANC Youth League.*) Social history: No*
> *personal political history. Good race*
> *relations, White/Black. Youth development*
> *programme. Property: Independent means.*
> *Property, 3 houses, Moroka, Meadowlands,*
> *Masinga (Z'land). Cattle owner. State*
> *Police Clearance. Category AAA.*
> **See Zulu Mandoma G.-ANC Transvaal.*
> *Ref. Youth League – Political File.*

Included with these cryptic notes were several transcripts from speeches, mostly of a sporting nature. The most notable was a transcript taken from a remark in parliament by the Minister for Sport:

> *That Nguni, he's a proper sportsman. I'm telling you, he's a good black man, the sort of native you can talk to if you want something done in the townships. Not a political type, but he's a natural leader, a chief in his own right. If we had more like him things would go better with the native people all round.*

Among the black people, even most of the township people, Peekay's first title defence became a deadly trial to see whether Mandoma would beat Peekay and so lay claim to being the *Onoshobishobi Ingelosi*, the Tadpole Angel. For them the fight had a mystical importance well beyond boxing and it became the major topic of conversation in the weeks and the months leading up to the fight. The trial against Geldenhuis and the police colonel Klaasens had convinced many of the blacks that Peekay was their leader. No person had ever taken a Special Branch policeman to court on behalf of a black man, not even an important black man. The very fact that Tom Majombi had been a nobody was proof that the *Onoshobishobi Ingelosi* was there to protect and to fight for them. A great many of the fans came to the fight wanting Peekay to win.

When Peekay entered the ring, the Chant to the Tadpole Angel thundered around the old Jabulani stadium where the fight was held; and now even a great many of the white supporters joined in. They had learned the lyrics on Springbok radio where, after Peekay had won the world championship, it had risen to number one on the hit parade. It was a magical moment which brought Peekay close to tears. He stood together with Mandoma in the centre of the ring as the Chant came to an end and Gideon suddenly moved and lifted Peekay's hand and held it aloft.

This was a different kind of fight. Even those who had come to see the white man smash the kaffir or the other way around, now realized that what they were going to see were two boxers with enormous pride who wouldn't give an inch, a white man and a black one who respected each other, who openly referred to each other as brothers, so that in some parts of the Afrikaner press both were actively despised.

Both had motive enough to win. Peekay wanted to retire the undefeated champion of the world and Gideon Mandoma, the herd boy from the hills and mountain peaks of Zululand, who had used his fists to get to the pinnacle, wanted to fight a man who, after beating Jackson, had been described by *Ring* magazine as the greatest boxer pound-for-pound in the world. If Gideon became the world champion he would be the first black boxer out of Africa ever to have done so.

The referee, a New Yorker who had officiated at two Joe Louis title fights, called the two boxers together and went through the usual ho-hum. The bell went and Peekay and Mandoma forgot that they'd ever been friends as they moved towards each other.

Mandoma was a natural fighter who came forward all the time. It had served him well against Geldenhuis, because he too fought off the front foot, but against Peekay it wasn't such a good idea. A straight-line fighter is easier to hit, he doesn't bob and weave and move about. Peekay's speed was such that he could nail Gideon more often. In the first round Peekay moved off the back foot as usual but he was making Gideon miss and nailing him in reply, though because he was moving back his punches lacked real steam. However, in terms of points he won the round quite easily.

In the second round Mandoma's timing was still out. He was trying too hard, trying for a big punch, and Peekay was too elusive and too fast. Peekay was beginning to put his punches together, working the familiar pattern to Mandoma's body. Mandoma hit Peekay several times with a good straight left and a right upper-cut coming off the ropes, the best punch of the fight so far. Peekay grinned, a sure sign that he'd been hurt. Mandoma came after him and received a beautiful straight left on the nose, making it bleed. The second round, despite the harder punching by Gideon, was also clearly Peekay's.

The third and the fourth round were the same. Gideon seemed to be no match for the hugely skilled world champion. Peekay was boxing beautifully, his feet a miracle of economy, lovely to watch. Mandoma, who was also a very fast boxer, was being made to look slow. The fight was going perfectly to plan and Hymie and Solly were delighted.

When Gideon came in after the fifth, a round which Dutch thought he'd probably shared with Peekay, the English trainer spoke to him. 'You're doing all right, son, but Peekay can dance all night. You've got to slow him down, get him on the ropes, clinch him, hold him as long as you can and, when you come off the rope, try to hit him first. He nails you going away. Go for him fast, a left-right as you come off the ropes. You have the shoulders, push him away; don't let him get away, you make the break for him then hit him on the break.'

612

In the sixth round the tactic worked well. Gideon would tie Peekay up as often as he could and move him onto the ropes. Twice he hit him with a glorious left-right combination as he pushed him away; once he thought he had Peekay going, but the bell saved the white fighter. The sixth round was Gideon's.

The tactic was working well for Gideon although he had to take a few torrid punches to get close enough to Peekay to tie him up. But once he had him on the ropes he was the stronger of the two fighters and he was doing a lot of damage close up, his short inside punches carrying more power than Peekay's. The seventh round was Gideon's too, and the crowd began to sense that the fight had evened up.

But the tactic couldn't last too long with a fighter as intelligent as Peekay and by the eighth round Peekay was starting to move forward, hitting Mandoma fast and clearing out, avoiding the clinch. Late in the round Mandoma walked into a left-right combination that put him on the canvas. Peekay would have stayed for the eight count, but Gideon was on his feet immediately, too proud to take the rest. It was a mistake. Almost immediately Peekay hit him with a long raking right, pushing him against the ropes; he wasn't quite quick enough from the recent knock-down to recover and Peekay planted three beautiful punches under his heart. Gideon went down again, this time taking the full eight count before he stood up. The bell went as the two boxers moved towards each other.

The ninth round showed the superb boxer Mandoma was. He came out on the attack and hit Peekay with a beautiful right cross, slamming into the side of the jaw. Peekay crashed to the canvas. At four Peekay hadn't moved and by seven he had only just managed to get to his knees. Peekay could only barely hear the referee counting and he felt himself slipping down the silver tunnel. At nine he was on his legs but plainly shaky. The ref examined him and allowed the fight to continue. Mandoma came in fast for the kill and Peekay managed to tie him up. But not for long; as the ref called for them to break, Mandoma pushed him away and hit him to the head with a good left-right combination. Peekay went down again. He was up at nine, but he knew he couldn't take very much more. *Dance klein baas, dance; when you dance they don't think you hurt.* It was Geel Piet's voice coming to him as a child.

Peekay didn't know where it came from. His legs felt like lead but he was on his toes, allowing his legs to do the thinking, years of training making them work instinctively. Gideon was trying too hard, trying to finish the fight. With twenty seconds to go he drew back on his right a little too far to follow a good left jab and Peekay, seeing the opening, hit him with a perfect right hand, smashing into his chin. Mandoma hit the floor so hard he actually bounced. He was up at nine and hung on grimly for the remaining few seconds before the bell went. Both fighters were exhausted. They'd fought each other to a standstill. Both sat in their corners knowing that they'd spent it all, that there were no more tricks. From now it was heart; there was nothing else to give.

Some people claimed that both fights against Jack 'Spoonbill' Jackson were Peekay's greatest, but there were others who were adamant that the last five rounds of the Mandoma versus Peekay title was the all-time great.

It proved to be one of the toughest fights ever witnessed in South Africa. Both men were exhausted, but they came out for the tenth. They started to fight toe to toe, too tired to move about the ring. Both went down during the round and got up and fought again. The fight had evened up, with perhaps Peekay just ahead on points.

There were those in the audience who'd seen Peekay's comeback against Jackson and who said to themselves that Mandoma couldn't withstand the courage of the white boxer, that he'd go before Peekay. But they reached round fourteen and Mandoma had been down seven times and Peekay six. They were still standing in the centre of the ring trading punches.

The crowd was hysterical. Something had to give. Each time one of the boxers went down there was a huge sigh, as though the crowd was sure it was the end; then there was a roar as the fighter got to his feet. Peekay had broken Mandoma's nose and closed one of his eyes, though Dutch had kept it working well enough for him to keep fifty per cent of his sight. Solly was not as skilled, and Peekay's right eye was completely closed.

Early in round fourteen Peekay put Mandoma down again with a left and felt a sharp pain in his hand. Mandoma got to his feet and Peekay tried to put another good one home but his left hand was hurting like hell every time he used it. Mandoma was gone, he was simply hanging on. Peekay was forced to lead with the right and Mandoma managed to survive, to keep his opponent's gloves away from his heart, for he knew that one more good punch under the heart and he was history. Peekay as usual had judged the fight to perfection; he was going to take him out in the final round. Towards the end of the fourteenth, Peekay landed another hard left and gasped as the pain shot up through his arm into his shoulder. His arm fell to his side and Mandoma hit him with a right just as the bell went.

Peekay was too exhausted to speak as Solly and Hymie worked on him. 'You just have to get through the round, you're ahead on points, just keep him off this last round, Peekay,' Hymie said, working on his shoulders.

'That's the ticket, my son, you don't have to put him down, just stay away,' Solly echoed.

'It's Jackson all over again,' Peekay gasped at last. 'I've broken my hand again.'

'Oh, Jesus, no!' Hymie gasped. 'Are you sure?'

'You've got the skill, just run, run from him,' Solly cried.

'I haven't got the legs, Solly.'

Peekay came out as a southpaw. It wasn't a surprise to Mandoma, they'd worked it too often sparring, but Gideon wondered why. He was so exhausted that it was all he could do to try to find the punch he'd need to take Peekay out. Time was running out. Halfway through the final round, Peekay put Mandoma down again with a good right hand, but there wasn't enough power in it to keep him on the floor. The Zulu had Peekay in the corner leaning on him when he heard Dutch shout, 'His hand, his left hand is broke!' Gideon came out of the clinch, moving back to the centre of the ring. Peekay's hand was broken; he couldn't hit him with a left. Peekay's left was the only hand that could put him down; he was safe. All he had to do was find the last punch. Peekay moved up to him and Gideon went onto the back foot, allowing Peekay to push him onto the ropes.

With thirty seconds to go in the fight, Peekay had Gideon on the ropes. He just had to hang on. The referee called for them to break and Peekay hung on. 'Break!' he heard the referee shout. He hung on a little longer. 'Break!' the command came again. The seconds were ticking by. Peekay stepped back but managed to drive a right under the black man's heart, then moved away. The black man's right upper-cut came from nowhere. Peekay didn't even see it coming. It connected flush to the champion's jaw and Peekay dropped like a stone to the canvas.

Gideon Mandoma moved two tottering steps to a neutral corner, barely able to stand. The final right hand from Peekay to the heart was catching up with him and he was blacking out in flashes. He held desperately onto the ropes, supporting himself, trying to stop his knees from collapsing under him. At the count of ten and as the crowd went wild Gideon tried to raise his glove, but releasing the rope was all it needed and his knees collapsed from under him. He pitched forward, face first onto the canvas. Both men lay unconscious but it was Gideon Mandoma who was the new Welterweight Champion of the World.

Still today there are white people and black who were present at the fight who argue that Peekay threw the fight, that he wanted Gideon Mandoma to be the next Welterweight Champion of the World. But it wasn't true. The young Zulu chief had just one more punch left in him and Peekay simply hadn't seen it coming.

The result of the fight should have settled the matter of leadership. Gideon was now champion of the world and the mantle of *Onoshobishobi Ingelosi*, the mystical leader of the black people, was expected to fall on him. It was what Mr Nguni wanted and had been careful to spread around before the fight. Initially it seemed that the people had accepted the new leader.

White South Africans love to think of Africans as predictable and simple-minded, though nothing could be further from the truth. The mantle which mystically befell the white boy as a leader of great importance was not lightly given away. A convocation of five of the country's most powerful witchdoctors, one each from all the major tribes, met in Moroka township to discuss the matter. These *abaNgoma* were not only men of the dead spirits, they were also astute elders of their tribes, and it did not escape them that Gideon Mandoma was a Zulu, the tribe which had successfully conquered all the other tribes excepting the Xhosa.

In the matter of tribes it was always the Zulus who differed in opinion or who thrust their point of view to the front. The fact that a white boy had been chosen to lead was so remarkable as to be beyond their doing and even beyond their magic, for none of them would have willingly brought such a thing about. On the other hand, assuming that the leadership was now taken from the white and returned to the black, this was not a decision to be made in haste. Many pots of beer would need to be consumed and much looking into the entrails of freshly slaughtered animals and throwing of bones and reading of the smoke and re-telling and examining of the ancient prophecies and legends must take place first.

The elders met during the day on a soccer field. It was more a patch of bare earth with two rickety posts at either end, but it was large enough for the people to come and sit as the old men discussed the way of this thing between the white *Onoshobishobi Ingelosi* and the young Zulu chief, Mandoma.

Finally, after many days they signalled that they were ready to give the verdict. A feast was prepared for that night and Mr Nguni supplied three oxen to be roasted.

Thirty male members of each of the tribes were invited to be present at the feast, to carry the decision back to the people. The feast again took place on the dusty soccer field under the stars, although the soft coal the people burn in the townships creates a haze that blots out the sky and cancels the stars nightly. The five old men sat on *indaba* mats covered with jackal-skin karosses around a fire built in the centre of the field. In a semicircle around them sat the tribal representatives and behind the old men, roasting on three great wooden spits over beds of glowing coals, were the three oxen. The smell of the slowly roasting meat filled the night air.

One by one the old men rose to speak. They spoke of the beginning of the mystery; of how a small white boy had brought comfort to the prisoners in the country's most notorious prison, how he had made tobacco appear where there had been no tobacco before and how the words of the prisoners had flown through him to their kraals to bring comfort to their women and children; how on one great night he had brought all the tribes together and blended them by taking their tribal songs and making one great song of the people; and then he had made the stars fall from the sky. Finally they told of how he had fought the *amaBhunu*, the Boers in the ring, and had never lost to them. Not once. Now he was fighting for the black man, Tom Majombi, who was dead, but the white one was fighting the Boers for his shadow so that he might rest peacefully with his ancestors' spirits. Is this not the sign of a great mystical leader of great courage? He who will fight to restore the spirit of a dead man to him? These were surely the signs of greatness which cannot be lightly exorcised from the *Onoshobishobi Ingelosi*.

Mr Nguni, fortified with half a bottle of brandy, stood up and asked to speak. He was taking a tremendous chance, but his generous gift of the oxen and a constant supply of kaffir beer all week made him feel entitled to talk and gave him the confidence to do so. 'Was it not spoken once that the conquest by Mandoma of the *Onoshobishobi Ingelosi* was to be the principal sign that the power had passed over? Was it not true that the first time when the sangoma declared they must fight to see if the white one still has the power, they did so in Sophiatown and the *Onobshobishobi Ingelosi* defeated Mandoma in front of the people and so the greatness was still in him? Now again, they have fought and this time it is Mandoma who has won. This he has done again in front of the people. Does this not mean that the shadows and the spirits have spoken differently this time?' Mr Nguni sat down, satisfied he'd said enough, noting from the nods and 'hayas' emanating from the audience that most of them agreed with him.

There was a long silence from the old men until at last the great Swazi medicine man and high witchdoctor Somojo, who took his name from a witchdoctor who belonged to the great legend which began across the Zambesi when time was pale grey and not yet black with the age of things, spoke. Among the assembled doctors he was the most powerful. His peppercorn skull was white and the whites of his eyes were tobacco brown, bloodshot at the edges and watered with age. 'Was it not true that the fight was even, as of two well-matched warriors?' he asked.

'Haya! It is true,' the crowd answered.

'Was it not true that towards the end the *Onoshoh-ishobi Ingelosi* was beginning to win?'

'It is as you say!'

'Was it not true that the Zulu Mandoma unleashed a mighty blow which brought his opponent crashing to the ground where he lay *ukungezwa*, unable to get up?'

'Yes! Everything you say, great one, it is so, he was unconscious!'

'Was it not true that when the *Onoshobishobi Ingelosi* lay, a count of ten was made?' The old witchdoctor crouched suddenly, his long neck pushed forward like an ancient tortoise as he turned slowly to look at them all, his shrill voice counting to ten on his fingers. Then, shooting both hands above his head, his fingers splayed, he cried, 'Suddenly at the count of ten the Zulu Mandoma was struck by a blow unseen and fell to the ground and lay *ukungezma* beside the *Onoshobishobi Ingelosi*?'

'Oh, oh, oh!' the crowd moaned their amazement. 'He was struck and he fell forward. It is as you say!'

The old man looked around him, his rheumy eyes taking them all in and finally coming to rest on Mr Nguni. 'I ask you this then. Who was he that struck the last blow?'

A gasp of astonishment passed over the crowd. The shadows which guarded over the Onoshobishobi Ingelosi were so powerful that they could strike his opponent to the ground even when he himself was unconscious.

'The *Onoshobishobi Ingelosi*, he struck the last blow!' the crowd shouted. 'He is still *the one*!'

'It's the rule that at the count of ten the fight is over, he who is standing is the winner!' Mr Nguni shouted angrily, emboldened by the brandy.

There was a shocked silence as the crowd turned to look at him. Nguni towered over the diminutive witchdoctor. He was also a man of power who had many cattle and was said to have great wealth; he was also a chief, but to speak to the great Somojo in such a manner was inviting disaster.

'This rule? It is a white man's rule,' the old man spat.

Mr Nguni knew immediately that he was trapped. He had swallowed the gourd of quick anger and now was being made to vomit its contents up again. 'Yes, it is a white man's rule,' he said ruefully.

The old man stabbed his finger accusingly at Mr Nguni. 'Ho! In this black man's heart there rests a white man's rules?'

There was silence from the crowd as the old man waited for Mr Nguni to speak. Finally the huge Zulu looked up. 'It is not a rule in my heart,' he said slowly.

The old man raised his fly switch, his voice a shrill warning, 'Who wishes to challenge "the power" of the *Onoshobishobi Ingelosi*? Who would have us pass "the power" on to the Zulu chief, Mandoma?' The old man glared at the crowd, waiting to see if anyone would respond.

'We have read this in the smoke and in the throwing of the bones. It is also in the entrails as it was told in the great legends.' He looked at Mr Nguni. 'He who would change this will be struck dead by the same unseen hand that struck Zulu Mandoma at the counting of ten.' He directed a toothless grin at Mr Nguni. 'That is the black man's rule!'

'Haya! Haya!' the crowd exclaimed, shaking their heads in fear and wonderment.

The old man was a high witchdoctor, the highest of the high, who had taken the leopardskin and the jackal kaross of the greatest of them all, the ancient and venerable Inkosi-Inkosikazi. But more than this; on his deathbed the great medicine man had passed the gold

622

coin of ancestry to Somojo the Swazi. The title of high witchdoctor is not a capricious decision, it comes to him who is the most worthy and it is decided by the ancient coin of gold about his neck.

Somojo began slowly walking up and down in front of the *indaba* mats and glaring at the assembled men. 'There is more to this matter than the business of the fight, which is merely an affair between young men of equal valour.' The old man's arthritic, simian claw reached into the leopardskin cloak and withdrew a leather bag which hung about his neck. His hands trembled as he withdrew a small gold coin not much larger than a blazer button. He displayed the ancient, slightly misshapen coin in his open palm. With an excited murmur the crowd surged forward, compulsively drawn to the tiny gold object. The old man's fingers snapped over the coin and the crowd drew back as though rebuked. 'This is the coin of the *strange ones* from that time; this is the magic coin of the high witchdoctor which speaks only the truth for those who hold its power in their hands. About this coin there is a legend that dips its ancient hands deep into the cornbasket of time, each grain of corn a year, until two thousand grains have run through the dark fingers of time.

'At this time there came to the land of the Zambesi huge canoes with oars that stuck from their bellies like the skeletons of a great fish and from the centre of these grew large poles, higher than the centrepole of the king's great *indaba* hut, and from the poles hung great white karosses to catch the wind. From the belly of the great canoe a hundred times the size of even the biggest war canoe came the *strange ones*. Their skin was pink and their eyes were the colour of the sky and their hair

623

was long and fell to their shoulders, some as pale as flax and others like the gold of ripe corn and yet others with hair as red as the deeper glow of breath on embers. Some wore beards while others were smooth faced, but on their arms and legs grew the same fine thick hair which shone in the sun.

'Upon their heads they wore close-fitting helmets of metal of a kind unseen before, the tops of which were shaped like the beak of the hornbill, pointing both front and back, with plumes of hair and sometimes feathers. Over their torsos they wore scales of metal rings extending to a metal flap which hung like a small apron over their private parts and which jingled as they walked so that it was always known when they were coming. Under this flap of metal their hips were girded with a skirt of cloth or soft leather and on their feet they wore leggings to their knees, these extending down to form sandals of strong, thick leather. Strapped from a broad leather belt which further protected their intestines hung a sword of a metal never seen before, harder and sharper and stronger than any stone or copper, and sharper than shaved hippo bone or flinted rock. About their wrists they wore bracelets of tooled leather studded with shining metal studs to ward off the blows of knopkieries and each carried a mighty axe of the same metal as the sword, shaped like a slice of a melon with the shaft set into two metal shafts set into the concave side of the axe. The blade of this great head-chopping instrument was sharper than a young lion's teeth.

'These strange pink creatures came with their women and children and they subdued the black tribes and took slaves and some left in their ships and returned again and again, each time taking slaves and bringing others of their kind back with them when they returned, until they made a great empire. With the black people as their slaves they dug deep into the earth for copper and iron,' the old witchdoctor opened his hand to show the coin, 'and the precious yellow metal which they prized above all else.'

A low moan escaped from the crowd, like the dry crackle of a man's dying breath. They all knew of the white man's greed for gold and the tyranny the precious metal had brought them all.

Somojo the high witchdoctor stopped pacing and hopped from one leg to another as though the ground beneath his feet was hot and he could only bear to stand for so long on one spot. 'The empire of the *strange ones* who came and lived as rulers became known as the *Ma-iti* though it was commonly known that they called themselves the "Children of the Star". They claimed to have descended from a star that fell to earth and took a young woman of the *strange ones*, mated with her and had many sons of a great fierceness who spread across the earth. The shining blueness of their eyes was the light of the stars burning through a daylight sky and it was this which gave them power over all the dark-eyed people of the world.'

A man drew closer to the fire carrying fresh logs and a bundle of branch twigs. He moved forward stooped as though trying not to intrude into the ambient circle of witchdoctors. He hurriedly placed fresh logs onto the embers and then threw the armful of branch twigs atop the fire, brought from who knows where, because there are no trees in Moroka township. The fire snapped and crackled as the twigs flared in short fierce blazes of yellow flame, snatching at the smallest twigs at the tributaries of each branch then, as suddenly, dying away, a twist of white smoke where a moment before the flame had been. Beneath the brief pyrotechnics of dry branch and twig the embers licked slow tongues of flame over the surfaces of the new logs, slowly wrapping them into themselves, turning the mute wood into heat and flame and life.

'Like all things based on murder, oppression and theft the empire of the *strange ones* fell into corruption. Their great empire was drifting on the canoe of time towards the rapids of oblivion when a slave was born among the *strange ones*. His eyes were of the bluest hue, like the clean, high winter sky, but his hair was dark and his skin the colour of tanned leather. He was the son of a black slave woman and a male from the *strange ones*, though he too was a slave, for such was the corruption and decay of the empire that they had made slaves of some of their own people who in the past had questioned their wrong ways. This child, born of the black and the white, was named Lumukanda and it was he who when he was still young rose up and brought the miserable remnants of the people together and destroyed the two empires of the *strange ones*. A child of the star led the desperate starveling tribes against the *strange ones* and be conquered them and utterly destroyed them. Then he set fire to their great cities and wiped out the marks of where they had been, like a man's foot wipes out the mark of an overnight fire in the dust of the new morning.'

The crackle of fire, as the new wood caught and grew the flames, was the only sound to be heard as the people listened to the words of Somojo the great witchdoctor. The flickering light from the fire lit his wizened monkey face as he brought the great tale to a close. 'Then Lumukanda the *strange one* gathered all the remnants of all the tribes and moved the people from the Zambesi, south to the river of the Limpopoma; and when he reached this and came to a deep gorge which led to a place to cross he called the tribes to himself. Behind him rose a great cliff and he stood with his back to the cliff and he pointed to the land across the river. "Go into these lands where the grass is sweet and make it your own; multiply and live in peace," he commanded.

'Then the witchdoctor Somojo came to him. "Great one, will you not come with us?" he asked. Lumukanda turned and pointed to the great cliff where a small waterfall fell to its side. "High on this cliff to the right of that waterfall there is a cave. I shall climb to its entrance and dwell there with the great Snake God where my spirit will remain to watch over you. If the *strange ones* should return with their blue eyes and their hair the colour of ripe corn and they would take you into slavery, I will come down from the cave and return to all the tribes and I will deliver you from their bondage and the tyranny of their greed." Then Lumukanda placed a gold coin into the hand of Somojo. "This is the coin of your ancestry and the sign that I, the child of the star, will come when I am needed," he said.'

The high witchdoctor paused, waiting for the weight of the words of the great legend to be felt upon the bent backs of the hushed crowd seated around the witchdoctors on the soccer ground. Then slowly he pointed to the night sky and in a shrill, high voice asked, 'Did not the stars fall from the heavens when the *Onoshobishobi Ingelosi* brought the tribes together for the singing of the great song of Africa?'

There was a gasp from the crowd as they finally comprehended what the old man was saying. Many of the men grabbed handfuls of dust and wiped it on their foreheads; others rocked on their haunches at the awesomeness of the prophecy. Somojo the great Swazi witchdoctor folded his spindly legs down slowly to sit on the jackal-skin kaross under a sky where the heavens were shrouded by the smoke of the township fires and the night smelt of roasting meat and the slightly sour odour of fermenting kaffir beer.

Mr Nguni didn't remain behind for the feast, he was fiercely disappointed at the outcome. 'The fly-blown old fart in his tattered leopardskin cloak has ruined everything!' he thought bitterly. His immediate plans were in disarray; had Gideon been given 'the power' then he, Nguni, the one who controlled him, would have seen his own power and prestige spread throughout the land.

But Mr Nguni knew better than to try to change things or, from this point on, ever to openly oppose Peekay. By morning the whole country would know of the decision to retain the white *Onoshobishobi Ingelosi* and there would be no way he could confound it. His mouth was dry with the coppery taste of defeat on his tongue. Somojo the great witchdoctor, the old Swazi pimp, had openly rebuked him and made him eat the meal of humiliation in front of all the tribes.

But Mr Nguni was also an African. In his head he might well reject the old man's silly warnings, but he felt the expensive brandy in his stomach turn sour and in his heart he trembled mightily. He would have to step on the surface of this problem with great care, or he would sink into oblivion.

Twenty-nine

On 7 March 1960, almost exactly three years after Magistrate Coetzee had concluded that Peekay had a prima-facie case against Colonel Klaasens and Lieutenant Geldenhuis for the abduction and murder of Tom Majombi, the last of three verdicts was handed down by Mr Justice Petzer of the Court of Criminal Appeal.

In an editorial the day following the court decision, the *Cape Argus* summed up the general feeling amongst the black people and also the fair-minded element of the white South African public by writing:

> *Over a period of three years we have witnessed two police officers, Lieutenant Geldenhuis and Colonel Klaasens, receive a trial by jury which resulted in a murder conviction. Since this original sentence we have seen two further trials, in which no jury sat, where murder has been reversed to manslaughter and finally manslaughter to a misdemeanour which has been further trivialized by a fine of ten pounds. Justice*

is not only blind in South Africa, it has
also become totally deaf; finally, it is senile.

Two days after Judge Petzer's decision Geldenhuis was returned to duty, and just twenty-four hours after returning to his post at Special Branch in Pretoria he was transferred to the police district of Vereeniging, some thirty-five miles from Johannesburg.

The period over which the Majombi trial was conducted had not proved a happy one for Geldenhuis. He'd been placed on clerical duties away from the real action of the Special Branch and his promising career had suffered accordingly. His only consolation had been that he had access to the Red File which concerned itself with the movement of the principals of Levy & Peekay. His transfer to Vereeniging was, in effect, a censure for the young policeman who, despite his acquittal, had become too hot to handle and needed a period in the comparative wilderness to cool down.

Though nothing was ever said, his defeat by Mandoma had also affected the way his senior officers regarded him. From a potential world champion he'd become just another boxer, and one who'd made a series of unfortunate headlines over a protracted murder trial. In addition he'd suffered a second defeat, this time at the hands of Togger Brown, when he again boxed as the undercard to the world title fight between Peekay and Mandoma. In all, he'd caused too much embarrassment even for a police force which is not easily embarrassed.

The posting to Vereeniging was ideally suited for a career censure when you don't want it to look that way. To a prying media, the move could be explained as an important posting for a promising young police officer while, in truth, it amounted to several steps down the road to oblivion.

Geldenhuis was no fool and saw the move to Vereeniging for what it was. Outwardly he'd recovered from his extreme angst and inwardly from the almost suicidal frustration which had culminated in his vomiting fit and collapse in the toilet. But his bitterness against Peekay consumed him. He was famous for being able to keep his feelings under control but now his rage was always near the surface and he would lash out at the slightest provocation.

In his tunic pocket Geldenhuis kept a single gold-plated pistol bullet with the nose suitably filed into a dum-dum configuration and when his inner anxiety grew too unbearable he would finger the bullet, reminding himself that it was reserved for his mortal enemy, that sooner or later the time must come when he held Peekay squarely in the sights of his police revolver.

In his imagination they would be alone and he would make Peekay go down on his knees and beg for his life. They would make a deal and he would insist that Peekay fight him, properly in a ring, and he would fight Peekay until he'd knocked him unconscious. Then Peekay would recover and the place would be in darkness and he'd stand up in the boxing ring as the lights went on. Standing in the ring would be a huge, ugly, syphilitic black whore in the nude. He would force Peekay to undress and then he would hold the gun to the back of his head and make him go down on the mountain of black kaffir flesh. When he was down there with his head in the hair and the stink of her thighs he would pull the trigger, blowing away the back of his enemy's head with the gold dum-dum bullet.

In his sick mind he would savour the scene that followed. He could see the homicide squad arriving. After surveying the scene they might even suspect it was him, but as he'd killed the black whore as well, there would be no clues. He'd ordered the gold-plated, .45-calibre bullet from an American mail-order company in Jacksonville Alabama nearly three years ago and he'd never shown the bullet with its filed nose to anyone, preferring it to lie warm to the touch and secret in his pocket where he could reach down and finger it. The boys in the murder squad would look down at the blown-away white man's head between the black whore's thighs and smile, and one of them would be sure to smirk and make the obvious crack. Forever afterwards people would talk about Peekay the rooinek lawyer ... *whose brains were wasted on useless black cunts.*

Jannie Geldenhuis found himself head of the Vereeniging Special Branch in charge of nothing in particular. Although there was a great amount of unrest in other parts of South Africa over the government's infamous 'endorsing out' laws, Vereeniging's model African township was quiet as always.

As a member of the Special Branch Geldenhuis wasn't involved in regular police duties, his brief being essentially political, concerned with demonstrations, sabotage and anti-government activity.

The murder trial had knocked him about severely and he would have been almost happy to be away from the spotlight had, for instance, someone else rather than Peekay been involved in his prosecution. What ate at him was not the original conviction for murder, but the fact that his trial and the publicity it had caused had allowed Peekay to rise to prominence as a brilliant young barrister while, at the same time, leading to his own ignominious demise. Added to this, the new posting had removed him from daily contact with the Red File and the long-planned revenge the meticulously researched details within it represented for him.

From the inception of the law partnership Geldenhuis had been keeping tabs on the daily movements of Levy & Peekay. The two young barristers were under constant surveillance and for the past year this had also involved Gideon Mandoma who'd joined as an articled clerk. Mandoma and also the 'coloured whore', Tandia Patel, who'd graduated from law school in Durban to join Red as a junior, already had secret police files of their own which were as carefully annotated and updated as those of Peekay and Hymie. Hymie was proving the most difficult to keep tabs on; he was involved more in the world of business and finance which was by its very nature secretive; also, he seemed to exercise a natural caution which often made his movements hard to follow.

After he joined the secret organisation, Geldenhuis was given the assignment by the *Broederbond* to 'investigate' the black Christmas party Solomon Levy held in the grounds of his palatial home. 'It is not in the interests of our people for an event like this to take place,' was how Cogsweel put it. 'Take your time, not this year, maybe not even next, it could be in ten years' time, but you will know yourself when the time is right. Then call me.' Geldenhuis was delighted; it was God's will that he should destroy not only Peekay and the Jew, but Solomon Levy, the money pot itself.

'Cogsweel, is he, you know, the top man in the *Broederbond*?' Geldenhuis asked, as he and Colonel

Klaasens left after dining in the private room of a restaurant in Pretoria. 'I mean, he's a rooinek isn't he?'

'Irish. His grandfather fought in the Boer War on our side. No, he's not anything very high up. But he's high enough, don't you worry, man.' He punched Geldenhuis on the arm. '*Jy is in die oog*! That's all you have to worry about; the *Broederbond* looks after its own.'

Peekay was different. His work was in the courts and he seemed to attract publicity without necessarily seeking it. The cases he took on were often considered hopeless and his clients unlikely to be able to pay, although Hymie would see to it that the firm always had one big corporate litigation case going. 'Peekay, you've got to help finance our legal charity work with a bit of corporate robbery,' Hymie would tell him. Peekay proved to be as astute and tough in this area as he was in the other and, more and more, large companies involved in litigation were seeking his services.

It infuriated Geldenhuis when large corporations, some even run by Afrikaners, such as the Volkskas Bank, would retain Red. On more than one occasion, accompanied by Colonel Klaasens, he would pay a discreet visit to such a company and sometimes with good results, though often enough it was the two men's connection with the *Broederbond* which made more of an impression on the company directors than their official status as police officers.

Despite these efforts Peekay and Hymie seemed to have more legal work in the corporate sector than they could conveniently handle. Sometimes, to their enormous chagrin, the board of directors of a large company would find themselves unexpectedly facing a coloured woman who chain-smoked as she asked them rapid-fire questions and who showed a grasp of the problems involving their brief which confounded her beguiling looks, leaving most of them in open-mouthed disbelief after she'd departed.

Peekay and Hymie would wait for the inevitable phone call to come through on the day after Tandia had visited a company to report on the initial brief given to Levy & Peekay. The reaction was almost always the same. The chairman was disappointed, the company had expected a principal of Levy & Peekay to represent them.

Of the four people who most obviously represented Red – Peekay, Hymie, Tandia and Gideon, Jannie Geldenhuis concerned himself perhaps the least with Tandia. He still had the original 'confession' he'd forced out of her at the Cato Manor police station, admitting that she was a whore. When the time came it alone would be enough to completely discredit her. He also had the personal matter of Bluey Jay to resolve and this too he would bring to a head when the time was right. But, after Peekay, Gideon Mandoma was Geldenhuis's most constant source of concern; though once again, it wasn't the Zulu boxer's well-documented and rapid rise in the ANC which concerned him most (the police informers, planted as moles within the ANC, could be relied upon to keep him informed). Rather, it was Mandoma's ambition to be something else. This aspect of Mandoma's life completely puzzled the young police lieutenant. Gideon Mandoma was apparently seriously concerned with the job of being a law clerk with Levy & Peekay and with part-time university attendance to gain his LLB degree at Witwatersrand University.

Geldenhuis prided himself that if you stuck with an apparent conundrum long enough, eventually the riddles in a plot presented their solutions politely to you. People were predictable and if you studied them sufficiently you could discern their personal patterns. Everything has a pattern, every human being has an intellectual thumb print. 'Why?' Geldenhuis would ask himself. Why would Gideon go to work every morning when he'd successfully defended his title five times? By most white standards and by all black ones, he was filthy rich. Most boxers, even the white ones, squander their money and when they're not in training have a good time. Mandoma's actions were against everything he knew about African behaviour. Gideon had everything he needed to be powerful among his own people; he was a folk hero and he was rich. Africans saw education only as a means of achieving the kind of status Gideon already enjoyed a hundred times over.

Geldenhuis didn't believe that Africans were altruistic; history had showed that the tribes killed each other for power and material possession – cattle and land. In modern black society this had become money and influence. If Gideon already had all these things, including a rapidly growing respect in the ANC, why then would he make things hard for himself by working as a humble clerk in a law firm?

Geldenhuis turned his attention to the riddle of Mandoma's involvement with Red. And then it came to him. Of course! Gideon was thinking long term. The Zulu chief was thinking way ahead to when he was much older and an African lawyer with many years of service to his people. Geldenhuis gasped inwardly at the audacity of the idea. Mandoma was preparing to be the first black prime minister of South Africa!

The idea shocked him beyond belief and later he mentioned it to Colonel Klaasens. 'I think I've worked it out. Why would a world boxing champion want to be the kaffir boy who makes the tea and carries messages around the place?' He looked steadily at Klaasens. 'You want to know why? I'm telling you something for nothing. Mandoma sees himself one day as the first black prime minister of South Africa and what's more, so does Peekay and the Jew!'

Klaasens laughed but then stopped abruptly and suddenly looked serious, as though he too had come to a realization. 'No, Jannie, you're wrong!' He paused. 'He wants to be the president. We going to be a republic pretty soon, they're all talking about it in Pretoria. Verwoerd wants the British off his back. The black bastard thinks eventually their side will win in this country and he's making early plans, he wants to be the first black president!' He paused, his finger raised dramatically. 'Not just him, that *kaffir boetie* bastard, Peekay, *he's* the one who sees himself as the fucking prime minister!'

Geldenhuis was almost bowled over by the logic of the remark. It was all the more surprising coming from Klaasens, an impulsive and therefore dangerous man, but not a deep thinker. Geldenhuis simply hadn't thought it through; the pattern fitted both men perfectly. The Zulu chief who rose to the top of the black nation and won the respect of the other tribes as a boxer and later as a lawyer; brilliant Oxford-trained advocate who'd always been the champion of the black people. In a multiracial South Africa with a white minority which, initially anyway, possessed the wealth and industrial muscle, it made almost perfect sense! Geldenhuis secretly blamed his senior officer for preparing him incorrectly for the Mandoma fight. They'd concentrated on working for Mandoma's head, believing he cut easily around the eyes, that if hit consistently they would pump up and close down. But Mandoma took everything Geldehuis managed to throw at his head and in the end was able to see clearly enough to slam the policeman clear through the ropes. He flushed just thinking about the humiliation. He was going to nail Mandoma, but the case against the Zulu boxer would be tighter than a nun's twat. He wasn't stupid and he wasn't Klaasens. He'd do it by the book and he'd put the bastard away forever where they could break his spirit and turn the would-be president of South Africa into a gibbering black monkey.

Jannie Geldenhuis found some consolation in the fact that in Vereeniging he'd run his own show and be away from the day-to-day contact he'd endured for almost three years with Klaasens. But he'd make sure he kept in touch with and on the right side of the big bastard. The police colonel remained his only direct access to the Red File. Geldenhuis gained a great deal of comfort from the fact that Klaasens hated Peekay almost as much as he did himself; he would happily help to put Mandoma away as well, so he'd take a special interest in the surveillance of the people involved in Red. Tandia he could handle himself. And as for the Jew? Well, he had a special surprise for him. Furthermore, Klaasens could be relied upon to respond to 'suggestions' by the more imaginative Geldenhuis when it came to tactics against their common enemy. In the end Vereeniging might not be such a backwater after all.

Thirty

Monday, 21 March was a bright highveld late summer morning with just a hint of autumn in the air. Juicey Fruit Mambo didn't need to get up early so he slept in late. He'd had a bit too much beer the night before and when he'd wakened as usual at six his head was sore; so he'd turned over, pulled his blanket over his head and gone back to sleep, waking finally around eight and feeling somewhat better.

Madam Flame Flo's house girl had left him a pot of meat and *phutu*, maize meal cooked light and fluffy with plenty of salt, and she'd added two ears of roasted corn. When Juicey Fruit got up, he sat in the sun in the back yard eating quietly and reading the *Sunday Times*. He looked for things in it to talk to Tandia about, hoping also he might find a court case in which Red was involved. He'd followed the Geldenhuis murder trial for three years, searching the papers every day for news. When Peekay secured a verdict of guilty (which was later overturned) he'd simply helped himself to a bottle of Mama Tequila's brandy from the Bluey Jay supply and wandered off down to the river and got himself joyfully plastered, keeping the entire African village awake all night. When he'd returned about noon the next day Mama Tequila had chastised him, 'It was a rotten party without you, you hear! We all got drunk with happiness and here you are doing it on our own down by the river, you got no consideration, Edward King George Juicey Fruit Mambo!'

About mid morning when he'd finished reading the paper, he went out to inspect the Packard. The beautiful pink car gleamed under an open-sided car port which Madam Flame Flo had had specially built for their visits.

Juicey Fruit Mambo realized that more people than ought to were passing the house. It was a Monday; the people should be at work and the children at school. Why were so many of them walking towards the centre of the township? He stopped and leaned over the roof of the Packard. 'Where are you going, what is all the excitement?' he called to a passing group of high-school students dressed neatly in their freshly pressed uniforms.

The group stopped and a boy of about sixteen raised his arm and gave the thumbs-up, freedom salute of the Pan-Africanist. '*Izwe Lethu!* Our Land!' he shouted, clearly excited. 'Have you not heard, Bra? We are going to the police station without our passes! Maybe they will arrest us,' he added, puffing out his chest, 'but we don't care. Sobukwe says they can't arrest everyone, so we must all do it all at once, then the police can't do anything, man!'

Juicey Fruit Mambo grinned, showing his two pointed gold incisors, then he shook his head. 'Haya! haya! Sobukwe, he said this thing? The police they can always do something. Maybe they will beat you with a sjambok, or they will bring in the dogs or even tear gas and the water gun machine!' He pointed to an aeroplane flying high overhead. 'Maybe they will bomb you!' he laughed. 'The *amaBhunu*, they can always do something!'

'*Izwe Lethu!* Today is the first step to freedom!' a young school girl in the group shouted out. Then she started to giggle, so they all began to laugh, though Juicey Fruit Mambo could sense there was hope in their laughter; they really believed. 'Kids, they're all crazy!' he thought to himself.

Like Tandia, Juicey Fruit Mambo was an ANC man though privately he also thought of them as a bunch of nohopers. He was also surprised at the demonstration; he'd heard Madam Flame Flo tell Mama Tequila that the township was always quiet, even when there was trouble elsewhere. He'd first heard Robert Sobukwe's call to action on the car radio, then, only an hour or so before, he'd read an editorial in the Sunday paper. It was one of the subjects he'd tucked away in his mind to talk to Tandia about. The editorial had suggested there would be trouble in the Western Cape, near Langa and also in some areas of the Southern Transvaal, particularly Orlando township in Johannesburg where Sobukwe himself would lead a group to the police station. The paper anticipated the whole thing would be a bit of an anti-climax but that the police, given seventy-two hours warning by Sobukwe himself, would be heavily armed and ready for anything.

Juicey Fruit Mambo set about waxing the Packard and soon forgot about the people heading for the demonstration.

In his mind he was rehearsing the conversation he would have with Tandia later when they'd drive to Alexandra township for supper before returning to Vereeniging.

Juicey Fruit Mambo missed Tandia terribly. For nearly five years he'd taken her to school and later to university and back every day. She'd sit up in the front seat of the old Packard with him and chat all the way home to Bluey Jay. Because she'd been shy and a misfit and so somewhat isolated both at school and later at Natal University, she would use Juicey Fruit Mambo as her sounding board. They always spoke in Zulu, which he had taught her. She'd talk to him about her lessons and later her lectures and Juicey Fruit, whom Tandia had taught to read and write, took these conversations very seriously. And because he was the only one who actually wanted to hear her talk, Tandia developed a technique of explaining her studies to the huge Zulu so that he could, at least in part, understand them. He was probably the only chauffeur in South Africa who could recite the complete legal torts as a Catholic might recite the catechism.

Tandia didn't know it at the time but these daily lessons with Juicey Fruit Mambo had taught her to explain often quite complex ideas in a simple and direct manner. Many of her clients were illiterate and for the most part completely ignorant of the law, and she became famous for her simple and articulate explanations. She was known among them as *umlomo ubomvu ocacisay*, the red mouth who explains. Like so many African nicknames it was a clever combination of ideas; it told people Tandia was a member of the Red team, at the same time it gave them a physical characteristic to latch onto, the bright lipstick she always wore, and finally it told them what she was famous for. Not bad in four words.

Juicey Fruit worried daily about Tandia's safety in Johannesburg and had no trust whatsoever in the boxer

Mandoma, even if he was a Zulu. He reasoned that Gideon was a midget and that he could crush him with one hand. What use was a midget when half a dozen tsotsis came at her? Now he grinned at the thought of how he'd solved the problem of her safety.

His love for kids had paid off when, after three days of the previous week spent driving around Meadowlands, Orlando and Moroka townships, stopping and asking teenagers everywhere, he finally located the whereabouts of Johnny Tambourine.

He didn't recognize Johnny Tambourine when he drew up in the pink Packard outside a shop in Moroka, but he had no need to worry. The moment he opened his mouth to speak Johnny stepped forward. Juicey Fruit Mambo didn't have the sort of face you forgot in a hurry. The tall young man who stepped up to the car had a serious expresson on his face.

'Long time no see, Bra.' He spoke quietly with no animation.

Johnny Tambourine was now a tall, lean teenager of sixteen who wore the familiar baggy pants cut down to nothing at the ankles, open-necked floral shirt and cardigan of the tsotsi. On his head he wore the ubiquitous 'tsotsi' itself, the English working man's cloth cap. Juicey Fruit Mambo hid his disquiet at finding Johnny Tambourine was a tsotsi, but after his initial surprise, he realized that it had been inevitable and was, now that he thought about it, perfect. That is, providing he could get the gang to go along wth his plans.

Juicey Fruit Mambo broke into an enormous smile. He was dressed in a dark grey suit with a white shirt and brilliant pink tie to match the Packard; he was looking sharp. 'I see you, Johnny Tambourine!' He stuck his large hand out of the car window and Johnny

Tambourine took it, his own hand disappearing into the huge black fist.

Johnny Tambourine didn't return the traditional Zulu greeting, nor did he affect the two-phase grip. He didn't go in for that shit ... I see you, you see me, everybody sees everybody, then the cows and the hens and on and on for ten minutes or more before any business you've come for takes place! That sort of talk was for the peasants. He remembered the huge man standing in front of him clearly but that was a long time ago when he'd been a little snotnose with a bicycle wheel hoop. He wondered what the big bastard wanted after all these years? His expression remained sober as he spoke. 'I hear you want me, Bra?'

If Juicey Fruit Mambo felt insulted by Johnny's poor manners he showed no sign. He'd lived in a township himself and knew the kids had no respect for the old ways. He released his grip on Johnny's hand and waited while the three other tsotsi youths moved up to the car. The handshake had broken the ice and the three others seemed more friendly.

'Remember me, Dog Poep Ismali?' a light-skinned youth asked cheekily and then grinned at Juicey Fruit Mambo, taking his hand and shaking it silently. Juicey Fruit Mambo also offered his hand to Flyspeck Mendoza, who was the smallest of the three by far and dragged one leg slightly as he walked. He wore spectacles and seemed a very serious type, not at all the kind to be a tsotsi. Too Many Fingers Bembi hung back a little, but when Juicey Fruit Mambo extended his hand his face broke into a huge white smile and he gripped it in the African manner, the only one of the three boys to do so.

Juicey Fruit Mambo scratched his head as though

thinking, his fingers tapping down the length of the long jagged scar which crossed his shining pate. Then he suddenly patted his scalp, indicating hair. 'The white one. Where is the white one?'

'Kaas Kop? He crossed over,' Johnny spat.

Juicey Fruit clearly didn't understand the expression and looked querulous. 'He is in gaol?'

'No, man, his skin, it was white like his hair, so he crossed over. He went to Cape Town where nobody knows him. He's white shit now, dog shit dried in the sun!'

The other three laughed, it was clear that Johnny Tambourine was still their leader. Juicey Fruit considered this news for a moment. 'That is enough punishment, now he must live with that fear.'

'I hear you been asking all over the place for me?' Johnny said, kicking at the dirt. He seemed ready to talk and as he looked up he brushed a fly from his face. Juicey Fruit Mambo noticed that three fingers of his left hand seemed deformed, as though they'd been badly smashed and hadn't been properly set again.

'This is true, Johnny Tambourine, I have come to make you keep your promise.'

'Promise?' Johnny Tambourine laughed, drawing his head back arrogantly, 'We are tsotsi, we snatch bags, pick pockets, mug and rob. Sometimes we get in a bit of housebreaking and theft, but we never make promises,' he boasted. 'That is why we are tsotsi, you can never trust us!'

Juicey Fruit Mambo opened the door and stepped from the car. 'First you are a man, Johnny Tambourine. Then you are a tsotsi. Is it the man or the tsotsi who does not keep promises?' He towered nearly a foot above the already tall youth.

The movement from Johnny Tambourine was amazingly fast. The knife came from somewhere, he opened the blade with his teeth and the thrust of it came towards Juicey Fruit Mambo, seemingly in one smooth lightning movement. But it wasn't fast enough. Juicey Fruit Mambo grabbed him by the wrist and appeared simply to turn him upside down. One moment he was standing with a knife in his hand and the next the knife spun from it and Johnny Tambourine hit the dirt as though he'd suddenly, on a whim, decided to dive into the dust head first.

'Ho!' Juicey Fruit Mambo grinned. 'Now I have seen the tsotsi, can I please talk to the man?'

Dog Poep Ismali, Too Many Fingers Bembi and Flyspeck Mendoza took a step backwards, ready to run. Nobody had ever seen anything like Juicey Fruit Mambo before. He'd 'flipped' Johnny Tambourine without even appearing to move from the spot.

Johnny Tambourine rose slowly, dusting his pants with both hands, his eyes downcast. He walked over and picked up the long open-bladed pocket knife and snapped it closed, dropping it into a pocket of his neatly pressed tsotsi pants. Finally he looked up, measuring Juicey Fruit with his eyes as though nothing had happened. The look showed he was still not afraid. Juicey Fruit Mambo liked what he saw a lot. Maybe he'd come to the right place.

'The *man* will keep his promise,' Johnny Tambourine said quietly.

Juicey Fruit asked for a meeting the following day, promising to bring beer.

'Carling Black Label, that's what we drink, Bra. Bring a case, tsotsi are big beer drinkers!' Flyspeck Mendoza chipped in.

The following day they met again under one of the few remaining large trees in Moroka township. Someone had built a crude bench all the way around the trunk of a large old leadwood tree. It was strange to find a leadwood at this altitude but the old tree looked well set, its dark grey bark rough looking with its characteristic longitudinal furrows and irregular transverse cracks. In fact the entire tree had a grey appearance which suited the bleak landscape of the township.

The five of them sat under the tree. There were a few other people about, all of them youths of roughly the same age. 'Don't worry, those guys are my operators, real cowboys; they'll watch for the police.' Johnny Tambourine looked at Juicey Fruit Mambo and nodded his head towards the Packard. 'The Black Label?'

Juicey Fruit Mambo's mouth fell open. 'Haya, Johnny Tambourine, here in the open? We will drink here under this tree?'

'I told you man, those are my men, we'll know long before a Black Jack can come near.'

They sat down under the tree drinking beer, Juicey Fruit opening the bottles in a flash with a gold incisor. Flyspeck Mendoza produced a large zol and they shared the joint between them, the marijuana making them feel cool and relaxed. When they'd each drunk a couple of bottles of beer and the zol was down to a finger nip, Juicey Fruit Mambo opened up the subject of why they were there.

'Johnny Tambourine, Flyspeck Mendoza, Dog Poep Ismali and Too Many Fingers Bembi,' Juicey Fruit Mambo spoke each name slowly and with great respect, as though they were men of substance and purpose, and the gesture was not lost on the four boys. 'You remember Tandy?' Each of them nodded, smiling at his own memory of the days in Sophiatown when they'd met what they thought must be a beautiful film star.

'She was a great *unine*, we talk about her still sometimes,' Johnny Tambourine confessed.

'She is a member of your gang. It is a long time now but she agreed, you agreed also. Time does not change these things, my brothers,' Juicey Fruit said rather ponderously.

Dog Poep Ismali laughed. 'She will be the prettiest tsotsi in tsotsidom!'

This sent them all into gales of laughter. The dope was having its effect and the giggles had set in. 'Now she is a lawyer in Jo'burg.'

'Yes, we know, Bra. She is called "the red mouth who explains", and she is the world champion Gideon Mandoma's sweetheart,' Flyspeck Mendoza said; then he added, 'He is still our friend.'

'Haya! You have seen them together, you have spoken to her?' Juicey Fruit asked.

Too Many Fingers Bembi shook his head. 'No, he is big time now. We do not see him, only in the movies or when he rides in a big open Cadillac.'

'He has a Cadillac, a big open car?' Juicey Fruit said, impressed.

'No, Bra, it is a car that belongs to other people, big-time gangsters I think, but when he wins he drives in the back of this car and people come from all over to see him,' Dog Poep Ismali said.

'He is the best world champion of any weight any time in world history!' Flyspeck declared.

'I think maybe Peekay, the *Onoshobishobi Ingelosi*, he is better,' Juicey Fruit Mambo said mischievously.

'Never!' they all chorussed. 'He beat him hollow! He knocked him out!' Too Many Fingers Bembi protested, getting quite upset.

It was Johnny Tambourine who brought the meeting to order again. 'How must we help Tandy?' he asked, the whites of his eyes red from smoking the zol.

Juicey Fruit Mambo opened four more bottles of beer and handed one each to the boys before de-capping another for himself. Then he told them the story of Tandia and why she hated Geldenhuis. The treatment of Tandia at the hands of the police officer was a familiar enough story and each of them understood how such a thing could happen. They only really became deeply interested when Juicey Fruit spoke of the murder trial and how Peekay had nailed Geldenhuis and gotten a conviction for murder against the policeman which, naturally, had subsequently been quashed. But Geldenhuis was determined to get Peekay and with him Tandia.

'She is fighting for the rights of the people and she knows too much about him. He will try to kill her someday; she must be protected.'

'How can we protect her?' said Johnny Tambourine.

'She is living in Meadowlands. You can watch her house. If they are going to get her they will come to the house. They will not do anything in public, except maybe in a crowd. If she is in a crowd at a protest or maybe at an ANC meeting, you must be near her, you must watch the people around her, that is when they will try to get her!' Juicey Fruit Mambo put his hand into his pocket and withdrew a wad of banknotes held together with a rubber band. 'Here is two hundred pounds, it is all the money I have.'

Two hundred pounds was nearly four years' salary for the average black working man and it represented a fortune. In fact it was everything in cash money Juicey Fruit Mambo owned, his entire retirement fund put together one note at a time.

Johnny Tambourine removed the rubber band and counted off sixty single one-pound notes. He handed ten to each of the boys and put ten into his own pocket. 'Expenses! Ten pounds each for expenses, Bra,' he said, being practical. 'You do not have to pay us, but there will be expenses.' He held up the remaining pound notes. 'We will need a gun and some ammo.' He returned the rubber band to the roll and handed what remained of the stash back to Juicey Fruit Mambo. 'We will do this job, we will keep this promise.' They all solemnly shook hands on the deal and arranged to meet at Tandia's house in Meadowlands the following Monday evening when Juicey Fruit Mambo would drive Tandia home and reveal his protection plan to her and reacquaint her with the four boys.

It was nearly one o'clock by the time Juicey Fruit Mambo had finished polishing the Packard. People had been passing all morning and his curiosity had grown. The township police station was no more than a fifteen-minute walk from Madam Flame Flo's house and Juicey Fruit Mambo enjoyed the stroll in the sun. It was one of those marvellous high veld late summer days when the air is polished clean and sits warm on your back and the sky is blue, the colour of a much-washed cotton shirt – though it was the time of year when a storm could build up in minutes. Seemingly from nowhere the big cumulus nimbus clouds would build in the late afternoon. If you went indoors for a moment you'd sense from the change of light that something had happened and then when, minutes later, you came out again, there were the towering castles of grey tinged with white, real estate for Gods and fright-ening giants to live in. Rain would come down in tor-rents. First a sharp 'ting!' like a pellet on the iron roof, then half a dozen more and the preliminaries were over; down it came, crashing, so you couldn't hear yourself speak, filling the gutters and flooding the dirt roads, each drop heavy with malice, washing away the red topsoil and generally behaving badly. Then, as suddenly, it would stop, leaving the whole place polished in the bright evening sun, the sky even bluer than before. That was a high veld rain storm for you, full of braggadocio but not very big in the long-term department.

Juicey Fruit Mambo was surprised at the size of the crowd as he moved down Seeiso Street towards the police station at the top end of the township. Everywhere people were singing and dancing and shouting '*Izwe Lethu!*', raising their arms in the thumbs-up salute and generally having an excellent demonstration. If you wanted a peaceful demonstration with a bit of class you couldn't have asked for a better one. People were carrying placards, neatly printed by schoolchildren. You could see everyone had been up late by lamplight the previous night, parents exclaiming in astonishment at the work of their kids, who had made placards not just protesting against the pass laws – when you had a good demonstration going there wasn't much point in reserving it for just one thing when there were so many inequalities available. Placards covered the whole gamut of protest: *Down with Bantu Education. We want BETTER homes, Free Education, Equal Work for Equal Pay, Down with Unjust Laws! We want Freedom of Speech, Down with Removal of People! Down with Bosses, Freedom for All, Let our leaders Speak of Freedom now! Down with Passes, Passes must go! Passes put people in gaol. Pass laws Break Family Life. Pass laws are Enemy No 1 of the People.* Juicey Fruit

Mambo observed that the 'down with' posters were the most popular.

The demonstration was unusual for another reason; no police with leashed Alsatian dogs walked among the crowd. In fact, not a policeman, black or white, was to be seen anywhere on the African side of the high-security fence which surrounded the squat red police station building. It was not until Juicey Fruit Mambo broke through to the front that he saw the two Saracen armoured vehicles with machine guns mounted on their turrets. Here the police station was surrounded by policemen carrying Sten guns and an occasional rifle; there looked to be about two-hundred-and-fifty or so white constables, although there may have been others inside. Some were dressed in ordinary everyday police uniform while others wore the not-yet familiar combat fatigues and soft cloth caps which gave them the look of German Panzer troops. These were obviously the police recruited overnight from outside the area in anticipation of trouble in the township; they looked young and inexperienced. Most of the police were chat-ting, smoking, and watching the crowd. They carried belts of ammunition around their shoulders and you could just see they thought they looked tough. It was obvious they'd decided the crowd was peaceful and that nothing unforeseen was about to occur.

Near the gate on the right leading into the police station compound was an area of no-man's-land about ten yards wide. Every once in a while, to the cheering of the crowd, a young man would run into the clearing, place his pass on the ground and set it alight. This was sheer bravado; the PAC instruction was for the men to leave their passes at home and offer themselves up for arrest as not having their passes on them, an offence which led to imprisonment. They were to stand with hands held out, waiting for the police to walk over and handcuff them and take them away. But by the time Juicey Fruit Mambo arrived, too many people had been arrested this way and the police were simply ignoring the gestures and even the foolhardy burning.

After each such burning a white police sergeant with a blond crew cut would pick up a megaphone and say, 'That's all right, burn away, man! We have your pitcher on our camera and we will get you another time. Without a pass we will find you because, man, you going nowhere, no job, no place to live, you a nobody!' The crowd would laugh in response to this warning and even the police sergeant seemed to be enjoying himself.

But he was right of course, and the crowd grew less enthusiastic about destroying the one document that at least allowed them to stay in the township and work. The peaceful demonstration was beginning to fizzle a bit, though everyone seemed happy enough. Overhead the planes circled and every once in a while a Sabre jet would dive, coming in low over the crowd, the ground trembling with the shock waves it made, but it had the opposite effect to that intended and seemed to add to the carnival effect of the demonstration. The people remained unafraid. The big bad wolf had huffed and puffed to no avail. Everyone was a bit pleased with themselves; the point had been made and nearly five thousand people had turned up in a township that never protested. It was a show of strength, some claimed, far more significant than that shown in Langa or even Evaton, where a crowd of twenty thousand people had been dispersed earlier in the day when the same Sabre jets and Harvard bombers dived menacingly low over them. 'Those Evaton people scare easy, man! There will be no more peaceful townships, the government has been warned!' people were saying to each other as they prepared to go home for a late lunch.

It was about half past one when an old man, using a long smooth stick to lean on, hobbled into the clearing in front of the police station. He was diminutive and so old and poorly dressed that many of the people started to laugh. He approached the gate, nearer to the police station than most of the pass burners had ventured and, in the manner of very old people, he came to a slow halt and turned stiffly, looking over his shoulder at the crowd. Then he took his pass from a threadbare coat which hung well below his knees and slowly brought it up so that eventually he held it aloft, above his shoulders.

Juicey Fruit watched fascinated. The old man must have been in his eighties, and he had a scrawny tuft of white beard and snowy white hair. He looked like a country person, his clothes clean though in rags and his body bent from the sort of work a man does in the fields or walking all his life behind a plough, his bones welded stiff by arthritis and the years of sleeping hard on a grass mat. Now the old man lowered himself into a crouched position, leaning heavily on the stick. He placed his pass on the ground and then the stick; and, taking a box of safety matches from his coat pocket, with trembling hands he tried to set his passbook alight.

The crowd were enchanted by the sight and were cheering and chanting 'Afrika!', showing the thumbs-up sign and shouting '*Izwe Lethu!*' A small group near the fence on the left of the police station, where a couple more Saracens were parked, their machine guns trained on the crowd, started to sing *NKosi Sikelela i' Afrika*.

But, as so often happens with gestures, the old man's

hands trembled too much or the breeze which had suddenly risen was too strong, for he was unable to light the document. Juicey Fruit Mambo, observing his predicament, rushed forward and bent down beside him.

'You are brave as a lion, my father. You have the courage of a bull elephant, but your hands are old, I will help you. Give me your pass and I will add it to my own and together we will light the fire which will show the white devils our contempt!'

Juicey Fruit Mambo took his passbook from the inside pocket of his jacket and, picking up the old man's grubby pass, he helped him back to his feet. Then he stooped to pick up the stick. It was of a dark wood and smooth as satin to the touch. This is a stick which was a very good friend to this old man, he thought, and turned the stick around so that the more pointed end reached his shoulder. 'We will hold this burning of our passbooks up to the heavens, my father.' The old man barely came to Juicey Fruit Mambo's waist as the huge Zulu punched a hole through the passes so they rested on the end of the beautiful old stick.

The crowd were showing their delight at the sight of the huge black man, with his front teeth missing and the two pointed gold incisors flashing in his mouth, and the ragged little man. It was a metaphor not lost on them; the age and endurance of Africa taken together with the hugeness and strength of the African people. At that moment they knew they could win. If it took a hundred or even a thousand years they would win. The roar from the crowd was becoming deafening.

The mood of the white men guarding the police station changed and they hastily stubbed out their cigarettes and held their Sten guns at the ready, releasing the safety locks. The machine guns fixed to the turrets of the Saracens arced over the crowd in a silent warning. There was nothing except the increased noise level to suggest the crowd was getting out of control; the two kaffirs in front burning their passes seemed to have captured its imagination. The big guy with the bald head in the well-tailored suit, he must be somebody important, a PAC organizer or something. The sergeant who'd been on the megaphone entered the police station and in an immortal statement not intended in the least to be funny, reported to Lieutenant Geldenhuis, 'Sir, the natives are becoming restless. Better you come and speak to them. They are expecting someone from Pretoria, a senior person. Is someone coming?'

Jannie Geldenhuis finished the last of his coffee before rising and walking out of the station. He was pretty sure that the crowd was under control, there were none of the usual signs that political agitators were working them up. No stones had been thrown and few among the crowd even carried sticks. He was anxious to keep the status quo; he didn't want it to appear on his record that the quietest township on the Rand had erupted into chaos almost immediately it had come under his control.

In fact, he'd been unhappy about the extra recruits and the presence of the Saracens. These new men were raw, not accustomed to crowd control. It was the usual overkill by the people in Pretoria. The last thing he wanted was a senior officer from Pretoria trying to take over. He removed his revolver from his holster and slipped off the catch, more as a gesture to his own men than as an intended threat to the crowd.

Juicey Fruit Mambo produced his zippo lighter and, removing the top, he poured a little lighter fluid on the

656

passbooks. Then he replaced the top and, activating the lighter, held it carefully to a corner of the passbooks, waiting until he was sure they were well alight. Then he lofted them high into the air above him to the delight of the crowd. 'Look, my father, your gesture is not wasted, the people, all the people they salute and respect you,' he shouted down to the old man.

At this precise moment Geldenhuis stepped out of the police station. He would later replay in his mind what had happened, but in truth he was never quite sure. Something in his brain snapped and he was suddenly standing naked and back in the pink room at Bluey Jay with a screaming Tandia crouched over the pink satin bed in front of him. Blood ran from his penis and he was in terrible pain. The door into the room crashed down and a huge, snarling black man with two gold incisor teeth, his eyes popping with madness and his great hands stretched out to reach for his neck, was coming towards him. He reached for his police revolver on the carpet, knowing he was about to be killed. The explosion roared in his head as he fired in a crouched position. The firing seemed to go on and on and when the mist cleared in front of his eyes the crowd was fleeing and bodies lay everywhere. A machine gun from one of the Saracens was still raking the bodies lying in the dust. They jerked, animated by the impact of the automatic fire as the hot ballistic teeth ripped into them. Some black people sat in the dirt, still alive, screaming from their wounds. One huge woman held her hands cupped in her lap; they were filled with her own intestines. She didn't scream; her shoulders shook as she sobbed, a small private sobbing ceremony for the death enveloping her in the hot afternoon sun.

Juicey Fruit Mambo lay face down, his body covering

the old man's. Part of his head had been torn away by a dumdum bullet which would have killed him instantly. There was a stir, as though miraculously the huge black man still moved; then the ancient little man rose from under him and brushed the dirt from his ragged coat. With one hand held to his back, he stooped to pick up the stick which had fallen from Juicey Fruit Mambo's grasp; the passbooks still burned and he brushed them off the end of the stick where they continued to burn, a tiny sacrificial fire. Then he rested the stick on Juicey Fruit Mambo's heart, holding it upright. 'I invite your spirit to enter the sacred stick,' he said quietly. 'Come, I will take you home.' Then he stood upright again facing the Sharpeville police station. Slowly, his neck stiff as a turkey cock, his rheumy eyes passed along the line of white policemen as he raised his clenched fist into the air, his thin reed-like voice cut through the silence. '*Lumukanda ehla!* Come back, Lumukanda!' And the white men who stood wrapped in the silence of their slaughter, their guns still smoking, knew something had happened, something had changed in Africa for ever.

It was quarter to two on a cloudless late summer day in the once peaceful township of Sharpeville. The world would never be the same again. Somojo, the greatest of all the African witchdoctors, leaning heavily on the spirit stick which carried Juicey Fruit Mambo back to his shadows, hobbled away, picking his way through the dead bodies, most of which had been shot in the back. Around the old man's neck hung a tiny leather bag. He could feel the comforting thump of it against his chest cavity as the ancient gold coin within it knocked against him. He spoke to the stick in his hand. 'You have not died in vain, spirit of a brave man, I have called and it is time! It is time for Lumukanda, the child of the morning star, to return.' Somojo the Swazi, the greatest of all the living witchdoctors, made this promise to Juicey Fruit Mambo.

Later that afternoon, when they'd loaded the sixty-nine dead into the back of two trucks for the mortuary, holding them by the arms and legs and swinging them, then letting them go so they landed on an awkward pile of arms and legs and blood-soaked torsos, a thunderstorm struck. The usual thing: quick as anything, big clouds arriving out of nowhere, a typical late summer high veld storm. It did what such a storm always does; rushed in, a fearful conniption of water, wind and muddy fuss. When it was over, all the blood which had soaked into the hard ground in front of the Sharpeville police station had been washed away.

That night the sky was more beautiful than usual with the stars so close you could almost reach up and touch them. This was unusual; the soft coal the people burn in their cooking fires in the townships mists the evening sky with smog which blocks out all but the most determined stars. But the rain had somehow washed the sky clean and the stars above Meadowlands were as bright as they are in the bush. Johnny Tambourine, Too Many Fingers Bembi, Flyspeck Mendoza and Dog Poep Ismali waited outside Tandia's house for Juicey Fruit Mambo to bring her home in the Packard. Too Many Fingers Bembi suddenly pointed upwards and shouted excitedly, 'Look! Over there, a falling star!'

Thirty-one

Peekay was utterly devastated by the news of Sharpeville. For him it was the end of hope and the beginning of a deep fear that insanity was going to win in the beloved country. The killing fields had come back to South Africa; hostilities had broken out again in the three hundred year war based on greed, fear and revenge.

Peekay found himself facing a terrible moral dilemma. A liberal South African who believed in justice, a sense of fairness and the rights of every man, woman and child to an equal place in a society based on freedom of opportunity – in the post-Sharpeville South Africa it could only be thought of as the ridiculous credo of a hopeless dreamer.

The black people had had enough, and Peekay's love for them was swept away in the torrent of hurt, anger and betrayal they felt. Now they demanded the right to avenge the injustice and to play by the same cynical rules of vengeance as those used against them.

On the day following the massacre, Peekay accompanied a distraught Tandia to the mortuary near Sharpeville. When they arrived hundreds of people were waiting around the squat red-brick building to claim their dead. They were mostly women, their eyes swollen from weeping, some with their men and rather more with small, runny-nosed children clutching at their skirts.

Under similar circumstances, a white crowd would have been loud and demanding, impatient with the tedious paperwork performed by a battery of clerks recruited from elsewhere who sat under the bluegum trees behind portable tables. It was well into the morning yet none of the bodies had been processed for release and some of the people had been waiting since dawn. But Africans are familar with the despair of waiting and they'd come expecting no less. The people of Sharpeville had not yet indulged in the luxury of anger; overcome with grief they waited, confused and beaten in the still hot autumn day, for the white man to restore their dead to them.

Peekay, who'd phoned earlier for an appointment, arrived with Tandia at precisely eleven o'clock to be met by the white mortuary official, Klopper.

Klopper had a nickname among the Africans, who called him 'Inkosi Asebafa, Lord of the Dead'. He liked this name a lot and lost no opportunity explaining it to any white person he might meet. Klopper was about as big in the dead-body business as you could get and held absolute power in Soweto which, he was fond of pointing out, housed Africa's largest mortuary.

His presence in Sharpeville on temporary transfer from Soweto to take charge of body sorting was an indication of how seriously the government regarded the matter of the previous day's massacre. Klopper was not easily intimidated and he wouldn't stand for any nonsense. He was just the sort of man to have on hand when you were thinking of having a massacre and wanted a calm, orderly aftermath.

Peekay had met him before when he'd been a witness in the Tom Majombi case. Klopper seemed to him to be a man obsessed with death, though in his mind he seemed only to equate it with the black people. He had witnessed so many violent and unnatural deaths – the stabbings, mutilations, muggings, ritual murders, clubbings and domestic beatings which make up the daily count of the dead in the black townships – that he seemed to have forgotten that people die of natural causes, or for that matter, that white people die at all.

He didn't see the Sharpeville massacre as any more than destiny catching up with another sixty-nine kaffirs. It wouldn't have occurred to him to blame the white police officers involved for the incident. White men do their duty and sometimes kaffirs become dead as a consequence. There was nothing wrong with that.

He was standing outside the mortuary scratching his balls and enjoying the late morning sun when Peekay and Tandia drew up. Klopper was an obese, ruddy-complexioned man who, despite being completely bald, gave the impression of being overly hirsute. He affected an untidy beard roughly trimmed about two inches below his chin. Coming up to meet it, as though it was stuffing spilling out of a rent in his chest, a wild tuft of white hair mixed into his beard. His arms, too, were covered with thick, almost matted black hair and the short sleeves of his open-neck shirt were rolled as far up his arms as they'd go so his biceps appeared to balloon out of them like Popeye arms. He was at least six feet tall but possessed the legs of someone a foot shorter, so his ballooned torso seemed precariously balanced, as though it was always about to topple from its unsteady and undersized pinning. This impression was reinforced by a strong smell of brandy, suggesting that he might be somewhat tipsy. Klopper looked dangerous, as though he had been designed for violence.

He drew his right hand from his trouser pocket and raised it casually in greeting at Peekay and Tandia's approach. '*Goeie more, advokaot*, it's a nice day after the rain last night, hey?' Klopper's voice was cheerful, though his greeting seemed to ignore Tandia completely.

'Good morning, Meneer Klopper,' Peekay said, smiling, though his voice was formal. He turned to Tandia. 'May I introduce you to Miss Patel, my legal partner.'

Klopper offered his hand to Peekay, still ignoring Tandia. The two men shook hands briefly whereupon Klopper's fat fingers plunged back into the interior of his khaki trousers to resume their jiggling. His head slightly to one side, squinting, he examined Peekay, as though trying to read his thoughts. Finally he smiled, showing a lot of gold in his mouth but no laughter in his small, black eyes. 'If you want trouble you must go some place else, you hear? The trouble here is over yesterday already. Today is all peace and quiet.'

Tandia felt the anger rise up in her. It wasn't Klopper's rudeness – she was prepared for that – but this mocking tone. She'd cried for Juicey Fruit Mambo most of the previous night and by early morning she was back in control of herself. By the time Peekay picked her up in Hymie's Mercedes for the drive to Vereeniging, he'd been surprised at her composure.

But now, simply by opening his mouth, this huge, stupid Boer with his fat guts spilling over his belt and his fingers working his elasticized testicles brought back her distress. He seemed to typify everything Juicey Fruit Mambo despised. Even in death this gross human had dominion over him. She struggled to fight back her tears, but the anger she felt threatened to overpower her. 'Tonight!', she comforted herself, 'tonight Gideon meets to launch *Umkonto we Sizwe*, Spear of the Nation. Please God let them allow me to be the first woman to join!' she prayed silently.

She'd left Peekay's flat in Hillbrow very early that morning. Gideon had been called to an all-night ANC meeting and Peekay had taken her to his flat in Hillbrow from the office soon after the news of Sharpeville had come through. He'd spent the night trying to comfort and calm her. Tandia had been too distraught to resist when Peekay had held her in his arms and rocked her and soothed her with quiet, reassuring words.

At one stage he'd tried to sing her to sleep with a Zulu lullaby. He had a nice voice, clean and unselfconscious and the melody with its beautiful Zulu words was so hauntingly familiar that she fantasized that her own Zulu mother must have used it, sung to her when she was an infant.

Later, when the sparrows were beginning to chirp in the eaves directly above his top-floor window, when Peekay thought she'd fallen asleep, he stretched her out and covered her with a blanket and slipped a pillow under her head. Then she'd felt his lips touch her brow as he whispered, 'Sleep now, sweet Tandia. Sorrow has a season, but it will pass.' Then she'd heard the squeak of a loose floorboard under the carpet as he tip-toed from the room; soon after, she'd heard the shower running.

With Peekay out of the room, Tandia started to cry

again, this time not knowing whether it was for Juicey Fruit Mambo or herself. Peekay's barely sensed kiss and the manner of his words were the gentlest thing she could ever remember happening to her. They contrasted so with Gideon's words when, less than an hour after the news of the Sharpeville massacre, Madam Flame Flo had phoned to say that Juicey Fruit Mambo was among the dead. Tandia had become almost hysterical and Gideon made very little attempt to comfort her. 'Tandia, Mambo was a Zulu. He died like a Zulu should die. I would be happy to die like him. He will be happy, his shadows will be happy and the people of his *isigodi*, they will be happy. There is no need for grief!' He'd spoken as though he was giving her an instruction, a lesson in how he expected her to behave; and then, without touching her, he'd left her for an urgent meeting at Moroka township.

Soon after dawn, despite Peekay's protests that he must take her all the way to Meadowlands, Tandia insisted he only drive her to Johannesburg Central where she proposed to take a non-European taxi home. When Peekay had looked upset, she'd explained, 'Peekay, they rise early in the townships. By now the place is bustling with people hurrying to catch an early train. What do you think my neighbours will think if I arrive at my doorstep at dawn dropped off in a big black car by a white man?'

Peekay grinned, suddenly understanding. 'About what my neighbours would think if they'd seen you leaving my doorstep at dawn?'

'No wonder you're such a crackerjack barrister!' Tandia said, trying to sound cheerful.

Tandia needed to go home to bathe, to change into a black dress, and to pick up a brief she'd been working

665

on. Peekay would pick her up around mid morning, using the intervening time to get a court order to have Juicey Fruit Mambo's body removed for burial in Zululand. This would normally have been extremely difficult, if not impossible in the time, but it had been quickly arranged after a phone call to Magistrate Coetzee.

The taxi had only just pulled away and she was fumbling in her bags for the keys to her house when a youth of about sixteen appeared suddenly at her side. Tandia gave a start.

'Hi Tandy, long time no see.' The boy had a nice smile and it was obvious he was friendly. Then Tandia recognized him.

'Johnny Tambourine!' Despite her distress she was glad to see him.

'When we heard about Sharpeville and you didn't come with Juicey Fruit Mambo last night, I told the others to go away. I thought, for sure, something bad has happened.'

'Oh, Johnny they killed him. They shot him!' She began to cry again.

'Don't cry, Tandy,' Johnny Tambourine put his hand on her shoulder and, taking the key she was holding from her hand, he opened the front door of her little house. 'Sit, I'll get you some water or something.' He looked about him, trying to decide where the kitchen might be.

'Thank you, Johnny, I'm fine,' Tandia sniffed, rubbing her swollen eyes. 'I must look a mess,' she smiled through her tears. 'I didn't know you'd seen Juicey Fruit Mambo. Please sit, I'm being rude.' She moved to sit on the edge of a small sofa and pointed to a chair.

'Ja, only yesterday, we made a deal, we done some business.' Johnny sat casually on the arm of a chair that matched the design of the sofa, crossing his legs to show a pair of bright red socks which matched his cardigan. He seemed a young man very much in control.

'Business? You had some business with Juicey Fruit Mambo?'

Johnny Tambourine scratched his head, then realized he was still wearing his cap. He removed it from his head, placing it on the chair beside him. 'Ja, we got a contract to look after you. Me an' Dog Poep Ismali an' Flyspeck Mendoza an' Too Many Fingers Bembi, all four, we going to protect you from now on; it's all agreed and signed for.'

Despite considerable effort on her part, Tandia was unable to persuade Johnny Tambourine that she was perfectly safe on her own. Exhausted from lack of sleep and in some exasperation, she'd finally agreed to a trial week under the protection of the four boys. It was another wonderful, typical ham-fisted Juicey Fruit Mambo scheme wrought out of his love for her and the least she could do was pretend to go along with it until the boys grew tired of the game and went back to loitering, three-card scams, mugging and petty theft.

Johnny Tambourine considered that his job had started right there and then and he'd come with her in the car to Sharpeville, sitting quietly in the back seat of the car while she and Peekay confronted Klopper.

'We've come to identify one of the deceased and to arrange for the removal of his body, Meneer Klopper,' Peekay said politely to the large man.

Klopper removed his hands from his trouser pockets and to their surprise came to attention; then he lifted himself onto his toes, which caused him to wobble dangerously as he leaned over them. The entire performance was meant to intimidate. 'I must say, man, you don't look like a relation of anybody we got here, Advokaat.' Klopper stabbed a blunt finger in Tandia's direction, acknowledging her presence for the first time. 'Not her too! We only got black kaffirs here. Who was it who died? The garden boy or the house girl at your place, hey?'

Peekay removed an envelope from the jacket of his suit. 'He was a friend,' he said quietly. He handed the envelope to the big man. 'It contains a court order entitling me to make a positive identification and gives me authority to remove the body.'

Klopper smiled. Taking the envelope and holding it by the corner he tapped it several times into the open palm of his left hand. 'That's nice. A friend, hey? A white man who has black kaffir friends,' he squinted down again at Peekay, 'That Tom Majombi, you know the kaffir who become dead in the Geldenhuis trial, he was your friend also, hey?' He laughed suddenly and turned to Tandia. 'I would be careful if I was his friend, you hear? All his kaffir friends, they become dead!' He stressed the word kaffir, making it obvious that it included her. He continued to look at Tandia, a thin smile on his fat face. 'You hear what I'm saying?'

Tandia held his stare. It was an impertinence she might not have been allowed had they been alone. Even now, the years of conditioning made her feel guilty. Guilty for what? She wasn't sure, for being born? Why was it she felt this life-or-death need to hold the fat white man's insolent stare? How could this animal intimidate her? Klopper ignored the flap of the envelope he was holding and, without looking, nipped a corner with his thumb nail and began tearing about a quarter of an inch off the top, his fingers working deliberately as though he was in no hurry to open it. Tandia held his gaze, though the need to look away was becoming almost irresistible. She felt like a small bird mesmerized by a snake and, inwardly, she was screaming for the eye contact to come to an end. When Klopper had torn a thin sliver of paper off the top end of the envelope he finally dropped his gaze, inserting a fat thumb and forefinger pincer-like into the envelope to withdraw the court order. He unfolded the paper and appeared to look at it for a moment. 'Edward King George Juicey Fruit Mambo?' He read it slowly and aloud. Then without looking up he added, '*Here*, man, some kaffirs got blerrie funny names!'

'*Inkosi Asebafa*, Lord of the Dead! That's not a funny name?' Peekay shot back.

Tandia grinned and Klopper looked at him coldly, his small dark eyes hostile. His voice was clipped as he spoke. 'You done your homework as usual, I see, advokaat. Most of the dead here, you know, they haven't got any papers.' He grinned, seeming to brighten up. 'They left their passes at home, that's what this whole kerfuffle is all about, man! Do you have papers for the kaffir who has become dead?'

'No, I don't, but we can identify him quite easily.'

'Identify him?' Klopper looked surprised. 'You can't identify a kaffir without papers, man!'

Peekay sighed. He could have kicked himself for making the crack about Klopper's African name. 'The deceased is quite distinctive looking, he has two gold-capped incisor teeth and a large zig-zag scar across his skull.'

'Gold teeth and a zig-zag skull? We got no one who become dead who looks like that!'

Klopper's response was clumsy. Peekay knew instantly that the Boer knew all along that they'd come for Juicey Fruit Mambo.

'I'm sure you have, Meneer Klopper, he's very large, six eight, six ten maybe? You couldn't miss him.'

Klopper's voice was casual, almost uninterested as he spoke. 'Oh, that one? Ja, I remember now! It was the zig-zag head, when you said about the zig-zag head, that got me mixed up.' He paused just long enough for the effect, looking directly at Tandia. 'That part was blown away when he become dead.'

Tandia gasped and Peekay put his hand around her shoulder and squeezed her lightly. It was an involuntary action and a mistake and he saw the triumphant smirk on Klopper's face. 'We have an ambulance coming, Meneer Klopper,' Peekay withdrew his arm from around Tandia's shoulders and looked at his watch, 'any minute now. I'd like to sign for him please.'

Klopper shook his head as though he was genuinely regretful. 'I'm sorry, any other one you can have. Just say a name and you can have any other kaffir who has become dead yesterday, but not this one. The kaffir with the sharp gold teeth, I definitely got strict instructions from high up not to release him.' He handed the court order back to Peekay.

'This is ridiculous, Klopper!' Peekay said, dropping all pretence at politeness. 'I've got a court order, until it's rescinded it's valid. Who gave you the order to retain the deceased?'

Klopper seemed not in the least upset by Peekay's pointed manner. He could quite easily have told Peekay to mind his own business, but instead he smiled, 'As a matter of fact a friend of yours, advokaat. A good friend of yours,' he grinned, enjoying the moment.

'Lieutenant Geldenhuis, it was him, he personally left the instructions.'

'Jannie Geldenhuis? Lieutenant Jannie Geldenhuis?' Peekay corrected.

'Ja, I think it will soon be Kaptein Geldenhuis. It was a brave thing that he done yesterday against all those drunk, *dagga*-smoking, murdering black bastards!'

'Brave thing!' Tandia could contain herself no longer, 'Jesus! Can you believe it?'

Klopper turned surprisingly quickly for a man his size and stabbed his finger at Tandia, 'Hey! You! Kaffir! You shut your mouth, you hear? You take God's name in vain again you in lots of trouble!'

Tandia looked at him defiantly then turned and walked back to the car, too distraught and angry to remain with Peekay. Johnny Tambourine opened the door from inside and she sat beside him. Inside the car she gave vent to her feelings. She was snorting with indignation: her nostrils flared as she fought to keep down her anger, 'I'll kill him, I'll kill the fat white pig!' she hissed.

Johnny Tambourine put his hand on Tandia's shoulder and chuckled pleasantly, 'That's why you got us, Tandy, he said quietly. 'Hey man! I told you, we got a contract.'

From the seam running down the side of his shaped tsotsi trousers Johnny Tambourine withdrew a sharpened bicycle spoke. 'Me, really I'm a knife man. Flyspeck Mendoza, he's the professional, he can use a spoke, cut spine with it better than a surgeon. When the time comes, Flyspeck will do it for you.'

Tandia shuddered, 'Johnny, you mustn't do it! Klopper's just an ignorant Boer, there are thousands like him.'

'He's dog shit in the sun, Tandia!'

'Johnny you're here to protect me; that doesn't mean you've got to kill everyone who insults me! *Here*, I'm a coloured person, a black like you; if we did that, in one month all the white people in South Africa would be dead!'

Peekay knew better than to follow after Tandia. He'd already compromised himself earlier by physically touching her in the presence of Klopper. The fat mortician would have seen it as a weakness, even worse, a perversion, and would have totally lost respect and become wholly recalcitrant.

'Can I get Geldenhuis on the phone? Do you have a number?'

Klopper indicated the mortuary building directly behind him with a jerk of his head. 'He's in there; wait here, I'll go and ask him if he'll see you.'

A few minutes later Geldenhuis came out of the building, adjusting his cap as he walked into the sunlight. 'Howzit, Peekay?'

'*Goed*, Jannie,' Peekay answered, equally casually, in Afrikaans.

'What do you want?' Geldenhuis asked bluntly, reverting to that language.

Peekay produced the court order and held it out to Jannie Geldenhuis. 'It's a court order giving me authority . . .'

Geldenhuis cut across him impatiently. 'Ja, Klopper here told me. But why do you want this kaffir, what's he to you?'

'He was a friend, he's also a Zulu, I want to give him a proper burial.'

Geldenhuis looked directly at Peekay. 'Don't play games with me, you hear? You know he was a terrorist!'

672

Peekay laughed, surprised. 'What? Juicey Fruit Mambo? Don't be bloody ridiculous!'

'I know this kaffir, he works for a coloured woman called Mama Tequila. Do you know her?'

'Ja, I know her. The deceased was her chauffeur, that's not a crime.'

'No, man, before that, in 1947 he was in a gang that tried to blow up a pylon for the main power line from Durban to Pietermaritzburg. We keeping him for fingerprints, also we got a photographer coming down from Pretoria to take his picture.'

Peekay laughed. 'Jesus, Jannie, you people never give up, do you? Tandia's told me about the case. The police were made a laughing stock! It turned out to be a group of white guys. Juicey Fruit Mambo happened to be nearby on his way to a hospital where he worked!' He paused, 'But it didn't stop your lot from smashing in his skull when they threw him down a stairway and knocking out his front teeth in an attempt to get him to confess!'

Jannie Geldenhuis looked up at Peekay, 'I wouldn't believe everything that coloured bitch told you or, for that matter, hasn't told you! The police case was badly prepared, he, whatzisname, Juicey Fruit Mambo, was guilty all right; today that wouldn't have happened, I'm telling you, man!'

Peekay brought his forefinger to the tip of his nose. 'Hey, wait a minute, Jannie, what are you saying . . . hasn't told me yet?'

Geldenhuis laughed. 'You think you know everything, don't you? You always so fucking smart! Well you don't, you hear? You know nothing!'

'Miss Patel is a colleague, a partner and a lawyer with an impeccable reputation, that's all I need to know about her.'

'Miss Patel? Who are you calling miss? Miss, like she's a somebody, like she's a white person! The black bitch is a whore and I can prove it,' Geldenhuis spat.

Peekay was suddenly terribly angry. 'Who are you calling a whore, Geldenhuis?' A tiny voice in the back of his head told him to stop; danger lay ahead. But he couldn't leave it there and just back down. He suddenly knew he was in love with Tandia, that he wanted to smash Geldenhuis's face in, defend her against his vile accusations. He gritted his teeth, fighting for control, his entire body shaking with the effort.

'You fucking her!' Geldenhuis grinned, pulling his head back slightly, delighted. 'Jesus! Peekay's fucking a black whore!'

Geldenhuis was fast enough to see the left coming, but it was only a feint. Peekay's right hand smashed into his jaw, almost lifting him from the ground, and he sat down hard and then rolled in the dirt. There was a cry of astonishment from the Africans waiting under the bluegum trees and a solitary black constable came running up. The people, alerted by Tandia's return to the car, had been watching; someone in the crowd had recognized her and the *Onoshobishobi Ingelosi* when they'd arrived. Now they saw the Tadpole Angel knock the hated Lieutenant Geldenhuis down and they were too astonished to do anything but gasp. Had it been anyone else they would have scattered, running from the trouble to come, but they now saw Peekay's presence as a sign and they held their ground.

Geldenhuis lay still as Klopper ran over to him but before the big man could lift him up he sat up and shook his head. '*Is jy okay?*' Klopper asked anxiously.

Geldenhuis pushed him arm aside and waved the black policeman back; then he rose a little unsteadily to his feet. The policeman ran over and retrieved Geldenhuis's cap and, dusting it first with the back of his hand, handed it to his superior who placed it back on his head. A bright trickle of blood ran from the corner of Geldenhuis's mouth. He wiped at it with the back of his hand and then looked up, grinning triumphantly. 'I've got you, Peekay!' He turned to Klopper, 'You witnessed it, an unprovoked attack on a police officer!'

'Ja, I'm your witness, I saw the whole thing, Lieutenant.' Klopper's voice was unctuous, anxious to collaborate.

'You know what is the stupid part, Peekay? You hit me for nothing, I can prove it. I can prove she's a whore.'

Klopper's arm went around Peekay as he stepped towards Geldenhuis. 'No more, you hear!' The fat man's strength was enormous as he held Peekay. Some of the Africans had moved closer and the men among them were starting to look angry.

Geldenhuis hadn't slept the previous night. He still couldn't quite believe that he'd been responsible for the first shot, the fatal shot which had killed Juicey Fruit Mambo. The whole thing had a dreamlike quality. He'd realized later that in the subsequent chaos nobody seemed to know he'd started the massacre. What had kept him sleepless was the certainty that his career was finished. He'd been the Special Branch man on the spot, responsible for maintaining order during the protest and he'd failed. Coming after everything else, he was certain that this time he was doomed.

But he showed none of this anger outwardly as he fixed his pale blue eyes on Peekay who was being held in a bear hug by Klopper. At the very least he should smash his fist into Peekay's face. In his imagination he could hear the crunch of bone and cartilage as he flattened his nose.

But this moment too passed and he was back in control. He was too good a police officer to waste the opportunity with a piece of gratuitous revenge when Peekay had so much more ultimately coming to him.

'You'd better come inside, man.' Geldenhuis paused, 'Into the office . . . or I can place you under arrest here, you can suit yourself.' He was still panting a little from the shock of the punch though the blood had ceased to run from his mouth. Tandia and Johnny Tambourine came running up. Klopper still held Peekay, who'd made no attempt to struggle. 'Let him go, man,' Geldenhuis said to Klopper, 'I can defend myself.' He turned to Tandia, 'Get back to the car and wait, you hear? Take the kaffir boy with you!'

Tandia looked questioningly at Peekay. 'It's okay, Tandia, we're just going to the office for a chat; wait for me, I shan't be long.'

Geldenhuis grinned, his voice over-familiar, 'Do as you told now, Tandy.'

Tandia, pale and frightened, stood her ground. 'What's going on, Peekay?'

'Lieutenant Geldenhuis said something to me and I took exception to it. What I did was stupid; it's okay, just wait for me in the car.'

Tandia knew immediately that Peekay had come to her defence, that he'd hit Geldenhuis because of something he'd said about her. 'Lieutenant, do you intend to press charges?' She was surprised at the firmness of her voice.

Geldenhuis gave a short, dismissive laugh. 'I'm a boxer, I should have known better, man. I thought he was going to hit me with a left hook!' His voice was almost friendly as he added, 'I just want to talk with Peekay, in the office, do you mind?'

'If you're going to arrest him he's entitled to a lawyer,' Tandia persisted.

'Then if he's arrested, I'll call you, you hear?' He turned to Klopper, 'You too, stay outside, calm these kaffirs down, get things going but don't let anybody in the mortuary while we're there, we got things to talk about.' He turned and walked towards the door, Peekay following him. Geldenhuis stopped before entering the building, brushing the dirt from the back of his pants. He turned again, looking back at Klopper. 'Nobody comes in, you hear? Not even you!'

The big Boer nodded and, turning to Tandia and Johnny Tambourine, indicated with a dismissive sweep of his hands that they should return to the car. Then he did the same to the Africans who'd gathered around, '*Buyela emuva*! Go back!' he yelled. It was an expression he used a lot and it was one of no more than a dozen instructions he'd learned in Zulu in over thirty years of dealing with black people on a day-to-day basis.

Peekay followed Geldenhuis into a small office. 'Close the door, man,' Geldenhuis said. 'Sit down.' He indicated a bentwood kitchen chair, one of two beside a table. He removed his cap and placed it on top of a brown manila file lying on the table. He hadn't been quite quick enough and Peekay read the single word 'Mambo' scrawled quite large on the cover.

Peekay hadn't addressed Geldenhuis directly since he'd punched him. Now he said, 'That was a bloody stupid thing to do, Jannie, but I don't wish to apologize; understand, I'd do it again under the same circumstances.' He should have left it at that, but he was still angry. 'You bastards think you can say anything, do anything, but you can't. Miss Patel may just be another kaffir to you, but she's a colleague and a young advocate with a brilliant career ahead of her. You can hide behind your policeman's badge as much as you like, but she's the future and your bullets and your bullying and your *baasmanskap* isn't going to change that. When you pulled the trigger you put an end to hope for a reconciliation. You declared war!'

'Who said I pulled the trigger?' He spoke calmly enough, not giving anything away, but instantly Peekay knew that it was Geldenhuis who had fired the first shot and who had killed Juicey Fruit Mambo.

'It doesn't matter who pulled the trigger; Sharpeville was your operation.'

Geldenhuis grinned. 'Like you, man, I'd do it again under the same circumstances; my men were in danger!'

'Ja, that seems clear, three hundred men armed with Sten guns, two Saracen armoured weapon carriers with machine-gun turrets, an eight-foot high riot fence between you and the crowd, which consisted of as many women and schoolchildren as it did men. The dangerous weapons they carried were sticks attached to protest banners. I imagine you were in mortal danger!'

Geldenhuis looked over at Peekay calmly. 'You talking shit! You wasn't there, man, I was. Save your questions for the inquiry, we going to charge all the wounded for inciting violence. I have no doubt you and that black whore will be in court for the defence.'

Peekay gritted his teeth, but this time he didn't react to the policeman's taunt. 'We'll be there,' he said quietly.

Without thinking, Geldenhuis rubbed his chin; then he took his wallet from the pocket of his police tunic.

He opened it and produced a small square of paper. He handed the square to Peekay, 'Here, read it, now let's see who's telling lies.'

Peekay opened the tiny square of paper carefully and slowly read the confession Geldenhuis had forced out of the frightened teenager at the Cato Manor police station all those years ago. Peekay folded the page again and without saying anything he returned it to Geldenhuis.

'Tandy and me go back a long time,' Geldenhuis said smugly, enjoying the effect of the innuendo as he replaced the paper into his wallet.

Peekay leaned on the table and brought his fingers up to his lips. He was silent for a while. 'Tell me, Geldenhuis, this confession. I see it's typed; was it part of a statement of arrest?'

'Ja, you could say that.'

'I see, but there is no record of Miss Patel having been arrested and charged with prostitution. Had there been, she could never have been admitted to the bar.'

'Ja, well, there were no charges.'

'Why not? Thirteen is the age of consent for Africans and coloured women. If that is a voluntary confession she should have been charged for prostitution.'

'Ag man, I forget now, there were other circumstances, she wasn't charged, just brought in for questioning.'

Peekay's forefinger touched his nose lightly. 'Other circumstances? I take it there is a record somewhere, a transcription of these other circumstances? An adequate reason why a young girl prostitute is allowed to go free after signing an official admission of guilt?'

Geldenhuis sighed impatiently. 'I'm not stupid, Peekay. You know the police make deals all the time.

That document is signed by a police officer and a black police constable witness. Maybe, because it's not official, in a court of law you can make mincemeat of it! Inadmissible evidence and all that.' He leaned back in his chair, fanning himself with his wallet. 'Who gives a fuck! It's got Tandia's signature on it and mine and a reliable witness and, published in a newspaper, people will draw their own conclusions! The first female black lawyer, she's big news, man! And I can destroy her credibility any time I like.'

'Why?' Peekay asked, his manner almost absent-minded.

'Why what?' Geldenhuis returned.

'Why, all those years back, would you have gone to that much trouble?'

'Simple! I already told you. Young girls like that. She was pretty and not stupid. They go on the game, sooner or later they shack up with an important gang leader and suddenly you on the inside, you got a reliable informer.'

'So Miss Patel is your personal informer?'

Geldenhuis realized too late that Peekay had him trapped. It was so quick, none of the niceties he'd expected, just one sharp, deadly verbal thrust: *So Miss Patel is your personal informer*? If he lied and claimed that Tandia was his informer then Peekay would confront her and she'd be forced to clear herself by telling of the incident in the pink room at Bluey Jay. If he told the truth, that Tandia had never been in his service as an informer, Peekay would become equally curious as to why he would blackmail a schoolgirl who was making a few bob on the side as a prostitute. There was only one obvious reason and you didn't have to be Sherlock Holmes to figure it out.

Jannie Geldenhuis felt as though he was going to choke; both ways he ended up being seen as a sexual pervert. It was the one thing he couldn't bear anyone to find out, least of all Peekay. He felt a sudden chill come over him, a bone marrow coldness as a sudden vision of the childhood experience in the cold room of his father's butcher's shop etched itself sharply in his mind.

Peekay looked up, his face without expression, waiting for the policeman's reply. He was suddenly terribly confused; he couldn't believe that Tandia was a plant, a police informer, it simply didn't make sense. Yet he'd seen the note, and Geldenhuis was in a perfect position to blackmail her. 'Are you telling me Miss Patel is in your pay?' he asked again.

Jannie Geldenhuis smiled blandly at Peekay, concealing his emotions. He was in charge here, not Peekay. He was not here to be cross-questioned by the rooinek lawyer. 'No more questions. Save your questions for the courts, advocate. Let me ask *you* some questions now. This man, Juicey Fruit Mambo, why was he at Sharpeville; this person comes from Durban. He has a record as a terrorist; why does he suddenly show up at Sharpeville which is a small township, not even important and thirty-five miles from Johannesburg?'

'That's quite easy to answer. His employer, whom we both know as Mama Tequila, has a sister who lives near here. She was visiting her sister and no doubt he was curious and went along to the demonstration for a look.' Peekay paused, shrugging his shoulders. 'The rest you know.'

If Geldenhuis was surprised by this news he didn't show it. 'Have we not got a wider conspiracy here? Funny how the visit comes about just when there is a major demonstration planned isn't it? A demonstration in a township that is known for being peaceful, for not normally joining into this sort of thing?'

'Hang on! What are you trying to say? That Mama Tequila is a covert terrorist? Or that Juicey Fruit Mambo is an agent provocateur? Or that someone else is pulling the strings and made it convenient for him to be up here when the protest was planned? Which is it to be?'

'The law is the law, if people break the law they going to get into trouble.' Geldenhuis pointed his finger at Peekay, stabbing it in the air several times to make his point. 'You know what you are, Peekay? You're the lowest type there is, the kind of white man who wants to destroy all that we've built up, you want to tear down a decent God-fearing people. You want to hand back to the dirty, ugly, stupid and primitive black man what my ancestors fought three hundred years to win. I'm warning you, man, that kaffir with the gold teeth in there was number one. And if you're fucking Tandia Patel, you're number two!' He lifted his head, looking up at the ceiling, 'Jesus! Imagine the headlines!' He looked back at Peekay, 'Please, man, do it! Please give me the chance to string you up by your balls in front of the public. It would be the best day of my whole fucking life!'

'You know what your problem is, Jannie? You could never beat me in the ring. You simply weren't good enough.' Peekay pointed to the policeman's gun. 'And now, because you lack the skill with your head and your hands, you want to even the score with that!' He felt a little foolish taunting him, but he hoped it would work.

Geldenhuis jumped to his feet, kicking the chair away

from behind him. 'Any time, you hear? Any place! You name it, I'll be there, with or without gloves!' His face, contorted with rage, was two inches from Peekay's.

'Christ, Geldenhuis, back there with Klopper you fell for the oldest trick in the book, a feint with the left hand followed by a right. Don't insult me! Go pick on some defenceless black man and gun him down at a peaceful protest!'

Peekay got ready to block the punch he felt sure was coming. Geldenhuis's face had gone white as chalk and his pale blue eyes made him look as though they were fitted into a porcelain mask. It was not the first time Peekay had witnessed naked aggression; he'd faced hate and rage in the ring often enough, but this was different. Strangely he felt better for it. Now he knew what he was up against, he'd flushed the enemy out. He'd have to keep scoring off the Afrikaner, try to keep him off balance. That way the police themselves would watch him, tie his hands, afraid that if Geldenhuis came after any of them too openly the media would cry foul and Red would make a fool of them in court. As long as he could keep alive the policeman's determination to vindicate himself utterly in everyone's eyes, to show the world he was the better man by trying publicly to humiliate Peekay, they were all more or less safe. He had to keep needling him in public so as to keep the enemy in the open. Geldenhuis hunting them without the need to vindicate himself in public was much too dangerous.

But Geldenhuis had one more surprise for him. He pulled back, suddenly smiling, and Peekay could feel the tension leave the policeman. Peekay realized that the lightning ferocity and the incredible calm, all within moments, was what made the policeman such a remarkable and feared interrogator, this schizoid ability to be hot and cold, two people at once.

Geldenhuis quietly resumed his seat and, pushing his cap aside, he opened the manila folder. 'Do you have a good picture of the deceased?' he asked calmly.

'Not personally, but I'm sure we could find one easily enough,' Peekay replied.

'In that case I will release his body to you. We have a photographer coming from Pretoria to take the pictures of all the dead, that's why the relatives are having to wait outside. He's late, he was supposed to be here by eight o'clock.'

'You mean we're going to have to wait?'

'No I just said, get me a good picture. Even if we took a picture of this person,' he tapped the manila file, 'it wouldn't be any good, he's only got half of his head with him.' Geldenhuis said this sotto voce, not attempting to score a point; he was a police officer doing his job. He rose from the chair. 'C'mon, you'll have to officially identify him. I'll take his fingerprints at the same time.'

Predictably, the first thing that hit Peekay as they entered the mortuary was the smell. He had no idea that human bodies could develop such a stench in so short a period. The smell of putrefaction filled the room. He clutched at his stomach with one hand and covered his nose and mouth with the other as he turned to rush out again, but Geldenhuis grabbed him by the shoulder halting him.

'Dead kaffirs stink, hey? Just stand still for a moment and breath normally.' Peekay turned back again to face the room and, reaching for his handkerchief, he placed it over his nose. Geldenhuis showed no reaction to the stench.

684

The room was in semi-darkness, like being under a heavy canopy of trees. It wasn't large and if you looked carefully you could pick out most of the detail, though it contained no windows. Light entered from two skylights in the roof, both of which had been painted white in an attempt to insulate the heat coming in; two large extractor fans whirred on either side of the skylights.

The room seemed completely filled with the dead, laid out side by side on the polished cement floor, each corpse touching the other with a narrow corridor running down the centre and another, even narrower, along the wall leading to where they stood at the doorway. The corpses which were identified were covered with a green sheet from which two naked feet extended into the centre isle. On each left big toe was tied a manila label bearing the dead person's name. Those of the dead who had no identification, those who'd done as instructed and left their passes at home, were also covered, though this time their feet were covered and their faces exposed awaiting identification by their relatives. It was all very neat and tidy; Klopper obviously ran a tight ship.

The far wall appeared to be made of glass insulator bricks in the centre of which was set a white enamel door about twice the size of a normal oven door. Set in line with the door and extending about eight feet out into the room was a ramp of the sort you sometimes see in loading depots where cases are pushed along metal coasters set between rails. The oven-like structure was obviously the incinerator for the unclaimed dead, and the ramp was for the smooth delivery of a body through the enamel door into its interior. Near the oven door, completely covered by several of the green morgue sheets, was what appeared to be a mound about five feet high.

'Can we do this quickly, please?' Peekay gasped.

'Ja, but we have a problem,' Geldenhuis pointed to the green mound. 'Klopper didn't have room for everyone, you know, to lay them out all neat. These are crisis conditions, this place is only built for a few stiffs. So, well, man, some they still in that pile. If Zulu Mambo, the Bantu you looking for isn't here,' his hand swept along the row of bodies, 'then you going to have to find him in that pile over there. Mostly over there is the bits and the bad sights. A machine gun, it can cut right through a person, also some of the guys, they used dum-dum bullets.'

Peekay removed the handkerchief; his expression was incredulous. 'You bastard, Geldenhuis!'

Geldenhuis shrugged. 'I'm sorry, we can't let anyone in to help you. No black people are allowed in until we taken all the photographs. Maybe you'll be lucky, maybe he's here, all neat in a row,' he paused, rubbing the point of the chin where Peekay had hit him, 'but I don't think so.'

Peekay was trapped and he trembled as he walked down the centre aisle looking into the faces of the dead. There was a constant hum of flies in the room which he hadn't noticed as he'd entered and now he saw them clustered about the eyes and crawling around and into the open mouths of the dead who, apart from being covered with a sheet, had received no special attention. The blood from their internal haemorrhaging had caked around their mouths and necks. Peekay brushed a bloated fly from his face.

Peekay came to the end of the long lines of the dead, knowing Juicey Fruit Mambo would not be among them but nevertheless forcing himself to look at each face. Here was the legacy of hate, the ultimate punishment for mothers and fathers and children who'd dared to hope they might be free in the country of their birth. Finally he reached the cloth-covered mound of the dead. The green sheeting was heavily stained with large brown patches of dried blood and in one place the brighter red of a fresh seepage. Peekay stood trembling, lacking the courage to pull back the sheets. Finally he did so and what he saw would be part of a recurring nightmare from which he'd wake screaming for the remainder of his life.

On the top of the pile lay a huge woman, her legs wide open; her crotch and stomach had been blown away and viscera had been pushed back into the gaping wound. The elastic bottoms of her pink crêpe-de-chine bloomers with tattered fragments of bloody cloth attached still dug into her thighs, though her dress and the rest of the bloomers had been torn away. Except for the bizarre garters, her enormous body lay naked from the waist down. Propping it up were heads and arms, legs and torsos – though piled up the way they were, at all angles, they didn't look like bodies, more like components, a junk heap of rejected human parts.

Peekay knew he was going to be sick and he grabbed at the oven door set into the wall, only just managing to swing it open and lean over the delivery ramp before vomiting into its interior. He remained like this for some time, continuing to heave; when at last he withdrew his head he was totally distraught, his body bent forward almost double, shaking violently.

Geldenhuis watched Peekay as he threw up into the interior of the cremation oven, then he slowly withdrew his Smith & Wesson .38 calibre service revolver from its holster. Pushing to the left, he opened the chamber, removing the bullet in the chamber nearest to the barrel. He reached into his trouser pocket, his hands closing around the warm, familiar shape of the single gold square-nosed bullet. He slid it silently into the vacant hole in the revolving chamber of the revolver and carefully pushed the chamber back. When he cocked the gun the gold dumdum bullet would line up with the barrel to blow half of Peekay's head away.

The coldness had come back, the terrible cold that seemed to seep down into his marrow. This place; the plan was working perfectly, it was even better than his fantasy of finding a boxing ring. He hadn't planned to kill him, just to humiliate him. But now as he saw the way things were turning out, he knew it was a certain sign from God that he was right. He was alone with Peekay; the black whore lay there ready for him on top of the sides of beef, just like the vision he'd been given. The cold grew more intense. Things were becoming mixed up in his head, blurred. He was in the cold room behind his father's butcher's shop. It must be a Tuesday, the carcasses were stacked up against the end wall. It was only right, his father must be punished, what he was doing was terribly wrong, he was committing a mortal sin, he was doing it with a black woman and so he must die. It was the only way to save South Africa, to do his duty as an Afrikaner and as a white man! But he was too cold, his finger was frozen on the trigger, slowly he lowered the gun and tried to still his shivering body.

Peekay stood stooped over, panting, his hands resting on his knees. 'I'm a coward, I can't do it!' he gasped, without looking up. Then he began to sob softly, a great sorrow welling up in him, a terrible sadness for his whiteness, for his pale eyes and hair like straw which marked him as a vicious killer, a member of the *strange ones*. Slowly his fear began to leave him; the great hollow places it left behind were filled instead with grief. His grieving was for the mother, the great, warm mother of Africa with a washing basket on her head filled with freshly laundered clothes smelling of sunlight, the flash of her white teeth as she laughed and gobbled up the gossip of the day, the slow perambulation of her massive thighs. He mourned for the woman who cradled her soft brown children in her massive arms, her skin like velvet and her song sweet as goats' milk mixed with honey. He pulled her as gently as he could from the top of the pile and laid her on the ground. Then his grief turned back as he lifted a child, no more than eight years old, his small, innocent face serene in death, as though he'd fallen asleep and was being carried in the arms of a loving father to his bed. Peekay laid him down as well, not even seeing the gaping hole in his chest. His grief moved the people one by one and laid them gently down. At last, at the very bottom, lay Juicey Fruit Mambo, his two gold incisor teeth intact in his huge broken head. Peekay bent down and lifted his shoulders off the ground and then he sat and cradled Edward King George Juicey Fruit Mambo in his arms and wept and wept.

Thirty-two

In the days and weeks immediately after Sharpeville the country was in an uproar with strikes and protest marches occurring everywhere. This time the world sat up and took notice and the Johannesburg stock exchange hit an all-time low. Whites in their thousands mobbed travel agents and the United States, Australian, Canadian and New Zealand embassies were flooded with requests for immigration papers.

A week after Sharpeville, with the country almost brought to a standstill, Magistrate Coetzee called Tandia from a telephone box near the Magistrates Courts. From where he stood he could see the dilapidated building with its four windows on the first floor where Red had its offices. He could as easily have walked across but he couldn't take the chance of being seen. Besides, there wasn't much time; he had to take a chance that the Red telephone wasn't tapped.

When Tandia came to the phone Magistrate Coetzee spoke urgently. 'Listen, man, Tandy, the government has declared a state of emergency! This morning I signed warrants for the arrest of ninety-seven so-called activists here in Johannesburg,' he paused, 'you know I don't take sides in these things, but Gideon Mandoma's name was among them. Geldenhuis came personally to pick up the warrant for him, *jy moet gou maak*, there is not much time.' Then he added, 'I don't know how to advise you, but like I suggested might happen, in a week's time they are going to ban the ANC and PAC, they will become outlawed organizations. For your own sake perhaps you should resign now. Later, who knows, it might be useful to have done so?' He replaced the receiver without saying goodbye.

Tandia called Johnny Tambourine to her office and told him to meet them with an unmarked car from Levy's Carpet Emporium at the usual place. Months previously the four boys, who as tsotsis knew the city drains well, had located a manhole in the centre of the small rear courtyard to the Red building. They entered it and found it led to a main storm-water channel that was almost dry when it wasn't raining and easy to walk along. They'd checked all the manholes out until they'd found one in a quiet back street four city blocks away which they'd marked; another was marked nine blocks away. The four of them, Hymie, Peekay, Tandia and Gideon were the only people at Red to know about the escape route which, except for several practice runs, had never so far been used. A small storage shed was built over the manhole with a permanent covered walkway from the main building to the shed so that they couldn't be observed from the roof of a surrounding building.

Tandia went through to the tiny cubbyhole which served as Gideon's office and asked him if he'd come through to Peekay's office. Gideon saw the look of concern on her face and rose immediately, 'What is it, Tandy?'

'Trouble. Come quick, you may have only minutes.

There is a warrant out for your arrest. Geldenhuis!' She was shaking slightly and Gideon could see that she was scared.

Tandia quickly outlined Magistrate Coetzee's conversation to Peekay. 'I've organized a car and we'll use the drain. Johnny Tambourine will be waiting at the manhole in half an hour.'

'Not *we*, Tandia. Just Gideon!' Peekay said.

Tandia was shocked. 'I must go with him, Peekay!'

'No! You cut down his chances. If he's caught you're implicated.'

'He's right, Tandy,' Gideon said.

'Bullshit! The government have declared war, they're going to ban the ANC, Coetzee told me. If you have to go underground I'm in this fight too!'

'Tandy, you're more useful where you are. We have to have some people who are clean. We've discussed it, remember?' Gideon said.

'You can use Peekay. I'm a member of *Umkonto*. We have to fight, you can't stop me.'

Gideon spoke slowly. 'I am the head of *Umkonto*, its chief. You will remain here and you will not come with me, you hear?' It was a different Gideon talking; he was perfectly calm but there was no mistaking the authority in his voice and Tandia actually took a step backwards.

Her head downcast, looking at her fingernails, she said softly, 'Yes, sir.'

Peekay looked at his watch. 'You better scram.' He embraced Gideon. 'I see you with my heart, Gideon,' and drew away. 'You two would like a few moments alone, I'm sure.' He walked over to the door and closed it behind him.

'What will you do? Where will you go?' Tandia asked.

Gideon smiled. 'We have planned for this moment a long time. I will be in touch, but don't worry if you don't hear from me for a while. You can tell Peekay anything you hear from me, but no one else, not even one of us, not even *Umkonto*. You understand?'

Tandia nodded. 'Please Gideon, please let me fight.'

'I must go,' he said, as though he hadn't heard her. He moved towards the door then paused. 'There will be lots of time and lots of pain. The Boers are going to give us a terrible hiding at first. Your time will come, Tandia.'

Tandia ran over and kissed him, but Gideon pushed her away. 'No, Tandy, that's over. When we come to the end of this thing, we'll see.'

'Gideon! I love you,' Tandia cried.

'Tandia, you promised you would do my hating for me. I need your hate now. Don't love me, *hate for me!*' He closed the door and was gone.

'You Zulu bastard!' Tandia spat at the door. 'You think a woman can't fight!'

Gideon moved around the country evading detention and addressing young black South Africans who were being recruited to *Umkonto we Sizwe*. These meetings were known as 'the midnight cadres' because most of them took place in secret after midnight and never involved more than fifty young men and women, selected to attend a freedom lecture with 'General' Mandoma.

The title of general was an honorarium given to Gideon by his young recruits who spoke of him as 'General Mandoma, the undefeated champion of the world'. It was stirring stuff and with his own charisma and undoubted power with words, Gideon was quickly seen as the head of a terrorist army in the making.

But Gideon was a general without experience. The ANC had not anticipated guerrilla warfare with the white South African regime, believing right up to the time of Sharpeville that one day soon they would sit around the negotiating table. Gideon had not been given permission to recruit or train and no meaningful retaliatory infrastructure existed. The techniques of urban and rural guerrilla warfare were practically unknown to them. The ANC were strictly amateurs coming up against a hardened and highly experienced paramilitary police force led by the Special Branch whom they knew shot to kill.

After having been on the run for nearly eight months, Gideon was to be sent to Algeria to learn how to organize guerrilla groups and urban fighting units. The Algerians had offered to train the ANC in the business of fighting a superior and better organized force, using all the technique and know-how they had gained fighting the French for their independence.

Peekay arranged to see Gideon just before his departure. This last meeting, which would follow a typical midnight cadre talk so that there would be no suspicion of Gideon's departure even among his own people, was to take place in a church hall in the heart of Wesselton African Township on the outskirts of Ermelo, a smallish town in the Eastern Transvaal.

Peekay hadn't seen his friend for nearly two months and, as it was a week into December, among other things he carried with him several Christmas presents, though his most important reason for seeing Gideon was to give him the British passport prepared in Kenya for him. Peekay's visit to Gideon also concerned Tandia. In the aftermath of Sharpeville she had become hopelessly overloaded with work. The South African government was prosecuting the Sharpeville wounded and even members of the families of the dead. Several days before his final meeting with Gideon, Peekay had confronted Hymie, questioning his priorities.

Hymie had remained very quiet while Peekay talked and Peekay soon realized he'd spoken thoughtlessly. Hymie looked at him steadily. 'Have you any idea what you and Tandia bring into this company in fees every year?'

'Not really. Look, I'm sorry, Hymie, I spoke out of turn. You're right, I guess I don't think about it much, there's so much bloody work to do.'

'There was a time when money was important to you, Peekay, when you were too conscious of not having it. Now you've gone the other way. Why is it that you can never do anything more or less moderately? Let me tell you how much the two of you earned last month; about sufficient to keep the switchboard operating!'

'I'm sorry, Hymie, but you know the nature of the work. These people can't pay!'

Hymie brushed the comment aside. 'I have two talents, old son: I know how to make money and I reckon I'm a half-decent sort of a barrister. You appear to only have one: an ability to fight injustice without any thought of material gain. Our other partner, the pretty one, is so preoccupied she wouldn't even bother to eat if we didn't insist on her having a square meal once a day here in the office so we can talk. She thinks a statement is something the police take down, not something we send out. It was great when you were both doing some corporate work, the firm actually made a bob or two, enough on several occasions to pay for the electricity and maybe even the stationery and lunches!'

Hymie sighed. It was more a quick intake of air than a sigh, for Hymie never sighed. 'However, that all ended with Sharpeville. No legal firm was ever more aptly named, we have been in the *red* since the day we opened our doors.' Hymie's monologue was delivered with typical machine gun rapidity and now he slowed down. 'Peekay, altruism costs a great deal; we also serve who only stand around and make money! The fight for freedom in this man's republic is a very expensive business; every time you lose a civil case your client has costs awarded against him.'

Peekay was deeply ashamed and he hugged Hymie, apologizing. 'You know Hymie, I forget sometimes that without your genius I'd probably be a hack lawyer in a small town somewhere, another Don Quixote tilting at windmills, fighting cases for washerwomen.'

'So what's new? Talking about washerwomen, your clothes . . . how long is it since you bought a new suit and all the stuff that goes on under it?' Hymie pointed at Peekay's somewhat shabby attire. 'I recall you bought that grey suit at Macey's in New York after the first title fight!'

Hymie dressed beautifully. His suits were made by a short, rotund Jewish tailor in Saville Row known as Mr Emms, who believed that with the invention of the belt to replace what he called 'suspenders' the art of tailoring had come to an end. 'You're a successful barrister and you dress like a tramp!'

Peekay gave Hymie a wry grin. 'Some successful barrister! I have a string of noteworthy, even glorious defeats against my name. No barrister ever earned a bigger reputation with a poorer record. Christ, I sometimes wonder what the hell we're trying to do, Hymie? Yesterday, as I was walking back here from court a young guy stopped me. He wasn't any older than Johnny Tambourine; he asked me for a light. "Sorry, I don't smoke," I replied. "That's okay, I don't want a light anyway. I just want to say something to you. My mother, she thinks you are a hero, because you defended my father. Last night, the police, they came to my house. "Your father is dead," they say, "He committed suicide. He jumped from the fifth-floor window of John Vorster Square, you must come an' fetch his body!" The young guy was suddenly crying, "Fuck you, white man! Why you come to help him? Maybe if you don't come they would have beaten him and put him in Johannesburg Fort, but one day he would have come back to us!" Dammit, Hymie, I feel as though I'm achieving nothing. Pretoria is laughing at us, that is if they even notice the Jew, the rooinek bastard and the coloured bitch.'

'The fat Jew!' Hymie corrected. 'You're wrong, Peekay. There is a belief in the Jewish faith that in every generation a "just man" is born, someone who is incorruptible, the perfect innocent. The just man is sent to keep the chosen people on the rails, to prod their consciences and allow no compromises with the faith. By all definitions he's probably a perfect pain in the arse, but the Jews believe that without a just man they would not survive, that the light of Judaism would go out.' He paused. 'That's what we are, the last of the just men in South Africa. If we give up then the light goes out. They must be made to feel remorse.'

'Ha-bloody-ha! Do you think Geldenhuis feels remorse? He thinks of only one thing, vengeance! They're obsessed with blood, *bloed reinheid*! blood purity. If we are watchdogs of justice they don't hear us yapping at their ankles. I sometimes think Nguni has

697

more influence on the outcome of things than we do.'

'I've been meaning to talk to you about that, Peekay. Nguni is getting increasingly difficult to handle. He arrives at Angel Sport board meetings pretty sozzled on brandy. He's getting more and more rapacious, he keeps demanding a larger share of the action but isn't prepared to put up any capital. I must say, he seems to have rather a lot of clout with the various quasi government committees.'

Peekay laughed. 'Hymie, you're beating about the bush. What you're saying is that you think Nguni is in the pay of Pretoria. The share we gave him in Angel Sport after the Jackson fight was supposed to be the carrot to keep him close to us. What if he's using his position to spy on us? Tell him to go to buggery!'

Hymie nodded. 'His share in the firm is what's financing a Soweto bus company he started three years ago without us knowing. Without the income from Angel Sport he'd be up the spout.'

'Transport? He'd need a government concession for that.'

'Precisely. It's not the sort of thing they hand out willynilly.' Hymie sighed, 'I'm glad you agree we get rid of him.' He paused momentarily, 'What about his friendship with Tandia?'

Peekay knew precisely what Hymie meant. Nguni had used the excuse of Gideon's absence to start squiring Tandia, saying that he was responsible for showing her the ways of the African people. Tandia had been happy to go along with him. While she claimed at every opportunity to be unashamedly black, carrying a pass like any other black woman, she was conscious that her looks prevented her from being wholly accepted by the important echelons of black male society. Peekay watched in dismay as she seemed to spend most of her infrequent spare time with Nguni, seeming almost to see him as a father figure.

Peekay shrugged. 'Tandia's a big girl, she'll understand.'

'I hope you're right,' Hymie said.

Peekay knew Hymie too well not to realize what he was saying. He was asking him whether there was something about Tandia he ought to know. He'd shared his doubts about Mr Nguni for this very reason. Peekay knew he was abusing Hymie's trust by not confiding his concern about Tandia to him.

After Sharpeville, Peekay knew he was besotted with Tandia. It was only by supreme willpower that he could maintain his concentration in court when the going grew tedious. Sometimes he would sneak into her courtroom and sit in the gallery and listen to her. Tandia in a courtroom became transformed; she moved around in a black gown as though it was the costume of a queen, her form elegant and her gestures beautiful to watch. Her mind was as sharp as a whiplash and she commanded great respect from men who would spit on her rather than light her cigarette outside the courtroom.

Peekay would wake in the morning his whole mind filled with her. He'd lie still, hardly daring to breath, so that the notion of her lying in his arms remained undisturbed. At night his last thoughts would be of her and often he would find that his cheeks were wet with tears he hadn't even felt. Peekay was profoundly in love and there was nothing he could do about it.

Tandia sensed his feelings towards her and they filled her with fear. Her emotional defences were infinitely greater than Peekay's, besides which the thought of loving him was so fraught with danger and self-destruction that her mind couldn't entertain an idea so positively futile. She had believed herself in love with Gideon but over the weeks he'd been away from her, while she worried enormously for his safety, she found that she missed him less and less emotionally. She had decided that love for a man was something she could never have, that it had been eliminated from her psyche, that her brutalized past had branded her, searing the tenderness and love in her and leaving only scar tissue. In addition, the idea of sex with a white man, any white man, filled her with revulsion.

Nevertheless, sometimes when she looked at Peekay and he was unaware of her, she felt a strange compulsion to touch him. He was so strong and so vulnerable at the same time. His was a kind of innocence she couldn't believe possible in a human being. Tandia didn't know whether she wanted to shake him or hold him, but she knew he was different, different to any person she'd known – and that the difference was extraordinarily attractive while at the same time infuriating.

Peekay was in a high old mess with nobody to turn to, not even Hymie, who'd warned him off on the very first day they'd seen Tandia crossing the football stadium towards the boxing ring in the centre of Ellis Park.

Peekay's love for Tandia and his knowledge of Geldenhuis's letter tore at him remorselessly. He even thought to confront Tandia and tell her that Geldenhuis had shown him her signature on the statement and that he didn't care, that it didn't make the slightest difference. But, if he was mistaken, if there was some other explanation, his suspicion was such a blatant sign of mistrust in her that she would have every right to despise him for it, a thought he couldn't bear.

Suspicion feeds upon itself like a cancer and Tandia's relationship with Magistrate Coetzee now seemed to take on a sinister new meaning for Peekay. He found himself watching her with Coetzee and with Mr Nguni, as much as he was privy to either of these relationships. He became confused, not knowing whether he did so from jealousy or to spy on her. Either way he hated himself, hated what it was doing to him.

Doc had said, 'Every fact has two sides, it depends always from what side you are coming!' Peekay knew this to be true. Looked at from one side, Tandia had always shown the utmost dedication to the cause of justice for the black people and had been totally loyal to him and Hymie, while Magistrate Coetzee had proved a just and marvellous mentor.

Peekay was too good a lawyer not to examine the second interpretation, the facts seen from the opposite perspective. These could also be made to make almost perfect sense if you thought of it as a clever, patient and determined police operation designed, in the end, to trap Hymie, Gideon and himself and bring about their destruction.

But, much as he respected Geldenhuis, he couldn't bring himself to believe that the young police captain (Geldenhuis received promotion after Sharpeville) had the necessary clout to put something like this into place on his own. He thought about Klaasens, but quickly dismissed him too; the publicity the police colonel had received at the Tom Majombi murder trial would have made him too high on the suspect list. Any half-competent lawyer, using revenge as the true motive for their capture, would leave the police case open to ridicule in ten minutes in front of the bench.

And then, on the way to Wesselton township to see Gideon and to bid him farewell, driving along a stretch of road betveen Bethal and Ermelo, it struck Peekay. General Van Breeden, Police Commissioner for Johannesburg. He was the missing ingredient!

Almost from their first day back home Van Breeden had been involved with them. He'd been the influence behind allowing Ellis Park to be the venue for the fight and it had been his interference which had allowed an equal black audience to attend. Over the years the likeable and capable police commissioner had maintained a friendly relationship with both of them, though more particularly with Hymie, who maintained an unlisted telephone in his home where the two men could contact each other at any time.

Tandia, Mr Nguni, Magistrate Coetzee and Van Breeden, with Geldenhuis playing the overt role of hunter and later to distract attention from the others; these four made an almost perfect flip-side of the coin.

'Jesus! Stop it Peekay,' he commanded himself. South Africa had become such a place of hate, suspicion and fear that his imagination was running away from him. Why was it that the most demented, the most evil scenario always seemed to be the most likely? People were always seeing a conspiracy where none existed, making connections which were dubious to say the least. He spent half his life in court disproving conjecture. The police prosecutors could see connections which were so completely tenuous as to be absurd, yet they'd often spend days building on them, heaping them with innuendo and often helping them along with false witness. He was indulging in the behaviour of a Geldenhuis, the Special Branch mentalities which believed everyone was guilty until proven innocent.

It all hinged on the original confession by Tandia to being a prostitute. Peekay decided to ask Gideon whether Tandia had ever talked to him about it. He thought it was unlikely, but people in love will often clear the emotional deck; it was too important not to try.

It would be tricky trying to maintain his loyalty to both Gideon and Tandia and not to send Gideon away disenchanted or to provoke him to an emotional defence of his woman. But Peekay was desperate for some sort of reassurance and he felt he had to try. He told himself there were other reasons as well. Because it had been a natural assumption after Gideon's escape that Tandia would be watched by the Special Branch it had been suggested that he make no attempt to contact her. But love takes enormous and often foolish chances and Peekay didn't know whether Gideon had tried to see her despite this warning. Tandia also knew about Gideon's departure to Algeria. Perhaps Gideon himself was in terrible danger and should be warned. If Geldenhuis knew of his imminent departure, he would strike immediately, pulling out all stops to find him, issuing a border and airport alert and sealing off the borders to South Africa with extra men and helicopters.

In actual fact, two of the half-dozen Special Branch black men delegated to watch Tandia since Gideon's disappearance had been hospitalized by unseen assailants, believed to be tsotsis. In each case robbery had been assumed to be the motive, and as the muggings had taken place several miles from where Tandia lived and when the men had been off duty, it was assumed by Geldenhuis to be a coincidence, though nonetheless one to watch carefully. Peekay noted this as yet another contradiction to Tandia's guilt. If Johnny Tambourine and his boys were active, surely this was another sign of her innocence?

Approaching Ermelo and Wesselton township, Peekay stopped to pick up a small barefooted kid of no more than twelve who'd been waiting by arrangement on a lonely strip of road outside the town. The small, serious-faced boy, who wore only a pair of ragged khaki shorts, looked at him a little fearfully from the side of the road as he responded shyly to the password Peekay gave him, his eyes showing big in the bright moonlight as Peekay asked him his name. 'It is Simon, sir,' he answered proudly in English. Peekay later learned from Simon's father that his son had been waiting for him beside the road for eleven hours and had gone without supper. Simon climbed into the front of the car and seated himself on the edge of the seat, his back straight as a ram-rod with both his hands holding onto the dashboard. He gave Peekay shy directions to a place under a willow tree beside a small river, really more a *spruit*, where he could conceal his car. From there they walked the mile or so into the dark township.

General Mandoma, the undefeated champion of the world, had just risen to speak and the kids, some no more than fifteen, rose to their feet chanting, 'General! General! General!' as he stood ready to address them. He saw Peekay enter and silently motioned him to sit at one of two vacant chairs set at the back of the room. Gideon held his hand up for silence and when they'd quietened down and seated themselves, sitting cross-legged on the floor, he opened up with a huge smile. A Gideon Mandoma smile was something to see; it had the effect of the sun coming from behind a cloud and it immediately transferred to the people around him, so that the kids resumed his smile spontaneously, leaning forward, drawn impulsively towards him.

Hymie called Gideon's smile his secret weapon. 'If they ever catch you, Gideon, our defence will be a piece of cake. We'll say nothing and simply have you smile at the jury once every hour!'

Now Gideon began, his expression one of mock seriousness. 'Yes, I am a general, that is true. The white authorities already accept this, they call me, "The General Nuisance"!' The smile came again and, coupled with this simple corny quip, it brought the house down. Gideon could count on another fifty soldiers joining 'The Spear'.

Now his face grew serious. 'I am a general whose army is made up of barefooted amateurs. My automatic weapons are flick knives and sharpened bicycle spokes, my artillery is stones and, in a battle charge, my bayonets are sharpened sticks!' He paused, looking at his audience. 'But we will learn, my brothers! We will learn, my sisters! We will sharpen your teeth, comrades, and make your hands familiar with the explosion 'plastic' and we will show you how to make a bomb from an old alarm clock and stuff found on this town's junk heap and how a beer bottle filled with paraffin and an old rag can be your hand grenades against the police.'

There was a murmur of excitement around the room. Gideon changed tack suddenly. 'This unlikely force, this barefoot army of freedom, it can run partly on courage but it also needs money. We are not rich, we do not have taxes and goldmines to finance our fight, but we will ask the people to give.' He paused. 'The white people!' Mouths fell open in surprise and a murmur rose from the small crowd. 'There are those amongst you who are already skilled at helping white people to give; your fingers know the feel of pockets and crawl as quickly as spiders into handbags.' Gideon looked over at the dozen or so young tsotsis in the audience who stood together in a bunch at the back. 'Gentlemen, from tonight you are our bankers, from Wesselton native township,' he raised his hands and wiggled his fingers, 'from your fighting fingers, *Umkonto we Sizwe* need one hundred pounds a week!'

The crowd gasped. This was a great deal of money, the weekly wages for twenty-five families. A tall, gangly youth stepped forward. He was dressed in typical tsotsi fashion. 'We will bring you two hundred, General!' he called. The crowd cheered and beat their hands against the cement floor and the dozen or so tsotsi boys glowed with pride. It was the first time these tough street waifs had felt needed in their lives; the idea of fighting for freedom by simply 'doing their own thing' was enormously appealing.

Gideon looked serious. 'Some of you will be caught and go to prison. If you find yourself in prison look for the ANC leader. If there is no ANC leader there,' Gideon shook his head, 'Haya! I don't think this is possible, but if there isn't then ask for the PAC, it doesn't matter, *Umkonto we Sizwe* or *Poqo*, we are all fighting for the same thing, we all eat with the same spoon.' Gideon quoted an old Xhosa proverb, '*Umuntu ngumuntu ngomnye*, People are people through other people. In prison you will learn things, new things you can use. You will also teach things, things you already know how to do on the street. If you go to prison you must use the time well, so when you come out your teeth will be sharp with malice for our oppressors!' Gideon made the act of going to prison seem a worthy one. 'Prison for our soldiers is like going to the white man's boarding school, a private college; the *amaBhunu*, the Boers, will supply the food, the clothes and the classrooms and we will all go willingly to our daily lessons.'

There was a great deal of laughter over this, though it was laughter mixed with fear. Everyone knew how brutal existence for a black man was in a South African prison. Peekay marvelled at Gideon's way with the people. 'Some of you will die,' Gideon said simply. He turned his palms up in an elegantly simple gesture, which looked more like a blessing than a shrug. 'It is in the nature of a soldier to die.' His voice changed and grew soft. 'But dying is not easy. You will sit alone in the death cell when the great dawn of no tomorrow comes and you will think, "I am alone! My brothers have forsaken me!" But you will not be alone; soon you will hear the singing, the singing of those around you who have wakened with the dawn to thank you and bid you farewell.' Gideon's voice was now only a whisper, 'People are people through people.'

The room was silent and unabashed tears could be seen in the eyes of many in the audience. 'This is no time to cry, my comrades, we are going together on a journey,' Gideon smiled his wonderful smile once more. 'One day we will be free. We will come out of our houses one morning and the air will be sharp and clean and we will smell the wood smoke of the morning cooking fires and we will fill our lungs with the breath of freedom! And you will say, each one of you, "I remember, I was there when it all began".'

Gideon changed the mood as abruptly as he had done before, turning to Peekay who sat mesmerized. What a great barrister Gideon would make; what a tremendous leader he was becoming.

'We have with us tonight a friend,' Gideon gestured to Peekay at the back of the hall. 'I went against our custom and did not introduce him to you at the beginning, this is because he isn't here!' The crowd laughed, but only the youngest amongst them turned to look at Peekay.

'I know it is difficult for some of you to understand, but not all whites are against us. There are some who work with us. Some of you will know of the work which is done by my friend Peekay for the people, the work which is done by Red. Peekay has put himself in danger by coming here tonight, but now you can see his face and see his heart. If you are in trouble in the fight for freedom and the police catch you, because you have joined *Umkonto* and because you are a freedom fighter, you can call Peekay. He will come to you in prison and he will fight for you in the courts.'

The tall youth who had volunteered to double the weekly tithe for the township now asked, 'How will we let you know, how will we tell you we have been caught?'

Gideon chuckled, 'You are not alone now. You are *Umkonto we Sizwe*; we will know and then the *Ono-shobishobi Ingelosi* will know,' he snapped his fingers, 'just like that!'

Gideon brought the meeting to a close and a great many of the audience came up to him simply to touch him before they departed, their fingers touching his hand or some part of his anatomy lightly, briefly, not expecting a response. It was as though by actually touching him they gained the power and confidence they needed; the concept of *people are people through people* was operating instinctively in them. Gideon's was a rag-tag army based on trust and not on fear.

'Come, my brother, we can talk now. A woman here has cooked some food, we must go now to that hut.' The two men walked together through the township in the moonlight, the people who had attended the meeting gliding past them silently. They came to a small shack and Gideon knocked politely at the door. A large woman opened it quietly and they entered. Inside the shack was divided by a curtain behind which must have been the sleeping quarters for whoever occupied it.

Gideon pointed to the curtain, an eyebrow raised in question. 'It is only me here. My husband and my two boys they are in gaol,' the woman said. 'I have cooked food and I will go now.' She touched them each lightly on the hand and left the shack.

A tiny table was set in the centre of the room lit with a hurricane lamp. On it sat a pot of *phutu*, stiff meal-iemeal porridge, and a smaller one of meat and gravy together with two enamel plates and spoons. A pot of tea, a can of Ideal milk, a cup without a handle used as a sugar bowl, and two tin mugs were placed on the centre of the table. Both men began to eat in the African way, spooning meat and gravy into the plates and taking the stiff porridge from the pot with their fingers, dousing it in the gravy before bringing it to their mouths. They were both ravenous and neither spoke as they ate.

After they'd eaten Peekay produced several packages from his bag. He handed one to Mandoma. 'Here, it's your Christmas present. It's something I own which I want you to carry with you always.'

Gideon took the parcel. 'Who knows where I will be on Christmas day, may I open it now?'

'Of course!'

Gideon unwrapped the small parcel. Inside, resting in

a beautiful handtooled leather scabbard, was the hunting knife Gert had made for Peekay.

'My sincerest hope is that you never have to use it, but if you do, my hand is on it with you, Gideon. When you strike, you strike for me as well.'

Gideon withdrew the blade from its scabbard and felt the balance of the knife in his hand. 'It is beautiful, but the skull, the skull on the handle, it means it is a killing knife.'

'I am sorry, Gideon, it's not much of a Christmas gift.'

'It is a gift of concern and protection, that makes it a gift of love, I will keep it always with me, Peekay.' Gideon put the remaining gifts from Hymie and Tandia aside to open later. Peekay withdrew a passport from the inside pocket of his jacket and offered it to Gideon. 'It is a British passport obtained through Kenya. Hymie brought it back with him from London yesterday. You'll have to get used to your new name.' He handed Gideon an envelope. 'Inside you'll find your new birth certificate, it indicates you were born in a mission hospital and educated at a mission school in Kitale which is a northern outpost of Kenya's white highlands.' Peekay put his hand on Gideon's shoulder. 'Well, you old bastard, at last you're going off to a very selective boarding school to be educated.'

Gideon chuckled, deep down in his throat as though it came from his stomach. 'Tell Hymie thanks, the people will honour him some day for this.'

Peekay interrupted. 'Please Gideon, Oliver Tambo is organizing your travel details outside South Africa. I don't want to know how you leave or how you get to Algeria.'

Gideon shook his head and laughed softly. 'Haya,

haya, Peekay, there is so much to learn about being a freedom fighter.' He looked at Peekay. 'In the boxing ring it's so easy, so clean, one on one, your fists, your heart and your head. The bell goes, you fight and in the end the man with the most skill and the most courage,' he laughed softly as though thinking, 'maybe even the man with the last punch wins.'

Peekay grinned, 'That's all it took, you bastard, you saved it up special!'

Gideon laughed, 'I have not told you about this punch, from where it came. When I was very small, I was a herd boy and every morning we would go out and milk the cows and bring in the milk. I longed to grow up and come to the big city and be somebody. Every afternoon when it was time to bring the cattle in we would take them first to the river to drink and then we would have the competition for the boots.'

Gideon looked down at his shiny shoes and wiped a spot of dirt off his left toecap with a casual brush of his hand. 'There was an old man who worked in Durban and every year he would come back to his home on holiday for two weeks and he would bring a pair of boots. His baas would give him these old boots to wear on his holidays and he would give the herd boys the old boots the baas gave him to wear before, the last time he came. These boots they had done a lot of walking and there were big holes in the soles, but they were city boots, the guy among us who wore them, he was the king of the herd boys, if only for that day.

'Every night when we came to the river for the cattle to drink, we would put one of the boots up on a rock and count fifty steps and each boy would take two stones. The boy who hit the boot wore them home and

711

all the next day until sunset, then we would come again to throw stones for the boots.

'All day, while I watched the cattle alone on the mountain, I would throw stones. I would put a small rock, the size of a boot, on a big rock and count fifty steps and throw at it.

When I could no longer lift my arm because it had become very, very sore I would start with my other hand. Always I would throw until I could not lift this arm also, then I would start on the other again. Soon I was the one who almost always wore the boots.

'I was very proud and all the other guys respected me because I always won fair and square. When I beat you, Peekay, for the title, that last punch, I had nothing left, but in my head I said, "My arms they are stronger than his, he has never thrown for the boots, he has already got the boots. I have one stone left, one last throw." That's what won the title for me.'

They sat in silence for a moment, two friends who knew each other well. Then Peekay cleared his throat. 'Gideon, there is something.'

Gideon replied softly, 'Haya, Peekay, yes, I can feel this thing, your heart is heavy, heavy! What is this something?'

'It's Tandia.'

Gideon chuckled. 'You are in love, I have known this thing a long time.'

Peekay looked shocked. 'I cannot deny this, Gideon. But I know it is impossible! You are my friend and even if I fought you for her, the law says I cannot have her.'

'The law cannot stop a man and a woman. The law of nature is stronger than the law of the *ama-Bhunu* ... At the mission school when I was young, once the teacher was reading from the Bible. It was a hot afternoon and I was nearly asleep, but I remember the words so very well.' Gideon paused and then, almost as though he was a schoolboy again, started to recite: '"Show me the way of an eagle in the air, show me the way of a snake on the rock and show me the way of a man with a maid, when I know these three things, then all things are known unto me!"'

Peekay grinned, 'Thank you, Gideon, but I am not in the woman-stealing business. You quote from the Bible and I will quote you a Zulu proverb, "The heart is a hunter who does not seek permission from the herd to hunt." I think it means roughly the same thing but, nonetheless, unless Tandia herself decides otherwise she will, I'm sure, be waiting for you when you get back.'

Gideon shook his head. 'Peekay, I know Tandia and I know Nguni. That Zulu, he was my manager since I was an *umfana*. Since I fought you that first time in Sophiatown. That man, he is a big pain, he would give a headache to an Aspro!'

Peekay laughed. Gideon was trying to put him at ease and now he continued, 'I cannot be angry with Nguni, he is very greedy; to have a beautiful woman on your arm is good for business. The people they look at you and they know you are rich and have a lot of power, that's what a beautiful woman can do for a guy. I have done this also, but when the time comes I will take a woman from my own kraal, it is the Zulu way. A woman from another *isigodi* but from my own tribe who can give me sons, the sons of a chief. When I return, Tandia will not be waiting for me, that is for sure, my brother.'

Peekay had never heard Gideon speak like this before. It had never occurred to him that Gideon might take a village woman for his wife. Gideon had the potential to be a future leader of South Africa and Tandia, a beautiful and intelligent wife of mixed blood, would have been politically perfect as his partner. Peekay now realized that it was precisely Gideon's grass-roots personality that made him so effective as a leader. He had a foot in both camps; he was a sophisticated and highly successful urban African who had not forsaken his tribal roots. He could reach his people at any level without having to pretend to be anyone but himself.

Now Gideon looked at Peekay and shrugged, 'Tandia too, she wants something from Nguni, she wants acceptance, the respect of the elders, it is important for her to climb into her black skin.' He looked up at Peekay, his eyes filled with concern for his friend. 'This time I am glad there is a bad law which says a black woman and a white man they cannot make love.' He paused again, biting his lower lip. 'Tandia cannot love a man, Peekay. Inside her something it has happened, I don't know what is this thing. Even if the law was not there, she is not the woman for you. She cannot make you happy, man!'

'Gideon, I can't think about her, but I also can't stop thinking about her; it is a nightmare and now there is something else.' Peekay took a deep breath and told Gideon what had transpired with Geldenhuis.

'. . . And then he showed me a statement, a piece of paper signed by Tandia when she was just a kid. Geldenhuis is in a perfect position to blackmail her, to ruin her life and therefore to force her to be an informer.'

Gideon looked at Peekay. He spoke quickly, but there was anger and hurt in his eyes. 'I don't want to hear this! Not from you, Peekay. If Tandia was a white woman, would you believe this? Because she is black,

714

you think maybe ... maybe that white policeman he is right?' He made a fist and clenched his jaw. 'You believe this dog shit when he shows you a piece of paper!' By now Gideon was shouting, his shoulders shaking with rage.

Peekay was shocked. He put his hand on Gideon's shoulder but the black man knocked it away. He tried again, and again Gideon pushed Peekay's hand away. 'Please Gideon, listen to me! I ... I don't know what to believe! I'm in love with Tandia, I'm a white man and if I fall in love with her I destroy her! Destroy everything! So it's simple. I'm a big boy, I know what to do. I can handle that. I *have* to handle it!' Peekay paused, catching his breath. 'In the end it concerns only me and I can learn to live with that. But now there is this thing, this statement. This isn't just me any more. This is everything I care about! You whom I love, Hymie whom I love, the things we are fighting for. Those people in Sharpeville who died. What do I do? Say nothing? Keep hoping it's all bullshit? Another Geldenhuis trap?' He paused again. 'But what if it isn't? If that bastard has got her nailed down? Tell me, what the fuck do I do? If I remained silent, said nothing and it all happened? What if Geldenhuis does have Tandia on a string?'

Gideon's voice was cold and angry and he spoke in Zulu. 'Every black woman is a whore in the eyes of people like Geldenhuis! Every little black girl ever born is supposed to be waiting to spread her legs the first time she sees near a white boy. That's what we're fighting. When it comes down to it, that's what apartheid is all about! This single, terrible fear within the white man's mind that the black whore will tempt his sons and destroy his bloodline.

715

'But what about temptation? Well, Afrikaners know all about temptation, they tell us all the time they are a deeply Christian people. Temptation is the work of the devil, temptation is evil. And what colour is evil?' Gideon gave Peekay a bitter smile, 'Evil is black, of course. So when the white man feels his temptation, he knows it is the work of the devil! And when he rejects temptation, separates himself from it, what is that?' Gideon laughed scornfully. 'That is God's mercy. Separation . . . apartheid, is therefore the work of God!'

The anger had left Gideon's eyes, but now there was a sadness and his voice remained urgent. 'Can't you see, Peekay? Can't you see, what we're fighting is *your* fear. And when *you* think Tandia may be guilty, it is *your* own guilt you are feeling.' He stabbed his finger at Peekay. 'You say you love this woman? This black woman? What is it you love? Her body? Her long legs and nice tits? Her arse? Her beautiful face? Her smile? Or is it something else? Something that makes her Tandia? Her dedication to truth and honesty? Her courage? Her desire for fairness and justice for all of the people? Her ability to fight like a tiger for all of these things? Her determination to be better, stronger, quicker in her mind than those who oppress us? Even her hate? Sometimes you can even love a person's hate! Tandia is black. *She* knows *she* is not a white, she is not afraid of herself; that piece of paper she signed when she was a child, it is not *her* guilt on that piece of paper, it is the guilt of Geldenhuis. Geldenhuis is carrying his own guilt around on that piece of paper.' Gideon's voice grew suddenly strident again. 'It is not possible for him to use it against her, blackmail her, because, listen to me, Peekay, she is not guilty!'

Thirty-three

Peekay picked up the *Johannesburg Star*, turning quickly to the classified section. For the past three weeks he'd been doing the same thing each morning and now he saw what he was looking for:

> *This little piggy went to market*
> *This little piggy had a beer alone*
> *This little piggy climbed a peak*
> *And this little piggy came home.*

Gideon was back! The coded message conveyed that Gideon would be crossing the border from the Portuguese side into Swaziland and that Peekay should be alone at the market-place at Pigg's Peak, a small town in Swaziland. He would indicate his presence by placing a case of Lion beer in the back of the car and the assignation would take place in four day's time at four o'clock in the afternoon.

Peekay worried about Gideon's return. He'd tried in his letters to persuade him to stay away, to lead from the outside. The courts were full of ANC and PAC men who'd been captured, who'd shown themselves no match for the Special Branch. Informers were everywhere and Peekay feared his friend's life would be wasted on a senseless act of terrorism.

But Gideon was coming back. Coming through Swaziland was a peculiar route. His face was famous in the Portuguese territory, he'd fought twice in Lourenco Marques so he'd be easily recognized by the locals. The only advantage was that it was less than four hours from the border to Pigg's Peak and from there they could cross at Bulembu and come into South Africa through Barberton, country Peekay knew intimately.

Still it was chancy. Then it occurred to him that Gideon was travelling without the knowledge of the ANC. This would cut down the likelihood of informers alerting the Special Branch. Coming through Lourenco Marques also had the added advantage that Gideon would come straight off a ship and be across the border in less than two hours.

Peekay still hoped to convince Gideon not to return when he met him face to face. The three partners had all but concluded that what Peekay and Tandia were doing, in terms of achieving justice, was very nearly pointless, that by going overseas and beginning the task of working for sanctions against South Africa they would, in the long run, have a far greater chance of bringing the apartheid regime to its knees. When the whites saw their way of life being eroded they would be less inclined to support a fanatical racist regime. Greed is nearly always the best persuader.

Peekay wanted only one more thing, a second crack at Jannie Geldenhuis: an opportunity to get the infamous police captain on the stand again, preferably on a charge of murder.

This time Peekay was vastly more experienced and,

while he expected to lose the case regardless of how blatantly he proved the policeman's guilt, he was confident that he could use the courtroom as a stage to expose, for the entire world to see, the perfidy, cruelty and moral corruption of apartheid. He simply needed to trap Geldenhuis one more time.

Peekay knew this wouldn't be easy. The policeman was watching him as carefully as he was waiting for Geldenhuis to make an error of judgement. Hymie tried desperately to persuade him that it was a foolhardy plan. Hymie was getting close to despair; he'd calculated the odds of their remaining safe from the new laws which seemed specially designed for their demise and he'd concluded that time was running out for Peekay and Tandia in particular, but really for all of them.

Just a week before Peekay read Gideon's message in the *Star* he'd tried to force Peekay to look at the case rationally. 'Listen to me, this isn't like last time when we nailed the bastard with Tom Majombi! The law has been doctored to the point where as long as Geldenhuis kills black people in the name of the Special Branch he's safe as a house. He isn't going to do anything he can't justify as police work.'

'Ja, I know, Hymie, but sooner or later he has to do something we can nail him on personally. You can't just be evil in one way and good in all other respects; sooner or later he has to act on his own, do something which he can't justify in the name of the law. Guys like him always do.'

Peekay looked anguished. 'Hymie, I know you think part of it is getting even for Tandia. But I promise it isn't that! I mean, if it was, I dare say, with the contacts we have, we could plan some sort of ultimate revenge, then we could all leave South Africa and in the best of all worlds I could try to persuade Tandia to love me enough to marry me legally. You could marry Harriet and we'd all live happily ever after, spreading truth and justice and persuading the world to bring sanctions against the government in Pretoria.'

Peekay stopped, rubbing his forehead with the butt of his hand as though he was trying to expunge what he was about to say next. 'But that's just what it isn't! I want the world to see what *we* see, that Jannie Geldenhuis isn't an isolated madman, but a part of the logical offspring of a country where one section of the population has gone mad! We may not all be like Geldenhuis, but in any other country he would be either in prison or under severe psychiatric treatment in an institution. In our country he is a God-fearing citizen, who reads the lesson in church on Sunday and who is about to be promoted to colonel by a grateful government. He is a media personality, a famous policeman who keeps our children safe from the pathological fears of their insane parents. Geldenhuis is there because we appointed him; it is our collective insanity which allows him, and the thousands like him, to be who they are!'

'Peekay, I tremble in my very boots when I hear you talk like this. Let's at least put a deadline on leaving South Africa.' Hymie laughed grimly. 'My people have an instinct for knowing when to move. The only time we denied that instinct we paid too big a price. Let's put a time on leaving and I'll get Red sorted out so we don't lose too much. What do you say?'

Peekay shook his head. 'Hymie, I don't know. I don't know that I can leave just like that with nothing to show for ten years as a barrister. Less than nothing! My country is in ten times worse shape now than it was when we left Oxford. We have contributed bugger all!'

Hymie grew suddenly angry. 'Arsehole! You're show-ing all the signs of being a martyr. You know what you want to make me do? You want to make me puke! You've done everything a man can do for his country except die for it! If you want to do that, then go ahead, most of the whites will breathe a sigh of relief because you're no longer there to prick at their collective con-sciences. The blacks will mourn you for a day or two and then you'll just be another white liberal who got swallowed up in their plight. You won't even be useful dead! A white man dying for the cause of South Africa's blacks wouldn't even make a useful martyr!'

The conversation had ended there, but Peekay knew Hymie was right; it was only a matter of time before the government delivered the blow which would put them out of the game. Geldenhuis was holding all the aces. Now as he sat reading the paper and thinking of Gideon's return he wondered how he might persuade Tandia to come with them. She agreed that they'd become a useless appendage to the justice system but she wanted to go underground to fight. Perhaps if he could also persuade Gideon she'd see the need to get out, but Peekay was fairly certain both would elect to stay and fight even knowing that the odds were stacked against them. He despaired at the thought of Gelden-huis on the loose with Tandia on her own without the protection of Red. He simply couldn't see how he could possibly leave without her.

Peekay left for Barberton after breakfast on the day he was to meet Gideon at Pigg's. He stopped briefly at the library to say hello to Mrs Boxall and then drove up to the Berea to see his family.

He received the usual joyous reception from the black twins. Even his mother seemed delighted to see him;

she'd mellowed considerably since he'd obeyed the Lord and given up boxing. Peekay now supported the family financially and she no longer needed to sew and had grown quite plump from all the morning and afternoon teas she attended witnessing in His name and generally doing the Lord's work. If only he would stop wasting his talent on black murderers and terrorists and become a judge, a born-again judge, she would have the perfect son. She, in conjunction with the Lord, was working on this during their 'quiet time' every day.

Peekay explained that he could only stay a couple of hours and was on his way to Swaziland, news which was met with a great deal of consternation, particularly from the twins who'd rushed to the kitchen to rustle up a batch of pumpkin scones. Peekay wasn't going to chance bringing Gideon over the border, he'd bring him back over the mountains on foot, and so he got the twins to pack two sets of bush clothes. Then he told Dee and Dum to take food enough for two meals out to Eendrag farm where they would find a motor car parked outside the old house. 'The boot will be open; put the food in the boot.'

'We will wait for you, so we can cook you a proper meal,' Dum said. Peekay forbade them to do so and their bottom lips dropped simultaneously in an exact and unconscious duplicate expression of dismay.

Peekay called Gert at the prison and asked if he could borrow his half-ton utility and if he'd meet him at Eendrag farm. Gert didn't question him when they met, he understood that if an explanation was necessary Peekay would have made it. Peekay arranged to have Gert pick up his bakkie at an Indian store two miles into the border on the Swaziland side in two days' time, the keys left with the Indian storekeeper. Dropping Gert off at the prison, he left just after two in the afternoon for the drive over the mountains to Swaziland.

The road to Havelock is winding and not well used, so that Peekay felt he had the mountains to himself. It was an early spring day in September and the sky was an intense blue, turning the crags and bluffs around him to grey. The winter tussocks which grew on the high slopes shone silver with the late season, making a dreaming landscape around him. He imagined the still-ness beyond the whining engine of the truck: the crystal cave of Africa was no more than a few miles from the road he travelled and he thought of Doc, the knight errant of Africa, his long thin body stretched out on his white throne.

Sudden tears welled in Peekay's eyes. 'Doc, the madness has won in the beloved country,' he said, looking up into the mountains. He pulled over and cut the engine, his tears making him unable to see the winding road. The total stillness swept around him and enclosed him as though drawing him into the dreaming time where Doc lay in his cave. 'Doc, please help me to fight the madness,' he whispered.

Peekay crossed the border and the road deteriorated almost immediately so that it took almost forty minutes to reach the little town of Pigg's Peak. He drove to the general store, bought a case of Lion beer and a carton of cigarettes and returned to the car. Then he drove to the open marketplace where twice a week the women from the villages brought produce for sale. He placed the beer in the back of the truck and the cigarettes in the glove compartment, got back in and waited. It was five minutes to four in the afternoon.

A few minutes later an African, wearing a shabby khaki army greatcoat, perhaps in his fifties, opened the door on the passenger side and climbed in. He smelt pretty ripe and Peekay extended his hand. The black man took it, and they shook hands in the traditional African double-grip manner. 'My name is Julius,' the black man said slowly in English, pausing between each word.

'Peekay, my name is Peekay. Thank you for being on time to meet me,' Peekay said in Siswati. The older man was delighted and threw back his head and laughed, showing only four yellowed teeth in his mouth. 'Now I know you are the *Onoshobishobi Ingelosi*, you speak all the languages of the people!' He pointed to four young men who stood outside waiting. 'Please, we can give for these boys a lift, they go to the same village.'

Peekay readily agreed and the four young guys, laughing among themselves, climbed into the truck.

Peekay turned on the ignition. 'Where are we going, Julius?'

'We are going to see Somojo. It is near the great mountain Bulembu, I think maybe one hour.' Julius held up his forefinger. It was almost back to the border he'd just come from, though Julius had no way of knowing this.

'Somojo? The Great sangoma?' Peekay was surprised, the greatest of the living medicine men seldom saw whites.

'He said we must bring the *Onoshobishobi Ingelosi* to him.'

Peekay had expected that Gideon might be in hiding in a friendly village where they would have to deal with a clan chief and he'd brought three good white collar-less cotton poplin shirts with him. The shirts were of the old-fashioned kind intended for starched collars; worn collarless, with a traditional stud to hold the neck

724

together, they were much favoured by older African men of some standing. They were not a gift worthy of the great Somojo, Peekay thought; he would need to apologize profusely when he presented them.

They arrived at sunset and Peekay was taken to a reception hut, a round beehive construction made of woven grass held into a conical shape by saplings, known as a *guga*. A woman brought him a huge old Victorian porcelain basin and jug filled with water for him to wash. The floor was covered with a freshly woven grass mat; a small three-legged stool in the very centre of the room was the single piece of furniture in the round hut. At the door was an earthenware water pot of dark clay with a small drinking calabash floating on top of it.

The four young guys brought out the case of beer, his canvas overnight bag and sleeping bag and placed these within the hut. Then they squatted beside the doorway, talking in an animated manner, enjoying the importance of the occasion. From their conversation they appeared to know nothing of Gideon but had simply gone along to bring Peekay to Somojo's kraal. It seemed unlikely that they'd simply cadged a lift or they would have moved on after they'd arrived. Then it occurred that they were there to guard him in the event that they had been followed.

Julius, too, hadn't mentioned Gideon. Peekay walked out to the bakkie and retrieved the carton of cigarettes from the glove box. He broke out a pack and he handed it to the boys who were delighted and divided the pack between them, each lighting a cigarette and keeping the remaining four, sticking two behind each ear.

Using his rolled-up sleeping bag as a pillow, Peekay lay on the grass mat which was new and still smelt of the sweetness of the meadow. When it had grown dark in the hut and Peekay had been kept waiting an hour or so, sufficiently long for the old witchdoctor to assert his importance, a small boy came to fetch him. Carrying the three white poplin shirts, Peekay stepped out into the early evening. The village was a big one with perhaps fifty beehive huts built around a cattle kraal enclosure of wooden stakes and thorn-tree scrub. The cattle were being driven into the safety of the kraal for the night by the herd boys, one of whom was cracking a whip and really acting the boss. Outside the huts, fires were beginning to crackle and snap as women fed green thorn-bush branches into them. The smell of smoke, cattle dung and dust, the sound of the lowing cattle, the barking and yapping of the scrawny yellow mongrels and the laughter of the women as they prepared the evening meal filled the air and seemed to Peekay to be an altogether fitting way to end a long and tiring day.

The small boy ran ahead of him, moving between huts, scattering chickens who'd not yet flown to their roosts for the night. They came to a path on the edge of the village and Peekay followed the child down it. It was getting dark, as it does quickly after sunset in those parts where the high mountains snaffle the light. They came to a clearing completely enclosed with a high wooden fence made of heavy stakes. The child stopped at the opening to the enclosure and pointed inwards; then he turned and ran for his life back down the way they'd just come. Peekay turned and watched as the darkness swallowed the child up.

The small compound contained three beautifully constructed traditional conical huts, one large central one and a smaller one to each side of it. A fire burned outside the large hut and two jackal-skin karosses were spread over grass mats beside the fire. Almost immediately a young woman appeared from one of the smaller huts and silently invited Peekay to sit, pointing to one of the karosses.

Peekay removed his shoes and sat cross-legged, placing the white shirts on his lap. Outside the compound a frog began to croak and almost immediately the night was filled with the the sound of frogs responding. Peekay had seen no water but guessed there must be a dam or stream nearby. He heard the sound of coughing coming from the large hut, then hawking and the pause of someone spitting. Then he made out the irascible voice of an old man saying something he couldn't quite hear.

Moments later the great Somojo stood at the entrance, being led by a second young African woman. He was a little man, bent over with age, wrapped entirely in a bright purple blanket. He allowed himself to be led to the kaross next to Peekay where the first young woman waited for him. Together they placed him on the soft warm fur and pulled the blanket around him so that only his ancient head appeared above the purple mound. He sniffed and smacked his toothless gums; his rheumy eyes appeared not to see and his chest wheezed so that he gave the impression of someone who wonders where he is and is completely confounded as to how he got there.

The Swazis are small and lightly built, a mountain people, but Somojo was positively tiny and took up hardly more room than if the blanket alone had been carelessly dropped to the ground. It was hard to believe that this old man was one of the most powerful black men in Africa, the greatest of all the medicine men alive, the wizard of all the wizards. When the drums of Africa carried his name, kings and paramount chiefs trembled for the power of his witchcraft. It was said that he could turn day-old chickens into hawks and hawks into mighty eagles with wings that cast a shadow over the sun. Stories were told of how he could make the great black mamba dance on the last three inches of his tail, how he had reached through the king's chest, when King Sobhuza II was just a young boy, and pulled out his heart, making an incantation and putting it back in front of the eyes of all his counsellors, how the king had fathered seventy sons in the ensuing forty years and each year came more, each a mightier warrior than the last. At night, late, a white owl came to sit on the roof of his hut and if any man saw this great white bird, in seven days he would die of a madness which would make him take a knife and tear his own entrails from his stomach. Somojo's cures were legendary and his prophecies so profound that no great tribal decision from the Congo River down could take place until he had seen the sacred smoke, thrown the bones, examined the entrails of a red jackal and given his approval or sanction. The curse of Somojo the great was worse than death because it meant when death came there would be no return to the shadows of the dead man's clan. The dead one would become a ghost who wandered alone in the spirit world, howling in crags and mountain peaks, cursed and utterly forlorn, never again to sit beside a fire drinking beer in the company of his shadows in the spirit world.

Like Inkosi-Inkosikazi before him, Somojo was very rich and had travelled throughout the country in a great black Mercedes 600. He no longer travelled now, though, and the last time he had left his home in the mountains of Swaziland had been when he appeared at Sharpeville. His great black car had been given to the king and now he lay each night on his jackal-skin kaross between two young princesses from the royal kraal who kept his old bones warm and attended to his every need.

One of these young women brought two gourds of *mqombothi*, maize beer, and handed one to Peekay.

'I thank you, *inKosuzana*,' Peekay said, addressing her by her title of princess. The young woman smiled shyly, surprised at this expression of respect coming from a white man. Then she kneeled and held the second gourd of beer to the great Somojo's mouth, feeding him the thick concoction as one might a small child. Peekay wondered if the old man was senile, for he'd given no sign that he was aware of his presence. He drank the sour beer, trying desperately not to pull a face and waited, for he dared not say a word until he had been formally recognized by the great medicine man.

One of the young women appeared with a tin plate piled high with stiff maize porridge, known as *iPhalishi*, a small bowl of meat, and another bowl of peppered yams and greens picked in the wild. She placed these in front of Peekay. The second maiden appeared with food for Somojo and together the two young women proceeded to hand feed the old man, rolling the stiff porridge into tiny balls and chewing his meat for him before placing it in his mouth.

There is a moment in the high mountains that is like no other experience on earth. It comes when a full moon rises suddenly from behind the black outline of the high crags and peaks and lights the night world. It is a moment of moments, a sudden great golden orb that hangs so close above the peaks that the women in the mountain kraals rush from their huts to sing a song to encourage it to remain where it is and not to roll down the peaks and set the world on fire. The song is like a children's nursery rhyme and is meant to show proper respect as well as flatter the Lord New Moon so he doesn't get any crazy ideas about coming down the mountainside to have a look at how things are going on earth and, in the process, do all manner of damage.

> *Lord, Full Moon*
> *Stay high in your mountain sky*
> *Great eye of bone and golden light*
> *watch the wily demon night*
> *Stay high, stay high!*

Peekay finished his simple meal and waited for the great Somojo to complete his own. It was now quite dark and only the embers from the fire threw a little light, though only sufficient to outline the old man and his two hand-maidens. A grunt came from Somojo; the two women rose and, taking the plates, returned to the cooking hut. At that moment the moon came up and the young women came out of the cooking hut again, sang the rising moon song and then returned.

The moon hung huge and golden above the great Bulembu which rose up in front of Peekay. A voice came from Somojo, a thin, clear voice; though of an old, old man, it contained no cackle of infirmity. 'I see you *Onoshobishobi Ingelosi*, you have been witness to our dead and your tears have been our tears and your voice our voice and now your seed shall be our seed and you shall father a son and he will be a man for all

Africa and his name shall be Lumukanda, child of the morning star.'

Peekay was deeply moved by Somojo's unexpected words. 'I see you, great Lord Somojo and I thank you for allowing me to sit on your kaross and beside your fire.' He rose to his knees and, crawling over to the old man, he placed the three shirts beside him. '*Makhosi*, please accept this unworthy gift.' The fire spluttered as old fires sometimes do, catching up into a few moments of licking flame and lighting the old witchdoctor's tiny simian face. Peekay saw Somojo's eyes were rolled back and he appeared to be in a deep trance. Somojo's hands, like dry twigs in winter, emerged from the top of the blanket and he withdrew a leather cord to the end of which was attached a small leather bag not much bigger than the top half of a man's thumb.

The old man held the tiny bag in front of him so that it dangled from the leather thong. Slowly his eyes rolled back until the whites disappeared and he was looking directly at Peekay, his eyes like soft, bright raisins.

'Take it, wear it, it is the golden coin of Lumukanda.'

Peekay was astonished beyond belief. This was the most sacred of all the things that ever were to the black people. 'I cannot, Somojo, it is an honour beyond me, too great for my status, much too great for a white skin, I cannot take this from you.'

The old man's expression didn't change. 'You are not taking it, it is bringing you. It will come back to me, you must do as I say and wear it around your neck, it will know when to come back,' he repeated.

Peekay took the small leather bag, cupping his hands in the African manner to receive it. Somojo dropped it into his hands. His tiny, skeletal hands fluttered briefly in the air and then, like trapdoor spiders, they retreated back into the blanket. Somojo closed his eyes and Peekay knew he was dismissed.

Peekay crawled back to the kaross and put his shoes on, stooping low until he judged that he was sufficiently far from the old man to rise with respect. Then he made his way in the moonlight along the path back to the village.

At dawn Peekay was awakened by a cock who seemed to be crowing on the roof of his hut. He stooped to get out of the guga and felt the unaccustomed tug of the leather bag around his neck. He crawled out into the light, feeling a little stiff from having slept on the floor in his sleeping bag. Outside the mist hung low over the village and he could barely make out the outline of the cattle kraal, though he heard the bell of a lead cow and the soft cries of the herd boys as the cattle lowed, ready to be taken out to graze. He removed the leather thong from his neck and gently pulled the drawstrings of the tiny bag, tapping the contents into the palm of his hand. The coin was heavy, nearly a quarter of an inch thick, and smooth with generation upon generation of handling, so that it was only roughly round and resembled a pebble in shape. On its face were the very vaguest markings, which appeared almost as tiny scratches on the surface. The gold coin shone in the early morning light and Peekay was totally awed by the sight of it, he'd been afraid to remove it from the bag in the dark and now as he looked at the most precious relic in Africa, south of the Congo River, he began to tremble. It was the most powerful magic he had ever been near and the soft morning light catching it seemed to give the tiny coin, no bigger than his thumbnail, a heartbeat of its own. Peekay was frightened about its meaning. He put the coin back into its tiny bag and tucked it under his shirt. If any African knew he possessed it he would kill him instantly; it was unimaginable that it could ever come into white hands, no matter what the circumstances.

A fire burned low outside his hut and he placed a couple of pieces of wood onto it adding a few twigs to make the embers flare. Peekay stood hunched over the fire, rubbing his hands above the flames. He was grateful for the padded anorak he wore. It was an old one he'd bought for Pike's Peak when they'd trained in the US for the first title fight and he'd often used it in the mountains at home and when he'd first returned. Now he was glad to have it on, a familiar garment to cloak his terror and his awe.

He'd returned to his hut the evening before hoping he might receive news of Gideon, though he wasn't sure that after his confrontation with the ancient witch-doctor he could go through the emotional reunion of a meeting with his friend. Now, standing in the dawn light in the mist-shrouded mountain village, he wondered to himself what the day might bring.

The woman who had brought him the basin and jug the previous day now brought him a mug of dark tea sweetened with honey. 'Ngiya bonga, Mama, I thank you, mother.' Peekay said, taking the steaming mug from her in both hands. The woman left quietly, melting into the mist.

Peekay looked up from his cup to see a man wrapped tightly in a blanket approaching him in the mist. It was only when Gideon was within twenty feet of the fire that Peekay recognized him and, dropping the cup so that the tea spluttered furiously in the hot coal, he rushed to embrace his friend. Gideon brought his blanket around both of them and hugged him, the village echoing with their laughter.

733

'I see you, Gideon,' Peekay replied; then he glanced quickly at the black man beside him, though he could hardly see him through his sudden tears. 'I have missed you, with my heart, but in my head I wish you hadn't returned.'

'I am a soldier now, Peekay. I have no choice, comrade,' Gideon said softly, his voice also showing his emotion.

Peekay sniffed, then laughed. 'Comrade? That's a habit you'd better get out of bloody fast, kaffir. Just the word itself could get you twenty years!' As he'd expected, Gideon was dressed in old clothes, dirty and heavily patched, and on his head he wore an ancient grease-stained felt hat, misshapen and tattered, which he'd pulled almost over his eyes so he had to raise his chin to see Peekay. While the clothes he wore were perfect for the anonymity he needed on the road, Peekay said, 'Jesus, Gideon. You smell like a gorilla's armpit. How long have you been travelling rough?'

Gideon chuckled. 'Not long, my brother. I exchanged them for my suit when I got off the boat. The old man who wore them thought I had gone mad. But it is good for me to feel like this, it will do me no harm; it is like wearing the skin of my countrymen again. Algeria and Europe spoiled me; I was beginning to think I was a somebody.'

'Welcome home then, and take off that bloody hat. You're talking to a white man you understand!'

Gideon pulled the tattered felt hat off his head. 'Shit, I'd forgotten, it's too easy to die where we are going.'

'I thought you went to Algeria to learn how to survive in a war zone?'

'They taught me twenty ways to kill a man, but nothing about surviving amongst killers. It's not going to be easy being a kaffir again. I can't even be Gideon Mandoma, Welterweight Champion of the World. I'm just a kaffir like I was when I was lashing coal for the furnace.'

'That's good, that way you *may* stay alive; your anonymity is everything now. I have brought you clothes, old clothes for the mountains, but clean at least.' Peekay looked down at Gideon's feet. Gideon wore a pair of tackies, the sandshoes well scuffed but still durable. 'Your tackies will last going over Saddleback. We really ought to make an early start. We'll stay the night in the old farmhouse outside Barberton, the place Magistrate Coetzee left Tandia in his will. Then tomorrow morning you will drive as my chauffeur to Johannesburg. If I cannot do it right now, I warn you that on the mountains and at Eendrag I will try to persuade you to go back, Gideon. I have money and a plane ticket out of Lourenco Marques to London with me.'

'Haya, haya, Peekay,' Gideon said, shaking his head sadly, 'we cannot go back. It is too late to turn back now. I have come to fight, there is no other way the *amaBhunu* can be made to understand.'

Thirty-four

In December the Solomon Levy Carpet Emporium held its annual Christmas party and Solomon Levy gave the entire first three weeks of the month over to the preparations for it.

Hymie called Peekay early one morning in the second week of December. 'Have you read the papers, old son?' he asked. Peekay had been out early for a run and confessed he was only just out of the shower and hadn't.

'Simon Fitzharding, you know, the BBC producer guy I told you about who's doing the thing on the old man's Christmas party, said something dumb on a radio programme yesterday and it's on the front pages of all the morning papers.'

'Dumb? What did he say?'

'The stupid prick announced over the air that the Solomon Levy Christmas party was the only true example of Christianity and the true spirit of Christmas to be found in South Africa.'

Peekay laughed. 'He's probably right.'

'Well the shit's hit the fan! That bloody Christmas party! It's too high profile anyway. Did you see the stuff in the *Outspan* and *Die Huisgenoot*?'

'Ja, Tandia showed me in the office, it was pretty spectacular. But, so what's new? It's the same every year, your old man has a natural instinct for getting publicity. Have you called him about Fitzharding's gaff?'

'Ja, before you. He thinks it's the greatest publicity ever. He's besotted with the idea of this BBC documentary. He spends most of the day in that ridiculous little engine going around the garden blowing its steam whistle and shouting, "Camera, action!"'

Peekay laughed. 'Sorry Hymie, I know it isn't funny, but there's something very bizarre about the BBC choosing to show a Christmas bash by one of South Africa's foremost Jews in order to demonstrate to the world that the African Christ has been put back into Christmas.'

The big party as usual was to take place on the last Saturday before Christmas and the preparations for it started at daybreak on the first of December when an army of workmen moved in. For the next three weeks there would be a great deal of coming and going. The tracks for the miniature railway had to be laid, the fence which divided the black from the white needed to be built, *braaivleis* pits prepared and the huge spits where several whole oxen would be roasted set up. In the final week two identical carnivals with flying swings, a big dipper, dodgem cars and all the usual side shows would be erected.

To Solomon Levy the toy train was the most important of all, and the tracks for the miniature railway were the very first thing to be done on the estate. These followed around the complete perimeter of the gardens except for a detour through his prize-winning dahlia garden on the black side and famous rose garden on the white.

The old man was determined to make the Christmas of 1966 the best ever. The BBC had selected his party for the Africa segment of its Christmas day programme, 'Christmas with Children Around the World'. He was tremendously excited about this, and imagined at once that the Queen of England would be watching the programme on Christmas day, seated on her throne with Axminster on the floor, and there he would be, driving the train in his new lightweight Father Christmas outfit.

Simon Fitzharding, a rather pompous Englishman who was known at the BBC as an awful hack, had been the only director available to cover the Africa segment of the documentary and he couldn't believe his luck. Solomon had insisted he move from his second-rate, BBC-budget hotel, and take over an entire wing of the large house, where he found himself treated like royalty.

After this splendid reception he simply hadn't the heart to tell the excited Solomon Levy that Africa had been allotted exactly five minutes of the one-hour programme and that, furthermore, because Africa started with an 'A' it would appear at the opening of the documentary – a nice compliment in one way, but also the scene over which the title and opening credits would appear.

Simon Fitzharding also had a BBC budget which gave him very few options. He'd settled on the Solomon Levy Carpet Emporium Party almost immediately because it was a single location – a splendid one at that – it was multiracial, it cut down on expenses, it offered unstinting cooperation and, in fact, it had everything he needed to succeed.

He made the decision to put most of his efforts into one grand opening sequence. The opening shot, he decided, would be Solomon in all his glory as the Father

Christmas engine driver coming towards camera in the little engine with all its carriages loaded with toys. The sequence would culminate in Father Christmas Solomon Levy drawing his engine into the station where all the children waited for their presents. The final shot would show two little girls, a black and a white, holding their appropriate dolls and looking wide-eyed into the future.

Simon Fitzharding, though perhaps not a very inspired film maker, was nevertheless a perfectionist and with Solomon Levy he had a willing actor on his hands. Over the final week they'd practised the action at least fifty times until the timing was perfect.

Jannie Geldenhuis was in his office in John Vorster Square at his usual time of half past seven when he read about the proposed BBC documentary of the Jew's annual party in the morning papers. He'd also read the recent *Die Huisgenoot* article with rising apprehension. It was seven years since he'd been sworn into the *Broederbond* and had vowed to fix the fat Jew's Christmas party. Now it had finally got out of hand and, he knew, in the eyes of the *Broederbond*, that this could be seen as partially or even entirely his fault. The matter of the Jew's kaffir Christmas party should have been settled years ago.

In the intervening years Solomon Levy had become one of South Africa's leading philanthropists. He gave equally to both English-speaking and Afrikaans-speaking charities, as well as many African and coloured ones, though notably never to the Indian community whom he regarded as deadly competitors in the carpet business. In short, Solomon Levy had become an extremely difficult target.

Geldenhuis picked up the phone and dialed a number in Pretoria. Finally, after the phone had rung more than a dozen times a voice at the other end simply said, 'Ja?'

'*Jakkals*,' Geldenhuis replied.

'Your number?' The voice demanded in Afrikaans.

'*Een en tagtig.*'

'*Jou moeder se voorname?*'

'Anna, Sophie,' Geldenhuis replied, giving his mother's christian names.

'*Wag*,' the voice said, instructing him to wait.

He held on for ten minutes before the original voice returned, still speaking in Afrikaans. 'Are you calling about a certain kaffir Christmas party?'

'*Ja.*'

'*Wag*,' the voice instructed again.

This time he didn't have to wait long before there was a new voice, which he thought he recognized, though it had been a long time since he'd been briefed. '*Jakkals?*'

'*Ja, meneer?*'

'You may proceed with maximum impact.' The phone went dead.

Jannie Geldenhuis felt his heart pounding. Shit! They wanted Solomon Levy killed! Jesus! And he'd been afraid he'd get a negative response. Censured for not having undertaken the task long before. At best he thought they'd simply tell him to create a disruption and make it look like an attack from religious fanatics or an extreme right-wing element: create enough of a disaster, kill a few kaffirs.

Geldenhuis was delighted with his Christmas present from the *Broederbond*. Maybe he could work it so he got Hymie and Peekay as well; also, why not Tandia? At one stage or another they had to be standing together. A bomb in the right place, that's all it would take.

But Jannie Geldenhuis knew he was daydreaming. He could get a couple of his men into the grounds, that wouldn't be too hard – there were carpenters and technicians everywhere, even planting a bomb with a timing device wouldn't be impossible. But on the day the place would be crawling with children, white children. His chances of getting the four people he most wanted to kill all together on the black side was negligible.

Besides, while he didn't care particularly about killing Hymie, he wanted Peekay and Tandia alive for two reasons. He hoped they would lead him to Gideon Mandoma. The sudden increase in terrorist activity and rumours from his informers gave him reason to believe that Gideon was back in South Africa. And, most importantly, he had a personal vendetta to settle with both Peekay and the black bitch.

He'd already broken Tandia as a teenager; what had happened then was child's play. Now she would be really something to work on, all the old fears to bring back, new ones to work on. Breaking down her beauty alone, that would be something. Now, when she was so terribly guilty, breaking her now would be a most exquisite pleasure. His brains against hers, his arrogance against her fear, his hate against her hate. The re-enactment of that day at Bluey Jay, only this time with his ending.

But, more even than her, there was Peekay. He could taste Peekay like blood in his mouth. Geldenhuis dreamed of reducing both Peekay and Tandia down to shit, for he knew both were guilty of the most terrible crimes against his Afrikaner nation for which they must both die. He also believed in his heart that they were guilty of miscegenation, the most heinous crime of them all, that struck at the very roots of the survival of the white tribe in Africa. With Peekay there was the physical thing as well, the man on man.

Just as Peekay dreamed of getting Jannie Geldenhuis into court for a showdown in front of the world media, so Geldenhuis dreamed of getting Peekay into the ring. The need physically to get the better of the hated rooinek had never left him. He knew that while most weeks Peekay kept himself in reasonable shape with a couple of hard games of squash and two or three long runs in the early morning, he worked much too hard to be in the really top condition he needed to fight. Besides, he hadn't put on a glove since the night he'd lost the title to Mandoma. He was probably ten pounds over the welterweight limit and not nearly as strong or in the same sort of shape as Geldenhuis knew himself to be.

Geldenhuis spent most of the day after his phone call to Cogsweel at the *Broederbond* working on how he might eliminate Solomon Levy without leaving any trace as to the identity of his assassins. And when he opened the evening paper he couldn't quite believe his luck. In the paper was a picture of the little engine. In the background, on what appeared to be a door, was the name of an engineering company, J. Poulos Pty Ltd. Beside the photograph of the train was a plan of the Levy gardens showing the entire topography of the estate and the exact layout of the train tracks. The plan had been prepared to scale by a qualified draughtsman so that the grounds could be correctly laid out for the Christmas party and for the film crew to work from. Apparently the train had gone in for some last-minute repairs and there was some concern as to whether it would be ready in time.

The idea of sabotaging the toy train had already occurred to Geldenhuis but he'd quickly dismissed the idea. He couldn't be sure of blowing up the engine without killing the white children in the carriages. Now, as he read an interview with one of the cameramen hired by Simon Fitzharding, his excitement increased. In the interview the cameraman explained the opening film sequence for the BBC documentary when Solomon Levy would be alone in the train filled with toys during one complete loop of the tracks.

Geldenhuis had all the information he needed to formulate a plan. The newspaper had presented it to him on a plate. Checking the Pretoria telephone directory he located the address of the engineering company. Geldenhuis had long since learned to trust simple ideas and he knew if he could get into the engineering works for less than twenty minutes he could go a long way to bringing the assassination of Solomon Levy to a successful conclusion.

With most of the equipment he needed in a small canvas sports bag he left just after three in the afternoon in an unmarked car for the forty-mile drive to Pretoria. With him he took a plainclothes black detective from the Special Squad who had no idea as to the purpose of their journey and who was simply required to act on instructions when they got there.

They arrived in the general area of the engineering works, which was in one of the older industrial suburbs of Pretoria, just before five o'clock, having stopped along the way at three hardware shops where Geldenhuis sent the black detective in to make several small purchases. The factories in the area closed at four and now the dirty back streets were completely deserted.

Geldenhuis stopped the car half a block from where

the engineering works was situated and, with the black detective, he went to work on a well-rehearsed routine. The police captain grabbed a tyre iron and spanner and slipped the hubcap from the rear driver's side wheel. He started to undo the nuts while the black man removed the jack and spare tyre. The detective quickly seated the jack and raised the tyre while Geldenhuis removed the tyre nuts and finally the tyre itself. Together they fitted the spare, tightened the nuts again and lowered the jack. When the weight of the car was taken by the spare tyre it was shown to be almost completely deflated, with only sufficient air in it to keep the tyre from riding directly on the wheel rim. It would drive safely enough for the half a block it needed to travel.

Geldenhuis wiped his hands on a piece of cotton waste and removed a pair of blue workman's overalls from the back seat of the car which he climbed into and quickly buttoned up. Then he reached back into the car for the canvas sports bag in which he'd placed their several purchases.

With a cursory nod to the black man, he slid the canvas bag over his arm and held up both hands, fingers wide, indicating ten minutes, whereupon he started to walk in the direction of the engineering works.

He soon found the place he was looking for, a large iron shed or workshop, roughly the height of a three-story building with the name 'J. Poulos Pty Ltd. Industrial & Heavy Engineering' in large white letters painted halfway up and across its entire windowless front. A massive set of double sliding doors, perhaps twenty feet high and almost as wide, were set into the centre of the building and opened by sliding along heavy greased steel tracks fitted above and set into the cement floor below the doors. Cut into the farthest corner of the left-hand door, like a pet's door in the kitchen, was a small door raised about a foot from the ground and only large enough for a man to enter the huge workshop if he stooped right over. It too was made of corrugated iron and was obviously only used when, as now, the large doors were closed. To his surprise the small door stood slightly ajar; it must be used by the night watchman, who was seated rather grandly in a crude imitation of a heavy old squared-off club armchair, made entirely from packing-case planks. The black man sat in the evening sunlight and appeared to be mending a pair of trousers which were draped over his knees.

'God is on my side,' Geldenhuis thought, observing the open door, 'the fat bastard was meant to die.' He waited out of sight against the wall of an adjoining property until he heard the car approaching. The road ran some fifty feet from where the watchman was seated and, as the black detective drew to a halt, the watchman looked up from his sewing.

The plainclothes detective got out from behind the wheel. Geldenhuis could see that he had one arm in a sling as he walked over to examine the rear tyre. 'Shit!' the detective said in a voice loud enough to carry to the watchman.

The watchman rose and put down the pair of trousers he'd been repairing, walking over to the car. 'You have a puncture,' he said in Zulu, pointing to the offending tyre.

'Haya, haya, I have a big problem!' the black detective tapped the sling on his right arm, 'My elbow, it is cracked, I can drive, but this tyre, I cannot change this tyre, my arm is not so strong.'

The night watchman scratched his head and looked somewhat bemused. 'It is a big problem, my brother,' he said rather sheepishly. 'Also I do not know this thing for changing tyre.'

The detective laughed. 'Give me only your strength, brother, I will show you, then next time you will know. It is good to know this thing.'

'Ja, it is good,' the night watchman agreed, 'you will show me, I will help you.' It was still completely light and, in his mind, his duties as a night watchman only really started after dark. He liked the idea of learning how to change a tyre. You never knew when such a skill could be useful, maybe one day he would work in a garage?

Geldenhuis watched as, using his left hand, the detective opened the boot and indicated the spare tyre. He waited until the night watchman was crouched beside the flat tyre; the detective stood directly behind him so that if he turned suddenly his view of the engineering works would be blocked by the black policeman's legs.

Geldenhuis threw the canvas bag over the wall and vaulted it himself, dropping lightly to the other side. He covered the distance to the small door in less than ten seconds, walking quickly on rubber soles. He pushed carefully at the door which opened easily without a sound; stooping, he entered into the interior of the building.

To his surprise, once inside he could see quite easily. Sixty feet above his head, beyond the steel crossbeams from which hung six set-ups of heavy block and tackle equipment, were several large skylights. Almost immediately he saw the small engine standing directly outside a small works office built at one end of the building. Geldenhuis approached the tiny locomotive and as he drew closer he noted the name, 'Poulos Pty Ltd.' painted in fairly large letters on the door of the office directly behind the engine. This was the sign he'd seen in the newspaper photographs, saving him the need to make any enquiries as to the whereabouts of the engine and thus avoiding anyone remembering a telephone call at some later date.

Geldenhuis worked quickly. From the canvas bag he removed a six-inch aluminium single cigar canister which had been packed with plastic explosive and was already fitted with a fuse which protruded about six inches from a hole cut into the rounded top of the cigar container. It was about a twelve-second fuse, its detonator buried deep within the plastic explosive.

In Geldenhuis's hand the small cigar bomb didn't look much but it packed enough wallop to blow the engine in front of him sky high. He removed a lump of cotton waste and a small tin of lighter fluid, and doused the waste with the fluid. Then, lying on his stomach, he pushed his hands behind the left-hand front wheel of the engine until he could run his fingers along the front axle. He wiped the axle clean, the lighter fluid removing any film of grease there might be on it. He waited a few moments for it to dry before he removed from his pocket a tiny tube of a new Japanese instant glue which had just come onto the market. He spread a thin line of glue along the side of the cigar canister, pressing down hard and emptying the entire tube as he traced its point along the length of the canister. He then attached the canister to the centre of the hidden side of the front axle, holding it for a minute or so until the instant glue attached it, leaving his hands free. He wiped the silver aluminium canister clean, using a freshly doused wad of cotton waste. He then removed a roll of electrical tape and taped the canister firmly to the axle, making it impossible to shake loose. Finally he led the short fuse along the axle, taping it completely so that the dark electrician's tape concealed the white fuse, allowing only the last teased end of the fuse to rest no more than a quarter of an inch from the inside rim of the front wheel.

It was awkward work and he skinned his knuckles several times, cursing quietly to himself. He wasn't unduly worried about being discovered; if for any reason the night watchman became suspicious and attempted to investigate, the black detective had instructions to kill him – simply rendering him unconscious would mean someone would know they'd been there. Geldenhuis was a professional and he knew not to hurry a job as critical as this one. The charge would lie hidden for more than two weeks before it was to be exploded and, in the meantime, it had to be capable of withstanding dozens, perhaps hundreds of trips in the little train.

Next Geldenhuis removed a small tin of Estapol, a clear plastic lacquer, and using a new one-inch paintbrush he painted the inside rim of the wheel with the lacquer. Reaching into the bag, he withdrew a flat tobacco tin which he opened to reveal about fifty two-inch strips of highly flammable magnesium tape, which he began to lay carefully into the wet plastic lacquer until they covered the entire inside circumference of the train wheel. By morning the plastic lacquer would be dry, fixing the strips tightly to its surface. Finally he doused a fresh wad of cotton waste in lighter fluid and wiped the surface of the electrician's tape carefully, as well as any metal areas he may, inadvertently, have touched to leave a fingerprint.

Geldenhuis remained on his stomach and, using the torch, he inspected the outside of the wheel he'd doctored. Even from a distance of a few inches nothing showed on the outside of the train. The job was complete. He rose confident that unless someone with a probing torch lying on their stomach as he had just done knew exactly where to look, the engine would have to be flipped onto its back with its wheels in the air to see where the tiny bomb was concealed.

He tidied up quickly, returning everything to the canvas bag. Finally he inspected the floor to see whether he'd left anything behind. Returning once more to lie on his stomach he pointed the torch to shine it under the engine. His eye caught a single magnesium strip which lay on the floor directly under the inside of the wheel. He recovered it and slipped it into the pocket of his overalls.

Geldenhuis glanced at his watch. It was almost fifteen minutes since he'd entered the building, less time than it required to get a novice to change a tyre, but time to leave. He took one final glance at the shiny little green engine with *The Solomon Levy Magic Carpet Express* lettered in gold along its side. Christ! The fat Jew bastard could have anything in the world and he spent his time playing engine driver! To Geldenhuis there was something sinful about this. A man ten times richer than the president who dressed up in a Father Christmas outfit to play toy train driver and give kaffirs expensive presents was definitely sick. Bastards like that deserved to die.

He moved quietly over to the door. The two black men were still hunched over the wheel with his back to him. Stooping, Geldenhuis let himself out. He moved quietly along the front and then down the side of the building and quickly crossed the back area of the works and scaled the wall. He set out to walk to the pick-up point he'd arranged, about a mile away on the main highway.

Geldenhuis was delighted with the way things had gone. It was copybook stuff and he hadn't even had to break in to do it. Now all he needed to do was to find someone who'd been invited to attend the kaffir Christmas party so that he could prepare the bomb's triggering method at the right moment. He grinned to himself. God was good, it was payback time. He knew just the man for the job.

Thirty-five

Just after midnight on the day of the Solomon Levy Carpet Emporium Christmas party the *braaivleis* barbecue pits were lit. By dawn, with the wood reduced down to beds of glowing coals, the huge spits, each carrying a whole ox, were moved into place. By mid morning the delicious smell of roasting meat filled the air.

The air crackled with the excitement of the carnival, the screams, whirrings, whooshing and thumping of the dodgem cars, the flying swings, the big wheels and the calliope music of the carousels. Everything was for free as many times as you liked and the very thought of it pumped the heart full of good-time juice. The children rushed around in circles and chased each other about, just to wear off a little energy so they wouldn't completely burst into tiny pieces from the happiness of things.

Just on three thousand employees and two hundred other guests attended the Solomon Levy Carpet Emporium Christmas party. Lorries and buses began to arrive from dawn onwards on this day of days and the people in the upper-crust suburb surrounding the big house were wakened early by the singing of black people packed like gaily papered chocolates into the back of open lorries and rickety buses passing their clipped, manicured and aloof properties. To the indignant people who lived around the Levy estate the day was known as 'Kaffir Christmas' and each year they signed a petition to the council and the police to abolish it.

Many families had travelled hundreds of miles overnight to get to the party while others had been on the road since long before dawn. Shower blocks and marquees were set up to headquarter these distance travellers and to provide a little early morning respite for already exhausted parents.

The baby-feeding and medical clinic, staffed by a dozen nurses and two doctors, opened at six and already waiting as the day's first patient was a five-year-old from Germiston named Tiger Joe. Fat tears streamed down his little black face as a young female doctor examined him while his ma, a giant woman wearing a huge mauve picture hat, puffed out her cheeks and continued to scold the little boy for causing the neat pink gap where he'd lost three front teeth falling off a stationary carousel pony.

Breakfast, an unofficial event which the caterers had learned over the years to provide, was served to the early arrivals. There were mugs of scalding sweet white tea, a couple of hundred loaves of white bread, a hundred yards of cold sausages, huge brown pots of soup-bone gravy and, of course, to go with it, mountains of stiff white mealie pap, steaming in giant black three-legged, round-tummied kaffir pots.

The experienced mothers among the early arrivals dressed their children in their second-best outfits for the morning mayhem, hauling them back in by the ear around eleven for a good scrub and general repairs in the shower block where they changed into their party best, outfits which had taken months to pay for with every spare penny the family could scrape together. The children wore socks as white as driven snow, patent-leather shoes like Shirley Temple's, a flutter of petticoats and pretty organza dresses in limes and yellows, pinks and greens with huge ribbons to match. Little boys in sailor suits walked stiffly in unaccustomed shoes that creaked with newness. Older children in their school uniforms, pressed and starched, with trouser creases and gym frock pleats perfect, concealed little pieces of flannel cloth in their pockets to keep their polished shoes up to optimum presentation at all times.

A few minutes before noon the people on the black side of the fence started to converge on the tiny train station, where a microphone had been placed on the platform. The five hundred or so children and parents on the white side were drawn to the toy station as well. It was from here that Solomon Levy would officially declare the festivities open and, much more importantly, announce that lunch was ready to be served from a dozen great marquees and roasting pits.

They all knew the routine; a shorter-than-short speech from Solomon who, on this one occasion every year, always seemed lost for words; then the world's most sumptuous feast; and at precisely two o'clock, to a shrill 'toot-toot!' from the little engine, the most successful Jewish Father Christmas in creation would circle the grounds bringing with him the most wonderful gifts imaginable.

This year though, to accommodate the needs of Simon Fitzharding's endlessly rehearsed documentary, the open train carriages would be filled with Christmas gifts instead of children and Solomon would arrive at the station to the final chorus of 'Hark the Herald Angels Sing', performed by two hundred children of all the colours of Africa.

In the matter of security Hymie had ignored his father's protests and instigated a huge security operation. Upon arrival at the gate every guest, regardless of colour, was required to show a specially produced employee or guest identification disc. Finally, to the embarrassment of many of the white employees and the good-natured laughter of the black, who were more accustomed to the indignity, every guest was searched by uniformed security men and women. The high-walled estate was ringed with a private army of security men, who also mingled freely with the crowd, watching for a would-be assassin.

And, of course, the little engine came under the scrutiny of Hymie's team who wanted it pulled apart but Solomon, whose final week of rehearsals in the little engine had been constantly disrupted by the security men working on the track, wouldn't hear of it. He was heartily sick of his son's paranoia and agreed only to an inspection of the train.

Mama Tequila, too fat to move more than a few yards on her own, stayed sitting in a huge old swing chair in the rose garden where she could quietly watch the children passing in the train without having to attempt to carry her huge frame about the place. The children and lunch was all she cared about – and the fact that Solomon Levy had sent her a personal letter inviting her to come. For lunch she could rely upon Madam Flame Flo to dart into the food marquee like a cheeky sparrow and emerge, chirping excitedly, with a couple of plates piled high with the choicest titbits. She'd practically starved herself at breakfast: six pieces of toast and three eggs, with a pot of coffee. Flo had fussed and worried for her, but she was reserving extra room for lunch. Solomon, who referred to food as 'nosh', knew almost as much about pleasing a person's stomach as she did.

Mama Tequila was wearing a red sequined gown and a huge red Laughing-Cavalier picture hat festooned with two magnificent white ostrich feathers. Her chubby fingers were a vulgar splash of diamonds as she fanned herself with a delicate little Japanese paper fan. Where she sat among the roses, with the swing chair moving back and forth, she glimmered, glittered, sparkled and shimmered in thousands of tiny bomb-bursts of light. The swing chair was situated close to a long and beautiful rose arbour festooned with climbing pink roses to make a natural tunnel of blossoms through which the train travelled. Children would see her as the train emerged from the arbour and squeal with delight. It was as though she was an unexpected sideshow placed in amongst a bed of roses to surprise them. Halfway through the morning a rumour started that Mama Tequila was Mother Christmas, after which the children waved and smiled and cheered and blew kisses at her. The presents had yet to be given out and they reasoned that if Mother Christmas was anything like their own ma, it was just as well to be nice as pie and show no disrespect.

Mama Tequila was beginning to feel decidedly peckish. She was happy when noon came, the funfair stopped abruptly and the train was halted for Solomon Levy to make his welcoming speech. She knew Flo would soon be chirping at her side with the first of several plates piled high with her favourite food.

She listened as the public address system whistled and then crackled. A voice said, 'Testing, testing, one ... two ... three ...' and then with a final tear of static grew silent. The next voice she heard was that of Mr Nguni who spoke in Zulu to the crowd, though only for a moment. She couldn't understand him but she guessed he was simply calling the crowd to attention for Solomon's welcome. Trust him to get in there somewhere. She didn't like the big black man, nor did she trust him. More than once she'd chastised Tandia for going out with him; he was creepy, a black man you couldn't read, who laughed too much and showed too many white teeth. That would be a one-eyed snake that would be very cruel and careless with a girl, you could tell just by looking at the bastard. Tandia had told her that nothing had ever happened between them, that he was like her father. 'A father you don't need, a Big Daddy, yes, that more like it, but only if he likes to give diamonds, you hear? Does he give you diamonds?'

'He takes me places, I meet people I couldn't normally meet, people who are important to me,' Tandia protested.

'Meeting kaffirs is never important to anyone, skatterbol,' Madam Tequila had said, ending the discussion.

Now she heard Solomon Levy clear his throat briefly and she imagined him standing at the microphone in his blue blazer with the bright brass buttons and beret. Flo had left ten minutes earlier to get a good place in the lunch queue.

'My friends, happy Christmas!' Solomon Levy's voice suddenly boomed out over the loudspeaker. 'Thank you for comink to my house. Thank you, also, for helping me to make the business. This year you are gettink a bonus, one month's pay!' Mama Tequila could hear the loud cheer from the crowd and Solomon Levy waited for it to die down. 'My pleasure,' he said quietly, 'you are all makink me very proud.' His voice brightened suddenly, changing tack. 'Also, children, I got here a letter Father Christmas, comink direct the north pole!' Mama Tequila heard the scrunch of paper over the microphone and Solomon began to read. *'Dear children at Solomon Levy Carpet Emporium. Thank you all za nice letters you are writing. Don't vorry, I got for sure everything. I hope you are being also good boys and girls because two o'clock sharp I'm coming wit' my train by Mr Solomon Levy's house! Maybe you can be zere?'*

Mama Tequila could hear the squeals of delight from the children and she imagined how they'd be hugging each other. Their parents too, with the knowledge of a double pay packet coming in at Christmas time, would be feeling very good. Solomon Levy now ended the letter, 'Yours sincerely, Father Christmas. North Pole, za world, za universe!' There was a great deal of clapping and laughter and he concluded simply by saying, 'Okay, my friends! Now we eat. Enjoy please a little lunch.'

Simon Fitzharding's film crew had hardly been noticed during all the morning's excitement and the cameramen had used the time for pick-up shots, filming the oxen roasting on the spits, the chefs preparing the tables groaning with good food and generally keeping an eye out for a 'cute' shot.

Now the cameramen, grips and sound men stood by for a final briefing from the BBC director who, in a manner of speaking, had caused the entire security kerfuffle. The plan was simple and had been rehearsed a hundred times. The unit stood by, bored; they'd long since stopped listening to the Englishman with the hot potato in his mouth. There was very little that could go wrong. Both cameras would be mounted on platforms; there was a small one that allowed the cameraman to operate six feet above the heads of the crowd and looked directly into the train station. It was fitted with a four-to-one zoom lens so it could pan as Father Christmas Solomon Levy made his triumphant arrival from the direction of the rose garden. This same camera would also be used for the medium and close-up shots of the choir. The second unit, placed on the black side, was mounted on a much higher camera platform with the latest twelve-to-one zoom lens to pull focus and follow the entire progress of the little engine around the estate.

The platform on the taller tower had been built fairly high so that Hymie's security men could man it as well, with radio contact to their plainclothes people in the crowd. Solomon Levy's train ride was the next obviously critical moment in the entire security operation. For six minutes he would be alone and totally exposed with a crowd of three thousand or so people lining the tracks.

Peekay had permission to share the platform as he wanted to take pictures to send to Doris and Togger and Harriet in England. Later he'd also get the snaps for Mr Rubens, the schmaltzy shots the old man adored, showing wide-eyed kids hugging their Rubens-Kellerman dolls, which Solomon Levy specially ordered for all the children.

Peekay was as anxious as everyone else involved in the security operation, but he played no active role in it and the team had been so thorough that, as the day wore on, they'd all begun to relax a little. Hymie had given him a Nikon with the very latest telephoto lens for his birthday a year previously and he found he enjoyed messing about with it. He'd spent a lot of time taking pictures with Doc's old Hasselblad as a child and privately he fancied himself as a bit of a photographer. How the old man would have loved this Nikon, Peekay thought as he set the camera on its tripod and squinted through the powerful lens, deciding on the mandatory shots he would take when the little train finally got under way.

Now, with a few minutes to go, he watched the crowd through the camera's telephoto lens. The little green train would start in the dahlia garden on the black side where it was concealed from the crowd. Below him he could see Solomon Levy in his Father Christmas outfit flapping his hands about and, Peekay imagined, being a general nuisance to the security men who were loading the train with the pretend Christmas packages. This year Solomon needed no padding for his Father Christmas outfit and Peekay thought to himself that the old bugger really ought to go on a diet. The carriages were almost loaded with the beribboned boxes and assortment of bicycles, scooters, tricycles and dolls sticking out among them.

Peekay turned the lens towards the station. The platform was crowded with the children's choir which spilled over onto two stands, one on either side of the strange-looking little building. Next he turned the tripod and camera to face the distant rose garden. This was a shot he didn't want to miss; the little engine at this point was a hundred yards from the end of its journey when it entered a long arbour of brilliant pink climbing roses. He began to focus when he realized that Mama Tequila was in the background slightly to the side of the rose arbour. He adjusted the lens to bring

759

her into sharp focus. The huge woman appeared to be asleep. Peekay grinned to himself, he'd seen Mama Tequila tuck in before and he had no illusions about the size of the lunch she would have consumed. Even at the distance of some two hundred and fifty yards he imagined he could see her huge bosoms heaving under her shimmering red dress. He fired off a shot of the dozing Mama Tequila and flipped the camera ratchet to the next frame.

There was a sudden excited roar from the crowd as the little engine gave two shrill whistles and emerged from the dahlia garden. Peekay pulled his camera tripod around and checked his pad, quickly adjusting the lens of the camera by hand without bringing his eye to the lens. When he looked into the camera, to his satisfaction he saw his focus was bang-on as he fired off the shot. He removed the camera from the tripod and followed the little engine around, pulling focus and taking random shots. Then he suddenly realized that he'd been so intrigued by Mama Tequila that he hadn't completed focussing on his third set-up, the little train emerging from the rose arbour.

There was still a couple of minutes to go and he positioned the camera tripod and fixed the Nikon to it. He brought his eye to the camera and worked the powerful telephoto lens. The lens sharpened into focus and to his enormous surprise he saw Mr Nguni on his haunches beside the track halfway down the rose arbour. Peekay sharpened focus on his crouching figure; the big man was fairly deep into the arbour and it would have been almost impossible to see him by eye at the distance Peekay was standing. Peekay fired off a shot. The shutter blinked and in the fraction of a second it went from light to dark and back again he knew with a blinding realization what Mr Nguni was doing.

Peekay turned from the camera tripod and reached the top of the ladder leading up to the platform in three steps. He half climbed and half skidded down the ladder, jumping the last ten rungs to hit the ground running.

'What is it?' he heard one of the security men call from the top of the platform.

'A detonator on the track!' Peekay yelled, but already he was yards away, running hard. He had to run around a small copse of trees and down a sideshow alley. Two teenage girls, walking between tents, didn't see him coming and his shoulder collected one of them and knocked her spinning. He reached the open lawns and made for the rose arbour. People seeing him coming jumped out of his way, though some he dodged and others he pushed aside as he ran. His head was pounding and he could taste blood in his mouth where he must have bitten his tongue. The sound of the children singing in Zulu came to him clearly, like a car passing suddenly with its radio on too loudly; then he lost it, his own furious panting drowning out all sound. By the time he'd reached the centre fence the little train was behind the big house and heading for the rose garden. He reached the front of the arbour just as the engine entered the other side. Seconds later he heard two shots go off, one a split second after the other. A moment later a dense white smoke came from the front wheel of the engine, which seemed to be flaring with an intensely bright blue flame.

'Jump!' he screamed at Solomon Levy. 'Jump!!'

The old man was too shocked to respond and he flapped his hands wildly, beating at the magnesium smoke billowing into his face. Peekay ran towards him and, turning so that he was running with the train, he tried to pull Solomon Levy from the carriage. But Solomon wearing a bullet-proof vest was a snug fit, and in his panic he held onto the sides of the cabin. 'Stand up! Try to stand up!' Peekay screamed. The old man was gulping for air, his eyes popping out of his head; he was totally panic stricken and beyond response. Peekay beat down at his fists which were white-knuckling the sides of the engine, but still Solomon clung on. Peekay brought his hands around Solomon's thick throat and started to strangle him. With a cry Solomon brought his hands up and Peekay released his grip, slipping his arms under the old man's armpits and jerking with all his strength against the movement of the train. With Solomon's foot now off the throttle, the train started to slow down. For a few desperate moments nothing happened and then Solomon Levy was dragged clear of the cabin. They hit the ground hard at the same moment that the engine emerged from the arbour; then Peekay lost his hold on the old man. Both of them seemed to bounce and then roll wildly, the momentum of the fall hurling them over a small embankment and clear of the engine. With a deafening roar the bomb exploded, sending the little engine high into the air. It landed on its snout and somersaulted three times to land on its back in a rose bed fifty feet away.

Peekay was already on his feet by the time the first of the security men reached the scene. He was bleeding slightly from the mouth but seemed to be all right, though his head spun furiously and the sound of the explosion at such close range had momentarily deafened him. Had they not been below the sound when the explosion went off it might well have burst their eardrums. He was also finding it difficult to focus, catching only glimpses of a man moving towards him. He felt the man grab his shoulder; the man's mouth opened like a fish under water but he made no sound. Peekay nodded, unable to speak and the man turned and ran towards Solomon Levy who lay motionless against a small tree. The top of his Father Christmas outfit had been torn away by the explosion, showing the bullet-proof vest, half on and half off his hairy stomach. Peekay's eyes were beginning to focus a little better, though they still seemed to snap-shoot the scene around him, like a cinema projector with its speed out of synchronization. People seemed to be running from everywhere.

His vision cleared, but now it was as though he could see everything with the clarity of slow motion. Hymie moved up to him, touched his face with the flat of his hand, sobbing; he said something which Peekay couldn't hear then moved towards his father. Tandia rushed up and grabbed him; she seemed to be sobbing in little gasps, grabbing him about the waist and burying her head in his chest. He tried to bring his arms up to embrace her but they wouldn't work. There was no pain, but they simply wouldn't respond to the message his brain was sending to them. Solomon Levy's legs seemed to be at strange angles and Peekay wondered vaguely whether they were broken. Nothing made a lot of sense. Hymie returned and hugged them both, tears streaming down his cheeks, his lips moving soundlessly. Someone threw a blanket over his shoulder and he tried to hold it but his arms still refused to move. Then, as though someone had thrown a switch in his head, the sound came back on and he could hear. It was the most fortuitous piece of timing in his life, for Tandia was looking up at him, her green eyes bright with tears, 'Peekay, I love you,' she said and started to sob quietly, her head against his chest. Then he was looking into the pale face of a blond woman in a white coat with an untidy wisp of hair across her forehead who had the same pale blue eyes as Jannie Geldenhuis.

'Let me take a look at you?' the woman said in Afrikaans. Then she let out a short expletive, '*Here, jou been*!' She pointed to his left leg.

Peekay's head was almost clear and he realized he hadn't imagined Tandia's words. He glanced almost casually at his leg, looking down over Tandia's shoulder. He felt no pain whatsoever so he was surprised to observe that the bottom half of his khaki trousers had been torn and below it the knee was totally soaked in blood.

The woman doctor was on her haunches, ripping the material away. A deep gash ran from just under his knee to his ankle and looked as though it had been sliced open with a boning knife, the top layer of skin folded back to expose the tendons of his ankles and his calf muscle. With a sudden rush, the pain appeared in his shoulders as though his arms had been jerked out of their sockets, though there was still no pain from his leg. 'I can't stitch it here, you'll have to go in the ambulance,' the doctor said rising. 'I'll give you a tetanus injection, also one to kill the pain.'

'*Dankie, doktor. Hoe goan dit met die ou kerel*?' Peekay asked. He had a violent headache but his mind was now lucid and his concern was for Solomon Levy.

'Both his legs appear to be broken and his collarbone. We'll have to watch his heart, that's all,' the doctor replied. She looked directly at him and sniffed; with an almost imperceptible nod of her head, she indicated Tandia. 'It's none of my business, you hear, but people are looking,' she said, loud enough for Tandia to hear.

Shocked, Tandia pulled away from Peekay. 'Don't! Please don't go!' Peekay cried. He tried to stretch his arm towards Tandia but the pain was too great. Tandia stood three feet from him, her hands covering her face in shame.

The woman doctor stepped between Peekay and the distraught Tandia, blocking her from his view. 'Come now,' she said, 'You can't stay any longer on that bad leg.' She called over a couple of medics carrying a stretcher. '*Kom hier, maak gou, jong!*'

Whatever the doctor had given Peekay to kill the pain was making him feel very woozy. Johnny Tambourine had appeared just as they were putting him into the ambulance. 'Look after Tandia, Johnny!' he shouted up at him.

'She's a mess, man! Mama Tequila is dead,' Johnny said, making no attempt to soften the news.

'Stay with her, Johnny, take my car, take them home to Madam Flame Flo's house in Vereeniging. Stay there, I'll call tonight or get over.' He had to fight to keep his concentration and his eyelids were becoming impossibly heavy. The ambulance attendants were trying to close the door. The news of Mama Tequila's death was suddenly too much and his mind shut it out. He suddenly remembered the camera on the tower, his lawyer's mind asserting itself. 'Johnny, my camera! It's on the tower, get it!' he shouted; he was too woozy to realize how callous and unfeeling he must have sounded to Johnny Tambourine.

'Shit, why is it always us who die,' he heard Johnny Tambourine say as the ambulance doors closed him from view.

Peekay awoke just after dawn and lay listening to the sparrows chirping outside. The nylon curtains were drawn but the window showed as a contrasting square of pale light in the dark hospital room. The bird noises told him he was probably on the ground floor. 'Good, I can walk out,' he thought, 'walk out and find a phone box and call Hymie.' This thought was, of course, a nonsense but his mind was still blurry from the sedation he'd received and it had taken up more or less where it had left off with Johnny Tambourine in the ambulance. A thought formed in his head. 'Tandia? She said she loved me?' Then he wondered if it was something he'd dreamed. His mind began to clear, the outline of his thoughts sharpening. He could vaguely remember arriving at the hospital, the strips of pale purple neon light passing above him as he was wheeled down a long corridor, then nothing more. Now it was all coming back to him, like animated bits of a jigsaw puzzle falling into place by themselves. He felt the shock of Mama Tequila's death for the first time and sudden tears blinded him and ran down his cheeks. He tried to move his hand up to wipe at them and realized both his arms lay across his chest cradled in a sling which was tied around his neck. He was feeling lousy; he tried to sniff away the tears and his head still ached, but the pain was familiar. His body had been badly battered before and he knew he'd be okay in a week or so when the bruising and stiffness worked out of his muscles. His left leg was stiff and sore but it wasn't throbbing.

He was propped up against a pile of cushions in a half-seated position. He tried to look for a call button; his throat was dry and he needed a glass of water. He became conscious that his neck was in a brace and that he couldn't move his head either to the left or right; his entire torso was a slab of dull pain. Then Peekay felt a hand touch him gently on the right shoulder. 'You all right, old mate?' Hymie rose from the chair beside the bed where he'd dozed off and moved over to look at Peekay. He needed a shave and his eyes were red with dark rings about them; they seemed set back too far into his pale face. He'd never seen Hymie looking so exhausted.

Peekay tried to smile. It was difficult to get the first word past his lips; his throat was dry and sore from swallowing blood where he'd broken a tooth in the fall. 'You look like hell, Hymie,' he croaked at last.

Hymie grinned. 'Look who's talking.' He walked round to the console on the other side of the bed and poured a glass of water and held it for Peekay to drink. The water felt wonderful and though it hurt a little to swallow, it cleared his throat.

'How's the old man?'

'I checked an hour ago, he's sleeping. He's off the critical list.' Hymie grinned again. 'He's so swathed in bandages and plaster of Paris that he looks like the Michelin man. The doc says all that blubber and the stupid vest we made him wear probably saved his life a second time when he took the fall.' Hymie was talking too fast, trying to over-ride the exhaustion in his voice.

'Hymie, you're beat. You're going to have to get some rest. What's the time?'

'No, really, I'm fine, I've been dozing most of the night.' Hymie looked at his watch. 'Ten past five.'

'You've got to get some sleep,' Peekay insisted. The need to concentrate was making his head throb. 'We've got a hell of a day ahead of us.'

'We? That's a joke, you're going nowhere mate, that's for sure!'

'Hymie? Have you contacted Tandia?'

'Ja, I called late last night. The doctor gave Madam

Flame Flo a heavy sedative and she was asleep. Tandia was pretty broken up, but having to look after the old girl was probably a good thing. Johnny Tambourine is still with her.'

'My camera? Did he pick it up?'

Hymie looked quizzical. 'Camera?'

'I'm not sure he heard me, I asked him to get my Nikon from the camera tower. It holds a picture of Mr Nguni placing a detonator on the track.'

Hymie's head jerked back in surprise. 'Nguni? Jesus!'

'He placed a couple of detonators on the train track. They set off some sort of highly inflammable material, probably phosphorous. No, the flame was blue,' Peekay recalled suddenly, 'magnesium! It was probably magnesium. It would have fired a short fuse and set off the bomb.'

'We've got to get him before the police do. They'll want to interview me today and if I don't tell them it was Nguni, when we get him into court as a witness it will be obvious I withheld evidence from the police.'

'Witness? How do you mean, you just said you saw him?' Hymie's usually quick mind was a fraction slow, but then he realized what Peekay meant. 'Shit, you don't mean Special Branch? Geldenhuis?'

'It's not such a leap to take. Nguni was paying back a favour to someone. Why otherwise would he be implicated in a plot to assassinate your old man? He wouldn't do something like that on his own.'

Hymie drew breath through his teeth. 'If you're right and Geldenhuis realizes Nguni's been identified, he's going to be one dead black man before nightfall,' he said.

'Exactly.'

Hymie looked at his watch. 'I'll call Tandia and ask

Johnny Tambourine about the camera; it's still early but I guess she'll understand. I'll also call Pretoria; if Johnny didn't get it, let's pray it's still on the platform.'

'Hymie, I've got to get out of here. Don't put up a fuss, can you send a car around for me?'

'Ja, okay, but only late this afternoon. You've got to get a little rest at least.'

'You too, we'll meet at five o'clock at Red. If Tandia's in any sort of shape she ought to be at Red with us.'

Hymie nodded, then stopped at the doorway. 'Peekay, about yesterday, my old man . . .'

Peekay cut him short, 'Don't, Hymie, don't say it!' he laughed. 'I can't stand a mawkish Yid!'

Thirty-six

People talked about Peekay's incredible rescue for months afterwards and they told of how the bomb could have killed hundreds of children, exaggerating his bravery and suggesting somehow that he'd not only rescued Solomon Levy, the famous Jewish multi-millionaire, from certain death, but had somehow diverted the train, preventing the bomb from exploding in the dead centre of the children's choir.

But only rarely, when the story was in the hands of a more responsible teller, and even then always as an afterthought, would they mention the incredible fluke: how the sheared-off head of a tiny bolt, no bigger than the pinkie on a man's hand, had flown off the exploding engine, entered the right eye and lodged in the brain of a fat old coloured woman who was sitting in the rose garden. Some storytellers would even add that she'd brought her bizarre death upon herself, pointing out that there was a notice put there, as plain as the nose on your face, which said nobody was supposed to go in the rose garden.

There were never less people and more flowers at a single funeral. Mama Tequila's grave was piled fourteen feet high and ten yards across with the most expensive wreaths you could imagine, though few of the cards accompanying these floral tributes carried names on them. People who didn't want to be remembered, remembered in their hundreds.

To everyone's surprise, except Tandia and Madam Flame Flo, Mama Tequila turned out to be Dutch Reformed Church. The young *dominee*, not long out of Stellenbosch University, where he'd scored high on theology and zero for street smart, didn't know what to make of the whole thing. The entire front of the church and the extensive lawns on either side were covered in floral tributes but only thirteen people and an Indian photographer came to the funeral service and only twelve to the graveyard.

The six girls were there of course, with Hester hiccuping with grief throughout the service and Rachel elbowing her in the side, though she too had a good cry with all the other girls; and so were Doctor Louis Rabin and Mr Dine-o-mite, who'd done his crying previously and whose eyes were red with grief. Then there was the projectionist from the Odeon cinema, Ismail Naidoo, who nobody had ever seen before but who told how Mama Tequila had brought a double-chocolate ice cream cone to his projection booth every Wednesday for twenty-five years. Madam Flame Flo, Tandia, Peekay and Hymie made up the thirteen, or fourteen if you counted Sonny Vindoo's driver – who would have counted himself but didn't know whether he had a right to do so. And of course there was Mr Dine-o-mite's son, who took pictures of the floral tributes which he tried to sell to a newspaper syndicate. Photographers can't really be counted in these things, you can't be a serious mourner with a camera stuck up your nose.

Mama Tequila turned out to be enormously wealthy and left a diamond ring for every one of the girls, including Tandia, and a trust fund which granted the girls an income for the remainder of their lives. They also received the money she'd invested on their behalf, which was enough to buy them houses and set them up in good marriages. However, in her will, which had been dictated to Tandia at Red, in a part Tandia didn't read to the girls on the day, Mama T, the realist to the end, said, 'I'm telling you, man, I'll be very surprised if they all go straight and narrow. A working girl is a working girl, it's very hard to make a new life standing on your feet all day in front of a hot stove, to keep a man, when you can make him keep you on your back in a warm bed.' Finally, in an announcement which shocked even the girls, but when you thought about it was a pretty good thing to do, she placed Bluey Jay under the trusteeship of Dr Louis Rabin and Sonny Vindoo together with a trust fund to run it as a private drug, alcohol and VD clinic for the treatment of coloured and African street women. Mama Tequila hadn't forgotten her beginnings or forsaken her less fortunate sisters, though she was buggered if she was going to help those white sluts.

The meeting at Red scheduled at five o'clock on the day after the explosion had finally taken place at eight in the evening, Peekay having taken a little longer than he'd expected to sign himself out of hospital and Tandia having been unwilling to leave Madam Flame Flo until she'd given her supper and put her to bed with a strong sleeping potion.

Hymie opened the meeting, the first part of which was attended by the two senior security men who'd

772

been responsible for the overall surveillance of the Levy property and who had wanted to strip the small engine. One was an ex-Pretoria CID detective named Swart and the other an ex-Scotland Yard Detective Sergeant named Brown who had been on the London Metropolitan Bomb Squad before migrating to South Africa. They were briefed on the significance of the Nguni identification and its implications that the Special Branch might be behind the plot to assassinate Solomon Levy.

Brown gave a low whistle. 'You've got the perfect lead and you can't use it. These Special Branch chappies are usually pretty hard to nail anywhere their sort operate. It's always tough going in against the police, but it's twice as hard against the political bods, they've got carte blanche. You're going to have to find this Mr Nguni and get him to confess before you hand him over.'

Peekay laughed. 'That won't be sufficient to get an indictment. The chances are he'll never get as far as the witness box and we won't be able to prove the tape wasn't obtained under extreme duress. Besides, a black man's evidence doesn't carry a lot of weight with an all-white jury. The Special Branch are heroes to the whites in this country and, if it's the guy we believe who's behind Nguni, he's practically a national hero.'

'We need to have Nguni on the day in court so he can be cross-examined,' Tandia added, 'and we need to have his confession on tape. Somehow we need to keep him from the Special Branch in the meantime.' She paused, then added, 'Or he'll die falling out of a window trying to escape.' Tandia was mortified by the Nguni incident and although she had been enormously distressed by the death of Mama Tequila she had made a point of phoning both Peekay at the hospital and

Hymie at home to say how she regretted not taking their advice to stay away from him. They had both repeatedly warned Tandia that they believed Nguni was not to be trusted, but she'd persisted with the relationship, declaring that he had never done anything to deserve her mistrust and had been having a tough time with his transport business lately. This was true and both Hymie and Peekay had reaffirmed this in an effort to comfort her.

'Mr Nguni left his house in Moroka township about four o'clock yesterday afternoon and he hasn't returned. I have the information from Johnny Tambourine whom I have asked to put out feelers in Soweto,' Tandia said. Peekay was gratified; despite her distress she'd been acting as a professional and doing her share of the work.

'Do you think he'll go bush?' Swart asked.

'I don't know,' Hymie replied, 'while I can't elaborate, there are a lot of people out there looking for him. Nguni's face is pretty well known among the black people. He may try to get out of the country.'

Peekay turned to the two security men, changing the subject. 'Have either of you had a chance to take a look at the engine. Can you tell us anything about the bomb?'

Hymie interjected. 'Just a moment, Peekay, before our friends answer, I'd like to say something. I know you must be feeling pretty rotten about the bomb, but I want it made perfectly clear that you *did* warn me about the engine, you *did* want to take it apart and you did not guarantee its safety. I am entirely to blame; the decision not to take the engine apart was mine.' Hymie looked over at Tandia. 'The death of Mama Tequila is on my conscience, Tandia.'

Tandia looked up shocked. 'You mustn't, Hymie! You are not to blame for the evil, the terrible evil in people that makes them do things like this. I am the stupid one, I refused to listen to your warnings about Mr Nguni.'

'Nobody is to blame for anything; now *please*, can we get on with my question?' Peekay was being deliberately insensitive. This wasn't the time for self-recriminations. Peekay was proud of the way Tandia was holding herself together. Apart from a wan smile when he'd commiserated with her, she'd contained her emotions when she'd arrived. How he ached to hold her in his arms, to stroke her and tell her he loved her.

'Thank you for your remarks, Mr Levy, though I must say I feel pretty upset with myself,' Brown said. He then explained how the bomb had been devised and how the detonator had ignited the magnesium strips glued to the inside of the train wheel and how they'd flared, lighting the fuse and setting off the plastic. 'It was extremely clever because it was so simple: a pot of glue, magnesium strips and a bit of electrician's tape. The whole thing could have been put together in less than twenty minutes by a relative amateur. The bomb must have been placed when the train was sent to the engineering works for spray painting and modifications.'

'Do the police know this?' Hymie asked.

'I couldn't say so, sir. Certainly they didn't hear it from me. They cordoned off the entire area and threw me off the site as soon as their own explosives men arrived. Which is fair enough, I would have done the same thing myself. I'm pretty sure it won't take them long to come to the same conclusion.'

'We should try to get to the engineering works first,

sir,' Swart said. 'It's a long shot, but he or they may have left a calling card.'

'How are we going to get to look around the engineering works without a warrant to make a search?' Hymie asked.

Mr Swart answered, they'd obviously already worked out a plan. 'Tomorrow we'll be there when the place opens. I'll walk in and I'll simply act like the police officer I used to be, ask if I may look around and if my partner,' he turned towards Brown, 'can ask the engineers a few questions.' Swart grinned. 'If it doesn't work or if the police have already been, well we haven't broken any law I know about, man.'

Despite the fact that the ANC, through Gideon's people, were alerted, Mr Nguni simply disappeared into thin air. A security man at the gate on the day of the picnic could recall him leaving, but he wasn't sure whether it was before or after the explosion. After three or four days Peekay began to suspect the worst, that Geldenhuis had got to him and Mr Nguni was dead.

A week after the explosion Peekay received a call from Mr Nguni's wife, a timid country woman named Martha who was well-born and therefore acceptable where it mattered in African tribal society, but who had no place in his public life and who played the traditional and subservient role in his household. Peekay had met her a few times over the years when he'd been at Mr Nguni's home and he'd always made a point of going into the kitchen and talking to her.

'*Ninjani*, Martha,' Peekay said, using the more common township greeting.

Martha resumed his greeting shyly, 'I greet you, baas, Peekay,' and then added in a soft, concerned voice, 'My husband, he has not come home, we have not seen him for one week.'

'Ja, Martha, Hymie too, he has been worried, your husband missed a board meeting yesterday. When did you see him last?'

'He came home in the afternoon when he came from baas Hymie's house in Pretoria, but he left again soon in his car.'

'Did he not say anything to you?'

'He does not tell me when he is going, but when he is going far away he tells me,' the woman answered simply.

'But this time he didn't tell you?'

'That is why I am worried. When he goes far away he always tells me. When he goes only one day or two, he doesn't tell me. Now he has gone away one week already!'

'Did he pack a suitcase or take anything?'

'No, everything is in the bedroom.'

'Money, did he take any money?'

'Haya, haya, I cannot say this, I do not know where he is keeping his money.'

'Do you want me to call the police, Martha?'

There was a pause at the other end of the line before Martha Nguni answered, 'He will be very, very angry, baas Peekay, but I think also you must call.'

As a matter of course Peekay identified the time and date of his conversation with Martha Nguni on the tape recorder plugged into the phone and then called the Phomolong police station and reported Mr Nguni missing.

Two days later two detectives from the Special Branch in Pretoria arrived to interview Peekay and Hymie and asked them if they had any reason to suspect Nguni might have been involved in the explosion. Hymie pointed out to the two men that Mr Nguni was a business partner with a great deal to lose and absolutely nothing to gain by such an act, that to suspect him was ludicrous.

They then asked why Peekay hadn't informed them at the same time he'd informed the police at Moroka township and Peekay said he hadn't connected the two incidents, but that now obviously the police had. 'Is Nguni, for some reason, under suspicion?' he asked. One of the detectives replied that this wasn't the case, that they were simply exploring every possibility. The two Special Branch men left apparently satisfied and Peekay hoped to hell he'd been convincing. The official report that he was missing now made it possible for the police to instigate a real, if only pretended, search for the black man and as long as this wasn't connected with the explosion by Hymie or himself, or openly by the police, Geldenhuis would feel relatively safe, even if Mr Nguni was genuinely on the loose and trying to escape from the Special Branch.

Several weeks and then a couple of months went by and Mr Nguni still hadn't surfaced. By this time Red was convinced he was dead and the best chance they'd ever had to get Jannie Geldenhuis had been frustrated, probably by Geldenhuis himself. The Nguni connection had not been made by the newspapers and so the disappearance of the well known black man had only been paid minor attention by the media. Nguni had a relatively low profile to the whites and was only really known in boxing circles. In due course the police announced they had no new information but were pursuing their enquiries, the usual official euphemism for a case book which was about to be closed or at least given a low priority.

Peekay's shoulders mended quite quickly to the point where he could use his arms, but the muscles still pained him a good deal and had grown weak from lack of use. He decided to go back to the gym to build up his strength and to regain a modicum of fitness. The Rand Club to which he belonged had a small gym which would have suited this purpose perfectly but he chose instead to return to Solly Goldman's boxing gym.

The two men embraced warmly when Peekay arrived at the sleazy downtown gym. 'It's good to 'ave ya back, my son,' Solly said. Then trying to cover his obvious emotion he rubbed his hands together. 'Right, Champ, give us a couple months and I'll 'ave ya ready for a shot at the bleedin' title.'

Peekay smiled. He saw Solly from time to time, but not often enough. The inventor of the Solly Goldman thirteen-punch combination had been one of the more important people in Peekay's life. Now he held Solly at arm's length pretending to examine him. 'You know, Solly, when I started with you at fifteen you wore that same frayed brown striped tie to hold up those same baggy grey flannel trousers. I'm not sure it wasn't even the same sweatshirt, I swear I remember that egg stain!'

Peekay started working with weights trying to build up his shoulder muscles where they'd been torn by the explosion. But one thing led to another and in a couple of months he was spending time with the young fighters in the gym most nights after he was finished at Red, boxing with them in the ring, demonstrating punches and correcting their technique. He was never one to do anything by halves and he began to put a lot more into his early-morning road work, building his wind and his legs. Pretty soon he was back to the welterweight limit and his body was hard and fit again.

Almost four months after the explosion and the death of Mama Tequila, Tandia got a telephone call late one afternoon from Madam Flame Flo. 'Listen, Tandy, I know you already coming over Thursday but something funny has come up, jong. Do you think you could come and see me tonight?'

'It will have to be late, Auntie Flo. About nine o'clock, I'll get Johnny Tambourine to drive me. No I won't, I'll drive myself and stay the night.'

'No, man, bring him, he can stay in the room in the yard. What I got to say, maybe he can help.'

Tandia was working on a case with Peekay and she'd set aside two hours that evening to go through the briefing with him. She glanced at her watch; it was nearly six o'clock, he'd be coming in any minute. She fumbled in her handbag for her compact. Peekay was the last guy in the world who would notice whether she'd put on fresh lipstick or not, but the operation of fixing her make-up helped her confidence. Ever since the death of Mama Tequila she'd been awkward; no, not so much awkward, but on edge, nervous, when she was alone with Peekay.

Nothing had been said about the afternoon of the explosion when, in her panic and distress, she'd blurted out her love for him. In fact, later when she'd had the courage to face the incident herself she was genuinely surprised at her outburst. Her love for him was so fraught with impossible implications that she'd buried it deep in her subconscious.

Tandia was not a dreamer. Mama Tequila had taught her to keep her eyes focused on the hard edge of reality, only to gamble with resources she was prepared to lose. Loving Peekay, no matter how covert, was well beyond any such resources, and when she'd declared her love for him immediately after the explosion, it was her heart and not her head which had betrayed her. She was determined that this should never happen again.

Peekay had tried on several occasions to talk with her when they'd appeared to be alone but she'd resisted, either leaving the room on some hastily fabricated excuse or talking over him about some or other legal concern. She could see his frustration, but she had to lead in this matter. She was stronger than him and knew that even the smallest declaration of his reciprocal love, the merest suggestion, would lead to disaster.

Mama Tequila's death had had a surprising effect on her. She found that she'd relied on the old woman more than she'd ever thought possible. Mama Tequila was like an old coastal freighter; battered and weathered by the storms of life, it always knew the quickest way to a safe port or the best way to ride out a storm. You could focus on her, knowing that she'd calculated the odds and prepared for the disaster at the slightest sign of a change in the barometer reading.

The old girl had also been proved right about Nguni. The black tycoon's demise had shattered Tandia's confidence in men even further and added to the awkwardness she felt with Peekay and Hymie. There hadn't been the slightest suggestion from either partner that her friendship with him had delayed Angel Sport's disassociation with the black businessman, but she now knew this to be true. Nguni would not have been present at the Solomon Levy Christmas party had Hymie acted when he'd first decided to do so. Tandia tormented herself with this and with the fact that Mama Tequila might still be alive had she not been so stubborn about her relationship with Nguni.

It concerned her that she was still looking for Patel's

approbation, that she'd never been able to do without him in her life, that she'd always needed a father figure, an older man; Juicey Fruit Mambo, Dr Rabin, Magistrate Coetzee and finally Mr Nguni. The little girl who had been starved so early of the love of her father seemed to spend her life trying to regain it, the wonderful safety of a love that was protective without being physical.

Despite his outward appearances of gentleness, Peekay was a man with needs who would want to possess her for herself, body, mind and soul. He was a possessor of a one-eyed snake she couldn't ignore.

All the other men, the father figures in her life, had wanted something from her, Juicey Fruit Mambo to protect her, Dr Rabin to assuage his Jewish guilt and feed his intelligence, Magistrate Coetzee to confound his own racist beliefs and, finally, the ambitious and calculating Nguni who wanted her to sharpen his aspirations and show off in front of his peers.

Peekay would want nothing and everything and everything was much too much. Tandia told herself she would not give herself to Peekay ever. It was making him understand this without coming out and declaring it bluntly to him, making him somehow understand that what was going on between them was unrequited love, that she would not be going to England with him should they decide to leave, that she had already been drawn into the fight for freedom beyond the passive and almost useless pursuit of the law. She was tired of tilting at windmills and the time had come for her to join Gideon and to take direct action.

Tandia now realized that her love for Gideon had been an infatuation which she had allowed to grow into a habit. Now that this pressure had been taken from her she liked him even more as her leader. Though she'd only seen him once since his return, his work was everywhere and, under his command, *Umkonto we Sizwe* was beginning to look like a concerted and determined force.

Tandia told herself that her need to hate was infinitely more important than any other emotional commitment she might have in her life and that with Nguni she had finally sloughed off her need for even a father figure in her life. She was on her own and her teeth were sharp. For the time being this was enough, she had all the emotional baggage it was possible to carry.

She made sure that the briefing to Peekay filled the two hours she'd allowed for it and when they concluded and Peekay asked her if she could stay a little longer she was able to plead her visit to Madam Flame Flo.

'Tandia, we must talk. You've been avoiding me ever since the explosion.' They'd taken to referring to it as 'the explosion' to avoid the pain of Mama Tequila's death. 'I want you to know that I . . .'

'Peekay, it was a mistake! An emotional outburst brought on by my anxiety at the time; my relief that you were alive was such that my mind found the wrong words. Please, Peekay, as a friend I cherish you more than I can say.' Tandia took a deep breath, looking directly at him. 'But that's all there can ever be between us.'

Johnny Tambourine picked her up at eight o'clock and they set out for the hour or so's drive to Vereeniging. Madam Flame Flo gave them the usual big welcome. She set the table for supper and invited Johnny Tambourine to join them. The little woman always prepared a feast and he'd been thinking about it most of the way from Johannesburg.

Madam Flame Flo allowed them to eat before she talked, fussing over Tandia, making her eat more than she would have done on her own. When she'd served coffee she relaxed for the first time and began to talk.

'You remember the Taj Mahal night club?' she asked Tandia.

Tandia smiled. 'How could I ever forget it; that's where I met Gideon.'

'Well I never told you, but Mr Nguni and a woman named Baby Shabooti and myself, we owned it. I don't want to go into the details, but it never worked, the three of us. I was convinced that Nguni, who was responsible for the hard spirits we bought from outside and smuggled in, was taking a cut and not sharing it, so I sold my share to Baby Shabooti. She and Nguni, they had a thing, so it was okay between them. When Sophiatown was no more she opened a lot of shebeens in Soweto and made a lot of money and built a big house, the biggest in the whole place, double storey with everything hot and cold. I'm telling you, man, you name a convenience she got it, even two of it! She and Nguni, they broke up I thought after the Taj Mahal. But yesterday she calls me on the telephone. Maybe she calls me once a year, maybe not even so much. She tells me she wants me to sign a paper.' Madam Flame Flo looked up. 'A long time ago we bought a garage, you know a service station, and when we broke up they paid me my share okay, but I forgot to sign the paper. Now she wants me to sign. "Ja, of course," I say, "no problems, I'm going over to Meadowlands Friday, I'll come by your house and sign." "No!" she says, like I caught her by surprise, "I'll send it over to you."'

Madam Flame Flo looked at them expectantly. 'Is that all?' Tandia asked. 'She didn't say any more?'

'Tandy, that's enough, man! That woman she spends her life showing off her house. She is the biggest brag artist in Soweto! It wouldn't surprise me one of these days she sells tickets! Guided tours to see the bathroom taps! If she didn't want me to come to her place so she can rub my nose in what she got, the new velvet curtains, maybe a new lounge suite, everything matching, then there is something wrong, man. I'm telling you something for nothing, there is something very funny going on, jong.' She took a deep breath, 'You know what's going on?' Tandia and Johnny both looked at *her* expectantly. 'You go in that house, you find Nguni!'

'That's a big leap in logic, Auntie Flo,' Tandia said.

'Never mind logic, you hear? I'm telling you I'm right! But I also did something else. I called two friends who see her sometimes, you know once a month maybe. We talked about this and that, then I asked, "How's Baby Shabooti?" They both said the same thing, they haven't been to her place for four months!' Madam Flame Flo clapped her hands together gleefully, 'You want to make a bet I'm right, hey?'

The four boys waited until Baby Shabooti left in her big Pontiac convertible, sitting in the back with the hood down, her chauffeur even wearing a cap, before they approached the house. Johnny Tambourine walked round to the back door, tapping politely on the wire screen door. Directly behind it was a burglar-proof door of steel bars and he could see a fat woman, no doubt the cook, working at the stove. She turned at the sound of his tapping to look at him.

Johnny stood with his cap in both hands. 'Please mama, I am looking for work?'

The big woman wiped her hands on her apron and approached the door. 'There is no . . .'

Johnny Tambourine removed the cap with his left hand so that she was looking directly into the gun. 'Open the door, mama, you will not be hurt.'

The woman, eyes big with fright, unlocked the burglar-proof door. Johnny whistled sharply and entered. Flyspeck and Dog Poep emerged from the side of the house and entered the kitchen with him. Dog Poep was carrying a canvas bag and both were wearing balaclavas over their faces. Too Many Fingers Bembi had been left outside to warn them with a sharp whistle should anyone approach.

'Are you alone? Who else is here?' Johnny asked.

'A man, he is sleeping in the big bedroom. Please do not kill me,' she pleaded.

'Take her and tie her up, not here – someplace, maybe the bathroom,' Johnny said to Dog Poep. He said to the woman, 'Please mama, do not scream or make a noise and we will not harm you, you understand?'

Johnny and Flyspeck found the room they were looking for after the third try. They opened the door quietly to see Nguni fast asleep on a double bed. Both waved at their noses; the room smelled of brandy and sick and Nguni was either asleep or passed out on the double bed. He'd kicked the blankets off and lay in the nude, his huge stomach raising and lowering with each breath. He was snoring horribly and seemed to have gained weight since the last time they saw him. The boys looked at each other, grinning. They couldn't believe their luck. Nguni was out to the world and there would be plenty of time to set up.

They crept to either side of the bed and Johnny Tambourine nudged an old-fashioned porcelain chamber pot half-filled with sour sick under the bed with his toe. He whispered to Flyspeck to set the tape recorder up. An empty bottle of Cape brandy stood on the console beside the bed and another half filled, but there didn't seem to be a glass.

When Flyspeck was ready, Johnny Tambourine reached over and slapped Nguni hard across the face. To his surprise the huge man grunted but remained asleep. 'Jesus, he's unconscious, man,' Johnny said in a loud whisper. Flyspeck brought back his hand, indicating that Johnny should hit him again. This time the blow was even harder. Nguni jerked up and his eyes opened, though his face showed no surprise and his eyes were unfocused. Johnny hit him again with the flat of his hand and, grunting, Nguni came to.

'Who? Who are you?' he said thickly, not yet seeing the gun.

'Sit up, Nguni!' Johnny said.

Nguni opened his mouth, about to protest when he saw the gun and gave a start, his eyes suddenly huge in his head. He pulled himself up into a sitting position, his eyes never once leaving the gun Johnny Tambourine held. Then he looked up slowly, his lips gibbering with fright. But then, just as quickly, his expression changed.

'It's you, Johnny Tambourine! I thought it was Special Branch. Put your gun away, man, we can talk.' He snapped the gold Rolex off his fat wrist and handed it to Johnny Tambourine. 'Here, take it, I am your friend,' he smiled.

Johnny took the watch and handed it to Flyspeck. It felt heavy, people said it was real gold. 'We are not friends, Nguni.'

The large black man must have had the constitution

of an ox for he seemed to have recovered instantly, though his eyes were completely bloodshot and his skin puffy from drink. 'Johnny, Tandy is my friend, you are my friend.'

'No more, man! You killed Mama Tequila.'

Nguni actually chuckled, his stomach wobbling. 'Why would I do that?' he said, his voice amused.

'No bullshit, Nguni. We have proof.' Johnny was bluffing. Tandia had simply told him that he was the prime suspect.

'What proof?' Nguni said, raising his head slightly and sticking his jaw out. He was gaining confidence by the second. 'You are lying, Johnny Tambourine! If this was so, they would have said it in the newspapers.'

Nguni cursed himself. He was still drunk, he'd slipped, his mind wasn't working fast enough, he'd virtually admitted his guilt. He tried to recover, hoping the boys were not very bright. 'I left that place before the explosion.'

'Why did you run away? Because you are guilty!' Johnny replied for him.

Nguni shook his head slowly. 'Haya, haya, Johnny, it was my business. There were people who wanted money from me, I couldn't pay them.' He spread his hands. 'That is the simple reason, man. I am hiding from these people.'

Johnny sighed, 'Nguni, we are tsotsi, not lawyers or the police, we do not ask how is a thing? Why?' He pointed the muzzle of his gun in Flyspeck's direction. 'My friend here has been hired by Tandia. He is a killer, a hired gun. But Tandia doesn't want to kill you. "Don't kill him, Johnny," she says. "Tell him only, if he makes a confession we will let him go. If he does not, we will tell Geldenhuis where he is."'

At the mention of Geldenhuis's name Nguni jerked backwards hitting his head hard against the bedhead. It was so sudden as to be almost ridiculous. The giant Zulu was suddenly out of bluff, unable to hold himself together any longer.

'That whore!' he spat.

Johnny and Flyspeck froze, not believing what they'd heard. 'What? What did you say?' Flyspeck said. It was the first time he had spoken.

'Geldenhuis has a paper, a confession, when she was a schoolgirl she was a whore, *isiFebe*!' He started to laugh. 'That Geldenhuis, he is a very clever man, so clever he got me a bus transport licence for Soweto. It is not possible for a black man to have a licence, but he fixed it for me.' He spread his hands, squinting up at Johnny Tambourine and Flyspeck Mendoza. 'You can work for me, I will pay you well. One day I will be the richest black man in Africa!' He seemed to find this last statement very amusing and started to laugh again, his laughter turning almost immediately into a fit of coughing.

Nguni leaned forward, his head bent towards his knees. Flyspeck didn't even think, the spoke came out of the seam of his trousers and entered the first and second vertebrae, his wrist turning to sever the nerve and cut through the soft, pulpy tissue. Nguni was dead without having moved. He simply sat slumped over his huge black belly.

'Shit!' Johnny said.

Flyspeck shrugged and grinned. 'He bad-mouthed Tandy, man!'

Dog Poep heard them and came running into the room. 'What happened? What's the matter?' He stared at them both. Johnny Tambourine and Flyspeck

Mendoza were pointing at the huge buckled shape of Mr Nguni and pissing themselves with laughter.

Johnny Tambourine, Dog Poep Ismali, Too Many Fingers Bembi and Flyspeck Mendoza, with the help of Gideon's people, crossed the border into Mozambique to join a terrorist training squad. Or that's what Tandia thought, but halfway across the Komati River Flyspeck Mendoza lost the grip of the guide who was holding him and panicked. He couldn't swim and, being the smallest, the water came up to his neck. He disappeared under the swift-flowing current, came up thrashing and disappeared again as the river current carried him off. Several minutes later and several hundred yards downstream he was washed up unconscious on a part of the bank covered with reed. The villagers guiding the boys across called him with the soft hoot of a river owl, which was the signal to keep them together in the dark. Two of them came back and searched the riverbank to no avail, and they assumed he was drowned.

Flyspeck Mendoza regained consciousness just before dawn and climbed up the riverbank, not knowing which side he was on. He started to walk and skirted the lights of a town, which unbeknown to him was Komatipoort. When the sun came up he slept, and travelled all of the next night. At dawn, hungry and footsore, he came to a farm where he waited until sun-up and then asked the farmer for work. The farmer asked him for his work papers and when Flyspeck said he'd lost them the farmer grinned and said he could work for his food, but no pay. And so he became a slave.

Flyspeck was a city boy, a bad guy who stayed up late and rose around noon, a hired gun. He had a bad leg from a knife fight and he'd never worked a day in his life. The farmer took the gold Rolex he was wearing and then beat the living shit out of him. He continued to do so daily with a sjambok until Flyspeck was working quite well for a city boy with a bad limp.

But at night in the dark cell, no different to a prison, where the farmer kept all the vagrants – who turned out to be just about everyone who worked on the farm – he sharpened the end of a bicycle spoke he'd stolen, using a small slab of slate-stone. Though he was exhausted from the dawn-to-dusk work and the others around him fell asleep within minutes of eating their evening meal of mealie pap and watery gravy, Flyspeck forced himself to stay awake long enough each night to do a little honing.

For almost two months, night after night, he worked in the pitch blackness until the point of the bicycle was smooth and narrow and sharp as a needle and the sides felt like satin to his touch. The time had come for Flyspeck Mendoza to depart.

Two days later the tractor broke down in a field where they were sowing potatoes and the Boer climbed down and buried his head in the engine. Then he sent his boss boy back to the shed for something. The boss boy laid his sjambok over the back of the tractor and walked quickly away. Suddenly the Boer was alone in the field with only his slave workers, his head in the tractor engine and the top three vertebrae deliciously exposed on the base of his red, sunburned neck.

The spoke went in so cleanly that the Boer let out a soft 'pffft!' like a long sigh. To anyone watching, he would have appeared just like before, on his knees with his head in the tractor engine. Only this time he was dead and the beautiful spoke was already back down the seam of Flyspeck's ragged trousers. Flyspeck reached down and unclipped the Rolex from his wrist and put it in his pocket. Then he picked up his bag of seed potatoes and walked to the end of the field and he just kept walking. Two days later the police caught him on the outskirts of Barberton where he was arrested and thrown into gaol to await trial.

Flyspeck Mendoza confessed readily to the murder of the Boer, but he'd not used his proper name when he'd asked the Boer for employment. His fingerprints were sent to Pretoria to the Department of Native Affairs which keeps the fingerprints of every African over the age of sixteen. A month later he was indicted for murder a second time, this time under his correct name which, because it showed up on a computer check of wanted persons, was also sent to the Special Branch. Finally it arrived on the desk of the youngest colonel in the history of the South African police force.

Colonel Jannie Geldenhuis didn't take long to make the connection between Flyspeck Mendoza, the death of Mr Nguni, and the disappearance of the four boys. The Rolex watch found on Flyspeck was instantly identified as having belonged to Mr Nguni. The Boer who'd been murdered on a farm about twenty miles outside Komatipoort had died in exactly the same way as Nguni had done. He was also sure that Tandia was behind the murder somewhere – otherwise why would all four boys, Johnny Tambourine in particular, have found him when a national manhunt had failed? Johnny Tambourine was her chauffeur and minder; she had to be involved somewhere. Even if Tandia was only aware of the murder and hadn't reported it to the police she could be indicted.

The more Geldenhuis looked at the file on Johnny Tambourine, the more excited he became. Flyspeck

Mendoza was a lifelong friend, they did everything together. The four boys, he discovered, all worked for Tandia. He had to find out if Nguni had said anything before he'd died. Geldenhuis grew suddenly cold. He had to find out whether she had anything and if she did he had to compromise her so that it couldn't be used.

How Geldenhuis handled the kaffir on the murder charge at present in Barberton gaol was critical if he was to compromise Tandia. He picked up the phone and a voice answered, 'Constable Vermaas.'

'Vermaas, look up your prison directory and tell me the name of the Kommandant at Barberton prison.'

'Yes, colonel,' Stoffel Vermaas answered. A couple of minutes later he called back. 'Colonel Smit, sir. Do you want me to call him for you?'

'*Asseblief, ja*,' Geldenhuis thanked the operator and waited for the call to come through from Barberton.

There was a click in Geldenhuis's ear. '*Smit hier*,' a voice said on the other end of the phone.

Geldenhuis identified himself to the prison officer. 'Not *the* Jannie Geldenhuis, the boxer?' Smit asked.

'Ja, I boxed a little,' Geldenhuis laughed, 'a long time ago.'

'We take our boxing pretty seriously down here, colonel. What can I do for you?'

Jannie Geldenhuis explained to Smit what he wanted.

'Ja, of course, colonel, we will make everything available and ready for your arrival. But, just one thing; prison regulations state that a prison officer must be present if an interrogation takes place within the prison. I cannot allow you to interrogate with only your own people in the room.'

Geldenhuis cursed under his breath; he was dealing with a small-town yokel who played by the book. 'This is a Special Branch case, Kommandant, we do not require supervision with the work we do,' he said, a hint of sarcasm in his voice.

'Nevertheless, colonel, I must insist.'

Geldenhuis was too good an operator to push it any further. He sighed heavily so that Smit would hear him on the other end. 'As you wish, Smit.'

'Colonel Smit, Colonel!' Smit corrected, his voice suddenly hard.

Geldenhuis realized at last that he wasn't dealing with a fool and softened his voice immediately. 'I'm sorry, Colonel, here in Special Branch we do a lot of undercover work, we get a bit careless with titles. If you will make a man available we'd like one who has been involved in getting information out of a prisoner himself, if you understand what I mean?'

Geldenhuis wasn't too worried. He'd have preferred to have Flyspeck Mendoza on his own with a couple of his own men, but Barberton prison was a place with a notoriously tough reputation and, anyway, in his experience, warders in country prisons didn't exactly play by the rules. He'd sweet-talk the prickly kommandant when they got there.

Smit called Gert immediately after the phone call. 'We've got Jannie Geldenhuis, the boxer and Special Branch Colonel coming down from Johannesburg tomorrow early to interrogate the kaffir who murdered the Boer from Komatipoort. I've told him you will attend.'

'Yes, Colonel,' Gert replied, 'Do we want the interview on tape?' Though he and Smit had been friends for twenty years they generally kept things formal during working hours.

Colonel Smit looked up at Gert. 'You know who called yesterday?'

'No, sir?'

'Peekay. He's going to defend the kaffir murderer. He phoned to say he's coming down the day after tomorrow to see this Flyspeck kaffir.'

'*Here*, man, why?' Gert asked, amazed. 'It's open and shut, the man has confessed.'

'That's just what I said. He wants to expose the conditions on the farms. Blacks without papers used as slaves. This guy who got murdered, he says he's been doing it a long time.'

'Jesus! So what's new? It's been going on three hundred years!'

Smit looked up again. 'You know, Gert, I love Peekay like my own son, but I don't think he's going to make old bones, he doesn't know where to draw the line.'

'That's what made him champion of the whole world, he never knew when he was beaten,' Gert said, though it was plain he was as concerned for Peekay as Smit was.

Smit cleared his throat. The subject of Peekay was too painful to discuss even with Gert. Peekay was the only truly innocent man he'd ever known and he found it a distressing experience coming to terms with this kind of truth. He admitted to himself that if he hadn't known him as well as he did he would despise him for it. Smit knew about fanatics; his own people, the yolk, were often as fanatical and totally unreasonable and unreasoning. But you couldn't put Peekay in the same category. Peekay didn't hate the Afrikaner people or the kaffirs or anyone for that matter, he hated injustice. He couldn't see the grey shades, the reasons, the necessities for things to be as they were and this made him dangerous to a system which Smit himself supported. But it made him doubly dangerous to people like Jannie

Geldenhuis, and Colonel Smit knew how people like Geldenhuis were and how they reacted when they were threatened.

'Ja, on second thoughts, we'll let Colonel Geldenhuis and his people in alone with the kaffir. If he's going to have to smack him round a bit to get whatever he wants from the bastard we don't want to be the people to stand in the way of justice. But tape the interview, Gert. Put a two-hour tape on and let it run; if he does something stupid and the coon dies, we want to be covered. But also, man, if they ask if we taping, just look stupid, let him think the *japies* from the *platteland* don't go in for that sort of thing.'

Thirty-seven

Tandia was arrested in the early hours of the morning and given five minutes to dress. It was the second time in her life she'd been roughly pushed into the back of a kwelakwela, a police van, and taken into custody. In the ensuing years the frightened teenager had become a great beauty and a famous barrister, yet nothing, she told herself, had changed. She was still a kaffir and Geldenhuis, her original tormentor, still had his boot on her neck.

The back of the police van had the sharp pungency of African sweat and the sour smell of beer mash as though earlier in the night a drunk had vomited. In fact, Tandia concluded, this was precisely what had happened, for the floor and the wooden seat on which she sat were wet, suggesting that the back of the van had recently been hosed out. The wetness now added to the cold, though she was not sure whether she shivered from the damp, dark cold interior of the van or from her own sense of misery.

For some reason the siren on the van would wail intermittently, for fifteen seconds or so every few minutes. She wondered if it was intended to intimidate her; there couldn't be much traffic at this time of the morning nor, she imagined, was her arrival urgent.

After a while they slowed down and stopped. She heard the police driver talking to someone. They must have arrived at the gate into the huge, grey granite structure of the John Vorster Square police head-quarters. The van moved off slowly again and pro-ceeded for what seemed like only a few yards before it stopped. Moments later Tandia heard the passenger door slam and then the sudden rattle of the lock on the rear door of the van. The door opened and the detective sergeant who'd arrested her stood waiting. 'Get out now, please, miss,' he instructed. Tandia half stooped and climbed out, the air outside cold and fresh on her face after the smell of the van. He held a pair of hand-cuffs. 'I've got to do this, it's procedure, I should really have done it when we arrested you.'

Tandia nodded, holding up her wrists. It was dark but if the policeman had looked carefully he might just have made out the slight discolouring around her wrists which were the scars from the last time she'd worn handcuffs.

She expected to be finger-printed and formally charged but instead she was led down a long corridor into a brightly lit room which, under normal circum-stances, would have seemed like a joke. It contained a powerful light with a larger than usual frosted bulb in the centre of the ceiling. A single wooden upright chair stood directly under it. A polished honey-coloured cork linoleum covered the floor and muffled her footsteps as she entered. The walls of the fairly large room were painted a light apple green. It was so obviously an inter-rogation room that it seemed to belong in the pages of a Dick Tracy comic book. The door was painted a glossy brown and on it was lettered in white:

Interview Rm. 1. Europeans only.
Onderhoud Km.l. Slegs Blankes.

Tandia pointed to the door. 'You've brought me to the wrong place. I do not suffer from the affliction of being white, constable.' She was using the last of her courage, for she could feel her bowels beginning to constrict; the well known barrister was quickly dissolving into the small frightened teenager sitting in the play chair at Cato Manor police station.

The white female constable who'd taken over from the detective sergeant when they'd arrived at John Vorster didn't bother to reply. 'You can sit if you like,' she said, standing at the door and pointing to the lone chair. She was so nondescript in appearance that she almost defied description; she was twenty pounds over-weight and the hem of her light-blue drill skirt was a good four inches higher on one side than the other.

'I'd like to use the toilet, please,' Tandia asked.

The female constable looked confused, then annoyed. 'The non-European toilets are on the other side of "C" block. There's no time, man.'

Tandia pointed to the chair. 'If I can sit on that white person's chair, why not on a toilet seat?'

The woman seemed to hesitate again; then she jerked her head. '*Kom, maak gou, jong,*' she said, telling Tandia to hurry. Tandia followed her down a corridor to a women's toilet. 'Leave open the door,' the female constable instructed. She stood directly in front of the open door looking into the toilet, her heavy brown stockinged legs slightly apart and her hands clasped behind her back.

They returned to the room and Tandia seated herself on the chair. The constable closed the door and left her, having first made her remove her shoes and confiscated her handbag and wristwatch. Placing the watch into the bag and taking both shoes and bag with her she placed them in the corridor directly outside the door. Then, using both hands, she pulled at the door which closed slowly. Tandia realized it was nearly six inches thick and must be sound-proofed. As the door clicked to a close a small red light went on above the lintel and she noted a telephone receiver fixed to the wall where it had been hidden by the open door.

Tandia longed suddenly for the calming effect of a cigarette. 'Hold yourself together, nothing's happened yet,' she said to herself, though she could feel the constriction in her chest and the leaden feeling in her stomach as her terror began to mount. It was oppressively hot in the room and she rose from the chair and removed the cardigan and then the sweater she wore under it. She was wearing a fashionably short green woollen shift which, she now realized, showed her figure. Soon this, too, became too warm and she was conscious of her clammy overheated body. Her scalp itched as the perspiration gathered on her brow.

She wiped herself down with a discarded sweater but the perspiration soon returned as she paced the room, fanning herself with both hands. She was becoming increasingly distressed. Finally after what seemed like an hour or more, with a rattle and a soft 'phffft', the door opened and Geldenhuis stood framed in the doorway.

'*Here*, but it's hot in here,' he said, blowing through his teeth and fanning his face with his right hand. He turned and spoke to someone in the corridor, 'Tell them to take down the heat, you hear?' Then turning to her he smiled, 'Good morning, Tandy. I'm sorry about the heating, I told them they mustn't let you get cold.' He grinned, 'You know cops, they always over-react!'

Tandia sniffed, 'That was considerate of you, Colonel Geldenhuis.' She was surprised at the hint of sarcasm in her voice.

Geldenhuis took a step into the room, 'Now don't be like that, Tandy!' There was a grin on his face but his pale blue eyes were cold and seemed not to move, as though they were permanently locked into place. He turned. 'Bring a table and another chair!' he called at the open door.

Almost immediately two black constables appeared, one carrying a table and another carrying a chair. It was obvious to Tandia that they'd been waiting outside for permission to enter. The single chair placed directly under the light had been a ploy to unsettle her. Jannie Geldenhuis was dressed in full uniform, though he wore no cap and he carried a flat plastic zip-up folder under his left arm. He put the folder on the table which had been placed away from the light with the original chair moved to one side of it and the second chair placed on the other side.

Tandia was surprised. She hadn't seen Geldenhuis in uniform for several years and in it he took on a different dimension. If the uniform was meant to intimidate her it had slightly the opposite effect. As a uniformed policeman he tended to be the Geldenhuis who had terrorized the child. As long as she could hold on to her adult status, her lawyer's mind, Tandia told herself she could overcome these old fears. The uniform he wore would help her to keep this in mind. What she needed to fear far more was the plainclothes Geldenhuis where the evil and the private madness lay.

Had she known why Geldenhuis had appeared in

uniform she would have recoiled from him in horror.

'You know why we've arrested you?' Geldenhuis asked suddenly, though his voice was still relaxed.

'On a conspiracy charge,' Tandia said. 'It won't hold up.'

'Ja, that's right. But you're wrong, it will.' His voice tightened a fraction. 'Sit please, Tandy.' He pointed to the chair and waited for her to sit. 'So, after all these years here we are at the beginning again, hey?'

'Only in one respect, colonel. This is the second time you have placed me under wrongful arrest. I would like to make a phone call please.'

'Maybe later, it's still early in the morning,' he glanced at his watch. 'Hey man, it's only six o'clock; your boyfriend, Peekay, will still be out running.' It was the first hint of animosity and Tandia braced herself.

'My partner is in Barberton today. I would like to call Hymie Levy.'

The policeman's lips puckered, 'Ja, that's right, I remember now. I was down there yesterday, they told me he was coming.'

'I've read the warrant, colonel, could you please explain how it involves me?'

Geldenhuis held Tandia's eyes. 'Very simple. We have incontrovertible proof that you were aware of the killing and the identity of the killer of Samuel Nguni.'

'That is not true!' Tandia burst out, the volume of her protest betraying her nervousness.

'That is not for you to say, the court will decide.'

'Will you show me your supporting evidence?' Tandia asked, trying to keep her voice calm.

'Ja, maybe I will, maybe I won't, it all depends . . .'

'On what?'

'What do you think?'

'On whether I cooperate? I am no more implicated in Samuel Nguni's murder than you are.' Tandia was feeling safer; if Geldenhuis kept it to legal matters she could cope.

From the time he'd placed the plastic folder on the table Geldenhuis started to pace the length of the room, his arms behind his back, his whole attitude seemingly relaxed, never actually looking at Tandia. His manner was almost courtroom procedure, with her seated in the witness box and him prowling the floor as he cross-examined. Now, for the first time, he moved up close and placed his hands on the edge of the table opposite to her, leaning slightly forward so that he was almost directly above her, dominating the space they occupied, forcing Tandia to keep her eyes downcast. 'Cooperation, in our business that's a very important word, wouldn't you say, Tandy? Without cooperation we would be in a lot of trouble. But mostly, people, they're good, they cooperate with the police. Sometimes they need a little help, but mostly they're pretty good.'

Tandia realised that Geldenhuis was using standard authority structure, a slightly patronizing, though initially impersonal manner backed by an acute awareness in the victim of the authority behind it.

She told herself she would need to keep the dialogue on an equal footing as long as she possibly could. 'I cannot cooperate by pleading guilty, colonel.'

Geldenhuis moved even closer to her, raising his voice suddenly, so that she jumped involuntarily, looking up at him. 'I am not a fool, Tandy. I know that!' The expression on the policeman's face changed instantly and he smiled. 'There are lots of sorts of cooperation.' He paused. 'And each kind has, you know, its reward.'

'And what sort of cooperation did you have in

mind . . .' she paused for less than a second before adding, 'Colonel Geldenhuis?'

Geldenhuis realized that she was up to most of his tricks, that Tandia wasn't some ingénue with whom he could toy. But he had a long way to go yet and if she thought she knew where he was coming from, all the better. 'Well let me see now, Tandy, first we have to put our cards on the table. I show you the cards I got hey? Then you show me what you got.'

Tandia forced herself to smile, 'I'm afraid I'm not very good at card games, colonel.'

'Ag, man, it's easy, I'll teach you how to play. It's very simple, really. The one with the best cards wins.' He walked over to the door and closed it.

Tandia followed him with her eyes, noting again the small red light that went on above the door the moment it shut. 'I am not aware of having any cards,' she said, raising her voice so Geldenhuis could hear her.

He turned and walked over to the table. 'No, man, that's not true, you will see when we play the game you have a good hand.' Geldenhuis picked up the plastic folder on the desk and unzipped it. He withdrew two neatly typed pages and, leaning over, placed them in front of Tandia. 'I am putting my first card down. This is known as an ace. Take your time . . . read it.' He turned and started to pace again.

Tandia began to read the transcript which was headed up in the standard manner of a confession notice. After a few paragraphs she looked up and waited for Geldenhuis, who had his back to her, to turn. 'This is a police verbal, Colonel Geldenhuis.'

'Ja, and that's just the start.'

Geldenhuis dug into the folder again and produced a newspaper photo of Johnny Tambourine taken when he had been written up as the boy who had saved Tandia and Magistrate Coetzee's lives. 'We have positive identification from the cook.'

Tandia ignored him. She read through the documents, trying to seem the lawyer she was, although inwardly she was filled with misgiving.

> '... and then man, my Bra comes to me.
> We are going to hit Nguni he says.'
> P: 'How do you mean hit? To hit with
> your fist?'
> Mendoza: 'No, baas, hit is like a hit-man.
> We must kill this Nguni guy. He is a bad
> cat, man.'
> P: 'Why must you kill him? Did he tell you
> why?'
> Mendoza: 'For what he did to Mama
> Tequila.'
> P: 'Why would he do that? Was this Mama
> Tequila a relation or something?'
> Mendoza: 'Ja, my Bra says because he
> killed Mama Tequila ... Tandy's friend,
> when he exploded the bomb.'
> P: 'Did he say she knew what he was
> going to do?'
> Mendoza: 'Ja, I think she knew.'
> P: 'Think?'
> Mendoza: 'She knew.'

When she came to the end, Tandia looked up at Jannie Geldenhuis. 'Colonel Geldenhuis, I don't know what you're trying to do, but this verbal isn't worthy of you. Peekay was in Barberton today interviewing Flyspeck Mendoza. If the prisoner has been over-enthusiastically interviewed by your people this will come out in the evidence. Even the South African courts don't like police verbals obtained under duress and that leaks like a sieve. I never knew of Nguni's murder until after it happened. What you're trying to do is clear up Nguni's murder and implicate me in some sort of treasonable conspiracy.'

Geldenhuis rose from the chair, and perched on the comer of the table. He reached down and retrieved the two pages in front of her and resumed them to the plastic folder. Finally he leaned over and patted Tandia lightly on the shoulder. 'You're good, Tandy,' he chuckled, 'But I already knew that. I admit, maybe we had to do a few things to get this kaffir boy to talk, but the lowveld court where they're going to hold the trial won't worry about a little thing like that. We're giving them a double murder confession – that's not something that happens every day, a kaffir who has killed two white men. Magtig! What a trial for the district court! Don't you worry, I can make this confession stick all the way, man.' Geldenhuis paused. 'Your boyfriend can do what he likes, I've got a signed confession.' He reached into his pocket and withdrew the gold Rolex watch. Tandia recognized it immediately. Nguni would brag about it to everyone who would listen; it had cost him six thousand American dollars. 'This was found in the pocket of the accused, it is Nguni's watch.' He leaned over and touched Tandia lightly under the chin, grinning. 'And now I've also got you, skatterbol. What do you think your boyfriend can do about that, hey?'

Tandia was repulsed by Geldenhuis touching her and she wanted to jerk her head away, but she didn't have the courage to do so. This was the third time he'd referred to Peekay as her boyfriend and she couldn't continue to ignore him. 'Please, colonel, do not refer to Peekay as my boyfriend, it's not true!'

Geldenhuis opened the folder and withdrew a ten-by eight-inch photograph, the size which would normally be submitted as evidence in court. He tossed it carelessly in front of Tandia, not saying a word. Tandia looked down at the picture without picking it up. The black-and-white print was grainy, having been blown up quite a lot from the original sixteen-millimetre negative, but it clearly showed Tandia with her arms around Peekay and her head on his chest.

Tandia's mouth fell open. 'The explosion! It happened after the explosion. Peekay is my friend, I was terribly upset!' she protested.

Geldenhuis's hand shot out and grabbed her by the throat. 'You are fucking him, you hear? Fucking him! You fucking him at the Jew's house. The Jew bastard who loves kaffirs, he should have died! That bomb should have killed the fucking bastard!'

His voice had started low but now he was shouting, his eyes wild, as though he'd gone suddenly mad, and the corners of his mouth twitched. It was all so astonishingly quick that pure fright had not yet caught up with Tandia. Geldenhuis was choking her and she clawed at his hands, but they were enormously strong for a man his size and the clamp around her throat grew tighter until she started to black out in flashes. As suddenly as he'd attacked her he released his grip, standing up and walking away from the table. He cleared his throat, lifting his chin slightly and adjusting his tie. Then he produced a folded handkerchief and dabbed at the corners of his mouth.

Tandia's head was bent over the table and she was coughing violently, trying at the same time to regain her breath. Tears streamed from her eyes, blinding her. Geldenhuis turned suddenly and pointed his finger at her, taking a step towards the table again. Her tears prevented her seeing him clearly but she instinctively flinched, expecting another attack. But he moved no closer to her. When he spoke his voice seemed to have gained a level of control, though it was still angry. 'You think you so bladdy clever, you two. Two big-time lawyers always in the papers. To me you just a kaffir, you hear? A stinking black kaffir! You think you can do anything you like, that we just all *japies*, hairy backs, stupid Afrikaners, you think it's a joke. You think keeping our blood pure, it's a joke, don't you?'

'It's not a joke,' Tandia rasped, her voice barely audible.

'Hey? What did you say, kaffir?' Geldenhuis took another step closer to the table, his voice menacing. Tandia pulled back, involuntarily bringing her hands up in front of her face.

'It's not a joke, colonel,' Tandia repeated. She was having difficulty speaking.

'What do you mean by that, kaffir?'

Tandia was frightened and her throat burned terribly. She realized dimly that what was happening was not part of the way Geldenhuis had planned things, that he'd lost control. 'Nothing, Colonel Geldenhuis. I meant nothing,' she whimpered.

He sniffed, wiping his nose with the back of his hand, turning away and then immediately turning back again, 'What would you know about racial purity, hey? You part a kaffir and you part a bladdy *charra* and now you want to do it with a white man so your children will be part of us too! Your filth will come into our blood!' He took a step up to the table and reached over to retrieve the photograph, waving the picture in Tandia's face. 'You fucking him, you bitch, and you got to be punished!'

It was the word 'punished' which acted as the trigger. The vision of his father in the butcher's cold room, his large hairy white flanks bent over the huge buttocks of a black woman, suddenly overwhelmed Geldenhuis. It was his duty, his sacred duty before God to keep the purity, to prevent the blacks from turning them all into bastards and half-castes, into the scum of the earth! His hand shot out to grab her again and Tandia jerked back, over-balancing her chair and landing hard on her back, hitting the back of her head on the cork floor.

For a moment Tandia lay stunned. Then she felt the boot on her neck. The fear rose up in her, a dark animated ghost which started from nowhere and filled her entire being. She was back in the cemetery at Cato Manor; in her mind she heard his voice, a younger voice, but still his. *You report this you dead meat, you hear?*

'Get up, you black bitch,' she heard Geldenhuis say, though his voice seemed to come from a distance. Tandia lay perfectly still, his boot still on her neck. Then it lifted but she still didn't respond. 'Up!' he shouted and the toe of his boot landed in the small of her back. The pain drove up her spine but she managed to stifle the scream so that it came out as a choking, gasping sound. Still she didn't move, her fear rendering her totally powerless. Now it was a huge wave washing over her senses and drowning them in its roar.

Geldenhuis reached down and grabbed Tandia by the hair, jerking her head from the ground. 'On your knees, kaffir!' He pulled hard and Tandia felt an explosion of pain in her head as it was drawn upwards. Her eyes remained tightly closed, her traumatized mind still obeying his order in the cemetery a dozen years before. Tandia had no sense of time, she was no longer aware of where she was, her body simply responding to his commands.

Geldenhuis released her hair and still she kept her eyes closed. His words in the graveyard repeated over and over again like a gramophone record stuck in one place. She could hear him panting above her and then his voice again, 'Open your eyes, kaffir!'

Tandia opened her eyes. Geldenhuis stood in front of her, his legs slightly apart; in one hand he held his police revolver and in the other his deformed erection. 'Kiss it better!' he commanded, bringing the barrel of the gun to her forehead. Tandia moved her head forward, her lips touching him. 'Properly better, man!' She felt the barrel of the gun push into the side of her head. Tandia opened her mouth and took him in. Above her Geldenhuis began to whimper; then she felt his body shudder and then he pulled away from her.

Geldenhuis walked halfway across the room, adjusting himself and replacing his revolver. Then he took his handkerchief out and, without unfolding it, wiped the sweat from his face. He walked over to the phone beside the door. Lifting the receiver he waited, then spoke into it. 'Bring water, drinking water and a glass.' He turned, remaining beside the phone. 'Get up, pick up the chair and sit down!' he commanded.

When the water came he walked over to the table, placed the glass down and filled it, pushing it across the table towards her. In a solicitous voice he said, 'Drink, Tandy, it will help your throat.'

Tandia drank greedily, though the glass chattered against her teeth and she had to hold it in both hands.

Her throat hurt to swallow. She put the glass down empty, not looking at Geldenhuis who had brought his chair back to the table and now sat opposite her. He took the empty glass and removed his handkerchief; unfolding it, he wiped the interior of the glass, then he half filled it, drinking himself, though only half the water in the glass.

'That's the difference between us an' you people, *we* always get even. We never forget. That's why we on top and you on the bottom. Now you and me, we even again, quits.' Geldenhuis paused. 'What's the matter? You think something terrible happened? When you bit me in Durban, that's when something terrible happened. What happened just now, that was fair, you hear? Very fair. I should have killed you for what you did to me. I thought about it a lot. But in the end I am a Afrikaner, we are a fair people. I got even, but I did it fair. You can count yourself very lucky you not dead, man.'

Tandia looked directly at Geldenhuis. She spoke slowly at first, her voice coming out slightly hoarse. 'Since the first day you came into my life you've tried to make a whore of me, Jannie Geldenhuis. But it won't work, you'll never do it.' She sniffed, 'You can't make a whore out of someone who isn't one. But what you just made me do, that won't make you better, because you can't make a man out of someone who isn't one!'

Geldenhuis laughed but Tandia could see in his pale blue eyes that she'd struck home. It was the first time she'd seen confusion in them and she wasn't afraid of him attacking her again; the demon in him was temporarily spent.

'I suppose you think Peekay is a man? Sies! A white man who does it with kaffirs!' he said, but the smile on his face wasn't secure and he lowered his eyes, unable to hold hers.

'I know nothing of Peekay's sexual proclivities, Colonel Geldenhuis, but I now count you among the kaffir fuckers!'

The shock on the police colonel's face was enormous. It was as though he'd walked unexpectedly into a right thrown from way back behind the shoulder; his face seemed to physically crumble, his jaw went slack and he grabbed onto the edge of the table with both hands as though he was preventing himself from falling. Tandia panicked, his sudden reaction triggering the delayed shock of the past hour of horror. She knew suddenly that he was going to kill her and she jumped from her seat and flung herself at the door, hammering at it with her fists. 'Open the door! Open the door! Please! Please!' she screamed. Then she saw the phone on the wall and grabbed it, 'Open the door! Please open the door!' she screamed again down the receiver. She turned, weeping with shock, expecting Geldenhuis to leap upon her and instead saw him seated at the table looking at her, the expression on his face benign.

'Come and sit down, Tandy,' he said quietly. 'No one will open the door.'

Her heart still beating violently, Tandia returned to her seat. Geldenhuis seemed perfectly relaxed, one hand on the table the other on his lap. 'Sit, we haven't finished talking yet.'

Tandia sat, avoiding his eyes. 'Look at me,' he said. Tandia lifted her head to look at him and his hand shot up from his lap and pushed the gun against her forehead and pulled the trigger. The empty gun clicked a fraction before Tandia's scream, her hand grabbing at her neck in fright. Geldenhuis was even prepared for this and slapped her across the face, cutting the scream cold and preventing the hysteria rising up in her. 'See, there are no bullets,' he said.

Geldenhuis put the revolver back in its holster and then looked up at her again. 'You have broken your neck chain,' he said, pointing to the thin gold chain lying on the table. He reached over and picked it up, examining the two small pointed gold teeth attached to it. 'There is no escape, we always get even in the end,' he said impassively, then placed the chain back on the table in front of Tandia. 'Tandy, look at me.' Tandia raised her eyes slowly, expecting anything and was surprised to see that Geldenhuis wore a hurt expression. He shook his head slowly, 'You don't understand, do you? You have cooperated with me, Tandy, even if we didn't play our game of cards, hey? Never mind, some other time; now you must get your reward. Jannie Geldenhuis reached over for the plastic folder and withdrew the two foolscap pages of transcript. 'I could have made it stick,' he boasted and tore the manuscript in half. Then he tore it again and again until little squares of paper covered the table in front of him. Finally he looked up and Tandia knew instantly that the policeman had returned. His eyes were hard as he spoke. 'I'm going to get you, Tandy. You and Peekay. But fair and square. Also Mandoma and the Jewboy. All four. You are trying to destroy my country and my people and you will hang for treason.' He pointed to the bits of paper scattered over the table. 'Tonight we fixed one more thing; you and me, we quits now.' Geldenhuis turned to Tandia. 'Will you do me a favour?'

Tandia was exhausted and enormously distressed, but she held herself together, not sure that they'd come to the end of the bizarre and terrifying night. Gelden-huis could as easily snap again and so she was careful to mollify him now. 'I will try, what do you want me to do?'

'Tell Peekay about what happened.'

Tandia looked at Geldenhuis in alarm. 'Why?' she asked, astonished.

Geldenhuis spoke impassively. 'Ja, well, you see if you try to bring a charge against the police for molest-ing you, Detective Sergeant Koekemoer and his two coons who brought you in will swear to the court you resisted arrest. A bruise like you going to have on your neck and maybe a mark on your back, that's consistent with resistance and necessary subsequent restraint.' Gel-denhuis seemed to be smiling to himself as he placed his elbows on the table and began to gather together the tiny pieces of paper, pushing them into a neat pile between his cupped hands. Finally he looked up at Tandia, the smile still on his face. 'So, tell Peekay he can have his revenge in the boxing ring. Tell him he can come any time, you hear? Any time he likes. I'm ready.'

Thirty-eight

Peekay had been in Barberton on the night of Tandia's arrest, seeing Flyspeck Mendoza at the prison. He'd arrived to find that Flyspeck had been brutally tortured by Colonel Geldenhuis the previous day so that now one eye sagged half an inch lower in the eye socket, his nose was broken and most of his teeth were missing. But the little guy swore to Peekay that he hadn't confessed to Nguni's murder, which is what Geldenhuis wanted him to do. Peekay had spent most of the day seeing to it that Flyspeck received adequate medical attention and so decided to remain overnight and leave for Johannesburg at dawn the following morning.

Though Gert and Colonel Smit had been helpful, they had little sympathy for Peekay's client. In their book a self-confessed murderer takes what comes to him, even if it ends up being a bastard like Geldenhuis. Peekay got into town by nine in the morning and went directly to Red. Chronic Martha met him with a message to call Tandia at his Hillbrow flat. Tandia had a key, for she would often go there to work on a case when she didn't want to be disturbed. It was convenient, no more than ten minutes by taxi from the office. Peekay called immediately and Tandia answered.

'Peekay, I thought you'd be here,' she sounded distressed.

'I spent the night in Barberton. What's wrong Tandy?'

'Can you come please, Peekay?' she said in a tiny voice.

'Hang on, I'll be right there.'

'Tandia, you look bloody awful, what's happened?' Peekay said, dropping his briefcase and running towards her as he entered the flat. Tandia had attempted to smile as Peekay walked in but the sustained effort to remain in control of her emotions was too great and now, for the first time since she'd left Geldenhuis and John Vorster Square that morning, she was unable to push the horror of the night sufficiently away from her and her bottom lip began to quiver.

The detective sergeant had put her into a non-European taxi just after half past seven that morning. He'd paid the driver and instructed him to take her home to Soweto. A block along she'd re-directed the driver to Hillbrow, to Peekay's flat. The taxi driver took one look at Tandia and without saying a word changed direction. Ten minutes later she arrived at the flat. 'He gave me too much money,' the driver said.

'Your lucky day,' Tandia said, crossing the road. She'd rung the bell and when there had been no reply, she'd let herself into Peekay's flat. He'd obviously not returned from Barberton. She panicked suddenly. Why had she come directly to him? She thought about retreating, returning home. Nobody need know. She was strong enough. Mama Tequila would have told her to get off her sweet arse and go to work.

She went directly to the bathroom and turned on the shower, scrubbing herself from head to toe, washing the lather off her body and starting again until she had repeated the process three times. She felt sure she would never feel clean again in her life. She'd taken a spare toothbrush she'd found in Peekay's bathroom cabinet into the shower with a tube of paste and she did the same thing, cleaning her teeth three times and spitting the foam violently at her feet in the shower.

She was still dry-eyed as she towelled herself and fixed her make-up; then she called the office just after half past eight when Chronic Martha opened the switchboard. Her concentration kept lapsing and her attention span grew shorter and shorter as her panic grew. She'd been pushing it away ever since she'd left Geldenhuis but now it began to seep through her fingers. She thought again about running away, keeping what had happened to herself. She'd learn to live with last night, she always had in the past. It was one more hate, one more score to settle. But this time she knew it was more than this. The police colonel's threat to destroy them was real; they were all in danger. She must talk to Peekay and in doing so she would have to tell him what had taken place at John Vorster Square.

How would Peekay react when she told him what Geldenhuis had done to her? How could she begin to tell him? She didn't have those kinds of words, she'd never shared an intimacy in her life with a man. Only once with another human being, Sarah. In Sarah's bed all those years ago. She'd never forgotten the touch, the loveliness of the touch of someone else's hand caring about her, gentling her spirit. It was a warmth she'd felt for a few stolen early momings and then never again.

Gideon had been Tandia's only lover. His lovemaking was masculine and direct; she expected no more, it suited her and meant she didn't have to pretend. She hadn't allowed Nguni to touch her and he, in turn, hadn't persisted; this had been one of the main reasons why she had continued to go out with him.

Peekay had kissed her just once, thinking she was asleep, after Juicey Fruit Mambo's death, and the touch of his lips on her brow was like nothing she had felt before. Now she wanted it again, like a little girl who wants a hurt kissed better. When she'd called him from Barberton hospital after the fire bombing at Magistrate Coetzee's farm, he'd been barely able to reply, his voice choked with emotion and relief at her safety. It was then that she had begun to realize he was fundamental to her life. When she'd seen him lying dazed in the smoke and chaos of the explosion at the Christmas party her heart, empty for so long, had suddenly filled, like water rising up from an underground stream, rising from the bottom of an empty well and splashing over the lip, all in a time frame faster than her mind could comprehend. In that moment she was totally without fear and she'd run to him and held her head against him and brought her arms around him. For a few dazzling minutes before the doctor's asinine voice had torn her from this completeness, she'd known what it felt like to be totally in love.

Now Tandia waited for Peekay to return, not knowing what to expect, not knowing what to do, but returning blindly to him, knowing instinctively that if she pushed the hurt and the anger and the loathing back into her one more time it would corrupt her spirit to the point where even the hate she felt couldn't sustain her need to live.

Peekay sat beside her and put his arm around her and pulled her into his chest. She couldn't look at him, dared not look. 'Tandy, please, tell me?' He pushed her gently away from him, took her face in his hands and made her look at him. At last the tears came, the tears for what Geldenhuis had done to her, the tears for Patel and the tears for herself as Peekay held her in his arms and stroked her and started the healing of her with his strong hands.

When finally Tandia was able to control herself sufficiently to speak she looked up at Peekay. 'Last night I was arrested by Geldenhuis.'

The shock on Peekay's face was enormous. 'Arrested? How? Why?'

'Peekay, we are in danger. He tried to indict me for complicity in Nguni's murder. He had a verbal supposedly taken from Flyspeck Mendoza, accusing me of ordering the murder.'

'It's not true, Tandy. I spoke to Flyspeck yesterday. They tortured him, but they got nothing!'

Tandia sighed. 'It was only an excuse, Peekay. It is a long, long story, but you and Hymie are in danger so I must tell it.' Tandia looked up at Peekay and burst into tears again.

'Come Tandy, you don't have to say anything.'

'No, I must.' She began to talk, telling Peekay of the rape after Patel's funeral. She spoke quietly going through every detail, as though the words were in braille etched into her mind and she was running her fingers over them and saying them aloud. There was a flatness to her voice, as though by keeping it in a monotone she could hold the emotion she felt at bay. She spoke without looking up at Peekay, until she paused to blow her nose, and then she saw that tears were running down his face as he looked at her, his love for her so intense that she could feel it burning into her. He felt a terrible shame that he'd doubted her, that Geldenhuis had so easily conned him with the confession.

Tandia talked on and on, finally coming to the arrest, despite her distress not sparing herself or working shy of the sordid detail.

Peekay felt a deep, dark presence rise up in his soul, a need to destroy so great that his entire body shook. He grew so pale that Tandia grew fearful. But what Tandia was witnessing was the coming of hate to Peekay, the destruction of innocence. The power of hate roared into him like a white-hot furnace, consuming everything; he disappeared into it, a silent scream of vengeance shouting in the flames. Nothing of him was spared by the consuming fire; only the scream remained, the single violent scream of hate. Slowly he started to control it, to hold its gnashing teeth from his heart.

It was the same feeling he'd experienced when suddenly confronted by the Judge in the mines. The hate which had been bottled up in him all the years of his childhood had burst like a ripe boil and he'd beaten the huge man senseless. He'd pushed the incident back into his subconscious; never allowing it to surface. It was the single moment in his life of which he was monstrously ashamed, knowing he had been no better than his oppressors, that within him there was a darkness.

Now the need to strike out blindly, to inflict a physical hurt, senseless and violent, had resumed. If he allowed it to grow it would bind into a knot that would fill his being, a giant serpent of hate writhing within him.

Tears ran down his cheeks as he fought to control the desire to smash Geldenhuis, to take a club to him and pulp his head for all the hurt and suffering his kind brought upon others. But Peekay knew that the spirit of an evil dragon slain in this way simply enters the heart of its slayer where it eats from the inside to destroy him. That the killing had to stop in the beloved country. That men and women must see that the world is not simply the domain of the cruel, vicious and rapacious. That good can grow from the killing fields and that justice was a mighty sword that could work for their side.

'Geldenhuis wants a fight, Tandy. Nothing would give me greater pleasure than to beat the shit out of him in the ring, if only to try a little to make up for the brutality and humiliation his kind have imposed on others, on you! But it won't do anything of the sort. When I step into the ring I accept that his way is right, that violence is the only revenge. But we have to stop believing in the right of might, we must get him on our own terms. Just once, in this wretched country's history, I promise you, justice will be seen to be done!'

A week later, Gideon was captured along with six other *Umkonto we Sizwe* terrorists attempting to blow up a govemment fuel depot on the outskirts of Johannesburg. The depot wasn't of particular strategic importance but was located close to a very up-market white suburb and the explosion was designed to shatter windows for a mile around and to burn conspicuously, a part of the campaign designed by Gideon to undermine the confidence of whites in the ability of the police to ultimately protect them from black aggression.

But, as so often happened in the past, the Special Branch, under the leadership of Colonel Jannie Geldenhuis, proved worthy of this task and the six terrorists were allowed to disarm the three guards patrolling the depot and to cut the wire and enter. Police waiting inside caught them with fifty pounds of common mining gelignite, cordtex for linking up the explosives, half a pound of semtex plastic explosive and two fairly sophisticated timing devices in case one failed. They were totally surrounded and out-gunned. Gideon conceded without a fight.

Geldenhuis personally arrested Gideon, pulling his arms behind his back and borrowing a pair of hand-cuffs to do the job. Gideon was unarmed except for a knife on his belt which Geldenhuis now removed. 'You had your chance, Mandoma. I told you in the ring to kill me; now it's my turn. But first I have something to return to you.' The police colonel's head drew back and he spat in Gideon's face.

Gideon laughed, spit running down his cheek. 'I am sorry I spat at you, Geldenhuis. You are not worthy of a black man's spit.' Gideon saw the police colonel's face contort and the left hand coming, but there was nothing he could do to avoid the fist which smashed into his face. Gideon steeled for the second blow; a boxer instinctively follows through and the right now smashed into the side of his jaw. He stood panting, waiting for Geldenhuis to hit him again, but the policeman held back. Gideon's nose was bleeding and he could taste blood in his mouth. He grinned. 'Your right hand was never any good, Geldenhuis!' He paused momentarily. 'Not like Peekay, he's got a right you have to respect, man!'

The morning papers, having completed printing at midnight, ran an additional two-page supplement on Mandoma's capture which was on the streets by half past seven. Though Gideon wasn't the official leader of the ANC, he was looked upon, particularly by the young blacks, as the man who would eventually lead them to victory. To the whites his arrest represented a high water mark in the campaign against terrorism and they applauded the brilliant Colonel Geldenhuis who'd brought it about.

Hymie called Peekay, who had been at Johannesburg Fort since three in the morning trying to get access to Gideon and had only just returned home. 'Peekay, we've got Geldenhuis just about nailed down, let's move now. With Gideon's capture the bastard has become a national hero. Two of the morning papers speak of him as a future general.

'If we move quickly and bring a charge of murder against Geldenhuis it should force the state to postpone Gideon's treason trial until the court has heard the murder charges against him.'

Their case against Geldenhuis for the bombing of Solomon Levy's train at the Christmas Party was almost complete. Mr Bottomley-Tuck, the chief legal clerk at Red, had obtained a set of Geldenhuis's fingerprints simply by applying for them through the cryptics department in Pretoria. These were sent to London where they were found to match those on a tube of glue found by Brown during his search at Poulos Industrial & Heavy Engineering. The glue type also matched the glue used to attach the bomb to the metal surface inside the train engine.

Another piece of proof surfaced closer to the trial. Peekay obtained a warrant to search Geldenhuis's flat and Swart and Brown discovered a pair of overalls hanging behind the kitchen door. In the left pocket lining of the overalls was a thin piece of wire about three inches long, resembling the filament which runs through the centre of magnesium tape. This exactly matched the tiny sample taken from the train engine. On further examination in a laboratory a small part of the hem of the pocket lining was found to be stained a pinkish colour; this was analysed as magnesium of the same type used to fire the wheel of the little train.

Red was ready to pounce.

Thirty-nine

Colonel Jannie Geldenhuis was arrested by two of General Van Breeden's men leaving the office just after six in the evening. The warrant charged him with the murder of Sophie Van der Merwe (Mama Tequila) and the attempted murder of Solomon Moshe Levy.

The arrest of Geldenhuis was a bitter blow for *die volk*, who regarded the police colonel as *Die vuis van regverdigheid*, the fist of righteousness, a white knight who single-handedly stood between them and the black hordes. Churches throughout the country asked their congregations to pray for the safe deliverance of Colonel Jannie Geldenhuis from the forces of evil and from the anti-Christ whose hand was so clearly in evidence.

On the afternoon of the day following the arrest, General Van Breeden was summoned to Pretoria by the Department of Justice and from there he was taken to see Balthazar Johannes Vorster, the Minister for Justice and of Police and Prisons.

Bul Van Breeden was ushered politely, though almost silently, into the minister's office by his male secretary. Vorster was a large, thick-necked man. He sat at his desk signing documents as the secretary tapped lightly on the door. '*Kom!*' the minister said; then, still not glancing up, 'Sit!' as General Van Breeden entered.

Bul Van Breeden had known Vorster for a number of years and, had they met on a casual basis, they would have referred to each other by Christian name. But Vorster, who was widely tipped to be the next prime minister, was a stickler for procedure in his ministerial capacity and it was obvious to Bul Van Breeden that he was on anything but a casual visit.

'Good morning, Minister,' Bul Van Breeden said, taking the chair at the desk. The fact that he hadn't been ushered into the minister's lounge to wait for a formal interview boded badly. Vorster was an impatient and outspoken man with the usual politician's long and spiteful memory.

'Colonel Geldenhuis, why have you arrested him?' he asked suddenly.

'Because I was satisfied that a prima-facie case exists that he has committed a murder.'

'Prima facie! That's hardly proof positive! And you didn't think to inform me first?'

'No, Minister. Colonel Geldenhuis is not of sufficient rank to have made that necessary.'

'Good God, man, must I remind you that I am the Minister for Police also! The man is a brilliant young police officer. He exemplifies the best things in the force. He stands for something important in the white community. He has just captured, at great risk to his life, the most wanted terrorist in the country! He's a national hero, man! And *you* go and arrest him as a *murder* suspect!' The minister brought his fist down hard. 'How do you know that this so-called murder wasn't an accident brought about in the course of the man's official duty?'

Bul Van Breeden's voice was very quiet when he spoke. 'I hope you don't mean that last statement, Minister?'

'Grow up, Van Breeden!' Vorster shouted.

Bul Van Breeden rose up from his chair. 'Is that all, Minister?' he said, standing to attention. He was having difficulty controlling his anger.

Vorster clicked his tongue in annoyance and then sighed. 'Sit down, we are not finished yet.'

Van Breeden resumed his seat in the overstuffed high-backed chair in front of the minister's desk.

'I want you to make an arrangement, General,' Vorster said.

'What sort of arrangement?' Van Breeden was still angry.

The Minister for Justice ignored his question. 'The arrest of Colonel Geldenhuis, taken together with the treason trial of Mandoma and the five others, is going to have international ramifications.' He leaned back in his chair. 'It's a delicate time for the republic, you understand? Britain and America and some of the more important European countries, Germany in particular, are talking of imposing trade sanctions. The treason trial will be bad enough, but if it is held in conjunction with a murder trial involving Colonel Geldenhuis it would greatly enhance the cause of our enemies over-seas and has the potential to do great harm to the republic. London reports people gathering outside South Africa House – and it's the middle of the blerrie night in London!' Vorster picked up a pencil from the desk and pointed it towards Van Breeden. 'Tell me, General, how compelling is the prima-facie evidence against Geldenhuis? Can this whole thing not be pinned on the kaffir, what's his name?'

'Nguni.'

'Ja, Nguni.'

'I don't think so, Minister. The evidence outlined to me by Advocate Peekay is precise and very detailed and seems to implicate Geldenhuis categorically.'

Vorster grunted. 'Him again! Why is it always him! Can we not bring some sort of injunction against the man?'

'Not one that would stand up in court.'

'Well, what then? What do you recommend?'

Bul Van Breeden looked surprised. 'Recommend, Minister? I am a police officer, I deal with the law. Advocate Peekay hasn't broken the law!'

'Yes, yes I know that, man,' Vorster said impatiently, then adding, 'when something involves the security of the state we all have to expect a few twists and bends in the straight and narrow road of legal precedent.'

'I could arrest Advocate Peekay on a DWT, detention without trial, but Minister, I don't recommend it. You would be adding a great deal of fuel to an already blazing fire,' he said.

Vorster appeared to be leafing through a file in front of him and Van Breeden realized it was his own dossier. 'Hmm, I see here you are a known friend of Hymie Levy, the partner of Advocate Peekay, himself an advocate?' Vorster looked up. 'Can we not do business with this Jewish friend of yours?'

'I'm sure you can talk to him, Minister.'

Vorster seemed to be thinking for a moment, tapping the end of the pencil on the edge of his desk. Finally he looked up at the policeman. 'I want you to arrange a meeting, a casual meeting that never took place, you understand?' He straightened up and closed the file in front of him. 'I want Advocates Peekay and Levy and the coloured girl to be present.'

'You mean Advocate Patel, Minister?'

'Ja, her. Make it a private dinner, at your house. One of my people will be there to brief you.'

'Brief, Minister? We will be receiving orders?'

'To put a proposition to your friends,' Vorster corrected. 'And, General, I charge you with the task of making sure no record exists of it having taken place, if you know my meaning?'

'Certainly, Minister.' General Van Breeden rose.

'Oh, and let my secretary know the venue first thing in the morning. Can you see yourself out, General? I think you know the way.'

Bul Van Breeden called Hymie on his return to Johannesburg an hour later and arranged for dinner the following evening, simply saying it was important and inviting Peekay and Tandia as well.

The three partners arrived promptly at eight. Van Breeden met them at the door of his modestly stylish home in a suburb called Saxonwold. 'We have a "guest" from Pretoria,' he said in an undertone. 'I'm afraid everything's "Mr" tonight, the complete protocol.' He ushered them down the hall into the living room. 'Hettie is visiting her sister and it's the maid's night off. I hope you don't mind a cold collation?'

A tall thin man with rimless glasses on a head roughly the dimensions of a shoe box standing on its end stood up as they entered the living room. He was dressed in a blue pinstriped suit, a white shirt and a light blue rayon tie. He appeared to be about forty, though his perfectly square crew cut was already quite grey. 'I'd like you to meet Mr Cogsweel from Pretoria.'

'Graham Cogsweel,' the tall man said, shaking hands all round.

Supper was a finger affair eaten on their laps and it

passed quickly enough with Hymie and Bul Van Breeden keeping the conversation going. Tandia offered to make coffee and after she'd poured for everyone Van Breeden addressed them briefly.

'Frankly, I'm not totally sure why I've invited you here tonight, though I have some idea.' He looked at the tall government man enquiringly.

'It serves no practical purpose for you to know,' Cogsweel answered, smiling thinly. His accent suggested one of the better private schools somewhere in Natal and though he hadn't been exactly talkative during supper he'd kept his end up and was obviously an intelligent person. Judging from his slightly didactic manner, Hymie concluded that he was probably a lawyer.

'Okay, just as you wish,' the general said, 'I haven't a lot more to add other than to suggest we listen to what Mr Cogsweel has to say.' He leaned forward and recovered his coffee cup from the table beside him.

Cogsweel took a hurried sip from his own cup, then placed it on the coffee table. 'I'm sorry we have to go through all this cloak-and-dagger stuff, it isn't really as it seems,' he said, immediately confirming to them all that it was indeed what it seemed. 'It's just that this is an unofficial meeting, no notes are being taken and no record kept.' He spread his hands. 'If we can't make any progress then I'll . . .' he smiled, 'slip silently back into the night!'

'A very cloak-and-dagger expression,' Hymie laughed. Peekay and Tandia smiled; the man from Pretoria was making such an obvious attempt to play it down.

'I'll come straight to the point,' Cogsweel said. 'We are led to believe that the case against Colonel Jannie Geldenhuis is substantial?'

'Surely that's for the courts to decide,' Tandia said quickly.

Cogsweel looked over, obviously surprised that she'd spoken. In talking he'd looked mostly at Hymie, on whom Pretoria had directed him to concentrate. 'Well, we'd hoped to avoid this, you know, happening.'

The people in the room were stunned. 'What? The case coming to court?' Hymie asked astonished.

'Ja, it's not in the ultimate interest of the state.'

Peekay started to laugh. 'I'm bloody sure it isn't,' he said.

'Gentlemen,' Cogsweel said and then quickly added, 'and Miss Patel, I am appealing to you as South Africans. This case has the potential to damage our overseas relations at a time when things are very delicately poised for the government. The prime minister himself is involved in this matter.'

Peekay snorted. 'And what if we refuse you, Mr Cogsweel?'

They all waited. Cogsweel turned his hands upwards. 'It's still early times, let me talk some more. You will note that we haven't questioned your evidence? At a preliminary hearing we could examine your evidence *very*, *very* closely!'

'We are *very*, *very* used to that happening, Mr Cogsweel,' Tandia shot back.

'But we want to negotiate in good faith,' Cogsweel continued. 'We are going to accept that your evidence is compelling and try to reach a compromise before we find ourselves lost in a legal wrangle.'

'Hold it right there!' Peekay said. 'We are appearing on behalf of two parties. The sister of the deceased victim and Mr Solomon Levy! We are quite used to legal wrangles and certainly we believe our evidence indicting Colonel Geldenhuis is compelling. But it *isn't* open for discussion or for bargaining! We are *not* prepared to discuss anything, with you or the minister for justice or even the bloody prime minister or anyone else outside a court of law!'

Cogsweel looked at Hymie, who shrugged. 'I guess that's the end of our discussion, Mr Cogsweel.' He raised one eyebrow. 'Time to slip silently into the night?'

But the man from Pretoria was made of sterner stuff and wasn't to be denied. 'I respect your point of view, Advocate Peekay. Your encounters with our government over the years may have left you somewhat disaffected. I admit it isn't always easy to understand the ways of Pretoria.'

'Please don't patronize me, Mr Cogsweel.'

'Oh but I'm not! Politics and politicians often confound me as well. Can I change the subject for a moment?' Cogsweel said suddenly. Then without waiting for their agreement, he continued, 'Let me talk about the other case, the treason trial. You people in this room are the defending lawyers. It's interesting isn't it how in this case it is the government who has the compelling evidence. There appear to be no mitigating circumstances; the six men have already been charged with treason and they will certainly be convicted.'

Peekay moved forward in his chair as though to speak and Cogsweel held up his hand. 'No, please, advocate, there is no possibility of any other verdict.' He paused and they all knew what he was about to say. 'The sentence for treason is death. Gideon Mandoma and the other five men will certainly die; your defence, no matter how provocative or brilliant, is purely academic. Nothing will prevent Mandoma going to the gallows.'

Peekay started to rise. 'I think we've heard enough, Mr Cogsweel.' Hymie and Tandia also began to move out of their seats when Tandia saw Peekay bring his forefinger up and lightly touch his nose.

'Jesus, Mandoma in exchange for Geldenhuis!' His voice was barely above a whisper, but they all heard him.

'A simple swap,' Cogsweel said, rising and pulling at the lapels of his suit jacket, and then flicking at the left-hand lapel with his hand. 'You have twenty-four hours to decide. There can be no discussion. Mandoma will be allowed to escape, providing he undertakes to leave the country. The other five will receive ten-year sentences. You will agree to withdraw all your evidence against Colonel Geldenhuis.' Cogsweel glanced towards Bul Van Breeden and, putting his hand into the inside breast pocket of his suit, he withdrew an envelope and handed it to the police general. 'This is an instruction from Brigadier General du Plocy. In it he asks that you carry out the government's wishes in this matter as though the instruction had come from him personally.' Cogsweel smiled his thin smile, 'Which, I suppose they have, in a manner of speaking.' He turned to the others. 'Please convey your decision to the general here before eight o'clock tomorrow night.'

Cogsweel stooped and picked up a brown felt hat from beside his chair. He placed the hat on his head, adjusting the brim. 'Please, don't anyone get up,' he said. He moved over to each of them and shook them formally by the hand, only just touching the tips of Tandia's fingers. Then he walked to the doorway of the room as Van Breeden rose to accompany him to the front door. 'No, no, I can see myself out, General.' Cogsweel looked over at Hymie. 'Now it's time for me to slip silently into the night, Mr Levy.' He smiled, turned and was gone.

'Mama Tequila always said, a man who wears a brown hat has trouble with his one-eyed snake!' Tandia said, not sure why she'd made a statement so entirely inappropriate, though they all laughed, which somewhat eased the shock they felt.

Van Breeden shook his head, '*Here*, man! You must believe me. I had no idea.'

'Bul, you must excuse us, it looks as though it's going to be a long night,' Hymie said as they heard the sound of Cogsweel's car driving away.

The three partners left soon afterwards and went directly to Hymie's apartment where Hymie perked a large pot of coffee. They hadn't spoken much in the car, each involved with their own thoughts.

'First,' Hymie said, 'we ought to set the rules, decide what constitutes a decision from all of us? Or do we have one already, are we all prepared to simply say yes or no?'

'No, I've got problems. I need to talk them out,' Peekay said.

'Ja, me too,' Tandia added.

'Well then, do we decide by unanimous vote, or what?'

'We've always resolved things unanimously, why should we change now?' Tandia asked.

'Because I'd be bloody surprised if it doesn't get personal,' Peekay grinned, 'and I want to leave here still loving you both.'

'Ah, I see, you are not inclined to vote with a simple "yes" to the government's offer?' Hymie asked.

'No, I have to talk. It isn't that easy.'

'Okay, but it has to be unanimous,' Hymie said. 'Peekay, you start.'

'I know I'm going to sound like a bit of a prick, but swapping Geldenhuis for Gideon is too easy. When we went to Oxford it soon became clear to me that the law E.W. taught wasn't the law I was going to find when we returned. Our law has never been colour blind, it has always judged pigment. But in the ten years we've been practising we have seen a madness come into it. Innocent people die every day on the gallows and murderers go free to kill again, to kill in the name of the law! That a man as vile and loathsome as Geldenhuis, the man who fired the first shot at Sharpeville, can become the youngest colonel in the history of the South African police force proves my point. If it was simply a matter of letting him go free to save Gideon's life, a swap, it would be easy. But it isn't! That's precisely what it isn't!' Peekay's voice was filled with emotion. 'It's joining the madness! It's allowing ourselves to be a part of it, part of this dreadful conspiracy!'

'Hang on a mo, Peekay! This decision involves just the sort of universal integrity that makes man decent. It allows us to return life to a man who has gone to war and is prepared to die to defeat an evil system, to replace it with your kind of justice,' Hymie cried.

'Let me finish, Hymie! Then you can go for your life. Man's highest single collective achievement is the application of natural justice to society, his greatest defeat is when he destroys it. If that sounds didactic I don't apologize. If mankind forsakes this single premise, then we are doomed as a species!' Peekay looked up at Hymie. 'You're right, Gideon is at war, a righteous war, but nevertheless one in which the consequences were dear to him. He has always known that if he was captured he would die. By swapping him for Geldenhuis we are making a mockery of the very principles for which he is prepared to die. I don't think Gideon would find this acceptable. I'm not at all sure I do either.' Peekay's voice trailed off, full of emotion.

'You'd have made an excellent God, Peekay,' Hymie laughed. Then he turned to Tandia. 'I am going to take the position of Solomon; hear all the evidence first and then capitalise on it. Your turn next, Tandy?'

Tandia sat with her shoes off and her legs curled up under her. 'I don't share Peekay's respect for the law. But then I have never seen it operate so that the scales of justice gave me and my kind an equal weighting. Frankly, the law stinks! I use it because, though a blunt and stupid weapon, it is the only one we have – the country of the blind where the one-eyed man is king. My other choice would be to do what Gideon is . . . was doing. And you both know that I've thought more than once about that! All my life I have seen evil triumph over good. Even when we win a case against the state it isn't because justice has triumphed, or good has beaten evil, it's because our proof is so overwhelming that the state can't afford to be shown up for what it is, or some corrupt or incompetent magistrate or judge will be exposed – and that's only when, despite the best efforts of the bench, we manage to get away with a jury who don't suffer from collective brain damage. From where I sit, hate always wins! Always! Geldenhuis's hate beats me, beats you, beats Gideon! The only way we're going to destroy his kind – and that means the white racist regime in South Africa – is by using the same weapon they use, hate and fear! It's the only thing they understand! But to do this we need leaders who are prepared to take up arms and wage a relentless and ceaseless war of attrition until the last racist is burned out of the system. Gideon Mandoma is a charismatic leader who can get the people behind him and he's not afraid to take up arms, not afraid to kill! For once the black people have a leader who doesn't want to sit on the *indaba* mat and talk platitudinous crap with the hairy backs! If we manage to get a murder conviction against Geldenhuis, and even that isn't certain, all we do is create a vacancy for the next bastard from the queue stretching from Pretoria to Cape Town! Quite apart from Gideon being my loving friend, my country cannot afford to lose him. You can stick your principles, Peekay. I want him released so we can wage war!'

Tandia was shaking by the time she was finished and very close to tears. She had never spoken like this in her life before. All her life her hurt and her hate had been folded up and locked away inside her heart.

Peekay wasn't surprised. Tandia's uncompromising feelings were no less rigid than those of Gert or Colonel Smit and he told himself he had no right to expect that they should be.

'Phew!' Hymie said. 'And you, Tandia Patel, would have made an excellent Old Testament prophet! I think I'm going to have a good brandy after that. Will you join me?'

Tandia attempted a smile, though she was still somewhat overwrought. 'Yes please, Hymie, I need it more than you do.' She was conscious that she might have alienated Peekay, even lost his affection, and she felt a stab of actual pain in her breast at the thought of this. But, for the first time in her life, she'd spoken the burning in her belly, she'd released the fist that clamped her heart, she'd let the hate surface. More than this, she'd shouted it. She had opened the doors of the dark little room and spread the carefully folded sheets of her hate out so that they billowed in the wind. Hate was the driving force which had kept her going through the years of despair and misery, through the deaths of Juicey Fruit Mambo and of Mama Tequila; now, at last, she'd articulated the source of her power and she felt suddenly whole and strong.

Hymie handed Tandia a brandy balloon and Tandia brought it up to her lips. The sharp, bright fumes of the brandy struck her nostrils and then she felt the warm glow expand throughout her as she took the first sip. Even brandy tastes better, she thought to herself. She ventured a glance at Peekay who sat with his eyes downcast. She was in love with a dreamer, an impossible dreamer. He actually believed in good as a force, despite everything, he still believed. How did he do that? Tandia didn't know whether to laugh or to cry, all she knew was that she loved him and that, curiously, she could keep her love in a separate compartment to her hate, that both could co-exist within her.

'Well, we're in trouble. We're split. My task is to convince one of you to change your mind,' Hymie said, coming to sit on the arm of the leather couch beside Tandia. He looked into the brandy balloon as he started to speak, as though he saw within it a truth he was about to pronounce. 'I think you're both missing the point,' he said quietly. 'We have been placed in a position which will decide the lives of two men. That pompous idiot Cogsweel was right in one thing, our chances are almost nil in terms of saving Gideon from the gallows. If he is found guilty of treason, as he almost certainly will be, there can be only one result. Our case against Geldenhuis, despite what Pretoria may try to do, is strong enough to get a conviction, particularly if we've got the world media watching. In other words, if things remain as they are, two men are going to die. Or, if we agree to the swap, two men remain alive.' Hymie looked up from the brandy balloon. 'Don't you see? We've been given the power over life and death! Don't think of these two lives as belonging to Mandoma and Geldenhuis, a freedom fighter and a cruel, corrupt member of the secret police. See them as two men, any two men. We are being asked to sentence them to death or release them. Can we honestly put on the black cap and pronounce sentence so as not to damage the precious principle of natural justice? In the end natural justice has to exist in the hearts of man! That means in my heart, your heart, Peekay and yours, Tandy! It doesn't begin in a society, it begins with each of us. Is Mama Tequila's death paid for if Geldenhuis dies? If my father had died, would I feel recompensed when they strung Jannie Geldenhuis up on a piece of rope? I don't think so!' Hymie gulped at his brandy and then continued, 'When the British liberated the death camp at Dachau they found scribbled on one of the latrine walls these words, *Together since the world began, the madman and the lover*. The concept that we can prevent murder by murdering is barbaric and strains the quality of natural justice so that it is rendered useless! I violently disagree with Tandia's point of view, though I think I can understand it. I know a great many Jews feel the same way about the German people. But, Peekay, I cannot reconcile *your* justice with the qualities of mercy and compassion, which are surely the very cornerstones of natural justice? If we make the decision not to make the swap between these two nameless men, we deny the very principle on which your case rests.

Our choice is not between justice or tyranny; it is far more fundamental, we must choose between the madman and the lover in each of us.'

The room was very quiet for what seemed like a long time, then Peekay looked up. 'I agree,' he said simply.

Hymie walked over and kissed his friend on the brow. Then he brightened suddenly. 'Why don't you both sleep here tonight? Tandia, you can get up early and take a taxi home. I have a special reason.' He paused and then pronounced the single word, 'kippers'. He turned back to Peekay. 'I've had half a dozen of the loathsome creatures flown out from Fortnum & Mason as a special treat.' He turned to explain to Tandia. 'They're a predilection he learned from Doris with the wonderful tits and I'm even willing to have the whole place stink for days. After all, what are friends for, if they can't tolerate the odd *really* nasty habit between each other?' Hymie grinned, and Tandia knew that what he was telling her, despite having heard how she felt, was that he loved her.

'What are kippers?' she asked.

Peekay looked at her. 'Taken together with eggs and tomatoes, the ultimate breakfast experience. If you will share my kippers, Tandy, all is forgiven!'

Forty

The one good thing about escaping from custody with police permission is that you don't have to run for your life expecting a bullet in your back. Gideon escaped from the police kwela-kwela which was taking him from Pretoria Prison to court (or that's what they told him on the morning). He hadn't been told of the plan and was more than a little confused when the police van stopped and appeared to be making a complicated turn in a narrow road, moving back and forwards several times before coming to a halt in an opposite direction.

He could smell dust in the interior of the van and the scrunch of tyres told him they were off the tarred road. Next he heard the rattle of the chain as the back doors were unlocked, flinging bright daylight into the dark van.

'Get out, *maak gou, jong*!' a white police officer ordered.

'What for?' Gideon asked, remaining seated.

'*Uit, kaffir*!'

Gideon looked out of the back of the van to see they'd pulled up on a lonely dirt road, in what looked a little like a *kloof*, for there was a *krans* rising steeply on either side of the road which stretched back to the end of two *koppies* then turned abruptly to the left.

They're going to kill me, was his first thought as he sheltered his eyes, stooping and stepping out into the blinding December morning.

'What are you going to do?' he asked querulously, convinced he was experiencing the final minutes of his life.

'Here, man.' A second officer handed him the large padlock lock from the back door of the van, 'hold this so your fingerprints are on it, make sure, also your thumb, okay?'

'What are you going to do?' Gideon asked again, taking the lock in his cuffed hands and doing as the officer required.

The officer took back the lock carefully and placed it hanging open on the hasp. 'Okay, fuck off kaffir!' the first police officer instructed.

'Then you will shoot me!' Gideon cried.

'You escaping officially, man! Go on, *voetsek*!' The officer pointed down the dirt road with a sweep of his hand.

Gideon held up his hands showing his handcuffs. If he was going to die he wanted to die unshackled. 'Can you make loose my hands, please? You can put them back after you have killed me,' he said to the policeman.

'No way, man! You can't escape with your hands free, it's not right if you got no handcuffs on, it makes the police look blerrie silly. Now run, jong! Or I bring the sjambok, you hear?'

'How can I pick the lock and escape when I'm wearing handcuffs?' Gideon asked sensibly.

'Hey! You trying to be cheeky, kaffir?' The second

officer stepped forward, his face menacing, his fore-finger held under Gideon's nose. Gideon backed away, then turned suddenly and started to run down the road, zig-zagging frantically, expecting the bullet in his back any moment. But all he heard were the two policemen laughing. He couldn't leave the road; the rocky slopes on either side of it would have slowed him down and made him a sitting duck as he attempted to climb to safety.

'Hey, kaffir! You drunk or something?' Peekay stepped into the middle of the road, grinning broadly. Gideon looked fearful; there was no recognition on his face, his memory was smudged with fear. He glanced backwards to see the police van pulling away, moving in the opposite direction. 'Whoa!' Peekay caught him at the same moment as his mind snapped out of panic. The two men embraced, Gideon panting frantically, his head on Peekay's shoulder. 'I see you, my brother,' Peekay said, patting Gideon on the back as though he was a small child who needed comforting.

Gideon pulled away at last. 'I don't know . . . how is it . . . this thing . . . Peekay?' he said in English, gasping out the words.

They reached the car and Peekay opened the door on the passenger side, taking a pair of bolt cutters from the floor. 'I hope to hell I know how to use these things. The guy in the hardware shop showed me, but I couldn't exactly explain to him why I wanted them. So here goes!' With some trouble Peekay finally managed to remove the handcuffs and, placing them in the glove compartment, said, 'We'll throw them into a river somewhere.'

Gideon rubbed his wrists, 'When I'm prime minister, remind me not to make you Minister for Industry!'

They both fell about laughing, their tension escaping like a suddenly punctured inner-tube.

'There's a cold chicken, some fruit and two cokes on the back seat. Help yourself, I even brought paper napkins!'

They drove directly to Swaziland crossing the border at Havelock where they showed the travel permits Peekay had obtained in Johannesburg. After this simple formality they continued on down the road for about a mile when Peekay saw Julius. Despite the heat he was still in his ancient army greatcoat, standing waiting for them beside the road.

Peekay drew up beside the little man. Julius stood to rigid attention and gave the thumbs-up salute. '*Sakubona, uJenene! Amandla!* Greetings, General! Power!'

'It is twice now you have helped the people. You are now an officer in *Umkonto we Sizwe*,' Gideon announced solemnly, placing his hand on Julius's shoulder.

Julius, overcome, started to cry. 'Officers don't cry!' Peekay said, trying not to laugh. 'You've lost another tooth, old man! You better be careful, you don't have too many to spare.'

'It's okay, officers in *Umkonto we Sizwe* are often toothless,' Gideon laughed.

'Usually after they've been interviewed by the Special Branch.'

Julius seemed to think this was enormously funny and cackled a great deal, though the tears continued to run down his cheeks. 'Haya, haya!' he said at last, 'The woman who shares my blanket buys only gristle, my teeth are not good fighters!' He got into the back of the car, immediately filling it with rich pungency. Then he produced a Swaziland passport from somewhere inside his army coat and handed it to Gideon. 'Your passport, General, it has also in it a visa for Tanzania.'

Gideon examined the passport which looked well used and had a number of exit stamps as well as the entry and departure stamps of several African countries. His name and picture looked as well worn as the rest of the document. It was an excellent forgery.

They stopped at Pigg's Peak for Julius to get off and catch the bus to Bulembu, back to his village. Peekay got out of the car and walked around to the boot where he removed a large box with a cellophane window forming most of the lid. It was a cashmere blanket in a brilliant scarlet. 'It is for Somojo, Julius. Last time I came with empty hands.'

'*Ngiya bonga Inkosi*, Thank you, Lord. You are well remembered in the village. I am always there when you need me.'

Gideon and Peekay arrived at Matsapa airport on the outskirts of Manzini in plenty of time for the three o'clock Heron flight to Salisbury, the capital of Southern Rhodesia. Peekay handed him a ticket, several loose bank notes and a small book of travellers' cheques. The two friends embraced. 'Here we go again, my brother, *hamba kahle*, go well.'

Gideon was too moved to reply and his eyes welled up with tears. He turned and walked towards the small plane, not looking back. Even from the back he looked like a fighter. 'So long, champ,' Peekay whispered, 'keep punching, you hear?' The lump in his chest was about to burst and he hurried back to the car.

Peekay drove into Manzini to call Tandia long distance from the post office. Then he called home to Barberton to tell his mother to expect him for the night. Dum answered the phone, picking up the receiver and immediately announcing in slow monosyllabic English, 'We are very, very sorry, the missus is gone for having tea by Missus . . . Oost . . . Oos . . .' She hesitated, obviously having trouble getting her tongue around the name of the lady Peekay's mother was visiting.

'Missus Oosthuisen! It's me, you silly *umFazi*!' Peekay laughed, feeling suddenly better as Dum squealed with delight at the sound of his voice. The news of Gideon's escape would be on the evening news and he was grateful he wouldn't be in Johannesburg to deal with an over-excited press. A dose of Dee and Dum innocence was just the sort of cheer-up medicine he needed before the farce of the Geldenhuis murder trial which was to begin in two days.

The less said about the trial the better. Geldenhuis was acquitted and the judge granted his lawyers permission to sue Red for wrongful arrest. Jannie Geldenhuis was restored to his rank and was back on the job a week later. In church congregations throughout the land prayers of thanks were offered to a merciful God who had once again demonstrated that, in crucial matters, He was prepared to step in and see that the right thing was done by His children. Colonel Jannie Geldenhuis was booked for nearly a year's church appearances.

Flyspeck Mendoza was found guilty and sentenced to death, but his case exposed the slavery and brutality on many white backveld farms, and the government was forced to open an inquiry.

Just before dawn, on 15 January 1967, Peekay, Tandia and Hymie stood silently outside Pretoria Prison. As the moon began to fade and the first light appeared Peekay heard the words of Inkosi-Inkosikazi in his head. 'You can see the moon rising over Africa and you are at peace with the night, unafraid of the great demon Skokiaan, who comes to feed on the dark night, tearing its black flesh until, at last, it is finished and the new light comes to stir the sleeping herd boys and send them out to mind the lowing cattle.'

As the light came to the dark prison so came the voices of the black inmates as they began to sing their brother to his death. The marvellous voices of Africa, sometimes soft and low and sometimes thundering, carried down the cold, polished, disinfected corridors of iron as the inmates sang the hymns of praise in their cells. Then, as six o'clock approached, their voices rose in the final choruses of the *Concerto to the Great Southland*. First the Sotho, then the Ndebele, followed by the Swazi and the Shangaan, and finally the Zulu voices rose, huge and awesome as they sung the victory song of the great Shaka, using the flats of their hands to bang on the steel doors of their cells as the mighty Zulu impi had done with their feet to make the earth thunder. Then, as the hour struck, all the tribes came together, humming the glorious finale, the refrain of each of the tribes. The huge prison vibrated with the deep, haunting male voices and the wardens stood in silent awe as the kid, who had no tribe, was sung to glory by all the tribes. At six o'clock precisely, little Flyspeck Mendoza's neck was snapped and he was torn from the tree of life.

With the star missing, and the anti-apartheid world celebrating the escape of Mandoma, the international media stayed away from the treason trial of the other five men on the truism that nobody comes to the pantomime to see the fairies. Thus the government almost achieved its aim as the trial chugged to its inevitable and pre-arranged ending. But on the final day the prosecution dropped a bombshell. One of the prisoners had turned state's witness and they asked permission from the bench to put him on the witness stand.

The prisoner who'd decided to sing was an ex-mine boy named Samson Mungazela, who had served as boss boy to a diamond driller on Randfontein Consolidated Mines and was the explosives expert on Gideon's team. He'd been hurt in an accident underground several years previously and had been given a job in the High Explosives Depot on the surface. It was he who had supplied Tandia and Johnny Tambourine with gelignite when Tandia visited the mine compound once a week in her capacity as free legal adviser to the migrant black mine workers.

Tandia had always parked in the same spot, reversing her beetle-backed Volkswagen into a small alley between two mine buildings which could be approached from the rear without being observed. The smuggled sticks of gelignite would then be placed under the rear seat while she was away from the car.

Tandia had never told Peekay and Hymie that she had been actively transporting explosives for *Umkonto we Sizwe* for three years, and that apart from being its first recruited female member she was the highest-ranking woman in the resistance movement.

The prosecuting barrister, a brilliant contemporary of Peekay's named Martinus Kriel, asked for permission to put Mungazela in the witness box. 'The accused has evidence, your honour, which we believe is pertinent to this trial.'

Peekay rose immediately. 'Objection, your honour, the witness has already testified to this court and my learned colleague for the prosecution has commenced the summary of the state's case against the accused.'

Tandia had passed a note to Peekay as he sat down. It said, *Object! Mungazela could implicate me!* Peekay's heart stood still. What had Tandia been involved in?

Kriel picked his words carefully. 'Your honour, we believe that by cross-examining this witness again we can prove that a member of the counsel for defence is directly implicated in a culpable way in the indictment for which we are prosecuting counsel.'

'Objection!' Peekay called. But he was hardly heard in the uproar which followed Kriel's statement.

'Order! Order!' Judge Boshoff shouted using his gavel repeatedly, but it was nearly a minute before the court-room was brought to silence again. 'There is no need for you to object, Advocate Peekay. I will do so myself. What the counsel for the prosecution is indicating is highly irregular and should not be handled in this manner.' He turned to the jury. 'I require the jury to retire from this court until they are recalled. Both senior counsel will then approach the bench.' He brought his gavel down once again. 'This court is adjourned for fifteen minutes!'

Peekay and Kriel stood before the judge's bench. 'We will retire to my chambers for ten minutes at which time, Advocate Kriel, you had better have some answers,' Boshoff said.

'Yes your honour,' Kriel said.

'Kriel, you dirty bastard!' Peekay hissed as they followed Boshoff. 'If you had something like this on me you should have taken it to the Public Prosecutor!'

Kriel smiled, 'It's not on you, Peekay, it's on your partner!'

The judge asked them to enter and told Peekay to close the door. 'I ought to report you to the Law

Society. I may still do so, Counsellor Kriel. Explain!' he demanded.

'Your honour, the police prosecutor presented us with evidence during the luncheon adjournment which implicates Peekay's colleague Miss Patel strongly in matters that could be construed as treasonable and relate directly to this case. It seemed appropriate to give notice of this in court today.'

'The police prosecutor? Was this the arresting officer Colonel Geldenhuis?'

'Yes, your honour.'

Kriel was too sure of himself, Pretoria was clearly behind him. Peekay had to play for time and try to abort Mungazela's evidence. 'Your honour, I believe my learned colleague has designed this entire affair to engender speculation. He knows this is unacceptable evidence in your court. It's a cheap shot at my colleague and I take enormous exception to it! He knows the correct procedure is to take his accusation to the public prosecutor!'

Judge Boshoff looked hard at both men. 'I am giving you until nine o'clock tomorrow morning, an hour before this court convenes. You will both of you report to me in my chambers, you hear? You, Kriel, to satisfy me that you can substantiate the testimony of your witness. And you, Peekay, to assure me that your junior counsel is not, to the best of your knowledge, involved other than as your second counsel in this trial.'

Peekay saw the tiny smirk on Kriel's face and he knew that the barrister had achieved what he'd set out to do, to give himself a little more time, and more importantly, to have the evidence against Tandia accepted at the treason trial. Geldenhuis would have his revenge.

850

When he and Tandia stepped out of the court fifteen minutes later, bulbs flashed everywhere and reporters crushed around them, shouting questions. Fortunately they'd both wanted to work in the car that morning so Hercules, the Red driver, had brought them to Pretoria. Now he waited for them outside the court and they were able to make their escape.

Tandia broke down in the car, not because of what she'd done, but because she'd deceived Peekay and Hymie. Gulping back tears, she told Peekay of her work as a member of *Umkonto we Sizwe.*

Peekay handed her his handkerchief. 'Tandy, dry your tears. One stick of dynamite or a thousand, it doesn't make any damn difference, the charge is still treason if it can be proved you supplied Gideon's people, your people. You're a terrorist, so the deception of both Hymie and myself is academic.'

'Peekay, you and Hymie are the only two people I've ever entirely trusted and now I've betrayed that trust,' Tandia cried.

Peekay held her hand. 'Tandia, we're all fighting for the same thing. The question now is not one of recrimination, it's whether we fight or flee. Nothing else matters. What are our chances of discrediting Samson Mungazela when I cross-examine tomorrow?'

'When you cross-examine? You're going to tell the judge in chambers I'm innocent? Peekay, if it comes out you perjured yourself it'll be the end of your legal career!'

'Tandia, listen! If there's a good chance I can get the judge to dismiss Mungazela's evidence we can kill the thing stone dead tomorrow. Jannie Geldenhuis is panicking. If he'd done this the slow way and used the proper procedures it could be a bloody sight worse.'

Tandia shook her head. 'Peekay, if Mungazela has talked, and we know he has, it couldn't be any worse. When we get into Red I'm going to have to use Hymie's clean phone to make at least ten calls, if it isn't already too late. Geldenhuis will be able to bring in fifteen, maybe twenty, men in the explosives cadre of *Umkonto*; some are going to crack, they always do! And like Samson Mungazela I'm the ace they hold, the only thing with which they can bargain. If they know Samson's confessed, why would they hold back; they don't know their collaborating evidence is the vital difference! Jannie Geldenhuis must be convinced ...' Tandia's voice trailed off and she shivered involuntarily, though as much from disgust as fear, '... that he's got me on a plate.'

Hercules coughed politely. 'What is it?' Peekay asked him in Zulu.

'The police, they are following us, sir.'

Peekay didn't bother to look through the rear window. Hercules had an uncanny instinct for police. The old black man was more than a chauffeur to them all. He'd been in Solomon Levy's family since Hymie's childhood, driving Hymie to kindergarten and ever since, and finally becoming the driver for Red where he was greatly beloved.

'Hercules, listen carefully, you're going to have to go shopping when we get to Johannesburg. When you drop us at Red go straight to John Orrs.' Peekay turned to Tandia. 'Write down your shoe size for a pair of tackles, the size of jeans you wear, two shirts, a warm sweater, also a couple of changes of underwear – practical stuff, cotton, that won't rub you – enough for two days. Add three pairs of thick woollen socks. You've got toilet things in the office, haven't you? Write anything else you're going to need. Cigarettes?'

Tandia nodded and, taking a yellow legal pad from her briefcase, started to write. 'Put two blankets and two towels on the list as well,' Peekay said. Tandia didn't ask any questions; she knew there could be no possibility of going home, that all their places would be under twenty-four hour surveillance by men from the Special Branch. Peekay was making plans for her to get away immediately. She knew he wouldn't talk in the car; Hercules wouldn't blab but he was an elderly man and, under interrogation, could break.

Peekay added a few items of food to the list and handed it to Hercules, adding a fifty-rand note with it for the food. 'Hercules, give this list to the manager and tell him to give you the stuff immediately and to put it on my account. I have written all this on the note as well. Then when you've bought the food take the car to the carpet depot and exchange it with a Solomon Levy Carpet Emporium car, but make sure it doesn't have anything written on the door. Put all the stuff in the boot and bring the car to the manhole. Make sure you fill it with petrol first. Don't go back to Red. Go straight to the manhole and be waiting at the usual place by a quarter to six tonight. Do you understand?' Peekay said all of this in Zulu.

'I understand. What sort of food do you want me to buy, baas Peekay?' Hercules asked.

'I've writ . . .' Peekay hesitated for a fraction of a second, realizing Hercules didn't want to say he couldn't read. 'Get a cold chicken, some bread, salami, maybe a tin of canned peaches, Nescafé and condensed milk. Don't forget a tin opener and matches.'

'I hate salami!' Tandia said.

Peekay grinned. 'Okay, no salami, Hercules. Get a tin

of bully beef, two tomatoes and an onion, also a small billycan, make it two, one for water.' He turned to Tandia, 'I'll make you Doc's favourite, you're in for a treat.'

Tandia didn't want to tell Peekay that she hated bully beef even worse than salami. The light banter had eased the tension a little and she tried to prepare her mind for what lay ahead.

Hymie was waiting for them in the boardroom when they arrived. 'Christ, the place is surrounded with cops. I've phoned home, there are a couple of guys watching the block, I imagine it's the same with your places.' He took Tandia in his arms and hugged her.

'We're going to have to get you out, Tandy.' Hymie had heard the story from a reporter on the *Star* who'd called him for comment and he'd obviously reached the same conclusion as Peekay.

Tandia nodded. 'But look, my own people can try to get me out, it's crazy for you two to be involved!'

'We are your own people, Tandy, and we are involved,' Peekay said quietly. 'If I thought you had a better chance of getting out of the country with them I'd agree for your sake, but I don't. Your face is well known and Gideon isn't here to see things go right.'

'There's no chance of an international flight, Tandy. Jan Smuts will have been alerted.' Hymie glanced at his watch. 'If we could find a private field perhaps a small plane over the border, but it's nearly four o'clock, it would be too dark to get off the ground by the time we get there. Besides, air traffic control would have been alerted. But if we can get you to Swaziland we can have a Heron waiting for you on the ground at Matsapa to fly you to Nairobi; from there you can catch a flight to London.'

Peekay glanced at his watch. 'If we leave soon we may make it to the lowveld by car, but from the Nelspruit turnoff to Barberton we can anticipate a police road block; it's a side road and the only logical place to stop traffic without disrupting a major highway.' Peekay paused, thinking. 'Geldenhuis will expect us to try to get out by light plane so he will already have covered the smaller airports but he can't put out an alert or road blocks on the national highway, until we're officially wanted, which will be after you appear in court tomorrow. By that time we'll be into the mountains.'

'What about the other way through Hectorspruit, the Matsamo entrance?' Hymie asked. 'It's quicker, isn't it?'

'Too risky, I don't know where they'd put the road block and it's unfamiliar country for me if we have to try and go through the bush to get over the border. If I can get us across the de Kaap valley I can take Tandy over the mountains. It's only eighteen miles or so, but it's tough going. Tandy's unfit and not used to climbing; it may take us two days, but once we're into the high mountains, it's going to be bloody difficult for anyone to follow us.'

'Two days! Shit, Peekay, that's a long time for a city girl to be roughing it!'

Tandia laughed. 'I love the mountains, man! Juicey Fruit Mambo and I would often spend all day in the Drakensberg.'

'It's going to be a bit tougher, you didn't smoke forty cigarettes a day in those days. Hymie, there is no better place to hide, I'd rather we took a little longer and were sure, don't you reckon?'

'Well, as far as we know, Jannie Geldenhuis is no mountain man,' Hymie replied. 'Frankly I'd feel much better if Tandy was in the first-class section of the four fifteen BOAC flight to London.'

Peekay went over to the phone, called Barberton long distance and asked to speak to Colonel Smit. Smit's secretary put him through. '*Hoe gaan dit*, Peekay? What can I do for you?' he asked.

Peekay took a deep breath, hoping his voice would sound casual. 'Colonel, what I'm asking you to do tonight will be illegal by tomorrow morning.'

Smit was silent on the other end of the phone. '*Here*, Peekay, I just heard the four o'clock news on the radio.' There was a pause. 'Is it true what they saying?'

'Colonel, it's a Geldenhuis trap, a conspiracy. I need a favour.'

There was another longish pause and then Smit said, 'Peekay, tomorrow is a long time in a man's life. What is legal today is all the information a man can act on. What is it, man?'

Peekay sighed with relief. 'Colonel, could Gert meet me, us, in the prison van with half-a-dozen black warders dressed as prisoners already in the back?'

'Ja, I suppose that can be arranged, where?'

'At a small place called Schagen, it's a little railway station, about eight, ten miles up from Nelspruit.'

'Ja, I know where is Schagen. What time?'

'Around ten o'clock tonight.'

Peekay knew that Kommandant Smit and Gert would have to wrestle furiously with their consciences. Just about any way they looked at it they would see Tandia, if the allegations were true, as a traitor to their country. A black traitor. He was asking them to give aid to a terrorist. Peekay would not have been surprised if Smit refused, though he knew he'd keep his mouth shut. But he also knew he had one thing going for him. An

Afrikaner with Smit or Gert's background valued and honoured friendship above all else.

'I will ask Gert, Peekay,' Smit said, then paused for a moment. 'If he won't do it, I'll be waiting for you at Schagen tonight, son.'

'Thank you, Colonel.'

Smit's voice came back over the line. 'Peekay, you're a bloody fool, you hear? Don't do it, man! You are risking your life for a kaffir girl!'

'No, Colonel, for a friend,' Peekay said softly and hung up.

Next he called home and spoke to his mother briefly. Then, somewhat to her chagrin, he asked to speak to one of the twins.

'You know, I sometimes think you love them more than your own mother, son,' she said in a hurt voice.

'Mum, it's just a bit of business.' He heard the receiver being put down and his mother calling. A minute or so later Dee, breathing heavily from having run, answered. 'You are coming to see us, ja?' she asked in Shangaan, her excitement coming through.

'Listen Dee, I can't explain, but pack my rucksack as if I was going away for two days into the mountains. Put in everything for a high climb. Also my boots and mountain clothes. Don't forget the medicine box and the square torch, the one that fits on my belt. Then both of you meet me at four o'clock tomorrow morning at *Itshe Ingulube*, where you used to turn back for home when you came with me part way into the mountains.'

'There is something wrong, Peekay. I can feel it, my skin is sore with your trouble. There is something wrong, you must tell me!' Dee repeated, her voice was urgent.

'No, Dee, just do as I say. Meet me at the place we

named Pig Rock before dawn. The path is good up to that point and you can use the torch in the dark. Oh, and bring extra drinking water! I must go now, I'll see you in the morning. Go well, Dee!' Peekay put down the receiver and turned to Tandia. 'I think we ought to be going soon.'

Peekay had anticipated Geldenhuis pretty accurately, the policeman had indeed assumed that they would attempt to get Tandia out by light plane, though, in case they tried the obvious, he had his men alerted at Jan Smuts Airport. Before Kriel had even stood up in court he had men headed for every private or municipal airport within a hundred miles of Johannesburg. Flight Control had been alerted to report any private or small aircraft flying out of the Transvaal, Natal or the Orange Free State filing a flight plan which took them within fifty miles of any South African border.

He'd also anticipated the Swaziland plan and had arranged for road blocks from six o'clock in the evening onwards, three miles into the Barberton turn-off from Nelspruit and two miles out of Hectorspruit on the road to the border post. Though it seemed unlikely that Peekay would choose any of the further six entrances into Swaziland he'd nevertheless alerted the local border police at each of them.

He'd done the same thing for Basutoland and Bech- uanaland. The border into Rhodesia and Portuguese territory was already well guarded and here he'd simply issued an alert. This time Jannie Geldenhuis believed he had Tandia boxed in, trapped at Red or within the confines of the city or Soweto. Three police cars sur- rounded the block ready to tail her should she leave the building. All these precautions may have seemed over-elaborate but he knew Peekay was as clever as trick shit and he wasn't taking any chances.

Geldenhuis cursed himself for not having done the initial interviews with the Treason Six. But because of his suspension from the case after his own arrest, he only got back to the prisoners after his acquittal and Gideon's escape. He quickly saw his mark among the five remaining prisoners; it was the kaffir with the withered arm, Samson Mungazela, who seemed to lack the resolve of the others and responded a lot quicker to pain. When he implicated Tandia, Geldenhuis quite simply thought all his Christmases had come at once. He had the kaffir girl at last! Now all he had to do was get her boyfriend!

Samson Mungazela also spilled a dozen other names and Geldenhuis followed this up with four arrests within hours; by dawn, after a little physical persuasion, he had collaborating evidence from two of his suspects, which was all he needed. He was confident that Tandia would be forced into court in the morning where the world would witness her humiliation and also see Peekay's reactions as Kriel tore his girlfriend to pieces in the witness box.

Peekay and Tandia left Red five minutes apart, walking under the cover-way across the rear courtyard into the tiny storage shed and down into the stormwater drain below. Both of them were dressed in the white overalls of the Johannesburg municipal maintenance workers. Ten minutes later they emerged onto a back street two blocks from Red and walked to a vacant building lot where Hercules sat in an unmarked brown Chrysler sedan.

The evening traffic was heavy all the way along the Rand to Pretoria and Tandia hid on the back seat with a blanket covering her. They repeated this performance through every small town they went through until they reached the tiny deserted station at Schagen at a quarter to ten that night and parked the car under a large kaffirboom tree. A few minutes later they heard a truck slowing down as it turned off the highway and changed up from low gear as it gathered speed again. A couple of minutes later the prison van loomed up and drew to a halt beside them.

Both Colonel Smit and Gert got out, though only Gert was in uniform. They could hear the black warders chatting in the back of the van and Gert shouted to them to shut up. Peekay greeted his two friends quietly as they shook hands, indicating Tandia who stood a little apart. It was bright moonlight and she could see the two men quite clearly. To Peekay's surprise they both stepped up to her and shook her by the hand. '*Goeienaand, Tandia*,' Smit said formally while Gert, smiling easily, took Tandia's hand.

Tandia smiled. '*Baie dankie*,' she said simply, thanking the two officers for coming. She had changed into jeans and blouse and wore the new socks and sandshoes Hercules had bought for her, putting the suit she'd worn in court into the boot.

Peekay still wore his business suit, though he'd removed the jacket. It was almost a full moon and the subtropical evening was warm, but he knew that towards dawn it would get very cold and he'd added his jacket to the stuff they'd piled onto the hood of the car to take with them.

'You were right, Peekay, there's a road block about three miles in along the Barberton road. They're Nelspruit guys, but none of the police we know, probably Special Branch,' Gert said in an undertone. 'We stopped and talked a bit; they're stopping all incoming traffic.' He glanced over at Tandia. 'They know who they looking for and showed us a magazine picture.'

'Okay, let's get going, man. You never know what eyes are around, even in the dark. Where are we taking you?' Smit asked.

'Gert knows, Colonel. To the farm, Eendrag, you know, Magistrate Coetzee's old farm.'

Gert opened the back of the large van, shining his torch into the interior where half-a-dozen black warders dressed in prison uniform sat. They immediately stood up as the doors opened, grinning into the torchlight.

Gert explained to them that if the van was stopped by the police and opened they were to stand up and conceal the presence of Tandia. To Peekay's enormous surprise, he used the name *Onoshobishobi Ingelosi*. There was a murmur of amazement from the men at the mention of the mystical Peekay, who was the special legacy of Barberton prison.

No more than about twenty minutes after they'd left, driving down the escarpment into the valley which Doc had named 'God's toe print', the van slowed and drew to a halt. The men in the back of the van stood up immediately, pushing Tandia and Peekay to the back of the cabin end where they crouched. They heard a voice say in Afrikaans, 'Police!'

Then Gert saying, 'Ja, we saw you before coming out.'

Then the second voice again, 'No, man, we the new shift. You from Barberton prison?'

'Ja, ten prisoners from the lock-up in Nelspruit. A fight in the location over a shebeen woman. Kaffirs are crazy, man!'

'We'll have to look,' the policeman said. Peekay held

Tandia's hand, squeezing it in the dark. The sound of his heart seemed to fill the whole van. He pulled Tandia close to him so that her body touched his and he felt her trembling.

'What for! Don't be blerrie ridiculous, the kaffirs in there are some of them still drunk!' Smit said.

'This is Colonel Smit, our kommandant,' Gert said, then added, 'we don't want a shooting, man! Kaffirs like this are dangerous.' He paused 'Here, you open it!' Gert must have offered the keys to the back of the van to the police officer.

There was a pause; then a second voice, one they hadn't heard before said, 'What's going on here?'

'I've got ten kaffirs in the back, they been arrested after a fight in the Crocodile River valley native location and they mostly still drunk. If you want to open the back, sergeant, you better take your gun, you know what kaffirs are like when they been drinking skokiaan!'

There was a sudden banging on the side of the van and Tandia nearly fainted, but it came from the inside. 'Haja Policeman! *Buya lapa*! Come here!' one of the black men in the van shouted and the others all laughed and began to bang on the side, shouting obscenities. Moments later the van pulled away and after a short while the men all sat down again convulsed with laughter and congratulating Peekay on his magic as they all chatted on happily. A few miles further on they heard a hand banging against the back of the driver's cabin; it was Colonel Smit telling Peekay they were approaching the turn-off to Eendrag.

'We must go soon, my brothers,' Peekay said to the men in the van. 'I thank you for what you have done and my ancestors thank you also.' They all responded,

862

'Haya, *Onoshobishobi Ingelosi*, it is a great honour.' Then one of them, starting slowly, began the first high single note that begins the chant to the Tadpole Angel, when the boss boy in a gang calls them to the song. He held the note which deepened down and down as it neared its end until it vibrated in the back of the prison van. Then the voices of the others came in to pick up the first words of the chant. Soon the van was filled with the haunting melody of the great fighter who came for the people.

The van stopped and Peekay and Tandia got out while the men still sang. Then their leader called them to a final chorus and their voices ended with a sudden thud, an expulsion of air from deep within their chests as though a hundred picks had hit the ground at the same time.

They stood in the moonlight, the two Afrikaners, the coloured, the rooinek and the black men, all the colours of Africa for one moment in perfect harmony. Colonel Smit shook Peekay's hand, then suddenly the huge man embraced him, pulling the little welterweight into his chest. 'My God, little *boetie*, be careful!' As quickly as he'd held him he let him go, his voice tight with emotion.

Gert took Peekay's hand. 'Go quickly into the mountains, Peekay. I'll only feel safe when I know you're up past the foothills.' He squeezed Peekay's shoulder, 'You the best, you hear?' Peekay was too overwhelmed to speak, but it wasn't necessary for him to say anything; they both knew how he felt.

The two men both shook Tandia's hand, wishing her luck. She wondered what was really going on in their heads. They obviously loved Peekay so much that the fact that she was placing him in danger must have made them feel enormous animosity towards her. But they showed none of this to her. Both men climbed quickly into the van and with a scrunch of tyres they pulled off the shoulder of the road and went on their way. The back of the van was now open and the men called, 'Hamba kahle, Inkosi, Inkosazana. Go well, my Lord and Princess.' Peekay and Tandia watched until they could no longer see the tiny wink of the red tail-lights and then turned down the dirt road leading to Eendrag half a mile away.

The bushveld lay silver in the bright moonlight and they could hear the sound of the river in the distance, where it took a bend and the water flowed over rock to make the rapids. Tandia had only been here once, she'd not even come down when the old man had left the property to Peekay in trust for her. But now as they walked up the rutted road, each on a tyre path with the grass on the centre island grown high and almost to their waists, she felt as though she was coming home.

They passed the burned-down cottage where the walls stood naked and sheets of twisted corrugated iron collapsed inwards, like a toy box filled with untidy bits and pieces. They continued over the small rise and there stood Tandia's ghosted house of Africa against the ridge, its white gables and the sweep of the steps leading up to it clear in the moonlight. As they approached she smelt the moonflower blossoms and the frangipani which hung in the still air as if to perfume her arrival home. They climbed the steps and stood on the stoep looking out at the silver ribbon of river where, in the moonlight, the water turned white as it took the wide bend and turned into the rapids. Tandia, who was running for her life, had suddenly never felt safer. Peekay stood at her side and Africa was all around her, clean and perfect. Calm flooded her and seemed to invade the very bones in her body. Though the African night was filled with sounds, it was also perfectly still. Peekay, as though instinctively understanding, turned and took her in his arms. His mouth closed over hers. After what seemed like her whole life he lifted his head. 'Tandia, I love you,' he said.

Tandia suddenly wanted this man with a fierceness that physically hurt. It was a feeling she'd never experienced and it rushed into her hands. The calmness of the moments before Peekay had taken her into his arms was gone; now an urgency grew in her as she tore at her blouse and then her jeans. Tandia made no attempt to calm the feeling within her, or to delay in getting her clothes off and then helping Peekay to remove his own. She pulled at his shirt, breaking a button as the others came loose. Around his neck he wore a leather thong with a small bag attached to it that she'd never seen before. Getting his shirt off, even though he was attempting to help her, almost brought her to panic, as though the moment would pass and she'd be left with nothing. Peekay spread the blankets they'd brought and suddenly he lay with her and was loving her, his lips moving over her, his hands urgent and caring, trying to gather up all of her at once. Then he was inside her and she rose up and was carried away, floating on the perfumed air over the distant rapids which roared white water over rock. Then they were quiet again; she lay perfectly still, perfectly silent, bathed in the perfume of frangipani and moonflowers in the shining African night. Tandia cried softly and Peekay kissed her tears and held her and sssh'd her, kissing the lids of her eyes until he'd magicked her into a deep exhausted sleep.

Forty-one

At about the same time as Gert and Colonel Smit were turning the prison van into the short road leading to Schagen station Jannie Geldenhuis left John Vorster Square and went home. The police colonel was dog-tired; he'd been interrogating the four black men they'd brought in that afternoon. He badly needed sleep and when a report came through at half past nine that the lights were still burning in the Red boardroom he was confident he'd won the first round and forced Tandia and Peekay to appear before Justice Swart in the morning.

At a quarter past four in the morning Geldenhuis was awakened by Koekemoer, the duty sergeant on the phone. 'Sir, we have a report in from the Nelspruit police.'

Geldenhuis was instantly awake. 'Ja, quick, what?'

'They've found a brown sixty-five Chrysler with "TJ" plates parked at a place called Schagen, which is a small railway station about eight or ten miles before you get to Nelspruit.'

'Have they forced it, looked inside, checked the registration?'

'We've done that, sir. It's registered to the Solomon Levy Carpet Emporium.'

'Shit!' Geldenhuis cried.

'They've forced the boot and discovered a woman's skirt and jacket and high-heeled shoes. It seems pretty certain. The suit fits the description of the stuff Tandia Patel was wearing in court today, I mean, yesterday.'

'They may have transferred to another vehicle. Have you checked the road block on the Barberton road?'

'Yes, sir, every vehicle coming in since six o'clock last night has been stopped and searched.'

'I'm coming in. What's the time? Okay, it will be light by six o'clock, call Police Air Command. I want a Piper Cherokee with pilot on standby and cleared for take-off to Barberton by seven o'clock. Call the Barberton police. No, don't! That whole fucking town thinks Peekay is Jesus Christ! Call Nelspruit, it's only thirty miles away, they can make it in plenty of time.'

Geldenhuis had made his first big mistake. He was a city boy and he'd assumed that two towns so close and both in the lowveld would share the same sort of environment. But Barberton is a mountain town, its topography quite different from the savannah grasslands and undulating hills of the Nelspruit area. He was recruiting a bunch of plainsmen for territory that even mountain men respect. 'Tell the senior officer I want ten men, if they've got them, and a sergeant, all white and fit and fully armed; also a good kaffir tracker, explain they're going to be climbing, to wear fatigues. If they've got dogs, bring them also, we can let them get a scent off the clothes *the terrorist* left in the car.' Geldenhuis no longer referred to Tandia by her name but by the words *the terrorist*, in the same way as a hunter might refer to '*the lion*': she was something he was hunting to kill.

Her personality dimensions no longer existed for him; his task was to destroy her. In his mind she was already dead meat. 'What time did they find the car?' he asked.

The sergeant was reluctant to tell Geldenhuis the truth, but his superior always found out. 'Just after midnight, Colonel.'

'What? And you called me now! Four hours later?' Geldenhuis was suddenly furious, 'Jesus fucking Christ, Koekemoer! We could have been in Barberton by now!'

'Colonel! The call came through the main switch and wasn't transferred to the operations room. I didn't know about it! They filed it for your morning report.'

'They? Who? Find out who took the message!'

'I've done that already, Colonel. Officer Stoffel Vermaak. He came onto the switchboard on the eleven o'clock shift and didn't read his standing instructions until just before I called you.'

'Put him on report, he's a boxer isn't he? Yes, that's right, a middle. Still, put him on report! Bladdy idiots like that don't belong in the police force! I'll be in in forty minutes. Call off the other road blocks. Jesus no! Don't do that! The car near Nelspruit could be a decoy. Call Nelspruit again, tell them to put a road block on the Havelock road, halfway up between Barberton and the Swaziland border. If they say it's not their district, tell them we've cleared it in Pretoria.' Geldenhuis changed the subject. 'Has Hymie Levy left Red?'

'Yes, Colonel. We followed his Mercedes home about midnight. We have people in the front and back of his place and the car is still parked underneath the building.'

'Jesus, how much does that mean? You had people front and back of Red and Peekay and *the terrorist* managed to walk out under your bladdy noses! What about the driver, what's his name, Hercules?'

'We haven't seen him since he dropped the two of them off at Red at fourteen hundred hours yesterday.'

'Check his home, I don't remember his surname. If he isn't home, bring him in when he gets in.'

Sergeant Koekemoer was surprised, it wasn't like Jannie Geldenhuis to forget the surname of the Red chauffeur, Hercules. The police colonel was so well versed in the three Red partners and every circumstance of their daily lives; forgetting the surname of the black man who drove them regularly was definitely not a good sign.

Koekemoer worshipped Jannie Geldenhuis and was, perhaps, the only person in the police force who did. He was worried about him. Lately, Geldenhuis had complained occasionally of a headache and hadn't seemed quite as sharp. He hadn't been near the boxing ring, or even into the police gym since his acquittal. It was as though the anger in him, which these days always seemed at the point of boiling over, was clouding his judgement. Increasingly he'd lash out violently and several black prisoners had died at his hands before they'd confessed. Which wasn't like him at all.

Geldenhuis came back on the line. 'One last thing. Make a note to call a guy named Cogsweel in Pretoria at eight o'clock. I want authority to talk to the army base commander at Komaatipoort. His number is in the code book in central security, I'll phone through now and give them my clearance number.' Geldenhuis slammed the receiver down.

Peekay woke Tandia at half past three in the morning. She tried to sit up but discovered she'd been wrapped in a cocoon of blankets. The moon was still bright in the sky and there was as yet no sense of the coming morning. Peekay unwrapped her blankets. 'It's very cold, Tandy, put on your sweater when you dress.' Tandia realized with surprise that she was naked and clung to a blanket, pulling it up over her breasts as she sat up. Peekay laughed. 'Too late for that, darling. You are quite the most beautiful woman in the world anyway, you shouldn't be allowed to wear clothes!'

'You're supposed to love me for my brains, Counsellor!'

Peekay knelt down beside her and kissed her gently. 'But I do! Good morning, beloved Tandia. Your brains, body and spirit, all of you, I love with a deep passion.'

Tandia couldn't quite believe she'd made love! Physically loving Peekay had played no part in her romance-scape. Physical love wasn't an aspect of her life she cared to remember. With the exception of Gideon, her body had only ever been violated by a man. Now, inexplicably, all that had changed.

'Peekay, last night was? We did ...? I'm not still asleep?'

Peekay kissed her again. 'No, but you've got to get up, we have to be gone in half an hour.' He rose, turned and walked over to the end of the stoep where Tandia was surprised to see the embers of a small fire. He returned moments later with a small billycan which smelled of onions. Tandia was ravenous, she hadn't eaten since the luncheon adjournment the previous day. 'No plates! Hercules remembered a spoon and a fork, two tin mugs, but no plates.'

Tandia ate from the can, a mixture of bully beef, tomato and onions. She hated bully beef, but the concoction Peekay had prepared for her was delicious. Perhaps being in love makes you like bully beef, she thought. She ate half the contents of the can and handed it to Peekay.

'No, please, finish it! I ate during the night, cold chicken. There's still some left, would you prefer it?' Tandia shook her head, getting stuck into the remaining bully beef with gusto. 'There's a small running stream behind the house, get dressed, you can wash and I'll put on water for coffee.'

By the time Tandia returned from the stream the sky in the east was beginning to show the faintest indication of light, a narrow strip against the horizon, as though the night had developed a silver rind. Peekay handed her a mug of coffee, white and sweetened with condensed milk. Putting his arm around Tandia, he pointed to a star just above the horizon. 'See the big star on the horizon, that's the morning star. As a kid I would sometimes wake up just before dawn and frantically climb the path up the hill behind our house and sit on a big rock at the top and wait to see if I could catch the exact moment when the morning star went out. But I never could. I'd watch and watch until my eyes started to water. Then always, when I couldn't stand it any more and blinked, when I looked again it was gone!' Peekay laughed softly, 'But it was back again the next day, squatting there just above the horizon and due east, always in the same spot waiting to disappear on me again. I used to think it knew all about me and was playing a game it was very good at and which it was determined I would never win.'

'Peekay, do you think one day we can rebuild this house and you and I could live here in a South Africa where it isn't a crime for a black woman to be terribly in love with a white guy?'

Peekay turned Tandia towards him and pulled her

into his chest, almost spilling her coffee. 'If I didn't think that, Tandy, I don't think I'd want to live. I don't want to make our life in England. We are African, this is where the sweetness and the bitterness lies for us. This land has been sick for so long I sometimes think it will never recover, that the sickness is terminal. But I know it will. My nanny, Gideon's mother, used to say, "There is a season for sorrow and then it will pass." When it passes we'll come back and restore this house; like the beloved country it has solid foundations. It will be our house, the house for all Africa.' He kissed her again.

It was nice hearing the words. Tandia could almost believe them when Peekay spoke them. Dreamers are like that, they can make you believe things. They believe the morning star is playing with them. She found it was nice believing, even easy, if only for these few moments.

Peekay pushed her gently from him, his tone lighter as he spoke. 'Okay, kid, let's kick the dust. It's half an hour's walk to where Dee and Dum are meeting us; drink your coffee and let's vamoose!' He stooped down and, picking up a blanket, started to fold it, gripping the edge of the blanket in his mouth and bringing the two ends together.

Dee and Dum were waiting for them when, just after half past four, they arrived at Pig Rock. It had been light for twenty minutes but was still cold, the early sunlight not yet bright enough to warm them. The twins saw them coming and ran squealing to meet them, each of them grabbing Peekay by a hand and dancing about him like young girls, though they were women in their mid thirties. 'Stop!' Peekay said laughing, 'Where are your manners? This is Tandia, who I have talked to you about many times.'

Dee and Dum stopped and turned to Tandia, both

held their arms out and they hugged her simultaneously. The gesture was one of total openness and generosity; they were including her into their circle, for they instinctively guessed that Peekay loved this beautiful woman. 'Welcome, our sister,' they said simultaneously, as though they'd rehearsed the line. But Peekay knew it wasn't rehearsed; he'd seen them do it all their lives, as if they shared a collective brain, or at least a connected one. He doubted very much if the two girls could exist apart from each other for more than a few hours, though he couldn't remember them ever apart for even this long.

Tandia liked them immediately; she was amazed by the process of falling in love. She found that she was able to let her defences down and allow the warmth of Dee and Dum to come straight through to her. It was like a rebirth.

'Thank you, my sisters,' she said, hugging them back.

'Come on, you silly *izaLukazi*! Tandy and me must be gone, the sun will be high in a minute. Where are my mountain clothes?'

'We have brought everything. More than you asked!'

'We can't carry more. We have to travel light. Tandy isn't accustomed to the mountains.'

'That is why we are coming,' Dee said.

Peekay looked stern. 'No, Dee, you can't!'

Dee stood directly in Peekay's path, her legs firmly planted, slightly apart, arms folded. She seemed suddenly like a big woman, though he could not remember ever seeing her like this. Dum now stood beside her, unconsciously striking the same pose. 'You are in danger! You who belong to us, who is our flesh and our heartblood, you cannot tell us a lie!' Dum cried.

'No, you cannot tell us a lie. It is in our skin, it is

hurting us all over!' Dee said and both of them started to rub their folded arms and roll their shoulders, moaning softly.

'We will carry for you!' Dum said suddenly. She pointed at Tandia. 'Tandy is beautiful, but she has no legs for the mountains. Her ankles, look at them, pfft! They could snap like a chicken bone! If she falls, if she hurts her leg, who will carry her?'

Peekay had to admit they had a point. Tandia was both unfit and unaccustomed to the sort of climbing they would need to do. The likelihood of her spraining her ankle or falling was considerable. Peekay knew the twins could walk all day, that even if they had to carry Tandia in a stretcher, they'd make it over the top.

'What about the missus?' Peekay asked, thinking of his mother's objections.

'We have written a letter!' Dee spoke in English, 'Gon wun day missus pliz, Dee, Dum,' she said proudly, repeating the exact words in the note they'd left for his mother.

'She will be angry,' Dum added, 'but you are our heartblood! There is danger in our kraal, we *must* be with you.'

'Okay!' Peekay said, making his mind up suddenly. If they could distribute the weight between them so that Tandia carried nothing they would make better time and there would be less likelihood of her injuring herself.

The twins wiped tears away, dabbing their eyes with identical gestures, as though they'd been choreographed. 'Thank you, Peekay,' they said, their voices soft and loving, 'we will protect you.'

Peekay loved them both fiercely, but now he frowned, hiding his feelings. 'Now! Where are my mountain clothes?' He looked down with distaste at the rumpled grey pinstripe lawyer's suit he was wearing.

'They are on the Pig Rock,' both girls shouted.

Peekay went up to the rock to find his mountain clothes laid out on it, his old shirt and khaki pants ironed and starched. His anorak too had been washed within an inch of its life with precise creases down the centre of both sleeves. His thick grey socks were laid side by side, lined up perfectly with both toes pointing in the same direction. His climbing boots were water-proofed with fresh dubbin and his old khaki cloth hat, torn and mended a hundred times also bore the signs of having been starched and ironed. Even his belt and the worn and scuffed sheath of his hunting knife were polished. He climbed into the clothes which were not uncomfortable despite the liberal starching they'd received, but he felt stupidly neat in the perfectly creased khaki trousers which had been patched in a dozen places.

The girls took the blankets Peekay had brought along and quickly redistributed the stuff in Peekay's rucksack plus the provisions they'd brought, folding the blankets around it so that they ended up with two neat bundles tied at the top. These they lifted to their heads, where they balanced easily, leaving their hands free. Peekay's rucksack now contained only his mountain gear, spikes, climbing hammer, and small axe as well as a torch and Doc's battered binoculars. Hanging over the top of his rucksack was a coil of rope. It all felt light and com-fortable as they set out.

Peekay allowed Dee and Dum to set the pace, placing Tandia between them. They were both experienced bush walkers, accustomed to the mountain terrain and would set a pace which would allow Tandia to continue far longer without a rest than if he attempted to do the same thing. By the end of the day they would have travelled further than if he tried to hurry them along the easy bits and nurse Tandia up the steeper slopes. Mountain climbing is like digging; you end up with a deeper hole if you go at it at a steady pace.

By half past six they were over the foothills and about to begin the climb into the high mountains. Tandia had kept up well, but Peekay could see she was tired and needed a rest. Dee and Dum seemed simultaneously to reach the same decision for they stopped. Dee took a thermos of tea out of a bundle and Dum a flask of water and a couple of cups. She poured water for Tandia first, filling the tin mug. 'Drink it all, Tandy. You have lost much water already.'

Tandia drank gratefully and handed the empty cup back to Dum. 'Thank you, Dee,' she said.

Dum held the mug out allowing Dee to fill it with hot, sweet tea. She handed it to Tandia, 'I am Dum,' she said.

'I will call you both, "Dum-dee-dum!" Then I won't get it wrong!' Tandia laughed.

As they'd set off Peekay had spoken to the twins in the Shangaan language with which Tandia was not familiar. 'We have five, maybe six hours' lead; you must take this city woman as fast as you can, but do not break her. We are going over Saddleback to Swaziland.'

'In one day?' Dee asked.

'It depends how well Tandy lasts. But as far as you can take her.'

The twins nodded, knowing their task, knowing that how they judged the journey could mean Peekay's life, for they now felt the danger around him strongly. It smelt of death and of hate; they knew their heartblood was running from a great and calamitous evil.

The climb to Saddleback normally took five hours from the end of the foothills. On the very top of Saddleback there was a small plateau, about three hundred yards across, like a bald patch, torn by the wind from the leeward side of the mountain. It was composed mostly of rock and scree and tuft grass and the wind usually blew at gale force across it. It was totally exposed but it was the only way across the high mountains on foot. After they were across it Peekay knew they would be safe, they'd be on the rainy side of the mountains and, if necessary, could leave the path and conceal themselves within the dense mountain scrub and even in the rainforest in the high kloofs.

Ten minutes later they started to climb again, this time in earnest. Two and a half hours later, with stops of five minutes every half hour to rest Tandia, they reached a spot where Peekay could see the valley for the last time. He took the binoculars from his rucksack and focused them. In the deep blue distance the de Kaap valley looked peaceful; in one or two places smoke rose straight up where a small bush fire burned and a scud of low cloud lay just below the far escarpment. Then he heard the faint sound of a small aircraft, a buzz like an angry bee rising in the clear morning. Sound carries remarkably far in the mountains. He looked carefully, scanning the length of the valley until he finally saw it, a Piper Cherokee still fairly high but heading towards the town which was concealed, tucked below the foothills. Geldenhuis had arrived.

If it took the police colonel an hour to get underway, they had about three and a half hours' lead. Peekay made a rough calculation; if Tandia didn't crack they would make it over the top, but only just. His only concern was to get over Saddleback; concealed in the deep mountain scrub the police would be no match for him unless they had a bloody good black tracker, and even then he felt confident that he could avoid his pursuers.

A police transport vehicle and squad car was waiting at the small airport when Geldenhuis arrived. Beside them stood seven white police constables and a sergeant, formed into a rough squad. The sergeant brought them to attention and saluted. 'Sergeant Maritz, Colonel!'

'Stand your men at ease, Sergeant,' Geldenhuis said. He was dressed in fatigues and carried a police semi-automatic rifle slung over his shoulder. He wore no pistol on his webbing belt; in its place was a hunting knife whose leather handle was topped with a death's head. Some knives rest peacefully on a man's hips, mere decoration or affectation, used for cutting fishing line or sharpening twigs. Even though its blade wasn't visible this wasn't that kind of knife. It was purpose built, the kind of knife a man would give a name and would also speak to, but always with respect in his voice.

'Is there anyone here who knows this country?' Geldenhuis asked.

'Yes, sir, we have a black tracker who says he knows it well. He looked over to a middle-aged African who was seated under a nearby syringe tree. '*Buya lapa*!' he called in Fanagalo. The man scrambled to his feet and came running over. He was a little man dressed in an old army greatcoat and he smiled, showing only four yellow teeth in his mouth. 'He's a Swazi and he says he comes from up near Havelock on the Swazi border; he says he knows the mountains round here very well.'

'You mean he's not your regular police tracker?'

'No, Colonel, this isn't our area; the Nelspruit area is flatter country, our trackers don't come over this way.'

'What about the local police?'

'Well, Colonel, if I may say so, they're not too pleased about this. I mean, us people from Nelspruit police taking over an' all.' He pointed to the little Swazi who now stood fifteen or so feet from them, waiting to be asked to step forward, 'They sent this guy.'

Geldenhuis said, 'Okay, fuck them!' He ignored the little black man and turned to the map. 'Let's see if the kaffir knows what he's talking about.'

'There are several paths up through the foothills but they all seem to eventually converge going through this gorge; after this it's straight up over the top, a single path. We have to get to them somewhere between this gorge and the top of Saddleback. If they get over the top the kaffir says you can forget it, it's dense bush and scrub and from what I understand, Peekay knows the country well from when he was a kid.'

Geldenhuis turned the map upside down and called the little Swazi over. 'Show us where to go,' he demanded in Zulu, pointing to the map.

The little Swazi looked at the map. 'Even if you turn it the right side up I can't read it, baas,' he said in Siswati, 'for reading maps I am no good.'

Geldenhuis grinned despite himself, at least the bastard wasn't a fool. 'Explain then how we go,' he demanded.

'There are four ways, baas. One is longest, but it is shortest, because the path is good. All the paths they come to a gorge, then same path all the way over the mountain.'

'How many hours to the top?'

The black man seemed to think for a moment, counting on the fingers of one hand. 'Six, six hours I think, baas. It is very, very hard.'

'The top of the mountain where the path crosses, is it very rocky?'

'No, baas, by that mountain is only grass by the top,' Julius ran his hand over his head. 'Like the baas head.'

'Well, the kaffir seems to know his way. It's six hours to Saddleback.' He turned to the men, 'Have you brought enough food and water? Remember you've got to come back as well.' Geldenhuis grinned, looking up at the high mountains, 'Have a good climb, you hear.'

'You won't be coming, Colonel?' Sergeant Maritz asked, surprised.

'Ja, I'll see you up there.' Geldenhuis didn't explain any further. 'Okay, man, now I want to talk about *the terrorist*.' He cleared his throat. 'You already know there are two of them, a woman and a man who is supposed to be a pretty big hero around these parts, you all know who I am talking about. I don't want to mention his name because when a man turns against his country the only name you can call him is a dog. A fucking mongrel! I'd like them taken alive. But I'd rather they were dead than free.' He sighed, 'Okay, you know how I feel? That's why I'm not using the local police for this job. If we kill their hero, it's bad public relations for the Barberton police and I don't want the whole fucking town up in arms. But someone who aids a known terrorist to escape is a terrorist too! If any of you feel differently about this then say so now, you hear?'

Geldenhuis looked at the men standing in front of him. 'This isn't police work, man! This is fighting for your country! You are helping to rid South Africa of the scum!' He waited, looking at each of them, but the men kept silent, most of them with their eyes downcast. 'Okay, I'm waiting for a helicopter to come up from the military base at Komaatipoort. We're going to try to squeeze the bastards between me and you guys coming up. I'll land on Saddleback and ambush them if they manage to get that far before you reach them. Okay, you better get going. Good luck.' Geldenhuis turned to the sergeant beside him and shook his hand, 'Thank you for your cooperation, Sergeant Maritz. If we pull this one off I'll see all your men get a commendation from Pretoria.'

The men marched off and one of them, a corporal named Shorty Bronkhorst who was known as the station wit, snorted, 'The bastard thinks he's John fucking Wayne!'

Captain Julius Dube had come down from Bulembu, crossing into South Africa to do some serious shopping in Barberton. It wasn't quite as close as Pigg's Peak on his side of the border, but he wanted a double bed and inner-spring mattress. To go with his newfound military status he'd paid the *lobola*, bridal price, for a second wife, a young and nubile *intombi* from a good family. Their wedding gift to themselves was to be the bed, a status symbol probably closer to a general than a captain, but Julius was ambitious.

However, the choice of double beds with inner springs in Pigg's Peak was decidedly limited. Barberton was three times as close as Mbabane, the Swazi capital, and also likely to prove a better shopping venue. Julius was fairly careless about borders and while his papers were in order he failed to get a required stamp from the police station on the South African side of the frontier.

He'd come down from Havelock in the bus and had passed a police road block on the road but had thought nothing of it. Later, having selected a bed and mattress and arranged for it to be brought up by lorry to the Bulembu border post in two days, he'd celebrated at a shebeen in the native location where one or two jam tins of *mqombothi* too many had made him conspicuous. He'd been picked up by the local police and accommodated in a cell for the night.

The routine for being caught was standard, he'd be sjamboked (five lashes to discourage future temporary immigration) then put on the bus to Havelock, handcuffed to the bus seat and the key given to the driver. When they got to Havelock the bus driver would deliver him to the local police sergeant who would come out and officially unlock him, give him a stiff kick up his already very blistered backside and escort him to the border.

Julius had been waiting at the sergeant's desk to be released and his wallet and sundry shopping returned to him before being taken out into the yard of the police station to get sjamboked and put on the bus. Then the call had come through to the front desk from the Nelspruit police asking for a black tracker who knew the local mountains.

Captain Dube was not a man to be easily daunted. He was a mountain man born and bred. He'd once been a tracker in the Swaziland police; besides he knew these particular mountains like the back of his hand. He'd also heard Peekay's name mentioned in the conversation and details as to why a tracker was required. The *Onoshobishobi Ingelosi* was in a great deal of shit and Julius wasn't the sort of officer who walks away from a crisis. The rest was astonishing, even to a smooth operator like himself. He wondered fleetingly whether Somojo had a hand in it somewhere, seeing as the *Ono-shobishobi Ingelosi* was involved. The white police sergeant seemed angry with the police from Nelspruit and when Julius, who like all Africans kept every official paper he'd ever received, had shown him his honourable discharge notice from The Royal Swaziland Police Constabulary he'd given him the job of taking the police contingent from Nelspruit over the mountains. The sergeant had also let him off the mandatory sjambok on the basis that it might inhibit his walking speed.

Thus Captain Julius Dube's finest hour had been thrust upon him as though miraculously. He could already see his next promotion and wondered to himself whether a rank existed somewhere above a captain but below a general. Julius knew one thing for sure; it was going to be a very long day in the mountains for the Boer policemen, and their chances of reaching Saddleback were about the same as his of growing a fresh set of molars.

Though nothing untoward happened, the six hours it had taken them to get to the gorge had been very difficult for Tandia. They'd stopped for ten minutes every hour and reaching the gorge they had taken half an hour for lunch. Tandia had by this time just about had enough. Peekay removed her shoes and allowed her to bathe her feet in the icy mountain stream before he examined them for blisters. In choosing sand-shoes for her to wear he'd shown his experience. Tackies are the best walking shoes for this kind of country, they're comfortable, don't need to be broken in, are soft enough not to cause blistering and will accommodate swollen feet simply by adjusting the laces. To his surprise, though her feet were swollen, the skin wasn't broken. He smeared her toes in vaseline before putting on a pair of fresh socks for her. Peekay knew that if her feet could last, she could, though clearly she was close to a state of collapse. They had two hours' climbing to go and Geldenhuis would be closing in fast. The twins too were tired; they'd put on a fair bit of weight over the years and while they often went into the mountains this was serious climbing for anyone. He noticed that Dee was limping as she walked to the water to fill their water bottles and discovered she'd cut her foot when she'd slipped on a section of miner's blue shale when they'd passed an abandoned mine digging; she'd jammed it against a sharp outcrop of rock. She'd continued on, ignoring the cut and not wanting to delay their progress. Peekay cleaned the rather nasty three-inch wound, picking the tiny bits of shale out of it with a pair of tweezers and finally dousing it with iodine to kill any infection. The iodine stung horribly and tears ran down Dee's cheeks, but she never said a word, simply biting her lip. Dum suffered with her; tears also ran down her cheeks and she stood by her sister biting her lip as well, seeming genuinely to be experiencing the same pain Dee felt. Peekay padded the wound thickly with gauze and wrapped it tightly, using almost the whole spool of two-inch wide elastoplast. Though Dee limped slightly he knew she wouldn't let her foot slow them down, and she refused to lighten the burden on her head.

Peekay made his calculations. If they could cover the slope ahead in two hours, a climb which usually took a little over one hour from the gorge, they'd be over the top at half past two, half an hour ahead of Geldenhuis and his men. It wasn't much of an advantage, but it would be enough if he was careful.

Halfway up the slope was a place where he could stop and see into the valley approaching the gorge below them, where the three good paths to the gorge began to converge. Anyone coming along any of them would be clearly visible through the binoculars. If the valley was empty, he knew they were in trouble. Geldenhuis would have made it through the valley and into the gorge. The maximum pace he could expect from Tandia wouldn't get them over the top; the police trackers would reach them twenty minutes before they could achieve their goal.

They set out once again to climb out of the gorge and onto the final slope, the twins in front with Tandia just ahead of Peekay so he could steady her. Despite the cold her body was soaked with perspiration and she was forced to stop every twenty feet to gain her breath. Though nothing was said Tandia was conscious that they were losing ground rapidly and that Geldenhuis couldn't be too far away. But her legs simply wouldn't carry her more than twenty paces at a time and sometimes far less. Her chest hurt terribly and on several occasions she was sure she was going to have a heart attack. At first she'd cried softly, but soon she didn't even have the energy for that and became convinced that every step she took would be her last.

Halfway up the slope to the top and more than an hour after they'd left the gorge Peekay halted them. Focusing his binoculars he pulled the valley beyond the gorge into focus. He saw almost immediately that it was empty and his heart sank. Geldenhuis had made it into the gorge below, they were finished.

Then Peekay caught a tiny glint of metal on the edge of the vista contained within the glasses and he swung the binoculars to his right. He gasped as his eyes adjusted to the sudden movement. Then he started to laugh, his laughter building until it echoed against the hills about him. Finally he turned to the three women, his face creased in a huge grin, 'God is good, children, if we can just keep on our feet we're going to make it. The opposition, God knows how, has become confused!'

Peekay had seen the police trackers coming down a valley parallel to the one which worked its way to the entry of the gorge. Ten years before there had been access between the two valleys through a second narrow gorge but it had been filled with a massive rock slide. In about ten minutes Geldenhuis and his men would find it impossible to continue. Though the two valleys were less than half a mile apart a sheer cliff face separated them and it would take nearly two hours for the men to retrace their steps. He couldn't believe his extraordinary luck; the path to the mountain slide was well known locally, a favourite destination for hardened climbers. It was common knowledge there was no longer a way through to the big gorge and he couldn't imagine how such a mistake could be made, unless it was deliberate.

Greatly cheered, Peekay talked Tandia up the slope, sometimes it seemed by inches. Nearly two and a half hours later they sat within fifty feet of the top. 'The last bit is tricky, so we'll rest for half an hour before crossing, Tandia. It's a bit windy up top so we'll stop here.' Given the choice, Peekay would have liked to cross, just to know that they would be out of immediate danger where they had more than one option. But the final fifty feet was almost sheer and he was doubtful Tandia would make it without a rest. The luxury of the extra two hours they'd gained on Geldenhuis made it an easy decision. He chose an overhanging rock that cut into the side of the mountain as shelter. There was room under it to spread a blanket where Tandia could lie.

Tandia was crying softly, her courage completely exhausted. The fact that she was fifty feet from the top meant nothing; it might as well have been a mile. Peekay removed her shoes and her jeans; lying her on a blanket, he began to massage her legs. She cried out in agony at the touch of his hands against the knotted quads and calf muscles. Peekay continued to work on them for nearly an hour, a lot longer than he'd hoped to stop. But he realized that if he couldn't get her moving again they'd be trapped anyway. The mistaken path taken by their pursuers had most certainly saved them from capture and possibly saved their lives.

Captain Julius Dube led the Nelspruit police patrol right up to the rock slide, gasping in pretend horror when they'd come around a corner path and faced the mountain of rubble. 'Haya, haya!' he'd exclaimed, holding his hands to his head. The disaster was immediately apparent to them all and Julius had prepared himself for the thrashing he was about to receive. The men were tired and had been pushed at a hard pace by him as he'd deliberately attempted to wear them out.

'Jesus! What happened here!' Sergeant Maritz shouted. The rock slide, though a decade old, had torn most of the side of a mountain away. The rock fall had been much too calamitous for vegetation to have taken over and the slide they looked at seemed as though it could have happened the day before yesterday. But the men from Nelspruit, who were not even local Nelspruit guys, most of them transferred from all over the place, knew nothing of this and even less of the way of mountains, where it might take a thousand years and a million rainfalls washing silt into the rock to cover a fall like this one with grass and bush. Maritz, though plainly exasperated, judged the predicament they found themselves in to be an honest mistake and Captain Julius Dube began seriously to believe that the hand of the great Somojo was apparent in all of this. Everything he'd done with the *Onoshobishobi Ingelosi* had turned out successfully, as well as being very profitable. He also knew that the great *makhosi*, Somojo, had blessed the white man with the special gifts. He, Julius Dube, was having the one great day of his life which the spirits promised to every man who lives on this earth.

Maritz, trying to contain his exasperation in front of his men, took a swig from his water flask and, rinsing his mouth, spat it out. 'How far back is it to get onto another path?' he enquired of Julius.

'Haya, baas, it is very, very, far. I think two hours also!'

'*Fok! Ons moef nog twee ue loop tot die groot kloof!* Still two hours from the big gorge!' he said in dismay to his tired men, who'd already had about as much time in the mountains as they felt they'd ever need.

The men all groaned and Shorty Bronkhorst observed, 'John Wayne is going to have to hold the fucking pass alone.'

No one thought this was very funny. It was half past one and they still had three hours to go to the top. Peekay and his kaffir girl would be in Swaziland drinking a second cup of tea by then, Maritz thought to himself. 'We'll stop for fifteen minutes,' he said, 'it's not going to make that much difference now.'

Geldenhuis had waited nearly six hours for the

helicopter to arrive from the army base at Komaati-poort and he was getting worried. He wanted to be well in place to ambush Peekay and Tandia when they came over the top and it was nearly three o'clock already. He was cursing himself; the men would be closing in and he wasn't in place. He wanted Peekay and Tandia for himself. He hadn't yet decided whether he would kill them, but he wanted the option to do so before the men arrived so that he could claim they'd made a run for it. He was nearly crying with frustration when he heard the beat of the chopper's blades and five minutes later it landed. But then the pilot had to refuel and go through an entire checking procedure before they took off.

The pilot was a colonel himself so Geldenhuis couldn't pull rank, which was the usual procedure when the police and the army worked together. It's deliberate, he thought to himself, these army bastards don't like to take orders from a cop, they've deliberately sent a fucking colonel to checkmate me! What's more the shit is a rooinek! He felt like hitting somebody, but there were no kaffirs handy.

The pilot had introduced himself simply as Robin Winter, not observing his rank but not saluting as well, so that the police colonel knew from the start they were quits. He spread a map on the grass and Geldenhuis explained their destination. Winter was far from impressed, looking up from the map into the mountains as though he was making an instant judgement. 'The up-draughts in that range are notorious, Colonel. A chopper like this one can drop two or three hundred feet with no prior indication. Landing on top of Sad-dleback could be suicidal.' He checked the windspeed averages marked on his flying map. 'The winds up there are gale force.' He looked at his watch and then back at the high mountains. 'At least there's no cloud, though I expect it will come up soon.' He seemed to be making up his mind. 'We've got time for only one pass. After that I'm out of there, old son,' he said cheerfully, but Geldenhuis knew he meant it.

Geldenhuis wanted to hit the pompous bastard; almost six hours to get up from his base at Komaatipoort and he wasn't even guaranteeing he'd put him down on the top of Saddleback. Fuck it! He'd make the bastard do so at gunpoint. 'Thanks, Colonel Winter, let's go, man,' he said keeping his voice even; it was fifteen minutes past three.

Ten minutes later Peekay saw the helicopter approaching. They'd just prepared themselves to leave. The helicopter circled once above them at about five hundred feet and then disappeared. It came around again half a minute later, this time lower, and he could see Geldenhuis at the open door with his rifle pointed at the pilot. The chopper disappeared from view and they heard it faintly above the howl of the wind as its engines went into a higher pitch. Then they lost its sound, but it returned, the blades whining at an even higher pitch. Moments later the chopper passed low over them, banking sharply with only the pilot in it. They were only ten minutes from the top, fifty lousy feet. Peekay could see the panic in the eyes of the twins and Tandia looked at him. 'It's all over isn't it, Peekay?'

Peekay's mind was working too rapidly to grasp the despair they felt. He turned to the twins. 'Go over now. When the policeman stops you, he will ask if you have seen us. Tell him we are just ten minutes ahead, that you saw us ahead of you as you came up from the gorge. He will come after us, thinking we are ahead. Now listen carefully. The path divides into a fork on the other side. Tell him the one going to Swaziland is the right-hand path, then take the left one yourself. Wait for us after one mile of walking. Hide in the bush in case he comes.'

Dee and Dum picked up their bundles and balanced them carefully, though with the wind they had to hold onto them with one hand. Now that Peekay had told them what he wanted they were not frightened. They turned to leave and Peekay walked over to them and kissed them both. The last time he had kissed them he was five years old. Dee and Dum's faces lit up into a brilliant smile, for that's what it seemed like, a single smile on two faces, as though the smile came out of both of them. 'You are our heartblood, Peekay,' they said together.

Geldenhuis was surprised to see the two women coming across the open ground towards him. He was still searching for the path when they suddenly emerged over the top fifty yards from where he stood. They appeared not to see him and he shouted. '*Buya lapa, abaFazi*! Come here, women!' But his voice was torn from him by the howling wind, which was now buffeting the women's skirts as they used both hands to steady the bundles on their heads.

Geldenhuis ran towards them, covering the fifty yards fairly quickly, though it was difficult against the wind. He'd jumped from the helicopter six feet from the ground and Winter had put everything into the blades to get himself out. He stopped beside them now, panting. Both women looked amazed at seeing him, the whites of their eyes huge in their faces. They pulled back from him afraid.

'Do not be afraid of the gun, I am a policeman,' he shouted.

'We are afraid, Inkosi!' Dum shouted back.

'I won't harm you, I am in a hurry.' Geldenhuis was not conscious of the irony of this remark. 'Tell me, have you seen two people? One a white man? Maybe ahead of you?' He'd turned his back to the wind, standing parallel to the two women so that he could talk quite normally.

The two women turned to each other, talking rapidly in a language he couldn't understand.

'What is that you are saying, hey?' Geldenhuis said.

'We have seen him, Inkosi,' Dee said.

'He is with a woman, Inkosi,' Dum added.

'How long ago?'

The twins seemed to be thinking. 'I think not so long, Inkosi.'

'I think twenty minutes.' Each twin held up ten fingers.

Geldenhuis grinned; then his expression changed and he looked at them strangely. 'Are you two twins?'

'Yes, Inkosi,' the twins said together.

It explained the hands going up together. He'd heard of that happening with twins. 'Which way is it to the Swaziland border?' Geldenhuis asked.

'We will show you, Inkosi,' Dee said.

'Did you hear any men coming behind you?'

'No, Inkosi, we did not hear,' they both said.

It was amazing, Geldenhuis thought, they seemed to have one mind. They turned back into the teeth of the wind and set out for the other side of the plateau. Geldenhuis was jubilant. Peekay and Tandia would be exhausted and he was fresh; they couldn't be more than a few hundred yards away and the trackers hadn't caught up. He had them to himself.

When they got to the edge of the plateau and dropped over the side the wind seemed to stop. Fifty feet further on the path divided and the two kaffir women stopped. One of the women pointed to the right-hand path. 'It is this one, Inkosi.'

'To Swaziland? This path goes to Swaziland?' Geldenhuis repeated.

'Ja, ja, it is this one, Inkosi,' the second woman said.

They had nice manners, Geldenhuis thought, these bush kaffirs, not like the cheeky black bastards in the city. He was amazingly relaxed. He knew he'd come up to Peekay from behind. If he'd seen the helicopter he'd know it couldn't land in the wind and would have seen it fly away again. He set off down the path the two women had indicated. He wouldn't run, there was plenty of time.

Dee and Dum took the path to the left. Too afraid to stop and hug each other, they moved forward as quickly as their tired legs would take them, fearful that the policeman with the gun might return, fearful also of Peekay crossing in case the man came back. But they'd always done as Peekay asked and now they hurried to where they would anxiously wait for him.

Peekay and Tandia climbed to the edge of the plateau and watched as the twins reached the other side with Geldenhuis and disappeared. Peekay waited another minute before they set out. It took them nearly ten minutes to cross in the gale-force winds.

But by that time Dee was dead.

Geldenhuis had followed the path at a steady trot, covering a couple of hundred yards along the rocky descent in as many minutes. His mind was concentrating hard, but there was something nagging at him. He knew from past practice to listen to it. This was an instinct that was never wrong. He scratched at his mind, even stopping once to try to think the concern to the surface of his consciousness. A little later he passed a patch of soft sand, smoothed by the previous night's rain; it would have been impossible to avoid it if one were walking along the path, yet there were no footprints. He came to another a little further along and it too was virginal. Then it happened! Shit! African twins are very rare. Twins are regarded as bad *muthi*, bad medicine, and, even today, the weaker of the two twin babies is left outside the village. It was not uncommon to find a small black infant on a rubbish dump in the townships, a twin left to die. Then it hit him like a thunderclap! The two black women were Peekay's twins. It was in his file. He'd grown up with black twins! Geldenhuis turned and retraced his steps down the path. Turning down the second pathway he ran steadily until he saw the twins. 'Stop!' he shouted. Dee and Dum saw him and panicked. They dropped their bundles and started to run. Geldenhuis ran after them, not even seeing the bundles which had rolled off the path. He lost sight of them and then saw them ahead of him again, still on the path. The stupid women hadn't run into the cover of the bush. He stopped, went down onto one knee and, taking quick aim, fired. The bullet tore into Dee's back, killing her instantly.

Dum stopped and turned, screaming. She flung herself onto Dee's lifeless body, then rose and ran into the dense bush on the side of the path. Geldenhuis fired off three more shots, missing her. He ran up to the black girl's body; he could hear the second kaffir girl crashing through the bush. He kicked at Dee's body, knowing instantly that she was dead. '*Jou moel!*' He looked into the bush where he could hear Dum. Jesus, it's just a kaffir girl! he said to himself. I must be going crazy, thinking about going after a kaffir girl. He'd worked out Peekay's ploy. As usual it was shit smart. The two women had been sent ahead as a decoy and to misdirect him. He'd fired the four shots while Peekay and Tandia were coming across the plateau and the howl of the wind had killed the sound. All he had to do was wait. It was just how he'd imagined it would be; even the dead kaffir woman. He brought his boot under the hem of Dee's dress, lifting it. He'd make Peekay die the way he'd always fantasized it. *The terrorist* could watch and then he'd kill her.

Geldenhuis pulled Dee's body off the pathway, covering the blood on the path by kicking dust over it with his boot. There wasn't much time and he found an outcrop of rock just off the path and waited.

Peekay and Tandia came down the path glad to be away from the wind, Tandia walking slowly but a little easier. Geldenhuis saw them coming and steadied his rifle. Peekay was in front shielding Tandia. He aimed low at his hip just as Peekay saw one of the bundles lying at the side of the pathway. Peekay turned and dived at Tandia, knocking her over into the bush beside the path just as Geldenhuis squeezed the trigger. The bullet caught Peekay high in the shoulder, just below the collarbone.

Peekay felt no pain. He rolled off the path and leapt to his feet, grabbing Tandia's hand and pulling her. 'Up! Get up!' he screamed. Tandia somehow managed to get to her feet and they stumbled down the slope into the dense scrub, disturbing the boulders which clattered down the mountain slope in front of them.

Somehow Peekay managed to get Tandia a hundred yards or so down the densely wooded slope. Then he stopped. They'd come to an outcrop of rock in high grass which appeared to form a small hollow to one side. He pushed Tandia into it and crept in beside her. Tandia's breathing was coming in rasps and Peekay held her to him. Then he realized that blood was dripping onto her shoulder. He put his hand up, feeling the hole in his shoulder for the first time.

They could hear Geldenhuis crashing around some distance to their right. Peekay pushed Tandia from him. Seeing the blood, she brought her hand up over her mouth, stifling her scream. Geldenhuis was moving further away. He'd be quiet for a few moments, obviously listening for them, then they'd hear him moving again. It was impossible this high up on the slopes not to disturb loose shale and rocks as you walked.

Peekay knew Geldenhuis would go back to the path soon, not taking the chance of getting lost. Then he would see the blood and know he'd wounded Peekay and he'd come down more carefully, following the blood spoor. 'Listen, Tandia, we don't have much time. I know a place near here, maybe a mile and a bit where I can hide. I'm going to draw Geldenhuis away, make him follow me. Don't worry, I know the country, he doesn't, he won't get me, I promise.' Peekay tried to grin; his shoulder was starting to throb badly.

Tandia flung herself at him. 'Peekay, you're going to die! If you're going to die I want to die too!' She sobbed against his chest.

'Tandy! Listen, you can make it!' Peekay whispered urgently. 'When Geldenhuis comes after me wait five minutes, then go back to the path. You've got five miles to go, it's mostly downhill. In two hours you'll be in Swaziland. Ask the first person you see to take you to the village of Somojo, every Swazi knows where that is.' He reached into his shirt and removed the leather strap around his neck with the tiny leather bag attached to it. It was the gold coin of Lumukanda. 'Take this, Tandy.' Peekay placed it over her head so that it sat with the gold chain on which hung Juicey Fruit Mambo's gold eye-teeth. 'When you get to the village give it to one of the young women who serve Somojo. It's important, do you understand?' Tandia nodded, her eyes tearful again. Peekay took his wallet from his top pocket. 'There's money in there. When you get to the village ask for Julius Dube, he's one of our people, also a captain in *Umkonto*. He'll take care of the rest!'

'I don't want to go,' Tandia pleaded.

Peekay was suddenly angry. 'Go! You must go! Otherwise they win! You understand? Otherwise Geldenhuis and all he stands for wins!'

Tandia nodded, sniffing, and Peekay rose. 'It will be all right, darling. Move out with me, go to the right for fifty yards, then wait quietly. He'll come after the blood, after me. When you see him pass this spot wait five minutes then move back to the path.' He kissed Tandia, holding her with his good arm. 'I love you, Tandia. You are my whole life!'

Tandia started to weep. 'Peekay, I love you! Please, don't leave me.'

'Tandia, you must make it! You must hang on. Whatever happens, you must get through.' Peekay smiled, 'Tandia, about last night. If you're pregnant, you know, just if? If it's a boy, will you call him just one name? Just Lumukanda.' Peekay repeated the name, 'Lumukanda, child of the morning star!' He kissed her deeply. 'Goodbye, beloved Tandia,' he said softly. Moments later they set off together. Peekay squeezed her hand

and released it, Tandia moved to the right and he, making a fearful racket to hide her movement, moved downwards and to the left, away from the rock outcrop where they'd been hiding.

Geldenhuis had done just as Peekay had thought he might. He retraced his steps to the pathway and soon he discovered the blood trail; then he heard the two of them crashing to his left in the dense bush directly below him. He followed the sound for nearly ten minutes, soon finding more blood. Whichever of the two of them he'd hit wasn't going to get too far. He knew Tandia was exhausted but that Peekay wouldn't leave her. The madness in him made him feel totally confident, a lion stalking his prey. It was better this way, he had to work for his kill. He would enjoy it the more for the effort it had taken.

Peekay was no more than a mile and a half away from the crystal cave of Africa. As he walked he cut a length of rope from where it sat on the top of his ruck-sack and made a quick sling for his arm, cushioning the rope with a handful of tough mountain grass. He dabbed at the blood on his shoulder, laying the spoor for Geldenhuis until he judged he was sufficiently far from Tandia for her to get away. The men following her wouldn't reach Saddleback before nightfall, that was, if they'd been foolish enough to continue beyond the gorge. Trapped in the high mountains for the night they'd freeze to death even in midsummer.

After an hour it was time to lose Geldenhuis. Peekay had moved around in a large circle, climbing gradually higher. Geldenhuis would never find the path again. It was half past four, he had an hour and a half before sunset. The deep kloof of rainforest he was going to was hidden in a crease of a mountain abutting Saddleback and he worked his way towards it. Geldenhuis was managing to keep on his track and he could hear him coming up behind him.

The shrub was becoming more sparse as they climbed higher. Twice Geldenhuis caught sight of Peekay and took a shot at him. But it was almost impossible to fire up the mountain slope; his optical perspectives were out and he missed by a large margin. By now Geldenhuis realised that Peekay was on his own. But it didn't matter, it was Peekay he wanted. He laughed to himself. When the chips were down Peekay had deserted the kaffir girl, the white man in him asserting itself. Peekay's blood spoor had stopped but he could hear him and occasionally see him. His quarry was in country where it wasn't too hard to track him.

Peekay was beginning to feel slightly nauseous from loss of blood; he was growing weaker but enough strength remained. The wound was clean; under the collarbone and out the other side, smashing a hole through the shoulder blade. His arm was getting very stiff and painful but he'd torn his sleeve, plugging the bleeding, though he could feel his back was wet, sticky with blood. Peekay came at last to the narrow gap between the two high cliffs. It was here that he hoped finally to lose Geldenhuis. It was well concealed and in the shadow of the towering rock, a place you could pass fifty times and not see. He slipped into the darkness of the narrow opening, moving quietly. Soon he was on the other side looking down into the rainforest below. On the side opposite to him was the cliff face that contained the crystal cave. To the right of the concealed entrance to the cave the bridal veil fell, the fine white spray of water turning pink in the late afternoon sun. Below him the huge old yellowwood tree stood high above the canopy of trees, the way it had stood sentinel for six hundred years, maybe more.

Peekay moved slowly down the slope, his bad shoulder making it difficult and painful to do so. He was sweating, the sweat cold, coming from the pain. Twice he stopped to hear if he was being followed but he heard nothing. It took him fifteen minutes to get to the floor of the forest below and he stopped briefly at the stream to drink. He was growing weak but he knew he must somehow get to the ledge beside the cave, get into the crystal cave to Doc. Peekay knew that he was losing too much blood, that by morning he'd be unconscious and too weak to climb out of the kloof. He had somehow to find the strength to climb up to the cave, to lie beside Doc. He moved through the dark cover of the trees reaching the base of the cliff. 'Please, Doc, give me the strength,' he cried softly, looking up at the rock face towering above him. 'Just one more time, give me the strength I need.'

Peekay took off his rucksack, gingerly pulling its bloodsoaked strap off his left shoulder. His movements were slow, conserving his strength. He didn't panic; panic races the blood. He took half-a-dozen climbing spikes and the tiny hammer and fitted them into his belt. He also took the torch and attached it as well. He started up the rock face moving slowly, judging every move. His shoulder had started to bleed profusely as he demanded work from the arm; his teeth cut through his lower lip from the pain. Sometimes he was so dizzy he was forced to stand with his back to the cliff to prevent himself falling.

Geldenhuis lost Peekay. He'd caught sight of him for a moment as they worked across a ridge but then they approached a huge towering bluff and Peekay had vanished. He knew he must be in the vicinity; beyond the huge bluff the mountain fell sheer for a thousand feet. Peekay had disappeared into the rock. It was getting late, in less than an hour it would be sunset. Night comes quickly in the mountains. He wasn't even sure if he knew his way back. But he was past caring. Nothing else mattered to him now but the kill. He was so close, he could smell the death he was going to bring about. For forty minutes he searched, passing the entrance a dozen times before seeing the blood spot and looking into the dark, narrow fissure in the cliff face. He had to slide in sideways. At first the entrance didn't appear to lead anywhere, just a huge fissure in the towering cliff and then, as his eyes grew accustomed to the softer light, he saw another drop of blood. He moved on, squeezing through the narrowest bit which wasn't much wider than his body turned sideways. Suddenly he was looking down into a kloof of rainforest. In the centre a huge tree rose above all the others; at the far end, a cliff with a waterfall to its right held the kloof in its lap. He saw where Peekay had made his descent and then more blood.

Geldenhuis was able to follow the blood spoor down to the floor of the rainforest below. Once he reached the rainforest floor he lost it, but he kept going; moving along the stream he found another spot of blood on a rock. It was dark and still under the canopy of trees but he forced his way up the stream towards the waterfall. When he reached it he moved along the cliff face to his right, choosing it instinctively. He'd lost the blood trail but then he saw Peekay's rucksack and, looking up, he saw the blood on the cliff face above him; it was smeared over parts of the rock face where Peekay's shoulder had wiped against the rock. Geldenhuis could see clearly how to make the climb, but he would have to do so without his rifle. He placed it on the rock and felt to make sure the knife was on his belt. He began to climb, moving as quietly as possible up the blood-stained rock.

Peekay had finally reached the ledge. He was totally exhausted. The wound had torn further and he was bleeding profusely. He was too weak to do anything about it. He could feel the setting sun on his face as he lay there, trying to gather sufficient strength to venture onto the six-inch ledge which led to the cave entrance. He would have to wait a while and gather his strength, harvesting every little bit until he had sufficient for the last short journey, the precarious ledge, the crawl down the narrow tunnel into the bat cave and then into the crystal cave of Africa itself, where Doc lay waiting for him, his long body turning slowly into crystal, into Africa itself, the blood and the muscle and the spirit of him entering into the mystic land. He would lie with Doc, they'd be together again. If only he could find the strength. The ledge was warm and it seemed a nice place to be. He could see the dark smudge of mountains in the distance silhouetted against the red sky of a setting sun. Those mountains were in Swaziland, Tandia would be there by now. Tandia had made it.

Peekay must have passed out, or perhaps he was dreaming, because he wakened to see a face standing above him. It looked like Jannie Geldenhuis. Only it wasn't. It was a Jannie Geldenhuis who had gone mad. The face above him was going to kill him. He followed the face's hand and saw the knife Gert had made for him, the death's head knife. He'd given it to Gideon, but now it was on the belt of the mad face of Gelden-huis. The blade drew out, sharp and beautiful, as keen to strike as death itself, the blade made into a miracle from a Dodge truck spring, deadly and cunning in Gert's brilliant hands. A spring under a Dodge truck that had gone mad and turned into a killer blade. That was funny. The knife came up and Peekay began to laugh. The knife Gert made to protect him from hate; he'd given it to Gideon because the hatred against him was bigger, he needed Gert's blade more to equal the odds against him. But he should have known, hate cannot live in a good man's hands for long, hate has to find the fingers it knows. The knife had found the hate it needed in the grip of the white policeman's madness. Now Gert's knife was going to kill Peekay. In the end hate was going to win. You had to laugh. He'd been wrong after all. In the end, blind ignorant hate with a knife in its hand had triumphed over love and compassion which always came open-handed. The blade came up into a high arc, beautiful against a blood-red sky.

A shadow passed slowly over Peekay as Dum moved up the ledge behind Geldenhuis. She snarled like an animal, lifting him off his feet, her white teeth flashing as they sunk into his throat, hurling herself off the ledge with Geldenhuis pulled tightly against her body. Peekay heard him scream and then the crash of their bodies, the black and the white, as they smashed onto the rocks a hundred and fifty feet below where their blood mixed and flowed together at the base of the great altar of rock. *Together since the world began, the madman and the lover.*

Peekay lay still for a long time. The moon came up, full and glorious, a bright florin of light in the African night. He'd always liked the full moon. He was back in the night country. He stood on the rock above the top waterfull ready to jump. 'You must jump now, little warrior of the king,' he heard Inkosi-lnkosikazi say.

Peekay launched himself into the silver air. This time he seemed to float and the old witchdoctor's voice came to him again, but from a distance. 'You are wearing the skirt of the lion tail as you face into the setting sun. Now the sun has passed beyond Zululand, even past the land of the Swazi and now it leaves the Shangaan and the royal kraal of Modjaji, the rain queen, to be cooled in the great dark water beyond.

'You can see the moon rising over Africa and you are at peace, unafraid of the great demon Skokiaan who comes to feed on the night, tearing its black flesh until at last it is finished and there is light again and the people sing softly in the morning.'

Peekay saw the journey, the bittersweet journey from the beginning, from the soft black breasts that suckled him, the warm taste of milk, more than you could drink if you tried your hardest. He heard the click of the train wheels carrying him to the east, a small child frightened as a butterfly. *Small can beat big, you must remember only one thing, little boetie, first with the head and then with the heart.* It was Hoppie's voice coming to him as he flew higher and higher ... Grandpa Chook, Geel Piet, *Dance, klein baas, that way they think you not hurt.* Captain Smit, E.W., Hymie, who would love him now? Beautiful Hymie ...

Such a fortunate life ... Peekay rose higher and higher, floating on the silver night above Africa. He passed over a village, a high mountain village where the yellow moon clung to the peaks and the bluffs. Below him in a tiny mound of scarlet cashmere Somojo sat, his grizzled head clear in the firelight. He was in a trance. 'A woman has come into the village, Somojo, a woman of no tribe,' one of the princesses said quietly.

'She gave me this and told me she must bring it to you.' Somojo's tiny hand, bony as an ancient monkey's claw, rose from the scarlet blanket and she placed the leather pouch within it. 'You are wrong, my child,' the old, old man moaned softly. 'The mother of the morning star belongs to every tribe. Lumukanda is back with us.'

ALSO BY

BRYCE COURTENAY

THE POWER OF ONE

First with your head and then with your heart . . .

So says Hoppie Groenewald, boxing champion, to a
seven-year-old boy who dreams of being the welterweight
champion of the world. For the young Peekay, it is a piece
of advice he will carry with him throughout his life.

Born in a South Africa divided by racism and hatred,
young Peekay will come to lead all the tribes of Africa.
Through enduring friendships, he gains the strength he needs
to win out. And in a final conflict with his childhood enemy,
Peekay will fight to the death for justice . . .

**Bryce Courtenay's classic bestseller is a story of the triumph
of the human spirit—a spellbinding tale for all ages.**

April Fool's Day

In the end, love is more important than everything and it will conquer and overcome anything. Or that's how Damon saw it, anyway. Damon wanted a book that talked a lot about love.

Damon Courtenay died on the morning of *April Fool's Day*. In this tribute to his son, Bryce Courtenay lays bare the suffering behind this young man's life. Damon's story is one of lifelong struggle, his love for Celeste, the compassion of a family, and a fight to the end for integrity.

A testimony to the power of love, *April Fool's Day* is also about understanding: how when we confront our worst, we can become our best.

A powerful account of life and death from one of Australia's best authors

THE AUSTRALIAN TRILOGY

THE POTATO FACTORY

Ikey Solomon and his partner in crime, Mary Abacus, make the harsh journey from thriving nineteenth-century London to the convict settlement of Van Diemen's Land. In the back-streets and dives of Hobart Town, Mary builds The Potato Factory, where she plans a new future. But her ambitions are threatened by Ikey's wife, Hannah, her old enemy. As each woman sets out to destroy the other, the families are brought to the edge of disaster.

TOMMO & HAWK

Brutally kidnapped and separated in childhood, Tommo and Hawk are reunited in Hobart Town. Together they escape their troubled pasts and set off on a journey into manhood. From whale hunting in the Pacific to the Maori wars in New Zealand, from the Rocks in Sydney to the miners' riots at the goldfields, Tommo and Hawk must learn each other's strengths and weaknesses in order to survive.

SOLOMON'S SONG

When Mary Abacus dies, she leaves her business empire in the hands of the warring Solomon family. Hawk Solomon is determined to bring together both sides of the tribe – but it is the new generation who must fight to change the future. Solomons are pitted against Solomons as the families are locked in a bitter struggle that crosses battlefields and continents to reach a powerful conclusion.

JESSICA

Jessica is the story of a remarkable young Australian woman who defied the conventions of her time. She had a stubborn streak and the courage to act out her convictions, in spite of the consequences.

Jessica is a tomboy, the pride of her father, as she grows up on their farm. One quiet day, the peace of the bush is shattered by a terrible murder. Only Jessica is able to save the killer from the lynch mob – but will justice prevail in the courts?

Set in the harsh Australian countryside against the outbreak of World War I and the years beyond, this story is heartbreaking in its innocence, and shattering in its violence.

Based on a true story, *Jessica* is a testimony to the power of the human spirit triumphing over the odds.

FOUR FIRES

In a small town like any other small town around Australia live the Maloneys. They are a fifth-generation Australian family of Irish Catholic descent who are struggling to reach the first rung of the social ladder. The Maloneys are a family you won't forget: a strong mother, a father broken by war, three boys and two girls, one of whom has an illegitimate daughter. Each of their lives is changed forever by the four fires—passion, religion, warfare and fire itself.

Four Fires is unashamedly a story of the power of love and the triumph of the human spirit against the odds.

MATTHEW FLINDERS' CAT

The story of a drunk, a boy and a cat.

Billy O'Shannessy, once a prominent barrister, is now on the street where he sleeps on a bench outside the State Library. Above him on the window sill rests a bronze statue of Matthew Flinders' cat, Trim. Ryan is a ten-year-old, a near-street kid heading for all the usual trouble. The two form an unlikely bond.

Through telling Ryan the story of Flinders' circumnavigation of Australia as seen through Trim's eyes, Billy is drawn deeply into Ryan's life and into the Sydney underworld.

A modern-day story of friendship and redemption by an internationally bestselling author.

THE FAMILY FRYING PAN

Mrs Moses is a small woman with a big heart and enormous courage.

The only survivor of a Cossack raid on her village, she takes with her a big cast-iron frying pan, so heavy that she can only sling it over her back. Yet this is no ordinary frying pan—it's The Family Frying Pan, blessed with a Russian soul.

From this frying pan Mrs Moses manages to feed the various refugees who are travelling with her across Russia to freedom. In return, each of the group must tell a story around the campfire at night – stories of compassion and bravery, of human frailty and, above all, of hope.

SMOKY JOE'S CAFE

Thommo returns from Vietnam to an Australia that regards him as a mercenary guilty of war crimes. All who remain of his platoon who fought and died in the Battle of Long Tan are affected the same way. Now Thommo and his mates are angry men out for revenge. They're the 'Dirty Dozen', just like the movie. Only it's real life, and they're so screwed up they probably couldn't fight their way out of a wet paper bag.

That is, until a woman of character steps in. Wendy's infant daughter is dying and needs a bone-marrow transplant. Hell hath no fury . . . as she sets out to mould this bunch of ex-jungle fighters into a unit that will fight for justice, by fair means or foul.

WHITETHORN

From Bryce Courtenay comes *Whitethorn* a novel of Africa. The time is 1939: White South Africa is a deeply divided nation with many of the Afrikaner people fanatically opposed to the English.

The world is on the brink of war with South Africa electing to fight for the Allied cause against Germany. Six year old Tom Fitzsaxby finds himself in the Boys Farm, an orphanage in a small remote town in the high mountains, where the Afrikaners side fanatically with Hitler's Germany.

Tom's English name alone proves sufficient for him to be racially ostracised. And so begins some of life's tougher lessons for the small, lonely boy.

Like the whitethorn, one of Africa's most enduring plants, Tom learns how to survive in the harsh climate of racial hatred. Then a terrible event sets him on a journey to ensure that justice is done. On the way, his most unexpected discovery is love.

SYLVIA

'I am Sylvia Honeyeater; I think myself born around 1196, and this is the story of my life. I am cursed by folk as an optimist and a dreamer, which is a dangerous combination . . .'

From master storyteller Bryce Courtenay comes the colourful epic of Sylvia Honeyeater, a peasant born in the late 12th century into a Europe torn by religious intolerance. With a singing voice that can literally charm the birds out of the trees, and an acute and questioning mind that refuses to accept unreasoned beliefs, Sylvia leaves her birthplace to embark on a pilgrimage. Together with a band of larger-than-life characters, she sets out to form a Children's Crusade, who plan to travel to the Holy Land.

From a bawdy life as an entertainer in a whorehouse to an austere and frequently cruel existence in a nunnery, she fights to be true to her destiny. In an age when signs and portents were eagerly sought as indications of blessedness, Sylvia finds herself either cast as an instrument of Satan or adored as a miracle-worker. And her mysterious birthmark causes much confusion: can this peasant maid indeed be a chosen messenger?

This is storytelling at its very best. *Sylvia* is a tale of adversity and triumph, of adventure and crusades, and of a beautiful and gifted woman.

THE PERSIMMON TREE

In the heartwood of the sacred persimmon tree is ebony, the hardest, most beautiful of all woods. This is a symbol of life, a heartwood that will outlast everything man can make, a core within that, come what may, cannot be broken and represents our inner strength and divine spirit.

It is 1942 in the Dutch East Indies, and Nick Duncan is a young Australian butterfly collector in search of a single exotic butterfly. With invading Japanese forces coming closer by the day, Nick falls in love with the beguiling Anna Van Heerden.

Yet their time together is brief, as both are forced into separate, dangerous escapes. They plan to reunite and marry in Australia but it is several years before their paths cross again, scarred forever by the dark events of a long, cruel war.

Set against the dramatic backdrop of the Pacific during the Second World War, Bryce Courtenay gives us a story of love and friendship born of war, and the power of each in survival.